# TAWNY FIELDS

## A TRIED & TRUE NOVEL

## CHARLI RAHE

TRIED AND TRUE PUBLISHING

*For everyone who has made it this far. This is part one of the end.
And always for my husband and children.*

# Note from the Author

Scarlett's fantastical story follows a woman's journey through her magical heritage in which she encounters several dark scenarios. It is not intended for readers under 18 years of age and includes adult content.

While I'd prefer you to experience it as you go, your mental health matters. Please refer to www.charlirahe.com for a detailed list of possible triggers.

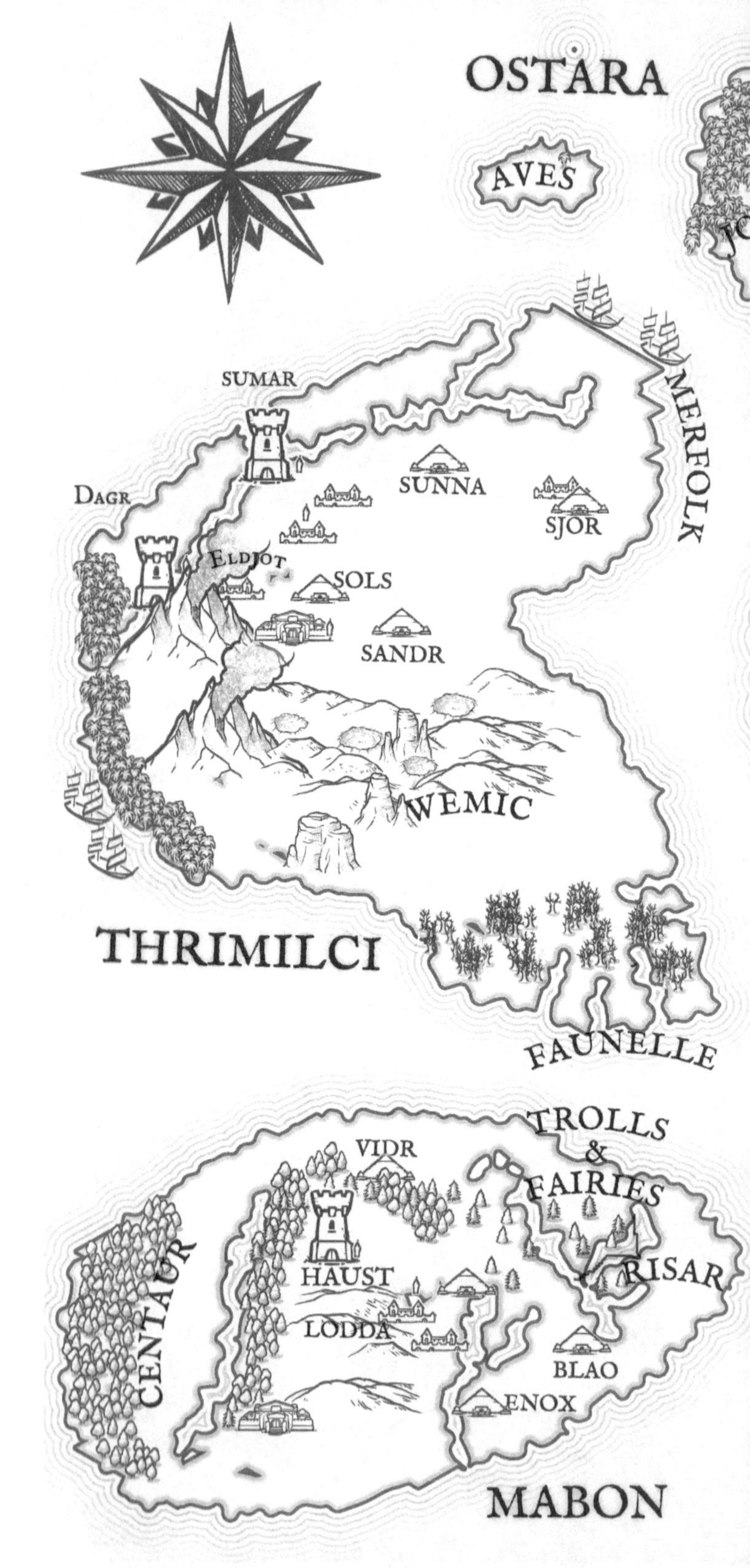
OSTARA
AVES
SUMAR
MERFOLK
DAGR
SUNNA
SJOR
ELDJOT
SOLS
SANDR
WEMIC
THRIMILCI
FAUNELLE
TROLLS
&
FAIRIES
VIDR
RISAR
CENTAUR
HAUST
LODDA
BLAO
ENOX
MABON

TIDINGS
ELIVAGAR
ANGUILLAN
ITR
REGN
ROT
AR
LYCANS
NATT
BIORN
CRATHODE
VETR
SVELL
GLITRA
MINOTAUR
KALLA
SNJAR
KALDR
JOTNAR
RGONS
STRAUMR
MOSSUR
TOWN CENTER
STOKER
HVALL
O
LLA
JARN
VALKYRIES

# PROLOGUE

White silken tents lined the side of Valla University's sprawling yellow stone walls on their big night. The girls turned two months old and their father would meet them for the first time.

They had names. After the Prime announced the year's theme — colors — the possibilities were endless. Without Alder's help, Wren would have been forced to name their three children on her own, but there was Lark.

The golden muscled man that towered over her with intense grey eyes that seemed to peer right into her soul would have intimidated most. His dark waves brushed his strong jawline as he turned to give Wren a reassuring smile.

He carried Jett, her beautiful boy with big turquoise eyes just like her grandmother. She could see Alder in him with his tan skin and flaring temper tantrums. Most of the time, Jett was the most lovable boy there ever was, but his fuse was a short one. Steel adored his little brother. There was never a good time to tell Steel the truth. His little four-year-old mind might not understand the sudden change from Wren, his sister, to his mother. Alder did not know the boy posing as her brother was their son.

Slate toddled along between Lark and Wren, holding Steel's hand. Slate had been a tricky one. The little boy would turn two in the spring and while they knew he could speak; he chose not to. They had been right in nicknaming him Stoic before his Ausa Vatni. He had an old soul. He reminded you every time his steel grey gaze fixed on you.

Then there had been Indigo, Wren's first daughter born with her father's tanned skin and powder blue eyes. Indigo had been easy to name. She was sure Alder would approve. Indigo would take after her father, with Wren's temperament. Indigo almost never cried; she was such a wonderful baby.

Scarlett, Wren smiled.

She'd looked so much like dutiful Steel and lovable Jett when she was born. The same turquoise eyes, her hair only a shade or two darker and full, pouty lips like Wren's grandmother. Lark had named her. Wren felt overwhelmed by the numerous choices.

Thinking about Sparrow alone in Chicago with Tawny made Wren's heart hurt. Wren knew Hawk would eventually pull Sparrow from her grief and help her heal. Then who knew? Hawk was still in love with Sparrow. He had never seen himself as the heir to the Sumar palace and the overseer of Thrimilci, but he would be whenever Flint stepped down.

In the meantime, Hawk would spend his time with Sparrow. So much sorrow for one woman. Wren didn't know if she could be as strong as Sparrow.

Now there were no heirs to Elivagar in Tidings. Tawny was thousands of miles away in Chicago.

Wren filed into the tent with Hawk at her side. He'd be all silver in no time, just like Flint. Hawk was the spitting image of their father; he'd even started wearing his hair in the same pompadour fashion. Though Flint had a thin mustache on his olive face and Hawk was clean shaven for now. They were even alike in temper and behavior. Both men were intelligent with dark eyes and lean dancer's builds.

They walked around the tables placed on the wood floors that had been set for the induction ceremony, garlands of pine tree boughs hung with glittering lights around the tent. Mistletoes and poinsettias decorated the tables and hung from chandeliers that cast an incandescent light over the milling crowd. Their tables were nearest the stage because they were a greater family. Wren could have sat with the Tios or even the Hausts now that she and Lark were married but decided to stay with the Sumar.

"You can go sit with your family," Wren told Lark, and he gave her a feigned look of confusion.

"Embarrassed of your husband?" he asked.

He looked dapper even with children hanging off of him — *especially* with children hanging off of him. Wren's relationship with him was effortless.

That was what would be so hard about the night. Wren would see Delta and Alder together for the first time in a year — their baby boy would be with them. Sage, they had named him. Even thinking about it sent pain shooting through Wren. Alder was doing his husbandly duties with another woman. Lark took the edge off.

He took more than the edge off for the last month.

Wren told herself it was the hormones at first. Their first night together *had* induced her labor, and the girls were born the next day. Once she was healed, Lark had arranged for Pearl and Flint to take the girls for the night, since the boys had begun sleeping in their own room. There had been no excuse that night. Nothing as a pretense or an excuse.

They had wanted to make love to one another. They had wanted to every night since. When her monthly arrived, he seemed disappointed. He casually mentioned how six children would be a *nice,* even number.

"As handsome as he is, I find that a difficult emotion to project," Wren said, giving him a coy smile.

Flint pulled out the silver chair for Pearl and Wren's mother favored him with a feline smile. Her mother had always reminded Wren of a cat; big emerald almond eyes with a wide mouth on her deep tan face. She could usually be found lounging languorously, pouring over the papers that dealt with the day to day running of Thrimilci. Her coppery hair fell in big curls to the shoulders of her voluptuous frame. Wren had not gotten any of those curves, but was the same short height as her mother. Scarlett fussed in Pearl's arms, trying to find a more comfortable spot. Pearl cooed down at the baby girl, whose little fists were moving jerkily in the air.

The silver sparkling table cloth caught Indigo's eyes the moment Lark pulled out Wren's seat while balancing Jett on his hip. "I will return shortly," Lark said, passing Jett to Hawk and bending down to her.

Wren tilted her head back and Lark's grey eyes glittered with barely withheld mirth. They had decided it was pointless to act like they hated one another as it seemed most the married couples in Tidings did. Wren was still trying to get used to their public displays of affection. His full lips met hers she and was a girl again.

Lark withdrew and smiled a dangerously handsome smile. "It is getting easier," he said in his smooth, deep voice.

"Not quite as awkward as two fifteen-year-olds with dirt on their knees and leaves in their hair," Wren mused, looking up at those grey eyes.

"I always liked you with leaves in your hair," Lark said before he gave Indigo a kiss on her head and walked to the Haust table where his family sat watching.

"I always liked that Lark," Flint said, lowering himself into the seat next to Pearl.

Wren rolled her wide, dark eyes. That had been the mantra ever since Lark had petitioned Flint for her hand in marriage.

"Lark is a good man... always has been," Hawk said.

"Can I hold Jett?" Steel asked, swinging his legs in his seat beside Pearl.

Slate shared the seat that was big enough for both of them to sit side by side.

"I will hold Jett, and you can play with him," Pearl said, and Hawk handed Jett over the table, giving Flint Scarlett.

Wren did what she promised herself she wouldn't do. She looked for Alder. He was hard to miss. He was as tall as Lark and just as powerfully built. He sat at the Var table with the blonde, statuesque Delta. Her cool blue eyes watching the stage, the boy Sage had her same cool eyes and pouty mouth. She didn't see any of the Alder in the boy. Alder's chiseled face was hard. It had grown much harder since she last saw him and Wren knew he must be horribly unhappy.

Their eyes met over the crowd and Wren's heart lurched. Alder missed her. She knew it didn't matter that they had been apart, their love could survive anything. They would have to speak tonight. She couldn't be so close to him and not steal a moment away from the others. Nearly all of Tidings was gathered for the Valla U induction ceremony. Surely Wren and Alder could sneak away for a few minutes.

A new kind of apprehension grew in her. When Lark suggested their marriage, he'd said it was because they understood that they were both in love with someone else. That was before they had become intimate. Before he started hinting at her having his child. She was still in love with Alder, but she loved Lark, too. There was a potential for more with Lark, and now she wasn't as sure of where things stood with Alder in her heart.

Canis and Cygnus Var sat at the table, looking as dour as ever. Canis, the twin brother of Alder's father, looked years older. His blonde military cut hair on his round head was streaked through with white, his blue hooded eyes took everything in with a measuring gaze. The Var's were all big men. Cygnus was no exception. His blonde hair was neatly combed, Alder had gotten his coloring from his father, not a single feature from his mother, Ruby.

Jackal Var sat with his raven haired mother at the Geol table. Alder's lanky younger brother preferred his mother's company to his father's. Wren could never blame him for that. The floppy haired boy was a prankster and there was no room for that as a Var male. Ruby doted on her youngest son.

In contrast to her sons, she was a slender woman with fair skin and dark, high brows over wide, dark eyes. The Var genes had been stronger. Wren and Ruby had always gotten along, but Wren didn't think Ruby had any idea about Wren or Alder's other children.

The scent of cinnamon hung in the air, mixing with the pine sap as

Moon Straumr climbed the steps to the stage. The Prime of Tidings and Overseer of Valla University for Guardian Mastery flashed his wife a smile where she sat with her sister Ruby and Robin, Lark's sister and the youngest of her three sons. Opal Geol returned his smile as their daughter Amethyst bounced on her knee. The three Straumr boys were all much older than the toddling girl, and eight-year difference separated Amethyst from her baby blue eyed brother, Fox. The other two boys were both older than Wren.

The ceremony inducting the newest students would begin soon, and then it would be obvious if Wren moved about. She glanced at Lark. He sat with his parents, Peak, and his family and seemed to sense her gaze. He turned his head and curled his lips at Wren and she returned his smile.

Out of her periphery, she saw Alder stand and start towards the exit. Wren didn't think. She stood and followed him without preamble. Indigo fussed in her arms and Wren almost laughed aloud, better now than missing her chance.

Alder had noticed Wren following him and made a point of crossing behind the tent so she would see him. He stood there, tall and handsome, his powder blue eyes full of a warmth he only shared with her. Oblivious to the baby, Alder grabbed Wren by her waist and slanted his mouth over hers, making butterflies beat in her stomach. She had lived each day so that maybe one day she'd receive another one of those kisses. Then Lark had begun to give her his kisses, and only her.

"By the Mother, Wren. I have missed you," Alder breathed, unable to stop touching her.

Wren didn't dare try her voice; the lump that had risen would choke any words she attempted. Alder looked down at the blonde baby girl in her arms and he raised his brows. Wren knew what he must have thought if not Alder's then Lark's. While Alder consented to go along with her plan to marry Lark, he was not convinced feelings would not develop between the longtime friends. He may have been right.

It was now or never. "Indigo. Your daughter," Wren strangled out, and Alder's eyes went wide.

"I had no idea. You did not write." Alder gaped at the baby in her arms.

"I did not want to risk Delta intercepting the letter. It was better this way," Wren explained.

"I missed the birth of my daughter? Was Lark with you?" Alder asked, face stony, and Wren smiled wryly and stood on her tip toes pressing another kiss to Alder's lips and he gripped the back of her head, deepening it. "Well?" he asked, breathless.

"Lark has been good to me. Do you wish to hold Indigo?" Wren asked, her warm dark eyes searched his.

Alder nodded and opened his arms, unable to speak, and Wren placed Indigo in her father's hands for the first time. She settled in, blinking those big blue eyes at her father until someone screamed. More voices joined the first and the sounds of crashing started from within the tent. Wren's heart lurched when people began to run from the tent and the crackle of a lot of *calling* being used infused the air.

Steel, Jett, Slate, and Scarlett, she had to get them.

She spun to Alder. "Keep her safe."

Alder reached for her, but she picked up her skirts, running headlong back into the tent.

It was as if her worst nightmares had crawled from the recesses of her mind to play before her eyes.

Part of the tent was on fire behind the stage and Crathode, seven feet tall with clawed hands and beady eyes, were attacking. Screams sounded all around her as people ran from the front of the tent.

Her breaths came in short bursts as she pushed past people to the Sumar table, Delta ran from the tent holding Sage and Wren thanked the gods Alder's other son was okay. She reached the Haust table and saw Lark's parents had been killed, but no sign of Peak or Lark. Smoke was starting to fill the tent and Wren pushed against more people, *calling* as she went to fight off the attacking Crathode.

Tears sprung to her eyes when she spotted her table. Pearl was holding Jett, *calling* with her other hand and Steel holding onto her skirts, trying to keep the Crathode from gaining ground. Hawk was doing the same with Scarlett in one arm and Slate burying his face in his pants leg. The babies screamed in fear from all the noise and the snarling Crathode. Flint was injured and at the front of the line with Moon and her uncle Reed, keeping the Crathode from the escaping families.

Then she saw Lark, blood soaked and roaring as he dispatched Crathode after Crathode. Wren ran to Hawk and took Scarlett from his arms, and scooped Slate off the floor. Hawk's relief at seeing her was palpable.

"Where is Indigo?" he shouted.

"With Alder," she confessed as she gaped.

Moon's wife was laying across the shimmering silver table cloth that was quickly turning red with her blood. Robin's body was next to her with the son she was holding, her youngest, Silver.

Wren stifled a sob. "Hawk! The boy!" She shouted and Hawk darted forward and scooped up the boy half hidden in his mother's skirts from the floor.

None of the other children remained, and Wren said a silent prayer of thanks. Her heart hurt for all the losses of life. There were dozens of dead around them.

Flint turned over his shoulder, dark eyes blazing. "Hawk, Lark, get the women and children out of here!"

Pearl's emerald eyes went as wide as saucers as it happened. Before Flint could turn back, a Crathode bigger than all the rest broke through the line and clamped its claw down on Flint's arm. Pearl and Wren both screamed as Reed Tio attacked the Crathode to try to free Flint.

Lark was at her side, pulling her away and she gripped Scarlett tight to her chest. Hawk lifted up Steel and was pulling Pearl away from the carnage. Lark and Hawk were fighting their way through the tent while the women held onto the children and *called* to help when they could. Robin's husband ran into them and Hawk passed him Silver and began to cry, understanding what that meant.

"Go save your son, Regn," Wren heard Lark ground out.

His sister was dead.

More screams filled the smoky air as part of the tent collapsed at the front and Crathode poured through. Lark sliced a hole in the billowy tent and Hawk led the way through pulling Pearl through. Lark gripped Wren at the tent.

"Wren, I will catch up. Take care of our children."

"Come with us now," Wren pleaded with tears streaking her face.

Lark smiled, creasing his cheeks, and he gave a kiss to his son's head and then Scarlett's. "I fear that I would have come to fall in love with you, Wren." He pulled her against him and kissed her like he never had before, then pushed her through the slice in the tent.

She ducked her head back in, the last image of Lark forever etched in her mind as he grew. His skin darkened and horns begun to push through his raven waves. He turned around and met her eyes, offering a frightening smile. Still, he was Lark, she would never fear Lark, monster or not.

"Go, Wren. Our children are meant to be together. Sea said it was so," Lark rasped before charging into the melee.

Wren hesitated before running to catch up with Hawk and Pearl and whispered. "I could have fallen in love with you, too."

Scarlett watched her mother silently, as if the baby understood that crying now would give them away while Slate had pulled himself up so he could watch over her shoulder towards the tents.

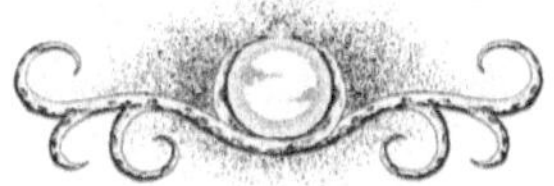

They ran through the night until they reached the Tio palace. Everyone looked dazedly unseeing as Wren, Hawk, and Pearl walked to their portals.

Once they were in the safety of the Sumar palace, Hawk began to lock the portal door. Wren's eyes widened.

"What are you doing? How will father and Lark get back?" she asked in a voice so high and panicked she hardly recognized it as her own.

Hawk straightened with a sympathetic look in his eyes. "If they make it through, nothing will stop them from getting here. I should go to the Dagr palace and lock it. I need a staffer so we came to notify the townspeople we are shutting down the portals. We cannot risk an attack—"

"What are you saying? Lock down the island? You... you do not think they survived, do you?" Wren accused.

Hawk blinked at tears. "Wren... I would not lock out Lark and father."

"You do. Ye of little faith." Wren choked on tears of her own.

She'd seen how few of the men had stayed behind to fight the Crathode. Flint had not been visible when they fled. Lark was part beast. He would be stronger than those monsters.

"Stop arguing. You are both leaving tonight. Sparrow is alone and vulnerable. I have an entire staff to keep me safe," Pearl reminded them.

Steel had buried his face into her neck sobbing and Jett was wide eyed and staring at them, too young to understand what was going on.

"Indigo is with Alder," Wren said weakly.

"Then he will take care of her," Pearl replied firmly, but what Wren heard was *if* they were alive.

"Put the boys to bed, Wren, and get ready," Hawk said before the white light of the portal swallowed him whole.

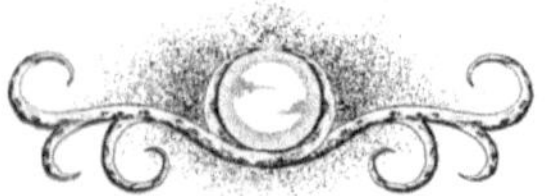

Wren could not stop her tears.

"You will raise them as brothers?" Wren asked as she brushed Steel's head and then Jett's while they slept in their room.

"Steel thinks he is his uncle, but like brothers, darling," Pearl soothed her.

Wren sighed. "That will have to be good enough." She bent down and pressed a kiss to each boy's head.

Slate was awake and sat on his bed, staring at her. She moved to sit beside him and pulled him into her embrace.

"My little stoic. I am so sorry," she whispered, kissing the top of his head.

His scent reminded her of Lark, and her heart twisted.

"I want to take you with me, but I know nothing of what you are. I do not know what triggers your change, or if you could hurt yourself or someone else. You are not made for outside Tidings." She murmured through her tears.

"He is their brother. He will be raised as such," Pearl reassured her. "If Lark comes back, I will send the children with him to you."

"He knows where the houses are," Wren said, nodding. "Maybe I should take Slate, anyway. He has such a hard life already."

Pearl sat down beside her. "Best to keep the boys together. I know you want to claim Steel as your own, but now is not the time. We leave things as they are. I have the ability to care for the boys and the resources. Hawk will have his hands full with Sparrow and Tawny..."

There would be no one to help Wren with Scarlett.

Wren nodded and pried her fingers from Slate, giving him one last kiss.

"Time to go, Wren," Hawk said.

His dark eyes were red rimmed, and she stood and walked from the bedroom where her sons slept and took her daughter from Pearl's arms. She left the wing she shared with her husband for only a few months and Hawk wrapped a reassuring arm around her shoulders as he led her to their new life.

# CHAPTER 1

# INDIGO

*Forewarned is Forearmed*

Scarlett's fur trimmed dress fluttered in the biting breeze of perpetual winter. She wore a grey sleeveless robe with white trim and a matching Yggdrasil for Valla University embroidered on her back since she wasn't the Tio Matriarch. You couldn't tell it was frigid out by looking at her because she didn't feel cold. She'd gone full great family. Everything she hated about the upper crust — she embodied. She stood as Second to the Prime as Ash Straumr addressed the crowd gathered, before their family members ran their last challenge, before they were proven tried and true.

Real Guardians — every child's dream come true growing up in Tidings.

Her paisley embossed teal velvet dress was fitting for a woman of her position. I barely recognized her. One did not get on Scarlett's bad side these days. She *used* to be forgiving. She *used* to be slow to anger. Now you tried to stay out of her line of sight because her wrath was quick and severe. At least, she was still kind to family. She had built a wall around her heart that was impenetrable.

All of us knew Slate and Scarlett had one hot interlude that ended strangely. He had suggested, in a colorful way, that she was having an affair with Ash. Slate was not the good guy. He was more volatile than ever. It was best not to make direct eye contact with Slate at all when she was around because the more she showed in her pregnancy, the more he was a rabid lion off its leash. All her time was spent with Ash did look suspicious. Scarlett refused to address Slate's allegations, making her look guilty.

Then there was Brass. By all the Gods, what a disaster! If anyone other than Brass had told us Scarlett slept with their grandfather, I would have called them a bold-faced liar, but Brass *was* the good guy. He was the best guy. He's stopped coming to the Sumar palace and completely cut her off. We'd all been shocked by the news. Scarlett refused to speak about it.

Ash addressed the crowd looking every bit the Overseer of Valla University for Guardian Mastery and the ruler of the Guardians, and he was only twenty-one. Scarlett's ex-fiancée was tall and one of the most handsome men to grace the gods' green earth. His lightest green eyes didn't miss a thing as he spoke to the stadium at the top of the mountain. It was really a half stadium, one half being completely open to the forest before it. The stadium was heated, the seating warm. It was nearly empty. Nervous parents waited for their children to come out the other end.

Ash had changed Scarlett. *Something* had changed her. Tawny sat with Steel on the stage. They were the Vetrs now. Tawny was the very last Vetr. She wore the scarlet robes of the Vetr matriarch trimmed in white with an embroidered auseklis on the back. Steel and Quartzite would be the last two staying on the stage. None of the other Vetr daughters were on the platform. Tawny had gone to great lengths to keep Cassiopeia Natt from undermining her authority in Elivagar lands.

The Natt castle was in Elivagar lands where my step mother Delta lived with her mother. She had begun testing Tawny's reign over the lands the moment Orion died. While Ash and Scarlett worked to reunite the lands, Cassiopeia and Tawny were divided in one, but no one would blame Tawny. Her grandmother was as vicious as she was frostily beautiful.

Just like her daughters.

Delta and Willow Natt sat with their mother and Diamond Natt in the stands like everyone else for the first time in their privileged lives. Both of their sons were doing the challenge today.

Sterling Haust and Sage Var were teamed with Ash. Three greater family sons together... with Scarlett. The original plan was supposed to be Scarlett, Silver, Slate, and I, but since their interlude, it had all changed. Jett had insisted she join him, Tawny, and Cherry's group, but she declined, saying she was the Prime's Second should be with the Prime. How would it look if she chose to run the course with someone else?

Who cares what anyone else thought?

Ruby Geol was there as well with her husband, Cygnus; my grandparents. My great uncle sat next to Cassiopeia. Canis's long time affair with her was not as carefully hidden. It was a great surprise to all who didn't have empath abilities or could read minds. Since I could absorb powers, I had a taste of how they regarded one another well before now.

The start was also the end of the course. You traversed the snowy mountain and back again using the tracking skills learned at Valla U. There were twenty obstacles and subsequent flags to collect in order to complete the course. You were allowed teams up to four. You weren't competing with the other course runners; it was designed for you to utilize every skill you could muster however you could. If it was easy for you, excellent. If not, then you didn't learn enough at Valla U, and you would try again at the biannual retake under a fog of disgrace.

As soon as the pronouncements were finished, Ash, Scarlett, Slate, and Tawny would all descend the stage and change into their armor for the Ragnarök challenge.

"When was your last monthly, Dove? Should we be extra attentive to your wellbeing during the challenge?" Silver asked hopefully, as he ran his palm under my cloak.

"Just because you use your endearment for me does not mean it is an endearing question. Mind your own business, Regn," I said, fighting a lunatic smile.

Silver was sex on two feet. Devilishly handsome and he knew it. The way his body moved, even with his clothes on, hinted at hedonistic nights in which I was intimately familiar with. Silver didn't think I knew he was trying to get me pregnant from the moment I signed our marriage contract, but I did. I told him six months of fidelity and I'd consider it, but he had barely waited six days before trying.

Six weeks in, and he wanted to start planning for a wedding that might never happen. We both knew we were not a typical couple. I would always have Sterling, and every passing day was the longest Silver had gone without being with another woman.

Silver turned to me with his dreamy, chocolate eyes flecked with gold, and my lips twitched to curl. Damn the handsome bastard. I couldn't help stroking my thumb along his clean-shaven jaw. I wanted to muss up his dark coiffed hair, kept short and styled gentlemanly, but resisted, knowing he hated it. I'd save it for later in the privacy of my bedroom.

He was tall and broad with hard packed olive muscles. His left side was covered with black, jagged Celtic tattoos that ran from his neck to his ankle. A curve of the tattoo always peeked up from under his collar. I knew those tattoos by heart.

"Humor me. Did you buy new teas?" Silver asked.

I did smile then. "Oh, my betrothed. You know I just had my monthly and I can taste the difference when you switch my teas. Naturally, I had to get more since I couldn't find where you hid the latest batch."

Silver smiled the smile that caused grown women to throw themselves at him, absent of their undergarments. It was an amazing smile, but I'd never tell him that.

"I know you want my children, Dove. Why fight it?" Silver's impish smiles did terrible things to my will power.

He couldn't help his lecherous ways or how badly he wanted to plant his seed in my belly. It was something primal in him that needed to stake its claim in me. If I hadn't let Sterling do it in six years, I wouldn't be letting Silver do it until I was good and ready.

"Because I said six months, and I meant it. I don't have a problem having children before the wedding. That should be enough for now."

Silver looked thoughtful as Brass walked from their older brother with his family and Spinel Regn, Silver's grandfather and the reason Silver was the way he was. The young woman with him couldn't have been much older than I was and she was the third girl I'd seen him within two months. He was handsome. With Brass's good looks and Silver's coloring, he had aged extremely well.

Brass embraced me, careful not to touch my skin or I would absorb his mind reading abilities. "How are you, Indigo? You look lovely. Still putting up with my brother, I see. I just wanted to wish you both luck before I sit in the stands."

"Brass! How was your trip? Back for good?" Jett asked, swaggering up with his usual arrogant demeanor that was somehow flattering on my older brother.

Jett was several inches taller than the Regn brothers, who were inches over six feet themselves, but all the Var's were tall and almost all of them powerfully built like Jett's tan sculpted physique. Jett's dark blonde hair was cropped short, his turquoise almond eyes identical to Scarlett and our uncle Steel's. He had a way of always having his lids slid low and looked impossibly smug as his square chin jutted out.

Brass and Silver were just as broad as Jett. They had all trained together as youths in Valla under Cordillera's direction. The Grand Mistress of the Shadow Breakers and Silver's aunt was also there with her lover Chafer. He was nearly twenty years her junior. Scarlett had made him the director of the arena in Valla, but he was a front. He had no interest in running anything, but Cordillera did. It was her only legitimate business to cover for her assassins' guild they generously called a mercenaries' guild.

Brass's soulful amber eyes looked past Jett to the platform and back. Having constant contact with Scarlett's empath abilities made me attune to other's emotions. Brass wasn't very good at hiding his. They were all over the place.

Jett followed Brass's gaze and made a face. "*Uh*...Yeah, I would steer clear."

"She is kind of a bitch," Silver said, and I slapped his chest. "My favorite one, though."

Jett leveled his eyes at Silver, who held his hands up in surrender. Brass gave up the pretense of his casual glances and let his eyes hitch on Scar.

"Is she unhappy? Ash and her..." Brass asked.

Jett shrugged. "Who knows?"

He twisted a two-toned titanium and black plated ring that he wore over his ring finger. A tear shaped black diamond was inlaid in the ring. Scarlett had sent it to him before his trip to gain access to the arenas. He'd gone to stay in the cottages in Valla, away from it all. Rumor had it that Gharial had gone with.

"Did she send you the list of arena heads?" Silver asked, thumbing his own ring.

Scar had gotten his wedding band linked to open the arenas for him, too. Slate's wedding band was the fourth key to open them and the fifth had gone to Cordillera. No one else. Not me. Not Jett. Only those related to the arenas and her estranged husband, whose ring currently resided around her neck because he'd given it back. In the words of Scarlett, that cache hole.

"She did," Brass acknowledged coolly.

"She'll ease up once the arenas open. Things have been tense since she was attacked," Jett said with a shrug.

Brass's normally open face hardened at hearing of her attack and was glaring at Silver. "You did not think to mention it?"

Silver ran his thumb over his sensual lips. "There was nothing you could do once it was over. Besides, there was a whole gang of men planning to do her serious harm and not a hair on her head was hurt. Pewter and Siren tore them apart. All of them are dead. Not a single threat has been issued since."

"There have been more threats?" Brass asked, incredulous.

I winced. "Typical of such an unprecedented change. Nothing you wouldn't expect. Death threats and such. Ash never leaves her alone at Valla University. She's well taken care of. Ash was furious that someone would try to hurt his Second and put out a notice that anyone plotting to attack the Second would be convicted of treason, punishable by death." It took an effort not to roll my eyes. "He's had his own fair share of threats, mostly from women he's misused in the past. Otherwise, they love him and the few masochists will come around to Scarlett. Most are impressed with her."

Brass turned his head back to Scarlett. His thick, dark hair fell just past his shoulders and had it knotted at his nape with a few narrow braids threaded with ebony and bronze beads. From his profile, I could see the only two characteristics Brass and Silver shared; their thick masculine brows and anvil jaws. Brass was bearded with a short stubble which leant a roughness to the softness of his eyes that seemed to draw you in and make you want to trust him. Silver had a smile you knew you couldn't trust — not with your virtue, anyway.

"I should go sit. I only wanted to greet you and wish you luck. This will be a cake walk for you all." Brass turned back to us and gave one of his genuine warm smiles I'd seen girls melt for.

"We'll see you afterwards at the Tio's tonight?" Jett asked.

Brass's smile faltered, and he looked away. "Gigi's Ausa Vatni? I heard Scarlett came through on the precious stones for this year's theme."

Jett smiled broadly whenever he spoke of his daughter. "Opal. It'll take some time to get used to it, but it's exciting to announce her a name. You'll come to the party, right? You're family. You have to, Quick and Coyote are coming and Scarlett and your grandfather are thick as thieves, though he hits on her more than I would like." Jett scowled and Brass didn't so much as crack a smile.

Not everyone knew about Spinel and Scarlett. Jett and his wives didn't, and neither did Steel. Tree-gold had promptly informed Gypsum with his zoolinguist abilities about her affair and Tawny had been the driving force behind their first date.

"Spinel is going as well?" He rubbed his plump, defined lips together and averted his eyes. "I will."

"Just a head's up. Gypsum and Rosasite are a thing. Not a serious thing, but he's bringing her to the Ausa Vatni." Jett shrugged. "Whatever was between her and Scar is over, at least for Scar if there ever was. She doesn't give the girl a second glance much less a first." Jett sighed. "She doesn't give anyone much of anything anymore unless your name is Ash. I never saw this coming."

"Me neither," I added hastily.

Slate caught sight of Brass and prowled towards them. As tall as Jett and just as broad and powerful. A silver scar ran from his hairline to his bronze cheekbone over his left eye. Midnight waves threaded with Celtic silver beads and ivory fetishes fell to his chest. Grey eyes peered out from narrow eyes framed with thick long lashes so it looked like they were lined with kohl. Scarlett had been smitten with him. I didn't understand it. He radiated danger and a savage sensuality that would've made me hide under the bed.

He clasped a corded forearm to Brass's. "Good to see you have returned," he rumbled in a deep baritone.

"She has not been with him. He has not even tried," Brass said without preamble and Slate's full lips pressed together as a muscle flexed in the hard plane of his face.

"What an odd way to greet someone. I do not give a shit who she lays with. How was Gharial? We do not all have the luxury of running off for a week of lying about these days," Slate said coolly.

I looked away. It was so unlike Brass. Gharial was unhappily married and had only seen Brass a few times a year before. Those times had increased exponentially over the last month. Slate had no room to judge. Last time I asked, he had found his solace in the khoraz brothel in Thrimilci, specifically with a woman named Lynx.

"Judge all you want," Brass told him cavalierly.

Slate nocked up his strong clean-shaven jaw and looked down his nose at Brass. I reached out and brushed Brass's hand while he was distracted.

*... She can fuck her way out of any problem she may have. Do not tell me she is not fucking the Straumr boy. They are together every night until late. She has started sitting with him during classes as well as eating lunch with him. She fucked your grandfather. The woman has no line she would not double cross...*

"Have you caught his scent on her even once?" Brass asked. "Have you been following her? Is that how you know where she is at night?"

Slate's eyes tightened.

*... Do not defend her. Pewter and Siren have been reporting to me since you have been between the blonde's legs...*

"I would like to apologize to our future Guardians. Twenty-one years ago, we suffered a great tragedy. In my uncle's grief, he shut down our one way to prove those of you tried and true. I offer this biannual opportunity to those of you who wish to rectify his mistake."

Ash's caramel cheeks were flushed from the cold. He didn't wear a hat over his cropped espresso hair. Slate did have a point. Scarlett and he acted like a couple, but then if Moon and Reed had been a man and woman, they would've looked that way too.

Her caramel waves were curled and pinned back from her tan face; her brows were darker than her sun lightened hair. Her eyes were cool. Lush, full lips pressed gently together as she accessed the crowd. Her cheekbones were high and rounded when she smiled, which didn't happen anymore, above a narrow chin. Her turquoise eyes hitched over Brass and Slate.

*... Don't look at him. Don't look at him. Of course he's here. His brother is going to be tried and true. Surprised he can peel his cock out of that floozie long enough. Does he ask about our sons? No. Nothing. I made a mistake not them. Fiddlesticks. Don't think about my blood oath to Ash...*

I blinked and rubbed my fingertips to my temple. Brass arched a thick masculine brow at me.

"What do you have to say about that?" he asked.

I pulled my lips between my teeth and shook my head. "Say about *what?*" Silver asked, looking between us.

"Nothing," Brass and I said together and Silver leveled his chocolate gold-flecked eyes at me.

"Future Guardians, please ready yourselves," Ash said and lent Scarlett his elbow as they descended the stairs.

Slate turned around to watch her walk regally to the tents with Ash to change.

"Come on. We have to convince her not to run the course with Ash. She's family. She belongs with us," I urged.

Jett nodded and looked to Brass and Slate. "I have business elsewhere," Brass said stiffly, and Slate was caught up our little parade.

I gave Silver a kiss, he would stay back with Cherry when we went to speak with her.

Scarlett's thick white tent was fringed in gold next to Ash's whose was fringed in silver with matching stakes. The rich gold panels were closed when we approached and I pushed them aside as I walked in.

Scarlett lifted her head, pushing her hair from her face. She'd tossed her teal dress over a chair and was removing her boots. Slate followed in behind me with Jett on our heels. She pursed her full lips and banded her forearm across her breasts but made no other effort to move or hide herself.

Jett started apologizing profusely and turned to face the wall of the tent. Slate had obviously not seen her undressed in weeks. Her belly extended nearly as far as her breasts now. Her breasts were half again their original size and rested lightly on the top of her belly. She crossed her long lean legs.

"Indi, could you help me with my boots, please? I can't do anything with this gut." She sighed and ran her palm over the sphere of her belly.

Slate was kneeling at her feet before I could shift my body. He began unlacing her knee-high boots and rolled her thigh-high stockings down her leg. She looked down at the top of his head unspeaking.

"I want to protect my brother's bairn," Slate said flatly.

"I can protect myself, thank you. I'll be with three men as opposed to two. Two of which I trust with my life to protect me, and the other I trust will do as Ash tells him." She shifted her legs and Slate began on the other boot, he froze for an instant and began again.

Scarlett's lips curled as she looked down at him.

*... It's only a body. You've seen all of it many times before...*

"You do not need the Straumr boy's protection," Slate growled.

Scarlett rested her elbow on the armrest and ran her thumb under her chin, her forearm still placed over her chest. "They've quickened. Do you want to feel my sons kick? They've been especially active today," she asked, and Slate's face paled.

Scarlett laughed knowingly; it made me grimace as he slid her stocking off her pink painted toes. "I need to make sure whomever I'm with today is invested in my well-being. That's not you, there's nothing in it for you," she said icily.

"Silver and I will watch out for you, or Jett, Tawny, and Cherry," I told her.

She waved a hand dismissively. "Jett and Tawny have another pregnant woman to take care of. I won't burden them further. Ash, Sterling, and Sage are the strongest team that can offer me the most protection and support. It's not personal, it's business."

"Sage doesn't give a shit about you and Ash is only expressing interest because he's hoping you'll be grateful enough to sleep with him. Sterling might be the only one who is worth a damn, and that's because he's in love with Indi!" Jett shouted at the wall.

"I am invested in the lives of the bairn," Slate growled. "I would not want something to happen to you either."

Scarlett chuckled throatily. "How very *generous* of you. Thank you."

She got to her feet and Jett cursed leaving the tent. "You know where we'll be when you change your mind. We'll only have three so you can join us during the challenge if you want."

A frigid breeze streaked through the tent, but Scarlett wasn't affected by it. She let her arm fall as she walked to where her gear was on the table. She shifted the black scaled corset on the table. Intricate gold lacework matching her wrist blades and sheath stretched across the breast of the corset. It led to the dragon scale stomach that had a curve to it. Brass had gotten it for her birthday.

She cast a glance at Slate who, despite his obvious fury with her, had been taking in her curves. "I could use some help readying. If one of you doesn't mind helping me. Please."

Slate was there again picking up a black seamless thong and kneeling at her feet. She braced a hand on the table and I could see now how it would be hard for her to bend over, she'd have to bend sideways around her belly.

"Indi, you're staring," she said, smiling at me with none of the coolness she reserved for them two men in the room.

I smiled back. "You're pregnant."

She rubbed her bare belly biting down on her lower lip. "I know. Every morning I wake up in disbelief."

Slate raised her underwear to her hips and his hands stilled to the sides of her stomach. Her face went blank, and she held her breath. She banded an arm around her chest again and slowly turned her head to him.

*... Not that look. I know that scent. I'm not strong enough to deny him. Tender Slate gets me every time...*

"How are you, Scarlett?" he asked softly, running his palm over her skin.

I could almost see the walls being reinforced in front of my eyes around her heart. "Very pregnant and cranky if you must know. I want this challenge over, the next two weeks really so we can get the seventh piece from the Lycans and figure out how I'm going to get the last two from Canis." She slid her gaze to Slate, every bit the Prime's Second. "I only have five months left and twins tend to come early. I need to be carrying the Grar Dyr's son, the clock is ticking for us to save the world."

"Take the Ragnarök challenge in the summer," Slate said abruptly.

Scarlett's imperial gaze hung on Slate. "The Prime's Second needs to be a Guardian. This isn't a debate."

"You are my wife and you are with child. I am telling you to think of them first before your petty ambitions and the expectations of your lover." Slate had taken steps, so he loomed above her scowling down at her.

Her hand snapped out and grabbed his wrist bringing it to her stomach. She held firmly as she closed the distance between them, her belly pressing against him.

"Feel them then, *husband,*" she coaxed, only slightly mocking in her tone. "I've done more for you than you know. I'd do anything for you," she whispered.

Slate's tongue slid along his lower lip. "What have you done?" he rumbled.

*...What would you do tonight if I came to your bed? Fuck, she smells delectable...*

I felt like an intruder watching my sister with her estranged husband. I didn't want to leave though; I couldn't help but feel like she needed me. Her nude pregnant body didn't bother me in the least. I thought it was beautiful. We Guardians were immodest that way.

Scar's brow knit.

*... I can't tell you...*

"I'm going to stay in Ash's group. I don't think Sage will let anything happen to me while Ash is there to dictate to him." She released his wrists.

She was undeterred. Scar leaned over Slate's arm brushing her heavy chest over his bicep to pick up the corset.

"Do you need help?" Slate rumbled as if she had not just mentioned it.

"Yes," she said, handing Slate the corset and unabashedly raising her arms.

Slate moved behind her and began to lace the corset and she smiled ruefully at me as she adjusted her chest.

*... If Indigo was not here, I would bend her over that chair...*

He moved and began to buckle on the wrist blades.

"Are you having an affair with Ash?" Slate asked as he pulled her hair back over her shoulder.

"No," she answered simply.

"What aren't you telling us?" I asked in an even tone.

Scar's cleavage was pronounced in the tightly fastened corset. Slate couldn't seem to control the way his fingers traced along her collar bones. He knelt down with her black leather pants that had rectangular plates sewn over the front of her thighs.

*... I don't think he's ever dressed me before...*

"Good luck buttoning, I haven't seen my belly button in anything but a mirror," she said with a sigh.

"Do not dodge the question," Slate said.

Slate took Scarlett's hand, and she laced her fingers through his and the giant man started. She didn't acknowledge his surprise as he led her to the chair and he crouched in front of her to pull on her boots and buckle on black matte greaves.

"Ash asked me to consider being his second wife. He hasn't tried anything at all," she said leaning forward to try to take her blade belt from me, but I was frozen.

Slate hadn't moved. "What did you say?" he rumbled.

"I didn't say anything. I'm already married," she said, lifting her chin.

I grabbed her hand scanning her memories, and she tensed trying to yank back her arm.

"Let go," she said in a whisper.

I threw down her hand. "You didn't. Please gods, tell me you didn't, Scar."

Slate was watching me more upset than I'd ever seen him. Scarlett snatched the blade belt away, but stayed seated as she buckled it around her waist. She picked up her short seax as long as her forearm. Black handled carved into Freya and etched in gold, its black hand stitched scabbard had gold embossed wings and gold buckles. She clasped it around her right thigh.

Slate caught her chin and lifted it. "Explain yourself."

Her face was stony. "I swore a blood oath to spend three days after my sons are born during my first ovulation —"

"With Ash," Slate finished. "What did you get? Is that what you promised in return for becoming the first female Second?"

Her jaw clenched and her eyes blazed into two dark pits with burning hot coals in her sockets. She'd lost control of her anger, it happened more since she'd gotten pregnant.

"Get out," she ground through clenched teeth. "It was a mistake for you to come here."

Slate leaned forward and ran his palms over the scales of her stomach armor. "I will never let Brass's or my children be raised by that Straumr boy," Slate growled. "Tell him you will never be his second wife."

She leaned forward in her chair until her nose almost brushed his. The surrounding atmosphere seemed to charge with their chemistry. It was like he couldn't control his urges with her. He was supposed to be angry; he shouldn't have looked down her corset and stared at her lips. I couldn't ignore the bulge in his pants.

"Is the beast rattling in its cage? How does he feel seeing me heavy with pups?"

She reached her hand out and cupped him between his legs. A deep growl vibrated in Slate's broad chest.

*... Thank the Gods Indigo is here...*

*... Take her now...*

"As much as you loathe me, you are still drawn to me. You can't help yourself. Neither can I," she purred and reached for his hand.

Slate snarled like an animal and took two steps back. He looked at Scarlett like she was some kind of witch, casting a hex on him and hurried out of the tent.

She let her face fall into her hands. I rushed to her side and rubbed her back.

"Can I tell you a secret and you promise not to tell Quick?" she asked, her voice muffled by her hands.

"Of course," I said soothingly.

"I'm in love with Slate and with Brass, but Ash would only agree to remove the block on Slate's mind if I gave him an elemental child. Every time I see Slate I think this is the day, he'll get his memories back today. Every day I'm disappointed when he looks at me and I don't see love in his eyes. Ash told me it would take time. It's been three weeks." She sighed. "I slept with Spinel. I didn't know it was him. I thought his name was Balas, he never corrected me. Brass walked in on me in his room. You know I would never do anything to hurt Brass intentionally, don't you? I *never* would have slept with his grandfather."

She pulled her head up from her hands and her cheeks were damp, but still she gave a small smile. I hugged her, and she sniffled.

"I know." I couldn't believe she admitted to it. I realized I hadn't believed Brass until her confession. "Sterling will make sure you get through safely, so will Ash if he wants you back. Beware of Sage though, he wouldn't blatantly hurt you, but accidents happen every day." I told her stroking her hair.

"I'm drowning. I don't where the surface is anymore to find air and I'm flailing. I don't trust myself to make the right choices. I don't know who to trust. I feel so unbearably lonely, but there's always someone around —"

"Scarlett, my love. Are you ready?" Ash's deep cultured voice came from behind the panel and she started to wipe away her tears.

*My love?* I mouthed to her, and she gave me a self-deprecating smile.

"Just a minute," she called.

Old Scarlett was gone again. The one who fiercely loved and always fought for the right thing. Even if she wasn't sure what the right thing was.

It was wounded Scarlett. Show no weakness, bottle it all up, barrel through it, Scarlett. I couldn't believe this Scarlett had chosen Slate's memories over happiness. She should have let go of her pride and took a gamble on trying to win Slate back. She'd done it once; she could have done it again. The chemistry was there, it had been like a third body in the room with them.

Ash pushed open the panels as she clasped their mother's fur lined black cloak around her throat. Ash smiled when he saw me.

I aided Scarlett in buckling her black leather pauldrons with gold filigree buckles. She rose to her feet and gave Ash a lopsided grin.

He hadn't even waited to enter.

"You are ready. Indigo. Scarlett, we should be going," Ash said, and she nodded before pulling her hood up. She bent sideways to put a blade in each boot and straightened.

"Sage is ready whenever you two are." Sterling's rasping voice came through the tent just before he did and my breath caught.

We hadn't been so close since his father's funeral when I'd turned him down for the first time. Sterling's glossy chocolate hair was stylishly tousled, he was adjusting the belt over his broad chest so I only saw the top of his head. He was an even six feet, a couple inches shorter than Ash. His slanted brows rose above beautiful violet eyes, the same shade as his mother's, when he caught my scent. He was boyishly handsome with a pink pout and a straight nose. He didn't share many attributes with his cousin, Slate, but for his nose and those high chiseled cheekbones. Silver and Brass were also his cousins. They bore no resemblance whatsoever.

"Indi," he said in a rush. "Hi."

I swallowed. "Sterling." I tried for my most formal voice.

Scarlett saved me and crossed between us to break our locked gaze. "We're ready. Indigo has to go meet Slate and Quick now."

She slid her sorrowful gaze to me. If anyone knew what it was like to love two men, it was Scarlett. Her empathy was palpable.

"Activate your bond?" she asked, and I nodded *calling* to the elements so a blade of air cut my skin just above my laguz rune tattoo.

It activated my bond with her and Jett. I dabbed a little of my blood on the skin between her index finger and thumb where her kenaz rune was. Ours were in the same spot. She was anxious and exhausted, but under all of it was a crippling emotional pain. No wonder we hadn't activated the bond since we went to the Gorgon lands. She was so incredibly miserable.

"Are you coming to the wedding?" Sterling asked, breaking into my thoughts.

I blinked at him. Scarlett saved me again.

"I'll be coming, I'm not sure what my husband will be doing. You've got that thing, right Indi? Back in the States? I'm sorry Sterling, I asked her to make a run for me for the babies before Christmas even though we don't celebrate it here. I'd like one of those ornaments with the year. They only sell those for a limited time and I'm just so busy. I'll see you at the end of the race." She turned and embraced me tightly. "I'd wish you luck but I know you don't need it. I love you. Be careful," she said, and I mustered a smile for her before my eyes flickered back up to Sterling's.

"Sorry I won't be there." *Sorry, I'm not sorry.*

I'd rather die than watch him get married. I wouldn't expect him to come to mine and Silver's wedding. How could he expect me to?

"Tonight, though. I shall see you at the Tio's palace," Sterling said.

Ash was in the tent; couldn't Sterling at least pretend not to want to see me in front of his betrothed's brother? "It's my niece's Ausa Vatni. Silver and I will be there, of course. Good luck to you all. I'd better get going."

"Good luck, Indi." Sterling said placing a gloved hand on my padded cream jerkin.

It was the longest we'd gone without being together, but he had Diamond and I had Silver. Things had to change.

"Good luck, Sterling. Ash. Take care of my sister and her babies," I said looking into Sterling's violet eyes.

"I promise I will," Sterling said solemnly, and Scarlett nudged me from the tent.

*... Freya's burly boar, Indi. He might as well be wearing a sign shouting out how much he misses you. Don't get sucked in. Your future lies with Quick, nothing good will come from giving in now. The day after tomorrow he'll be married...*

That was sobering.

CHAPTER

# TWO

Every member of my family that wasn't competing in the Ragnarök was sitting in the heated stadium seats watching us with bated breath.

My half-brother was doing his best to pretend as if I didn't exist, but that was nothing new. Sage was tall with a wiry kind of strength like our uncle Jackal. He was his mother's son with big round blue eyes, ivory skin, full pouty lips and his blonde hair was slicked back in an undercut. Only Natts and Vars had that blonde hair. Only Vars and Hausts were as tall as he was in Tidings.

The men were dressed as I was, fitted pants tucked into fur-lined boots, thick fur-lined cloaks, greaves, pauldrons, and bracers. They each wore leather armor over their padded jerkins and supple gloves. Ash specialized in long seaxes that were strapped to his back. Sterling held a black spear with three more short spears on his back. Sage had a crossbow, bolts on one hip, and a battle axe on his other.

I only wore a cloak over my armored corset. I wouldn't feel the cold because of my elemental powers. Jett had activated his bond; he was

30

strong and focused. I drew strength from him. My silver haired uncle, Hawk, sat with Sparrow, Gypsum, and Pearl in the front row. My copper haired grandmother, who didn't look a day over fifty, gave me a nod. Pearl's emerald eyes glittered against her deep tanned face.

Steel had to stay on the platform as the Vetr representative with Quartzite. He was in full ambassador mode. His dirty blonde hair was carelessly styled, his tan cheeks flushed from the cold as he spoke to the curvy blonde. Steel could have been my brother, he looked so much like Jett and I and was only four years older. A rare late pregnancy. They happened, but the chances were minuscule unless you were a Geol descendent, so I was told. Guardians usually lost fertility sometime after their twenty-fifth year.

Brass sat with Spinel, Spinel's date, and his brother Coyote. Brass looked just like his handsome grandfather, but with Quick's short stylish hair and olive coloring. The front of Coyote's shoulder length dark hair was pulled back like Brass used to wear it. His espresso eyes were intense the times we had spoken. His son's Ausa Vatni was the first time I'd met him. His wife was one of my many red headed Tio-Rot distant cousins. Butterfly happened to teach Tribal Relations at Valla University for the Mastery of Guardians.

After the challenge, I'd no longer be a tyro there. I'd be a Guardian. Second to the Prime. I was the wife to the Dagr Patriarch and the delegate for the Grand Mistress of the Shadow Breakers.

My first wedding anniversary was in a few days and I was desperately trying not to hope that Slate would have his memories back by then.

Ash put his hand to my back. It was the first time the Prime and his Second would be running the Ragnarök course together. We were history in the making.

Behind us was Jett, Tawny, and Cherry. My brother's wife was as pregnant as I was, but with only one baby. Thus her tall slender frame wasn't as round as mine. In the last few weeks, my belly had popped. Cerise Kaldr had long raven hair like her wife, Amethyst Geol, my brother's *other* wife. Amethyst was mocha skinned with big dark exotic eyes and a wide mouth, while Cherry was fair skinned with cobalt almond eyes and full red stained lips. The polygamist trio had one daughter and a son on the way. It was their daughter's

Ausa Vatni tonight, a baptismal of sorts where Gigi would get her name.

Tawny's wide mouth smiled. Her big hazel eyes were sad. No one was happy about my choice in teams. Her thick arched brows bunched above her petite nose. I could tell she wanted to say something to me but couldn't with Ash there. She was the Matriarch Vetr and ruler of Elivagar, the island of perpetual winter since her grandfather died. Her true father had been Orion Vetr's only son. Hawk was her father in everything, but blood and her sire had made no difference to her brother Gypsum.

Gypsum would be inducted into Valla U this year. My chief. As tall as Steel's six feet, but more muscled. He'd started wearing copper beads threaded through his long raven locks like Slate. While Tawny was porcelain skinned as her my nineteen-year-old cousin was darker featured with had big puppy dog eyes and a killer smile complete with deep dimpled cheeks. Gypsum was heir to the Sumar family and all of Thrimilci, the island of perpetual summer. He was also having an affair with Diamond Natt while seeing Rosasite. Both girls knew about there was another girl just not who. He was nothing if not honest. He'd fallen in love with Diamond within two weeks of having moved from Chicago when our family revealed this whole other world to us.

Jett's tan, chiseled jaw was clenched, so the muscles leapt. He looked over his shoulder at the group behind them. Slate, Quick, and Indigo were the third group to go into the Ragnarök.

Indigo had held her own in the tent. Sterling and I had spoken more since I was spending so much time with Ash. He wasn't a bad guy, but he was traditional Guardian to the core. Marriage contracts, paramours, birthing as many kids as possible before you lost your fertility. He didn't come right out and say it, but he danced around having an elemental in his family line. Not with me of course, he didn't have to specify.

Indi was looking especially beautiful as of late. Quick made her happy, endorphins seemed to float around the air around her like fuzzy dandelion seeds. Her long corn silk hair had been tucked into her beige cloak, her cornflower blue eyes were always bright, and the beauty mark on her tan right cheek lifted when she smiled. Which she did often with pretty pink lips. She was classically beautiful and kind. The only reason she'd been single for so long was because our father misled others into believing she was adopted so his wife wouldn't know she was our mother's daughter. Sterling would've been walking down the aisle with her tomorrow if he'd known she was a true greater family daughter and a water elemental to boot. In that way, Sterling was a traditional Guardian. He never would have married for love.

I looked to Slate. Every time I looked at him I wondered if *this* was the time. That unconditional love that I'd taken for granted, I hadn't even understood what it was until it was gone. He'd never told me he loved me, but he had with his actions.

An alphorn blew once, long and low, and my stomach twisted. It had begun. I held no delusions of what Ash and Sage wanted. I was to be my best self and not to hinder them. Ash wanted to finish with the shortest time and I was not to hold them back no matter how kind Ash had been to me since becoming his Second, I would have to suck it up.

I took a shuddering breath, letting the cold air fill my lungs and felt my body's heat warm it.

"Better you stay in front of me," Sterling said, placing a hand on the small of my back.

I nodded absently and followed Ash and Sage into the tree line. It wasn't supposed to be like this, Brass was supposed to be the one who cared the most about our children, not Ash. I pulled up the reversible cloak that belonged to my mother and trotted behind them.

We were at the top of one of the many Frostfell Mountains that crested Elivagar. The Crathode caverns were the closest tribe. The half crustacean hybrids were one of the most volatile tribes in Tidings. Sage stopped at a fork in the snow crusted path. Pine and spruce trees, so thick I couldn't see past them, hid the twists and turns of the narrow paths.

As we approached a carved rock materialized.

"From a time when elementals were commonplace," Ash said, admiring the powerful *calling* abilities of Guardians long past.

"Elementals and Leshys," I commented, and Sterling grunted behind me.

The Leshys were the ones who made the first Guardian at the behest of Mother Nature. We were her Guardians. What she gave, she could take away. Two powerful Guardians that had been married, Storm Natt and Wind Dagr were the Romeo and Juliet of Tidings. He had become too powerful and to stop him, so Wind sacrificed herself. Storm saw what he'd created, what his love had died for and killed himself. Mother Nature took away our ability to become elementals. Indigo and I were the first elementals to be born in centuries.

"It is in Bjorn, the bear hybrids. It says to take the right fork, but first we must make a flash in fire. Silver or gold," Sage said in his honeyed cultured voice.

My half-brother had taken an instant disliking to me because of my mother's affair with our father. He didn't care that Guardian politics was all that kept them apart. Alder had loved my mother. He'd said her name with his dying breath. Our great uncle Canis had wanted to marry Pearl, but she chose our grandfather Flint Sumar instead. Canis never forgot her or the slight. Vars and Sumars never got along again. Orion Vetr and his family were the most prominent family in Tidings at the time. Delta Natt was his daughter. Our grandfather, Cygnus, had chosen the most advantageous marriage for his son.

Then the Red King massacre occurred and Tidings had been rife with suspicion. Most of the Crathode responsible were imprisoned, but the old jarl Moon Straumr had shut down the portals and the islands had been divided ever since. The year before Amethyst became old enough to go to Valla U, Moon reopened the university and marriage contracts became the hottest commodity. There weren't enough ambassadors, not as many children had been born. Guardians were a dying breed and my generation had to rebuild, reestablish bonds. Ash and I were working hard to that end.

"Here. Iron filings make gold sparks," I told them, detaching one of my links of my corset skirt.

I watched as Ash filed it down and sent it into Sterling's flames that flickered from his outstretched hand. Gold sparks crackled before dissipating and Sterling's lips quirked.

We trotted down the right path, snow crunching beneath our boots and we reached our first red flag. Ash plucked it from its stake and it evaporated.

"One down, nineteen to go. It is an ice field," Ash said, taking a careful step on the thick ice.

A frozen lake stretched before us. I looked for the catch. It was a time waster.

"Grab hold of one another. We can use air to blow us across the field," I said, taking a tentative step onto the ice.

Ash wrapped an arm around my back, Sterling took my arm and Sage held onto Ash's shoulder. I *called*. A bit of water helped speed us along and another flag appeared when we stepped onto the snow.

"Well done, Scarlett," Ash said, gesturing to the flag.

I felt a burst of pride and grabbed the flag. It was thick with stiff red threads and then it melted in my hands. A roar broke through my amazement and Sterling grabbed my elbow, yanking me back.

A seven-foot-tall grizzly bear hybrid appeared two feet from where I'd been standing and swiped at the air with a sharp claw. He wore long woolen tunics with cinched billowing pants and shoes that curled at the toe. His body was like that of a man but covered in thick brown fur. His human like eyes were savage in its furred face. Twenty more appeared behind it and fanned out. Polar, black, and even panda bears came charging at us.

I sprung my wrist blades as Ash *called* ice spikes that punctured into the Bjorn. Sage's cross bolts found human eyes and hearts one after another. I threw the blades from my belt over Sterling's shoulder and took a step back when he jabbed a Bjorn who had gotten too close with his spear. Sterling's violet eyes looked me over when the last Bjorn faded.

"You are good with those blades. Better than I would have suspected," Sterling said. "I have seen you compete at the Crash Course so I knew you were capable."

I collected my blades as Sage picked up his bolts. "When I need to think clearly or need distraction, I train. I've needed to train a lot since I've moved here," I told him, sliding my clean daggers back into my belt.

"This has been too easy by far," Sage said, starting back on the path that curved behind more trees from the ice field and picking up a red flag.

"You are never supposed to say such things. Now it will get harder," Sterling said with a boyish smile.

Sage shot him an irritated glance over his shoulder and his frosty blue eyes slid over me as if he just remembered I was there. At the end of the path, I groaned.

"Will you be able to climb with your belly?" Sterling asked.

I looked up the solid wall of ice to the winter storm brewing in the grey skies that painfully reminded me of Slate. "Yes. I can go first and create holds with my heat."

Sterling picked up the next flag and I watched it disappear. Ash looked to Sage and arched his brow. Sage gave me an irritated look.

"The wall is wide enough to save time all going at once," he said in his musical tone.

It was uncomfortable climbing straight up the ice, unable to flatten myself against it, but my fingers could get so hot it molded like dough to the shape of my hands making it easy to climb. For once, a break. Unfortunately, my awkward pose and extra weight made my legs feel strained on the long climb.

Ash lent me a hand when we reached the top and stood on the narrow lip of the cliff. A wall of trees stood before us. I cursed the Gods.

"Hope your arms are not tired yet," Ash said with a small knowing smile.

Ash lifted me onto the lowest hanging branch and I was on my own from there. I wished I'd worn gloves. I hadn't needed them, but now my palms were scraped from the bark and sore from lifting my weight. There was no clear path to the top, and the branches grew thinner the closer we got to the top.

The men's weapons kept getting snagged on the branches and curses rang around me. Pine needles bit into my cheeks when I slipped, scraping bark away and twisted so I would hit the branch on my hip instead of my stomach. I took steadying breaths and started again.

When I reached the top, I could *feel* Ash's anxiety with my empath abilities. He wanted to be going faster. The flag in Sage's hand was already fading. No healing was allowed until we finished the course and my muscles were already aching. Sterling and I spotted a boulder carved with words manifesting behind Sage.

I smiled at the words. I couldn't speak it, but I could read it.

"It's Aves. We take the path left after we collect black berries," I stated.

We picked up our pace trotting instead of walking until we came to a low six-inch-high bush between the trees with glossy black berries and a woody stem. I bent down and collected the berries and passed a handful to each man. Sage held his palm up as if he didn't want our skin to touch even though he wore leather gloves.

"Excellent. Well done." Sterling patted my shoulder.

We continued down the path to a river with a thin layer of ice over it. We wouldn't be sliding across it. Sterling placed a boot on the ice and it cracked beneath it. I picked up the red flag and felt the weight disappear from my hand.

"We will reinforce the ice and go across," Ash stated, and began *calling*.

Sterling, Sage, and I stepped alongside him and watched the river slow beneath the ice as it thickened. "We can use the same tactic as the last one," Sterling said, and I nodded.

The ice cracked around where we hadn't reinforced it and I staggered. Ash grabbed my elbow as he hurried across the ice in time for us to watch the ice we'd just walked over break apart and be swept away by the river. I kept watching as the river froze over again. The Ragnarök was like the Crash Course.

Another flag.

Ash read a Faunelle cipher, and we went right again. There was another flag and then one single tall tree.

"I hate trees," I whispered. "We each need to grow a tree."

Ash patted me on the back and gave me a boost under my arms like a child. "Take this one and grow it while you are on."

"Thanks," I said gratefully as the men began to collect seeds in order to grow a tree for each of them against the icy wall.

My tree was thinner and grew on an angle towards a frozen ledge above us. I grew it slowly so I wouldn't overexert my energy. Ash reached the top first and helped me up after having grown his tree at neck break speed. Sage and Sterling came up after and pulled the flag off the wall. The path along the cliff was only two feet wide high above a crevasse.

We didn't bother discussing it. Sage started with his back against the iced wall. Ash went next, and I followed with Sterling behind me. Wind ripped at our cloaks and I kept having to brace my feet so I wasn't pulled off the side. It whistled in my ears, biting at my cheeks and not for the first time, I was glad I didn't feel the brunt of the cold.

The cliff ledge opened up so there was a five-foot spot to stand and an engraving appeared next to the flag. Sterling took the flag and read the words. I stood in front of the circular gap in the cliff and frowned. I didn't think I needed to hear what Sterling read.

"Centaur. It says down the hole we go." He let out a breath and readied his spear. "Be ready for anything."

Sage went down first sitting on the ice and he disappeared into the dark. Ash went next lifting the pommel of his sword and letting it fall back into its scabbard. I sat on the ground and gave myself a shove. I slid about a dozen feet before I hit the floor I couldn't see a single thing in the pitch black. The ground was freezing beneath my fingers and I stepped to the side so Sterling wouldn't bowl me over.

Sage cursed when I bumped into him. "I'm sorry," I stammered and my body involuntarily shivered at the skittering sound in the dark around us.

I punched Sage once when he'd insulted my mother and me, but I had never touched him so much before. His fingers knocked my hands away like he was flicking away lint and I stepped back. Sterling's boot hit my leg, and I fell. Sterling grunted when my weight landed on him.

Ash pulled me up from around my waist and spun me so my nose rubbed against the leather of his armored chest. "Careful," he said. "Do you mind?" he asked.

I flared to life and screamed.

Jorogumo would always terrify me after they'd attacked me so many times. A pasty face with black shiny pinchers and six black eyes along its brow as its screeching rattle sounded inches from my nose. The spider hybrids swarmed over us. Some with only human heads on enormous spidery bodies, others had human torsos and faces, but all had pinchers and spindly legs.

I reacted on instinct and sprung my blade punching through the top of its head with a sickening thunk. Ash knocked me back and flames shot from my hands. The Jorogumo shrieks pierced my ears, and I cringed. Ash had pulled his long seaxes and slid through legs and torsos like a deadly dance.

Sage used his battle axe to chop and hack apart Jorogumo with impunity while Sterling stabbed with his spear keeping any from getting close to me. We worked surprisingly well as a team.

We were panting when the last Jorogumo faded and I used my

elemental light as a torch. My skin glowed red just below the surface offering enough illumination for us to see. Sage turned to take me in and sniffed before leaning over the edge.

Ice pedestals spanned into the darkness with no end in sight, but we couldn't see far. "I'll send globes of light out around us so no fire touches the ice and makes those things slick," I said, looking down to where the thin pedestals origin disappeared completely below.

I *called* four globes of light and sent them out in a diamond shape around us and took the first step. Each ice pedestal had enough space for a single foot.

I balanced my weight on a boot and wobbled. My legs felt weak from all the climbing and my center of gravity was off. Frost slid off the pedestal to be swallowed by the abyss and my stomach turned. I held onto my *calling* and taking each perilous pedestal at a time. When I took the final jerky step to the other side of the cavern, my body with stiff form the tension.

Ash grabbed my wrist to steady me while Sage was already picking up the flag and using one of my globes of light to read a carving on the frozen wall. "Anguillan. There is a tunnel."

We looked both ways and saw that off to the right, the wall curved. Ash's caramel cheeks were red in the white light of my globes. Sterling and Sage's nostrils flared with shallow freezing breaths. A chill seeped into me. I flared my elemental fire to life, knowing none of them would ever ask, and positioned myself to walk at the center of their three points. I thought I heard Sterling sigh as feeling returned to his fingers.

The wall curved into a tunnel that led down and around the outside of the mountain. The roar of the rapids echoed to reach us before we saw it. A flag waited for us on the frozen shore. Across the raging waters was another flag.

There weren't any trees to help us float across, the water moved too quickly to freeze and it was too deep to try to stop. "We are going to have to swim across." Sterling began to secure weapons to his person.

I took off my cloak so the waters wouldn't yank me under and tied it bulkily around my waist.

"I will go first, then Scarlett."

Sterling stepped into the water and staggered back even with the spear embedded in the river bed. He stretched his arm out for me and I was knocked back from the force of the water and my head went under. Freezing water flooded my mouth.

I had waited for hours for my mother to complete the Ragnarök. She didn't have a team to run the course with. She'd had to leave Valla U when she became pregnant with Jett. It was the first time I realized how powerful I was. It was how Orion found out that Sparrow and Tawny were still alive. That they hadn't died with his son, Ridge, out on the foothills of Valla.

So much had happened in the two years since we moved to Tidings. My parents had been murdered. That was what stuck out most in my mind. Ama and Shale had been killed in the capture and rescue of Slate. I'd lost Slate and my baby after I was almost murdered by the Stygian Knights. They were the ones responsible for the bounty placed on my head.

They'd captured me the night they'd killed my father. The next day I was delivered as payment to the Merfolk and drugged with rousen which prevented all thought, but that of pleasure. Giving and receiving it. Four days later, my family rescued me.

The clean-shaven masked man had never been captured, but Pepper and Spear, the Mint twins, had been until they took over Karkinos. They had imprisoned Slate on the back of the crab until Brass, Quick, Shale, Indi, and I freed him. Shale had died. Quick had nearly died, but I managed to heal them. Slate had eaten the head off of Spearmint. Pepper was still out there and had likely joined the few Stygians who had escaped the earlier raid I'd orchestrated with the help of Brass, Cordillera, and Moon. That was also the night I left Slate and moved back to Chicago.

His true ancestry had come out. He needed to propagate the Dagr line, and the Merfolk had left me incapable of conceiving. Little did I know that I just needed time to heal. By the time I had discovered I could have children again, Slate had married in a hand-fasting ceremony to Amber Lodda. We had a fling of sorts on a mission for the Shadow Breakers in Mabon.

Brass had been waiting for us with Amber on our return. Amber had found out she was pregnant and knew he'd been with someone else that night. Brass came to live with me in Chicago to make sure I was okay. The attraction I always felt towards him blossomed into something special. Slate had my heart, but I'd fallen in love with Brass, too. Then we'd found out I was pregnant with his twin boys.

I couldn't be with Brass while Slate memories hadn't returned. He'd come back from Karkinos that way. Slate had no recollection of our time together. Two years had been wiped from his mind and all of me.

Brass and Slate had come to me offering to make Brass my second husband and freeing Slate from martial responsibilities though he planned on having me carry his heir. If I married Brass and Slate got his memories back, there was no way to undo what had been done. I'd already gotten in too deep with them.

I wanted my Slate back. If he was okay with Brass being my second husband, we could address it then. My flesh was weak. Slate wanted my body and Brass had wanted everything. Slate had woken up after Ash removed the mental block and, I could admit, it looked sketchy. Then I discovered Balas was Spinel, Spinel was Brass's grandfather. I'd had two love filled nights with Brass's grandfather.

Now I had no one.

Sterling's grasp on my arm slipped, and I unfurled my fingers releasing him. I shut my eyes. I loved the water — always had. I never wanted any of it. I had been pushed through school by my mother. I had a bachelor's degree in fine arts and I'd done nothing with it. I wanted to have a boyfriend, get married, have kids. For my mother to be a grand-mother and bake cookies with my children like she'd done with me.

None of it would happen now.

Except for the kids. My mother and father may have died, and I had lost the men I loved, but I would have my sons. *My sons.*

I *called* a bubble of air over my mouth so I could breathe. Sterling's fingers were joined by another hand with a firmer hold and I felt us moving sideways across the river.

My boots only grazed the icy bottom. I couldn't straighten myself. My hand hit the biting air when Sterling dragged me out of the water. I fell onto my back and coughed up ice water. My wet skin prickled, and a hand pushed my hair from my face.

"What was that, Scarlett? Are you trying to get yourself killed?" Ash shouted at me.

"We should have teamed with Hunter," Sage said snidely, and Ash shot him a look over his shoulder.

Droplets from Ash's face splattered on mine and he yanked me to my feet. Sterling was drying himself off and Sage pulled down the flag. Ash lifted my tucked chin.

"Come. Only five more obstacles left. We will discuss this later."

His piercing light green eyes scanned mine, and I nodded, swallowing hard. Sterling took me under the elbow and pulled me close.

"Indi would never forgive me if you were injured or worse. You have survived too much to give up now," he whispered, but I could only nod in response.

Sterling released my arm and fell in behind me. Sage and Ash picked up their pace, and I dried myself clasping my damp cloak around my throat again. I'd been ready to give up. Part of me wished they'd left me to drown.

I placed my palm to the cool scaled armor over my stomach hoping I hadn't done my sons any harm. They were all that kept me going.

The path was leading back down the mountain to where our families waited for us. We'd been going through the Ragnarök for hours. Five hours was the average time, and we were doing extremely well despite my attempt to drown myself. I could tell the men were tired. Their steps weren't as sure and shoulders not as straight. We'd all take a nap before the Ausa Vatni.

Our peaceful jog lasted only an instant. Gorgons slithered out from the solid rock wall on the narrow path. Their undulating movements weren't as bad as the Jorogumo but sent shivers up my spine. I used my *calling* to send up spikes of rock into the sleek scaled bodies. The snake hybrids coiled and sprung trying to sink long pointed fangs into our skin. Venom flew through the air aimed at bleeding wounds that riddled our skin.

When the last Gorgon fell, I leaned against the rock wall. "There's something wrong about killing the tribespeople. Don't you think?"

My damp hair had frozen. It cracked around my head as I looked at the three men. Sage's fair face pinched.

"This coming from the girl kidnapped by the Merfolk? Perhaps you did not wish to be rescued. Those of us who have lived with the volatile tribes on our islands know they need a firm hand."

Ash ignored his jibe pulling the red flag off the wall as I shot daggers at Sage. "We need to hurry."

I trudged behind them to the end of the rocks and I cringed. There was only the climb down. We didn't have ropes to tie us to one another. We'd be hanging by our finger tips on the way down.

Sage swung himself over the edge and lowered his body down, the scrape of his boots on the rock, sending snow and dust into the wind.

Ash turned to me and caught my chin again. "Ignore Sage. He hates your family, that will never change."

"I don't blame him," I said.

"Sterling," Ash said without taking his eyes off me.

Sterling licked his chapped lips and gave me another look before climbing over the side. "Do not be long," he said in a low voice and disappeared below.

I gave Ash a curious look. "What is it?"

"I apologize if my treatment of you led to what you did in the river."

I sucked in a deep fortifying breath. "You haven't helped in the past, but nothing you've directly done besides said cruel words has made a significant impact. It's not you, Ash. We've been working really well together. I... had a moment of weakness. It won't happen again."

"I had no idea you were in such a fragile state, Scarlett," he said in a soothing tone.

I nearly laughed. Masking my constant vulnerability felt like a failing mission, but I'd done better than I hoped.

"I will take care of you, as I always should have," Ash said and ran his thumb down my cheek.

"When Slate gets his memories back, he'll take care of me. It's just hard waiting for that to happen," I confessed and stepped away from Ash.

Ash let his hand fall and I slung my legs over the edge of the rock lowering myself down. My life would only be ridiculously complicated if I gave into Ash's heartfelt apologies and sweet promises. As if I didn't know that so much of Tidings thought I'd slept my way into my position.

My whole body shook from the effort of the climb. There wasn't a muscle on my body that wasn't sore. My hands were raw and cramped from the stone. Hot tears of frustration at the awkwardness my pregnant belly posed as I made the descent steamed down my cheeks. Sterling had pulled the flag. Three left.

I was simmering with my elemental ability. Our clothes had frozen stiff and made moving rigid and clumsy. The heat my body radiated appeared to improve their moods as we went down the path until we reached another fork in the road.

"It's Wemic. Take the right path, they're winding us back around to the stadium," I explained, and trotted two by two until we reached the woods again.

I pulled the flag off a spruce and smiled. *Two left.*

Sage took a step forward and I could hear the whistle, smell the water. I jumped forward and yanked him back by his shoulder, but the ice spike caught his arm as it swung out to maintain balance and he sucked in a sharp breath of air. Suddenly, the woods became a gauntlet of impaling ice spikes.

"Run!" Sterling shouted.

The four of us divided and ran for safety jumping and dodging the sharp icicles. They caught in our cloaks, we felt them slice through our cheeks. I felt them snag in my hair that whipped out behind me. Sterling was caught by an ice spike so hard it spun him around. I barreled into him guarding my stomach and *called* air to roll us. Sterling used our momentum to push me back up, and he leapt to his feet beside me. Ash and Sage were ahead of us and had broken through a line of trees that separated us from the ice spikes.

Sterling and I were panting when we reached them. Sage gave me a cool eyed gaze, and I straightened. Sterling gave my shoulder a pat and exhaled heavily as he pulled down the red flag.

*One left.*

Forms materialized around us. They took the shape of the Crathode. Red and brown, some blue. All different kinds of crustaceans with beady eyes and giant razor-sharp claws. Their hard chitin exoskeletons were crusted and blotchy on their towering bodies as they closed in around us. I shifted into my elemental form, hair writhed around my head flames licked over my skin, and any Crathode that came close sizzled.

Sterling's spear found the gaps in their exoskeletons bringing the great tribesmen to their multiple knees. Ash's seaxes split heads from bodies, and Sage was just as deadly with his battle axe. I sprung my blades winking out my fire as we were pushed back-to-back in a tight circle. Blades flashed as snow began to fall. Sparks flew as claws caught on Sterling's spear tip.

Greater families were known for their breeding and politics, how strong we were in *calling*, but not our fighting abilities. Ash, Sterling, and Sage were extraordinary warriors, and I was proud that I more than held my own with them.

The last Crathode hadn't finished collapsing before Ash was picking up the final flag and grabbing my hand.

"We walk out together. The Prime and his Second. Head held high, smile, and look beautiful, as always." Ash said scanning my face and appearance and making small adjustments. "Curl your hair," he ordered, and I used hot air to twist my hair into big loose coils while he rubbed at my skin. "Good," he said and smiled.

He made me feel like a filthy child who'd been out playing in the mud. Luckily, he hadn't licked his finger before cleaning my face. Sterling stood opposite Ash at my side. I wanted to curl up on the snow-covered ground and go to sleep.

"We walk out, not run," Ash said, placing his hand at the back of my neck and we walked into the trees.

CHAPTER

# THREE

The stadium cheered when we stepped out of the trees. The Prime and his Second with the Haust patriarch and a Var son. Ash took my hand and raised it between us. The motion made me want to wince. My arms had been sliced by the ice spikes and raising my arm had made the cuts burn.

"We go into our private tents. No first aide for you or me," Ash said through his perfect smiling teeth and he *called* to check on the babies, healing me in the process so no one would know.

I did the same for him through our clasped hands. Ash was much better at the politics of Tidings than I was. Instead of letting our families greet us, Ash held my hand and led me to our tents beside the platform while Sage and Sterling went into the first tents for the care of the other Guardians.

*Guardians.* I was finally a Guardian.

Inside my warm tent, I started to struggle out of my clothing. I couldn't reach the back of my corset and had a rage quit. I sank down

46

into the wooden chair and choked on a sniffle. I swiped my tears from my cheeks and just breathed. I gasped as the panel to my tent opened.

"We should have made sure you had attendants. *Ah*, well. You learn."

Ash was wearing what he had before the course. His thick black sleeveless robe with its gold and silver trim that dusted the floors hung off his shoulders over his black leather jerkin with silver crescent buckles down the front. He crouched at my feet and took off my boots, setting aside my blades.

"Ash, you can get someone else to help me," I protested, leaning forward to knock away his hands.

He caught my wrists. "No one else will see you in a weakened state. Your husband will not support you; you will not take another. I have seen you weak, I have seen you undressed. We must hurry, if I know your brother, he shall be out soon."

"You saw me when we were together, not in over a year," I told him, shaking my head. "We're both married now."

"I am not making a request," he said sternly, and lifted me to my feet.

He spun me around by my shoulders and removed my cloak before he began to unfasten my corset. I was unbuckling my short seax, wrist blades, and belt until the corset fell free and I covered myself with my hands. Ash leaned past me and picked up my dress. A thin champagne dress went over my layers of petticoats in the Elivagar style. I didn't turn around as Ash helped me step out of my pants and pulled up my skirts, laced my corset, then helped me get the dress over my head.

I cleared my throat. "Thanks. I've got it from here."

"I will leave when you do. Time is of the essence, my love," Ash said, picking up my underwear and thigh highs.

"I can do that," I said, snatching away my panties and then made a joke of myself as I tried to wriggle into them.

Ash held up my skirts so I could pull them up and I gave in to him helping me with the stockings. He laced up my boots while he was down there and buckled on my short seax with lithe fingers.

"Is Quartz going to dump a drink in my face again because you've seen me undressed?" I asked.

Ash raised his eyes to mine as he laced my boots. "Quartz knows I have asked you to join our marriage. She prefers that we court publicly, so a scandal is avoided."

"You told her? Does she know about the rest of it?" I asked, fidgeting.

"Of course. I am not ashamed and it is smart for our family to have an elemental in our line."

He helped me stand again, and I held out my arms to slip on my paisley embossed teal velvet dress that was trimmed with a long brown fur. It was a gorgeous dress that Ash had chosen for the occasion. He had always enjoyed playing dress up with me.

Ash buttoned the crystal buttons up the length of my gown so the champagne skirts underneath peeked from the center split and at the plunging neckline. He slipped my Tio robe over my shoulders, and I crossed the room to put my jewelry back on. My oval emerald wedding ring with diamond arches around the stone, a diamond solar cross ring for the Dagr sigil, my silver Yggdrasil necklace, and silver torque. I never took off my silver chain of stone pieces that I tucked into my dress. I put on emerald drop earrings and ran my fingers through my loose light golden-brown curls.

A few swipes of mascara and a light pink lip gloss, I turned to face Ash ready to greet the newest Guardians. "Do I pass inspection, Prime?" I asked teasingly.

Ash was always in control. He knew how to manipulate people so you would give him what he wanted and think it was your idea all the while. He played politics better than anyone else our age. Only when it came to me had I ever seen him lose his self-possession. I had that effect on people.

Ash closed the distance between us grabbing the hair at my nape as he brought his lips just above mine. He looked down through lowered lids at me and I took in a slow breath.

"You have always had such a smart mouth, Scarlett."

"I'm still married," I whispered.

Ash's eyes flitted between mine and he loosened his fingers letting them comb through my hair. "We need to award our newest Guardians."

He offered me his palm, and I took it. He looped his arm through mine and we exited the tent. Sage and Sterling left the aide tents at the same time and followed us up to the platform. Steel and Quartz were there to greet us and we embraced each one in turn. A pedestal with a leather bound box waited for us and Ash stood in front of the podium.

I picked up the braided gold torque and stood before Ash. "Be strong when you are weak, be brave when you are scared, be humble when you are victorious. Congratulations, Ash Straumr. You are Mother Nature's Guardian."

I leaned forward and took Ash's wrist and put the golden torque on it. I kissed him on both cheeks. He plucked a torque from the box and lifted my wrist.

"Be strong when you are weak, be brave when you are scared, be humble when you are victorious. Congratulations, Scarlett Tio. You are Mother Nature's Guardian," he said, and I couldn't help the ridiculous smile that lit my face.

I shifted to stand behind him next to the pedestal. Sage was first. I handed Ash the torque, and he put it on Sage's wrist and clasped his forearm. I wouldn't clasp his forearm; I would kiss him on both cheeks as I had Ash. That was what we had decided on when we planned out the ceremony. Sterling was next.

Jett, Tawny, and Cherry had come through the woods while we were giving Sterling and Sage their torques. The urge to jump off the platform and check on them was overwhelming.

At first glance, Cherry looked worse for wear. Jett was carrying her in, but it looked to be from exhaustion, not an injury. Slate, Quick, and Indi were out of the tree line before Jett and the others had gone into the tents. Aside from superficial wounds, Quick was limping until they passed the point where they could receive healing and then he was walking right again. Indi looked for me on stage and gave me a little wave, I smiled back. Slate's grey stormy eyes skimmed me before he pushed into the aide tent.

Only Ash and I had the privilege of cleaning and changing before we exchanged torques. Slate was the first one to reach us. Ash put the torque on his wrist and had to grasp his forearm as he'd done with the other men. I swallowed and kissed him on the hard planes of his cheeks.

"Congratulations, Slate," I whispered.

"You changed," he rumbled and gave Ash a sidelong glance before walking off the stage.

He hadn't even asked how I was doing.

A hundred new Guardians crossed the stage. The last team took seven hours to complete the course, almost double the length it'd taken our team. Once the last Guardian crossed the stage, I said goodbye to Ash and wandered over to where my family was gathered. I was finally able to hug them as much as I wanted, which was a lot.

Then I started crying.

The day had been long and emotional for me.

Hawk's dark eyes caught my wobbly chin and embraced me, pulling me tight against his lean dancer's form. His dark trimmed goatee brushed my forehead as he soothed me.

"Wren would be so proud of you," he whispered.

I could smell the mint on his skin, he'd styled his prematurely silver hair as his father had in a pompadour away from his olive face. I buried my face in his shoulder as he stroked my hair. I couldn't find my voice. I missed my mother. I *always* missed my mother, but it was stronger than the usual dull ache.

Families had already begun to leave the stadium. Only a quarter of the stands were filled. We were to go back to the palace and get ready for Gigi's Ausa Vatni — *Opal's* Ausa Vatni. The day wasn't over yet. There would be a feast and dancing before the children born to the Tios and Jett were given their names.

I lifted my head looking for Indigo. Quick held her in his big arms making her look like a child. Today would be hard for her too. She'd been raised with Delta as her adopted mother, but since Delta found out our mother had birthed her, she'd disowned Indi. Our father to her, was what our mother was to me. Indigo would be having a rough day too, but at least she had Quick.

Sparrow took me from my uncle's arms. She was petite like Tawny with the same long dark wavy hair that fell down past her waist. Sparrow's dark exotic eyes gleamed as she gave me a squeeze.

"Let's go home and you can get a nap in before the party, it's still early," she said, angling me towards the path with her arm on my shoulders.

Tawny had her mother's mannerisms and fiery personality, but she must have resembled her father.

Tawny was barely two inches over five feet, but the Matriarch Vetr held herself as if she was eight feet even. She slid her arm around my other side and leaned her head on my shoulder. Steel had fallen back to hang out with Gypsum, the two men had become close. They'd even gotten over the strange uncle/brother-in-law relationship between them.

"You look so hot for a big fat pregnant woman."

I strangled a laugh. "I think that was supposed to cheer me up."

I could hear Tawny's smile. "It's true. You're lucky you've only gained weight in your belly. Are we still on for tomorrow?"

I groaned as we walked from the stadium and down the mountain trail to the Elivagar portal gate. "Trying on designer dresses with all of *this* is not what I would call a good time."

I rubbed my belly with a palm and Tawny laughed. She was my best friend, just as our mother's had been best friends.

"We always have a girls' shopping day during Yuletide. I'll help you pick something good for the masquerade and the induction ceremony. Unless..." Tawny trailed off and raised her dark brow at me with an amused smile.

I rolled my eyes. The town heart of Elivagar came into view, a quiet snowy town of brick and stone homes and storefronts which a constant flow of chimney smoke puffed up from. Women in rich thick fabrics and big bell skirts walked about with their men in padded jerkins and fur-lined cloaks. I loved Elivagar fashions even with the tight corsets and half dozen underskirts.

"Ash has not picked a dress for me," I said with exasperation.

"He went into your tent after the challenge," Sparrow hinted.

"No one would think twice if I was a man," I grumbled.

"But you're not a man, Scar. You're a married woman and your reputation means everything. Granted, my nephew is an errant husband at best. Nonexistent at worst. Still, because he does not show you the respect you deserve, doesn't mean you should compromise your values."

My husband and the khoraz brothel.

Try as I might, I couldn't face that truth. Now I didn't have Brass's love either. One day at a time, I reminded myself. Ash promised he'd get his memories back. Some insane part of me wondered if he'd gotten them back and had decided he didn't want me anymore so he kept on pretending he didn't remember. That was an awfully painful thought.

If Reed Tio resented the fact, I'd taken his position as Second, he never let on. We arrived at my great uncle's home, Pearl's childhood home, as dusk fell.

The walls were all cool grey stone, the top of the doorway was a large stained-glass clock. It was appropriate for the Tio palace. The door was blocky stained glass with a blazing sun peaking over wavy hills. Sunflowers stretched high on either side of the door.

Fern Rot had curves that rivaled my own grandmother's with fiery red hair met us in the portal room with Reed. The woman had a warm smile and hugged Pearl the second we were all through the door. She was the second-year tyros' headmistress. Fern had a rushed excited way of speaking. I couldn't imagine her ever being angry a day in her life she was so perky. Fern was like a classic southern woman without the accent, incredibly friendly and hospitable.

Reed's coppery brown hair was styled like Hawk's with a thin mustache that topped his mouth. His eyes were dark, and he was average height like Hawk, an inch or two under six feet. That was short for Guardians who had been bred for their looks, strength, and skills.

"The Straumrs are all here. Now so are the Tios, Rot, Dagrs, Geols,

Sumars, Vetrs, and all the provosts from Valla University. Mostly because they're all Rot and Tios." Fern laughed.

Fern fluttered around us like a red-headed humming bird, ushering us into their formal ball room. One wall was all windows, letting in bright sunlight. The other walls were paneled with mirrors making the room look huge, two-tiered crystal chandeliers hung from the ceiling above an elaborate polished wood table that stretched the long room until an open space designated for dancing was before a full band.

It brought back memories of the only other Ausa Vatni I'd gone to for Coyote Regn and Butterfly Rot's son who was currently running around the dance floor with his older sister.

I rubbed my own belly.

The room was bustling with all the red headed Tio/Rot offspring and the dark-skinned Straumrs. I spotted Ash and Quartz with the three Straumr brothers and their two wives. Novaculite was Fox's wife and Quartz's twin. She was also pregnant, but since Fox was just over thirty, everyone knew it wasn't his, but Ash's.

Nova had known when they married she wouldn't be able to have Fox's child, but relations to propagate the lines were commonplace. She was petite like Tawny, with the same coloring. They were cousins and must have both resembled Ridge Vetr, Tawny's face was heart-shaped, while Nova's was thinner, though the relation was obvious.

The caramel skinned, youngest Straumr brother had baby blue eyes and a playful demeanor. Nova was a lucky woman even if he couldn't have kids and from Fox's pleasant attitude, he must've not held any ill feelings towards Ash. He was probably grateful, though Guardians did things the old-fashioned way — no turkey basters.

River Straumr was trying to hold a conversation with the other adults while his three kids sulked and nudged each other. River was even keel, not as playful as Fox, but not as serious as Crag. He looked the most like their baby sister, Amethyst, with mocha skin and dark eyes. His tight dark curls were styled as Fox's were, in what we would have called a "fade" back in Chicago.

Crag Straumr was with my uncle Jackal, Alder's brother. Jackal and Sage looked a lot alike, but Jackal's blonde hair always had a floppiness to it after a long day. His features weren't soft but harder than my father's had been. Like most of the Var men. He was tall and wiry and stood a half foot again over his bald ebony skinned partner. An odder couple could not have been found.

The Tio provosts were there, the brothers Sky, whose red hair fell to his shoulders and matched his fiery beard, and Ford, who was taller than his brother and father with close cut hair and was always clean shaven. All the Tio/Rot offspring had sapphire eyes and fair skin except for Butterfly, the youngest of the brood who had her father's dark eyes. Their twin sisters stood with the Straumrs, Wisteria and Magnolia whose daughter Crimson had had an affair with Ash while we were together.

The pretty red heads shared a small smile with me and went back to talking within their circle. She must have hated me. I would hate. She was in love with Ash and wanted nothing more than to be with him, yet he had chosen me, then he'd chosen Quartz. Ash had made me his Second when she had Tio blood too.

Brass was there. I ached for his reassuring warmth. I wanted to flex my mind and let him know I was thinking about him so he could send comfort my way as we used to do. I hadn't seen him in weeks and it felt like an eternity.

It was quite the dynamic I had with him and Slate. Slate needed me, Brass wanted me, but I needed Brass and wanted Slate. The person I'd become was unrecognizable to me. Maybe I needed Slate too. I'd walked away from him before, but I had never been able to leave Brass. Gods, such a mess. I was a mess. I'd made my life a mess. I was sure he could feel me close by and chose not to meet my eyes.

"You are looking lost."

Spinel Regn had come up beside me and I hadn't even noticed. He'd probably seen me gazing like some love-struck teenager at his grandson, though Spinel did not look like anyone's grandfather except for the bit of silver in his dark meticulously coifed hair. Brass resembled him, but that's as far as the similarities went. Spinel's personality was much more like Quick's.

"I was hoping it wasn't obvious," I said, noting my family had all wandered off in conversations of their own.

It wasn't smart to remain friends with the source of Brass's betrayal, but the Regn Patriarch was persistent. He wanted to be close to me whether from a genuine attraction or simply taking me up on my previous offer to be my escort. The Patriarch was my only tie to the Regn now.

Gypsum had brought Rosasite, Brass's ex. It was new and casual, but he needed a buffer between him and Diamond. Ash's chestnut-haired sister was a female version of him. Same light green eyes and caramel skin. Rosasite bore certain similar attributes, like, the slender frames of their bodies, which still managed to be curvy. Rosasite had a mane of glossy, obsidian curls, and light honey eyes against enviable creamy coffee skin.

Spinel chuckled softly, "There are so very many ways to be lost."

"I don't think my kind of lost is typical for a woman my age," I said gustily.

"Yes, I can see that." He held out a goblet. "Sparkling cider."

"Thank you," I said, taking the glass.

Quick and Indigo had joined Brass, Slate had followed them. He was alone.

They were dressed up. Satin waistcoats with embroidered trim and shiny silver and gold buttons, their pants were snug and tucked into black polished boots reserved for special occasions. Slate was in all black without a hint of color, the metallic black threads of his embroi-dery being the only contrast. The other men wore long white sleeve shirts with their cravats or ascots.

Spinel cut an impressive form for any age, just like his grandsons. "Thank you," he said.

"For?" I asked.

Spinel turned his head to me and gave me a smile that made my cheeks flush. He was old enough to be my grandfather, worldly, and cultured. I was an impulsive twenty-one-year-old girl, he should not have been looking at me like *that*. Not again.

"Where did you think Brass got his talent from? Descendants from the Regn line are always powerfully talented," he said, and I knit my brows.

"You're reading my mind."

*Wonderful.* Just what I needed. Another person I had to guard my thoughts around.

Spinel was looking at Brass too and I could tell he was trying not to glance our way. "It is rumored you had to stop sleeping at Valla University because men were sneaking into your room."

I fidgeted. How had that gotten out? Three different times, overzealous men had found their way into my shared bedroom at Valla U so I had to go back to my wing at the Dagr palace.

"It has also been said that you are having an affair with the Prime, but we know that is far from the truth. He is in love with you." He laughed softly. "They all are. One must wonder..."

"Don't waste your energy. You already know the truth," I said almost wistfully.

I was in love with two men. I had entertained the idea of having a second husband for the sake of my public appearance. I made a blood oath with Ash.

As far as Tidings was concerned, I was a single woman because my husband had all but left me. I wouldn't entertain having a second husband any longer because every man who got close to me wound up hurt.

"You and I have a mutually beneficial working relationship. I am still the Second to the Prime and a married woman."

"Yes, I see your husband needs a reminder of that." He nodded to where Slate was giving one of the staff women a thorough look.

An embarrassing whimper squeezed from my throat. As far as I knew, he'd only been with Lynx, the Minotaur khoraz at the brothel, I wouldn't be surprised if I was wrong though. Before we'd gotten married, he'd had a constant flow of willing women.

"He's free to do as he wishes."

"I did not mean to rub salt in your wounds. My grandson is still not speaking to either of us," he said in that same low tone.

I slowly turned my head to him. "Can you blame him?"

Spinel flirted with me constantly whenever we were together. Jett hated it. I was still inexplicably flattered by it.

"I could still be your escort, Second."

"Perhaps." I heard the word come from my own mouth and widened my eyes in disbelief.

"I believe it would be... how did you put it? Mutually beneficial. You have certain inclinations; I have discretion and the means. I want nothing from you. No ties, no favors. You need nothing from me. It is the most balanced relationship one could have."

His eyes glittered at me. By the Mother, he looked so much like Brass.

"Spinel Regn. Ensnaring another generation of young women in your webs?" Jackal gave him a lopsided grin and put his arm loosely around my shoulders. "Reaching high this time. My niece is out of even *your* league. I have to admire your ambition though. Since her father and husband are not around to shoot you their glares of disapproval and I am not good at glaring, I will have to content myself with a forthcoming negation of your undoubtedly unscrupulous offers."

Spinel chuckled amiably; it creased his olive cheeks with smile lines.

"Don't worry, Jackal," I reassured him. "Patriarch Regn meant no offense."

*... Let me think about it. Brass will think we're sleeping together. I don't think I could stand seeing that look again...*

"Yes, I am sure you have grown used to being a novelty since becoming Second to the Prime. How many marriage proposals are you up to these days?" Jackal asked jokingly, but my stomach dropped.

Ash, Brass, and the Merfolk King were the only ones who had said the words, but Pavo the Aves, Niall the Lycan, and, most recently, the Sunna heir had insinuated that he wanted me to come live with them. The fact that Slate had made it clear that we were no longer a couple even though we were married in the eyes of the Guardians emboldened my unwanted suitors. I'd stopped entertaining the notion of having a second husband when Cory, one of the Shadow Breakers I'd recruited for Brass's team, was poisoned while on a mission with me. He had been my first and only suitor, though Brass could make a great case that he had also been courting me.

Less savory offers were too many to count. I had gone on three dates before I met Ash. He was my first steady boyfriend who ended up proposing, but I'd fallen for Slate. There were days when I thought maybe I'd fallen for Brass first. Aside from the few guys who had snuck into my room at Valla U, there had been the ones who cornered me coming out of bathrooms while I attended feasts and ceremonies and the like. Men who would never have approached me so blatantly, were showing too much interest. Jackal was right. I was a novelty.

There were other families I recognized there as friends of the Rot. Litr, Blomi, and Sandr, including Shale's mother and uncle who were also provosts at Valla University. Asp Sandr and Boa Sunna. Shale had looked like her mother. Pin straight raven hair and dark up tilted eyes, Asp was petite as her daughter had been and Boa's hair was slicked back with his usual severe expression. His family was there with my Sunna suitor whom I was avoiding.

Cordillera was sans Chafer for once, her dark waves grazed her the thin chin of her olive face. She inclined her head to me when her dark narrow eyes with a lift of her manicured brows. Her nails matched her crimson lips, but that was the only color on her since she wore a slinky black dress on her petite frame.

"Our young Second is a very capable woman. When all one has is power and responsibility, in her position it will make you hard, Scarlett. One must have something or someone to help you unwind. Relax. Remind you that there is more. Ask your great uncle Reed. He can tell you better. Find an outlet. A man... or woman who does not care about who you are," Spinel said, looking at me over his goblet.

Jackal sniffed. "What excellent advice. I would have to agree... much to my surprise. Though, as your uncle, I would suggest you seek comfort from someone you care about."

Spinel plucked my empty goblet from my fingers. "A refill, Mrs. Tio?"

"Please," I said gratefully, relieved I wouldn't have to leave Jackal's side.

"My dearest Mrs. Scarlett, I hate to inform you that your pupils dilate around Patriarch Regn. I fear I am too late to offer my sound words of warning. Does it make you wish you preferred the fairer sex?" Jackal whispered, bending down to my ear.

I snorted only slightly astonished I hadn't blushed instead. "I doubt women would be any less complicated. Different complications, that's all."

Jett came towards us. He was looking especially handsome in a midnight blue double-breasted waistcoat with a matching cravat. It was heavily embroidered with metallic black thread and obsidian buttons. Cherry was in a flowing blue silk dress that matched Jett's waistcoat and Amethyst wore a black off the shoulder number — both looked like goddesses on earth.

The proud papa was carrying Gigi who wore a long white dress. She had her mother's mocha skin and midnight hair and grandfather's powder blue eyes. She had my full lips, the poor baby. She was pulling on his obsidian buttons as he approached me.

"Ready, aunt Scar?" Jett had never looked so handsome. "Great uncle Jack?"

Jackal feigned choking on his drink. "Dear gods, never say that again."

The arboretum where the ceremony would take place was an indoor orchard, floral and citrus scents mixing in the sweet air. It had a calming effect. There was a small pond and a white plush blanket laid out in front of Jett, Amethyst, and Cherry. We gathered around the pond.

Amethyst removed Gigi's dress and placed her bare on the white blanket. Jett, stood over her and nodded. Amethyst, picked up the bare-bottomed little girl and dipped her in the water. Cherry cupped her hand in the pond and let the water fall through her fingers and onto her head. Gigi smiled and played with strands of Amethyst's hair that hung by her face. Amethyst smiled and took Gigi out of the pond and wrapped the soft white blanket around her before handing Gigi to Jett. Jett made a gesture with his fist across his chest in the shape of an inverted 'T'.

Jett then announced, "We own this baby for our daughter. She shall be called Opal."

Tears gleamed in Amethyst's dark eyes. Her mother's name for her own daughter. Ash and I had influenced the council for it. It was one of Moon's last wishes as Prime, tawe'd come up against no opposition.

I was crying again. I'd somehow found myself with Spinel and Jackal. The Straumr brothers walked around the pond and laid their gifts at the happy family's feet. Jackal had no qualms about squeezing my shoulders tight. Spinel was ever the gentleman and held out an embroidered kerchief with his monogram on it. I thanked him and took it.

Dahlia Natt and Basil Straumr, Ash's parents, went up together to wrap up the Straumr family. She had never liked me. It didn't help that she was Delta's aunt. The strawberry blonde had a pinched, ivory face. Her green eyes always seemed to scrutinize everything except for her perfect son. Having her as our History provost and first year Head-mistress was nerve wrecking.

Basil was the record keeper for Guardian history, the claviger. He was a creamy coffee skinned aloof man, who ironically had memory issues. Ash was extraordinary at mental manipulations and had been keeping his father's Alzheimer's at bay. Ash never said as much, but he was ashamed of his parents.

"Want to walk up with me?" I asked Jackal.

"Why of course, Mrs. Scarlett," he said jauntily.

We walked around the pond together and I smiled at my beaming brother and the girls. Jackal placed a small open white box with a diamond tree of life pendant inside, it was the sigil of the Var family. I had known her name, so I'd cheated and gotten a gold bracelet with her name engraved on it; Opal Geol.

I smiled and gave Opal's foot a squeeze as I passed on Jackal's arm. Ruby Geol was behind us, Opal's sister and my grandmother. She was crying. Her short onyx hair was pulled back. Her wide dark eyes were the same as Amethyst's with high arched brows. Her skin was porcelain and her pouty red stained lips trembled. It had been a rough year for her as well after losing Alder. Jackal stopped and gave me an apologetic smile. I released his arm with a pat and blinked when Spinel appeared at my side again.

"If I may escort you back into the ballroom for dinner?"

"Thank you, Spinel," I said, taking his arm.

We watched the Tio heir and his wife name their newborn daughter before the Ausa Vatni ceremonies were concluded and Spinel led me into the ballroom.

## CHAPTER 4
# INDIGO

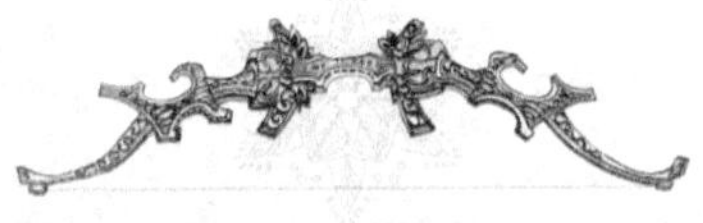

Dinner had been delicious. I sat next to Scarlett and Silver. His grandfather, Spinel sat on Scarlett's other side. He had been by her side all night.

"How many songs has your grandfather spent dancing with my sister?" I asked Silver as we stood with Brass, Slate, and Jett.

"I do not know. How many is all of them?" Silver asked, tapping his lower lip.

"He is very handsome," I said, watching Brass and Slate out of the corner of my eye.

Scarlett didn't look pregnant from behind, not even from the front in her dress. It was a spectacular dress. A flowing aquamarine empire waisted gown with heavy gold trim lined the low neckline and around the waist. Her light golden brown hair was all pinned atop her head with loose tendrils brushing her back and collar bones. Two narrow braids were over her shoulder, two silver Celtic etched beads, ivory pearl and carved starburst, and two feathers; one peacock feather from Pavo and a pure white one from Aeetus, the bald eagle hybrid and son of the Aves sachem.

"Spinel is old enough to be *our* grandfather," Jett said, eyeing the

61

dancing couple. "I think she has been taking dance lessons. She looks very confident on his arm."

"That has never stopped any of his girlfriends," Silver retorted.

"She's oblivious to how they look together," Jett said, shaking his head.

They looked like a couple. Not a bad-looking couple either. He was tall and in great shape, Guardians aged differently than other people. He guided her around the dance floor with ease and she was comfortable in his arms. The handsome older man had been treating her better than any one of his young girlfriends. I hoped Slate and Brass were insanely jealous.

"He does look an awful lot like Brass..." I said in disbelief.

Spinel guided her off the dance floor and led her over to get another cider drink. I caught Ash staring at them and he looked away. What was that about?

"And we all know how much Scarlett enjoys Brass," Slate said into his goblet as his eyes strayed.

"Look at that brunette staffer one more time and I'll pluck your eyes from your skull as you sleep," I said in a hiss.

Slate's brows rose. The scar through the left side was nearly white on his skin. Silver looked at me in shock. Brass and Jett didn't look surprised at all. Scarlett may have let herself be escorted, but she wasn't giving lewd looks to any of the men. There were enough men around who were looking at Scarlett like she was a choice piece of meat that she wouldn't have to try hard to get one of them to go home with her.

"He's keeping the wolves at bay," Brass said in a disinterested tone that wasn't fooling me in the slightest.

I gave him a sympathetic look that he ignored. Jett groaned.

Spinel's eyes kept flitting down to her neckline, but he was nonchalant about it unless you were staring right at them as I was.

Scarlett's eyes rose to ours and there was some foot shuffling. Spinel took her hand and kissed it before she started our way. Amethyst intercepted her with Opal and handed her off.

"Spinel Regn has taken an interest in you," Amethyst said in a coquettish smile.

"We have business together, he's one of the few men here I understand." Scarlett said, shifting Opal onto her hip.

"He is a very distinguished and handsome older man," Amethyst said, leading the conversation.

Scarlett never took her smiling face off Opal. "All the men in Tidings are handsome. Each one more so than the next, no matter their age. I find handsome men dull; I'd rather spend my time with interesting men that have a sense of humor. You hear that, Opal? Don't let those pretty faces trick you into thinking there's more than there is."

Jett turned around. "I am much more than a pretty face," he said, arrogantly jutting out his chin.

Amethyst laughed and walked towards where the red-headed provosts were speaking to one another. Scarlett brought Opal over to our circle and Jett made room for her. If it bothered her to be standing with Slate and Brass, but not *with* either of them, she hid it well. She was in greater family/Second to the Prime mode.

"That must be what all the ladies who want to get into your pants say," Scar said teasingly with a smile that made your heart swell.

"Damn it all, Indigo has said those very words to me." Silver flashed a smile that made weaker women toss themselves naked into his arms.

I snorted. "Get over yourself, Regn. All you are is pretty. *Now*. Smile and nod."

Silver tugged me to his side chuckling and pressed a kiss to my neck. My corresponding smile was moronic.

"Brass, may I speak with you for a moment?"

Scarlett's face was open and expressionless, but I had absorbed her empath abilities and hers were in a downward spiral. It'd taken a lot of courage to speak to Brass.

"No. I'm done with you," Brass said without even looking at her, and the tension between our circle grew.

"It's business, not personal," she continued bravely, not letting his chilly demeanor derail her mission.

"No matter," he said breezily.

A muscle above her right eye twitched. "Please be my arena commissioner. You don't have to see me except when I come to the arenas for shows otherwise you can relay everything through Quick. It's an excellent opportunity for you, Brass. Don't let your personal feelings get in the way of your future."

As far as we knew, Brass hadn't given up his position with the arenas. Brass was silent for a time then he downed the last dregs of his goblet.

"For once, you're right." I blinked at his curt tone and the hard set of his jaw. "What woman here would you approve of me bringing home, Scarlett?"

Jett made a strangled sound when he covered his mouth with his goblet. Slate's cool gaze slid to Scarlett's, curious on how she would react. Silver held me tight to his side as if I might involuntarily lash out and slap Brass.

Scarlett's eyes searched the side of Brass's face and she powered through the anguish. Her face transformed into an imperial mask. Her fingers flitted to her belly, but she stopped herself.

"In respects to the most suitable matches for child bearing and family status that are present, there's Crimson Rot who hasn't had any public suitors since she had an affair with Ash. Her family is Tio/Rot, so she's a greater family daughter. There's Orchid Litr, a lesser family daughter out of your home island who is still single and Sienna Clay, she's not associated with any families, but she's single and out of Valla. Her father is a wealthy merchant that I have contracts with for the liquor in the arenas so they're coming into some money. All three are Guardians four years younger than you and eligible," she said as if she was reciting a memorized speech.

Brass had turned to face her, disbelief coloring his features. He hadn't expected her to have really thought about who he should be with. Brass didn't know how badly she wanted him to be happy. She'd done the same thing with Slate when she thought she was barren. Those girls were ones that had happened by the Sumar palace before she fled to Chicago, they'd been thoroughly vetted by her.

"You have been looking for wives for me?" Brass asked, his defined lips stiff.

"Your happiness is important to me," Scarlett said softly and kissed Opal's head to break his gaze.

Brass froze over. "Pick one. One of the benefits of being a mind reader is that getting women is not an issue."

Scarlett kept her face partially hidden behind Opal's head. "Whichever you're attracted to, Brass. I've done my research, they're all nice girls from good families. Crimson got a bad rap but she'll be good to you. Tios are known for their fertility."

As if all the redheads running around weren't proof enough.

Brass looked over to where Crimson was chatting with Cyan Tio, her cousin and the fourth roommate to Silver, Slate, and Jett when they were at Valla U. A girl about my height, slender with a blunt cut fringe and deep brown soulful eyes was watching Gypsum lead Rosasite around the dance floor. Her cheeks reddened when Gypsum spun flashing a dimpled smile at no one in particular. Judging from her red hair, she was a Rot and very interested in our youngest cousin.

"Crimson it is," Brass said and left their circle to walk straight to her.

Crimson blushed prettily when Brass started speaking to her and he led her to the dance floor. Scarlett had watched openly and then turned back to us and offered a quick smile.

"Indi."

She offered Opal to me and I took her happily before Silver could take another chance to show me how great he was with kids. She ran her teeth over her lower lip and pivoted to Slate with her palm upturned.

"Would my husband like to pretend for three minutes that he doesn't loathe my existence and join me for a dance? I've been taking lessons." She gave him a drop-dead gorgeous smile.

Slate looked at her palm and walked through our circle so his chest pushed against her it as he went to the bar. Scarlett pulled her hand back and rubbed her palm over her belly and shrugged.

Jett, Silver, and I were too shocked to say anything. Silver took her hand from her stomach.

"I will take that dance." Silver said with his patented panty-dropping grin.

Scarlett's cheeks rounded when she gave him a grateful smile. Her eyes glittered with unshed tears.

"Thanks," she whispered, and they went onto the dance floor.

Jett moved up next to me and slung his arm around his shoulder. "You have changed him."

Opal played with my turquoise tree of life fetish in my hair. "Should I take that as a compliment?"

"Yes. You should."

"Indigo?" My stomach dropped as I turned around.

Had he been waiting for Silver to walk away? "Sterling."

He looked relieved as he smiled sheepishly at me. "How have you been? I have not seen you in weeks... other than that morning."

"I'm good and yourself? The wedding is upon you. You must be excited," I said flatly, and his violet eyes slid past me to where Diamond must have been standing.

"Have you set a date yet?" Sterling asked.

"Not yet," I admitted.

Jett took Opal from my arms and gave Sterling a nod. Sterling acknowledged him in return.

"I wanted to talk to you about earlier." Sterling said leaning in close.

"Oh? About what?" I asked.

"Scarlett."

"Thanks for watching over her today," I said, giving him a forced smile.

The ballroom was bustling with dancers and drinking. People were laughing and the constant conversation caused a steady hum amidst the ethereal traditional music of Tidings. Sterling wanted me to dance with him, but Silver was the jealous type. He would not be okay with a quick dance with Sterling.

Sterling gave me a lopsided grin. He'd given me that same smile after the first time we'd made love when he was supposed to be training with Sage. We were just two little kids in puppy love back then, but his shy smile tugged strings in me that brought me back in time even if it had been almost as painful as it was awkward.

"This is serious," Sterling said, sobering.

"Okay?"

"Scarlett let go. While we were crossing the river during the challenge. She let go of my arm...intentionally, Indi. She came around after that, but I do not think she wanted to survive. If Ash had not helped me grab her up..."

He trailed off. My stomach was churning. I worried something like this would happen one of these days. It'd been a long time since she was really and truly happy and the Norns seemed to be conspiring against her. I couldn't say *us* because the truth was... Silver made me happy. I lost myself in him. Forgot my painful memories and the fact that our father was gone, that the life I thought I'd live didn't exist. I was ready to make a new life with Silver, even if I was a bit reluctant to confess it.

"Does Ash really mean to marry her still? Do you think he'll try to kill Slate to accomplish it?" I asked in a hushed whisper.

Sterling looked past me again. "He thinks he is in love with her. When have you ever known Ash to walk away from something he wants? You know she offered up her next child to him in exchange for Slate's memories back? I cannot say it is worth it unless she plans to marry Ash. Quartz would rather have her as second wife than first mistress."

I tried not to crease my brow to let on how upset this news made me. Ash always got what he wanted by fair means or foul. Since the moment Scarlett set foot in his path, he'd wanted her and meant to have her.

I rubbed my exposed belly as I floated in the huge pool. The walls were the royal blue that matched the rest of the Sumar palace with gold patterned trim. The ceiling was done is golden landscapes, matching exposed rafters spanned it. Plaster sculptures of people lined the pool, as well as globe lamp posts. The pool itself was tiled in royal blue with blazing suns.

I was going to have to retire my sea foam green fringed halter bikini. The top wasn't big enough. I felt how Ama used to look. My belly balanced out the ample curves I'd developed so I didn't look *completely* ridiculous.

After I watched Brass leave with Crimson even though she lived in the Tio palace, and Slate was followed out by a brunette staffer, I'd decided to go home and sleep. The nap I'd taken in between the Ragnarök and the Ausa Vatni had only left me enough energy for a few hours of dinner and dancing. I made it to midnight and retired alone while the men I loved found women to warm their beds.

How could someone who was always surrounded by people be so

terribly lonely? Speaking of which, I wondered where Pewter and Siren hid when I changed out of my clothes. *If* they hid.

I had stopped training. That was the deal I'd made myself once I became a Guardian. I would focus on resting until the twins came. Swimming was my only way to release my stresses and since I was meeting the girls for a shopping trip later, I came early to the Sumar palace to swim before lunch. The others usually trained before lunch as well, but they'd be in the conservatory training grounds.

I'd finished doing my laps when the door to the prep room opened. Slate, Brass, Quick, and Jett came through the prep room doors in snug swim shorts that left little to the imagination. They were obviously not expecting me to be in there since the topic of conversation was last night's conquests.

Every time I saw Brass and Slate since our fall out, I felt another part of myself die. The deep laughter stopped when I was spotted floating on my back with my belly in the air like a submarine breaking the surface of the water. One of the babies must have thought they could help me stay afloat because he was kicking so much that the water rippled from my skin.

"Hey, baby sis. I didn't know you still come here," Jett said, jumping into the pool and wiping the water from his chiseled face when it was splashed from the other men hopping in.

"I don't. I've stopped training, but I'm allowing myself to swim. I'm going to torture myself with dress shopping with the girls in town so I thought I'd do my swimming here." I stopped short of saying I thought I'd be alone.

Floating felt good. The little bit of weight I put on unfelt as I drifted. I backstroked to the edge of the pool so they could so their laps. I couldn't stay in the pool. They always wrapped up their training with a swim. I had no idea Brass would be there. Him being cold to me made Slate's reprehensible behavior ten times worse.

"I'll get out of your guys' way," I said, climbing out of the pool.

I didn't make eye contact or even look their way, but I heard Quick grunt. "I have not seen you undressed in some time. I cannot believe you finally look pregnant."

I self-consciously touched my stomach and felt one of them kicking away. I chewed my lower lip. "Any success at knocking my sister up yet?"

I raised my eyes to where Quick stood his left half covered in black Celtic jagged tattoos from his collar bone to his ankle. Brass and Slate were next to him. Brass's hair was free from its knot for once and clung to his muscled shoulders. He was staring at my stomach as if he could see through my skin. He couldn't help the surge of paternal pride he felt, but it ebbed after only a moment.

Slate hadn't removed his dozens of narrow braids or the silver beads that threaded his long, wavy mane that dripped rivulets over his hard pecs. He peered at me from the corner of his eyes as if looking at me straight on would somehow capture his soul.

"Not yet. How are my nephews?" Quick asked with a laugh.

I stopped walking and bit my lip to stop a smile. "They like it when I swim."

Jett swam towards me and flashed me a killer smile as he pushed himself out of the pool from the side. He towered over me. He wiped a hand over the back of his short, cropped hair and over his tan face before placing his hands to either side of my stomach. His smile deepened causing a droplet of water to dangle from his nose.

"You know... I think they might be identical. I see one placenta and they share a sac." Jett's white teeth peeked from his full lips.

I beamed. "You're kidding? You can really see all that?" I cradled my belly.

"Calm and steady, like their father," Jett said, casting a wry glance over his shoulder. "Keep them away from my son. You don't want another Sumar and Regn pairing. The world couldn't handle it." He chuckled, and I forced a smile.

"That'd be nice," I said and placed my hands to my brother's. "I should go. The girls will be expecting me."

"They haven't swum their laps yet," Jett said, creasing his brow. "Hang out for a while. Ash is going to keep you busy, and we don't have classes anymore. Why don't you move back in so you're not alone?"

"Sparrow and Hawk are there. The babies will be born in a few months and I'll never be alone again. I'm savoring my me-time. I'll see you at the masquerade later." I gave him another forced smile and hoped it looked convincing.

"Are you coming alone?" he asked as my bare feet padded across the tiles.

I didn't stop walking. "No, I'm coming with Sparrow and Hawk."

"I meant a date," Jett called after me.

I stopped with my palms on the doors to the prep room and looked down at my belly. "No, big bro. I have enough on my plate, don't you think?"

After my swim, I went back to the Dagr palace for a nap. I napped whenever I had the chance. My energy levels always seemed to need replenishing. I met the girls in Thrimilci and bought three dresses with Tawny's help at the *Myriads of Murad* couture shop and a mask for tonight. The girls cajoled me into getting ready at the Sumar palace since my two favorite hairdressers would be there to help them get ready. The third hairdresser, and twin sister to the owner, had her baby two weeks ago, and I was going to their Ausa Vatni before Sterling's wedding tomorrow.

Cricket, the big-haired and serious blonde showed up with the busty brunette, Bronze. Katydid would be with her newborn and her husband Solder. I'd hired the three hairdressers to work for the arenas and roped Solder into providing the outfits for the competitors.

Bronze excitedly asked about my pregnancy as we took turns getting hair and makeup done in Indigo's bathroom. A huge bathtub sat in the middle of the room all done in pearl and iridescent tiles. The bathtub was two split sides so one person could sit facing the other in two separate tubs. Behind two low tiled walls, was a huge shower. Water sprayed from every direction, there was even a waterfall at the entrance that fell across the low wall so no one could see you if you were showering past it. The opposite side was a wall-to-wall mirror with double sinks trimmed is swirling champagne and silver mosaic.

I sat next to Indigo facing the mirrors while Amethyst, Cherry, and Tawny sat on the counters laughing and joking. It was a much needed pick me up from earlier at the pool. Quick had left before we had arrived so it had been a much needed double dose of estrogen. Between Ash and being alone... that was pretty much how I spent my days.

I'd lied to Jett about what I was doing for the masquerade. I had intended to go with Hawk and Sparrow, but I doubted it would work since Ash wanted me there early so we could have the first dance to open the masquerade together. Bronze gave me a light smoky eyes and shimmering pink lips before slipping my gold lacework mask over my eyes that did nothing to hide who I was. It went beautifully with the heather grey strapless dress I'd found that fit snugly to the floor but had a sheer skirt from an elaborate, gold beaded empire waist. Bands of intricate beading swept down the flowing sheer skirt train. Glittering combs to either side of my hair pinned back big curls to display my high cheekbones.

"I hope I look as good as you when I'm pregnant." Indigo pouted.

She looked gorgeous in a blush pink taffeta strapless mermaid dress. Its sweetheart neckline had textured taffeta and ivory pearls beaded over the breast until the skirt flared where circular taffeta rings wound around more ivory pearls. Her hair was in a glamorous up do low on the side of her head.

Tawny wore her favorite color, any shade of red really, in an off the shoulder fit and flare gown whose bodice and sleeves were heavily beaded in gold and red silk hung from the back of her sleeves. She wore even more red because of the Vetr colors, but it suited her beautifully.

Amethyst wasn't a bright color type of girl and tended to stay towards blacks and tans. She wore a glittering slinky dress that covered her from neck to toes with a small train. Cherry wore a cobalt blue flowing charmeuse strapless with a wide silver belt above her baby bump. Both girls wore their hair in loose long dark curls that fell to their slender waists. Cherry carried her weight in a small globe of a belly.

"You will," I reassured Indi.

The Sumar palace was on Thrimilci, the island of perpetual summer with the Dagr palace. Brass and Quick were from Ostara, the land of perpetual spring where the Var family reigned and Jett was the heir. Ostara was my father's home island. Mabon was where Sterling was the patriarch, the island of perpetual autumn. Valla was the fifth island and the only island to have all four seasons. I met a Leshy once who had told me to stay away from the sixth island, but in my two years in Tidings, no one had ever mentioned a sixth island.

"Are my parents going with you?" Tawny asked.

Cricket had curled her hair and pinned half of it up so she looked like a Greek goddess. I could *feel* her concern. Her wide hazel eyes were too anxious to be casual.

"No. I should actually be going right now. Ash is meeting me there. Since it's the first time there's a male Prime and female Second, he wants us to open the dance floor. He's been giving me lessons for the last month."

Amethyst was Ash's cousin and had chosen a side when she married Jett, though she was a Straumr through and through. "Ash may be the best dancer in all of Tidings. I am glad you two have made amends. He has his charms."

"I'm coming with, Steel can meet me there."

Tawny stepped into a pair of gold strappy heels identical to mine, except my feet were two sizes larger than her little pixie feet. We walked into the hall and wound our way through the Moroccan style palace with blue, white, and gold mosaics. Tiled mandalas spanned the tunneled ceiling to the ogee arched windowless windows. Sheer white panels blew into our path rasping across our dresses as we walked past, the smell of hot sand and summer permeating the air.

The sky was always clear in Thrimilci. It rained a few times a year and none of the windows had glass in them unless they were on the waterfall side of the palace and then it was all stained glass. We walked past royal blue clad staff until we reached the portal room.

The floor was mirrored tiles and it reflected the blue light from the ceiling, there were thousands of little blue lights in the cavernous room. Huge double doors on the opposite wall were mirrored with spokes radiating from a gold center circle, with white ovals around each spoke. It looked like a blazing sun.

Tawny looped her arm through mine as we opened the portal door and white light engulfed us, transporting us in an instant to Valla Univerity where I was the Second. I'd be dolling out punishments for tyros a year younger than I was and a constant staple there.

Every door that lined the yellow stoned castle wall was beautifully carved with vines as if each one was done with care. The university had a certain earthy smell to it that clung to every room. On either side of the long room, hung a tapestry that spanned the high walls. Pewter sconces between each arched door lit the room. Double doors led into the hall.

"I wanted to tell you first," Tawny said as we walked.

"What's that?" I asked.

Tawny's porcelain cheeks flushed. "Steel and I have started trying."

I stopped and beamed. "Oh my gods, that's awesome!" I wrapped my arms around her, and she smiled brightly back at me.

"I'm not pregnant yet. He's twenty-five but he turns twenty-six this year so we have to work fast if we want more than one, which we do."

"That's the best thing I've heard in a while. I'm so happy for you both."

The sprawling yellow stoned castle doubled as the main office of the Prime and his Second — me. Huge crystal tiered chandeliers hung from the high ceiling of the grand ballroom. Tiny, mirrored pieces were nestled into the stone walls reflecting the light from the chandeliers like starlight. Glittering pillars lined the enormous room with pedestal tables in between the pillars with platters of food being set out.

"Fairies are only a foot tall and look to be made of twigs and grass. You ladies are *much* more lovely," Ash said, leaning in close to my ear.

Ash had walked up behind Tawny and me the first night we arrived in Tidings. Those were the first words he'd ever spoke to us after Tawny had wondered aloud if we were fairies and not humans at all. He'd snuck up behind us again and a smile tugged on my lips as I turned to face him.

His eyes peered out from a black and gold half mask that looked like crocodile skin. His ascot and waistcoat were gold against his caramel skin and he wore black leather pants tucked into boots. His gold crescent belt buckle caught the incandescent light of the chandeliers. He took Tawny's hand and pressed a kiss to it.

"Matriarch Vetr, you look lovely as always," he purred with his patented cocky smile.

While I may have been on the mend with Ash, no one else in my family was. Tawny eyed him skeptically and looked about.

"Prime Straumr. My thanks. You remember that from two years ago?" Tawny asked.

Ash took my hand and pressed his soft lips to it, watching me closely, "I remember meeting Scarlett as if it were yesterday. You are breathtaking."

"Where's your wife?" Tawny asked curtly.

Ash smiled and straightened. "She is organizing the water pipe room as we speak."

A band was starting to set up at the far end of the ballroom with a variety of instruments I recognized and many I didn't know matter how long I lived in Tidings. Women with queenly bearings in swirling dresses glided into the ballroom on the arms of men in satin and leathers that cut powerful forms no matter their size. All Guardians vigorously trained, tonight was for new and current tyros to the university and all those who had been proven tried and true.

Guardians were easy to discern by their jewelry. Inductees would receive a silver Yggdrasil necklace that they could personalize, second-year students would have a silver torque bracelet, and all Guardians had a gold torque. You always wore all three if you had them.

"Are you ready for our dance?" Ash asked, still holding my hand.

Ash made me feel graceful and cultured when we danced. It reminded me of the good times while we were together.

"Tawny. Evening, Ash."

Steel slid in at her side. His turquoise almond eyes peeked from within with a jagged half mask that looked as though someone had clawed glittering red nails across its black surface. Steel smiled politely at Ash looking like a poster boy for Abercrombie even in black leather pants.

Steel was the only ambassador to the Thrimilci tribes, and he knew how to put his personal opinions aside in order to be cordial. Jett and

Slate were primed to help as ambassadors but had yet to make their decisions as far as I knew.

In the short time we had been standing there, the band had begun to play the traditional Tidings music, and the room was starting to hum with conversation. I pulled my hand gently from Ash's grasp when I saw Quartzite coming through the ballroom. Her long blonde hair spilled over her shoulder to her waist, her wide blue eyes peered out from a red jeweled rose mask. The mask matched her flowing dress clinging to her ample curves. Her rosebud of a mouth quirked as she approached.

"Good evening."

I greeted her with Tawny and Steel. "This is a tremendous year for Guardians. The first female second," Quartz said, wrapping her arm around Ash's trim waist. "The spouse dance is after your opening. I am so looking forward to it."

I nodded, averting my eyes and spotted Indigo in her blush and pearl half mask. Quick was with her in a gold studded off white mask that matched his cravat and waistcoat that's gold buttons were in the droplet shape of the Regn. Brass and Crimson were with them. Brass's mask was black and fissured with white like a cracked egg. He was in all black with white embroidery around the trim and black leather pants. Crimson was stunning in eye catching red.

Jett and the girls entered the ballroom and Cherry gave us a little wave. I waved back, but they walked over to where Indigo and Quick were getting drinks at the bar.

"I'll have to sit that one out," I said distractedly, I was *not* looking for Slate.

"Perhaps Reed will dance with you. That would also be a first," Quartz pointed out.

"Perhaps," I said, eyeing the bar.

"Come. It is time," Ash said, kissing Quartz on the lips, and offering me his palm.

Tawny gave me a small smile. "We'll probably be in the water pipe room."

"See you guys later," I said, ignoring Ash's slight frown at my casual dialect.

I'd be his Second, but I couldn't change who I was with those closest to me. Gypsum came in with the ravishing Rosasite on his arm. It was his and Rosasite's first year being old enough to come to the masquerade. Ash and I would induct them in two weeks into the university. She was in emerald green with a jeweled mask that looked like snake scales and Gypsum was head to toe black with a skeletal half mask.

He didn't spot us until Ash took my arm and led me onto the dance floor. Guardians began to clear away once they recognized that it was the new Prime and his Second. Lights caught on my gold beads as Ash held me out with a big, charming smile. *This* was the golden boy I agreed to marry.

The Guardians worshipped him.

Ash clasped my hand and our bodies made a "V" shape from our hips in a promenade position. Training helped me catch on to the dance steps quickly, I took orders well. I had better since Slate had been one of my trainers and never let me slack for any reason, then Brass had taken over outside of the University.

The music began in a slow graceful melody of string instruments and woodwinds. I began to recite steps in my head as Ash led me about in front of hundreds of sets of eyes.

*Step forward on inside foot, close with the outside foot.*

I could feel people waiting for the girl who was a khoraz to fail. Wondering if I had slept my way into my position. If I was having an affair with Ash under Quartz's nose. No one would buy that she knew he wanted me as his second wife once Slate passed. As if I could look to that and plan my life afterwards.

*Step forward on inside foot, hop.*

I caught sight of Slate as Ash and I circled and my heart soared. He was standing in the exact same position he'd been in when I first saw him. Mr. Dark and Dangerous himself hidden in the shadows of the glittering pillar standing stock still watching me with reflective silver eyes.

The song ended, and I curtsied to Ash favoring him with my very best smile. Ash twirled me around and the crowd clapped. I didn't care who saw. There was only one reason for Slate to be standing in that exact spot.

He remembered.

I picked my skirts and ran in my heels to where Slate stood. Maybe I wasn't running, maybe I was flying. His memories were back. My husband. The man who had loved me no matter what, and I didn't care about the past, I only wanted him back. To see in his eyes that love that scorched as often as it melted.

Guardians moved out of my way when they saw me coming with a megawatt grin on my face. Slate had moved behind the pillar deeper into the shadows. He wore all black with his black and gold wrist blades even now crossed over his broad muscled chest. His waves, heavy with adornments, fell over his satin paisley waistcoat.

"*Slate*," I squeaked as tears of joy burned at my eyes.

His body went rigid as I leapt into his arms.

I couldn't stop kissing him, my fingers curled in his hair, knocking his black leather bird mask off. It was a good five-seconds before I realized he wasn't kissing me back. I swallowed and slid down to my feet gazing up at him.

My chest heaved. "Slate?"

His bronze brow creased, the silver scar looking angry and vivid. "Have you lost your Gods' cursed mind?" He growled.

My lips parted with a sharp breath. "I thought...you are standing in this spot..." My mind reeled.

"The shadows are deepest here. Unlike *some* people, I prefer to go unnoticed," he growled as I searched his eyes.

My palms were still on his chest and I took them off as if he'd suddenly burned me. "My mistake," I whispered dropping my chin.

I balled my fists in the sheer fabric of my dress. Slate lifted my chin up, but I couldn't meet his eyes. I was embarrassed, rejected, crushed. I just wanted his memories to return.

"I have never seen you look at anything that way, much less anyone."

I pressed my lips together to keep anything pathetic from coming out. "I thought your memories returned. This was where I first saw you." I swallowed hard. "Forget it. I'm sorry."

Faces blurred as I withdrew from Slate and walked through the nearest doors. I'd grown accustomed to these long yellow stoned halls. I measured my steps so I wouldn't run. I just needed a little air.

I found a balcony inside one of the arched double doors and gulped the cold December air. It was the dead of winter in Valla.

I was the Second to the Prime. I couldn't be caught sobbing about a broken heart in public. Especially about my husband in particular. He was a known Lothario before we were together, so what did I expect when he had had his fill of me?

A rare few people had seen me and Slate as a true couple and how much he had loved me. For six weeks, I thought we were in love. What if that hadn't been real and the man he was now was who he was in truth? He always said I was oblivious of the game.

I leaned my forehead against the frosted stone rail as puffs of my breath trailed out into the air. It was the only balcony on that floor and it was only a matter of time another Guardian would join me out there. I desperately wanted to let my tears out, but they wouldn't fall as if they knew there wasn't time to indulge in a good cry.

"You should forget about him. Even when his memories return, will you be able to overlook all that he has put you through?" Ash closed the doors behind him and placed his hand on my back.

"I wish you could give me a certain date and time his memories will return so I can avoid him until then. I thought they were back, that's all. Things have been fine all month," I said, straightening. "Sorry I ran out like that." I sighed.

He pushed his mask on the top of his head and rubbed his palm over my back. "They will return when it has completely unwound. I have never done the like before, or I would have given you an estimated time. No one saw you leave. As far as they are concerned, a married woman jumped into her husband's arms. Nothing amiss there."

I turned my head and gave him a small smile. The tip of his nose had started to redden. Moonlight radiated so brightly between the university's towers; I imagined warmth from its rays like sunlight.

I let out a light scoff that was more like a quick exhale of air. "Thanks. I feel like a fool. This whole situation emotionally blindsided me." I rubbed my belly. "He avoids me. I've made so many mistakes." I shook my head with an apologetic smile. "This is not what you want to hear."

Ash placed his hands over mine facing me. "It must be hard since he is so close with your family. You have my word, if you stay by me, I promise you and your children will be taken care of."

The Norns must have been laughing at me. "Ash, I am sorry for how it all went down last year."

He looked out past the balcony, removing his chilled hands from mine. "The past. We are young, plenty of time to put things back on their proper paths." His lips curled as he looked at me out of the corner of his eye. "You know how patient I can be."

*Did I ever.*

We had been dating on and off for a year before he had grown tired of waiting, especially after I had been with Slate. He hadn't even known about Brass at the time.

"I do. We should go back inside and do our job before someone starts making up rumors. *More* rumors, I should say."

"Those will pass. We are new to our positions and younger than any other Prime and Second in our history."

Ash placed his palm on my back again and led me to the doors then stopped. I looked above to where his gaze had settled. A mistletoe hung above the doors. During the masquerade under a mistletoe was how Slate had stolen our first kiss.

"Did you know the goddess Frigga's tears changed the colors of the mistletoe from red to white, saving her son's life when he was poisoned? She kissed everyone who walked beneath it out of gratitude for getting her son's life back."

My voice sounded far away. Slate had told me that story when I turned him down, then goaded me into letting him kiss me. Despite it all, the memory made me smile.

Ash dropped his hand from the door's knob and turned to me. "I would not want to break tradition."

"Ash..."

My feeble protest ended when Ash slid his hand into my hair and slanted his lips over mine. Ash tasted like peaches. He always had.

He inhaled filling his lungs with my scent. His tongue skimmed mine testing my boundaries. Ash was a control freak, but I knew where I stood with him. He wanted me, always had, in a permanent way. No doubts had been in my mind about how he felt about me.

The little voice that should have been waggling her finger at me in disapproval was mute. His kiss transported me through time when my mother and father were alive, when I was innocent with few responsibilities beyond getting to classes every day. Before all the complications of Slate, and Brass, and death. The burden of doing the impossible and finding a way to get the two pieces of the works that I need from Canis to preserve our world. I didn't even know how it would end, how I would save it. All I had were questions and no answers. I wanted to be that carefree girl again. Not a jaded woman with the weight of the world on her shoulders.

I had hooked my arms around Ash's hard body firmly pressing myself to him. My tongue was tangling with his as I felt my back hit the stone of the castle exterior wall. After the Merfolk had given me rousen, the pleasure center of my mind was irreparably changed. I could smell Ash's pheromones; it stoked the fire inside me that never fully died out.

"Not like this," Ash breathed, tearing his mouth away from mine.

Shaking my head trying to clear it, I sucked in icy breaths. I had thrown myself at a married man. Ash had taken a step back and was straightening his clothes. I ran my shaky palms over my face and I fixed my mask that had been knocked askew.

"Sugarfoot, Ash. I'm sorry. I'll explain to Quartz. This is my fault."

As girls, Tawny and I never swore. We came up with our own substitutions and they stuck. I'd even heard Indigo use our substitutes a time or two.

Ash's piercing green-eyed gaze was unreadable, but his tone was stern. "Scarlett, I have wanted you for years. I only meant if we have waited this long, we can do it properly with Quartz's knowledge. This should not be a tawdry affair. Things between you and me —"

"We're both married. Slate will get his memories back," I said, rubbing my hands together trying to convey how inappropriate what we had just done was.

Ash straightened and scanned my face. His nostrils flared, and he offered me his palm.

"Come, we have to be seen," he said flatly, and I gave him my arm.

"That was a very nice kiss, Ash. Too nice," I said as he opened the door, and he paused.

"I am glad I am able to stir a positive emotional response in you," he mused.

We had left the balcony just in time. Guardians were spreading out through the hall mingling and greeting one another holding their drinks. I desperately wished I could have a drink.

Red curtains enclosed the water pipe room. Jett and the others sat at their usual table in the furthest corner from the entrance where they would have the most privacy. Wall to wall fabric draped in oranges, reds and yellows surrounded the room. Pillows lined the walls and the low tables. The younger crowd lounged about, splayed on the colorful pillows some had pushed their masks up onto their heads as they sucked in the flavored tobacco from the pipes on the tables. Lanterns hung off golden chains along the ceiling made to look like they were in a tent.

"I will not explain again," Slate growled from where he sat back with a goblet in his hand in the shadows.

Jett pushed his Iron Man mask back over his face as he leaned back on the couches putting his arm around Cerise and Amethyst. Cerise had a feathered peacock mask over her face, while Amethyst looked like a cat. Indigo shot Jett a nervous glance.

They'd all seen Scar running in her formal gown and leap into Slate's arms as if she'd forgotten how crappy he'd been to her. Indigo had slapped a hand to her mouth. She knew something, and she wasn't saying. Scar had disappeared then for a short while.

Ash had gone after her. The two came back together and gone their separate ways. Every man and woman wanted a chance to dance with the Prime and his Second since they were both so young and attractive. Many hoped they were inexperienced enough to be influenced.

Scarlett was sitting in the same spot that Jett had first seen her next to Ash and the rest of the great family brats. Diamond Natt now sat at her side on the vibrant pillows, her back to them. She'd done it intentionally; Jett knew and didn't blame her. Sterling, Sage, Garnet, Nova, Fox, and Quartz were also gathered around the table. Sage and Garnet at the far end facing towards them. Garnet, the giggling blonde Quick had been sleeping with while he and Indi were on the outs, kept casting looks his way, but then again, so were Diamond and Sterling.

Gypsum and Rosasite had come as a couple and sat with Quick, Indi, Slate, Tawny, Steel, Crimson, and Brass. Frigga's sweet grass, Brass and Crimson were acting like a couple. Crimson was the kind of girl that fell in love with the idea of love long before she'd met any man. Brass was like a white knight coming to her rescue after her destroyed reputation had prevented any suitors from courting her when she'd had an affair while Scar and Ash were together. Jett wondered what she would think about Ro having already been with her white knight.

Scar had been swimming when the guys had gone into the pool. Pearl had suggested their early training so they could help her in Thrimilci with something she didn't explain only to cancel after. It had been a plot to get them to see Scarlett that backfired. Scar looked like she wanted to be alone, that the sight of them had hurt her. It didn't help that not only was Slate being an asshole, but so was Brass. Would it have killed Slate to join Scarlett while Ash had danced with Quartz?

Rosasite and Brass had been and item until Brass found out Ash brought up taking a second husband to her. Then he'd dumped her, there wouldn't have been any bad blood between them except now Brass was being seen in public with Crimson.

He'd taken her back to the Regn manor in Ostara last night but hadn't slept with her even though she'd wanted to. Apparently, Ash was the only man she'd been with and they had been discussing what had been done when they'd walked in on Scar in the pool. It didn't help that

Slate had disappeared with that brunette staffer from the Tio palace in tow right in front of Scarlett. That bastard.

"What's the plan for your birthday this year?" Steel asked drinking wassail, the mulled wine had bits of fruit floating in it out of a crystal goblet.

"The cottages were fun last year. This year Ash and Slate won't get into a fist fight either."

Jett let his eyes slide from Slate to where Ash was practically waiting on Scar and Quartz on hand and foot bringing them both their drinks and taking turns dancing with them as if he was husband to them both. Quartz was even making a point to lean past Ash to join Scarlett in her conversations with Diamond. Diamond and Scar had always got on well.

Slate grunted. "A fight? How is it he still breathes?"

Hunter Snjar, Amber's brother, entered the water pipe room. His sleeves were rolled up and the veins in his arms stood out prominently. His skin was tanned which darkened his hollowed cheeks. His forehead seemed permanently furrowed above his hawk like blue eyes. He took one look at Scarlett sitting at their table, her body casually angled with her feet tucked under her and his lips curled. His intense gaze swept up to where they sat in the back as he walked up behind her.

Hunter ducked down and said a few words that made her cheeks flush and Ash's face hardened to steel. He raised his arm as if he was gesturing to Hunter, but what he was doing was putting his arm around Scar's shoulders. Hunter smirked and sat down on Scarlett's other side forcing himself between her and Diamond. Ash casually pulled Scarlett's long hair over her shoulder and Jett watched her curls bounce as his fingers slid through the sun lightened ends of her caramel waves.

Scarlett was in over her head. Hunter had a bone to pick with Slate after he hand-fasted Amber and cheated on her with Scarlett. Jett couldn't believe Scar was sitting at the same table with those people.

Crimson's hand rested lightly on Brass's thigh as she leaned against him where they sat on the cushions. She was from Indi's old crowd, Scar's current, and the two women got along. Jett got up to get Amethyst and Cherry fresh drinks and Scar lifted her eyes to him and mouthed *get me out of here.*

For some reason, the fact that she wasn't enjoying herself with them made him feel better. There was hope for her yet. Jett went to get drinks and brought them back to the girls.

"Amethyst, I hate to ask this of you. Could you distract the blue bloods so I can plot Scarlett's escape?" Jett asked.

"I knew she could not have fun with that lot," Quick said. "She looks bored."

Scarlett did indeed look to be suppressing a yawn. Crimson laughed.

"They are not bad people. I have heard pregnancy makes a woman tired. Two must make you twice as tired."

Crimson smiled at Brass. She had no idea that those were Brass's babies she so casually mentioned. It had to be the fastest a woman got around to talking babies before. Slate watched Brass over the rim of his goblet with a knowing curl of his lips.

Amethyst started to rise but saw a tall dark man heading through the room. It was not extraordinary, except that he was much older than anyone else in the room by decades and he had a commanding quality. He moved with a deadly grace indicative to the most skilled Guardian men from their years of training.

"Who is that?" Rosasite asked in a slightly awed tone.

Even with a bronze half mask on that matched his waist coat and ascot, you could tell the older man had an anvil jaw and lips women tended to stare at. Gypsum's dimpled smile parted his olive face.

"That is Patriarch Regn. Scarlett's recently added him to her collection of suitors. What is a pack of suitors called? A covet?" Gypsum chuckled at his own wit. "She seems to like him and wants nothing from her. Men always want something from her."

Quick snorted. "He wants something from her all right."

"Silver, you sound defensive. You care about her," Indi teased.

Quick arched his brow at her. "She is your twin. She has saved my life. I might not always agree with her, but she is like the sister I never wanted. Where do you think I learned it all, Dove?" His grin at Jett's little sister was salacious, it was a good thing he was making an honest woman out of her.

Scarlett had finally spotted Spinel, and she straightened. He noticed her eyes on him and a smile slowly grew on his face. She looked to where Jett and the others sat out of the corner of her eye and looked nervous. Spinel stopped in front of her and he said something to her making Ash go rigid.

Spinel offered her both his hands, and she spoke to those around her, giving Diamond a kiss on the cheek. Ash bent forward and kissed her cheek as well and her face flushed. Fox lifted his sky-blue gaze to where Slate sat. Fox had liked Slate and Scar together.

Scar took Spinel's hands and then she tripped as she rose sending her staggering into Spinel face first. Spinel caught her with a broad smile.

Scarlett was blushing right down to her neckline as Spinel pulled her upright from where she had landed against his chest, his hands slid innocuously from her hips and along her spine as she balanced herself on his body.

Brass cursed a colorful stream of expletives.

"Did he just...?" Indigo started to ask.

"*Call* and trip her? Yes, he did. Smooth. She does not have a clue either," Quick said, appreciating his grandfather's genius.

She didn't. Scarlett was apologizing and her face was still red. Spinel took advantage of her fluster and pushed her hair from her face reassuring her. Ash was looking up at them both, expression livid. Scarlett whipped her head down to him and she looped her arm through Spinel's, abruptly taking his hand off her face.

Spinel nodded to where Brass and Quick sat and Scar drew herself up. He led Scarlett over to where they sat and Jett watched as she put on her imperial mask, walling her emotions off from them. Spinel wore a permanent smirk when he came to a standstill in front of them.

"Good evening. I am off. I will see you at the manor. Crimson, you will have to join us for breakfast again." Spinel gave Crimson a smile, and she blushed. "Indigo, I do miss your lovely face in the mornings since you and Silver have been spending so much time at the Sumar palace."

"We see one another often since you have been spending so much time with my sister," Indigo said dryly.

"Your sister has graced me with her treasured attentions. I would be an utter fool to let her slip away," Spinel said smoothly.

"I know she has," Slate growled almost inaudibly.

Scarlett hadn't so much as blinked.

"Goodnight, Patriarch Regn," Crimson said. "Second."

Scarlett inclined her head like a superior acknowledging the notice of one beneath her. Which Jett supposed they all were given her new station. Spinel guided her possessively by the small of her back from the water pipe room. Ash followed them with his eyes as they went.

"When he said join *us* for breakfast..." Cherry asked with a giggle.

"He was implying he was taking Scarlett home tonight. I don't think she realized what he was doing, she's inexperienced when it comes to dating in Tidings," Jett said, wiping a hand over his face.

"There are worse men she could go home with," Indigo murmured under her breath with her eyes on Ash.

"I do not get it," Rosasite said in a bitter tone.

Tawny pursed her looks giving Ro a cool look and Steel patted her hand. Ro didn't get the message.

"She's gorgeous and powerful. A Guardian's wet dream," Cherry said wryly.

"That's my sister you're talking about." Jett gave Cherry a look and she giggled leaning in to press her pouty red stained lips to his.

"She is just a pretty *girl*," Ro continued caustically.

Crimson leaned forward to face Rosasite. "I heard she was sleeping with Patriarch Haust before Orion killed him. Rumor was *she* was the girl he caught Peak with. They say she has been sleeping with Patriarch Regn for months. That he's her only suitor now, and he's willing to give up his bachelorhood for her. They certainly look cozy."

Jett didn't keep many secrets from his wives, but Peak forcing himself on Scarlett was one. Orion was Tawny's grandfather who had been sentenced to death but died at the end of the trial. Few knew he had fallen on his sword for Scarlett.

A silence fell over all except Rosasite who gasped.

"I had not heard that! The Prime made her Second, anyway? That cannot be possible, the current Patriarch ran the Ragnarök with her. Unless he did not know." Rosasite sniffed. "Is there a man here she has not been intimate with in some way?"

Tawny's tiny fists balled and Steel rubbed her thigh. Jett raised his hand and laughed trying to ease the mood. Steel caught on and raised his own with a lopsided grin. Ro stared at Gypsum and her face darkened.

"She was on rousen. She's my cousin. Trust me, it sounds much worse than it was," Gypsum said defensively.

Jett's stomach sank at that and he didn't need to spare Steel a look to know he bore the same expression. Deep in a rousen stupor, Scarlett simultaneously used her *calling* to form a vortex of pleasure. Warm, wet swirling and sucking had caressed their bodies until Slate brought her in hand.

Slate was glaring at Quick who laughed. "It is a long story. You had me train her — the hard way to prove she could handle the patron rooms after the Crash Course. She was not ready; it was after she came back from the Merfolk."

"It wasn't her fault," Indigo said, shaking her head.

Crimson's eyes were the size of saucers behind her mask.

"You kissed my wife?" Slate growled.

Quick sat back and wrapped an arm around Indigo's shoulders.

"Now she's your wife again?" Brass asked, not looking at Slate.

"Lawfully," Slate growled. "Is she going to bed your grandfather?"

Brass's jaw clenched. "Not this time."

Jett tried not to seem too interested. Quick didn't call him out on the lie and everything Crimson had said was true. No wonder Brass was such an asshole to her, Jett thought.

Tawny sighed. "Daddy issues. She's chock-full of them. It was only a matter of time before a handsome older man filled that void with her left to her own devices. He's not so bad. Even I could tell he's out to keep other men away. Honestly, he's the lesser of the many *many* evils that have been throwing themselves into her path. She's ill equipped to handle men throwing themselves at her."

"Do you have daddy issues, Dove?" Quick traced Indi's jaw with a long index finger.

"No. I grew up with my dad. I have mommy issues." Indi's eyes slid to Quick who ducked his head to kiss her lips.

"I did hear that too. That is true? She was not sleeping at Valla U because Forest, Alexandrite, *and* Chrome snuck into her bed. Can you imagine? I was in the room next to hers and heard her scream until a man and woman carted them from the room. Those are her guards? I would be worried about those men who might force themselves on her. Luckily, the boy from Valla U left when she turned them down. She is so young for her position and vulnerable, being pregnant and alone," Crimson said with genuine concern. "I never really liked her, but that was not her fault. She has always gone out of her way to be kind to me and does seem a genuinely good person."

Jett stared down at his hands. Scarlett had gotten very good at hiding everything. He forgot how inexperienced she was and how sheltered she'd been. Fucking bastards trying to seduce her, sneaking into her bed. She was pregnant and married.

"She has guards," Brass said in a curt tone.

Slate growled and got to his feet, throwing his glass with a crash.

"Damn the gods."

Slate prowled from the room. Shadows seemed to stretch towards his body between the lanterns as if he called to the darkness and it sought to embrace him.

"Where is *he* going?" Tawny said, watching him leave.

"After our girl. He likes to pretend he doesn't care, but most nights I see him coming home late when I'm walking the halls with Opal during a feeding," Jett said.

"He's been... watching her sleep?" Indi asked, incredulous.

"Checking on her. She falls asleep outside; he brings her in," Brass said in that same dead curt tone he'd been using.

"What an idiot. He should just stay the night. She wouldn't tell him to leave, we all saw what she did earlier. She's still in love with him." Cherry shook her head. "Can't he see that?"

*"When you turn the corner, and you run into yourself, then you know that you have turned all the corners that are left."*

Jett sank back and watched Slate leave from the room.

Spinel was profoundly amused by my mental dance step counting but did say I had potential. I found myself preening like a complete idiot at his compliments. I spent the rest of my night with him helping me through a lot of obligatory conversations with Guardians I barely knew. Spinel knew everyone and because he could read minds like Brass could, I fell into old habits of speaking to him through my mind.

I missed Brass.

After many songs, and dancing with every person I knew in Tidings, Spinel walked me back to my wing at the Dagr palace. I had insisted the portal doors were far enough, but *he* insisted on walking me to the wing. The stone walls were lit by recessed lighting making it look like a cathedral as it lit the sculptures of the Dagr matriarchs along the walls like saintly beauties. Sparrow's statue managed to have an attitude. Slate's was yet to be commissioned. He would be the very first Patriarch of the Dagr line.

Groin vaulted ceilings with Corinthian grey stone columns and marbled tiles spanned the Romanesque halls. My heels clicked as we walked. If I was alone, I would've gone barefoot after all that dancing.

The Dagr palace was one single sprawling floor with a manicured cloister at its heart. I had redone a parlor as our wing just so Slate and I could have a wing off the gardens. I'd planted a blue morning glory vine that grew over a lattice there that I liked to sit with at night.

Lombard bands lined the stone monolithic columns that wrapped around the covered walkway and I was tempted to ask Spinel to join me on the stone bench so I could take in the night. It had become my favorite time a day. The few minutes I had before I fell asleep once all my daily responsibilities were handled and I could forget for blissful moments all the curve balls that had been thrown my way in the last two years.

Arched slatted doors spanned our wing, and I stopped in front of it. "This is me," I said stupidly.

Spinel reached past me and twisted the lever and opened the door with glittering eyes. He led me in backwards with one hand on my hip. It was dark in my wing; the only light came from the stars until Spinel reached out and found my energy plate turning on the lights without even looking. He must have gleaned it from my mind. He'd been touching me all night; he probably knew all my deepest darkest secrets if he was like Brass and could pick up memories through my willing touch.

"Balas..." I whispered, and immediately regretted the name all his lovers used, that I had only known him by until Brass revealed who he truly was.

"Give me the grand tour," Spinel said smoothly.

"Well, this is the front room," I said, my eyes flitting between his, and his lips curled.

Lips that were plump and defined like Brass's.

White marbled tiles spanned the floor of the light dusky blue front room, a soft beige couch and oversized chair occupied the front room throw pillows in varying shades of creams scattered across them. The sheer curtains framed the arched doors that led to the covered walkway before the cloister. A rectangular light wood table sat before it on a modern white and beige rug.

I took a step back from him and led him through the double doors into the dining room. It had enough room for a circular table that sat six and matched the coffee table. The chairs were upholstered in the same dusky blue as the living room with a white hutch. One of our mother's paintings hung on the wall across from the collection Moroccan lanterns hung in whites and blues above the round pedestal table.

A short hall had three doors. On the left was a guest bathroom and on the right the nursery. I opened the door and walked inside.

"The nursery, but I ordered new cribs from a troll in Mabon that will be ready sometime this week," I explained.

Sea foam green walls and a dresser complete with changing table had an off-white plush chair sat in the corner piled with stuffed animals next to a short bookcase filled with bright colored titles. A wood carved rocking horse sat to the side, a picture of my mother and I was framed of us picnicking at the lake.

Spinel walked into the room and began to look at the picture and the paintings. Above the first crib was one of the paintings their mother had sold right before we moved. Sparrow had tracked a bunch down; that one was my favorite. It was the tree of life with deep curling roots, a blazing golden sun shone down on a cat and a deer dancing next to a pond a mermaid leaned from.

I thought of the letter hidden behind its frame for the first time in months. An envelope with my mother's elegant lettering scrawl across the front that read *ALDER*. It was bloodstained, either my or my father's blood from when he had given it to me to read. I couldn't even look at the blasted envelope much less read my mother's final words. There was something so final about reading it, I kept pushing it off.

A second painting was above the next crib. It was a whimsical painting of a merman sitting astride a Centaur with the solar cross of the Dagr sigil in the sky and a lion hybrid with a charcoal barghest.

"Trolls make the best wood furniture."

"Pearl's dining room has such a beautiful table; I knew I had to have a troll made piece." I turned to go back to the front room.

"The bedroom?" Spinel asked with his hand on the doorknob.

My stomach heated. "I can have one of the staff bring a carafe of wine. I haven't had my glass for the day," I offered.

Brass, Slate, Chris, and Balas, *er* Spinel. The men I'd given myself to.

Try as I might, the occasional rogue thought of my nights with Balas snuck into my mind when he curled those lush lips of his at me, knowing what pleasure they could deliver. That he was old enough to be my grandfather and *was* Brass's grandfather held no bearing on how attractive I found the older man. It was sheer will power, propriety, and self-loathing that kept me walking a fine line, and him in my bedroom would be detrimental to those lines.

Spinel gave me a knowing look, and I rubbed my lips together. He opened the door and turned on the light. Two doors were in the left wall, one to the master bathroom and a closet as big as a bedroom that was half empty since Slate moved out. The bedroom was dominated by the big white bed. A modern down comforter laid across it and flowing sheer white panels that were swathed around the bed in a canopy. Piles of pillows ran along the white upholstered headboard. The walls were pale green with a white chaise. A long, distressed dresser had our mother's pictures in glass frames as well as intimate pictures of Slate and me kissing. The staff placed light pink peonies in vases to either side of the bed at the nightstands, knowing they were my favorite.

At least, if I had followed him into the room, that's what I would have seen. I didn't dare enter a bedroom with Spinel Regn. Now that I knew who he was, I couldn't be bedding the Regn Patriarch.

I heard Spinel chuckle and knit my brow.

"My wife let you into our bedroom?"

"Scarlett. You have a visitor," Spinel called.

My jaw dropped. What was Slate doing there? I barged into the room and watched Spinel give me a smirk before closing the bathroom door behind him. Slate was sprawled out in my big bed propped up on a mountain of pillows. His waves were free of its fetishes and beads that now sat in the ceramic bowl I kept in the nightstand for my own. My white blankets were pulled up to his hips, his bronze upper body was a masterpiece of countless sculpted muscles with the occasional silver scar that matched the long one that ran from his scalp to his cheekbone over his left eye. He narrowed his silver eyes that were framed by his long, lush lashes but there was no warmth there.

I crossed my arms. "I don't understand."

"Get rid of the geezer and come to bed, girl."

"You can't show up whenever it's convenient for you," I told him and lowered my voice. "He's not a geezer and you know it. That's why you're here. You thought I would sleep with him." I shook my head. "We'll talk about this when he leaves."

Spinel came out at that moment and raised an amused brow at me. "I'll walk you out, Spinel. Thank you for escorting me home," I said leaving the bedroom hoping he would walk out with me.

"Goodnight, Patriarch Regn," Slate said in mocking formality.

Spinel paused in the doorway. "She is a good woman. You would be smart not to let her get away. Four different men tried to take your wife home tonight with less honorable intentions than I, which is a feat in itself. Goodnight, Patriarch Dagr."

I walked in front of Spinel until we reached the slatted doors. "Do you remember your way back to the portal room?"

"Yes, Scarlett. Thank you for keeping me company tonight." Spinel leaned in and kissed my cheek.

"Spinel?"

"Yes, Scarlett?" he asked, already smirking.

"Why are you still interested in me?" I asked out of curiosity.

"Other than the fact that you are a sensational beauty and the most powerful woman in Tidings?" Spinel asked, and my cheeks heated. "There is a vulnerability to you, beneath your hard facade. It appeals to me. I want to nurture you, guide you, help you. A younger, less experienced man in the ways of life cannot do that for you. There are many other attributes I find very interesting about you, my criminally young Scarlett, but I do believe your husband is eavesdropping."

"Goodnight, Spinel," I said, giving his hand a squeeze before locking the door behind me.

I let my palm slide over the ridges of the slats before turning off the lights as I walked back to the bedroom. Slate hadn't moved. I went into the closet and pulled out a white lace baby doll nightie with a pleated skirt, it was one of the new lingerie dresses I bought to fit over my belly.

I walked into the bathroom.

It was similar to the one at the Sumar palace. Dozens of shower heads were built right into the tiffany blue tiles, the waterfall separated the shower from the rest of the bathroom was activated by an energy plate when you used *calling.* Two white ornate mirrors hung above the ivory sinks in front of the huge ivory clawed foot tub that would fit both of us easily. Bright pink floral accents decorated the bathroom giving it a feminine touch.

I readied for bed and piled my hair on top of my head before walking back into the bedroom. I let out a heavy breath and climbed into bed next to Slate.

"I saw that brunette yesterday follow you when you left last night," I said, pulling the blankets up as I sat up against the headboard.

"I did not bed her, if you are asking," Slate rumbled.

"She left right after you," I said playing with the down blanket.

"She did follow and threw herself at me. Desperation is not an attractive quality." He lifted his hand and his index finger caught on the thin sleeve of my nightie as he slid it over the curve of my shoulder.

"I feel desperate for you all the time," I said, swallowing. "Why are you here, Slate?"

"Did you bed the Prime?" he asked.

"No. Not ever. We kissed under the mistletoe tonight." I confessed. "They seemed to pop up from everywhere." I'd doled out three other chaste kisses to men before the night was through.

Slate slid his finger along my neckline and my skin prickled. "How often do men try to bed you these days?"

I watched his finger sliding over my cleavage. "At least once a day," I whispered.

"And how often do you take men up on those offers?" he rumbled.

I caught his hand. "Never, Slate. I've stopped looking for a second husband and I try very hard not to disrespect you or myself."

He shifted his hand out of mine and rested it on my belly. Warmth flooded through me as he delved to feel the twins. I shut my eyes and relaxed my muscles, sliding along the headboard to lean my head against his shoulder.

"Stay the night with me," I said softly.

I heard Slate swallow, and he removed his hand from my belly. "I have had a lover, girl."

He swung his legs over the side of the bed and I had to pull my head up before I collapsed onto the bed. I knew he had.

"Stay anyway. I just want to be held," I said and smiled at his back. "*See?* Desperate."

Slate stopped moving, and I scooted to where he sat and wrapped my arms around his waist, pressing my cheek to his back. Slate put one of his calloused palms over my hands and pushed them away.

I was getting really sick and tired of him leaving me.

He didn't though. Slate turned around and pushed me back against the pillows. He climbed over my leg and leaned his ear to my belly. Like an involuntary reflex, I slid my fingers into his hair and stroked through to the end. Soft silky waves fell across my lap and my insides pulled, making me want to tilt my hips up.

"You could have danced with me tonight... yesterday when I asked," I whispered.

"I know," he rumbled.

I could feel the babies kick at the deep reverberating tone of his voice and he froze. A little laugh escaped me.

"Did he kick you in the head?" I asked, knowing my sons were especially feisty.

Slate lifted my baby doll nightie up over my belly and ran his palms over it, *calling*. I let my head fall back against the pillows as he rubbed over my skin. He pressed his lips over my belly and I began to run my fingers through his hair again. I loved his long hair. I *loved* his long hair over my thighs.

"Come here," I beckoned.

He lifted his eyes. Slate practically dripped savage sexuality; it permeated my skin. He was the one who took care of me after the Merfolk had trained me on rousen. He weaned me off and made me his own personal khoraz. At his worst, I would still want him. The ties that bound us were tight.

"You could shift," I whispered.

A barghest could only take one human mate. Peak Haust, had drugged and forced himself on me, claiming me as his own when Slate was imprisoned. We had killed him and Orion had gone down for the murder. It was not a time I liked to think about.

"Do not..." Slate warned.

"Too late," I whispered, shrugging so the other sleeve of my nightie fell over my shoulder.

Charcoal grey fur pushed from his darkening skin; long pointed ears transformed from human ears with three sets of horns curling from his head. One set that curved from his jaw like tusks. His short snout was pulled back in a canine smile revealing teeth as long as my fingers. Slate's hair and those silver eyes were the only things about him that remained the same. The barghest man rippled with sleek bunched muscles ready to attack as he pulled his knees up between my legs.

"I do not want to hurt you," the beast man rasped as a low growl reverberated in his throat.

"So don't," I coaxed.

Slate grabbed my pleated skirt in two hands and with one hard tear, he ripped the nightie from hem to neckline. His growl deepened, and he placed his clawed hands to either side of my shoulders, prowling up my body. His lips were soft even in this form as he kissed up my belly and over my breasts. Long teeth scraped over my hardening peaks, his rough tongue swirling over me. His tongue traced my tendon, and I turned my mouth to his.

My back arched on the pillows and my belly brushed his sleek furred muscles. A barghest khoraz — one who desired. Khoraz was a negative term used for those who were sexually attracted to the tribes, or anyone specifically — like a barghest. Most of which were paid for the services they offered.

My insides pulsed as butterflies beat in my stomach. I wanted this. I needed him. I ran my palms over the sleek ridges of his muscles. I was panting, my body squirmed beneath his, and he rasped a chuckle.

"You are wanton, mate."

"Would it be cliché to say how badly I want you? As if you couldn't scent it." I grinned as I kissed over his jaw, careful not to slice myself on his razor-sharp tusks.

"The way you looked at me tonight..." he trailed off.

"You are him, and he is you. I always want you. That shouldn't come as a big surprise," I teased.

"I do not want you out in public. When men come near you, it takes a great deal of will not to tear their throats out. I do not want Spinel back in our bedroom."

*Our.*

"Yes, Slate," I breathed. "No more. I promise. I'll swear a blood vow this second if you want."

He chuckled, and I moaned in anticipation. Slate fisted his hand in the back of my hair, pulling me back so he could meet my eyes that were peeking out from lowered lids.

"What was Ash doing outside my bedroom that night?" Slate rumbled.

I blinked. Did he just play me? There I was lying bared before him, quite literally squirming with anticipation, and he was demanding answers.

"I made that pact with him for your memories. I knew you wouldn't let him touch you, much less *call* on your mind —"

Slate teeth snapped an inch from my face and his grip tightened making me wince. "You *called* me asleep, vulnerable, and let him into my bedroom? Had him *call* on my mind? Defenseless?" he growled.

My eyes were wide. He didn't have complete control in his half beast form and he was livid.

"I'm sorry. I thought it was the only way," I rushed out.

Slate roared in my face so I shut my eyes and fought the urge to cover my ears. He pushed off the bed and started grabbing his clothes.

"You violated my most private sanctum and trust for *nothing*. You traded your honor for *nothing* and lost Brass by fucking his grandfather whom you flaunt. What man does not want to fuck the Second?"

Slate was beginning to shift back into a man, his big powerful body returned to its bronze color as he jerked on his pants. I pulled the white sheet over me and scooted to the edge of the bed.

"He said it would come back in a few weeks. It's only just been that long. Any day now. Come to bed. Stay the night. Stay *every* night. I miss you. I miss *us*. I don't care who you've been with. I don't know how much longer I can do this without you."

My speech had started out confidently but had tapered into a pathetic mewl. He hadn't stopped dressing. My chin wobbled.

"Slate!" I called again, but he didn't turn around.

A hysterical cry bubbled up as I balled the sheet in my fists.

"I love you. I *need* you."

"Move on, Scarlett. This is not the life I want," he rumbled.

"But... before I went to the Merfolk. You were happy. You can't tell me you weren't," I said weakly.

"For a few days... I was blinded by lust." He tugged his boots on and made to leave.

"But that night... with Brass," I stammered out.

Slate turned around and poured his beads from the ceramic bowl into his hand. "Brass told me you would not be with him without my approval. He invited me to join you that night. Nothing more."

"You're lying. I can *feel* when your walls are down. Don't do this. Stop rejecting me and how you feel because of some stupid prophecy." I got to my feet; he was walking out of the room. "I make you happy. You just have to let me," I said, following him out.

"I am happy between your legs," he rumbled, walking past our nursery.

I was everything I ever hated in that moment. "No. I don't believe you. You can't fake that smile," I said, feeling like an elephant had parked its backside on my chest.

Slate stopped in the archway of the open slatted door. "I have no use for you."

"*Unless you can think, when the song is done, no other is soft in the rhythm; unless you can feel, when left by one, that all men else go with him; unless you can know, when upraised by his breath. That your beauty itself wants proving; unless you can swear 'For life, for death!' Oh, fear to call it loving! Unless you can muse in a crowd all day. On the absent face that fixed you; unless you can love, as the angels may, with the breadth of heaven betwixt you; unless you can dream that his faith is fast, through behoving and unbehoving; unless you can die when the dream is past — oh, never call it loving!*"

He had used my own favorite poets against me. I stared at the spot he'd stood in and closed my eyes, trying to imagine a different ending to the conversation. One where he told me his memories didn't matter, and that he loved me anyway. I pretended he never asked about Ash and we were actually making love in our big white bed. Slate was striking in white.

Tree-gold padded over to me rubbing herself along my calves. She was almost a year old and thirty pounds of pure white snowy fur with green eyes. Bee-gold was Indigo's cat, my cat's sister that had the same long white fur with blue eyes. She must have sensed how distressed I was, standing there staring into the night.

I bent down and scratched behind her ears. Gypsum was a zoolinguist and had bought her a glittering collar he said she liked. I let out a shuddering breath, unwilling or unable to digest what had just happened and crawled back into bed after I discarded my shredded nightie.

Never, while I was spending my high school nights, dreaming about the husband I thought I would settle down with and cramming for my expedited courses, did I think my marriage would end like that. I was divorced in all, but name. Alone and pregnant. I had thrown myself at him — begged him.

Had my mother ever begged Alder to stay? To not marry Delta? Had Indigo ever begged Sterling not to marry Diamond? It was his choice now, wasn't it? He was the Patriarch of the Haust. No one was forcing him to marry Diamond. Did Diamond want Sterling? She had been casting looks Gypsum's way all night, but *he'd* been with Rosasite.

I was starting to think that no one had it figured out.

Eating breakfast on the covered walkway with Sparrow and Hawk had become a daily tradition. I'd slipped the silver charm of a silhouette of a mother holding a baby onto my silver torque, the one I'd bought when I was pregnant with Slate's child before I'd known it. I would consider myself a widow until Slate's memories returned, and we'd forget this disaster ever happened.

I just had to hang on until then.

"Those dance lessons have paid off," Sparrow said, passing me a platter full of mushroom and onion omelets.

"I didn't feel like a complete klutz. Ash is a good lead," I said, trying to end the conversation.

Hawk and Sparrow were my only example of a functioning couple growing up. They were as much my parents as they were my aunt and uncle.

"Did he make sure you got home alright?" Hawk asked, glancing up at me.

For a split second, I forgot how miserable last night was with Slate. The staff had probably heard our argument.

"Spinel Regn escorted me back," I told them, and tried not to laugh when they both scowled.

"Patriarch Regn is seventy years old," Hawk said, his voice dropping as he held out a dish of bacon.

I thanked him for the bacon. "Sixty-six, actually. Spinel knows how to wade through all the politics and he knows everyone."

"Because he's been around forever," Sparrow said under her breath and I did laugh.

"If I said I know what I'm doing, that'd be a lie. He does mean well, and I have no intention of pursuing a romantic relationship with Brass's grandfather. He keeps the unwanted suitors away. I think it's his age, younger men find him intimidating so they don't challenge him for my attention."

I gave a small shrug and finished my meal. Sparrow and Hawk knew about the attack in Valla and the unwanted late-night visitors. Since they had eyes, they knew of my newfound novelty status.

Sparrow's thin hand clasped mine and gave it a squeeze. "Reject them long enough and the message will get out. You have those Shadow Breaker bodyguards, right?"

"Two during the day, and one while I sleep. I feel better knowing they're there even though I only see them when I need them."

Brass had trained and chosen Pewter and Siren as my bodyguards; two Breakers I'd recruited from a black-market dealer. Styg, or Civet, used to sell wares from the chained Leshy Orion had in his ice dungeon. Orion wasn't the man Tawny thought he was. I didn't know who my night guard was, it was better that way so I wouldn't subconsciously look around for them.

Steel had introduced me to Solder on our first trip to the Merfolk. Tawny and I met Katydid our first day in Tidings the night of the masquerade. The pretty blonde was Brass's only serious ex-girlfriend who also did hair and makeup with Bronze and Cricket for the Shadow Breaker competitions.

Tawny and Steel were joining me for their son's Ausa Vatni. I had never been to a Guardian's home that wasn't a lesser or greater family. Solder and Katydid were from Thrimilci so we could walk there.

Most of my dresses were empire waist gowns, the traditional Thrimilci gowns were my favorite, but I'd taken a liking to the heavy Elivagar styles that made me feel like Scarlett O'Hara in Gone with the Wind. My rose silk charmeuse gown crossed over my back and flowed to the white shimmering road as we walked through Thrimilci.

The Sumar palace was erected on the side of a cliff. The white palace covered the entire top, several pointed domes and turrets in metallic blue and golds glittered in the sunlight. It's hundreds of arched windowless windows were sculpted into the face of the palace. The rivers Mani and Sol flowed around and behind the palace that led to the water fall behind it. Hundreds of white pueblo styled houses were built along the side of the cliff in a slope, each one with a royal blue roof, some with gardens that were *call* assisted since vegetation tended not to flourish in Thrimilci. The town heart was at the base of the cliff where we came out of the fifteen-foot-high portal gate designed as a high mosaic arch done in whites and blues. Spiraling ironwork below it radiating from a blazing sun and below that an iron patchwork door.

The store fronts on the main road had wide open glass shop fronts white columns that lined the road. All signs were uniformly painted with royal blue signs and gold lettering. Tawny looked like a saucy doll with a flowing capped sleeved russet colored dress on. Steel wore traditional local men's clothing, a heather grey sleeveless linen 'V' neck with lapis toggle buttons. His shirt was tucked into snug black pants and wore supple boots. I could see the shape of his blades. Steel used the spear but carrying that thing around this time of day going to a baby's party would be ludicrous.

"Any luck with the baby making?" I asked her, ignoring the fact Steel was my uncle.

Tawny jumped on being able to talk about her marriage. All of us close to her were related to Steel. Cherry and she had grown close while I had run to Chicago and in her she had found a confidant. Her wide smile split her fair face.

"We are trying frequently enough," she said, quirking her brow.

I could see Steel's tanned cheeks redden. Steel used to be like the other guys, dating a lot of girls, no commitment, and then Tawny hit him like a ton of bricks, changing everything. He was hers and she was his from the moment they met and ever since.

"Did you sleep with Spinel last night?" Tawny asked suggestively.

I sucked in a heavy breath. "No. Your plan backfired. I went on a date with Brass's grandfather let myself do something horribly careless and now Brass wishes I was never born."

"I know. I take full blame for forcing you to meet him on your birthday."

Tawny looped her arm through mine as I explained what happened last night. Steel came to walk beside me running his hand through his tousled dark blonde hair in a gesture I recognized as being at a loss.

"Delegate... Second. I do not know what to call you these days." The smug woman's voice set my teeth on edge.

I came to a halt in front of Hopper's weapon shop and tried to control the sudden red blinding rage that assaulted me. Hopper was one of the captain's like Brass and Slate of the Shadow Breakers. His sister, Anthias, nicknamed Mirage for her projection abilities, was also a Shadow Breaker I'd recruited as a favor to Hopper. Brass had tried to whip her into shape, but she was a lost cause, not a team player.

She was tall and leanly muscled. Blonde hair fell over her shoulders framing her round face. Her wide mouth was pulled to the corner in a mocking smile and blue eyes glittered out at me from the shadows. Shadow Breakers and their shadows.

"*You* don't call me anything. Do you have something important to say or are you trying to antagonize me? I don't have time or patience for your crap today so tread lightly," I said, trying to pull free from Tawny and Steel's grasps.

Mirage stepped down from the store front and her smirk grew on her tan face. "Easy, tiger. I wanted to get a good look at you. That is all."

I narrowed my eyes at her and felt my nostrils flare. "I know projecting my image must be in high demand these days, Mirage, but I told you once. If you project me again, all bets are off," I threatened.

The glass door behind her jingled as it opened. Hopper was brawny with a dark blonde ponytail that fell over his back. He wasn't much taller than Mirage, just under six feet. His eyes were a midnight blue as he nodded to me folding his bright blue tattooed arms over his chest.

"Delegate. My sister giving you trouble again?" Hopper asked.

No more sweetheart. He hadn't called me sweetheart since Ash appointed me his Second. There was a certain wariness to his emotions that made the hairs on my neck stand. The secret he was hiding from me made him almost formal.

"Her mouth is getting her in trouble," Tawny snapped. "Keep that bitch on a leash. How many times does she need to get her fanny pack kicked before she learns her lesson not to talk sugarfoot to Scarlett?"

I was impressed with her usage of the "B" word which was only slightly diminished by her substitution for all the other curse words. Hopper put his big arm on Mirage's shoulder. She wore a tank top and snug pants; she wasn't much for dresses.

"I have got her," Hopper said, pulling her back into the shop.

"Is he afraid of you?" Tawny asked as we started back down the road.

"That was strange." Steel agreed.

"Everyone has been weird with me since I became Second."

Tawny gave me a rueful smile. "I know what you mean. I've been getting the same thing. You might want to think about getting a wig. I have one when I want to ditch my bodyguards."

Steel gave her a disapproving look, but I could scent the spike of interest in him. I didn't want to know any more about that wig even if I wanted to know what color it was.

"Take me to this wig shop."

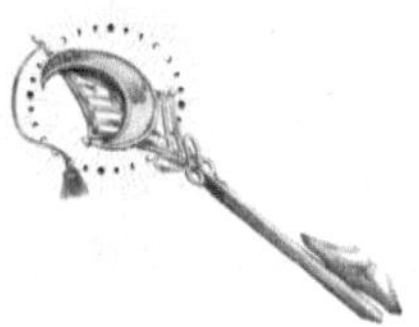

Solder's armor shop and Katydid's salon did very good business, with the addition of the exclusive contract I'd given them for my arenas, they'd bought one of the largest homes just outside of Thrimilci's town heart. It was a multilevel white pueblo styled mansion that started me thinking. I should move out of the palace. A palace was great, but their home had all the same amenities minus the portal door and indoor pool.

Their home had a rustic Tuscan vibe, I was more of a shabby chic girl myself, but it was still beautifully decorated. We stood around the lima bean shaped pool on the large flat stones as Katydid undressed her baby boy. She blew her blunt ash blonde bangs from her big blue eyes. Solder was almost as pretty as he was heavily muscled. He wasn't much taller than she was, with short brown hair styled like Quick's and full luscious lips. He had a scar through his brow which was rare for our people.

Katydid couldn't stop smiling as she dipped her son into the pool and out again and wrapped the soft white blanket around him before handing him to his father. Solder made a gesture with his fist across his chest in the shape of an inverted "T".

"We own this baby for our son. He shall be called Peridot," Solder announced.

What did a family do when there was no father? Would I be standing up there alone next year with a two babies?

Spinel would never let me do it alone.

I walked around the pool and placed the chest the Merfolk king had given me as restitution for my stay in my rousen stupor. Solder had been a gift for them when Steel visited. Merfolk were cold-blooded and loved warm blooded bodies. When Steel met Tawny, he stopped gifting himself and Solder took his place. I didn't need the pearls and baubles he'd given me — a new family starting out could.

Katydid gasped as I used my *calling* to float it over. A staff member from the Dagr palace had brought it for me. Solder understood and his big lips tugged at the corner. He had slept with Merfolk traitors and hadn't known it until I'd exposed them. He deserved the treasure chest more than I did. I'd made my peace with what happened and gotten Slate out of the deal.

We stayed for lunch and made small talk with Bronze and Cricket before leaving. It was an entirely different atmosphere than Opal's had been. Less formal, fewer people, and somehow more friendly. Not for the first time, I missed my simpler life in Chicago.

# CHAPTER 8
# INDIGO

Silver had kept me naked all day. We were eating our meals in my massive canopy bed and pretending the world outside my bedroom didn't exist. It was what I needed, and I hated admitting it to Silver, or having him know I was hurting because my first love was getting married.

Silver had decided he wouldn't be putting on any clothing either unless it was to retrieve meals from the staff. The champagne and sky-blue satin blankets were piled at the footboard so only a thin sheet covered us. My index finger traced the black tattoo over his left shoulder without looking. I knew his body better than I knew my own.

"The hard part is over, Dove. We could have dinner with the family if you are feeling up to it." Silver purred rubbing his nose along my ear.

At the opposite wall, heavy looking curtains hid a beautiful little nook. Sunlight no longer shown through the stained glass arched windows that went all the way up to the ceiling ending at an intricately carved nook, upholstered window seats circled around the little alcove.

I took a deep breath and took his hand from my stomach and raised it to my lips. "I don't know what I would've done without you today."

Sentimental wasn't my style. Not with Silver. We kept things light even though he'd cajoled me into getting engaged. I rubbed a thumb over the lapis stoned ring and the EH rune that hid beneath it. He'd hand fasted me as well. I wished I could pinpoint the moment I fell in love with the scoundrel. It had snuck up on me.

"You never have to wonder what any day would be like without me. I am not going anywhere." Silver purred pressing his lips to the side of my neck.

I smiled closing my eyes enjoying his kisses. Silver's kisses were remarkable. He could bring me to the cusp with those lips of his. His hand slid over my chest and gave my braid a pull. You always knew when Silver had taken a lover when we were at Valla U because the girl would have a single braid down her back. I agreed to the braids, but only in the bedroom. I turned in his arms to face him and he pulled my thigh over his hips.

"We could make a baby tonight. You and I, a piece of us both," he purred, kissing my lips lightly like the beat of butterfly wings.

"You made it twenty-four hours without talking about impregnating me. A new record."

I wrapped my arm around his back so our stomachs were flush. His body was covered in hard muscles, yet satiny soft and *mine*. Bigger than Sterling, greater family men tended to be leaner and not as heavily muscled. Quick was a lesser family man, the youngest son.

"I will ask every day until you say yes. One day you will, Dove." Silver's sensual lips curled into a devilish smile.

"You're right. I will, but not today." I swatted his backside with a satisfying whack before I rolled away.

A sky blue and champagne upholstered love seat and matching chaise lounge were in the seating area directly in front of the archway from the bedroom. On one side of the couches was the closet, and the other was the bathroom. I padded barefoot to it.

Scarlett had shared the bathroom with Tawny before Tawny moved in with Steel in the family wing of the palace. Scarlett had replicated it in her own colors at the Dagr palace. I slapped the energy plate outside the shower as I worked my fingers through my braid and climbed in to wash before we went down to dinner.

The sound of the water changed as Silver walked under the waterfall and joined me. Gods, he was criminally good looking and way too virile for his own good. He caught me checking out his backside as he ran his sudsy hands over himself and smirked.

"Get over yourself, Regn," I mumbled, smiling as I let the water stream over my hair.

"I will do that for you."

Silver ran his hands over my body relishing in washing me. We were one another's first real relationship. I was Silver's first love. Who knew a guy like Silver *could* fall in love?

"Okay," I whispered as he worked his fingers through my long hair.

"Okay, what, Dove?" he asked, guiding my shoulders, so I stood under one of the dozen streams that splashed around the shower.

"If you start treating me like Slate or your brother does Scar, I'll kill you. She should have killed Slate twice over by now. She *will* if she finds out about his affair. The only reason I haven't told her is because she's under enough stress as it is with her new position and trying to do right by Brass, finding him a normal, happy wife so he can stop hating her. All the while trying to win back Slate. It's not right. He hides it, but she flaunts it around headquarters, hoping Scarlett finds out."

Silver knit his brows. "You are right. He is a complete idiot. We all agree. He will not find a better wife, *woman,* than her. Neither of them will." His expression saddened, and I loved him all the more for it. "If Scarlett finds out, it will be a catastrophe. Spinel will have a good time building her back up afterwards," Silver said dryly. "I promise he will take care of her after that. I may have a new grandmother in earnest if she lets him."

I waggled my brows at him and he leveled his gold flecked chocolate eyes at me. "It's too bad Brass is his grandson or I would be rooting for them to become a couple. He's the kind of man who wants her to be a kept woman, she could really use that these days."

"Rewind a minute. What were you agreeing to?" Silver asked.

I was losing my nerve. Scarlett was positively ecstatic being able to have children again, and she loved the twins already, but her love life had crashed and burned. She allowed Spinel around her, but she wanted Slate back. Ash was creeping close, toeing her boundaries and she had pushed Brass away as hard as she could even though she was in love with him. Our mother had wound up alone until the end when our father rekindled their relationship after she reappeared from Chicago. He had thought she was dead for twenty long years.

Since a new class had been proven tried and true from Valla U, in nine months, another generation of Guardians would be born. I rubbed my lips together, a habit I'd picked up from training so much with Brass at Shadow Breaker headquarters since I'd been kicked out of Valla University for slapping Ash. I used to be thick as thieves with the inner circle until Alder claimed me as his daughter by blood. Then they shunned me. It had been a painful eye opener.

"Dove?"

He wiped a hand over his face pushing his short hair over his head. It was the only time his hair was disheveled. I clammed up. I shouldn't have said anything. Sterling getting married, that had to be responsible for my momentary lapse.

"Never mind," I said, giving him a smile.

He bent his knees so he could meet me eye to eye. "Did you... are you saying what I think you are?"

Silver's excitement was palpable, and I bit down on my lower lip looking away blinking at drops of water. He cupped my face and searched my eyes.

"Say it, Dove. *Please* say it out loud. For me," Silver urged.

I swallowed. "I want to have your child, Silver."

He sucked in a deep breath. "Truth," he said, using his truth detecting talent to discern my honesty.

I expected him to kiss me, but he slipped running out of the shower. "Silver?" I called out after him.

I stuck my head out from the waterfall and spied Silver totally nude and dumping my packets of tea that prevented pregnancy down the toilet. I started laughing, and he turned back flashing me a smile so bright and broad, I felt my heart swell in my chest.

"Silver, we can throw that out later. I'm not even ovulating. We're not physically able to make a baby today," I told him, unable to hide my amusement.

He flushed the toilet and straightened. My eyes widened. *He* was ready to make a baby. His body moved with an animal like grace, light on his feet despite his size as he prowled towards me. I was in his crosshairs.

"You are all mine, Dove. We may not make a life tonight, but we are going to practice all night. No dinner unless you are eating it off me, or vice versa."

He had earned his nickname because of his speed. "Quick" Silver Regn was before me when I blinked and lifting me off my feet.

I had to pull my mouth away to catch my breath. My back hit the cool tiles; shower heads were blocked by my body. I wrapped my arms and legs around Silver as he covered my face with kisses.

"I would never treat you how Slate does Scarlett. I promise. I am utterly besotted with you, Indigo. We can marry tomorrow... go the States... Vegas. I want you to be my wife, have my children. I want a life with you," he breathed.

He was saying all the right things. Silver didn't say things he didn't mean. He was a lot of things, but a liar wasn't one of them. I turned my mouth back to him and gasped when he pushed into me. He stopped and slipped back out. I could feel his bunched muscles beneath my fingers.

"Wait. I do not want to make our child up against a wall," he said, and I laughed.

"We're not going to tell them where we conceived, Silver. We can make a baby anywhere."

He was carrying me out of the shower, not listening to what I was saying. His hair was damp and flattened to his forehead, he'd never looked so young and out of sorts.

"I will know. I want to make love to you. That is how I want our child to begin, Dove. With love," Silver said, climbing after me.

I scooted on my back up the bed. I was melting beneath him. He was like a different man. I knew he wanted me to have his babies, but — he really meant it. His hands ran over me reverently, lips sliding along every inch of my skin. He was always a fantastic lover, this was different... I might've given in before if I knew he would be like this.

My damp hair wet the sheets under my head, his body was still dripping as he nudged my thighs apart with his hips. "I love you, Silver."

He moaned. "Dear gods, I have never wanted anything so bad," he whispered.

I smiled and placed my hands to either side of his face. Silver scanned my eyes afraid I was changing my mind. My smile deepened, and I slid my hand down his chiseled abs to wrap my hand around him and guided him into me with a moan.

It would be a long, scrumptious night and the only thing on the menu for dinner was "Quick" Silver Regn.

Silver yawned again at the dining room table; it was contagious. I started yawning too and Jett pursed his lips at me with narrowed eyes. Pearl was in a surprisingly quiet mood, her usual wide smile absent. Tawny, Steel, Hawk, and Sparrow had appeared for breakfast, which was unusual for a Monday, but they had missed yesterday's dinner because of Sterling's wedding.

"Where's Scarlett?" I asked and watched as mouths tightened around the table.

They'd all gone to the wedding, even Slate since he was Sterling's cousin and the Dagr heir. Sage's wedding was tonight. I wasn't invited, neither was Jett. Scarlett was going only because Ash had insisted.

Brass came storming into the dining room with Crimson's hand laced through his. We sat at a rectangular table that sat sixteen, made of a light-colored wood with delicately carved and painted in golds and silvers. The chairs were the same wood and upholstered in heavy gold and silver embroidery on white fabric. Lanterns hung from the walls in copper, blues, and gold in with intricately shaped metalwork framing the glass.

Its high domed ceiling had curved white beams trimmed in gold. It started out dark blue at the walls and faded to white at the peak of the dome with white birds painted in the segments between the beams. The walls were predominantly white but with smaller subtler mosaic patterns in teals and blues. On the north wall, a blue morning glory vine grew from a terra cotta pot. Scarlett had grown a clipping of the same vine at the Dagr palace. Her own private garden.

He pulled out the seat for our distant cousin and she smiled up at him, gathered her straight fiery red hair over her shoulder that fell to her chest. Brass was distracted as he took the seat next to her. Crimson greeted them pleasantly and Brass murmured a few words of pleasantries before brooding.

I looked to Silver who shrugged. "So... Scarlett?" I asked again.

Brass stiffened. Crimson fidgeted.

"She was at the Regn manor when we left this morning," she said in a small voice and suddenly everyone's odd behavior made sense.

Silver chuckled and slowly shook his head. "Another one bites the dust."

Slate went rigid.

"We already spoke with Scarlett about Spinel's interest in her, she's a grown woman and will make her own decisions," Hawk said in a measured tone. "Spinel has asked to formally escort her."

"We might have a new grandmother," Silver joked. "They have technically been dating since October."

I thought I saw Pearl's lips quirk, but Brass was enraged. "That is not funny, Silver," Brass growled.

"It is a *little* funny," Silver teased.

"Scarlett has my approval should she choose to seek it." Pearl said using a long nails hand to push her coppery coiffed hair over her shoulder.

"Mother?" Hawk sounded incredulous. "He went to Valla University the same year as you." He dropped his tone. "He came here with..." he trailed off, remembering Crimson.

Spinel had come with Brass to ask for Scarlett's hand behind her back when she was looking for a second husband. Hawk had given his approval providing Scarlett gave hers even though technically in Tidings, Hawk was free to give her away as he saw fit.

"Patriarch Regn has a manor, wealth, a full-grown family, darling. What does she have that he can ask her for? I cannot think of a single thing aside from her companionship. His grandsons all have advantageous matches and prosperous careers, some of which is due to Scarlett herself. He cannot ask her for anything that she has not already given happily of her own free will. While we are discussing such matters, I might add that men her own age have not been kind to her. He can offer her much and asks for little in return. I think she is making out quite well in the arrangement, should she accept." Pearl poured herself a second glass of tea.

I giggled and caught Jett's amused expression. Cherry and Amethyst didn't look to think much of Scarlett's beau either way. Brass murmured a curse and Slate lifted his head towards the entrance. Not a minute later, Scarlett breezed through the entrance. Tawny and Steel laughed, and she beamed a drop-dead gorgeous smile at them and twirled, pushing at the ends of a short black bob.

"You didn't!" I breathed.

Scarlett held her stomach as she laughed and took the seat next to Silver. "Dear Gods, no. I wanted to be able to go out without being recognized. You like? I told Balas, *um,* Spinel about it last night and he wanted to see how it looked. He hates it." She laughed with a flash of straight white teeth.

"The point was, so it was so far from your natural hair that you wouldn't be recognized. I say mission accomplished," Tawny said, brandishing her fork.

"Breakfast?" Silver asked with a knowing smile, and she waved the plate away.

"Spinel and I ate already at the Dagr palace. I invited him to join me here, but he was under the impression he wouldn't be welcomed. Any reason that might be? We usually host the Regn," she said coyly.

"None I can think of, darling," Pearl said with glittering eyes.

Jett gasped. "You're not wearing your wedding ring."

Scarlett looked down at her left hand then flashed her right hand. "I am. I was told explicitly to move on. So I have."

Under the table I watched Scarlett pinch Silver's thigh so he wouldn't call her out on her lie. All eyes turned to Slate whose jaw was clenched like a bear trap.

"You ate at the Dagr palace?" Sparrow asked, interrupting the stare off.

Scar leaned forward, Silver shot me a smirk when Brass and Slate's eyes fell to her cleavage with Cherry's. She plucked an apple out of a bowl on the table and bit into it so the juices flowed over the green peel. She angled her wrist and her tongue slid along the peel to keep it from dripping. Slate's eyes went from heather grey to glinting silver as she sat back.

"I stayed the night at the Regn manor, but I thought I would eat breakfast with you and Hawk. I'd forgotten about breakfast here today until you weren't there. We rode together in that gorgeous carriage he has to the portal in Ostara so I invited him to breakfast. I didn't want to be rude after he came all that way, so I stayed at the Dagr palace and ate there with him since he wouldn't come here. I'll see him soon; I asked him to be my escort at Sage's wedding."

She said it so matter of fact; I nearly missed the first statement. Silence descended on the table.

"Not many of us were invited to the wedding," Gypsum muttered.

Scarlett leaned forward to look to Gyps. "I know. I'm only going because I'm the Second. I think Ash made Sage invite me." Her mood changed at the drop of a hat. "I don't want to go." Her eyes got far away. "I don't —" She stopped short and her eyes slid to Crimson. "I have responsibilities. Spinel is good at maneuvering through the families." She perked up again and gave Crimson a knowing look biting into her apple again. "Mind readers have their benefits."

Crimson cheeks flushed to match her hair and Brass moved to say something, but Scarlett shot to her feet and straightened her wig. She turned her head to the entrance with Brass and Slate.

Spinel was a striking older man. He wore a forest green satin jerkin with pewter buckles down the front. Scarlett happened to be wearing the very same color caftan, an Ostara styled dress with a plunging neckline and heavy gold embroidered trim and wide belt. With her hair tucked under the wig, her elegant neck was displayed.

"I did not mean to interrupt," Spinel said, flashing Pearl a smoldering smile.

"Sorry, Spinel. I only meant to let them know I didn't forget about them." Scarlett said coming around the chair. "You didn't have to come all the way here."

"Ah, I realized how ridiculous I was being. Pearl has always been accommodating and Hawk used to spend a great deal of time at the Regn manor, so our families are like one and the same." He went around the table greeting them all in turn except for Silver and Brass then he turned to Scarlett who had moved to stand next to him.

His eyes slid over her approvingly, "I knew that dress would look lovely on you, but this must go before we leave."

Scarlett gave him a self-deprecating smile as he pulled the wig off her head and her long waves fell past her waist. "Let's go," she said, taking his hand as he raised it to fix her hair.

"Go where?"

Brass couldn't hold his silence any longer. He was positively squirming in his seat. The rest of us were watching the show. Scarlett ran her free hand through her hair and licked her lips.

Spinel was used to taking charge of situations and so was Scarlett, though her aggressive attitude was reluctant. With Spinel, she could sit back and let him make the decisions.

"I am helping her bring in my great grandsons' new cribs," Spinel said.

Eyes were back on Slate who's palms were pressed to the table top.

"New cribs? You have cribs already," I said, confused.

"Troll made is best," Spinel said, taking Scarlett's arm.

"When I was in Mabon for the feasts, I ran into a troll I know and she wanted to make my sons their cribs. Last night, I thought I would go check to see if they were ready. They were. We were too tired to bring them home last night—"

Spinel interrupted her. "We are going to get them now. We should hurry if we are going to bring them back to the wing and make the Var wedding in time."

Scarlett gave a little wave and left with Spinel. His hand moved from her arm to the small of her back as they turned the corner.

Silver let out a long exhale. "My new grandmother is well in hand."

"Shut up, Silver," Brass snapped.

"Gentlemen," Hawk admonished.

"Does that make your children, Spinel's step children?" Silver teased Brass.

I nudged Silver in the ribs, but Jett picked up where he left off. "My brother-in-law will be as old, I mean as *young*, as my grandmother."

"It's nice to not do things like to *think*," Amethyst mumbled.

"As if Ash would be any better," Cherry said, leaning past Jett to argue with Amethyst.

Tawny got to her feet and grabbed a startled Steel's arm. "I like him and he's mature, sophisticated, with those Regn good looks. Let's see if they want help. They're bringing back two cribs and Scar can't do it herself." Tawny dragged Steel from the dining room to hurry after them. "About time an honorable man treats her the way she deserves."

"How kind of Spinel to help Scarlett ready the nursery for her children," Pearl said, sipping her cooled tea.

Slate's fists hit the table, and he stormed from the room. I caught the smile on Pearl's lips as he left.

"I do not understand. Whose children does she carry?"

We'd forgotten about Crimson.

"Spinel thinks of Slate as a son. Our mother was his father's twin sister," Silver said, and Crimson went back to her meal.

Silver flashed me a look before meeting Brass's molten eyes. I wondered why Scarlett wasn't begging for his forgiveness, or had she already? She spent the night, but I doubted she'd be so cavalier if they had been intimate. No, it was Scarlett lonesome and grasping at straws.

I was really wishing Spinel wasn't their grandfather because she was smiling for once.

# NINE

After Spinel and Steel helped set up the cribs, Tawny readied with me for the wedding. I was dragging my feet. The morning had not gone as planned. I wanted to explain further about spending the night at the Regn manor. Spinel had wanted to take me to Mabon first thing in the morning and since I didn't want him staying at the Dagr palace, I stayed in a guest room. Spinel had taken me shopping on the way to the portal and picked out a flattering caftan that matched his jerkin. I had forgotten about breakfast with the family until I went to the Dagr palace so they wouldn't worry about my whereabouts.

Brass, Slate, and Amethyst were upset with me. At least Tawny and Steel had joined us in Mabon. Unfortunately, Spinel and Steel had nothing in common so Tawny did most of the talking.

Garnet was pregnant and walking down the aisle with my half-brother. It didn't stop me from wanting to strangle her. Ash was at the head table so I sat with Spinel, Gypsum, Tawny, Steel, Jett, and the girls, Sparrow, and Hawk. Indi, Slate, and Pearl weren't invited. The only reason Jett was, was because of Amethyst. Brass was there with Crimson at the Tio/Rot table.

We left the moment everyone started drinking. Spinel wanted me to spend the night again...not in the guest room this time. He was much too gentlemanly to come right out and say it, but his intentions were crystal clear. I hadn't so much as kissed him. Brass's face loomed in my mind, the face he shared with Spinel. I couldn't bring myself to be with him again and I was hanging onto hope with Slate by my fingertips.

Spinel was the kind of man I wouldn't even realize I was dependent on before it was too late. It would start with small things, then I would rely on him, after that I would give myself to him. I could see it happening.

For the next four days, I only saw Spinel briefly while making preparations for the opening of the arenas. It helped that Brass and Quick were the two men I spent twelve hours a day getting things ready with Indigo's help. Crimson would meet Brass every night and they would leave for dinner. Spinel was usually close behind her with dinner and an escort back to my wing which I appreciated far too much.

One arena on each island and our main opening was Friday in Valla. My nerves were shot. I wasn't sleeping and by Friday morning, I was regretting my decision to stop spending my free time with Spinel and needed the support he gave without having to ask and the company he offered with the sound advice that came with it. It didn't hurt that he was easy on the eyes.

When I stepped out of the shower, I wrapped a tiffany blue plush towel around my hair and around my chest. I wiped the condensation from the mirror.

I had bags under my eyes, I looked as tired as I felt, but at least the nausea stopped. I rubbed shimmering lotion over my body and swiped on deodorant before hanging my towels over the side of the tub and going out into the bedroom.

I had an Elivagar gown set out on the bed. Tree was purring as I came around the side.

"What are you doing here? Your stance was clearly made. If you want to live in the Dagr palace, I'll go back to the Sumar palace," I said, keeping my arms very still so I wouldn't cover my body with my hands.

Slate had a way of making me feel like a bug under his boot; so small and insignificant and alive at his leisure. Traitorous Tree was curled in his lap purring up a storm, Slate's silver eyes raked over me.

"I came to see the cribs you and Spinel brought for *your* bairn," Slate rumbled, looking like a Bond villain.

"Did you see them then?" I asked, shifting my bare feet.

"I did. I am coming tonight, I would like my access ring," Slate said.

I blinked. His wedding band was the access key. I wore it on a long silver chain with the stone pieces around my neck. I clasped a hand over my collection of pieces and remembered I was undressed.

"Allow me."

Slate slid off the bed sending Tree padding off and got to his feet. "You're not dressed for tonight," I said stupidly since he was in casual Thrimilci garb.

Slate stood before me and he reached around to the clasp of my necklace. I tried not to lean in and inhale his scent. The spicy scent of cloves, a crisp fall breeze, and man.

His hand grazed the swell of my breasts as he took the pieces off me. "Warm spiced apples and vanilla," he whispered as he clasped the necklace back around my neck. He ran his finger tip down my chest and over my belly. "No more Spinel?"

"I've drawn clear lines between Spinel and I," I said firmly.

Slate fell down to his knees and held my belly. He kissed the small sphere that housed my children. His hands skimmed over my belly and around my hips to my backside. He pressed his forehead to my belly, instinct kicked in and not the smart kind that should have shoved Slate off me.

I was stroking his hair, he seemed so lost to me these days and the desire to comfort him was stronger than anything else. "I'm glad you've decided to come tonight."

Slate kissed my belly again before he stood, towering over me. "Where is that wig?"

I knit my brows. "*Um*, in the closet. Why?"

Slate moved from me and went into the closet. He came back with the raven-haired bob. Slate *called* twisting my wet hair up and slid the wig over.

"I'm trying very hard not to be insulted by this," I said, covering my chest with a forearm.

Slate's eyes fell to mine. The hard planes of his bronze face, chiseled, his lashes so long and thick his silver eyes looked lined with kohl. His muscles bunched, and I held my breath. He scooped me off the floor, suddenly, his hands were clawed and sleek charcoal fur pushed from his follicles. His mouth elongated into an animal's snout full of fanged dagger teeth.

We were at the bed and he turned me around so my hands hit the mattress. I curled my fingers in the down comforter. Slate's fangs gripped the back of my exposed neck and I grit my teeth. His rough clawed hands grabbed a pillow and slid it under my belly before he gripped my hips.

"Slate, I thought you didn't have a use for me," I said, trying to drum up indignation.

He didn't speak. A growl from his chest rolled over my skin making my insides pull and twist deliciously and my back arched. Slate rasped a chuckle and his breath heated where his teeth scraped. I gasped as he rubbed himself between my legs. I felt him retreat, and I bucked against him.

Slate growled and gripped my neck tighter so I couldn't move my head so much as an inch. I moaned as Slate pushed into me to the hilt and stilled. His rasping breath was heavy.

"Fuck," he groaned. "I —"

"Don't you dare stop now?" I hissed.

Slate started to move and my face pressed against the cool down comforter. I couldn't move, it wasn't love making, it was claiming. His body thrust into mine, driving deep, picking up pace until he had straightened removing his teeth from my throat. My muscles clenched and squeezed around him. Slate shuddered with a low roar.

I grabbed Slate's hand at my hip as he withdrew. "You're not going anywhere." I panted, turning around shakily to face him.

He was shifting back, his clothes loosening after being stretched to the point of fraying. He was still fully dressed, his pants pushed just past his hips. Slate acted frozen in place so I used my *calling* to help me shove him onto his back on the bed. I swung my leg over his hips and he let his head fall back and shut his eyes.

I took his big hands and cupped my breasts with them. He sucked in a sharp breath as I pulled his linen shirt up and kiss along his hard ridges of muscles.

"Scarlett..." he began.

"*Shh*. I want you and I intend to take what's mine," I said, lowering myself onto him.

Three weeks was an eternity to a khoraz. Even if I hadn't wanted him, I needed him.

Slate hooked the corset that I had specially gotten to accommodate my belly. I stepped into the heavy petticoats using his shoulder to help balance me and he lifted it up to my hips and fastened them. I held up my arms as he pulled the black silk dress over my body so it fell to the floor and I slid my arms through the sapphire blue silk velvet dress that was trimmed in black fur. Its plunging neckline displayed my now ample cleavage. They received far too much unwanted attention. Slate had been on the giving end of that attention for the last couple hours.

He kneeled in front of me buttoning up the onyx buttons up the length of the gown that was only a little rumpled after Slate and I had rolled over it a few times. I traced my thumb over the scar that sliced over his left eye and he glanced up at me with a wry expression.

"Hard to button all of these blasted things without you blinding me."

I smiled down at him and watched him fight a smile of his own before returning to his work. I contented myself with smoothing his unruly midnight waves until he stood and I could no longer reach the top of his head. He ran his teeth over his full lower lip.

"Stop that or I'll tie you to the bed so you'll be here after I finish this arena business," I purred.

Slate sighed, something weighed heavily on his mind, but I didn't want to hear it. We'd gone three hours without saying anything hurtful to one another, everything else could wait until tomorrow. I had had to grapple my way free of him to get ready, I felt better overseeing preparations at the arena myself, though Slate had wanted me to stay.

By the Mother, how I wanted to stay.

I went to the dresser and plucked the emerald drop earrings from the jewelry box. Slate crooked a finger at me and pointed to the bed.

"You must wear undergarments." Slate rumbled and held up a pair of black seamless panties to me and a set of black thigh highs.

I groaned. "You can't see anything under all these layers."

Slate nocked up his chin. "It is not appropriate. Sit."

I sat on the bed and he pulled on my thigh highs. I stood so he could pull up my panties and then let down my petticoats.

"I have to do my hair and makeup." I told him as his eyes flitted between mine.

He held my jaw in his big hands and ran his thumbs over my lips. I puckered them to kiss the pads of his thumbs and he lowered his mouth to mine.

"They say you forgive me for everything." He whispered against my lips.

"I don't want to ruin this morning. We can talk about it tomorrow if you still want to. I'm not going anywhere, Slate."

I loosely wrapped my arms around his waist. I needed this morning. To be reminded of what I was fighting so hard to get back. It hadn't started out very romantic, but once our frenzied attacks on one another had finished, we made love. Sweet and slow. We hadn't made love since that first day he awoke after he regained consciousness — before I knew he didn't remember us.

He nodded against my head. "Get ready."

I smiled, and he came very close to sighing. I came close to asking what was wrong.

I walked into the bathroom and started to curl my hair, pinning it at my nape in a low, romantic up-do. I finished it with a thick braid across the crest of my head and tucked the end in with pins. After I completed my makeup, I walked out into the bedroom and Slate was gone.

The arena in Valla was at the eastern edge of the island. The River Ymir's east end poured into the ocean miles below the Straumr palace where we built the arena. The cottages were downstream where a diamond shaped slice of land housed the mini vacation spot for the Guardians.

The portable portal door Orion had his imprisoned Leshy built for me was placed in a white granite Roman arch that we'd built at the end of the bridge. Straight from the portal was the bisecting bridge that led to the massive arena. Two white, sculpted winged Valkyries stood as tall as the domed arena, pouring water from their outstretched palms and back into the river.

Corinthian columned porticos lined the several levels of the arena with hundreds of arched windows. Each level was topped by a molding of Valkyries and Mother's Nature, all topped by a coffered dome. It was quite a sight. I couldn't have done it without Orion and Brass. It had been Orion's idea to make the buildings framework out of the same materials used to make the nix torques. *Calling* didn't work on my arenas. You would have to take them apart stone by stone in order to destroy them.

I was alone at midday when I took the Dagr portal to the Valla arena. It was my largest one out of the five. Above the night club was a level that spanned an entire floor of bedrooms for the competitors if they needed them and for Cordillera's Shadow Breakers.

The entrance was a Roman arch that reached halfway up the white granite arena with two huge double doors that made them looked stretched from the average width and extraordinary height. Five slots were engraved in the doors. Brass, Slate, Cordillera, Quick, and I were the only ones to have access rings. I fit my wedding ring into an oval with tiny nearly imperceptible arches and the mechanisms begin to work. The doors slowly opened.

The inside was cool, but not cold and it smelled like stone, like dust and whatever they used to polish the black-and-white checkered marble floors. Shell-headed niches lined the curved hall, another set of double doors was directly across from the entrance that led downstairs to *Circus Maximus*; the nightclub under the arena. Built in shops would be setting up food, drinks, and souvenirs — nothing too extravagant. Hand held banners for younger fans to wave and keepsake coins.

On the opposite end of the curved hall was the access route to the preparation rooms. Stone steps to either side of the entrance led up to another hall that gave access to the arena seats, there was a third and fourth set built along the wall for the seats on that end. The entire arena kept in time with the Roman theme until you came to the course itself and the suites.

I ascended the stairs to my suite which also had an office next to it for when I was around. Brass and Quick had their own suite and shared an office, as did Chafer and Cordillera. My heels clicking on marble echoed as I walked through the empty halls. Soon the arena would be filled with thousands of Guardians and their children... or so I was praying.

My office was cream marble tiled with vaulted ceilings with gorgeous moldings and columns. A tapestry of Mother Nature hung behind a cream marble desk was piled with papers and Brass who sat at my cream plush chair. The matching marble fireplace had recently been lit, and the room was comfortably warm.

He lifted his gaze to mine when I entered but made no other move.

"Good afternoon. How are things going?" I asked, taking one of the two matching sofa chairs that faced my desk.

"Fine. I expected you here earlier," he said in a curt tone I would never get used to hearing from Brass.

I sighed and crossed my legs. "I had an unexpected visitor this morning. I'm sorry. I didn't mean to let you down."

He raised his amber eyes to mine and searched my face before looking back at the sheet of paper before him. He pushed it across the desk and I plucked it from the marble surface. Brass looked tired, his bronze jerkin was unbuckled to his chest to expose the silky dusting of dark hair that covered his skin and his sleeves were rolled up to expose his gold and silver torques and corded forearms. He ran his palms over his face to scratch along his stubbled beard.

The paper was an inventory of the liquors we'd ordered for Circus Maximus. The quantities were not the same as what we asked for, but it wasn't the end of the world. I set the sheet down and walked around the desk. Brass followed me with his eyes until I stood behind him.

"May I?" I asked, holding up my palms, and he waved at me to go on.

I reached down as I used my *calling* to finish unbuckling the jerkin all the way and pushed it off his shoulders. "What are you... *Oh, gods.*"

Brass's head lolled as I massaged his broad muscled shoulders. "Did you sleep here last night? The numbers aren't so off that we need to stress about it, Brass. Worst comes to worst, we'll send someone to raid the clubs at the arenas we aren't opening today. It's going to be great," I reassured him, rubbing my thumbs down his spine.

"Slate showed up?" Brass asked, his voice sounding muffled from his odd angle.

"He did," I said simply, and slid my palms down his arms so his jerkin was pushed off further.

Brass shook his arms out of the jerkin so it bunched behind him and he leaned forward. I kneaded his knotted muscles even though I could have used my *calling*. I was just happy he was letting me near him. He reached his hand up and pulled the leather strap from the knot at his nape so his hair fell free.

"You're not wearing your beads," I noted.

"It does not make sense since I no longer wear my hair loose. You no longer wear the ones I gave you. You're not dating my grandfather?" he asked, his voice dropping deeper.

I guffawed. "I was never *dating* Spinel. Like I told Slate, since I discovered who he really is I will never let it go past a close friendship. I wish it never happened, Brass. I like Spinel. He's a good man, if a terrible lech who sometimes has the morals of a dog in heat," I said in a playful tone.

Brass bent his head to the side to look up at me and back down again when I ran my fingertips over his scalp.

He moaned. "Frigga's sweet grass, that feels good. You shouldn't be doing this."

"Would Crimson be upset?" I asked, but secretly didn't care since she'd done much more with Ash while we were together.

"That was not what I meant. You are the most powerful woman in Tidings and soon might be the richest. Then you'll have the Prime's child and be unstoppable," he said dryly.

I reached down, running my palms over his chest and back to his shoulders. "We could start telling people the truth about our sons." Brass's hands gripped mine over his shoulders. "What are you doing in my office, anyway?" I asked nervously when he hadn't spoken.

"You want to claim my sons?" he asked in a measured tone, his thumbs rubbing my hands.

My heart started to race. "If Slate doesn't mind and Crimson doesn't. We only did it because of Peak —"

Brass was a love maker. When we were together, I could lose track of where I was completely until he was done with me. When he used his hold on my hands to whirl me around the chair and pressed his plump define lips to mine, the cool marble of my desk was against my backside.

I couldn't catch my breath. Brass had rucked up my dress and climbed on top of the desk with me. Papers crinkled under me and lazily floated off the desk.

Freya's burly boar, I was kissing him back. Blessed friction rubbed against me as Brass's muscular body moved. He tasted like cinnamon and smelled like spring; my tongue danced with his before my brain could catch up with my body.

"Slate," I panted, finally remembering how to use words.

"He said I could court you... marry you. For the sake of the gods, he has seen me make love to you... participated," he said, capturing my mouth again.

*Good point.*

My stomach was awkwardly smashed between us and Brass was trying to accommodate the added shape. His stubbled jaw scraped my own as he slid his palms up my thighs.

No. I couldn't risk it. Things were going to well with Slate when I was with rousen and took Brass to my bed in the Merfolk palace. That's when things got bad between Slate and I, I wasn't willing to test Brass's theory and jeopardize the bond we rekindled.

I laced my hands through his hair and twisted my face away. "You are with Crimson."

Brass leaned back, his dreamy amber eyes filled with frustration and hurt. "For *you*. Because of you. You are my world, Scarlett. Every decision I make is made with you in mind."

A crease between his thick masculine brow formed as he shoved off me and onto the floor. A throat cleared. I was too awkwardly shaped to move quickly while on my back, so I shut my eyes tight and prayed it wasn't anyone who could get me into serious trouble.

"I do not know what to call you anymore. I thought of you as a daughter, but perhaps you are to be my new stepmother...now it would appear you could be my niece-in-law," Cordillera said in a smoky voice.

Brass took my hand and helped me down from the desk knocking a dozen more papers to the floor. My cheeks were so hot, heat rays must have been blurring the surrounding air. What was going on today?

Chafer was with her. I raised my head as I smoothed my skirts, listening to his wicked chuckle. Chafer's dark hair was combed away from his sharp-featured face.

"I am not happy to see you, Chafer," I said, trying to distract from the immensely uncomfortable situation.

"That makes two of us," he teased, and I smirked at him.

Chafer's wide mouthed grin was just as wicked as his laugh. His eyes glittered below dark slanted brows. Cordillera wore a clinging, airy, red long-sleeve dress. The sleeves and back were a sheer glittering mesh with a sweetheart neckline. She gave me a scrutinizing look as Brass pulled his hair back; he'd shrugged into his open jerkin.

"Your dress is rumpled. Good thing I accounted for your fashion sense when I brought this."

Cordillera could insult me while being kind, it was her way. She gestured to the garment bag that was slung over Chafer's shoulder. If Chafer was ever a competitor, I would've nicknamed him Blade. His body didn't have an ounce of fat on it and he was lightening quick.

Brass was picking up papers off the carpet. I bent awkwardly to help him and he looked at me from the corner of his eye. I lowered my eyes. What had started between us wasn't over, Brass was simmering with aggravation.

An image forced its way into my mind. Brass and I on the desk. If we hadn't been wearing clothes, we would have been having sex on my shiny new desk. Just how long had they been standing there. I gasped and my vision cleared. Cordillera could project images she'd seen into other people's minds. I sharply inhaled and shut my eyes.

"Trying to bank that memory for later, delegate?" Chafer mocked, and I straightened.

"Could you two give us a moment?" I asked.

They had an office of their own they could wait in. "You can stay. They will know anyway." Brass murmured.

I let duty stack its frozen blocks around my heart.

*...This can't happen. I can't risk losing Slate again. I know what he said before, but while we're trying to mend things, I can't be having affairs with you. Crimson is a good match who wants all the same things as you. She can offer herself to you wholly, I can't. No matter what, you'd always have to share me...*

"One morning with him and you think everything is fixed?" Brass said, picking up the last of the papers and stacking them on the desk.

"Say it out loud. This telepathy nonsense does not offer the whole story. You bedded your errant husband this morning? By the Mother, that was a bad idea," Chafer said, taking a seat at one of the sofa chairs.

"Not fixed, but on its way," I said defensively.

"You are so naïve. How is that possible after all you have been through? The only kind of sex Slate has is the casual kind, this is not the same man you knew." Cordillera sounded sorry for me and I frowned.

"He might, but I don't. He knows that," I said firmly.

Brass scoffed and shook his head.

Chafer sucked on his teeth and leaned forward. "He has been with another woman —"

"I know about Lynx," I interrupted, not interested in hearing old news.

I started sorting the papers on the desk with Brass's help, things for tonight, things for the month, who would be in my suite. It would be a who's who of Guardian upper crust in my suite for the unveiling of Tidings first organized sport.

Chafer let out a low whistle. "You do not know. Some friends you have."

"I don't know *what*, Chafer?" I snapped.

"Your husband has taken up with a Shadow Breaker, right under your nose, delegate," Chafer said in a low, incredulous tone.

My proud shoulders dropped, and I looked at Cordillera. She shook her head... not her. Brass leaned past me brushing my arm to grab another sheet of paper.

"Slate doesn't sleep with Shadow Breakers." I wasn't sounding as self-assured as I had been a moment ago.

"She only sees the good. I need to go get a change of clothing and ready for tonight." His eyes slid to me and back to Cordillera and Chafer. "Scarlett, I need to go over things with you. You two have everything under control? The vendors need to be let in at three begin preparation, the competitors and the arena manager will be here then as well."

Cordillera steepled her red polished fingers in front of her lips that matched them. "I have done this before, nephew, but I thank you for your diligence."

"I have copies of these papers waiting for you in your office. We should be back in two hours," Brass said, taking my elbow with one hand and grabbing the garment bag off the back of the sofa chair Chafer sat at with the other.

It was a half-hour walk from the Ostara portal door to the Regn manor. The rounded arch was white marble chiseled to form two tree pillars on either end and a lacework of branches and leaves painted a metallic gold that fanned over the top. It was a long, silent trek with an irritated Brass over the glittering crushed stone roads that were lined with vivid beds of flowers. Ostara's town heart was bustling with women in pastel caftans and men in light jerkins walking in between wood shops and cottages with intricately carved trim.

The Regn manor was a sprawling French chateau. Elaborate baroque architecture decorated the interior. Brass took my arm, and we walked to where his bedroom was, I'd never been inside it. I'd only been to the manor with Spinel.

He paused with his hand on the doorknob.

"I should not have kissed you," he said, looking at his hand gripping the knob.

"It's okay. I've never had reason to complain about your kisses before," I said, trying to coax a smile out of him.

My reward was a quirk of his lips before he opened the door to reveal his sitting room. A gilt sofa of chocolate velvet greeted us and Brass moved further into the room of more gilt tables and sofas.

"Make yourself comfortable," he said, tossing his jerkin over one of the sofas with the garment bag.

"For someone who needed to speak to me, you've said precious little," I told him, following into a room I thought was the closet but turned out to be an exquisite brown marble bathroom.

Brass began undressing unabashedly before me. "Don't put much merit into what Chafer and Cordillera were saying. Slate cares about you, he needs... time. This other woman — he doesn't care about her."

Brass kicked off his boots before pushing his pants over his hips. I averted my eyes but caught sight of him in the mirror. The dark silky hair not only covered his chest but the rest of his muscled dark honey skin. His sculpted back flexed, and I watched his backside like I was under a trance as he climbed into the clear paned shower. He met my eyes as he turned around.

"I've never been in your rooms," I said cleverly, and he smirked.

My chest expanded with my heart. It was the most he'd looked like himself in such a long time.

"You saved me from an awkward conversation?" I asked.

Gods, shouldn't that pane be clouding with condensation? "Yes," Brass said, dunking his head under one of the several streams.

"Thanks, I suppose."

I picked up one of the bottles off his bathroom counter and lifted the lid. Cinnamon. Just the smell of it pulled cords in my belly that led south. I started going through his collection of toiletries, smiling and helping myself until I heard Brass chuckle. A roll of heat fell over me.

"Sorry. I'll just go change," I muttered.

"Or you could rinse off," Brass said in his smooth, deep voice.

I bit down on my lower lip; Brass swiped his dark hair away from his face with a big hand. This was my Brass. I walked back to the sitting room and started to snoop. Brass didn't spend much time at the manor and it showed. There weren't many personal touches. In the bedroom was a king-sized bed with a chocolate velvet gilt headboard. Long windows poured bright sunny light through the room.

I started unbuttoning the onyx buttons and pushed my sapphire dress off and laid it over the bed. I pulled the silk dress over my head and stepped out of my petticoats.

When I pulled back his brown and silver jacquard bedspread, I rubbed my palm along the sheet. I breathed deep. The whole room smelled like Brass. His gold sheets were Egyptian cotton and impossibly soft against my skin. I was only going to rest my eyes for a second. First, this morning things with Slate were righted and now Brass was smiling at me again. All was right in my world.

With the Ostara sun on my face, against the highest count cotton sheets I'd ever laid on, aside from Spinel's, I shut my eyes and spiraled into a deep sleep.

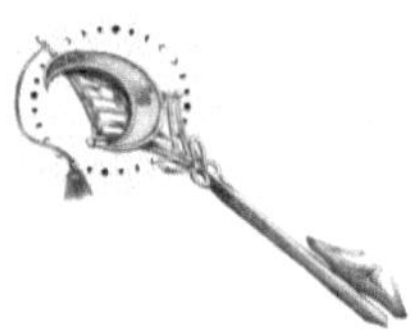

My eyes flitted open long enough to catch Brass's nude form climbing over me. He pushed tendrils of my hair away from my cheek and pressed his lips along my jaw.

"I have dreamt about you in my bed at home, but in those dreams, you fall asleep *after* I've made love to you," he whispered against my ear; his wet hair trailed across my face.

"Mm-hmm," I moaned, trying to hold on to consciousness as he wrapped his arms around me pressing his body close.

"Crimson. She's sleeping. Nothing happened," Brass whispered.

The bed shifted. "I believe you. Let us wake her. It is time we made love; I know you were with her before. She is beautiful."

Kisses punctuated her sentences, and I stirred. My arms were stiff at my sides. My next move was blind to me. Brass had shared me with Slate for a night, was I supposed to reciprocate?

I *never* wanted to share. I was way too possessive for it.

"We should go to the arena," Brass said, pulling his mouth away from Crimson's.

I fell off the bed onto my hands and knees. Crimson was making no effort to hide what she was doing on top of Brass, his hands on her hips as she...

I scrambled to my feet, yanking my dresses and petticoats off the bed. Brass was saying something, but I couldn't hear past the blood thundering through my veins. In my corset, panties, and thigh highs, I ran out into the hall, shutting the door behind me. I couldn't catch my breath as I slunk down the door to the polished marble.

Tears sprung to my eyes, and I blinked rapidly to clear them. Hands lifted under my arms bringing me to my feet and I staggered forward. Spinel caught me and held me close.

"I will have my staff get you ready in my rooms. We can retrieve your garment bag for you... and your shoes," he whispered.

I nodded with my chin tucked to my chest and Spinel lifted it. "The passions of youth. How I envy him. The most powerful woman in Tidings, weeping in her undergarments outside his bedroom while another woman tries to seduce him. Not that I am rubbing that in, my criminally young Scarlett."

I sobbed and Spinel lifted me into his arms. "Have I mentioned how soft your lips are when you cry? I have a variety of ways that you know well of that will stop those tears."

"*Please.* Just get me out of here."

My voice warbled and Spinel carried me further into the manor.

Spinel's bed was tufted teal velvet with silver tassels and intricately carved, it was massive and I felt like a child in it. Spinel had buried me under the jacquard blankets while he went back to Brass's room for my garment bag.

A headache pounded behind my eyes and my throat felt like it was closing on me. Spinel swept into the room and tossed the bag over a teal tufted chaise at the foot of the bed before coming to sit down next to me. He pulled pins out of my hair.

"I have the Second to the Prime in my bed and undressed, but I must be getting old since my only desire is to boost her mood," Spinel said in a soft soothing tone.

I'd been soothed by Spinel before and knew very well how good he was at it. As much as I wanted to let him, I would never do that to Brass again no matter how he'd hurt me.

"I'm so embarrassed," I whispered. "Thank you for bringing me here, I'm sure I would've crawled my way away from the door... eventually."

Spinel swung his legs over the side of the bed to face me. "You may take a fresh shower; I have women waiting for when you are ready to help you with your hair and makeup. I will escort you to Vanaheim and you can be my date for tonight."

"Slate is coming tonight, but I'll take you up all your other offers though," I said pushing myself up, holding the blankets to my chest.

"I will escort you until he can take my place. Come."

Spinel held out a thick silvery robe, and I slid my arms into it before helping me into the bathroom.

"Do you need help undressing?" Spinel gave me a smile worthy of Quick and left me alone.

I sunk down into a ball at the floor of the shower. Slate wasn't enough, now I had to have Brass too?

That wasn't it.

I loved Brass, but I could be happy for him and not have to see it. Seeing it made everything too real. Made everything I've given up displayed right there before my eyes. Brass and I had been happy in Chicago, just the two of us. He wanted to marry me and I didn't have to work for it. He was already there. We had been there. I had pushed him away as I always did, sabotaging things between us beyond repair.

I could hear the chattering of women and Spinel in the bedroom as I got to my feet and stepped out of the shower. Brass wasn't dressed. He wore a pair of pants slung low on his hips to display the "V" of corded muscle that disappeared under the waistband of his green drawstring pants.

I wrapped a slate grey towel around my body and rubbed my feet on the mat before padding onto the marble determined to ignore Brass. His amber eyes were gleaming as he followed my movements to the counter where I found moisturizer and other items I needed to get ready.

"Did you bed my grandfather?" he asked in a voice so low only Slate should have heard it.

I ignored him.

Brass hadn't even pulled back his hair before coming in there to... what? Check on me? Grill me with questions? Apologize? Spinel came to the doorway and didn't pay the uncomfortable situation any mind.

"I hate to rush you, Scarlett, but you are running late. As are you, commissioner. Do not give your employer reason to fire you on your first day," Spinel said wryly before leaving us again.

"Look at me," Brass pleaded. "She came in and disrobed before I awoke. I swear it. We did not—"

"Is she in your bed now?" I asked, drying my hair in the mirror as Brass stood at my side so close my elbow could feel the heat of his body.

He let out a noisy breath. "Yes. Scarlett, I was angry, so very angry when I found you here with Spinel. It didn't matter to me at the time that you never would have done it if you'd known the truth."

"Why are you apologizing to me? Go back to your room and the woman you're courting. You wanted to teach me a lesson? Lesson learned, Brass. Do not feel the need to repeat it and you'll have my thanks. We have a victor of Vigrid to declare tonight. Vanir versus Draugr at Vanaheim in Valla. You are my commissioner and I am the owner, that is all," I said coolly, and scrunched a handful of my light golden-brown waves.

Brass whipped me around, his hard muscled stomach against the swell of my belly. "Don't do that. I'm sorry, love. I should never have taken it this far. By the Mother, you make me crazy. I would never have done such a thing before. None of this is me!"

I had broken Brass. I'd known this for some time now. He had been wonderful and sweet. I was a better person just for knowing him, and I'd ruined that.

"Release me. From now on, our relationship is purely professional. As it should be," I whispered harshly. "I absolve you from any obligations you could feel for my sons."

Brass's chest rose and fell heavily, his eyes flitting between mine trying to find deeper meaning in my words. "No. I don't accept that. They're my sons, too."

"You should," I said taking a step back and yanking my shoulder from his grasp. "I'm not like you, I can't share. It's not in my nature and I won't apologize for it. You can have a wife and children with her. I am no longer needed and my reputation is already tarnished enough without adding the bastard children of a second son to the list."

Brass looked at me helplessly. "She was not supposed to be here. You were going to wake up, and I was going to make love to you, in my bed, for the first time."

Retorts and soothing words alike sailed past my mind, but in the end I settled on a good glare. Brass had a case of the *woulda shoulda couldas* that I could not indulge in. In was a blessing really, seeing him like that. The idea of touching him now made me feel ill, and that's what I needed to keep my eye on the proverbial ball that was Slate and my marriage. Having Brass trying to become my second husband while I was trying to mend things with my first would be a catastrophe.

I pushed back my shoulders and made a bee line for Spinel's velvet silk robe and tied it tight above my belly. I didn't spare Brass a second glance as I strode into the bedroom where a team of women awaited me with Spinel who looked past me to Brass.

Say what you would about Spinel being a womanizer, he loved his grandsons dearly. I looked at Spinel and knit my brow mouthing *I'm sorry.* The bedroom door shut, and I knew Brass had left us.

"My dear Second, I think you have broken his heart twice now."

I could not have predicted any of the events upon awakening that morning.

# CHAPTER 10
# JETT

Jett was wishing he wasn't an heir as he watched the Elivagar Draugr and the Valla Vanir walk through Scarlett's suite. Greater and lesser families mingled with a few prominent families around the cream marble floors. It led to a laurel patterned carpet that ran along the stairs and covered the seated platform where tufted wingback chairs were side by side in front of a two-way mirror that peered out into the arena.

It was the Valla Vanir Vanaheim arena, that was a lot of "V's". One heavily muscled man with a gold cuirass and gold mailed kilt walked with a leaner muscled man. They wore white wings to either side of their heads on a gold band and brown boots with golden greaves and gold arm cuffs. The female that strode between them looking like a goddess that had fallen down to earth in a short gold-plated dress designed to look like feathers and an exquisitely designed wide collar. The woman didn't have on greaves, but a golden metal damask pattern that extended past her golden boots to her knee. All three were oiled, blonde, and tan.

In contrast, the Elivagar Draugr were on enemy terrain. They looked as though they could handle it and more. The three Draugr competitors were clad in black and grey, their gear was made to look like their skeletons were on the outside of their skin. Each wore bone spiked pauldrons and spiked greaves. They were terrifying with skeletal painted faces like decomposed corpses come to life. The Draugr were fair skinned with dark hair threaded through with bone fetishes, except for the heavily muscled man who had short hair. He wore a shrunken skull necklace over his broad chest.

They traveled in a pack around Scarlett, Quick, and Brass. Ironically, the golden Vanir team was Chafer's team, the Vanaheim arena, his home base. Chafer and Cordillera would've been more at home with the Draugr in Elivagar.

Brass had taken a page out of Slate's book with his stony glower even though judging by Crimson's demeanor, he'd had finally plucked that rose. The red head knew what colors suited her and her emerald pleated gown made her look like a porcelain doll. Quick had Indi with him and were mutually nauseating. They matched, both in charcoal grey, hers, an off the shoulder lace gown that gave the illusion of nudity, and Quick in a charcoal brocade waistcoat.

Spinel and Scarlett were back together. They hadn't been spending much time together the last few days, so said Quick, but now they appeared to be back on. He didn't leave her side, nor did his hand leave contact with her for long at any point. His mannerism was both possessive and protective, but there was an element of soothing in it as well.

Jett could feel Scarlett slipping away. It was in the company she kept, her regal bearing, and the way she dressed. Her gown was shimmering feathers that graduated from a flared gold Medici collar to black with flowing black tulle that peeked out from the faux feathered long sleeve gown. Her neckline plunged to just above her baby bump with gleaming onyx buttons down the front. Her eyes were dark and smoky, her caramel hair curled and piled with her usual fetishes and beads. Her skin shimmered with a glittering powder that dusted every inch of her exposed skin. It was a far cry from the girl in the grey maxi dress that had shown up to breakfast the morning after her first masquerade.

"Fatherhood suits Solder," Cherry said, rubbing her belly.

Solder and Katydid looked on top of the world. Scarlett had Solder's armor shop manufactured all the Vigrid gear. Vigrid, the battlefield of the Gods and the official name for the arena competition. She had single-handedly handed him more business than he could handle and was opening up an *Armored Armoire* in Valla and Ostara. Every business that hooked up with Scarlett, she turned to gold.

It was contrary to what she did with men.

Katydid, Cricket, and Bronze now each managed a salon on Valla, Thrimilci, and Elivagar. They still did hair and makeup but it was exclusively for the Shadow Breakers, the Sumar and Dagrs, and for the Vigrid competitors. Solder and Katydid steered clear of Brass as if an invisible force field prevented them from penetrating his bubble. Katydid had dated Brass and Solder at the same time on and off for two years.

Gypsum sauntered over with Rosasite on his arm. Rosasite had a chip on her shoulder when it came to greater families, but it didn't stop her from seeing Gypsum whenever it struck his fancy.

"Shouldn't Slate be here?" Gypsum leaned in to ask.

Tawny and Steel glided over. They smiled broadly as they approached. It was hard to get close to Scarlett with Ash, Quartz, and her team of arena workers around her. Pearl, Reed, Fern, and the rest of the Tio brood were all there as were all the patriarchs save Cygnus. Ruby had made it out and stood with Dahlia and Basil making pleasantries. To think that Scarlett had brought this all together in the beginning just to find Slate when he was imprisoned when they'd all believed he was dead.

"Where's Slate?" Tawny asked, knitting her thick dark brows.

"The question of the night." Amethyst sighed. "The way Scarlett is looking around; she is wondering the same thing."

Amethyst was right. Whenever anyone wasn't speaking to Scar, her head swiveled. Spinel would change his hold on her to one of those soothing motions and she would refocus. Ash looked profoundly irritated at the older man's attention to her.

"He is at headquarters. I saw him before I left," Rosasite said plainly before taking a sip from her crystal chalice.

"What was he doing that could be more important than being here?" Tawny asked with irritation.

"More like *who*." Rosasite sniffed. "The Second is not the only woman in Tidings."

Gypsum's face darkened. "Don't be catty, Ro."

Rosasite's lips pressed firmly together. "I hear you, Gyps, but you men act like the sun rises with her smile."

"What floozie is this now? No more Lynx?" Cherry asked peevishly.

"He hasn't seen Lynx since his last competition," Jett interjected.

It was the night Peak tried to kill Chafer, Scarlett, and Jett. That night would forever be burned into Jett's memory.

"That was a while ago. I thought he didn't date?" Tawny nearly hissed.

"I would not call it dating," Rosasite muttered dryly.

A chime tolled three times, and the Guardians began to walk down the carpeted steps past the Corinthian columns to the cream jacquard wingback chairs. Scarlett's personal seat was sage green. Each chair had a name with a placard atop it. Scarlett whirled her finger in the air and placards shifted around her seat. One flew into her hand and she incinerated it in her palm.

Jett walked over with the girls and found that Indigo sat on Scarlett's left while Jett sat on her right. Tawny and Steel sat directly in front of them with Gypsum and Ro, Brass, Crimson, and Spinel alongside them. Ash, Sterling, and the others sat in the very first row with Pearl, Reed, and the older greater family members. Scarlett's green-blue eyes popped against the dark shadow as she offered them a smile.

"Slate said he'd be here and never showed. Did you guys see him before you came here?" she asked, calling over one of the servers that held her sparkling grape juice.

She grabbed two and handed one to Cherry who gave feigned exasperation as she took the chalice. "Nope. Forget him. Look at what you accomplished. You're amazing, baby sis." Jett swept his arms out to the arena before them.

Thousands of Guardians, young and old crowded the padded stone seats. The arena was a success. She smiled out at what she'd created.

"I only came up with it because I hated patrons buying time with people I cared about and it was the only thing I could think of that would help me find Slate at the time." It took an effort to smooth her brow. "He should be here."

"You won't get an argument out of me," Indi said under her breath. "Are you... okay?"

Indi's question appeared to startle her, and she looked to Brass in the row below her. It was like a slapstick comedy. Brass's head whipped around to her and she jerked it straight again.

"I went to the Regn manor for work with Brass and fell asleep. Crimson and Brass were kissing right there with me asleep," she said in a cool tone.

"Truth. What the *fuck?*" Quick bent forward to look at her and Scarlett's face turned to ice.

"I don't want to talk about it," she snapped.

"*Guardians and future Guardians, we welcome you to the Vanaheim arena and the opening night of Vigrid!*" A male announcer's captivating voice filled every nook and cranny. "*Tonight's matches of our home team of the Valla Vanir will face off against the Elivagar Draugr!*"

"Did you help pick out the names?" Gypsum asked over his shoulder.

"Brass and Quick helped, then each arena manager put bids in for a team. It went smoothly once Solder and I put together ideas for outfits," she explained.

"She's being modest, as usual. She had all the ideas, we merely refined them," Brass said, turning his head focused on Scarlett who wouldn't meet his eyes.

The lights went out so recessed lights along the steps and in the halls were all that lit the arena until the spotlights came on swirling around the stadium.

"*Our very first competitors... from our very own Vanaheim arena... CYCLONE!*"

American rock music played over the speakers and Jett laughed. One of the golden-haired, golden clad lean man greeted the crowd, walking up a ramp into the arena.

"It's like professional wrestling," Jett said.

Scarlett arched a brow at him with a smug full-lipped smile. "Each competitor picks his or her own song to play, radio edited versions only so it's not too harsh on the kiddies' ears."

"*And from the Elivagar Draugr... HUNDRED PROOF!*"

Gothic rock music started over the speakers in a highly edited version and Scarlett gave Jett a rueful smile. The leaner Draugr male competitor painted like a skeleton and sneered at the crowd as fitting his gimmick.

"I think I'm going to retire as heir and become a Draugr," Gyps said, flashing Scar a dimpled smile.

"Me and you both," Jett chimed in.

The two men stood on a stone platform and a boom sounded. The match begun, and the men were off. Blades spun and sliced at the men who jumped and dodged. Red clad Guardians stood to either side of the arena to safe keep the competitors. The men moved lithely, two big cats, muscles flexing, rippling as the blade whizzed past.

A narrow stone platform waited for them before pedestals that slowly stretched to the ceiling until they were jumping from the thin pillars twenty feet above a free fall. The danger was an illusion, the red clad Guardians ensured their safety with their *calling*. Rough ropes hung from the steel beams and the men swung across a gap until they reached a constant outpouring of water on a stone shoot.

The men were tossed and turned until they hit the bottom sopping wet and had to climb a wall to reach the next platform. The Draugr man rolled free of the colliding rock hammers a second before the Vanir man joined him on the platform.

The crowd roared as the Marilyn Manson song came back on. Black handheld flags were waved with *DRAUGR* embroidered across them in grey. The Draugr man spun in place to take in the cheering fans and even the booing ones and smiled. It was his first time competing and already he was addicted to the rush.

Scarlett left her seat with Chafer, Brass, Quick, and Cordillera. "I'll be back. I need to go let them know what a good job they're doing," Scar said with a smile.

Quick offered her his arm, and she took it with a grateful grin.

Scarlett returned with Cordillera, Chafer, and Quick at intermission. Guardians milled about the halls mingling and refreshing their drinks. Jett excused himself and went to the private men's lavatory. The bell started to chime and Jett hurried against the flow of men leaving the restroom and entered one of the stalls.

The door slammed open and Jett heard two men arguing. Well, one arguing, the other agreeing.

"I am here to protect her, but you know what hurts her the most. You and Slate. Pewter and Siren updated me when we switched shifts, they said Slate was in her bedroom for three hours. Now, I was at headquarters when he showed up. He did not act like a man who had spent the morning in bed with his wife if you catch my drift. Then, I find out you, *Captain,* tried to bed her right on her desk when you know Pewter and Siren would be hidden in the room with you. The worst part of today was that Siren said you slept with Crimson. That Spinel, whom *you* made out like he took advantage of her, was the one who made sure she was taken care of and here on time."

"Albacore, I understand —"

Jett guarded his thoughts as much as possible hoping Brass wouldn't pick up on his mind. Albacore, Cory, was the only man who had tried to court Scarlett when Ash urged her to take a second husband. It had lasted two weeks before he was injured and Scarlett wouldn't risk harm coming to any other man in her life so she'd stopped letting men court her except Spinel. Who knew what the real story was with Spinel and Scar.

"No, I do not think you do. I asked to guard her at night because I could not stand the idea of another seeing her at her most vulnerable. How can I protect her from the ones she loves? The ones who hurt her the most?" Cory accused.

"Her love life is none of your business, Breaker," Brass snapped.

"No one is there for her. She cries in the shower. Did you know she was still showering at least twice a day? She pushed you away, I get that, but what is Slate thinking? The Prime circles around her like a shark. All it is going to take a push in his direction. She wants to be strong, but she needs help. Mother's milk! She is drowning! How do you not see that?"

Cory's tone had changed, he wanted help for her. Jett had heard that tone before, the guy was infatuated with her. Scarlett had showered several times a day after Peak, every time Jett thought she was getting better, he was reminded of how much she'd gone through and far she had to go to return to normal, the new normal.

"*You* get back into her good graces. It is you or Spinel. I will arrange for another to replace you if you think she will let you close to her again," Brass said, all business.

"Slate?" Cory asked.

"Until he can admit to himself that he's in love with her and his prophecy will happen either way, he can't be trusted with her. Especially while he cavorts with *that* woman."

"Scarlett saw her the other day. Captain, she cannot find out."

Brass sighed. "While she thinks there is a small chance with Slate, she will never give up. No one else will stand a chance. That being said, I don't know what the answer is, Albacore. If you see an in with her, take it. I know your intentions are honorable. I won't begrudge you."

The lock clicked as the door unlocked and Jett heard the two men leave. Jett wiped a hand over his face trying to find an answer to it all. He didn't think he wanted to know who the woman was. There were three women that Slate had been with that were the unforgivable trifecta of Slate's exes, Cordillera, who was now one of Scarlett's confidants, but Lera wouldn't double cross Scar. Amber, who was murdered by Nirrin on the Wemic lands while she was pregnant with Slate's child. Which left door number three. Lynx bothered Scar, any woman did, but Lynx wasn't a threat to Scar, there were no prior problems between them.

When Jett returned to his seat, the final match had finished and the last Vigrid victor had won. Slowly, the Guardians began to file out and Spinel was back at Scarlett's side as if summoned. She didn't look when she offered her arm and he slid his over it.

Jett took Cherry and Amethyst's arms and began to lead them down to *Circus Maximus*; the night was just beginning.

# ELEVEN

I shouldn't have been surprised, but I was. How could he not come? It'd distracted me all night, and it vexed me that I couldn't enjoy my big night. For four nickel hunts and three copper skolls, Guardians got to see an organized sport for the first time. The night was a hit. The arenas were a hit.

"I have hardly seen you smile all night, darling. This is a proud night," Pearl said, catching me alone while Spinel got us another drink.

Her eyes searched mine. "I thought Slate would come, that's all."

My own honesty surprised me, instead of launching off into a grandmotherly lecture she embraced me. "Anything worth having is worth fighting for. He has always been a difficult boy, now he is a difficult man. I was very happy he had found someone; I am sorry it has been a difficult journey. I still hold out hope for the three of you, darling."

"Three?" I asked, confused.

Pearl didn't say a word but gave my hand a squeeze as she looked past me. I followed her gaze. Brass was speaking with Ruby and he pivoted his head to meet my eyes. He'd been doing it all night. I never wanted to see Brass again. Being in the same room with him and Crimson made me want to poke my eyes out.

"We older folks are leaving," Pearl said with a hint of humor.

Sparrow and Hawk came by to congratulate me. Reed took me aside to tell me how proud he was of how far I'd come since arriving from Chicago. I was having a hard time accepting all of their compliments. Ruby, the Straumr brothers, and all my old provosts spoke with me and we hadn't even made it out of my suite.

*My suite. My arenas. All mine.*

I was having a hard time wrapping my head around it. I promised myself I wouldn't cry about my parents or how Ama and Shale should be there. I would have made them managers of their own arena. There wasn't a day that went by that I didn't have the deaths of someone I loved on my mind.

*Circus Maximus* was on the lowest level of the arena. It kept in theme with the Roman architecture of the arena. A double circular platform of white granite was already bustling with Guardians dancing to a mix of the ethereal Tidings music tand modern mainstream music from the States. Glass pillar tables lined the walls where Guardians made conversation. A stone balustrade balcony lined three walls above the main floor where tables and sofas were set up for VIPs.

I sat at a table, looking down at the dancing people. Quick and Indigo stood out slow dancing during a faster paced song. They were so in love and it affected everyone around them. Tawny and Steel were on the top tier of the dancing platforms next to the DJ booth. Spinel gave my knee a squeeze, and I turned back to him with a ready smile.

"I think I'm going to leave," I stated.

"We have it all under control. The stands and suites are already being cleaned, and the Vanir and Draugr are signing flags, mingling with the fans. Go home, delegate. It has been a long day."

Cordillera sounded sincere. She hadn't even made any snide remarks about me and her father. When we'd gone to check on the competitors before the competitions they'd been nervous wrecks. Afterwards, they had stars in their eyes and thanked me profusely for hiring them. I decided I was way too young for all the responsibility I had heaped on my shoulders and felt uncomfortable from all the compliments I'd received.

I looked between the stone balustrade and saw Jett bringing the girls onto the first tier of the dance floor. I had to leave before Crimson groped Brass in front of me. She'd cornered me in the bathroom and had wanted to talk about it. I let my eyes glaze over and sang a power ballad from the 80's in my head until she finished. I had no idea what she'd said and was glad.

"Come. I will escort you." Spinel slid from the white tufted sofa and offered me his hand.

I took it and stood smoothing my faux metallic feathers. A green and gold laurel carpet ran down the center of the balcony.

"Going to tuck her in?" Brass said loud enough for us to hear him as we passed the sofa he sat at with Crimson.

"If she lets me, grandson. Crimson, goodnight," Spinel said smoothly.

Ash and Quartz sat with Sterling and Diamond; I'd seen the other Straumrs down on the dance floor. I gave them a nod before letting Spinel lead me away.

"I apologize for my grandson," Spinel said, leaning into my ear.

"If anyone should be sorry, it's me. I tend to get men who are interested in me hurt or in trouble."

I gave him an apologetic smile as we ascended the sprawling stone stairway. Spinel had a strong masculine musk that blended with the fresh rain floral aroma all men with Ostara roots had.

Spinel sat on the stone bench with me taking in the warm Thrimilci night air. I used my *calling* to help the morning glory vine grow. Lethargy made me not feel like moving from my spot, but Spinel was a dangerous man to leave to his own devices in my bedroom.

I stood and offered Spinel my hand. His dreamy chocolate eyes glittered in the starlight as he took it and rose to his full height. My whole day had been off. Spinel slid his hand slowly over my palm to lace his fingers through mine. His grip was sturdy and confident, everything I wasn't.

We stopped at the slatted doors of my wing and I became nervous.

"You are an extraordinary woman," Spinel said when I stopped to face him.

"So everyone keeps telling me," I murmured dryly.

Spinel smiled with defined plump lips. "You do not believe it."

"I'm skeptical at best."

"You want to invite me in, but you will not. Funny that my grandson was jealous of me when we left together, but I envy how much you love him. I have not known love like that in a very long time. Too many years to count since my wife passed."

Spinel lifted his hand to trail the back of his fingers over my cheek. I took his wrist and pressed my lips to it.

"Goodnight, Spinel," I told him, running my thumb over the top of his hand.

"Goodnight, Scarlett," he said in a low deep voice and took a step towards me.

He held me close against his chest and for a few moments I felt safe. It took much effort to push myself away from him. When I did, he bent his face down and sealed a kiss to my cheek before walking back through the covered walkway.

The staff had changed my sheets, so they didn't smell like Slate or sex. *Clean sheets, fresh slate.*

I was in the shower for nearly an hour before I dragged myself out and got ready for bed. I pulled on a pair of heather grey capri sweats that said *BEARS* down the left leg. My white tank top was big enough to fully cover my baby belly, and I wasn't sure if that was a good or bad thing. I should've been bigger. The stress of being the Second, the arenas, the pregnancy, the Ragnarök — it was taking its toll.

I didn't bother drying my hair before I climbed into my big white bed. Tree hopped onto the blankets and curled around my belly as I scratched behind her ears.

"I'm sorry. He is going to take a little longer to come around than I planned. He'll be back though, I promise," I whispered and drifted off to sleep.

I blinked in the dark. If Slate thought he could come into my bed whenever he wished, he was sorely mistaken. The electric crackle that accompanied him was absent. Tree hissed and leapt off the bed.

I couldn't hear past my own breathing. "Slate?" I called out into the darkness.

A gurgling noise followed by a choke made my blood run cold. A fist connected with my face in the dark and I tried to focus my eyes as the pain pulsed through my head. I saw stars. Maybe it was that my nose had been lodged into my forehead, but I couldn't see through the darkness. Fear inched up my spine as I thought about where my blades were set and if I could *call* them to me.

"Run, delegate," came a rasping wet voice on my left.

*Cory?*

A cold, smooth band snapped around my wrist as a man jumped on top of me. I screamed out and kicked and scream trying to do as much damage as I could with my one free hand. I groped for my short seax under my pillow and caught it with my fingertips. My left wrist was bound to the bed frame and my assailant grappled with me to capture my right wrist.

My elemental powers weren't working. My *calling* blocked. It was a nix cuff!

He backhanded me, and pain exploded across my cheek bone. My head pulsed, and I felt the cuff snap around my right wrist before he clasped the other end to the bed frame. He was panting, and I stopped thrashing. My *calling* was completely gone and panic joined fear along my spine.

He sat on my thighs and caught his breath. When he shifted his weight, I kicked wildly to throw him off. Maybe I could knock him unconscious and scream for help. Had that been Cory telling me to run or was I half asleep? My forehead hurt where I'd been socked and my cheek burned with pain. My mind felt jostled and my thoughts were foggy. He'd hit me hard.

His arm banded around my calves painfully and he wrapped them with my own sheet before tying it to the bed. He took his sweet time. I wouldn't give him the pleasure of hearing me struggle. I had a Shadow Breaker somewhere guarding me and they would be there any second.

The man hit the energy plate, and I gasped. When we rescued Slate from Karkinos, I'd watched him bite off the head of the man's identical twin. This man and his brother had sent me to the Merfolk, had helped kill my father, and had helped capture Slate.

Pepper; the last surviving Mint twin.

His bearded sneer wasn't as manicured as it had been. His brown hair appeared disheveled and long enough to curl behind his ears as if he'd been living under a rock for the last few months. I had hoped he died went Karkinos was injured. I should've known evil was much harder to kill.

The sight of his narrow dark eyes shining with malice wasn't what sent me into a near blind panic, but the body that laid in my doorway as if he had fought right up until my door to try to keep me safe. Cory would never flash that easy smile again; his hazel eyes would never crinkle in the corners. He wouldn't nervously call me *Delegate*.

Blood was pooling under him and his breaths rattled out of his chest. I couldn't tear my eyes off him. He was drowning in his own blood. I blinked at tears that stung my eyes.

"Hold on, Cory. Help will come soon," I said in a quavering voice that made me want to kick myself.

Cory's hazel eyes lifted as he tried to raise his head. I wouldn't let him die alone, I would hold his gaze until I saw the life leave his eyes, and I felt the Shadow Breaker bond snap between us. My vision blurred with tears when he offered me a smile as if he could read my mind and he dragged his hand to his heart. I watched his head go limp and his gaze go dark. I squeezed my eyes shut as the vision of what I just watched raced through my mind and the bond snapped between us. Cory was dead. I had distanced myself from him and he wound up dead regardless.

It was all my fault; I was death to men who loved me.

Pepper hadn't been idle as I was locked in Cory's eyes. He had unrolled a case of knives on the bed and was picking which one to use first.

"What do you want? If you're going to kill me, get it over with," I ground out, trying to stop the tears that rolled down my neck and collected at the hollow of my throat.

"We will need to rush. I imagine whoever set this boy up as your guard knows he is dead now and is rushing to your aid. First things first, I do not want you screaming, if you would be so kind?"

He gripped my face, and I tried shaking his hands off until he held my nose. I couldn't breathe, my mouth popped open to suck in air and he shoved tongs into my mouth. Pepper was always more in control than his brother.

Pepper pulled my tongue as I tried to wriggle it free, whimpering and drooling, as I fought against the nix torques. With one quick slice, pain exploded in my mouth as the resistance that held my head forward was gone. I watched with tears streaming down my face as he placed my tongue and the tongs back on the roll. My mouth was filling with fluid I guessed was blood but I couldn't taste it.

I fainted.

My mind protected me as best it could.

I choked on blood, startling myself awake.

I thrashed as I tried to stop him from grabbing a fistful of my hair and wrapping it around his wrist making the restraints dig into my wrists and bend my shoulders back. He leaned forward to see my face.

"This may hurt a bit. It may *all* hurt a bit, but at least no one is going to swallow your head," he said, and I felt the blade bite into my skin. "The Shadow Breaker tracker is usually at the base of the skull, yes?"

I screamed against in a horrific tone without my tongue as he used his momentum to pull my hair taut and slice skin from my scalp along with my hair in one quick slice. Hot blood ran down my neck and he let me fall back. I started shaking violently, the pain in my head and at my nape too much to endure. I kept wishing I would faint again so I could never wake up and that would be the end of it.

He held up two and a half feet of golden waves with a strip of flesh connected to it and I felt bile splash at the back of my throat. Blood was spilling over the sides of my mouth mingling with my vomit to run down my throat. He looked at the skin, inspecting it and sighed as he threw it at his feet.

"Not there. Oh, but I see your tiwaz tattoo. With your husband, yes? I seem to recall he had a similar tattoo. Success through sacrifice. You know nothing of sacrifice, you spoiled brat."

His tone went from mocking to harsh and barked. I knew there was no point in struggling, but I had to buy time.

My left hand was fisted above my head and Pepper nearly broke my fingers as he pried my hand open.

"Hold still. I do not want you bleeding out too soon. Everyone will be drunk at your Vigrid stadium, it dulls the bonds."

Pepper gripped my shaking hand, and he stuck his thin curved blade at the base of my ring finger. "This will expedite things. He will come running, or perhaps he no longer cares. We shall see."

He pushed. The blade slid between my joints and I screamed in a foreign tone coming from my throat until my vision blurred. Blood burst from the back of my throat with my garbled screams and sprayed over his face and my chest. Tree flew over me and latched on to Pepper's face hissing. The pain pulsed, and I felt more blood pouring down my restrained hand.

Tree was thrown, and she hit the wall and slid down to the floor and went limp. I groaned and cried unable to use a tongue that no longer existed. I coughed against the blood filling my mouth, splattering it over my face and the pillow behind me, it seeped into my ears.

I noticed for the first time that he was bleeding from his side, Cory must have stabbed him. Tree left claw marks along his face and over his neck. Blood was streaming from his shoulder too, another strike from Cory.

Was Cory my night guard?

Blood was pouring over my hand from my finger, the sheet behind my head was dampening with my blood, my body throbbed with pain that made it difficult to focus and think.

Pepper was gritting his teeth; he was in pain too. I could tell he wasn't going to use my body; he was going to torture me.

"My brother was all I had. Him and the Stygian Knights. You took that from me," he said and he snatched my hand again.

My head swam, and I hacked roughly without my tongue. Brass would feel the bond break when he took my finger, there was so much blood in my mouth it would be impossible for my EH rune not to be active.

"We were orphans. The Valkyrie sect raised me, as they do all unwanted children. They told us our mother and father were greater family. Could you imagine a scenario where a greater family would not want identical sons?"

I screamed as the blade slid into my knuckle. My eyes rolled in my head and sweat broke out over my skin. I prayed to faint. Pepper must have seen me start to fade into oblivion and pulled something from his pocket. He held smelling salts under my nose and I inhaled sharply, the pain more vivid than ever. I didn't want to cry, torturing me excited him.

I felt my skin give as he dug the point between my bones. I panted, trying to ignore the impossible pain, the Shadow Breakers would feel the bond break. I had to hold on. A Breaker would come. They couldn't all have been drinking at the Vigrid tournament, someone must've been sober enough to come.

"Ash thought he could protect you. Keeping you close. He was wrong. I was hoping you had started lying with him by now so I could finish off that arrogant snake."

Pepper ran his hand over my sweat-soaked skin as I violently shook unable to control any part of myself. I felt the moment my bladder gave at the sheer fear of being tortured to death and never meeting my sons... at the death of my sons.

"Do not worry. I have no interest in your flesh except to remove it. I think I will start here. Peel your breasts like an orange. I could take your babies from your body and let you watch them struggle for life before they die..."

Pure stark terror caused me to thrash again, tears streaking down my face. I choked on blood and vomit as my stomach cramped. His wickedly sharp blade was held to my stomach.

"Stop struggling. It is pathetic. *You* are pathetic." he snapped, sitting on my thighs.

The endless pain became worse by the constant throbbing of blood rushing. I knew I was going to go into shock soon.

The most ridiculous things kept flitting through my mind. My sheets were stained, I'd have to clean the sheer panels that draped over the canopy. My rug was likely stained too. It might all need to be replaced. My mattress would smell like urine forever.

Peppermint ran his hands over my skin, shifting my arms and moving my head. He was looking for more bonded tattoos. He hadn't seen the EH rune on my lower lip or the kenaz rune on the skin between my thumb and index finger. I couldn't think past the pain. I had to save myself, if not for me then for the lives I was responsible for. He pulled my ribbed tank top up and ran his blade along my skin, not enough to cut, but to remind me he was in charge. There was no way he was going to let me live.

"This has to go. The Stygians took Spear and I in the year we turned twenty. The one good thing about Tidings is anyone can go to Valla University, even orphans and abandoned children. My theory is, our parents were having an affair and could not risk the scandal. Not like your whore of a mother, she did not care who knew you were bastards."

He yanked my pants down, not finding any body art on my upper half, and was rewarded with the inguz tattoo on my hip. He tapped the Celtic roped "Xs" with the flat of his blade.

The blade bit into my skin where he'd found my Shadow Breaker rune, and a sob broke through. How much could he cut off before I fainted? Would he keep using smelling salts? How much more before I died?

"I may never have known my parents, but you will die knowing you failed yours. The man who murdered them is out there. You will die and no one will avenge them."

His eyes flickered up to my face, and he grinned maliciously at me. I was fading out again, my mind tried to preserve its sanity as he painstakingly cut at my hip. I was rubbing my fingers together trying to spread the blood to the bonded rune I had with Jett and Indigo. I'd moved my emerald ring to my right hand so at least it wasn't on my detached finger. My luck had finally run out.

# CHAPTER 12
# 1NDIGO

Silver's arm was wrapped around my waist as we walked leaning against one another from the Vanaheim arena. "We should have gone into one of the dozens of empty bedrooms."

I rested my head against his side as I let him guide us. "We have two perfectly good bedrooms, at your manor or my palace. There's no need to do the walk of shame in the morning."

"It was not fair that you were there while the Vanir were pretending to be Gods. A goddess in the flesh," Silver purred, lips brushing against my temple as he spoke.

Our footsteps echoed on the marble even with the steady stream of Guardians leaving the arena. The night had been a complete success, though the people who should have been proudest had left earliest. Brass and Crimson left shortly after Scarlett and Spinel. Slate never showed, and Scar made no effort to hide how much it bothered her for the first time in ages. She had been taking the stoic route, but it had gone out the window. It had to do with seeing Brass with Crimson, Scarlett had to know giving Brass up wasn't for nothing.

Jett, Amethyst, and Cherry were dancing when they left with Gypsum and Rosasite. Tawny and Steel left shortly before we had, *Circus*

*Maximus* was still filled with people. The party would go on well into the night. Cordillera and Chafer were managing things well, so we had decided to leave.

"You are trying to flatter me because you know I'm ovulating in a few days. I'm not changing my mind, Silver. I'm happier than I've ever been. It *feels* right."

Silver stopped and took my face in his hands. "Indigo Tio. How is it I have only been with you for a single year? We could have been together for several." He leaned in, slanting his mouth over mine.

I arched a brow at him when he withdrew. "Your memory is selective. We have been sleeping with one another for a year, exclusively for two months. Hardly a feat to celebrate," I said wryly. "Now I'll have to compete with all the Vigrid groupies who will inevitably form a following."

Silver's smile was positively sinful. "I love it when you get jealous, Dove. It shows me you fear losing me." He pulled me close, ducking his mouth to mine. "You never have to worry about other women again. I am yours if you want me," he whispered, and I couldn't stave off my smile.

"I want you, Silver," I purred back, and Silver groaned.

"Bed. Now. It would be best if you start undressing as we walk, it is a lovely dress and my teeth tend to tear such delicate fabric," he said as he pulled me after him.

I giggled like a thirteen-year-old myopic girl.

Silver froze and shut his eyes as if he was in anguish. "Oh, gods. Indigo," he ground out as a woman screamed in anguish somewhere behind us.

"What's wrong?" I let go of his hand and tried to lift his face up.

His brow drew down. "Run, Dove. Scarlett's in trouble."

He didn't have to say another word, and I was afraid to ask. We pushed against the Guardians leaving as we forced our way up the stairs. Silver held my hand in a vise-like grip. I had to ask.

"Tell me, Silver."

"Cory was the night watch guard for Scarlett and he is dead," Silver said in a thick voice. "Brass is at the manor; he will not make it there in time."

If she's still there.

The Valla night air was bitterly cold. Our feet pounded on the bridge and Guardians heard us coming stepping out of our way. My heart raced. The only reason Silver's bond with Scarlett would snap would be because someone had removed her skin from her body. With Cory dead, she was all alone.

Silver stumbled, and he stood there, head hanging. A rasping breath forced its way from his lungs.

"I am so sorry, Indigo," he rasped.

"What? What are you talking about?" I asked with a hysterical edge.

Silver's eyes were wide when he raised his head to me. "Your bond with Scar? It is intact?"

"Yes, of course. Why?" I asked.

"Run. Faster." Silver was pulling me so fast I was nearly stumbling as I tried to match his stride.

We staggered through the portal door; bright white light flooded the Dagr portal room. We weren't even sure she was there. It was a shot in the dark. If she ended up going home with Spinel, Brass would be with her. Maybe she was lucky, and they were at the Regn manor, that would mean Spinel was dead too.

I didn't know what I was hoping for. Beside the portal door sprawled the body of the Guardian who guarded the portal. Scarlett was there.

Silver cursed and he let go of my hand. He could reach her sooner without me.

"Just go!" I shouted, and his brow knit, but he turned around and ran at full speed.

They didn't call him "Quick" for nothing.

I turned the corner onto the covered walkway as Silver drew two blades from his boots before he entered the arched doors that led to Scarlett's wing. I picked the skirt of my dress up as I chased after him. The whole wing was dark except for the light coming from the bedroom. I entered the room in time to see Silver launch himself at a man, flying over Scarlett's bed.

My feet hit something solid, and I fell face first onto the rug. Sounds of Silver and the man fighting on the other side of the bed where I couldn't see them made my stomach twist. Then I saw what tripped me. My palm came away wet and bloody where Cory had bled out onto the carpet. He was on his back, head canted back as if he was looking at the bed. I scrambled to my feet. Those twinkling hazel eyes held no life in them.

A pile of golden hair laid on the floor and I gagged when I saw the strip of ragged flesh attached to it. A tremor sent my bones vibrating as I followed Cory's dead gaze. She wasn't moving. A sheet was bound around her calves to the bed and her arms were spread to either side of her. Her sweats were halfway pulled down her red stained hips, and her tan pregnant belly had a bloodied hand print to the side of it. I stumbled forward as my head swam.

Scarlett's head fell to the side, and she tried to focus her eyes. Blood seeped from her mouth as tears streaked her face. My throat constricted as I walked in a haze to her side. Nix torques. I unsnapped the torques from her wrists and pulled her arms down to her sides. A knife had outlined the shape of inguz rune that was almost flayed completely off.

The bed bowed as I sat next to her when I put a hand down on the sheets. My hand came up against something wet and warm and I looked down. I lifted my head to Scarlett's bleeding hand. The man had cut off her finger. The blood had not worked its way to my bonded rune yet. I didn't think I could tolerate the kind of pain she must have been feeling if her bond was active.

Blood soaked the pillow, the sheets, and over her chest. Her forearm was streaked with it to her elbow. Her throat worked, and I shrieked.

Where her tongue should have been was a jagged stump. I began frantically searching for her tongue and found it clasped in a set of bloody tongs near a roll of blades. The smell of urine, vomit, and blood caused me to gag.

The sound of flesh hitting flesh came from where Silver was straddling Scar's attacker as he grunted even though he was coming up against no defense. The man was dead, but Silver beat at him anyway, his sense and temper long lost.

I pried her tongue free of the tongs sobbing when a hand rested on my shoulder and I glanced up.

"Check on Quick. I have got her," Slate said, not taking silver eyes off her.

Upon seeing Slate, Scarlett's face crumpled, but she remained limp on the bed, too pained to move.

Slate took her tongue from my palm like it was commonplace and placed it in her gaping mouth to reattach it.

"Where were you?" she accused.

Her breaths came short and shallow as she gasped. Slate sat next to her and his finger traced the slices around her hip leaving a healed red trail behind it.

"I am here now. I will never leave your side again. I swear it." Slate's voice was thick with emotion, his deep rumble caught.

Slate picked up her chopped off hair. He sliced the hair from the piece of her scalp to reattach it before he could heal her. She was straight out of a horror movie the way blood was splattered over her face and coated her mouth down to her chest and into her ears. The little hair that hadn't been chopped off, matted in the damp blood over the back of her head.

"I thought I was going to die alone," she whispered through the tears and grabbed for him with a bloodied hand.

Slate saw her missing finger when she winced and started looking around for her pieces of flayed skin and finger. Silver straightened, panting, splattered with the gore of the dead man. It was on his face, his arms, over his satin waistcoat.

A shadow moved in the doorway and I whipped to it.

Rage washed over me. How *dare* she come.

CHAPTER

# THIRTEEN

Quick saved me. Indigo was here. Slate came.

I couldn't breathe.

Slate was healing my hip, Quick straightened from beside the bed and smeared the blood from his face with the back of his sleeve. My tongue worked. Indigo rose from the bed, her face a thunderhead. Her eyes shifted to a piercing ice blue. Slate pulled down my shirt over my belly and looked around.

That look. I had been waiting for *months* for Slate to have that look in his eyes. I could do without the pity and self-recrimination, but the love. I'd take it by the boatload.

I steadied my breathing and pushed myself up with my good hand. The pillow case stuck to the back of my bleeding head. My hair. It was all gone.

"Scarlett. You're alive," Brass croaked.

Brass pushed into the bedroom. He made a strangled sound and wiped his thumb and index finger under his eyes coming away wet. He

162

was shirtless and barefoot, as was Slate. Brass was in his pajama pants from earlier and Slate was in a pair of black fitted pants I'd seen him wear dozens of times before.

"Peppermint. He is dead now. Indigo. Enough," Quick said in a gruff voice I barely recognized.

Indi was inches away from Mirage's face, speaking in a harsh whisper. At Quick's voice they both swiveled their heads. Crimson appeared behind them in a robe made for a man.

"Get out. What are you doing here?" I managed to rasp out of my raw throat.

"Hold still, I am going to heal your scalp," Slate rumbled.

"Who cares about hair? Check the babies!" I snapped in a croak, hating being so vulnerable in front of Mirage. "I'll ask you again. What are you doing here?"

I looked at Indigo and Brass. I didn't need her to answer anymore. I knew why she had come; the same reason Crimson was there. She was spending the night with Slate.

"Get out and take him with you," I growled through clenched teeth.

I was completely drained of energy. The temptation to lay back down since I was partially healed was hard to ignore.

"Scarlett, *please*, I need to heal you," Slate begged in a whisper.

His voice hurt my ears. They felt like they were on fire.

I tugged up my urine-soaked pants and winced as it slid over my raw wound. I forgot about my finger, the crippling anguish in my heart numbed any physical pain. I held my good hand to my hip to stop the throbbing. I couldn't resist running my hand over my hair. Parts of it ended below my ears other parts were still long that hadn't been grasped in Pepper's fist when he sliced it off. A strand slid against my exposed bone and I grit my teeth. It didn't stop the high whimper that came from my mouth.

"Get out. Quick and Indi can heal me. The rest of you leave. *Now*," I said, feeling the blood rush to my cheeks.

I was bent trying to keep pressure on my hip and feeling weak. I was drenched in my own blood and probably looked like I'd dragged myself from a nearby grave. At any moment I was going to call out for brains.

Slate held the piece of my scalp in his palm. He grabbed my wrist.

"Scarlett. I do not want to leave. I want to stay with you. With your bairn," Slate pleaded.

My upper lip curled as I snatched back my hand. "Too little, too late. Get out of my room before I do something I might regret and have to tell my aunt I killed her nephew," I said in a slow measured tone before I turned to Quick. "Heal me. Heal me like this. I won't ever need that finger again. I don't want any Shadow Breakers knowing if I'm alive or dead. Pepper did me a favor."

Brass stepped forward with his hands out. "You don't mean that."

"Don't I?" I whipped my head to Quick, making my world spin even when I stopped.

"Truth," Quick said, coming around the bed towards me. "We can handle this. You all should go. She is losing a lot of blood."

"Wait. I have one more..." I glanced around the bed where Slate sat and *called* over Pepper's bloody blade.

It hit my palm and Brass shouted. "No!"

I pulled out my lower lip and stabbed the blade into it. The coppery taste of blood filled my mouth for the second time that night, and I didn't stop moving the blade until I had to spit, blinking against the tears from the pain. Slate held my wrists as I tried to cut the EH rune free. I didn't care if I hurt him anymore.

I blazed to life. Fire formed to where my body should have been, my short hair writhed around my face, hot coals for eyes in dark sockets. Fire churned within the invisible confines of my body.

"Get out!" I screamed as Slate let go with scorched palms.

The smell of his burnt flesh adding to the cacophony of disgusting scents.

The blade was on the floor and pain shot through my stomach. I bowled over, hugging myself.

"Get over it. Other than you having piss and puke on yourself, you are *fine* if a little bloody. Who else could he fuck that could project you, but *not* wind up killing him like being with *you* would?" Mirage asked smugly.

Crimson gasped. Quick wrapped his arms around Indigo's waist to keep her from attacking Mirage.

"He's yours. I never want to see his face again."

I pulled the emerald ring from my finger and threw it at Slate. I crooked my finger at Slate.

"My father's ring. Give it to me. You don't deserve it," I said in a disembodied voice.

My flames winked out. Slate pulled the ring off his finger and held it out. I *called* so it flew into my palm. I groaned again as more pain shot through my stomach.

"I am your husband," Slate said, taking a step towards me.

"Those are my children, love," Brass said pleadingly.

"I have no husband. These children are mine," I snapped.

Mirage sniffed. "Those children are no ones. Looks like you are off the hook, Captain."

Brass's head snapped to my stomach as did the rest of the people's in the room. My vision blurred, and I used my good hand to touch the warm fluid that had begun to run down my legs. I lifted my fingers in front of my face.

*Blood.*

Air rushed from my lungs. I watched everyone fall to the floor as the air blasted from me while they covered their ears. Fire raged along the ceiling. My fingers curled as I shouted soundlessly at the heavens.

Surely, I was never so bad in a previous life.

CHAPTER 14

# INDIGO

While everyone else ran to Scarlett as she fainted, I jumped on Mirage. I sucker punched her, and she went down like a sack of potatoes. I didn't stop hitting her until Silver yanked me off.

"You are just as crazy as your sister!" she screamed while on her ass, holding her gushing nose.

"Crazier! I have nothing to lose!" I shouted back.

Chafer barreled into the room and saw Cory. He closed his eyes and walked over to where Brass and Slate had laid Scar on the bed. Brass was reattaching her finger and knitting her skin back together. Slate's big hands were over her stomach, his face a mask of concentration and despair. All it took was him thinking her dead for him to admit he was in love with her.

*Too little, too late was right.*

Chafer walked to the bed and glanced over the side of the bed where Pepper's beaten body laid. "Good riddance." He sneered. "You two pathetic fools." He sniffed and shook his head.

Slate growled at him. Brass's amber eyes were molten.

"Does she want either of you here?" Chafer asked dryly.

166

"Do not presume to tell me what to do about my wife," Slate ground out.

I laughed. It wasn't a pleasant sound. Silver held me tight so I couldn't attack Slate as I wanted.

"She would rather die than let you touch her. Did you hear nothing she said? You're not her husband anymore. It's over. You've lost her for good." I looked at Brass and at Crimson who was healing Mirage. "Both of you."

I stopped struggling against Silver and he let me go. "Help me get her to Pearl. I don't want these people touching her," I pleaded, looking at Silver.

Silver ran his tongue along his lower lip and bobbed his head once. Chafer ran his palm over Scarlett's brow and sighed.

"You two should be ashamed of yourselves, and that says a lot coming from me. I have a fallen Breaker to tend to," Chafer said, hefting Cory up and left.

"No one is more ashamed than I am of myself," Slate rumbled once he left the room.

Brass looked at Crimson. "I cannot go back with you," he murmured.

"You are in love with another man's wife?" she asked in disbelief.

Brass turned away and pressed a palm next to Slate's on Scarlett's rounded belly. "I would stop if I could. I cannot risk losing her again. Those are my children she carries."

Crimson pulled herself up, obviously undressed under his thin green robe. "There is a reason I was so adamant about our love making today."

"She is in season," Slate said, raising his brow to look at Brass.

Brass's lips parted as he whirled to face Crimson. Silver stepped between Brass and Slate.

"I am taking her to the Sumar palace. Go take care of your baby's mama. The other one." Silver patted Brass's bare shoulder.

Brass was speechless. "We will know for sure in a few days," Crimson said in a small voice.

Brass nodded and looked back at Scarlett. "Take care of her. Thank you for being here for her."

"I will. What are brothers for? She and I are even now," Silver weakly joked and swallowed. "But I would follow her through anything."

"*I* will. If she asks me to help her remove those bonded tattoos and the tracker, I will. Make no mistake. As far as I'm concerned, both of you need to stay away from her," I snapped.

Brass didn't say anything as he walked past me, distracted by his possible impending double fatherhood. Slate rose from beside Scarlett and looked down his nose at me. I met his silver eyed glare.

"We saved the bairn. I would love to meet the person who thinks they can keep me away from my wife," Slate rumbled.

"Do you smell that? The scent of blood, vomit, piss, and death in your pregnant wife's bedroom? Where *you* should have been, but you were too busy bedding a projected image of her because you're a coward who can't handle the responsibility of being a husband. *I'm* the person who will keep you away as long as she wills it and if you try to come between us, you'll push her into running. *I* don't have a problem with killing you so I can keep my sister."

"Truth," Silver said, lifting Scarlett into his arms. "Take it easy. Let her sleep on it."

"Fine," I snapped and glanced down at the torn and saturated sheets.

Scar's hair was piled on the floor. Slate bent down and picked it up, rubbing his fingers over it. He *called,* braiding it so a rope a foot long and two fingers wide was formed and he tucked it into his pocket.

"We have to find a Guardian who can grow this back for her," he rumbled as his booted feet crossed the carpet, skirting the puddle where Cory had lain.

"Hair is hardly a concern when you've lost your heart," I spat.

"I can dispose of that vermin," Slate said, gesturing to the dead man's body.

He knelt down at the wall opposite the fallen man. No one had seen Tree's snowy body. Slate picked up the overly large cat and began to stroke her.

"She will survive as well. I will bring her to the Sumar palace."

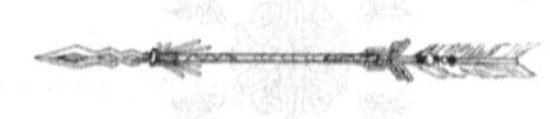

The well room was pristine white and mahogany. There were no rugs on the wood floors. A white triangular jacuzzi was paneled into the wall to the left next to a door that led to the rest of the bathroom. Against the far wall was the four-poster mahogany bed with all white bedding, heavy white paneling hung from the canopy on rings to shut with a flick of your wrist.

Scarlett laid back in the center of the bed, sweat glistening on her brow. She hadn't woken up in twenty-four hours. Pearl, Hawk, and Sparrow brought in two white chaises that they had taken turns watching over her. Jett and I sat across from them on a love seat. We'd been here since we brought her in. I had changed out of my dress and showered since she was safe.

Silver and the others waited just outside what was typically used as the birthing room. Wisteria Rot, the quasi nurse, checked on the babies every other hour. Tawny, Gypsum, and I had sided against letting Brass or Slate in the room. I wasn't sure who was more heartbroken about Slate's betrayal, but Gypsum was definitely in the top five. Slate had pressed his lips to Scarlett's unconscious body to deactivate the bond she'd activated from all the blood that had filled her mouth.

A stern knock sounded on the wooden double doors and I jerked against Jett's sleeping form. It was early on the second morning she'd been unconscious. No one had been told outside of the family and Shadow Breakers of Scarlett's condition. Cory's sister was distraught, he was the only one in her family she had left.

Hawk and Sparrow were curled up on one of the chaises together. Pearl had left a few hours earlier and Tawny had stubbornly taken her place. Tawny stirred and padded over to the door.

"Who's there?" she asked with a sleep thick voice.

"Prime Straumr."

Tawny craned her neck to look at me and I frowned. Ash seeing Scarlett in such a vulnerable state aggravated me to no end. Tawny shrugged narrow shoulders.

Tawny opened the door; Ash wasn't the only one waiting to be let in. Slate held a tray of food as if that would cajole us to let him in. Brass looked positively miserable, but I would not feel sympathy for him. He and Slate looked as if they hadn't slept since it happened, but I had seen them sleeping out on the couches in the waiting area. Crimson had joined Brass for a few hours the day before. Despite him wanting nothing to do with her, he was being kind and attentive.

"I received word that Scarlett had been wounded," Ash said in a nervous tone.

It caught me off guard. Ash was never nervous. He spotted Scarlett in the bed and brushed past Tawny. It was like letting down the flood-gates. Slate and Brass brushed past Tawny who gave an impressive scowl, and I shook Jett awake. Jett rubbed at his square stubbled jaw and gave me a smug grin until I nodded to the trio of men walking into the room.

Jett straightened, swinging his long legs over the side of the couch. "She's sleeping. We'll let you know when she can have visitors and only the ones she allows."

Jett's voice wasn't as guttural as our father's but it was a deep bass. He got off the couch and started to stretch. Ash was clean shaven with a spotless grey padded jerkin on. Ash crossed to Scarlett's side and ran his hand across her brow. His fingers trailed through her short hair and he pressed his lips together in a grimace. Without another word, he marched back to the doors and barked commands to someone unseen.

Slate put the tray down next to Scarlett, and mimicked Ash's actions before placing his hand on her belly and sighed. Brass sat down and ran both hands over his face and into his hair only just realizing how disheveled he appeared. Brass pulled his hair back tight and rewound the leather tie through it at his nape.

"No change?" Brass asked.

"Is your girlfriend pregnant?" Jett retorted.

I would not feel sorry for those men.

Ash returned to the bed eyeing Slate and Brass before sitting at Scarlett's side. "Whatever care she needs, whatever she needs, she can have the best Tidings has to offer. I refuse to lose her or for her to be less than herself," he said aloud. "You never deserved her. Perhaps I made my own mistakes, perhaps there have been a great deal of them, but the one thing that never changed for me was that I loved her and wanted her to be my wife. I doubt you can say the same."

My mouth had fallen open, waiting to see if Slate or Brass would engage the Prime, but they didn't. I wasn't even sure they heard him from the way they stared at Scarlett.

The color was back in her cheeks, but she looked weak and much too frail and thin in the big bed with her horrible short hair.

A knock on the door sounded and Ash smoothly rose from the bed to answer it. He led a woman by the elbow back into the room and brought her to where Scarlett laid.

"Her hair. It should be down to here." Ash pointed to Scarlett's elbow, ignoring Brass and Slate's irritated glowers.

Tawny sat back on the chaise with her eyes shut. She'd been up all-night crying because Scar hadn't woken. Our family had been put through a series of traumatic trials and the fractures were splintering into cracks that would shatter us all if we didn't get good news to balance it out soon.

The woman Ash brought in had a cool imperial demeanor as she laid her hands to either side of Scarlett's head. Slowly, Scarlett's hair forced its way from her scalp. I'd heard there was a way to grow back hair and nails, but I'd never seen it. Ash leaned Scarlett forward enough to pull the new growth of hair from behind her and the woman kept working. Her eyes shut as she *called*. In less than two minutes, Scarlett's hair was back. It was as if nothing had happened, not a scar or scratch on her.

Ash walked the woman back out and came back to the bed. His boots were polished to a gleam, he had an assertive way of treading over the mahogany that bespoke his command.

Seeing her back to her old self boosted everyone's spirits. The short hair was a hideous reminder of the atrocities she'd suffered.

"Mmm. That smells good," Scarlett said, wincing as she moved her stiff limbs.

Slate had to grip the tray, he and Brass had jerked so violently. "Chicken broth and buttered scones with chamomile tea," Slate rumbled in a rush.

Her eyes shot open and in them I saw loathing. Bloodshot turquoise eyes took in Slate and Brass. She slapped a hand to her hair and then looked at her reattached finger. They had healed her back to her original form. She finally saw Ash and her chin wobbled as she pressed her lips together.

"If these... *men* do not leave, I want them arrested," she ground out.

Ash blinked at her bewildered. "Them?" he asked.

"Scarlett, please don't do this." Brass shifted his hand to touch her, and she cried out.

"Stop! Don't touch me. Never ever touch me again," she hissed.

"I will not leave my wife. You cannot —" Slate started to argue.

"*GUARDS!*" Scarlett screeched.

I didn't know who was more dumbfounded. Ash went to the door and let in four Guardians in black cloaks with a silver valknut embroidered on the back.

"I meant to place you under protection," Ash said, watching as the Tidings Guardians marched over to Slate and Brass.

I was astonished not to find any smugness or even a snide smile on his face. He must still have been taken aback at her sudden vehemence towards men she claimed to love.

Sparrow and Hawk had woken up and got to their feet. "What's the meaning of this?" Hawk accused Ash.

"It's my decision," Scarlett interjected. "As Second, I order these men to be removed from my presence and kept a distance of five.... ten yards from me at all times."

"Scar, he's your husband," Sparrow said, smoothing her long dark tresses.

"I have no husband," she said with a sneer. "The next time I willingly gaze upon the man whom I married will be while I watch him burn on the pyre."

Tawny slapped a hand to her mouth. She was no fan of Slate's, but this shocked even her. Hawk came alongside Slate and put a hand on his big shoulder. Hawk wore traditional Thrimilci garb, a wrinkled sleeveless navy linen shirt and black pants tucked into supple black folded top boots. Strands of his silver hair had fallen from his pompadour and tickled along his olive face.

"Come, son. Give Scarlett time." Hawk ran a hand over his thin goatee.

"The babies?" Brass asked roughly.

Her hands wrapped protectively around her belly and a series of emotions passed over her beautiful face. "No matter how I feel personally, I'm not the kind of person to keep children from their father. My declaration does not extend to my sons once they are born. I can work out an arrangement. There is no reason for us to have to speak ever again," she curtly replied and pushed herself up against the headboard.

She wore a long white chemise with pearl buttons down the front. Brass watched her intently and rose from the bed.

"You're healed completely and totally. We didn't obey your wishes. What do you want to do about Vigrid? I can resign," Brass murmured.

"Don't be stupid," Jett chastised.

"Quick can relay anything I need."

She managed to look regal in her pajamas as she tossed back the thin white blankets to reveal her bared feet. Ash offered his hand, and she took it.

"I need to see Honeybee," she said.

Bee was Cory's sister; Scarlett had recruited them herself to the Shadow Breakers. "She'll not pay a copper skoll for Cory's funeral. I want at least three worthy suitors to be conveniently placed with shoulders for her to cry on. I happen to know she has not lost her fertility yet and now that she has lost the last member of her family she has a business to run on her own. She's a nice woman and deserves a family." She turned her face to Ash. "I could use your help, *please*." She swallowed. "Peppermint said you couldn't protect me, that if he had found us together, he would have killed you too. You should put extra guards on watch."

"Scarlett, I insist you come with me where I can see to your needs. I want to take you away from this place. Protect you and your unborn. Peppermint was wrong, you will be safe with me."

Ash hadn't released his grasp on her. He was subconsciously rubbing her bare ring finger and she ran her teeth over her lower lip. Her hand reached for her stone pieces and she found our father's ring there. Alder had been murdered at the Straumr palace on the night of Ash and Scar's engagement party. It was the night after Scar caught Slate and Mirage together.

"We are more than equipped to take care of her here." Jett rose to his full six and a half feet, his face hard.

"I'll be a portal away," she said, shifting her hand in Ash's, lacing her French manicured fingers through his.

"Please, Scarlett —"

Scarlett held up a hand cutting Brass off. "Don't," she wavered, swaying slightly as she took another step. "I don't... feel very well."

"Eat, Scar. You can stay for a meal," Hawk insisted.

Ash saw his opening and swept Scar's feet out from under her as he scooped her into his arms. She closed her eyes and rested her head on his shoulder.

"Take me away from this place," she whispered.

Ash raised his piercing celadon eyes to Hawk. Sparrow rushed to Hawk's side, and he clasped her wrist.

"We will come visit soon," Hawk stated helplessly.

Tawny crossed to where I stood with Jett in astonishment of the events that had transpired. Jett wrapped an arm around each of us as Ash carried Scar out with their four Guardians in tow. Brass sunk down to the bed while Slate stood like a vengeful statue looming with balled fists.

"I have to tell my mother," Hawk said, taking Sparrow with him.

Jett clenched his jaw. "I give it a month before he persuades her into marrying him. Looks like he gets what he wants in the end, it just took another year to get."

Brass fell back against the white knit blankets with his fists to his forehead. I watched his Adam's apple bob as he took a hard swallow.

"He is putting her in the room he designed for her. Less than a month, more like half that. We can forget about seeing her. He'll be trying to bed her before the night is through. She —" Brass broke off overcome with frustration.

I would not feel sorry for him.

"That boy told her I would get my memories back," Slate said almost to himself.

"You think that will make a difference after you slept with Mirage? Let me refresh your memory, you proposed to Scarlett, she agreed to it, ending things with Ash, you almost had sex with Mirage in the stall next to her while she projected Scarlett's image. She lost our father and her pregnancy in one night when she tried to salvage her relationship with Ash," I said peevishly.

Slate grit his teeth. "I never wanted any of this. Less than four months ago I woke up and two years of my life were missing. I had a wife; a lifetime of secrets were revealed and I remember *none* of it. I grow tired of your judgement. You do not know how you would have reacted. I regret my indiscretions. I should not have been so reluctant to be with her."

Brass didn't remove his fists from his face. "When I thought she had been killed... I can accept that she will not allow me to be her second husband or her lover, but I cannot... this distance."

Tawny and I had a soft spot for Brass. We all did.

"Space, time, and loyalty," Tawny snapped, holding onto her cool tone. "When she's done caring for Honeybee, she'll be lost. She always does better when she can refocus her comfort. She doesn't like to be pitied, something to do with how sad Wren was all the time." Tawny looked to me and Jett. "Maybe we can see if Spinel can weasel his way into the Straumr palace. She'll see him, and now that her and Brass are over... I vote Spinel."

"Words of wisdom for me?" Slate asked dryly.

"Stay out of her way," I snapped.

Jett ran his hands over his face and blew out a heavy breath. "I vote the geezer too."

I nodded. "I'll work it out."

Cory's funeral was held at the Vanaheim arena on the white stone bridges. Fifty Shadow Breakers were gathered around the pyre. Our family was invited because of Scarlett's previous relationship with Cory. Honeybee was a wreck. Scarlett stayed by her side the entire time and had two strapping, handsome men working as her attendants who were quick with kerchiefs and comforting words for Honeybee. Ash stayed on Scarlett's other side as if latched there.

It was the day after Scarlett woke up and no one had been allowed to see her at the Straumr palace. It was the closest we had been to her and her Guardian bodyguards prevented anyone, but Lera, Chafer, Honeybee, and Ash from seeking to speak to her far away.

Slate, Brass, and Spinel were in the crowd directly behind the

Guardian wall that separated the Prime and his Second from the masses. Pearl was none too happy with Scarlett's decision to leave nor Slate for his indiscretions. Mirage wasn't at the funeral, but her brother Hopper was and he looked to be trying to get Scarlett's attention, probably to thank her for not killing his little sister.

Two of the cream robed Valkyries waited patiently for the ceremony to complete. Their shaven heads were protected from the heavy snow by thick woolen hoods that hid their faces in their deep shadows. It was good that the Valkyries did homed the orphaned children because seeing them every time your loved one died made some people hate and fear them.

The fire was going out with nothing left to burn and the Valkyries would swoop in and collect Cory's ashes. Silver's reassuring arm around my waist did little for the cold in my heart. Scarlett belonged in the Sumar palace. Every minute she spent with Ash was another chance for him to take her away for good. His foot had been set in the door when he brought her into his inner sanctum, with her living in his palace she was with him every hour of the long day.

Silver had noted Quartz wasn't with them. Only one reason why that would be with them out in public. He was courting her publicly with his wife's permission. A Natt sharing a man... Thrimilci would sooner freeze over.

# FIFTEEN

Cory's urn was brushed black metal. Honeybee was as bad as I thought she would be, but my handsome blonde attendant had warranted a second look from her. I would have him bring her flowers as my messenger tomorrow. When she was ready, I'd arrange a dinner.

I had to be strong for Bee no matter how badly I wanted to let myself be reduced to a wailing wreck. My very soul ached. Pepper had been right about one thing, when it came to taking care of the ones I loved, I was a failure.

It was best for them to keep away. That was where Ash came into play.

Honeybee held the urn up to the grey sky. Grey winter storm like Slate's eyes. Heavy snowflakes fell from the cloud laden sky. Darkness would fall soon in Valla. Dark, like the abyss I'd fallen into. I was still falling with no end in sight.

*"Lo, There do I see my father. Lo, there do I see my mother. My sisters and my brothers. Lo, There do I see my people. Back to the beginning. Lo, there do*

*they call to me and ask me to take my place in the halls where the brave may live forever."*

Honeybee's voice warbled as she spoke. I waited for her at the base of the stone stairs that were constructed for the pyre. A stairway to the heavens. A lump the size of a Crathode claw lodged in my throat. I was grateful for the veil that hid the twitching of my features as I tried not to cry. I was Honeybee's rock, she had no one else. No husband, no children. Cory had been everything in her world. My life could always be worse. Death put things into perspective.

Honeybee had told me how much Cory cared about me. Cocktails, I'd nicknamed him when I had recruited him from the bar in Valla he owned with Honeybee. She said the main reason they had come to the Shadow Breaker recruitment that day many months ago was because Cory had wanted to see me again. He had been an omnilinguist. To demonstrate his talent in front of Lera, Brass, and the lot, he'd told me I had beautiful eyes.

The memory made the lump grow and I swallowed convulsively against it. My body shuddered as I drew a ragged breath and Ash's black leather glove wound around my back, offering me comfort. Quartz, Ash, and I had a sit down in their sitting room last night after dinner. Ash and Quartz hadn't waited a single day before broaching the second wife topic. Quartz had kept me company as I slept fitfully.

I was jaded after my encounter with Crimson and thought I would wake up with her tongue down my throat at any point. When I awoke unmolested, Ash brought us breakfast in bed. He laid across the foot as we ate with my cheeks on fire the entire time. Was this what it would be like? A woman I could confide in and a man to support me? That's how Jett, Amethyst, and Cherry made it look.

When we readied for the funeral, Quartz declined since she didn't know Cory and insisted Ash go with me. I knew they were testing the waters. Power sought power. I was powerful. A prized piece for their collection.

At least I was cherished, desired for more than my body. Ash was one of the few men in Tidings who could hope to have a balanced relationship with me. I was willing to bet Ash never thought he would be courting me again; I knew I didn't.

Honeybee descended the steps, and I caught the Valkyrie's eyes. Big, green, and gleaming deep within her cowl, she gave a slow shake of her head and disapproval wafted from her. Honeybee entered my line of sight and I moved from Ash to take her under the arm.

"Thank you delegate, *er*, Second. For everything." The brunette's nose was beet red from wiping it beneath her veil.

"Scarlett, *please*. It's me who should be thanking you, Honeybee. Your brother was a good man. I owe him my life." I insisted. "My attendant, Terne, can take that for you."

I couldn't do *nothing*. It wasn't in my nature. I felt the mutual attraction between the two and hoped I wasn't pushing too hard. Honeybee handed Terne the urn and offered her his arm which she took with a weak smile. The hardest step had been taken. The rest was up to them.

We helped her into the Vanaheim arena where we held the reception along the black-and-white marble and Corinthian columns. My family hovered just beyond my guards. They went everywhere with me. Four waited outside my bedroom at night, but I didn't feel any safer. I hadn't seen a soul outside of Ash and Quartz, but that was my choice. I wasn't up for visitors and their prying questions.

# CHAPTER 16
# GYPSUM

*Mistress needs me. There is no one left to comfort her and someone has to keep an eye on her before the Cocky One does her damage.*

Tree-gold would not stop with her incessant nagging. I couldn't be seen speaking to the bossy cat, or I'd be locked up in the Guardians equivalent to a rubber room. It was hard enough doing it in front of my family or Ro. Diamond understood, but she was one in a million.

Best bury that unwanted feeling, she was a married woman. She'd probably be pregnant within the next year.

*Move closer. Tiger Eyes is going to weep again if she does not look at him. Be wary of the Grar Dyr, he is ready to pounce. The Cocky One touches Mistress too frequently for his liking.*

Brass hadn't cried in front of me, but it was a safe bet that he had at some point. Animals talked. That's all they did. Sleep, eat, gossip. Animals saw all. Ash was touching Scar an awful lot. He seemed to be savoring the feel of her. She had spent her first night away from us. Ash may have exploited her weakness and slept with her, but it was so unlike Scar, I had a hard time believing it. Though, from what Tree and Brass said, Scar had been with the Patriarch Regn. Now *that* was unlike her.

Holding the cat carrier with a thirty-pound beast of a cat in the middle of a funeral for eight hours as Cory's body burned to ash had been no small feat. Now, as Guardians, namely Shadow Breakers, held somber conversations I felt even more out of place.

Cory had been a great guy. Loyal, honest, and infatuated with our Scar. She had that effect on poor men... and Shale. Shale had a crush on Scar until Indigo had one night with her. That had been for Ama. Gods, not enough time had passed to not to feel a stab of pain at the thought of them.

Honeybee was sobbing openly with Scar at her side in the arms of an unfamiliar blonde man with soft brown eyes, but Scar claimed he was her attendant. Scar felt responsible. The blonde she called Terne was probably one of the suitors she'd lined up for Honeybee. You couldn't hold yourself accountable for so many people's actions. It was Cory who requested her night detail. It was Brass who approved it. It was that psychopath Peppermint who had wanted her dead. We could be burning her up on that pyre too today if Quick hadn't hauled it and saved her.

I was spending all my free time with Ro at Shadow Breaker head-quarters. Diamond couldn't comfort me the way I needed, and I under-stood that. So did Ro. I trained with them under the radar. I told myself it was under the radar, but nothing happened in that place without the Grand Mistress's knowledge, not to mention Chafer, Brass, and Slate's.

Mirage had gone underground. Scarlett was well liked at HQ and news of Slate and her affair had gone over like a grenade. It was hard not to like Scar; she was modest and kind despite her power and influ-ence. It didn't hurt that she was a looker. That was why some women instinctually disliked her until they got to know her. It was a daily battle with Ro.

Rosasite was recruited by Brass and Scar and had a fling with Brass which should have been a big no-no because he was one of the four captains, the same reason Slate should not have messed with Mirage.

*That,* and she was a royal bitch. Mirage also slept with half of HQ and had no qualms about projecting other women while doing so. It was said Scarlett was a favorite.

Steel nudged me with an elbow. "Let Tree loose. That'll get her attention."

Tawny looked hopefully to me.

Steel and Tawny. Dear Gods, at one point I thought he was her uncle as he was mine, but Hawk wasn't her dad. That had been a tough one to stomach though it didn't change a stitch. Steel was good people, like my dad. Which was funny since he was unlike any guy Tawny dated in high school or college. I hung out more with Steel than any other guy on the islands. Who knew brothers-in-law/uncles could also be closest friends.

"Yeah. She might mow over a few people on her way," I joked, and my sister smiled.

Ro looked at the cat carrier poor Tree was crammed into. Ro was a fox. Exotic honey eyes, creamy coffee skin, and glossy obsidian ringlets. Brass liked blondes, everyone knew that, so when he started hooking up with Ro it was obvious to those who knew us he was doing the opposite of what Slate had who had found Scarlett's doppelgänger.

That was before. That was all before.

Slate had taken me under his wing; taught me how to fight and confided in me about Scar in a way I didn't think he did with anyone else. Not until Brass couldn't hide how he felt about her any longer. Then, it was Slate and Brass always watching over her. They had made a great team. Slate wasn't good on the emotional front having kept his distance all his life, and Brass didn't date much on account of his mind reading abilities. Women sucked. Scratch that. *Some* women sucked. Scar was different. The women in my life *period,* were different.

I placed the carrier on the marble floor and bent down. "Straight to her, no detours for appetizers," I whispered.

*There is always time for appetizers. Should I make a round and report back?*

I thought about it and nodded. Not very stealthy. Tree was light on her feet in spite of her size and she padded between people's legs without them noticing. A skill only a cat could accomplish.

She pranced back over to me and I bent down to hear what was being said.

*Tiger Eyes says the Cocky One and the Yellow-Haired made Mistress an offer she could not refuse. They want to court her. The Yellow-Haired was in Mistress's bed last night.*

Tree bristled at that. The bed with Scarlett was her domain. While Tree hadn't minded Scarlett's ex-boyfriend Chris, the only one she really loved was Brass until Slate healed her — she was coming around.

I figured that would happen. I didn't know what it was that rubbed me the wrong way about Ash. His entitlement, surely, but something else. It was probably that he wanted to own Scar.

"Report back to me when you can, Tree. Thanks," I whispered and straightened.

I watched Tree's long white fur tremble as she padded to Scarlett. She rubbed her body along the black velvet skirts of her gown and Scarlett exclaimed before picking her up. Scarlett's head swiveled around, it was hard to see her face with the veil on, but I thought I caught her smile. It was good being Scar's cousin. Few men could withstand the force of that smile and not buckle to her will. I buckled, but she was my cousin, so it was expected.

"Dancing to her tune," Ro muttered under her breath.

*Again with that nonsense.*

"If you can't say anything nice. Say nothing."

"Then I would never speak. However boring would that be?" Ro asked coyly.

"Get to know her. I promise she'll change your mind. You've never known a more selfless person. Unless you're still sore about Brass," I chided.

If Ro was a cat, she would've hissed. "I could not care less about who Captain beds. You greater families are all the same taking what you want, from whomever you wish."

"Are you implying that she stole him? If memory serves, she was with him first and you spend your nights in *my* bed on and off since he went to the Merfolk with her," I told her, giving her a smirk she quirked a brow at.

I knew my dimples worked wonders for me. I didn't have to try as hard in Tidings, the women were just as amorous as the men and no one bothered to hide it. Truly equal footing and no diseases to muck it up. Of course, then you ended up with rogues like Slate and Quick. Naturally, my two lovely cousins attempted to train them into husbands. Quick was still in training and Slate had failed miserably. Miserably for all parties involved.

Ro's eyes glittered, and she nodded to where Scar had been standing. "I suppose I should not be so hard on the Second. She does have the ability to ruin my life and kick me out of Valla University. I am surprised she did not kill Mirage. From her reputation, she sounded like she didn't tolerate insults."

Ro was speaking loud enough for Tawny and Steel to hear. Tawny took an immediate dislike to Ro. Ro could be catty at times and was close to Mirage. As good as the company she kept, Tawny had said. Tawny made a face as if some stench wafted through the room. Indigo had pummeled Mirage. I was there when she came into headquarters bloodstained and irate. Mirage hadn't kept what she was doing with Slate a secret. Being with Slate didn't matter to her, hurting Scar did.

Like I said, *some* women sucked.

"She'll get hers. Karma... or whatever we're supposed to believe in. The wheel of life. All that. She'll be reincarnated as pond scum," Tawny said peevishly.

"Scar was having a miscarriage. I think if she hadn't fainted, she may have killed her. I don't know who would've stopped her except maybe Brass or Crimson," Steel said, tugging on his ear.

We needed a subject change. All we'd done the last three days was talk about Scarlett and what was best for her, what she should do. She wasn't going to listen to any of us. In that way, she was stubborn. She'd do what she wanted, she always had.

"How's it going reading Orion's journals?" I asked Tawny who started. "Sorry. Was that a secret?" I whispered conspiratorially.

"No," she snapped a little too fast. "I can't really talk about it. He... wasn't always a good man. He wanted the journals to be found and there are no opinions in them — facts... as he saw them."

Steel was Tawny's rock. Without him, Tawny would've been a woman on the edge like poor Scar.

"What do you mean?" Steel asked, placing his palm to the small of her back.

Tawny pushed her long dark hair over her shoulder only to pull it back. "Orion was a dream beacon, like me. He shared in Cassiopeia's dreams. She had an affair... after Delta was born. Orion was cruel. Cassiopeia had babies two boys and was forced to give them up to the Valkyries. It gets worse," Tawny said, dumping her goblet down her throat.

She looked around suspiciously and noticed Indigo and Silver had breached Scar's wall of guards with Spinel. Pearl, Sparrow, and Hawk were waiting for their turn. Apparently, she was only allowed three at a time. Tawny felt helpless when it came to Scar. We all did.

"Orion confronted the father, it doesn't say who, but he had to promise his first-born son to Orion or he'd have destroyed his family. It must have been a somewhat prosperous family because they had much to lose. Why else promise not your son, but your nephew under blackmail? Orion made a blood oath. Either the nephew died or I have a forced uncle out there somewhere."

Steel's mouth was pressed into a firm line. "Frigga's sweet grass, Tawns. It's Alder. Alder is Canis's nephew promised to Delta. Canis has always hated our family because my mother spurned his proposal, but it seemed unlikely he carried a torch for her come decades later. Canis was the one who put the kibosh on Alder and Wren. I wouldn't repeat any of that out loud. Canis is not someone you want to cross."

Rosasite's eyes were as big as saucers. Juicy greater family secrets — celebrities of the Tidings world. I leveled my eyes at her and she smirked. Whenever she did, her lips pursed to the side as if she knew a fantastic secret.

"Scar was right, by the way. He captured a Leshy and forced it into the ice dungeons under the castle. The one she freed... it *had* been there for fifty years. My... sire died because... Orion was behind the Red King Massacre. The Crathode have always been his tribe. He has this list of targets. They all died except for Pearl, Hawk, Wren, Reed, and Moon. They were supposed to die. Wren seemed to be an afterthought, but how can someone's death be an afterthought? How could I be related to a man?"

Tawny ducked her head letting her long hair fall in front of her face. Steel rubbed her back soothingly, her shiny, thick velour shifting grain as he moved his hand.

"My father... Ridge. He must have known something for telling mom not to return to Elivagar. You know the bodies were so mutilated, they couldn't divide his from the Crathode that tracked us so they had to use the pyre ashes. My sire was never truly put to rest. It wasn't until then that Orion saw what he was doing and stopped his plotting. It was too late. Wheels were in motion. Flint, Slate's dad... grandparents, Quick's mom, Amethyst's mom..." Tawny dropped her voice low. "Orion was the head of the assassins guild that killed Alder, pushed Wren off the balcony... it feels like they're tying up loose ends. Moon's dead now, but he was an accomplished rider. For him to have been led off a cliff by his horse..." She shook her head.

"You are not the only person to think so," Ro confided.

Not so intrigued now. Ro looked like she no longer wished to be hearing the confessions that could get her killed.

"Sounds like the Stygians are cleaning house and Scar is in their target hairs. It could be good that Ash has put her under his protection. We should warn my mother and Reed. Is there anything else pertinent that we should know?" Steel asked, already zeroing in on where Pearl stood next to Scar.

"There are so many journals. I only picked up certain ones that I thought might have had Ridge in them or about the time I was born. The tone is so cold, as if he is making reports, not talking about murders. I hate seeing him this way, it's completely different from the man I knew. It colors everything he did for me."

"He loved you, Tawny. You pulled him out of his misery and gave him a reason to do better. Even mother came around to him, though I think she had her suspicions," Steel soothed.

"Gods, that reminds me. Orion said he thought Cassiopeia was the one who poisoned Sea Dagr. She was one of the few women invited there for the dinner party that helped with Slate's birth. Luckily, Slate was the strong silent type from birth. If he had cried, Cassiopeia would've known her poison had failed to kill him. I can't imagine living during those times," Tawny said, rubbing her forehead.

"Those times? Look around, Tawny. We're at a funeral because Scar's night watch guard was killed defending her. Scar is under attack. This is one of many times someone has tried to kill or capture her. It has to be because of this prophecy thing. Someone is either trying to keep it from happening or control her so they control whatever it is she's supposed to do — this *works* or project."

I said too much. Ro's gasp alerted me to how my angry tone had raised my voice. Steel and I looked about, but the others were too busy getting drunk or sharing memories of Cory. Some doing both.

"Remember how Scar hugged Orion after his trial?" Tawny asked, dropping her tone.

Steel and I bobbed our heads. "I think Scar knows most of what is in those journals. Orion and she spent a lot of time together at the end because of the arenas. He confessed while he was awaiting trial. I think he asked her to slip him the poison that killed him. She hasn't mentioned it, but who else? There's another thing."

"Freya's burly boar, how many secrets could one man have?" I cursed.

Tawny gave a rueful smile. "He was the Stygian Knight leader. His Leshy made all those portable portals. He's responsible for the tribes getting ahold of those doors courtesy of the Stygians."

Tawny wasn't smiling any longer. Those portals had done incalculable amount damage. They were the reason the Jorogumo had been able to invade Thrimilci. How Slate had been captured. How the Crathode were in Valla. The ripples of those events had touched everything.

"Scar has to know," Steel stated sternly and looked for her.

Scar was getting ready to leave, her wall of guards cut a path with their scowls through the crowd.

"She knows... most of it anyway."

Brass must have been listening to the entire time from afar. That meant Spinel could have heard too. Damn mind readers.

"I'd wait until Ash isn't with her to tell her about Cassiopeia. That information will mean more to her than to you," Brass said solemnly. "I see you sent your spy to her." Brass nodded over to Tree padding alongside Scar's skirts.

"Where's Crimson?" Ro asked dryly.

Slate would have gotten upset at the question, but Brass only looked resigned. "At home. She is upset with me."

"You're going to marry her if she's pregnant. She trapped you. What does she have to be upset about?" Steel asked coolly.

Normally, Steel was a sensitive guy who could bust out the ambassador diplomacy faster than a flea flick. Brass and Steel had gone to

Valla U together, roommates with Solder. It was hard to believe the three of them had been so close with the way Solder and Brass were with one another.

Women. *Some* of them sucked. Crimson should've known better.

Brass smirked. "Funny thing is two years ago; I would have been thrilled."

"B.S.," Ro said bitterly.

"Excuse me?" Tawny bristled.

I came to Ro's rescue, not that she ever needed rescuing. "She means Before Scarlett. That's her delightful sense of humor at play."

Brass actually chuckled and ended it with a sigh. "She's leaving," he said, sounding downtrodden. "I don't think she'll forgive me if she's carrying my sons and Crimson is pregnant."

They turned to find Scar being led out the high narrow doors by Ash. Slate had gotten ahead of them and was concealed in the shadows. Scarlett spotted him and flinched.

"She hates him," Brass murmured.

"When she has the twins, things will change," Steel said confidently.

"She's afraid by being their mother, their lives will be in danger. She is planning to give them up." Brass swept a hand over his trimmed stubble.

"What?" Tawny started.

"To Spinel so they can be raised as Regn. She's seriously considering being with Ash."

The helplessness of the situation was too much. I had to get out of there. First losing Ama and Shale, then Diamond, now losing Scar after so many deaths.

*Too much.* The appeal of running back to Chicago was enough to make me think twice, three times before dismissing it. I'd write to Scar. She had to know we would keep thinking about her and that she needed to come back and out of the lion's den.

# SEVENTEEN

My father had died in the room. Oddly, I hadn't slept in it before so its single memory of the Stygians attacking me and Alder here, didn't ruin it for me. On the contrary, I felt closer to Alder sleeping every night where he breathed his last breath.

A white chandelier lit the walls of my expansive room that matched Ash's eyes. Its furnishings were in matte whites and creams with a pink and cream floral bedding. An intricately carved bed crown had panels of fabric flowing over the plush bed. An upholstered bench was against the end of the bed and a sitting area with pillow topped couches that matched my bedspread. A writing desk was against the wall I shared with Ash's old room and a matching dresser with a huge mirror next to double doors led to a balcony.

Ash set down the fourth scroll I'd received with the other three still sealed scrolls on the white table that was the centerpiece of the semi-circle balcony that had been temporarily enclosed for winter.

I sat on one of the delicate white chairs. He sat next to me, picking my slippered feet up which I had folded up on the couch beside me. I gave him a lazy smile as he placed my feet in his lap. Marawacian rousen cocktails had been my drink of choice lately, all the pleasure feeling with none of the burning need to be touched. The marawacian made me numb. I needed numb. The downside was that it also made me feel heavy and sleepy with little to no appetite.

My head fell back against the floral cushion. "Who is it from this time?" I asked in an inflectionless voice.

Ash took my slippers off and let them fall to the floor. "Matriarch Vetr."

He began to rub my feet. 18k white gold and silver polish painted my fingers and toes. Ash had painted my nails for me before Quartz came to sleep. We slept every night in the same bed. Ash joined us for dinner in the bedroom and went to their wing afterwards. Quartz read in bed, as I did. I hadn't the energy for much else. My meals were small, and I rarely finished them.

I had one letter from Pearl, one from Gypsum, one was from Sparrow, and now one had come from Tawny. I knew I'd have to speak to them. Everyone would be at the induction ceremony. I just needed some time to... get over things. Ash had always been attentive and charming; we'd fallen right back into old habits minus the physical intimacy.

Ash's piercing eyes rolled down, and I smirked closing the luxurious, dewberry silk robe. Even that took a great deal of effort.

"If I wasn't going to see them tonight, we would get one tomorrow from Indi and the next day from Jett. At least they love me," I said.

"*I* love you, Scarlett Tio." Ash said, gliding the lace trim of the robe over my knee as his hands massaged higher. "You need to eat, no more cocktails. Thousands of eyes will be on us tonight."

I ran my fingers through my hair. Vainly, having my hair back after I thought I lost it made me feel better than anything else. I would've been okay with losing my tattoos, I didn't want any part of my old life. Finger included. I wanted to be free. I didn't want to get married. I'd rather hide out in my new bedroom.

Ash claiming to love me. I believed *he* believed it. "I should have a clear mind for the ceremony," I conceded.

Ash was anything but stupid. I never responded to his proclamations of love. They were just words. If I wanted love, I needed to feel it. With Ash I felt attraction and protectiveness from him. Ash was a gorgeous, charming man. Spending every day, all day with him like we used to, I was reminded of his considerable wiles.

"I shall have a light breakfast brought up and a dress since your belongings are at the Dagr palace. Whenever you want to move in, I will order the staff to have your things brought here." Ash's index finger circled my knee cap.

"You picked me out a dress? Just like old times, huh?" I said, taking his hand off my knee and lacing my fingers through his.

"Not that I mind you bare underneath this robe." Ash's eyes ran over my body.

"My pregnant belly doesn't hamper your ardor?" I asked coquettishly.

I should've had emotions, certain feelings about what we were speaking so casually about, but the cocktail of marawacian and rousen made it hard for me to muster up energy to even *feel* happy. I was nothing. Nothing was good.

Ash let his fingers fall from mine and onto my lap. I watched his fingers with interest as they peeled back my robe. They trailed to the inside of my thigh, and I quirked a brow at it.

"I have waited two years for you, Scarlett," Ash breathed as he gripped me under my thighs, pulling me down on the couch.

Idly, I wondered if I could feel pleasure.

# CHAPTER 18

# GYPSUM

"Did he give it to her?" Tawny asked, losing her temper.

Drill-tooth chattered down to me and I licked my chapped lips. Snow started heavily falling the moment we'd entered the woods behind the Straumr palace. The squirrel had climbed the nearest tree so we could be sure Scar was receiving our letters since she hadn't responded to a single one.

"We shouldn't have come. He has no reason to keep our messages from her. She's got them. I'm hungry."

I started to walk away when Brass let out a groan. Whose idea was it to bring the mind reader?

"What is it?" Slate growled.

"She's on something, like rousen, but not."

That's all Brass had to say, but Slate wanted him to spell it out. Slate looked up at the third-floor balcony. We could see Ash and Scarlett sitting in the couch before. Now, we couldn't see either. Tawny was up on her tiptoes, the four of them clad in white to blend in with their surrounding white capped forest.

Storm-pale swooped to land on my bracer. The Northern Goshawk confirmed what Drill-tooth told me.

"His mouth is on her," Brass ground out.

Tawny was shaking her head. I knew the feeling.

"She wouldn't. She doesn't even *like* him."

"I have bedded many women I do not *like*," Slate rumbled, and Tawny scowled at him.

"I can't stay here," Brass said, marching off.

"How does she feel, Brass? You said not rousen. Does she want him or is she indifferent?" Slate asked.

Tawny hadn't stopped shaking her head in disbelief.

Brass stopped. "Curious."

"What?" Tawny jumped on anything other than what was happening on the balcony.

"No, she's curious. As if she's performing an experiment." He cocked his head as if he could pick up a clearer signal. "There is another there. A man."

Slate whirled around and charged towards Brass, boots crunching in the snow with clenched teeth. "Another man with her?"

"No. The other man is... giving a report. Ash is angry," Brass explained. "They're leaving."

CHAPTER

# NINETEEN

That was unexpected.

If Sage hadn't interrupted us, who knew how far I would have let Ash go. Ash would not be a mediocre lover. He excelled at everything he did, and his mouth had trailed halfway up my thigh before Sage came in.

I should've felt ashamed or even embarrassed that Sage had seen me with my robe open, but I didn't. No more cocktails. It was impairing me in ways I couldn't put words to at the moment.

Ash had left with Sage to go over some pertinent reports. I knew they must have been important for Ash to have left me before he'd had a chance to consummate our new relationship.

I drew my robe up around my shoulders and got to my feet. I should shower. Ash said he'd send up food, and I'd force myself to eat. If I didn't want to pass out on the stage, I would need the energy. I had no delusions about sleeping arrangements tonight. I'd need energy for that as well.

I had missed the snow. I loved having the seasons back. Thrimilci

194

was beautiful, but I was a Chicago girl at heart; all four seasons in a single day sometimes. I walked to the back window and pushed it open. Thin glass planes encompassed the balcony. It was the only balcony to be protected from the elements. Ash had done it just for me knowing how much I liked being able to enjoy the sunlight.

A hawk with black barring and short wings dove and I followed it to its prey, only, it wasn't prey it flew to.

"Chief?" I called down from the third-floor balcony.

I leaned further, trying to make out the white shapes scrambling below. "Tawny? What are you guys... Are you *spying* on me?"

"Are you fiddlesticking that arrogant cache hole?" Tawny yelled back.

I laughed. The absurdity of the question broke through my haze and I found amusement.

"Do you want to come in? You don't have to stand outside like a stalker. I'll send someone down for you both," I explained and turned to leave.

"No!" Gyps shouted.

"When did you start hawking? This is ridiculous, come up and talk to me," I said, reaching for the pane's edge.

"You didn't answer my question," Tawny shouted again.

"By the Mother, Tawny. Who cares? Honestly, what difference does it make anymore who I sleep with?"

Tawny's face reddened.

"What are you on, Scar?" Gyps accused.

I smirked and flung my arms out.

*"O Romeo, Romeo! wherefore art thou Romeo? Deny thy father and refuse thy name; Or, if thou wilt not, be but sworn my love, And I'll no longer be a Capulet."*

I sighed as I pulled up a chair and sat, resting my elbows in the ledge. "Spinel appreciates my Shakespeare. I take it you're not coming in. I don't know what it's called. It lets me function without feeling. I rather like it and Ash says it doesn't affect my sons, so it's fine." I shrugged.

Gyps pushed back his white hood. His olive face looked darker against the pristine backdrop; his raven hair was tied back in a low ponytail. He drew down his brows in an expression that reminded me of Hawk.

"What is it called, Scar? You're acting like a lazy robot. Who says *not* feeling is the answer?"

I smiled fondly at my younger cousin. "When did you become such a man, little Chief? You of all people should understand why a little oblivion and a warm body would be welcomed."

"What are you on!" Tawny screeched, jumping in the snow like a toddler throwing a fit.

"Marawacian and rousen. All the pleasure, none of the pain." I sighed.

"Rousen! After everything you went through? You've lost it." Tawny was going to start tearing her hair out.

I shrugged again.

"You've lost weight, Scar. Are you eating?" Gyps asked, sounding concerned.

I stood and held my dewberry robe tight to my skin, twisting to show them my profile. "A proper bump and growing. I'm not particularly hungry."

My hair fell over my shoulder as I sat back down and started to braid it.

"Focus, Scar. Come down, put some clothes on. Let us take you home," Gyps said, moving his arm making his hawk fly off.

"I am home. I'm not going anywhere."

A white cloaked man stepped out from behind a tree and I pursed my lips. I should've felt something... anything.

"He's training you, love. Trained to his touch, to his opinions. When is the last time you disagreed with him? Rousen is rousen no matter how small the dose. It only feels harmless because you can function. Do you want to be addicted to Ash the way you are to Slate?"

It was Brass. My eye twitched. I was feeling... irritated. Yes. That was it.

*"Go, lady! lean to the night-guitar, And drop a smile to the bringer; then smile as sweetly, when he is far, at the voice of an indoor singer. Bask tenderly beneath tender eyes; glance lightly, on their removing; and join new vows to old perjuries — but dare not call it loving!"*

I exhaled heavily as I looked down at the trio. "Where is he? Tawny, you traitor. How could you team up with *them* after what they did?"

Tawny's brow furrowed. "I hate when you get all emo with your weirdo poems. Be normal and yell and curse like the rest of us! I needed help to see if you were getting our messages."

I slowly shook my head. "There's a good reason Indigo and Quick aren't here. You never would've brought them if you'd seen what Pepper did to me. Didn't Tree tell you, Chief?"

Brass cringed when Gypsum looked at him out of the corner of his eye. I stood and reached for the window pane closing and locking it. Tawny's mouth hung open. My best friend on the planet since birth. Gypsum was helping a squirrel onto his shoulder with a dark look on his face.

Why should it be that who I bedded was a big deal while they could sleep with whomever they pleased? The hypocrisy made me feel... angry?

A giant detached from a tree had must have been standing sideways behind it in order for it to hide him. He pushed back his white hood and raised his mirrored eyes to me. He and Brass both looked like hell. *Good.* They might have some infinitesimal of an idea of how I felt before the cocktails Ash gave me.

Slate's white boots crunched on the snow and he handed Gypsum something rolled up. Another scroll, narrower than the others and tied it to the hawk's leg. I unlocked the window and opened it again to let the hawk through. If I could feel, I wouldn't have done that, knowing nothing good would come of something from Slate.

The Goshen's claws locked around the thin ledge and I untied the scroll sealed with the snarling barghest head before a blazing sun. He didn't use the turquoise color I'd chosen for his seal, but black instead. I didn't read it but set it down with the others. I should have incinerated it. Brass's desolate expression stirred something in me I couldn't place.

"Find your happiness someplace else. I'm incapable of bearing further burdens," I said softly, knowing he would hear it anyway. "Damaged beyond repair. My mom and dad were wrong. Love shouldn't scorch, it should smolder so all of you isn't razed until nothing grows inside you anymore. Not even disdain."

Snow melted on my cheeks and I used a finger to clear the droplets. Brass looked as though I slapped him.

"You would be his whore," Slate growled.

*"Hold it up sternly! See this it sends back! (Who is it? Is it you?) Outside fair costume — within ashes and filth. No more a flashing eye — no more a sonorous voice or springy step; Now some slave's eye, voice, hands, step. A drunkard's breath, unwholesome eater's face, venerealee's flesh. Lungs rotting away piecemeal, stomach sour and cankerous. Joints rheumatic, bowels clogged with abomination. Blood circulating dark and poisonous streams. Words babble, hearing and touch callous. No brain, no heart left — no magnetism of sex; such, from one look in this looking-glass ere you go hence. Such a result so soon — and from such a beginning!"*

I shrugged feeling an altogether different kind of cold than the one coming in through the window. "Jealous that I'll no longer be *your* whore? Your barghest khoraz? There are better men than you that will hurt me less and please me more. My love was wasted on you." The door to the bedroom opened behind me. "I have to go; my lunch is here. I'll see you tonight." I shut the pane and left the balcony.

Eat. Shower. Dress. Simple enough.

# CHAPTER 20
# GYPSUM

We stared, dumbfounded, at the closed pane of glass waiting for her to reappear. The most emotion she'd shown they entire time was when she'd laughed at Tawny and told Brass not to wait for her to come around other than when she looked ready to set Slate on fire with his viperous words. That was promising. She looked like she was almost human.

*Almost.*

The walk back to Valla was a very long and quiet one. We arrived as Tawny cried tears of frustration while Brass took a page out of Slate's book and brooded. Slate had been the last to leave the woods.

*Too little. Too late.*

Part of me thought it was for the better, but there was always the other part that couldn't trust Ash. Scar was blind to it, always seeing the best in everyone. The world was spinning on its head. It had all gone topsy-turvy.

We trudged through the stone Urd gate and nodded to the black cad

Guardians who stood watch as we entered the town heart. Six roads from the star formation center led to three gates, Urd, Verdandi, and Skuld. Urd led to the Straumrs, Verdandi to the farms and cottages south of the town, and Skuld forked so south led to the Tio palace while north came around the cliff side to Valla U.

It was induction day so Valla was bustling despite the snow. Women clad in their thick Elivagar styled dresses and men in their padded jerkins and cloaks walked along the cobbled roads heading from shop to shop. Each shop had its own personality varying in material, but all had an old quaint European vibe and none were over three stories high.

I knew that that was deceiving. Shadow Breaker headquarters was in Valla and it had seven underground stories and three above, the only entrance was through a dead-end alley.

The hexagon center that housed the portal was completely void of the vendors that lined every stone wall in other sections of the town. Military purposes would've been my guess, though Valla hadn't need of a fortress or military in a long time. The free-standing stone portal gate had sculptured tree branches twisting up it. A sculpture of a woman, hands extended forming into branches crested the top.

Tawny rushed forward and grabbed Brass's forearm. "You have a chance to break through to her. We all saw it. We can't lose her to him," she said emphatically and Brass placed his gloved hand over hers.

"I know, Tawny. I won't give up on her that easily. I meant it when I said I loved her. There is Crimson. My hands are tied until I can sort through it."

I looked speculatively at Brass and saw his renewed faith. He had seen that he got through to her even in her drugged stupor.

"You won't give up?" Tawny pressed.

The corner of Brass's mouth tugged up. It was nearly a smile.

"I don't care how many are in between as long as I get to be the last." He looked to Slate and smirked. "One of the last two. Doesn't mean it does not hurt."

I walked alongside Slate. He was undoubtedly a bastard for what he'd done with Mirage, but at our darkest moments was when we needed our loved ones the most.

"What did you say in the message?" I probed.

Slate didn't look at me as we approached the portal, his mind was somewhere far off. "I told her I wanted another ceremony. One I would remember. I told her I wanted her to come home to me so she can make me pay for my miserable acts for the rest of my life. Her and the hellions we shall have." He raised a scarred brow at me giving me a sidelong glance. "I recited a poem. Walt Whitman is a favorite of mine."

I nodded and looked away. I wouldn't have pegged Slate for a poet lover. It was a good thing he had it up his sleeve. Women loved poetry. Pearl had hired a private tutor to give me extra lessons in the classic authors and poets.

The portal room in Valla University was packed like a can of sardines from tapestry to tapestry. The vine carved doors standing open with no need to shut them because as soon as you entered, another Guardian was right on your heels. Every Guardian that could physically make it out, did. The entire family had met in the Sumar portal room so we could arrive together, all save Scar. She'd be there already and likely devoid of anything resembling passion.

Pearl led the way down the staircase that spanned most of the wall across from a second set of stairs that was used to get to the first floor where all of our classes were, the dining hall we'd have our meals in was directly behind the wall of the stairs. The banners of all the greater families hung on the walls. I spotted the gold blazing sun on a royal blue field for the Sumars next to the gold banner with a silver starburst. The deep purple Straumr banner with a moon outline and a stark white crescent was placed beside the rich green Var banner, its golden tree of life crest curved with its roots.

The councilors wore sleeveless floor length cloaks of their banner colors, their sigils embroidered on the back. Tawny wore her scarlet red velvet robe with short white fur trim, the auseklis on the back like her banner. My mother's Dagr sigil was a yellow solar cross on a sky-blue field which clashed with her burgundy gown. It was why Pearl said she didn't like to wear hers.

Ruby Geol walked with the Natts before us. Ruby's purple robe and orange triad was vivid beside Cassiopeia's black that had a blue star inside a circle on her back. The largest banner was the grey and white Yggdrasil of Valla University. Scarlett had taken to wearing it.

A colored sundial symbol was tiled on the polished granite floor below the beautiful stained-glass windows that lined the room above the yellowed stone pillars. Night had fallen and a freezing wind whipped at our clothes. The constant file of Guardians descended the few steps down to the billowing white tents. The center tent would be reserved for the inductees and their families with the greater and lesser families where the stage would be.

Midnight blue and diamond white globes of glass and ribbons hung on glittered pine garlands that twinkled with white lights. The greater tables were arranged around the stage with table cloths that matched the ribbons and globes. Midnight vases filled with white peonies denoted Scarlett's influence on the decor. Crystal chandeliers with a dozen tiers dangled along the peaked ceiling.

Pearl gave me a wide smile, and I offered her my arm. It'd be her and I at the Sumar table. My mother and father would be sitting at the Dagr table with Slate. Steel and Tawny would be at the Vetr table and Indigo was Quick's fiancée, so she'd be at the Regn table. The Geols were the only greater family who didn't have their own table since Ruby was at the first Var table with Cygnus while Amethyst was at the second Var table with Jett and Cherry.

Our family had worked its way into almost every greater family except the Natt and Haust, though Slate was truly a Haust. Sterling wore their patriarch robe, the brown and gold with a jumis sigil embroidered on the back with metallic gold threads. Diamond was with him in a dusky pink taffeta gown and making an effort not to glance our way. Willow was the only other person at the Haust table, Sterling's sisters sat with the Straumrs.

The twinkling lights caught on a sparkling specter on the stage. There were over a dozen seats, Dahlia Natt sat in the fourth. Diamond and Ash's mother was the first-year headmistress and provost of History who had called me a myopic within the first five minutes of meeting me and I knew I'd never convince her I was good enough for Diamond.

Boa Sunna was next to her; Shale's uncle bore his usual stern expression. The first-year headmaster and provost of Nurture and Focus had a proud bearing, his up tilted eyes were made more severe by his slicked back, black hair.

Quartz was the only person on stage that wasn't associated with the university.

Ash wore the black sleeveless cloak with silver and gold, the silver valknut of the Guardians on the back. Beneath his cloak, he wore a silver brocade jerkin with matching buckles and a banded collar. A diamond crescent gleamed at his throat. It was obvious Ash had chosen Scarlett's dress. He had probably micromanaged her entire preparation for the night.

"I can only think of one time Scar has ever looked more beautiful," Tawny whispered.

I thought she had already sat down, but I saw no one in our family had. We were all entranced by Scar. It was strange to think that she had never had a boyfriend until Ash came around two years ago, she was positively stunning. Her caramel waves had been curled away from her face in an elegant up do that emphasized the delicate lines of her neck. She wore a band of sparkling diamonds around like a collar. Her diamond dress looked extraordinarily heavy. Under her grey Valla U cloak, was a capped sleeve floor-length gown with a sweetheart neckline. Diamonds were jam-packed along it until just past her hips where they were further spaced down to the train.

"I don't think I've ever seen so many diamonds on one person before," Indigo breathed. "She's lost weight."

They were real, Ash wouldn't allow her to wear anything but. A thick diamond cuff wound around her thin wrist. Her belly didn't look to have grown, but it could have been the dazzling diamonds distracting from it. It had looked fuller in her robe.

"When has she looked better?" I asked.

When Tawny took a moment to answer, I pivoted to look at her. She was looking at Slate who wasn't looking savagely angry for the first time all week.

"The day of her wedding ceremony," Tawny said wistfully, and she led Steel to their table sat for eight, but there would only be two.

Silver blew out a puff of breath as if he'd been punched. "Freya's burly boar, look at her finger."

Not on her ring finger which looked to have some kind of cover up on it to mask her tiwaz rune she had with Brass, but her middle finger. An enormous diamond was mounted on a diamond band. Talk about overkill.

"She is his treasure, his trophy, the crowning piece of his collection," Jett said in a sarcastic tone.

"Looks like a cushion cut to me," Cherry said matter of fact.

"She looks well kept, and that is the best we can hope for at the moment. Darling?" Pearl patted my hand with her long, elegant fingers and I escorted her to our table.

I pulled out the satin clothed chair that was tied with a big midnight blue bow for Pearl. She took a moment to fluff her copper waves. I took my beside her. I couldn't help stealing a glance at Diamond as I went to my own chair.

We met eyes and adrenaline shot through me like lightening. She had asked me once if I thought it was because what we did was forbidden that we felt that way. I hoped it wasn't. We both turned towards the stage, but that was worse with Ash and Scarlett acting as if their casual touches were commonplace.

Ash sat between Quartz and Scar like a king on his throne.

Wren would not have approved.

I sought out Rosasite.

We didn't have that thrill. It was comfortable and open, best of all, Ro didn't have the same expectations other girls our age did. She didn't want children and wasn't looking for an advantageous marriage. The parasites would try to lure me in once I was inducted. I'd been thoroughly warned.

The tables were seated, and the tent was humming with conversations. Ash stood, cocky as ever. I'd heard women say he was charming. The Guardians golden boy, everyone had known he'd be Prime one day. We thought that day was a long way off.

Ash made his way to the podium carved to resemble the Yggdrasil. "Welcome back to Valla, Guardians!" he said in a booming cultured voice.

There was a way I hadn't mastered yet, that you could amplify your voice using *calling*. The seated Guardians cheered their new Prime who embodied what they loved most, charm, an appealing appearance, strength, and intelligence.

"For those who do not know me, I am Ash Straumr. Prime of the Guardians and Overseer of Valla. Tonight is the fifth anniversary of the reopening of Valla University for Guardian Mastery. I would like to take this opportunity to have a moment of silence for our last Prime, my uncle, Moon Straumr."

The hum hushed to a deadened silence. Moon had shut the university down after the Red King Massacre, it had been closed for fifteen years. He had been deep in his grief with the death of his wife and the portal doors had been closed. No betrothals, fewer children, no Guardians were proven tried and true. It had taken five years of biannual challenges to catch up with the Guardians who had turned twenty the years the university was closed.

Ash continued, "During this time of gathering, I would remind you to stay strong. We are aware of the shortage due to the closing. New ambassadors are being reviewed for the available tribes and shall be awarded soon."

Greater families had first pick. Lesser families next pick. There was a slew of Guardians who had applied to become ambassadors and Vigrid competitors alike. Scarlett's arenas were a hit.

"I will now introduce this year's inductees to Valla University for Guardian Mastery, and the future of Tidings!"

The families cheered again, excited to watch their children cross the stage and receive their Yggdrasil pendants and leather bound class schedules.

Scarlett crossed from her seat to the pedestal beside Ash. Her body moved like a snake's, her hips rolling as she glided to him. Then she smiled. High cheekbones rounded; exceedingly lush lips spread over straight white teeth. Turquoise almond eyes twinkled like the night's stars.

It was a wonder Slate had ever left her. I supposed if I knew she would be the death of me it would make it easier. Ro was right, it did feel like the sun rose with her smile. There was a time when she looked sweet, she had always been gorgeous, but after the Merfolk took her she had a certain allure that attracted all the wrong men.

"Please come on stage when you hear your name," Ash said.

Ash began to call up the inductees one by one. Normally, it was a three-person operation. Moon had called the names, Reed gave them their folder, and Fern clasped on their necklace. This year, Ash handed the leather bound folders while Scarlett clasped on necklaces.

They sped through the list as if they'd choreographed the way it flowed without a hitch.

"Jade Kaldr."

Jonquil's younger sister, and Cherry's cousin, crossed the stage. She stood at a height with Scarlett, with the same build. By the way she moved, she was no simpering weakling. She knew how to fight. She had the classic beauty of Indigo with Scar's skill set — a deadly combo.

Ash smiled at Jonquil's sister in a way that suggested he'd known her in the nature that he'd known her sister. To my amusement, the blonde didn't acknowledge it and coolly stepped over to Scarlett who clasped the silver pendant around her neck and shook her hand with a radiant smile.

"Malachite Blao."

The only person other than Ro that I knew well in my year. He was a Shadow Breaker, almost as tall as Slate with a permanent smirk. Scarlett knew him as well. All the men she'd recruited had some sort of crush on her. When she smiled at Malachite a little brighter than the others, I knew I'd hear about it later. Malachite took advantage of her courtesy and snuck a kiss on her cheek, prompting a laugh from the crowd when Scarlett let out a rich, feminine laugh.

Malachite gave me a wink as he passed to the lesser family tables. Blao was a Mabon name.

Ash kept calling inductees, none I recognized until he reached our distant cousins.

"Mica Rot."

Another red head. Hair that fell to her hips with blunt cut bangs, her svelte figure glided across the stage to Ash. She didn't have the sapphire blue eyes most the Rot had, but brown like Butterfly's. She did have the porcelain skin all of them shared.

"Zircon Snjar."

Hunter Snjar's younger brother, another lesser family son. Taller than his brother and none of his clean-shaven, well-groomed looks. Zircon had long, dirty blonde hair pulled back in a low pony tail as I wore my own and dark tanned skin which was odd since he was from Elivagar. He turned aquamarine eyes on the crowd and I thought I heard a girl simper.

"Rosasite Sols."

Ro was lesser family though she wished she was anonymous. She hated the greater families, hated that there was any semblance of classes, she was an anarchist. I had no idea how Scarlett recruited her; it was likely Brass's appeal who'd joined Scar on her recruitments. Regardless, she was sexy as hell in her metallic bronze dress that brought out her eyes.

Scarlett endeavored to be friendly and gave Ro a megawatt smile. Ro's guard was down being excited to have been inducted into Valla U and smiled back. I chuckled when she descended the steps and was frowning to herself as if Scarlett had tricked her.

"Gypsum Sumar."

Ash called my name and my nerves evaporated. Pearl's emerald eyes glittered as she smiled at me and I bent to kiss her cheek before standing. I wished Tawny and my parents had been sitting with me.

I wound between the tables, breathing in the heavy pine smell of the garlands mingling with the vanilla from the occasional candle centerpiece and ascended the steps to the stage. It was much brighter than the rest of the tent. I would've been sweating up a storm in the heavy dress Scarlett wore.

I stood before Ash whose lips curled in that smug way most Guardian men had and he handed me a leather bound folder. "Be strong when you are weak, be brave when you are scared, be humble when you are victorious."

I shook his hand and before I could muster a smile for Scarlett she embraced me. "I forgot Rosasite was from a lesser family, she's always so nasty about us. You look handsome, chief. Get out of here before you make me feel old and I wind up crying in front of thousands of people."

I bent my knees down and lifted my ponytail so she could clasp on the Yggdrasil necklace. It fell into the hollow at my throat, the tiny Celtic tree pendant was only the size of a silver crescent.

"You're one to talk. You look so glamorous, I'm afraid to touch you," I murmured in a rush.

She hugged me again. "I'm sorry about earlier," she whispered and shoved me away.

I had told Diamond and Ro both I'd wave from the stage, but I had completely forgotten until I was back in my seat. She must have come down from the crap Ash was giving her. She was more herself than ever.

"Beryl Sunna."

A lesser family from Thrimilci and Boa Sunna's son. He had also been one of the few suitors Scarlett had when Ash asked her to find a second husband since Slate was a complete bum. The young man moved like a Shadow Breaker, deadly and lethal. Scarlett should have loved him. Granted, his was under six feet and was built more like Chafer instead of a brick house like Brass and Slate. He was definitely a long seax specialist like me.

Knowing Beryl had tried to court Scar, Ash chilled when the Sunna heir reached him. Beryl let it roll off him and kissed Scarlett's hand when she shook it. Scarlett's corresponding smile was extra bright. Ash didn't wait for Beryl to walk from Scar before he took her hand and pulled her next to him; an unwanted rival too close to Scar for Ash's comfort.

Ash inclined his head to Scar and her eyes widened. She stood in front of the podium and ran her teeth over her lower lip looking at the crowd through her lashes.

"Thank you everyone for coming. Let the merriment begin!" she said in her cheeriest tone, Ash held their gripped hands high.

Scarlett had a habit of biting her lower lip when she was nervous, all good signs that she was clear-headed again. Still, her and Ash seemed rather cozy. Scar stepped away from Ash as Quartz came over and took his arm. Crap. Everyone was filing off the stage.

Where would Scarlett sit?

Slate nearly knocked over his chair leaping up to pull hers out as she crossed to the Dagr table. Problem was, she wasn't heading towards the

Dagr table, but the Var. She was the Second and knew if she kept walking, or made a scene, it would reflect poorly on her.

Scarlett reluctantly sat in the seat Slate offered with her face an expressionless mask. Any step, no matter how small, was a step in the right direction with those two together and her away from Ash.

# TWENTY-ONE

Roasted goose sprinkled with oranges, apples, and lemon, mixed herb salad, creamed fresh spinach, and apple plum streusel dessert — I could've ignored the heaping helpings my soon-to-be-ex-husband kept piling on my plate, but it was the first time I'd had an appetite all week. I had no problem ignoring the man though.

My declaration was law and the four Guardians that guarded me from afar had stepped towards us to intervene until I shooed them off. I'd dismissed them for the night so they could be with their families. I wouldn't be setting foot outside Valla U grounds and when I did it would be to go directly to the Straumr palace.

Sparrow and Hawk sensed the awkwardness and filled it with small talk. "Did Slate tell you he's put in to become the Wemic ambassador?"

"I received his bid," I said, spooning streusel into my mouth.

Sparrow shook her head as if to clear it. "Right. Of course. What did you decide?"

"Given his relationship with the Wemic and residence already being in Thrimilci, he's an excellent candidate. I approved it and sent it along to Ash. He should get his confirmation letter tomorrow," I said, purposefully avoiding the fact that he was at the table.

"That's great news!" Sparrow beamed.

"Thank you, Scarlett," Slate rumbled and his big hand ran across the midnight tablecloth to reach for mine.

I put my hands in my lap. "Indigo was approved to work with the Aves and Jett with the Faunelle until he becomes patriarch. It'll work out well since Indi will marry Quick next year and they'll live in Ostara. Jett won't be moving there — for some time still, I think."

Hawk scoffed. "You're right about that. Steel is staying with the Merfolk?"

I shifted in my seat. I couldn't tell them I'd seen to things with the Merfolk to be sure Steel would be treated with the utmost respect there.

"The Merfolk are good with him. They're not particularly friendly with everyone. I don't think Tawny wants him trying to fix things with the Elivagar tribes. Delta and Cassiopeia resigned so now they don't have a single ambassador." I explained, stretching over the table for my goblet of water.

"Are we going to visit our friends in northern Elivagar?" Slate rumbled.

The Lycans. I'd completely forgotten. We were supposed to be there this past week. They'd gone in search of Slate and I, Grar Dyr and the Night's Child. We had promised in order to get the last piece that Canis hadn't gotten his hands on.

I was stuck. "Yes."

"This coming weekend?" he asked.

I *felt* hope. Slate usually went through lengths to hide his emotions from me. He had let his walls down on purpose. I would have to make things perfectly clear.

It was business.

I was putting on a show until I can put more distance between us and permanently cut ties. There was no hope.

"Yes," I said again, sounding exasperated.

As soon as the dancing started, I would escape the table.

The stage was dismantled while we ate and the moment the band set up, the music and dancing began. Ash wanted to do the opening dance again, so I stood, smoothing my diamond encrusted gown. What I was wearing was worth more than my mother had made in all her years working as an artist in Chicago.

Slate would always be faster than me.

His big hand wrapped around my wrist as he started to drag me onto the dance floor. It was either go with and walk like a woman or be pulled out and look like a child. I chose to keep up my act. He wanted to play house? I could pretend a while more.

The cocktails Ash had been giving me had almost completely run through my system and the hurt and the grief that threatened to smother me was trickling back. Slate took my hand and placed his other hand on my back as he brought me onto the polished wood dance floor.

"I have a dance to make up for, I believe," he rumbled, spinning me around so I faced him.

I kept my expression placid showing no weakness. My palm met his, the familiar feel of his callouses pressed to their usual spots. His hand rested on the small of my back as if the curve was made just for his hand. My belly rubbed against his black waist coat as we began to dance. My lessons had paid off.

"You are breathtaking, Scarlett," Slate rumbled.

*Breathtaking.* Slate and Brass had chosen that word to describe me on our first nights together. Lately, Ash had been calling me breathtaking without having had the body I'd surrendered to them.

I kept my face angled away from his like a ballroom dancer as we swept across the floor. "So I have been told half a hundred times tonight," I replied curtly.

Cloves, fresh fallen leaves, and the spicy scent of man wafted from him like a drug more mind-numbing than Ash's cocktails.

Rule number one with Slate: Never *ever* let your guard down.

"Did you read my letter?" he whispered, his breath puffing at my ear.

"No. There's nothing you could possibly say to change my mind. I won't be forgiving you this time."

"Because you feel foolish? Then we will run away. Go back to Chicago until forever or whenever you want. I do not have experience in making apologies. *Please*, do not leave me."

My mind went through a time warp. Slate had pleaded those words before and I had. That's how we ended up in this catastrophic mess.

By the Mother, how long was this song?

As if the Mother heard my cry, the song ended, and I tried to pull away. Slate held fast to me. His grey eyes were soft as he peered down his straight masculine nose at me. His black winged brows pulled towards one another as he waited in suspense for my answer. It was in vain.

"I've got to go," I breathed.

Show no weakness.

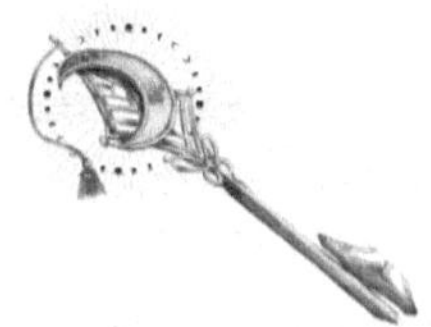

I had a surprise for Gypsum. I decided to tell him now because I had been such a cache hole earlier. That cocktail had done a real number on me. I wanted to hurt Slate, but I didn't want to actively hurt Brass, I just wanted him to stay away. It was the same story it had always been, I needed stability. Neither could provide it. They had too much influence over one another.

Better to have loved and lost and all that, but I couldn't gamble with my heart anymore. I was almost a mother. I didn't have the luxury of following my every whim. They had abandoned me that night and I had almost lost my life and the lives of my children. I couldn't forgive it.

"Gyps!" I called and brought the guys I'd rounded up over to him where he sat with Malachite and Rosasite.

Gypsum turned and started to get to his feet. I waved to him dismissively and smiled back at the two men who tailed me.

"Hey, Scar. What's up?" Gypsum put his goblet of wassail down and his dimples popped in his cheeks when he smiled.

"I don't think you've been formally introduced to Beryl Sunna, the heir to the Sunna family and Zircon Snjar, second son of the Snjar family from Elivagar. Gentlemen, this is Gypsum Sumar, future patriarch and Malachite Blao, heir to the Blao of Mabon. This is Rosasite Sols of Thrimilci, youngest daughter. You four men will be roommates this year," I said with delight.

Gypsum and Malachite stood and greeted Zircon and Beryl in a very manly way with lots of back slapping and firm shakes. Malachite was trouble. He had a cockiness between that of Quick and Jett. He was tall, with brown tousled hair and narrow brown eyes that crinkled when he smirked that reminded me of Cory.

Zircon was the strong silent type that would be mistaken for a dim bulb, but they'd be wrong. Hunter's younger brother had a savageness to him that reminded me of Slate without the hardness to his features. His eyes were pools of the lightest blue-green water that popped against his dark tan skin. He also happened to be Slate's hand-fasted wife's younger brother, but I didn't really know him at the time and, aside from Hunter, the Snjar's didn't appear to hold it against me.

I'd be lying if I said I didn't find Zircon attractive, but I liked my men how I liked the only car I ever drove; dark, powerful, and sexy with the potential for danger.

Gypsum and his three new besties took me out on the dance floor and I danced until my feet ached. Then I danced some more. Jett, Hawk,

Steel, and even Quick made their way out to where I spun and stepped with whatever man was bold enough to ask. Ash joined me for quite a few dances, checking in with me before mingling.

Steel was twirling me around when Spinel caught me by my waist. Steel gave him a courtly bow with a smile and left me to Spinel's devices.

"The Prime does love to show you off. I cannot blame him," Spinel said, holding me close as Slate had. "I keep waiting for your wall of guards to swoop down and steal you away."

I gave him a coy smirk. "I gave them the night of since I'm staying at the Straumr palace."

"I have heard. My grandson is heartbroken while he awaits news of his... friend's condition."

"How do you feel about that? Your grandson missing an opportunity to marry a greater family woman?" I asked.

"You are greater family," he said pointedly, and I glanced away at all the fancy people in all their fancy clothing.

"Giving up on me for yourself?" I asked, raising my eyes to his through my lashes.

"By the Mother, if I thought you would choose me over him, I may have to reconsider my stance on remarrying." Spinel's eyes glittered in the lights and I found myself captivated by him.

"Harassing or hitting on the woman I'm in love with, grandfather?"

I felt a twinge as Spinel pivoted us to face Brass. Two mind readers. No one spoke, Spinel handed my hand over to Brass before I could object.

"It is the same thing, is it not?" Spinel jested and Brass gave him a genuine smile.

Brass's hand clasped mine. "If you gave *him* a dance, I certainly had to try my luck."

The music slowed and Brass moved his body with mine. His dark hair was neatly combed back, his beard of stubble trimmed, he no longer looked like the weight of the world rested on his shoulders and I wondered what that meant.

"I blame myself for how things went down between us. I wish I hadn't born witness to it, but I hope Crimson is pregnant and you can have a chance to have more than one child with her," I said in a rush.

"You've always held me to a higher standard than anyone else. Why can't you accept that you didn't force me to do anything. Helping you leave, coming back to Chicago with you, making love to you — all my decisions. I should have kept my distance and let you be a wife to my closest friend. How could you still think I am remotely honorable when every chance I've had to back away, I didn't? I'm the reason Slate stopped speaking to you after the progress you'd made before the Merfolk. I will never forgive myself for what I have done. That and everything since his return."

Brass shook his head and a lock of hair slid over his cheek. He smelled like cinnamon and spring rain; fresh and sweet. I struggled with the urge to rest my head on his shoulder.

"He agreed to let you take me on as a husband because he thought it would rid him of his feelings for you... seeing us together. It backfired. I never wanted to push him away," Brass continued. "He never thought that he could allow you to be with another man." He smiled warmly, "But I am not any man."

"You're his brother in all ways but blood," I murmured.

"I'm his brother, his cousin by blood," Brass agreed wryly, "I hope he gets his memories back soon, Scarlett. Things need to go back to normal. I'll back off. Just don't shut me out. I beg of you."

I looked down at the feet spinning by. "I don't think we can just be friends anymore, Brass," I whispered. "Maybe I encouraged it, but you've hurt me too much by far."

"If you ever forgive me, I still won't forgive myself. Think on it. I'm not asking for an answer right this minute."

Brass released me and my arms were still held out when Slate took his place. I gaped at him. Mind readers and heightened senses made for a perplexed Scarlett.

I narrowed my eyes at him. Had he and Brass been plotting again? I wanted nothing to do with it. My pragmatic side knew eventually I'd have to work through things with Brass because we'd have children together... if I decided not to give them to Spinel to raise. I was having a hard time with it; I knew my children would be safer away from me. Where ever I was, death followed. When I had them, if I could stand to part from them, I would give them over. I'd still be their mother, but I had to put them before my own wants. Even if that meant leaving them.

"Your thoughts are dark. Not planning on killing me tonight, are you?"

It was his attempt at a joke, but I couldn't muster a smile. He was right, my thoughts depressed me and I could only imagine what kind of scent that gave off.

"Scarlett?"

"I was just wondering what pair of legs you planned on crawling between tonight and if dancing with me is some ruse to make said girl jealous," I said caustically.

Slate's jaw clenched; his full lips tensed. "Not unless you are offering."

I scoffed. "Oh Slate, you dream big. You have less of a chance than any other man in this tent. Six days ago you were with your lover while I nearly died and almost lost my sons in the process."

"So you say," he ground out. "I never made love to that woman, not even while she was you."

"Thank you for that lovely mental image. Why are you even bothering? Go back to your old way of life and leave me be. I don't want you anymore," I said, wishing I had more fire in my words.

My torture felt like a lifetime ago and yet like yesterday all at the same time. Slate touching me and looking at him made me feel like maggots squirmed in my belly, it felt an awful lot like disgust.

"I do not need to have Quick's talent to know you want me, girl." He paused. "Even if you hate me for the moment. You love me in a way I know I do not deserve."

I wanted to deny it and to say hateful things that would cut him to the quick, but I found no biting words at the ready. He was so smug.

"Time heals all wounds. My love for you is a festering ulcer I will keep clean so it may heal by staying far away," I said snidely.

"You may try, but I will never let you go," he growled in irritation.

I smirked; the conversation was not going how he hoped. He couldn't play nice for long. He mistook my smile and my breath caught when grey was swallowed by silver. Slate always did push too hard.

He stopped and slid his hand from my waist to my jaw, tilting it back. Slate's eyes flitted between mine until his shut. I heard his slight intake of breath a hairsbreadth from my mouth.

"You forgive him everything. Perhaps I will take another turn since you do not mind."

Garnet's voice cut through my fog and I snapped my mouth shut. When had I parted my lips? I had my suspicions about Garnet and Amber sharing Quick and Slate, but I never asked. I yanked myself out of Slate's grip and he growled. Garnet danced with her cousin Hunter whose mocking lip curl enraged me.

"In case you've forgotten, I am the disciplinarian this year. I'd watch myself if I were you." I snapped and didn't look back as I escaped the tent.

I didn't wait for her rebuke. I marched free of the dance floor, waving my family off and I left the tent.

A gust of wind jiggled my diamond drop earrings as I picked up my skirts and hurried up the steps into the university. I had no destination in mind.

Moonlight cast an array of colors from the stained class overhead onto the sundial below as I leapt onto the steps. No cursed elevators in Tidings.

Valla University was essentially an enormous castle. It even had its own little jail, not for tyro use thankfully or I would've seen the inside of those cells at some point.

I came to the office doors and turned the brass filigree knob, letting myself inside. I didn't hit the energy plate to activate the lights.

My office sometimes worked as a waiting area for people seeking audience with the Prime. Second was a glorified administrative assistant. I screened everything before passing it on to Ash if it was worth his notice. Ash was a micromanager; I wasn't the kind of person who was bothered by it so we worked well together. He wasn't the least bit passive aggressive, what he wanted, he said plainly, or perhaps manipulated me so deftly I didn't know it was happening. In any case, we were a good team. I didn't mind paperwork, and he was a brilliant strategist full of grand ideas.

I went through the side door and shut it behind me. From Ash's office was the only way in and out of Karkinos. The room that led to the portal door was always locked. I hit the plate beside the door so the gold sconces around Ash's office lit. He'd finished remodeling his office. It was like his old bedroom in the Straumr palace. Velvety black and metallic gold furnishings decorated the new Prime's room. Gilt black leather chairs faced a black marble desk and a chair fit for King Midas.

I crossed behind the desk and sat in the chair before I opened the top drawer and sighed with relief. A murky blue fluid sloshed in a large, gold-capped vial. Ash had promised it would be here if I needed it.

I did. I didn't think twice before twisting off the cap and downing the numbing cocktail.

I slunk down in the chair and shut my eyes. Garnet was right, I always found myself forgiving Slate. Love wasn't just blind; it was deaf and dumb too. Unfortunately, it wasn't mute.

It would've been easier if Slate and Brass had just given up and let me be. Why now were they trying so hard? Did the possibility of my death scare them into sense? Slate had pinpointed my obvious dilemma. How could I help run a nation when they all thought I was a fool?

Not for the even the hundredth time, I wished my mother was there to help guide me. Cut through the gloom and show me where to find my answers. Damned if I forgave Slate and tried to repair things, with a very strong chance of being in the same position months down the line and damned if I didn't because that meant admitting how badly I failed at my marriage.

I heard the snick of the door opening and pried my eyes open. If Slate or Brass had followed me, I'd scream. I felt like screaming anyway. Some days, I wondered how Sparrow did it. How she lost her parents, her sister, her husband, and now her best friend and kept on kicking.

My limbs felt heavy. It wasn't from the cocktail, but the melancholy that smothered me when I wasn't distracted. Choking and oppressive, in my heart I was already plotting out my life without Slate or Brass in it.

"I thought you would be here," Ash said.

His polished black boots gleamed even in the dim lighting. Silver crescent moon buckles were on the outside of each boot that matched the obsidian belt buckle at his waist. He stopped beside the chair.

"You took the marawacian and rousen again?" Ash asked.

I scooted back and straightened. "Yes. Better weak and vulnerable due to this than my untrustworthy emotions that have led me down the wrong path more than once. I'm fine. Go enjoy your night."

I rolled the vial between my fingers and pushed it over the desk watching its semi-circle trail until Ash stopped it with a finger. His insignia ring was the only piece of jewelry he wore aside from his Guardians torques and pendant. He opened the drawer of the marble desk and replaced the vial. I felt the heat and desensitized feeling roll over me and took a deep breath. I could breathe again, fill my lungs without the sharp choke of anguish like a noose around my neck.

Ash began unbuckling his silver jerkin and placed it over the back of the chair. "I do plan on enjoying my night." He told me, his lips curling as he looked down at me.

He wore a thin linen sleeveless white shirt tucked into his black pants, displaying his caramel corded arms. "You are in my seat," he said with glittering celadon eyes.

"Oh, sorry. I meant to return to my room. I was waiting for it to kick in," I said, rising from the gilt leather chair and skirted him to leave.

Ash placed his hands on my hips. "You do not have to leave. I want you to stay."

I knit my brow. The cocktail made it difficult to process other's emotions as well as my own. "Okay?"

Ash's thumbs ran over my jeweled hips and lifted me so I sat on the desk. Guardian men were all so fiddlesticking strong. The dress had to weigh twenty pounds, plus I'd gained five more just from the first half of my pregnancy. Ash sat down in his chair and rested his hands on my knees.

"Relax, my love. Let me take care of you. How it should have been all this time."

Ash's voice had dropped and his scent had spiked. His hands slid under the hem of my dress and his forearms pushed it along my legs as his hands glided ever north. They reached my hips and his fingers curled around the elastic lace of my panties.

"Lift," he ordered.

I braced my palms on the cool marble and did as he asked raising my backside off the desk. The chair scuffed on the granite floor as he shifted closer. My head fell back, and I sucked in a throaty breath as he placed my sparkling heel on the gilt of the top of his chair.

Ash's lips pressed along the inside of my thigh and my breaths grew shallow. He wrapped his hands around the top of my thighs and pulled me to the edge of the desk so my hands slid and I had no choice, but to fall back against it. The pins in my elegant up-do poked into my scalp, but I barely felt it. My diamond necklace weighed heavily on my throat as I drew in a sharp breath.

His tongue slid between my legs and he began to *call*. Slate hated *calling* when we made love, Brass did on occasion, but both of them were more about the physical feel of the action. Invisible fingers slid under my dress. Divided paths of heated air skimmed over my prickled skin. My back bowed on the desk; Ash's hands gripped my thighs firmly as his tongue swirled.

My insides pulsed, the coil pulled ever tighter and my fingers curled against the marble as I moaned. Ash stood and pulled my legs into the air.

"*Ah!*" I cried out as Ash pushed into me.

"By the Mother, Scarlett," Ash moaned as he thrust.

I gripped the edge of the desk above my head to keep from sliding off the desk. I could feel his invisible fingers unzipping my dress beneath me as he breathed harshly, my legs against his hard chest. My head rubbed on the marble as my neck craned back, pleasure crashing over me again. Ash grunted roughly as I went limp.

He was still panting when he helped me to my feet and pushed the dress off. It fell noisily to the floor. Ash pulled his own shirt over his head and bent down to suckle at my chest. I wrapped my arms around his head my eyes still shut as my head lolled. He spun me so my palms hit the desk with an audible whack as Ash kissed along my shoulder and forced my jaw to him kissing.

"Worth the wait, my love. We have much time to make up for," Ash said, running his fingers over the diamonds at my throat before bending me over his desk.

# CHAPTER 22

# GYPSUM

"The things I would do to the Second..." Malachite said with a smirk knowing I would say something.

Ro rolled her eyes and ladled more wassail into her goblet from the punch bowl they'd absconded.

"If you want to brave her husband and the Prime, feel free to try," I murmured dryly.

"I did. Granted, she politely declined our courtship, but I had to try when I heard she was looking for a second husband."

Beryl was from Thrimilci and had met Ro before, that he liked the Sumars counted in his favor. That he was easy going and quick with a joke made me think I'd made a friend for life.

Way to go, Scar.

Zircon grunted. "They say men who sleep with her fall into two categories; dead or crazy."

A man of few words, but very observant. You'd be an idiot to think that guy wasn't picking up on everything that was being said even if he didn't look like he was paying attention.

"Chief. Have you seen Scarlett?"

Indigo circled the table with Quick possessively wrapped around her. If Scarlett's dress looked like it was made of diamonds, Indigo's looked like gold beads over flowed her black strapless gown. Dangling gold earrings dripped from her ears, her corn silk hair was in a lavish braided up do.

"Not since she stomped off the dance floor."

Damn that Garnet. She was Diamond's best friend. Since losing Quick to Indigo she'd gotten married to Sage, but it didn't stop her from harboring a deep resentment for our family.

Malachite and Zircon both looked at her appreciatively and Quick's brow quirked at Malachite who glanced away. Slate was Quick and Malachite's captain, but they all knew Brass's little brother was up next to become captain. Indigo's eyes flitted to two girls approaching and her pink lips pursed.

Zircon stood. "Do you know Jade Kaldr from my home island and Mica Rot, Provost Wisteria's daughter?"

There was an instant dislike between the two gorgeous blondes. It didn't help that Jade looked at Quick as if he could be her new favorite toy.

"Jonquil's sister. We've met several times," Indigo said coolly, and turned to Mica. "We've met in passing."

Mica smiled shyly, and I stood to pull out chairs for the ladies since no one else had made a move. Rosasite placed her hand on my lap, claiming me when I sat again.

Mica nodded, her porcelain skin coloring at our attention.

She had a sweet, beautiful smile. Her mother was the one who Pearl enlisted to help birth Opal and now Scar's twins. Not exactly the friendliest woman I'd ever met, but her daughter radiated warmth.

I introduced the other men to Quick, and he removed his hand from Indi's waist long enough to clasp their forearms in greeting. Jade looked irked Quick didn't notice her.

"The Prime is gone and his wife looks ready to do some damage with that butter knife."

Malachite gestured to the buxom blonde twisting the blade on the table top sitting with Nova and Fox. Ash was gone... Scarlett was gone... Quartz was looking *stabby*... Gods, what was Scar doing?

"Silver!"

My eyes widened at Brass's slurred shout as he stumbled against Quick.

"Whoa! Drunk Brass. A rare sight indeed," Quick said, flashing a broad smile as he balanced his older brother.

"He blew it *again*. She's fucking him," Brass drawled out. "I can see what he sees," he said in a hushed tone that wasn't quite low enough for everyone to miss.

"Oh! I think it's time to get you home." Quick laughed nervously.

My new friends shared a few shocked and amused looks.

"I can take him home," Jade said suggestively, and Brass's glassy eyes ran over her.

"I bet you would," Indigo said dryly.

"I can read minds," Brass said suddenly, furrowing his brow at Jade. "I wouldn't if I were you. Tio women are worse than Natt. You don't want to find out the hard way."

Jade nocked back her chin and narrowed her eyes. Slate slid up beside Brass and put his hand on his shoulder.

"Come, brother. Misery love company," Slate rumbled, plucking the goblet from Brass's hand.

"Why do you always have to push her?" Brass slurred.

Slate's lips curled. "It is my nature. I do not have a slow speed."

He dropped his gaze down to the men sitting at the table, letting it skim over the women. I found myself holding my breath. Not many people knew Slate was a barghest shifter, but you knew there was something dark and dangerous lurking in him.

He downed the last of Brass's goblet and slammed it down on the table in between Malachite and Beryl hard enough to make the silverware clatter against the last of the plates.

"Strange that so many men have taken a keen interest in my wife." Slate rested his palms on the table's edge. "My fault I suppose, I have not made it clear. The Second belongs to me. Her body, her bairn... all mine. I am alive, it speaks for itself."

His vicious smile was all teeth. Indigo pursed her lips behind Slate's back and Brass stumbled forward. Slate straightened and put his hand on Brass's shoulder to keep him from stumbling.

"What —" Brass started to ask.

"*Ours*," Slate amended.

"Does she know that?" Ro asked without looking to either of them.

Slate's previous smile was almost friendly compared to the baring of fangs he gave to Rosasite. "She only needs a memorable reminder." He straightened and I could tell the others were questioning whether he had really had fangs. "Come. Let us get you home." He started to lead Brass away.

Indigo's blue eyes were glowing when she leaned forward on Malachite's other side. "Careful, Gypsum. You're the most eligible bachelor at Valla U now. The leeches will suck you dry." Her eyes took in Jade and Ro before Quick lifted her off her feet distracting her with a kiss.

"I like to think I bring it out in her. To think, she *used* to be sweet."

Indigo wrapped her arms around Quick with a smile and he carried her off. Diamond walked past and caught my eye in a swirl of pink ruffles that looked soft on her creamy caramel skin. I pushed back from my seat.

"Be right back."

Like a magnet, she pulled me in whenever she wanted me.

# TWENTY-THREE

Ash's fingers loosened their grip in my hair and I slowly sat back on my heels.

"Your mouth..." Ash cupped my face and ran his thumb along my lips, "it is fantastic."

No one wants to be the worst, but no one wants to be the best either. It implied practice or natural talent — no and no.

Ash hooked a finger through my stone piece necklace and held it up. "I keep meaning to ask you, what are all these? Did you not only have one?"

I took the necklace gently from his hand. "Pieces. I inherited them, you could say."

His hands roamed, but his eyes were hitched on my pieces. I changed the subject, uncomfortable with his attention to them.

"Do you think anyone missed us?" I asked, running my teeth over my lower lip.

"I am sure they did," Ash purred.

Books we'd knocked off the shelves, and the framed map of Tidings that had shattered on the floor had all been left as evidence to either a brawl or two careless people in an amorous way.

I heard the snick of the door open and sunk beneath his desk.

"Quartz." Ash sounded mildly surprised.

He wasn't dressed. He sat in his ornate chair like the emperor with new clothes.

"I missed you," Quartz said and let her eyes slide to my head that popped up from behind the desk.

Ash had always left love bites over me. They were everywhere. The little mouth sized bruises were along my breasts, thighs, shoulders, and probably my backside too.

"Ash must be pleased. You are the one that got away after all." She raised her big blue eyes to mine.

My cheeks were burning. The cocktail from earlier was nowhere near burnt off and still my embarrassment was palpable. No, it was worse than embarrassment. Shame. Guilt. Mortification.

I rose, picking my diamond dress off the floor with me and slid it over my arms.

Ash smirked at her. "Goodnight, Scarlett. I shall see you in the morning."

His voice raised at the end as if he wasn't sure. He looked at me and raised a brow. No, it was an invitation.

I bent down picking up the last of my scattered belongings and Quartz gave a knowing smile before she crossed the room to Ash where he hadn't so much as shifted a leg. I walked over to the door and shut it in case someone came in looking for them.

"How was she?" Quartz asked before my hand had left the doorknob.

I stopped in my office to eavesdrop, pressing my cheek to the carved wood.

"I understand why your father risked everything to bed her."

"And you prefer her for a second wife over Crimson?"

"Crimson was a passing fancy, though I appreciate you letting us try her out. In another month I believe Scarlett will be ready to join us," Ash told her.

"Until then?" Quartz pressed.

"Until then I intend to enjoy all of her wiles as often as I can."

"What about me?"

"There is more than enough ardor left for my wife. I will prove it."

I shut the door when the noises of their love making signified the end of their conversation. My stomach churned. Ash still wanted me, but Quartz had only been nice to me because she thought Ash would lose interest after we slept together. His cavalier attitude discussing me with Quartz made me disgusted with myself.

Which said a lot because the cocktail of poisons was at a high in my system only two hours in. I wouldn't know how I truly felt about things until my body flushed it out. All I knew is that I had to get out of there.

I crossed over the bench against the foot of the bed slipping on the dewberry robe and went out onto the balcony. The scrolls waited for me on the table. I sat on the floral cushions next to a sleeping Tree and pushed my hair out of my face. I still had on all my jewelry. Slowly, I took off the diamond earrings, the thick bracelet, and the choker.

I piled the scrolls in my lap and began to read through them, scratching Tree between her long, furry ears. Tawny wanted to go over Orion's journals, Gypsum wanted to talk about Ash, of course. The one from Pearl seemed the most serious. She needed to discuss the stone piece she'd given me. The first key to the puzzle. Sparrow was friendly and she danced around when I'd return. They all knew what had happened with Pepper. They replaced my bed and carpet.

I ran my thumb over the black wax that sealed Slate's scroll. I wondered where he found the insignia I'd made for him. I should burn it. I shouldn't read it.

I broke the seal.

*Torch,*

*I know you do not like me using that name, but I*

understand it now. We can marry in Thrimilci the proper
way and raise our children together.
I promise to never forget you again.
Come Home.

O me, man of slack faith so long! Standing aloof,
denying portions so long; only aware today of compact, all
diffused truth; discovering today there is no lie, or form of
lie, and can be none, but grows as inevitably upon itself as
the truth does upon itself, or as any law of the earth, or
any natural production of the earth does. (This is curious,
and may not be realized immediately, but it must be realized; I feel in myself that I represent falsehoods equally
with the rest, and that the universe does). Where has fail'd
a perfect return, indifferent of lies or the truth? Is it
upon the ground, or in water or fire? or in the spirit of
man? or in the meat and blood? Meditating among liars, and
retreating sternly into myself, I see that there are really
no liars or lies after all. And that nothing fails its perfect
return. And that what are called lies are perfect returns.
And that each thing exactly represents itself, and what has
preceded it. And that the truth includes all, and is
compact, just as much as space is compact. And that there
is no flaw or vacuum in the amount of the truth, but that
all is truth without exception; and henceforth I will go celebrate anything I see or am, And sing and laugh, and
deny nothing.

I need you.

I sucked in a shuddering breath and incinerated the scrolls. I hurried
over to my writing desk and pulled out a piece of paper and a pen.

*Thank you for the unforgettable night.*
*I went to visit my family. I'll see you as soon as I get*
*back.*
*Thank you for everything.*
*Affectionately Yours,*
*Scarlett*

I folded the letter on my desk and wrote *ASH* on the front. My feet couldn't move fast enough. I pulled on a cloak over my robe and slippers before picking up Tree and padding down the hall, glad I'd dismissed my guards for the night.

There was no need to look back.

The horizon was golden with the sun's slow rise into the sky. No one, but the staff was in the Sumar palace. I had made a brief stop to get clothing and the wig from my rooms at the Dagr palace and it was as if Pepper had only been a nightmare.

My life was a nightmare. My sons were the only thing I could think of that made me get up in the morning. I walked under the blue starry light of the portal room and into the palace halls. My flats swung in my hand as I traversed the mosaic covered halls to one of the side entrances. I followed the path with Tree padding along at my feet that led around the back of the palace to the River Mani; the spot of my favorite memory with Slate. We'd picnicked there with Quick and Indigo. It was the only time I'd tricked Slate into telling me he loved me.

I had brought the tan throw blanket we'd used and smoothed it over the flat sandy spot next to the river. I could see the waterfall a little ways away from where I stood.

I pulled off the plain white shift and stepped off the blanket digging my toes into the sand. I'd take off the gold polish when I was done.

A warm breeze caressed my skin, and I shivered. My feet scraped against the red gritty rock at the river's edge as I climbed in. The pool was an option, but I knew this was the only place no one would be to bother me.

The cool river water felt wonderful against my skin. I watched the sunrise floating on my back and whispered to my unborn babies about how I was going to stop being such a complete idiot.

Gut wrenching shame that was overpowering the hurt Slate delivered, made me feel regret like I had never known before in my life. Not even with Spinel.

A few good months had made me forget the year of miserable grief Ash and his cronies had caused me. How could I have slept with that man? At any other juncture, I never would have let myself be sucked into Ash's world. The man was charming, he knew when to hit and when to let it ride. It was a game. It was always a game. Slate had warned me my first week I didn't know how to play and he was right.

My skin was prune-like when I finally crawled out of the river. My shift stuck to my skin down to my knees. I hadn't bothered drying, the high sun in the clear blue sky would dry me fine. I laid down on the throw blanket and wrapped my arm around my belly as I rested on my side. Tree curled around me and began to purr.

# CHAPTER 24
# JETT

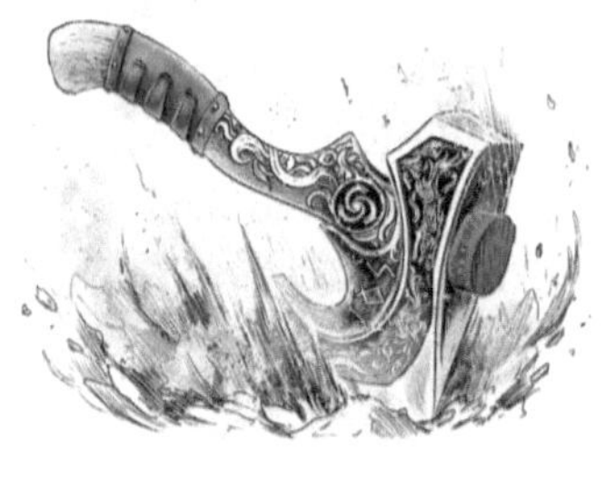

Brass looked like a wreck. Slate had dragged the drunk bastard home instead of taking him to the Regn manor. Indigo served him lunch; a ciabatta bread sandwich with Black Forest ham, mayonnaise, marinated red onions, tomatoes, provolone cheese and a side of pasta salad. Brass hadn't made it to breakfast.

There wasn't a need to ask why. Scarlett and Ash had disappeared and Brass got stinking drunk. It had only taken a week and Indi was warming up to Brass again. Slate had said something about Scarlett that had raised him in everyone's eyes. Jett wished he had heard it.

Opal tugged on Jett's Yggdrasil pendant as he ate across from Silver. They should adopt the Regn since they were always at the Sumar palace. Jett looked over his shoulder at the terra cotta pot and the blue flowering vine. It had finally reached the ceiling.

They could hear the footsteps marching down the fall before their unexpected guests entered the room. Ash's face was flushed, his green eyes darting to the faces that sat along the long-carved table. Brass was like a coiled snake ready to strike, his muscles bunching visibly under his shirt. Amethyst gently placed her hand atop Slate's which looked to be reaching under his shirt to grab a blade.

"I went to the Dagr palace. She is not there. Where is she?" Ash accused.

Pearl stood. Hawk and Sparrow were at the Dagr palace but would be coming later. Tawny and Steel were at the Vetr castle and would be there for the festival in Elivagar. Who knew what the Vars were doing, probably all staying in Ostara.

"Prime. How kind of you to join us for lunch. If you are referring to my granddaughter, I believe she was last seen leaving the tent last night. Has the Second left the Straumr palace?" she asked in a sickly sweet tone.

Ash's wall of Guardians had spread out behind him. Was he planning on arresting her? Gods, if it was anyone else the thought would have been improbable, Jett thought. It was Scarlett. Anything and everything was possible. Sage and Hunter flanked Ash bearing the same disdainful look Ash had.

"She said she was coming to Thrimilci. That she was visiting family," Ash answered curtly.

"In a letter, I presume?" Pearl asked.

Ash was getting more irritated by the minute. Amethyst stood and walked over to her cousin.

"I'll walk you out. She hasn't lived here since last spring. If she's here, I promise you, none of us have seen her. I would tell you, cousin." Amethyst's big brown eyes blinked innocently at Ash.

"When she shows, tell her I must speak to her at once," Ash clipped and spun on his boot to walk from the dining room.

Amethyst sighed. "Would Sparrow and Hawk lie to him? That would be bad. I'm sure he's going back now in case she hid from him."

Slate and Brass were already getting up from their seats. Jett kissed Opal's mop of sable hair and handed her to Cherry.

"Wait. We need to think first," Gypsum said, shooting to his feet.

"Gypsum is correct. Sit down, form a plan. You will need to find her before the Prime does. She must have a good reason for sneaking away and lying about it." Pearl said tapping a long nail to her lips as she thought.

"I can send out Storm-pale to see if she's wandering around Thrim-ilci," Gypsum offered with bright eyes.

"I can check headquarters. Shadow Breakers are like her family," Quick offered.

"Tawny might know," Indigo said.

"You three go on. Would she see Spinel?" Jett asked Brass.

"I believe a visit to Patriarch Regn is long overdue," Pearl said, rising from her seat in a swirl of emerald silk and left the room without further ado.

Silver and Indigo charged after her and Gypsum ran like he was on fire to the nearest window. Amethyst smiled warmly at them.

"I think I'll go check her old rooms and the upstairs wing, just in case. Cherry?"

Cherry rose with Opal on her hip and pressed her full red lips to Jett's. "When you find her, she may be out of sorts. She has been running a long time. I doubt she's very happy with herself this morning. I think we all know how that feels."

Amethyst looped her arm through Cherry's as Jett shook his head. "She constantly surprises me."

Brass was straightening his appearance, tucking in his linen V-neck, pushing loose strands back into the knot at his nape. Jett almost laughed and told him Scarlett wasn't going to magically appear, but who knew. It was Scarlett — maybe she would.

"I cannot stand sitting here useless," Slate growled.

"We're waiting to hear back in case she does come back. Sparrow is on your side. If Scar shows, she'll send word," Jett reminded him.

"What if she's gotten herself into trouble again? We couldn't put Breakers on her while she was at the Straumr's and he must not have thought she would run because she dismissed her guards last night without issue."

Brass started checking his blades concealed about his body to have something to do. Slate began doing the same and Jett balled his fists to prevent his hands from mimicking them.

Gypsum barreled into the dining room hitting the door frame as he came around the corner. His long loose sable hair clicked with the copper beads threaded through it.

"She's here!" he shouted.

"Where?" Slate asked.

Brass was already running having drawn the image from Gypsum's mind. "By the River Mani's edge!" he shouted, but there was no need, they were already on his heels.

Scarlett slept in a paper-thin shift that little girls usually wore to sleep in Thrimilci. Sparrow must have been very nostalgic when she gave it to Scarlett. The innocent look was only slightly spoiled by the trail of love bites over her throat and who knew where else. Her hair was dry but the trail of her footsteps in the sand led to the river. She must have been out there for hours. Tree was fast asleep against her until they'd bounded up, now she stared at Gypsum.

"Why would she be here?" Gypsum whispered, not wanting to wake her as the four men stood around her like the worst kind of creeps.

Brass crouched next to her; his fingers curled itching with want to touch her. "It's the only place Slate ever told her he loved her. They picnicked here with Silver and Indigo after she came back from the Merfolk. She's dreaming about it," he said wistfully.

"I fucking hate you," Jett muttered to Slate.

"Not as much as I despise myself. We have found her. She should get rest."

Slate was kicking off his boots before the others could get a word in. Brass rubbed his lips together and looked down at Scar. She looked so young. Not the *Glamazon* woman from last night, but the sweet girl who had arrived two years ago, bright eyed and hesitant at the new world. Her waves fell across the tan blanket, lips pursed as she cradled her belly in her arms. There was something bittersweet about her being at her all alone, as if she thought that was how she was safest.

"Do not ask me to leave," Brass finally whispered.

"I would not dream of it. Besides, she was very angry with me last time we spoke. Perhaps she will not run as swiftly from you when she wakes," Slate conceded and Brass began to kick off his own boots.

"We won't tell anyone until you bring her back to the Sumar palace," Gypsum started to say.

"And you will. Because if you don't, and Ash gets his hands on her. I'll kill you both. She needs time away from that bastard. He's brainwashing her, and she's too naïve to see it," Jett scolded.

Slate pulled his shirt over his head and tossed it at the foot of the blanket before he removed the blade belts that crossed over each shoulder. Brass was removing his blades he'd just checked and rechecked before he followed suit and laid down next to her. She didn't so much as shift an eye.

"She slept with him. I saw it in his mind. He was far from done with her. Quartz interrupted. Scarlett left around midnight and he hasn't seen her since," Brass said softly.

Slate swallowed visibly, teeth ground so hard Jett thought he could hear it. "We all make mistakes."

"She's here. I don't know how she normally is after she is with a man, but running off is never a good sign," Jett said dryly.

Brass smiled warmly at her sleeping form. "No. She likes to wake up next to them."

Gypsum cleared his throat awkwardly and signaled to Tree who hopped up and moved beside him. Jett started back down the path with him. The black barred Goshen he called Storm-pale landed on his forearm. Gypsum was nodding and then the hawk flew off.

"Gods, don't do that in front of the girls at the university, chief. They'll send you to the States and have you committed."

Gypsum laughed, his dimples popping on his olive face. The morning had turned out well after all.

# TWENTY-FIVE

I was cocooned by hot, bare skin. I saw red even with my eyes closed so I knew it was afternoon. Powerful arms were wrapped around me; one set of hands on my belly, the other set on my thigh. I shifted, trying to pull up an arm to block the sun so I could see and their scents wafted from them.

Cinnamon and cloves. Spring and fall. *Impossible. How? When?*

"Nothing is impossible, only improbable. Good afternoon, Scarlett. If you wish to keep sleeping, there is not much to do until the feast tonight," Brass murmured inches from my face.

The thigh holder.

"The Prime came looking for you, but alas, we found you first." Slate's breath tickled the hairs on the back of my neck.

I was speechless. Did I want to move? Could I live and die right there? By the Mother, was it tempting. I realized my arm was stuck because I was holding Brass under *his* enormous arm. I began to yank on it unable to find my words.

"Relax. We did not want you to wake up alone," Brass said in a soothing tone as he slowly lifted his elbow.

"And we did not want to risk Ash finding you. He seemed very upset that you ran out on him after last night," Slate purred in my ear.

"I didn't run out. I left a note. I need... space," I said, scrambling up into a sitting position. "Why are you both half dressed? I'm... not speaking to you."

"Me?" Brass asked amusedly.

"Neither. I already explained all of this," I stammered, pulling my legs up to my belly. "Why are you both smiling?"

"You read my message?" Slate asked.

I nodded once not meeting his eyes. "Words. Just words."

"*But* you came home," Slate purred again, that extra something in his chest from being a barghest seemed to vibrate deeply.

My cheeks heated. Was that what I'd done?

"*Home,* where my family is, you are..."

"Family? Your husband?" Brass offered, raising himself up to lean on his elbow.

"Not my husband anymore."

"Because you wish it, does not make it so or I would rewrite history this moment wishing you had never left to Chicago. Who knows? Perhaps I would have my memories then," Slate said, crossing his powerful legs on my other side.

I narrowed my eyes, looking between them. "I could have said the same thing to you last week. You want me to forgive you for sleeping around while I was sitting at home hoping and praying you'd come back? And you, you want me to forget how you started sleeping with Crimson when I was *right* there *and* not telling me before taking Rosasite to bed?"

They both had the grace to look uncomfortable under my steely gaze. Did I dare tell them I had been with Ash? No, not yet. I was punishing myself enough as it was, being abandoned again would do me in.

"I'm not saying I will, I'm only suggesting a path of redemption. And in no way do I mean so either of us will be together, I only mean that we can be friends again." I continued.

"Yes, we are following," Slate said in a too amused tone that made my lips pinch together.

"Prove it," I said before climbing to my feet, barefoot and all, and marching across the sand to the path that led inside the palace.

I could hear those two sun kissed, sculpted muscled idiots chuckling. They were not taking it seriously; it wasn't a joke. I wanted proof they could be trusted again and in the meantime, I needed to untangle the web I was caught in and pray they never found out about my night with Ash.

The fact that my love bites were gone made me pray I was first found by a kind, aimless wanderer that healed me before those two had stumbled upon me.

"Where's my cat?"

They were going to wait until I was asleep and sneak into my bedroom. Part of me, the raging lunatic, thought it would be like old times with Slate sneaking into my room. The sane part of me knew if they didn't show me things could be as they were, I'd always be suspicious. I needed that trust back.

"Indi, are you decent?" I asked cracking open her bedroom door.

"Dear Gods, not decent, but not yet indecent," Quick retorted from inside.

"Come in, Scar. Don't listen to this scoundrel," Indigo called.

I pushed the door open and stepped inside. They were in the bathroom getting ready for bed. I took my short black wig off and ran my fingers through my hair as I passed her sitting room to lean in the bathroom doorway.

"I have a big favor to ask. I won't be upset if you say no. I'll just try Jett next; he tends to hog the bed, so I thought of you first," I rambled.

"Yes," she said, brushing her teeth in the wall-to-wall mirror.

"Yes, what?" Quick asked.

Quick black jagged Celtic tattoos covered the left half of his body to disappear under his black boxer briefs and reappear at their hem. He was not a bashful man.

"Yes, she can sleep in bed with us tonight so your brother and that brute don't try anything she's not ready for." Indi flashed me a brilliant smile that lifted the beauty mark on her right cheek. "Of course you can stay with us."

Quick frowned and then smiled. It was his patented panty dropping smile and Indi quirked a brow.

"Not even in your wildest dreams, Regn," she said, scoffing.

"Perhaps in my wildest," Quick amended with a chuckle.

Indi ignored him and told me to borrow whatever I liked to sleep in, when I returned to the bathroom neither of them were there, but I could still catch the scent that lingered and knew they must've been in my old room.

I readied for bed and when I was on my way to the sky-blue satin swathed, massive bed, Indi and Quick reappeared. It was hard not to envy how the two of them looked at one another. They couldn't stop touching. Hopefully, they got what they needed to out of the way.

Quick climbed into bed first with Indi between us. He tucked her hair under her head and placed his face against the back of her head as he wound his arm around her waist.

"You were more yourself than I have seen you... I guess since before you left for Chicago," Indi said, tucking her hand under her pillow.

I bit down on my lower lip to keep me from the moronic smile that wanted to bloom on my face. The feast had gone extremely well. The dancing had gone even better. Everyone in town came out to the feast where the greater family mingled with the common folk. There were long tables full of platters of food and a dance floor with the ethereal dance music of Tidings blended with a folksier less formal kind that was my favorite.

Brass and Slate had made good on their efforts to redeem themselves. I hadn't told them about Ash. I knew the sooner I told them, the sooner I could deal with the repercussions, but... I needed time. Gypsum, Jett, and Hawk were hard pressed to get me on the dance floor and away from Brass and Slate. For the night, I'd put my anger and hurt away for long enough to just have fun.

"Even with the wig?" I asked, smirking.

"I think you were pretending to be someone else so you could enjoy yourself, like a costume," Indigo said.

The moonlight poured through the stained-glass windows beside the bed casting red and green light on her face. Quick lifted his head behind her.

"Did you see Brass and Solder make up? That was a grudge three years in the making. Perhaps you have stopped being a bad influence on my brother," Quick said.

My lips tugged at the corner. "Tonight was fun." I sighed. "Tomorrow I have to face Ash."

"Is it because he wants to marry you?" she asked.

"No. Well, yes. A story for another day. I can't marry Ash. I feel like I've given this speech before." I shifted to face away from them and cradled my belly. "Goodnight. Thanks for letting me stay here."

"Of course, Scar," Indi said, placing her palm to my back, and I felt the warmth of her *calling* put me to sleep.

"Rabbit."

My heart lurched, and I woke up with adrenaline pulsing through me. A hand rested on my belly and warmth rolled over me.

"Shh. You sleep like the dead," Brass teased.

I shoved back against Indi's intricately carved headboard, pulling the sky-blue satin to my chest. "Where's Indi and Quick?"

Those debauchees had probably ditched me to practice procreation in my old room. A smile pulled on Brass's lips and he held up a thick taupe dress in the Elivagar style with ivory lace trim and rose quartz buttons up the front.

"We knew you would need a dress for today," Brass said, laying it over my feet.

With Brass on my left and Slate on my right, I was trapped between to spectacularly muscled bodies. Luckily, they were both dressed.

"You raided my closet. Then I suppose you brought shoes and under garments?" I asked nocking up my chin and crossing my arms.

Naturally, Slate produced a pair of beige ankle boots with a practical heel and a lace fabric with as much material as an eye patch.

I looked dryly at the material and Slate's failure to suppress what could only be described as a proud smirk. "You forgot my corset."

"You will be very busy today; it will only make you uncomfortable," Slate rumbled as I snatched the items from his hand.

Slate's eyes hitched on my chest and I immediately stiffened. Brass shifted and climbed over my legs careful not to touch me and shoved Slate off the bed.

"We'll see you at breakfast. Pearl wanted you to come to her room before you go to Valla U," Brass said, ushering Slate out of the room.

I was astonished to find that Slate let himself be removed. "Alright." I answered, watching the two men. "Um, Brass?" I called when they got to the door.

Brass poked his head back into the room and I slipped from the bed to the sitting room and placed my hands on the back of the chaise. The modest nightgown I'd borrowed from Indi was similar to the shift I'd worn, covering me from my chest to my knees in a boxy shape except where my belly pulled it snug. His soft amber eyes glittered at me.

"Scarlett?"

His mouth caressed my name in a teasing, playful manner that on most days would have made me squirm. Today was not most days.

"Crimson?" I asked.

"No news yet."

I nodded, disgusted with myself. Men should come with a warning: *WILL CAUSE YOU TO DO UNBELIEVABLY STUPID THINGS.*

Pearl's room was at the highest level, at the very back of the gold and blue mosaic lined palace. Her double doors were exquisitely carved. A blazing sun was the centerpiece, half of which was on each door. When I knocked, the doors swung out and revealed her room.

It was sprawling. Her massive white bed sat under a recessed arch that was backlit. Ivory silk fabric draped on either side of the massive bed. She had an alcove that held a flight of stairs which led to the top of one of the many domed turrets of the palace. I moved to sit in an over-sized cashmere covered cream chair. Tawny's fair heart-shaped face turned with a wide smile and she stood to embrace me.

"You escaped. I'm so glad you're back," she said, pulling her long dark waves over her shoulder.

She'd overseen the Elivagar celebrations yesterday. There had been a twinge of sadness over how we were all growing up and changing. It had been happening in spurts and starts until we were miles away from where we'd started when we arrived in Tidings.

"You act like I was gone for months; it was barely a week... It seemed like the right decision at the time. Love makes fools of us all. The more love, the more foolish," I said with a rueful grin.

Pearl sat across from us, her curvy figure draped across the chaise lounge, her bare feet pulled up on the chaise next to her. She looked like a lounging movie star from the fifties.

"I am glad you got my message, darling. Considering the messengers, I was not sure if they would be thrown out before you heard it. Have you begun to make amends?" Pearl asked and held out a tray of scones.

I picked out a blueberry scone and sat back, nibbling on it. "I don't know what I'm doing. There. It's out. News flash: Scarlett Tio has absolutely no idea what she's doing. Do not tell the populace. I don't know how I'm supposed to help govern when I can't manage my own private life."

Tawny bit off a piece of a chocolate chip scone. "There's no shame in that, Scar. Are you and Brass or Slate on the mend?"

"Honestly, I don't know. I've decided to stop being hard on them temporarily because it takes so much effort." I let out a self-deprecating laugh and looked away. "I may have mucked things up worse than ever... spending the night with Ash. Just the one night and Quartz knows, but this whole thing is foreign to me. Now more than ever, I know without a doubt I could never spend my life with him," I said in a rush, and looked at them through my lashes.

I wished Pearl looked more surprised, and that Tawny looked less appalled. I sucked in a deep fortifying breath and Pearl's floral musk swirled in my nostrils. It was such a classic feminine scent.

Tawny swept a hand over her face. "Frigga's sweet grass."

"The Prime is not a man used to hearing the word *no*. Now that he has come so close to his goal, he may be reluctant to release you, darling." Pearl poured us both tea. "I shall think on the matter. That was only one of the reasons I asked you to come, darling. I have been helping Tawny wade through Orion's coded journals. *RIDGE* was used as the keyword cipher. We started with the year before and after Tawny was born and skipped to his most recent. Orion was a dream beacon as Tawny is, and he shared Cassiopeia's dreams... when they were on better terms."

She sipped from her teacup, placing the saucer in her opposite hand.

"It would appear that Cassiopeia dreamt of a crime she committed. You know that Sea Dagr died during childbirth, that I was there and masked Slate's life?"

Tawny was looking at me with a furrowed brow.

"Orion writes that Cassiopeia kept a deadly poison in her insignia ring. She emptied the powder into a glass of water she gave Sea, hoping it would kill her and the child she was birthing. It could only be one of the women who had been in and out of the birthing room. We cannot bring this to the Prime. The writings of a dead man's coded journal about an estranged wife's dream is not evidence to a crime. I bring this story up because Cassiopeia killed Sea because of her prophecy. She did not want it repeated and Slate would have inherited her prophecy, not the way we hear the words, but the images that accompany them. If she went through those lengths to murder Sea, I worry she may have hired the Stygian Knights to see to Slate's capture. I do not know what she is capable of, I only wish for you to be wary until she missteps and we can take further steps to handle her."

Tawny went into the things Orion had told us at the Valla jail. How he was responsible for the Red King Massacre, the attack on Ridge, Sparrow, and Tawny by the Valla cottages, and about Canis and the pieces. Pearl hadn't heard all of it before. The news about the pieces made her lovely face etch with concern. That Orion knew about Cassiopeia's affair with Canis and that Pepper and Spear were most likely the children sent to the Valkyries and how Canis promised Alder's betrothal to Delta as a consequence in an open-ended vow to do some dastardly deed when he was needed or else fall out of Orion's favor.

"Why would Orion have a hard time marrying Delta off?" I asked, frowning.

My stepmom was flawless. When you thought of a classic beauty, she was what came to mind and then some. Not to mention she came from the right family.

Tawny and Pearl shared a look. "Orion struck a bargain with Moon. Crag was supposed to marry Delta before they discovered he had no desire to be with women." Pearl sipped from her teacup.

"Dahlia is infertile. It was a dirty Natt secret. Moon demanded recompense for falsifying her marriage documents. That fell to Cassiopeia since she was already the matriarch. Delta was not yet married and since Canis owed Orion, Alder married Delta after she had her first child with Crag. Then Alder and Delta were to have an heir and afterwards—"

I held up my hand. "Crag and Delta are Ash and Diamond's parents?" I blinked in disbelief. "No wonder he lost it when he thought I was barren." My mind reeled. "What about Amethyst?"

Crag was old enough to be her father too.

Pearl gently shook her head. "Geols are known to have their last child a decade after their first as the rest of their eggs die. Jackal is much younger than Alder was too."

I wondered if Jett knew that. He seemed to be building his own army of children.

*Orion.* If he wasn't already dead, I would have poisoned him again. He set so many things in motion that had ultimately destroyed my mother's life. He said he was trying to redeem himself by helping me and Slate after all the harm he'd caused. It wasn't enough — not by a long shot.

"I always suspected Orion was behind so much of what happened. My instincts told me to hide Slate and to keep Sparrow and you from being found. Hawk would never have allowed Sparrow to be put in danger in any case and Lark was his brother, like Jett and Slate are now. Ash and Diamond were not told. None of us knew the truth, darling. They are of Natt and Straumr blood, only not the parentage they lived under."

She slowly shook her head in dismay. No wonder Delta was so vicious. She was a pawn — a broodmare. It explained Crag's reluctance to be anything other than a battle trainer. Fox and Nova's children would never be told their real father was Ash. I was starting to really hate Tidings.

"The Valkyries have raised thousands of children. When my mother disappeared, my grandparents believed the Valkyries might have found her and took her in. It happens. She would not have been the first child to be found wandering and taken in without question. The Valkyries believe if their parents want them, they will come in search of them. They keep meticulous record of the rare adoptions. Alas, she claimed to have been with the Leshys.

"I detest burdening you with this knowledge, Scarlett before sending you on your first big day running the university. You have problems of your own to deal with, but you are your mother's daughter. You will find a way to make Ash understand."

Pearl's words were reassuring, but her features creased with worry. Tawny looked guilty, as if she had committed Orion's atrocities. I offered her a smile.

"No one else has to know. It's over and done with, we'll make it right. You happen to be best friends with the Second. Once I return things back as they should be with Ash, we'll track down those stolen portals and put all those rogue Stygians on trial."

Pearl's brow smoothed, and she crossed the room to sit and embraced me. "Do not let the frivolities of love soil all the good you have done and all you have accomplished. Your mother and father would be awed by how much you have accomplished in the short time you have lived here. Be proud, darling. I am so very proud of you.

Pearl moved to take Tawny into her arms. "Matriarch Vetr, my how I never would have seen that coming. Orion was not always that way and in the end, he did what was right. The details matter not, but the efforts. He wanted to be a man worthy enough to call you granddaughter. To be worthy of Ridge. Orion and I were both agreed you shall make a grand ruler."

"What did you want to discuss about the piece?" I asked after Pearl withdrew from a weepy Tawny. "In your message, you said you had more information."

Pearl fixed her cat like gaze on me. "I overheard Steel and the boys discussing a puzzle you have been charged with solving. I believe they referred to you as, Night's Child?" She furrowed her deep tan brow with her sincere question.

"You know something about night's child?" I asked, feeling a burst of exhilaration.

"My mother called me Night's Child. She never did say why. As for the stone pendant, she never gave it to me. I thought that might be important. She placed it in my care before she died. She told me it was meant for a daughter taking the hard path. That that was what she had been told. I am assuming by the Leshys, but she never did say. Never once did she mention her time with them or her fifteen years lost." Pearl sighed. "She said when she left that she had a hallucination before she fainted. That a giant blue-eyed man carried her from the Leshy to Valla. That she never walked and when she awoke, she was simply there."

"That sounds like nonsense," Tawny said, making a face of consternation at not having clearer information.

"Likely so. I thought you might get use out of it all the same. Mull it over and maybe something will spark."

"Was she a good mother?" I asked.

I'd never gotten over having so much family when I thought It was just Tawny's family and me and my mom my whole life until two years ago. Any information no matter how insignificant I stored like a greedy squirrel.

Pearl smiled fondly. "My mother was a kind and loving woman, but she always seemed distracted. Come to dinner Tuesday night and I will tell you all the stories I remember from growing up if you want to hear more."

I smiled broadly. "It's a date."

# CHAPTER 26
# GYPSUM

The portal room of Valla University was more crowded than I had ever seen it. Second year tyros in all black and canary yellow belts brushed past us first years with our fire engine red belts. My mom and dad stood with Pearl beside me as we waited for the first-year headmaster.

Malachite came into the room a few doors down in a flash of bright white light and spotted me right away. A black jerkin with matching pants tucked into black boots. We could've been Shadow Breakers if we weren't wearing the ridiculous belts. The girls were just as bad, the belts not the dresses. They were forced to wear flowing black caftan dresses with wide red belts.

"Where are your parents?" I asked Malachite as he clasped my forearm in greeting.

His permanent smirk curled his lips. "My father drinks and my mother prefers the company of men who do not. They are glad I will be here year round."

I gave him a sympathetic smile, and he shrugged. I introduced the rake to my parents and Pearl. He majestically charmed them with little effort before Boa Sunna swept into the long room and began to gather the first-year male tyros to him.

Beryl stepped up beside me and nodded to Malachite. "My mother spends so much time coming to see my father, she is reserving her visit for another day."

Boa acknowledged his son's presence with a slight incline of his head. Malachite snorted.

"By Balder's brow. How do you know if he is happy with you? *Is* he happy you are here?"

"Balder's brow? I haven't heard that one before," I joked.

Beryl smiled wryly as Boa began to lead the fifty or so male tyros with their families through the yellow stoned castle. "He is a stoic man. His compliments are few and far between, but you know he means it when he gives them. He is fond of the Second. Not everyone is, I am sure you know."

I nodded. "Shale meant a lot to Scar."

And me, but I didn't know if Beryl knew of our relationship, as casual as it had been. Making sure Shale got a Mjolnir for her rescuing of Slate won over the Sunna and Sandr lesser families to Scarlett.

We walked up a set of winding stairs to an archway that Boa crossed through. It was a long wide hall with sets of doors to either side. Boa began to rattle off names and gesture to each room. Ours was the second room and as we passed in front of him to see to our things, I got the sense that he was proud of Beryl's roommates. I didn't think I would ever get used to people being proud of me for being born into the right family.

Across from the door were two beds nestled in a large arched alcove. Braided pillars divided the rooms three alcoves, another bed to the left, and one to the right. I hopped on the first bed on the left and my mom began to go through the trunk the staff had brought for me near one of the closet doors. The room was made of yellow stone, where there weren't pewter sconces, there were tapestries or narrow stained-glass windows.

Beryl took the third bed from me and Malachite plopped down on the one next to mine. "Not too shabby."

Pearl arched a brow, and he swung his feet over the bed and gave her an apologetic smile. I chuckled to myself. Malachite had a big mouth, but he respected authority and his elders. It was one of his best attributes as a Breaker. *That* and he could raise a force field.

My mom brought my own blankets from home and placed them in a folded pile on the foot of the bed. When she smiled her dark eyes gleamed with tears. If I had gone to college, they would have made me stay nearby like they'd done to Tawny and Scarlett. They hadn't pushed me as hard as they had the girls. I graduated high school a mere six months early, unlike the girls who had enrolled in college by the time they were sixteen. They'd been swamped with classes with zero social life. Tawny had gone a few dates with no one special, but Scar had been on a total of three ever and one was her prom before we came to Tidings. They had been too busy. Wren and my parents wouldn't allow anything but excellence.

Scarlett's complete confusion when it came to men and dating was understandable when you factored in her past. She was clueless. Wren had been busy when we arrived getting that priceless golden torque and if the rumors were true, spending her days and nights in Ostara with Alder rekindling their long-time affair. Scar had been on her own. Pearl had wanted to guide her, but you never knew how teenage girls would react to unsolicited guidance. I knew that and I was only nineteen.

My mom embraced me and I hugged her fiercely in return. Wren's death had broken her heart, but she was doing much better since Scarlett had married her nephew. Even if Slate was a complete bastard.

"You'll have to go down to the great hall. You don't want to be late; I hear the new Second is very strict," my dad joked.

Scarlett would be a just disciplinarian as Reed had been.

Zircon's savage face was stormy as he marched through the door and went straight to the last bed. A gorgeous strawberry blonde woman trailed him in followed by an older blonde man with hawk-like eyes. Hunter had inherited those eyes and followed whom I thought must be their father into the room. His older sister had been Slate's hand fasted wife. His parents were familiar with mine. Our family had insisted on taking care of Amber's funeral arrangements which had been orchestrated without Scar's knowledge.

"You are here, now you may go," Zircon said curtly and my mother's eyes widened.

Pearl was speaking to his parents. Zircon's mother was a Lodda from Mabon, and father the Snjar patriarch. Hunter smirked at Zircon, being several inches shorter than Zircon didn't have a bearing on their relationship. While Zircon was more heavily muscled, Hunter was nothing, but muscle and sinew. The Snjars didn't hold any ill will towards the Sumar or Dagr as far as we knew.

"I am leaving. I only wished to see who the Second had pulled strings for. This must be the heirs' room. Blao, Sunna, and Sumar. Unfortunately for you, Zircon. You are a second son," Hunter chided.

Zircon canted his head in a way that reminded me of Slate when he was ready to launch into an attack — the unmistakable challenge in his eyes.

"Boys," His mother, said and shook her head laughing nervously. "Please wait outside, Hunter."

Hunter skirted his mother and left the room, Hawk and the Snjar patriarch were exchanging greetings oblivious to his sons' roe. Malachite gave an exaggerated grimace as Beryl stood speaking to Zircon's parents. I'd heard the Sunna heir was always looking for ways to make connections that would promote his family and now I was watching it in action. Idly, I wondered if I should've been doing the same.

After we said our goodbyes until the weekend, we followed the flow of tyros down to the great hall. Long tables and benches were divided into four rows along its marbled floors. The walls were the same yellowed old stone, sculpted pillars lined the rooms and sculptured people lined the edges of the ceiling looking down at us. Chandeliers were on each side of the hall in pairs down the length of the hall. Between chiseled rafters were circular stained-glass mosaics depicting the phases of the moon. An homage to the Straumrs, no doubt.

At the head of the hall was a fireplace, the head tables for the provosts in front of them. The dining hall looked like an anthill with its scurry of motion.

"The left side of the hall is for first years. Do not sit too close, but not at the end either," Beryl said, nodding to the middle-left tables.

"So middle, you could have said middle," Malachite said wryly.

We sat where Beryl suggested and happened to find Rosasite and the girls, Jade and Mica, seated with an ebony skinned girl I'd never seen before. We greeted them and slid onto the long bench across from them.

Ash sat at the center most table with Scarlett, Fern, Dahlia, Boa, Sky, and Basil. Only the headmistresses and masters wore black robes with gold trim. Ash's had both. Scarlett was the only one in grey and doing her imperial face.

The second-year tyros were in classes so only the first two rows of tables were occupied.

Ash's cultured voice echoed over the hall when he stood. "Good morning, future Guardians. I trust you have all been settled into your rooms. I would like to introduce you to some of your provosts and other staff here at Valla University for Guardian Mastery. Those of you who have already been introduced, your patience is appreciated. First-year tyros have already been introduced to Headmistress Natt who teaches history, and Headmaster Boa Sunna who teaches nurture and focus." They inclined their heads.

"Second-year's Headmistress is Fern Rot, Mistress of Ceremony, and Headmaster Sky Tio provost of counter calling. To my right is Scarlett Tio, Second of Valla University. Our librarian and keeper of history is Claviger Bail Straumr. The other provosts you are sure to meet in time. First-year students have been divided into two classes. The tyros with schedule Vili please follow Headmaster Boa, tyros with schedules Ve will please follow Headmistress Dahlia. Your schedule names will be at the bottom of the page you received at your induction. Be strong, be brave, be humble," Ash said before he sat back down.

I opened my schedule folder and saw that I was in the Vili course. "Which course are you guys in?" I asked.

"Ve," Beryl answered.

"Vili," Malachite told us.

Zircon held up his open folder to show the Ve course. Ro was in the Ve as well, but Mica and Jade were with me and Malachite.

Boa and Dahlia stood; we began to group into our courses. Scarlett spotted me and smiled. She wore an Elivagar styled dress with so many skirts she looked like a bell. It was always strange to see the old fashions with a modern spin that had long gone out of style outside of Tidings.

Scarlett picked up her skirts and walked down the steps to me. Two golden Mjolnir, the highest honor awarded Guardians for bravery, were pinned to her grey robe Then she did something odd, she stopped and looked over her shoulder at Ash who was glaring at her. She ran her teeth over her lower lip and continued towards me.

"I promise I won't embarrass you. Are you settled in? Do you like your roommates?" she asked in a hushed tone.

"Yeah, they're great. What made you put the Snjar with us? I didn't think you cared for Amber or Hunter," I asked her.

Zircon was standing beside Jade and Mica. When Mica saw me looking their way her fair cheeks flushed.

Scarlett had seen her and smiled. "I think she has a crush on you. She *feels* so nervous around you. I thought you might be a good influence on him. I'd hate for him to go the way of Amber and Hunter. I've heard good things about him that makes me hopeful. Lure him away from the dark side," she joked.

Her teasing attitude didn't last long, the next second she leaned in and pretended to hug me.

"Ash is very angry with me. He's been weird all morning and I've been avoiding being alone with him. There's a storm coming. I can *feel* it. Keep your head down and try not to draw any attention until I can smooth things over. Same goes for your friends. Ro included." She gave me an apologetic smile and walked away, the white trim of her robe sweeping the floors behind her.

# TWENTY-SEVEN

After dodging Ash all morning, I knew we'd have our confrontation sooner or later. I found the report I'd been waiting all month for on my desk when I returned from an exceedingly awkward lunch. The Guardians that were assigned to look into the Jorogumo's massacre was reporting that the empress She'ik was killed by her own people. A civil battle.

*Complete sugarfoot.*

I'd seen the dead spider hybrids with my own eyes. Where were the survivors? It wasn't nearly enough to be all of them. It enraged me that it wasn't being taken more seriously. An entire tribe had gone missing, half of it dead and Ash hadn't gone to investigate it himself. Moon would have.

The door to my office opened, and I set down the Guardian's report. I frowned as Cassiopeia Natt, Canis Var, and Sage sauntered into my office. Cassiopeia must have been an amazing beauty in her youth. She was stunning even now, with shoulder-length blonde hair styled like a starlet from the fifties. Canis had not aged well for a Guardian. He looked younger than his seventy plus years but with his seamed tan face and hooded eyes and blunt, white hair cut so short it spiked, he was too severe to be called good looking.

"Ash isn't in," I said, not bothering to rise from my tufted rose velvet chair.

"We came to see you, *Second*."

Sage's honeyed voice made my skin crawl as he sat down in the wing backed seat across from me. Cassiopeia took the other seat as Canis rested his arms on the back of her chair. I laced my fingers on my rose marble desk top beside a picture of my mother and it was one of the few items that decorated my desk. I drew strength from my mother's smiling face.

"How may I help you, Matriarch Natt, Ambassador Canis, Sage?" I took no small amount of pleasure of not having a title for Sage.

Cassiopeia's frosty blue eyes scrutinized my office and then me. "I am here on official business as the Matriarch Natt since her father was brutally murdered. My granddaughter wants to know what your status is on Ash's marriage proposal. You have been living with them, bedding him, so she tells us. Married in all but name it would seem."

Her voice was sultry and breathless and matched her glamorous appearance. I couldn't believe what I was hearing.

"Quartz made it clear she didn't want me as a second wife nor anyone else for that matter. On top of which, I agreed to birth an elemental child for him. I think my part in their story is done." I leaned back in my chair and crossed my legs attempting to look bored.

"It is not up to Quartz," Canis said in his quick clipped tone.

I scoffed. "The point is moot. I'm still married."

"Accidents happen every day. A fall off a horse... over a cliff... over a balcony," Sage said, gesturing with his hand.

My insides boiled. I reversed the frame so my mother's face smiled at them with more warmth than all three of them were capable of combined.

"I thought you were too smart to be threatening the life of my husband to my face. So why don't you —"

"You have until tonight to decide," Cassiopeia said, rising from her seat.

"It took three of you to ask me if I wanted to marry Ash?"

"I would like to see those strange pendants you wear. Collecting them is a hobby of mine."

Canis was burning a hole to the spot under my dress where the stone pieces were nestled. It took all my will not to clasp my hand over my dress.

"Were you the one who wanted to keep anyone else from *collecting* them?" I asked.

Sage's head whirled up to Canis, his round eyes comically wide. Canis was unfazed.

"I do not like to share, but if you found them before me I would simply procure something you desired more and strike a deal. Has someone tried to stop you? Out of curiosity, how many have you gathered? One collector to another," Canis queried.

"Why would I *ever* tell you?"

*Shut up mouth.* My brain was trying to send whatever signals it needed to get my lips to seal. The controls were broken.

"I know where the project is located. I could show you sometime."

Canis's stiff upper lip never moved as he spoke. He knew where the works was, no wonder he wasn't in a rush to find the pieces. He'd probably thought he had time before I came along, snatching them out from under him. Most likely he hadn't had access because the portals were closed to him when Moon closed the university.

"No, thank you."

Mentally, I scratched off the islands Canis would not have had access to from Ostara from my list of possible places. That left Valla. *Thank you, Canis.*

"Pity," Canis said, taking Cassiopeia's arm.

"Sage, I haven't seen any requests to become an ambassador to the Ostara tribes. Indigo was approved to be the Aves ambassador. She's already made contact with them," I told him.

Sage rose from the seat. He was as tall as Jett and our father. He ran his hand over his carefully combed blonde hair.

"I have bigger dreams than babysitting ungrateful mutants. I am second in line to Ostara's seat after all and... accidents happen every day," Sage said smugly.

I felt my nostrils flare. The nerve of them coming in, threatening

Slate and Jett, and hinting at my mother and Moon's demise. Never let it be said, my tongue was bit.

"Third, once Jett's son is born this spring. I suppose one could hire a few Stygian Knights to absolve one of their problems. Fortunately for them, two of their most useless assassins have been disposed of. Pepper and Spear, the Mint twins? Have you heard of them? I keep expecting a thank you note for ridding the world of such incompetence, but it has yet to come," I said in a cavalier tone.

Cassiopeia's cool mask fell from her face and rage reddened her fair cheeks. "A half-wit. Just like her mother. Ash was wrong about you, girl."

At that moment, Ash opened the door to my office and saw my guests. He sucked in a deep breath and crossed to them. Canis waved his hand dismissively when Ash began to greet them.

"We await your response," Canis said, escorting Cassiopeia and Sage from the room.

Sage gave a slow shake of his head as he shut the door behind him.

Now that they had left I ran my hands over my face.

"Why do you let him dismiss you like that? You're the Prime, Ash," I murmured into my hands.

"You have no idea what it takes to procure the votes of the council. What sacrifices I had to make in order to get the position. You never play by the rules. You think these things get handed to me on a silver platter? You are wrong. You make me look like a fool," Ash said harshly.

I raised my head to him and furrowed my brows. "Ash, you shouldn't have to do favors. They should do *you* favors. The whole point of the Guardians is balance. Everyone knew you would be Prime one day. You're a bit on the calculated side, but it could be used to the nation's benefit. It came earlier than expected, I'm sure. I thought Moon would have another twenty years, but then you have always been the most logical choice."

Ash sniffed and looked at me with his piercing green eyes. "At times, I found your naivete endearing. Now I believe it is a nuisance. Moon was riding Canis's mount when he went over that cliff."

I rose from my seat and crossed to him. I couldn't begin to hide my shock.

"Ash, are you saying what I think you're saying? Canis had Moon killed? To what end? Moon was a good man. Maybe complacent and withdrawn, but good. Why haven't you had Canis arrested?" I stressed.

Ash looked down his nose at me. "Like I said, naïve. You do not get something for nothing in this world, Scarlett."

He lifted his hand to run his thumb along my jawline. I took a step back.

"Stop speaking so cryptically, say what you mean," I asked as suspicion creeped up my spine. "Tell me you weren't involved, Ash. *Please.* You are Prime, you have to be above all of that. He used you. You were born and raised to take Moon's place. If he told you differently, he lied. We haven't always gotten along, but with time, you would be one of the best."

"You make a good Second. You will make a better second wife."

"We need to talk about that. I don't think Quartz —"

"It is not up for discussion. I can only protect you if you are with me. Are you with me, Scarlett?" he asked, staring down at me.

"I'm with you, but only as —"

"Then I expect you to tell Cassiopeia you will be a part of Quartz and my marriage and we shall lay their doubts to rest," Ash interrupted me again.

"I'm already married."

I was feeling cornered. No one was listening to me and now I was being bullied. It was sugarfoot.

"You can and will."

Ash walked to his office and slammed the door leaving me bewildered on the other side.

It was Jett's birthday, and we were going to the cottages like we did the previous year. I needed to get away from Ash. He had lost it and Sage's threats had unnerved me. Would the Natts retaliate now that they knew I had been with Peak and now Ash? More than ever, I felt like I knew nothing about how the world of the Guardians worked.

Ash had left after dinner in the great hall. He gave me a meaningful look before leaving me in the office alone. The look said, *I had better see you in my bedroom in an hour.* He would be disappointed.

The others were waiting at the portal near the Vanaheim arena for me, it cut the walking time to a fourth of what it usually took to walk to hike from the Valla heart to the cottages. Jett was bringing a costume for me that they had picked up at a shop outside of Tidings with the girls. It was a seventies themed birthday party, so I would likely be wearing a tent.

I sighed as I checked Ash's office and turned the lights off. I *felt* anger and frustration when I shut Ash's door. I thought he had come back to force me to go with him, but Crimson sat at my desk. There was a crossbow on her lap, her legs crossed on top of my desk next to a bottle of clear fluid.

"Crimson," I said in a careful tone.

The pretty red head had a flushed face with a red nose. Her bright eyes were glassy, and hair limp.

"I am not pregnant. You must be happy," she said, sniffling.

"No, Crimson. You deserve happiness," I said, trying to step out of the aim of the crossbow, but she shifted it in her lap.

"Just not with any man *you* have ever met. You took Ash then you took Brass. Is it true, you slept with Ash?"

Her voice caught. On top of not being pregnant and having no marriage prospects, I had slept with Ash whom she was still in love with. Lying would only make her angry, and that crossbow pointed at my belly told me what kind of mind frame she was in.

Who let her in?

"Yes," I said, inhaling sharply bracing for the impact of the arrow if I couldn't thicken the surrounding air fast enough.

Crimson's face crumpled in her hands and the crossbow was unmanned. I *called,* snatching it out of her lap. She put up no resistance. It flew to me and I placed it on one of my mahogany shelves before I cautiously walked over to Crimson.

"You're too good for Ash. You always were. He only respects power and bloodlines," I soothed.

"You are only saying that because he chose you."

I opened the drawer and plucked a tissue for her. She blew her nose loudly and dropped it into the waste basket.

"But I didn't choose him. I know someone who is looking for a wife. An advantageous marriage, lesser family, but a good man." I leaned on the edge of my desk. "I'm terrible at my own love life, but I've been known to pair off some excellent couples. My night watch guard who passed recently, I paired his sister up last week and I received word today that she has moved in with a man I had conveniently placed in her path. I hate to take credit for my sister and young Regn, but I most definitely do."

I pushed the letter I received from Lera towards Crimson across my desk. Honeybee had asked to be released from her contract with the Shadow Breakers so she could settle down and start a family. I sent a messenger back to Lera putting in my vote to find Honeybee a position at the Vanaheim arena. Chafer had kept an eye on her and said my blonde assistant was smitten with Honeybee.

Things moved quickly in Tidings, especially when fertility was waning. If things went well, they'd be married and likely with child before the spring equinox.

She lifted her eyes to me from the letter. "It only took a week? I look like hell."

I felt her hope. She desperately wanted children and to find a good match before she lost her fertility.

"You're beautiful. I have a few things that can accentuate that beauty," I told her, and opened the drawer at my feet that concealed my last-minute beauty products.

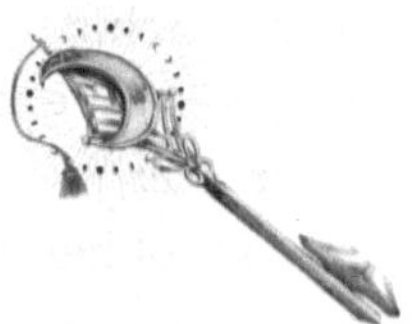

I knocked on the door of Gypsum's room and gave Crimson a reassuring smile. She looked dubiously at me. Malachite opened the door. He had a roguish quality most Shadow Breakers developed as if they all laughed in death's face and thought even the darkest storm clouds held a silver lining.

"Second, this is highly inappropriate. Taking advantage of such a young vulnerable man. Using your power and influence to seduce me when you have the ability to throw me out of the university. Ah, well. Do what you want with me, I will not breathe a word." Malachite held his arms out and threw back his head.

I let out a giggle and mentally kicked myself. Gypsum pushed Malachite aside who started chuckling at Gypsum's annoyed look. Gyps must have been getting ready for bed. His long, sable hair was still threaded with copper beaded braids, but he was only wearing a pair of brown plaid drawstring pants. More muscle than Steel, but the same height and build as the avid swimmer. I couldn't place the moment he became a man, but it seemed to have happened overnight.

"What's up, Scar? Crimson?" He smiled, dimpling his cheeks, and looked curiously at Crimson.

"I was on my way out and wanted to hear how your day went." I widened my eyes with a look that said, *let me in, idiot.*

"Yeah, cool. Come in. Everyone's decent, *er,* dressed." Someone laughed from behind him.

We entered the bedroom to find everyone in states of undress. They began to straighten up and looked more serious upon my entering. They greeted me with inclined heads and mutterings of, "Second".

I supposed if Reed had come into my room my first year I would have been nervous too. I introduced Crimson, technically an older, more mature woman from a Rot/Tio family and watched Beryl test the waters. It was easier with Malachite diffusing any tensions with jokes as he flirted with her. I quickly realized that she had not been flirted with much probably because the men in our course knew she was seeing Ash.

"Well, we should get going. You boys have classes tomorrow," I said, pulling Crimson away from Beryl and Malachite.

Beryl got to his feet with Crimson. "I would be happy to walk you out."

Gypsum arched a brow and smiled knowingly at me.

Gypsum walked alongside me as we made our way to the portal room. "So what happened with Ash?"

"Bad to worse. He's adamant about me marrying him. Like, tonight. I don't know. I had a weird visit today."

I told him about my conversation with Cassiopeia, Canis, and Sage, leaving out the part where they called me out on spending the night with Ash. Gypsum's brow drew down.

"Scar, no offense, but that wasn't too bright. Those things are trump cards. You don't lay them out so they see what you're holding. You've gotta wait and throw those suckers down when they're crucial. You've just pissed them off."

My little chief was lecturing me. It wasn't the first time I was told I had a smart mouth — a big, smart mouth.

"By the way, there's this guy here, Onyx. Keep an eye on him for me. I was told he was recruited by the Stygian Knights. I'm hoping we can bring him back from the dark side too so I haven't ousted him. Get a feel for him though for me, will you?" I asked.

"Sure thing. I gotta go." His big puppy dog eyes glanced away.

"Rosasite or Diamond, Gypsum Sumar?" I asked wryly.

He laughed nervously. "Diamond. Sterling is going to be at Jett's party."

I groaned. "*Great*. Quick will be in a fantastic mood."

"*Um*. I am going to hang out for a while. Tell everyone I am sorry I cannot make it," Crimson said, tucking her long red hair behind her ear.

Beryl's up tilted eyes glittered at me and I feigned surprise. "Oh, sure. No problem." I grinned before I walked through the portal alone.

On the west end of the Ymir River, Brass stood on a white stone bridge made luminescent by the moon's reflection as the Valkyries' hands poured water forth from the sky in front of Vanaheim.

He pushed off the stone balustrade and stood with a cat who ate the canary grin.

"I had a run in with Crimson," I told him as the breeze tugged on my dress.

"Where's your cloak?"

"Elemental, remember? She was not in a good way." I arched a brow at him when I reached him and folded my arms over my chest.

The taupe cotton dress had an ivory lace that trimmed the neckline and the hem. I left my robe in my office so the snow wouldn't dirty the white trim as we walked. The rose quartz buttons were ice cold through the thick fabric of my sleeves.

Brass's eyes scanned mine as I played the images of what happened for him. "She slapped me. You're the only other woman who's slapped me. She thought if we had... continued our intimacies that she would be pregnant. Quartz's pregnancy wears on her. I see you know Ash courted her for a second wife before dumping her again."

I started walking away from the arena on the north side of the bridge that spanned the width of the river and Brass hurried after me. "Don't worry. I introduced her to Beryl Sunna. He's an overachiever, always searching for his father's approval, *and* when they met there were definite sparks."

"You are always trying to marry everyone off, Scarlett. What about your own marriage?"

"Those who can't do, match, I guess." I shrugged my shoulders as I walked.

I'd worn half my hair pinned up in loose curls, the wind tangled them around my head as we walked. It was a bitterly cold night that would've frozen my lungs as I breathed, but thankfully I couldn't feel it.

"How did things go with Ash today?" Brass asked, changing the subject.

I told him everything, even the odd meeting with the snide trio after lunch. I wasn't ready to talk about my night with Ash and I carefully guarded it in my mind from him. The worst thing I could do was accidentally send images of it to him.

Brass was quiet as we walked and I went over the day. His steady breaths swirled out with every exhale. I stopped at the end of my story and looked at him.

"Are you cold? I could flare for you."

"He expects you to be there tonight?" he asked.

"I tried to tell him I wouldn't. I can't — he wouldn't listen."

"He might come looking for you," Brass said in a low tone.

"I know. I'm hoping he's going to sleep on it and see reason or Quartz comes clean and tells him she doesn't want a second wife."

"I'll take some of that heat now," Brass said.

I stopped and Brass pulled me against him so I was tucked to his side. I let my heat simmer through me and I felt Brass's muscles begin to relax.

"I'll go with him if he shows up. I don't want any of you getting arrested. It might take persuasion on my part to get him to back off. Do you think it's because I tell him no? I honestly don't get it."

"It's more than that, love. You make him feel good. When you shine your light on him, his world has never been brighter," Brass said as if he was reciting a weather report.

*Pure fact, no opinion.*

I fumbled for something smart to say and found that nothing came to mind. That was often the case.

We crossed over a frozen stone bridge, the Valkyrie compound was beyond the darkened trees, hardly anyone ever went there. We walked along the river until I could make out the cottages nestled against the bank. Jett reserved the Dagr, Sumar, and Vetr cottages all ready for the party. The cottages were private yet still within sight from one another.

I could see the flashing strobe lights in the Vetr cottage which meant Haarder, the spiky-haired DJ that I'd hired for the arenas, was spinning his music there. Everyone would be in the Sumar cottage.

Brass opened the door, and we found our friends and family sitting in the same spots they were last year on couches pushed around to face one another. They wore afros, go-go boots, leisure suits, vests, mini dresses, and platforms. Amethyst was bold wearing a halter neck catsuit.

"Where's Indi?" I asked, seeing her and Quick were both gone, but Sterling was there wearing something that looked like it belonged at a disco.

Jett was drunk wearing a huge blonde afro. "Hey foxy lady, no one speaks to you until you are properly attired."

Slate stood, and I covered my mouth with a hand. Jett had dressed him. He wore a torn Sex Pistols shirt and ripped jeans. His lips curled when he saw me trying to hold back my laughter. Tawny spotted me and hopped off Steel's lap wearing a bright mod flower dress with a wide white collar and white boots.

"I have your things upstairs. Come on."

Tawny grabbed my hand, and I gave Slate a small smile before I was whisked away. Brass would be filling in the others on my day because that's what they did whenever I got myself into a jam. I should be glad they all cared about me.

The cottages were medium-sized stone houses. The hall upstairs led to three different bedrooms that had all been claimed, so I would have to stay in the Dagr cottage.

Tawny held up a lime green and orange psychedelic dress with a low neckline and white boots. "I can help give you super big hair."

"Okay," I said skeptically.

Tawny produced a bra and suntan maternity pantyhose giving me a wink as I began to change.

"Where is Indigo?" I asked again.

Tawny started laughing wickedly. "Her and Quick are making babies." She waggled her brows at me.

Freya's burly boar, Tawny was drunk too.

"Okay... so they can't wait until after the party?" I asked in an exasperated tone.

Tawny shook her head drinking out of her glass. "Nope. She started ovulating."

"What? You mean like literally making a baby?" My voice had started to raise.

"Yes," she said, drawling.

Good for them, I thought and went downstairs feeling like a complete idiot in my platform go-go boots. They clapped and hooted making me feel even more ridiculous. Steel wore an identical wig to Jett's with a fringe vest and bell bottoms. Brass wore an all-black leisure suit and I couldn't hold back my laughter.

I held my belly as my body shook. Brass spun around for me and Tawny and I leaned against each other for support we were laughing so hard. Slate was at my side and took my arm. I sobered, my laughter tapering off.

"I have never seen you laugh like that before," Slate said, his eyes running over my face as if he was memorizing it.

"I guess we should put Brass in a sport suit more often." Another chuckle bubbled up.

"Hey!"

Quick came down the stairs, and I started laughing all over again. His polyester shirt was open down to his stomach with a pair of bell bottoms. Indigo wore a gold catsuit with flared bottoms and her blonde hair was curled to five times its normal size.

"You made it!" Indi cried as she hugged me, smelling like sex, honey and freesia.

Hints of Quick's cedar and patchouli cologne clung to her cheeks, and I didn't even want to know how. I was suddenly feeling bad for Sterling and couldn't figure out for the life of me why he would torture himself by coming alone.

The cottages were crowded, and the music had grown loud enough to hear across the sliver of vacation land. I sat down next to Cherry and the armrest Slate leaned on while the others drank and teased one another. If I didn't have my baby bump, it would have been just like old times. I could smile again and laugh.

It was contagious. I wanted to freeze time and live in the moments. Heaven, or whatever I was supposed to believe in as a Guardian, had to be sharing moments like these with those you loved.

Then I saw Ash walk in. My stomach dropped, and I leapt to my feet.

"Party pooper," Jett muttered.

"Take it easy. I'll handle this," I said quickly before Slate or anyone else could get it in their heads to talk to him.

He would rub what we'd done in Slate's face in half a heartbeat.

I walked over to him and he grabbed my elbow. "We need to talk now."

I didn't object, even if I had, he would've ignored me. He led me through the front room and up the staircase with everyone's eyes on us. His fingers pinched and would leave a bruise in my soft flesh. He opened the nearest door and yanked me in before him.

I rounded on him. "I understand you're angry, but I tried to tell you earlier. I can't be with you. I'm still in love with my husband. You must understand that," I said.

I'd never seen him so enraged. I thought he would strike me so I took a step back. His eyes pierced like blades, his face hard, muscles tensed as he closed the distance between us.

"This is your last chance. Leave with me now and I may be able to salvage this. If not, you have no one to blame, but yourself. Give yourself to me, Scarlett. Was it so bad, our time together?" he asked, wrapping his arms around me.

I gently tried to tug away. "Ash, you're scaring me. What are you talking about?"

"You want him back? After he made of mockery of you? Bedding khorazes in brothels and this last girl? Your love is *wasted* on him. Give it to me."

My calves hit the back of the bed and he pushed me down. I grappled with his hands.

"Stop, Ash. I mean it. The other night was a moment of weakness that can't be repeated. It wasn't bad, it just wasn't right," I said in a rush.

Ash was kissing my face and my neck, too much of his weight on my belly. "I was inside you. You want me, Scarlett. I felt it. I have held them off as long as I can. It is now or never."

"Held *who* off?" I asked, thrashing my head away.

"The Knights, you foolish girl. Who else? Come with me now, my love." Ash leaned on his hands which gripped my wrists on the bed to hover above me.

"Are you *with* the Stygian Knights?" I asked in a squeak.

I'd given up my fight or forgot that I was fighting and stared up at Ash. His wrathful face had an amused edge to it.

"You always tried to run from me. At Tawny's wedding, I saw one of my Knights and he alerted me as to what we had been contracted to do. I saw myself comforting a grieving girl, but you ran to that orphan instead. You tried to run again before our engagement party. The Knights notified me of another contract. Another opportunity to draw you in closer. Then those imbeciles took it upon themselves to give you to the Merfolk. How could I marry a woman who could not have children? If they had left you with the orphan's child we would have had a hostage, the orphan would have done anything to protect. They never saw the bigger picture."

Was I breathing? My chest was rising and falling, but it had nothing to do with my conscious thought because my mind was reeling.

"It forced you to run away, and we had lost the only weakness we had discovered aside from the Sumars themselves which were too smart to be caught alone. That was when word of a trip to the Wemic came. Amber was so cross she was left behind she went right to Hunter and told him everything. Sage had only impregnated her because your husband was drugging her so she wouldn't conceive and she, another incompetent, could not find a way to stop it. I blocked all memory of Sage from her so your mind reader would not see it. His weakness was back and pregnant — he would die for you. It no longer mattered if you carried his sons or not because we had ways around it."

"You *are* Stygian," I breathed.

Ash's anger boiled beneath the surface, but he gave me an exasperated look. "I prefer Knight. When you found him, I thought it was all over. Then, he did not remember you and you were heart broken. You would have let anyone between your legs and did. The middle Regn, Peak, Albacore, Spinel — even the orphan, though you knew he did not love you. Peak was always a liability. He knew you were supposed to be mine, but like all the Haust, he was more animal than man only out for their own desires.

"All he saw was his own petty revenge against his brother who stole Sea from him and loved only one other woman. Cuckholding his nephew, who happened to be the daughter of Lark's second wife, was far too much temptation. I would have killed him myself if you had not. It made it that much harder to draw you in close. But I knew, if I could prolong his recovery he would eventually misstep and you would run back to me. You did. Never once did you think that I would be capable of placing the memory blocker."

"What did you do the day you pretended to remove the block?" I asked, feeling tears of frustration bubble forth.

"Nothing. So you see, I am the only one who can protect you. Leave now with me. Keep your sons. It is the only way I can guarantee their and your safety. Do not come with, and gamble with their lives." Ash's vicious sneer was back.

"What about my family?" I asked, knitting my brow.

"I can save half. You, Amethyst, Indigo, and Tawny. The rest are on their own," he said simply.

My stomach turned; my dinner instantly curdled at his words. Ash had known about the contracts against my mother and father and the plan to capture Slate. He deceived me and I rewarded him. He could have saved all of them and didn't.

"Why?"

My throat felt swollen as I squeezed the word out. Foolish did not skim the surface of how I was feeling. Naïve did not accurately sum up just how flat out stupid I was.

His eyes slid down to my cleavage. "For the future of Tidings. Imagine the ability to control time. Do you know nothing of which you hunt for so blindly?"

"You already rule Tidings. They used you, Ash. They used your ambition against you. Who, within twenty years of us, would have been able to be Prime other than you?"

My words made his upper lip curl. "Not just Tidings. Do you not tire of how myopics destroy the Mother's world? With the project, we could go back and set things right. Make sure Guardians protected not just five measly islands, but all of Mother's earth."

"Kill millions of people to save the forests? Does that sound right to you?" I asked, incredulous.

"Not kill, those people would never have been born. Righting a great wrong. We should have always watched over the earth. The Mother never dreamed big. *Enough*. Do you care about the lives of your children or not?" Ash ground out, harshly jerking me on the bed for emphasis.

"After you stood by and let my mother, father, and countless other people and tribal folk die because of ruthless ambition? I would never have been with you."

Ash's face transformed. Big words from a girl being held down by a man who weighed nearly a hundred pounds more than her.

"Then it is Plan B, Indigo will have to be our key," he said in an inflectionless tone.

His eyes raised back up to my face. He was going to steal my pieces and the easiest way to do that was to tear them from me. I had felt the pewter bracelet that chilled my fingertips as we'd grappled. He wore a nix torque that prevented *calling* from working on him. I kicked and tossed my body; his one hand clasped my wrists above my head and the other enclosed around my soft throat.

"Do not make me hurt you. Give the pieces over," he ground out.

It was a revelation, the pieces had to be given. They couldn't be taken.

I could not die in white go-go boots. My dignity prevented it.

"Slate!" I tried to scream.

I'd felt him activate his bond the moment he stood outside the bedroom door. As if Slate would let me be in a bedroom alone with Ash. Never. I was sure at least Brass was with him if not the entire calvary.

The door crashed open and Slate and Brass burst into the bedroom. Ash spun off the bed pulling me up with him using me as a shield as he backed towards the windows.

"Let her go and you will have a running start before we kill you," Slate ground out.

Ash must have thought he was crazy kicking off his punk rock boots, but I knew he was making it less uncomfortable to shift. Ash still had my throat, my hand edged its way under my dress to my short seax.

"How does it feel? I can tell you earnestly, I had my doubts that she would fuck me so vigorously while married to you. I understand now why she is like a drug to you. You tell yourself you are not going back, that this is the last time and then she grazes your hand and flashes that smile. You think, I can say no. I know I should, but you do not. You want her again and again. No, now *this* is the last time. What were you doing when those lips were wrapped around my cock? How will it feel knowing the last man she was with was me when she died? When *you* die?" Ash said harshly.

I hadn't stopped struggling against Ash, even with my body feeling weak and watching Brass and Slate's faces etch with disgust and hate.

I should stop tempting the Norns. It could always get worse.

"No!" Brass shouted as Slate lunged.

Ash slipped his nix torque over my hand and shoved the back of my head so I hit Slate's knees as he charged forward. If Ash had pulled a blade, he might have stabbed Slate in the throat. He'd stumbled over my body and Ash placed a hand over Slate's head, freezing him in place for a split second. I heard Slate suck in a sharp breath and the air that beat past me from Brass's *calling*. Ash rolled out of the way as Slate fell to his knees.

I blinked dizzily as I watched Ash jump from the second-story window. Brass was at my side helping me to my feet and then turned to Slate.

"Go get changed, Scarlett. We leave now." Brass's tone was arctic.

I didn't say a word but ran from the room and went down stairs. The others had to know.

I stopped at the bottom step and realized the music wasn't playing from the other cottage any longer and everyone was smashed up against the windows.

"Scar, why is lover boy out there with one — *two* hundred men?" Jett asked.

I shoved him aside in the tight space between him and Quick. My heart skipped a beat then decided to make up for it by beating three times as fast. There weren't just men out there, but Jorogumo and Crathode. I spotted two Wemic at the front.

"Fucking Nirrin," Jett cursed.

Nirrin and his two brothers had turned on the Wemic. We had killed one cheetah hybrid, but Nirrin had gotten away with his injured brother when they captured Slate with the Stygian Knights.

"They're wearing nix cuffs. They want either me or Indigo, Amethyst, and Tawny. We've got to change and get out of here," I said in a distracted voice.

"Hurry, while they are still organizing," Steel said, pulling the wig off his head.

"*SCARLETT TIO!*" Canis's voice boomed from where they stood in rows outside of the cottage.

"*You are hereby stripped of your titles and stand accused of treason. You are charged with the murder of Peak Haust and Orion Vetr!*" Canis continued, "*Tawny Vetr and Indigo Var are charged as accessories!*"

"Send out the Tio twins and the Matriarch Vetr with Amethyst Geol," Sage shouted in a less impressive tone. "And the rest of you will be spared. You have ten minutes to comply."

I could feel my heart beat in my throat. Jett turned back to me; his brow drawn down. None of us could see a way out of this. Tawny blinked at me with a resigned look. Indigo's hands balled into fists.

"*Lie.* They'll kill everyone. They'll hunt down Jett, Slate, Brass, and Silver and make a spectacle of it. With Jett out of the way, Sage will be heir. They'll kill Cherry because she carries Jett's heir. They're purging the bloodlines. Tawny might be safe because she's of Vetr and Dagr blood, the two rarest so they'll want her children. Amethyst is safe if she doesn't put up too much of a fight because they'll need her to control her brothers. They won't need you though, Steel." Indigo's nostrils flared.

I looked behind me at the thirty other people who had just come for a party and the few friends we had in Tidings we'd led to their deaths and disgrace. Sterling stepped forward.

"Run. It is your only chance," he warned.

"Quick, you have your pack here from when we went to Ostara?" I asked.

"Yeah?" Quick asked, already taking his shirt off.

"Then you have the small raft. It will only fit five people. We'll divide," I said, following Quick's example and taking off my boots.

Brass and Slate were changed and armed to the teeth. "Brass and I have drank the least. Jett and Quick will go with Tawny and Scarlett on the raft and head east on the Ymir. You will get away faster and lead them away so we can get the others out of the cottages and to the Vanaheim."

"No. I do not like this idea. Indigo can take my place on the raft," Quick said, pulling Indigo to him as if that would protect her.

"Three of the four women they want in one location. No, Indigo has to go a different route," Brass said, clasping his black cloak at his throat.

I couldn't meet anyone's eyes. I wanted to give myself up and hope they ended my miserable life quickly if not in a humane manner. Sterling walked up beside those of us at the windows.

"A third group can head south into the forest to the Valkyrie compound. Indigo will be safe with me." Sterling's violet eyes had a weariness to them that made him look tired and older than our young twenty-one years.

Quick narrowed his gaze at him. "You *would* like that. I will go with you both, Cherry can take my place on the raft."

"If the raft is overrun, they'll need you to fight. No offense, Cherry," Steel said. "I'll go with Indigo and Sterling. Amethyst and Cherry will go with Brass and Slate. Jett, Tawny, Quick, and Scar in the raft. It makes the most sense. They'll expect the couples to stay together." Steel ran a hand over his face.

"Get changed," Slate growled close to my head, and Tawny looped her arm through mine and led me upstairs.

"I brought you these green khakis and a long grey sleeve with your mom's cloak. Don't ask me why I packed your blades, but I'm glad I did," Tawny said tossing me my pack.

"Thanks. I'd hate to die in lime green," I said with lackluster humor.

I buckled on my belt of blades and shoved a blade into each brown suede boot before buckling back on my short seax to my thigh. It was very difficult to do with my belly, but I managed it on my own. I buckled on my wrist blades and Indigo entered the room and began to change out of her catsuit in silence.

"Silver is very unhappy," she said thickly.

The door crashed open and Indigo covered herself with her arms. It was Quick.

"Get out, Scarlett, unless you want to see me make love to your sister," he said, already removing his last articles of clothing, his eyes locked on her semi-nude form.

I didn't need to be told twice. I didn't have anything worth bringing on the raft. I tucked my stone pieces into the ribbed shirt and picked up my beads, fetishes, and feathers and began to thread them into my hair. Alder's stone brushed band joined them in my hair.

My body was slammed against the wall and I winced as my head slammed back. "What are you doing?" I groaned.

Slate's hands were fisted in my hair pinning me tightly in place. "You fucked him. I cannot believe you fucked him. After everything. What were you thinking!" he growled.

I made a noise part whimper, part groan, all pathetic. He released me and turned away.

"I'm not the only one whose slept with someone reprehensible," I countered childishly.

"I cannot even look at you right now, Torch," he growled.

"Torch?" I squeaked, not moving from where he'd pinned me.

Slate grunted. "He wanted me to fully understand what I lost before one of us died."

Slate had his memories back. It was Ash all along. It was supposed to be a happy moment.

Instead, I watched Slate's back retreat down the stairs and my heart broke all over again. His bond was active and I could feel how disgusted and enraged he was. I could hear Quick and Indigo professing their love for one another and the sounds of love making that accompanied their proclamations. On a different day, I would have felt perverse. Today I needed to know the measure of love and why my love was unconditional, but Slate's wasn't.

"If we made a little Quick tonight, you had better take care of him," Quick said in between sounds of kissing.

"Take care of him yourself. You aren't shirking your responsibilities already are you, Regn?" Indigo responded, and my nose burned from the tingle of unshed tears.

Downstairs, everyone that had found a weapon, carried one. The rest had changed into the normal clothes, faces ranging from terrified to apoplectic. Sterling paced until Indigo descended the stairs, her hair braided in signature Quick style. I pulled my hair back into a ponytail and Tawny handed me an elastic band before doing the same to her own.

Cherry was crying and kissing Jett while Amethyst patiently waited for her turn. "Opal. You go straight there and get her and warn Pearl," Jett was telling her.

Steel kissed the top of Tawny's head and murmured as he held her. I didn't need to see what Quick and Indigo were doing, he was feeling desperate and helpless, trying to meld his body to hers as he kissed her. I crossed to the windows on the other side of the door from Slate and Brass.

My regrets mounted; if I hadn't gone to Ash's palace, if I hadn't slept with him, if we never had come to that cursed world in the first place.

"We need to get the last piece before Canis. We can all rejoin there. Someone has to go to Valla U and get Gypsum and to Thrimilci to warn Pearl, Sparrow, and Hawk," I said. "You might want to consider closing the portals. The arenas are safe from *calling* so unless they bring in bulldozers, get as many people as you can into them. They're all stocked with food and other amenities. Someone should get to Lera to help," I said as my exhale shuddered out from my body. "Spinel. Ash is jealous of the time I spent with him. He might not be safe either."

*Someone*, but not me.

Slate sniffed derisively.

If worst came to worst, I'd throw myself over so Tawny, Jett, and Quick could get away. It was the least I could do because if I had gone to the Straumr palace they'd all be safe; laughing and drinking and dancing. Not running for their lives, outlaws in the eyes of the Prime and the Guardians.

"My memories have returned. It was Ash who blocked them," Slate rumbled, and Tawny gasped.

"That's it? That's all you have to say?" Jett asked brusquely as he pulled away from Amethyst.

Jett looked fearsome in head to toe black. All the men wore black I realized except for Steel who wore dark blue and brown. Slate nodded and looked at me from the corner of his silver eyes. I glanced away. There were men and rogues everywhere. I would *call* at the ground and try to knock them all back to give us a fighting chance. Slate would be the last one out of the cottage and once I saw him, I was to set it on fire if the Stygians hadn't already.

Canis was Stygian. I couldn't imagine him answering to anyone. He had to be in charge. They'd been under our noses the entire time. I hated myself so much I couldn't stand it.

Indigo spun me around and hugged me so tightly I stifled a sob. "Take care of that pompous idiot. Don't let him be brave."

"Only I'm allowed to make sacrifices," I whispered, and she squeaked a laugh.

"Don't I know it. Take care of my nephews too. We'll meet you on the other side of the Igulbjorn Ice Cliffs in a few days," she whispered so no one else heard our destination, and I nodded.

"Ready?" Jett asked from behind me.

Indi threw her arms around his neck and I watched Jett swallow hard. I took the opportunity to say goodbye to the girls and Steel then looked to Sterling.

"I don't know how you ended up on this side of events, but your help is welcomed." I took him in my arms. "Please. If you're caught, don't let Ash hurt her because of me," I whispered in his ear.

"I swear on my life, I will not let harm come to her," Sterling whispered back.

I turned away from him and saw the dry look from Quick. I didn't have it in me to smile back. I smoothed my hand over my pony tail and held the doorknob.

"Get ready to run," I said so everyone would hear me.

"The nix torque. Give it to me and activate your bonds. All of you," Steel said, and I did as he told me.

I *called* air and sliced the skin just above my tiwaz tattoo. I rubbed it into the bond I shared with Brass, then on the skin between my thumb and forefinger to activate the kenaz tattoo between Indi, Jett, and I. Finally, I ran the cut along the inside of my lip against the EH rune for unity with Slate.

Jett smiled as he activated his bond with us, gebo, it meant gift and the one he had with Cherry and Amethyst. Indi was bonded to me, Jett with her laguz tattoo and Quick through their matching EH runes beneath their wedding bands. While Quick was bonded to Brass and Indi. All of us associated with the Shadow Breakers had our tracker tattoos used when we needed help, but we couldn't have them charging in blindly. They'd wind up getting themselves killed. Brass or Slate could activate their trackers once they reached the portal gate at Vana-heim. Steel was the only one in our group not bonded to anyone.

"Time is up, Scarlett. Are you coming quietly or do you intend to resist?" Sage asked, relishing in being able to speak to me with such contempt.

I opened the door and walked a few steps from the door with my hands up. Globes of light floated around where the men *called*. The bitterly cold air smelled like fear and violence. Hundreds of glittering eyes stared at me, from the three sets some of the Jorogumo had above pinchers in their human like faces, to the beady eyes on stems from the Crathode, and the glittering men's' eyes.

I noticed for the first time that over their black cloaks, they each wore a sickle behind a skull emblazoned in metallic red threads. It was the sigil of the Stygian Knights.

"Tell me one thing," I said in a clear even voice I hardly recognized.

"What is that, Mrs. Tio?" Canis asked as the bitter night breeze rifled the black furs over his shoulders.

"Which one of you killed my mother and father?" I asked, scanning the faces in front of me.

"Why that would be me, *sister*," Sage said in a honeyed tone.

The clean-shaven man who had been with the Mint twins was Sage. He'd been the one to deliver the killing blows to Alder. He'd killed his own father.

"I was the one in the pit when you were captured. Do you remember being stripped? Why, that was your dear Ash who could not stand for Spear to touch you even then. He *did* try to save you, but as most Tio women, you are set in your ways. Do you recall when I killed our father, how I terminated the life you grew in your womb? It is the memory that comes to mind when I need a pick me up. Murdering that sad excuse for a man and his whoring offspring's whoring offspring."

The roar from behind me was drowned out by my own howl. Sage had predicted my wrath and lifted his crossbow as I held out my hands. The earth crashed against itself, tossing me with it and the bolt cracked against my right collarbone. The cottage door exploded with people bursting forth and I held my right arm to my body as I used air to rip the doors of the other two cottages and into the Stygians so they would get the hint to leave.

I was right, the Stygians were wearing nix torques on their wrists and our *calling* was ineffectual against them. The good news was, they couldn't use it either and with their little regard for tribal folk, those they brought had no defense against it.

I flared to life, fire burned all around me and heated to a blaze so hot I melted the bolt. I kept *calling,* shifting the frozen earth in a constant earthquake until I saw Slate in my peripheral. Everyone was out of the cottage and it was time for me to go. Jett, Tawny, and Quick were lending their *calling* to mine, keeping the snapping claws and the puncturing of pinchers at bay.

My flames winked out and Jett placed one hand on my shoulder, his healing warmth flooded into me before he scooped me into his arms.

"Jett, what the hell are you doing?" I shouted as he charged along the cottages to the river.

I glanced over his shoulder to find Quick carrying Tawny in the same cradling manner while she pulled the raft out of his pack. She pulled the cord, and it began to inflate as they veered towards the river. Quick jumped as Tawny *called* the raft into the river. Rubber was not a material Guardians approved of under normal circumstances. Jett jumped in after them with me in his arms and I formed a wall of air to prevent their cross bolts and arrows from puncturing our raft. Quick was *calling* water to change the flow of the river around us while Jett gave us a strong push from the air. Tawny's arrows flew to shore at the enemies trying to follow us.

"Steel!" Tawny lurched in the raft, dropping her bow.

A steady line of Guardians were running down the river, some of the partygoers were running into the woods and still more tried to cross the river past the Crathode who waited in the water just for that purpose. Most of the fleeing partygoers fought their way through.

Slate was a seven-foot-tall monster all claws and teeth, gouging out furry clumps from Nirrin and his brother. I couldn't spot Canis; he must have gone after Brass at the forefront of the fleeing Guardians. I started to get the distinct feeling that they were herding us.

The cottage was on fire and Steel was limping just outside the door. The shadows of the inferno cast a gory backdrop over the already desolate scene. Steel raised his head to us and limped towards the river. I searched frantically for Indigo and spotted her long blonde braid swinging over Sterling's shoulder as he charged between the cottages towards the woods. I silently said a prayer more Crathode wouldn't be waiting on the south bend of the river.

Quick stood seeing Indigo slack in Sterling's arms and looked ready to jump out. I grabbed his hand and yanked him back down as Sage shot a cross bolt whizzing where his head had just been. His smile was wicked, and I threw up our barrier of air again.

Tawny screamed.

Steel had stumbled to the river where the Crathode were clamoring to get to him when Ash came to view from where he was fighting against Haarder at the Vetr cottage. Haarder clutched his side, thick red blood bubbled over his fingers. Ash searched for me and snarled when our eyes met before sending a fireball flying into Steel.

My intake of air caught in my throat as I gaped at the scene.

"We have to go back!" Tawny screeched as debris rained down.

The smoke cleared and where Steel had been only a crater. The air burst from my lungs unwittingly in a low groan that slowly grew higher and higher until I was shrieking louder than Tawny who was being restrained by Jett to keep from clawing her way out of the raft.

I forced more and more air from my lungs, far more than they could hold until I felt blood vessels bursting in my face and in my eyes. Then the Ymir rose before us in a tsunami thirty feet into the air high above the fires and fighting. Slate held Nirrin's throat in his jaws and shook his limp body. He stared up at the water and turned towards the west end of the river and fell on all fours.

Tusks jutted from its jaw, another set curved back from behind his ears while the third poked up from behind its pointed ears. A double row of off-white horns curved along its spine on a ten-foot-long frame. His muzzle was like a wolf's but his teeth, much longer. His body was bulkily muscled, thick across his chest and arms, but he moved with unnatural rippling grace. His long thick tail with a barbed tip trailed behind him as he broke out into a run.

There was no more air. I was empty. I released the wave.

Screams ripped through the night, but Sage and his troop were relentless. Water crashed over those near the cottages and I thought, if Steel had survived, I had given as much of an advantage as I could. No one swam better than Steel except for Indi who became one with the water.

The River Ymir no longer split around the sliver of land that housed the cottages. For a moment, I thought we were through the hardest part.

Sage lifted his crossbow with a malicious grin spreading over his face. My well of power was empty. I watched the bolt fly into the raft unable to stop it and the air hissed from the tear.

"Jump!" Jett shouted, and we leapt to the opposite side of the shore towards the woods.

My wall of air wavered as we leapt from the rubber raft that drifted flatly as we hit shore. From the moment our feet hit the frozen shore, we ran. Quick kept Tawny going with an arm on her back and Jett beside me using his long seax to deflect Sage's bolts. We ran blindly through the woods hoping to lose them.

Sage had our number. He had no intention of letting us go alive.

# CHAPTER 28
# GYPSUM

"Beryl and Crimson went to the greenhouse. He's attracted to her. I know that much. Who knows if it has staying power," I explained to Diamond as I dressed.

She had been quiet as of late, but tonight was different. The abandoned classroom we met in was a floor below my dormitory. We had to take extra precautions now that her and Sterling were married. It was officially an affair.

Diamond wasn't dressed for bed. I knew better than to ask for information she was unwilling to give. She wasn't mine. I grasped the crumbs she threw me and she begged me to take them.

"Walk me out?" she asked, pulling the taffeta dress over her corset and bustle; classic Mabon dress. She looked like she should be strolling the park with a parasol.

"Did you miss me?"

I saw her two days ago at the induction ceremony and we made love in a shadowed nook of the great hall. It wasn't enough. It was never enough.

Diamond smiled at me as she let her hair fall back from her hand to halfway down her back. "Of course. I always miss you, chief." She sighed. "It will be a longer break this time."

"Why's that?" I asked, annoyance making me bold.

She wrapped her hands around my neck and pressed her full lips to mine. "Because your cousin refuses to marry my brother."

It was my turn to sigh as I snaked my arm around her waist and led her from the room. "I don't know why you married him," I said for the millionth time. "You could have come to Thrimilci. I would have married you. You'd be wife to the Sumar patriarch. It's just as good as the Haust. Better, you have my word on that."

"It was arranged years ago. Your family cannot withstand another home wrecking scandal," Diamond said sadly.

"We could always run away together," I offered for the umpteenth time and she sighed anew.

The portal room was three floors above the classrooms. We walked in silence enjoying the closeness of one another as we went. Diamond paused before the room and licked her full lips.

"Kiss me one last time. I am sorry, chief. I would tell you if I could, but I swore a blood vow. This is the only way," she whispered.

Diamond pressed her mouth to mine. Her soft lips molding to mine until she withdrew and hastened away. I slowly withdrew to the wall and drew the shadows around me, sliding along the yellow stone as I entered the long room. I hid myself in the shadow next to the tapestry.

"We wait until they give us the word, then the university is under lock down. No one in, no one out except for pre-approved personages. Gypsum Sumar, Rosasite Sols, Beryl Sunna, and Malachite Blao are not permitted any access. I want a man on their rooms as soon as this is done. As for provosts, Every one of them is denied leave." Dahlia Natt looked to the black half masked men around her.

"Good. That goes double for Hawk Sumar, Sky, and Ford Tio. If any attempts escape. Kill them on sight."

My breath caught. Was this what Diamond wanted me to see?

Dahlia's pinched face turned to Diamond. "You are late. Your brother will be back soon and you do not want to get caught here if things go sour. You know your brother's temper," she said, looking more proud than I had ever seen her.

"Sour, how?" Diamond asked.

"Ash convinced Canis to give her one last chance to come willingly, if she does not, Ash will certainly make them feel his wrath. Sage went with as well."

Sage's presence made Diamond go rigid. "And Sterling?" she asked.

Dahlia looked at the men gathered. "We all have a part to play. Time for you to head home."

Diamond nodded and opened the vine carved door. With a flash of bright white light, she was gone.

"We shall need two men at every entrance and a patrol in all four wings to keep the tyros in order. The provosts will not become mutinous if the tyros are under guard."

Dahlia kept giving orders, but I had heard enough.

Never had I been more sure that I would die if I so much as exhaled too loudly. My path outside of the portal room was painstakingly slow. I wanted to run, to scream down the halls that we were all going to be prisoners if we didn't fight back. Scarlett would never agree to marry Ash.

Unless he threatened to kill us all. Which he was doing.

*Shit.*

I reached the stone steps and hopped on the stone railing, sliding down the flights of stairs to the men's first year wing. The halls were deserted this late at night, anyone sharing a bed would be in their throes for hours by now. I halted at the door to my room.

Zircon was Amber and Hunter's brother. A Snjar, and one of Ash's lackeys. A man was only as strong as his faith. I would have to lay my cards on the table and pray Scar's own faith was not in vain.

Malachite woke with unnatural alertness. Beryl hadn't returned from the greenhouse with Crimson. Unless he was walking her to the portal room. That certainly expedited matters.

"Odin's eye, Gyps," Malachite cursed. "What is it?"

"There are masked men guarding the portals. I think they're Stygians. We're on a list of people not allowed to leave the university grounds," I said in a hushed tone.

Malachite sniffed, but he was still smirking. "Your cousin is at the bottom of this. Zircon was right. Dead or crazy. Looks like the Prime went crazy. Are we waking the wildcard?" He nodded over to Zircon's sleeping form.

"No. We'll leave him and hope he isn't a Stygian. Come on. If Beryl is escorting Crimson home, he's headed right for them."

I opened my trunk pulling out my long seax and my short seax in its scabbard and my axe. It was my grandfather Flint's short seax and Scarlett had given me the axe for my eighteenth birthday. The wickedly sharp curved blade had Celtic braids etched along it, and a carved handle.

Malachite wore his two long seaxes crossed over his back and buckled bands of daggers around his biceps; Shadow Breakers and their blades.

**The halls were still vacant.** Malachite and I ran from the men's wing to the women's first year wing. Malachite knew exactly which room the girls were in and he looked at me guiltily when we reached the door.

"Gyps, I —"

"Ro and I haven't made one another any promises," I told him, cutting him short.

His nostrils flared as his usual smirk had a tightness to it. "I did not think you would mind since you were with Diamond tonight."

I cringed. "Best not say that again out loud. Ro knows there's another woman, but not who. For Diamond's sake, keep it quiet."

He mimed locking his lips and opened the door. The girl's room had the same set up as ours. All the rooms did with different scenes in their stained-glass windows.

"Ro. Get up." I shook her awake and started to explain what I overheard.

Malachite stood over Jade's sleeping form and their fourth room-mate, the ebony skinned girl. Mica was dressing after Malachite woke her.

"What about this one?" he asked, gesturing to Jade.

"Wake her. She will not like to be under anyone's thumb even if they say your cousin's husband killed her sister," Ro said, walking to her closet in her underwear and a cotton tank top. "That is Celestine. She is from Valla. We will need bodies." Ro said pragmatically as she tugged on her pants.

Mica walked over to Celestine and woke her while Malachite woke Jade.

I left them letting them know I had to go the provosts' offices and wake them before it was too late. Six tyros against the fifty or so masked men would mean a quick death for us. None of the provosts were on Dahlia's list to be spared. I hoped that meant we could trust them.

Fifteen minutes since I saw the group gathered in the portal room that felt like hours. I had to stop twice and hide when pairs of the masked men walked by on their way to bar exits. I thought it was strange that my dad was staying the night at the university. He never did, but now I saw the bigger picture. It had been planned.

They needed hostages and half the heirs would be at Valla U, the other half would be at Jett's birthday party. Anyone else left out was in on the scheme.

No one stood in the provosts' hall. I had only been once visiting my dad while he taught U.S. History. The Guardians thought themselves superior to myopics, or humans who didn't know about our world. At least some did like Dahlia Natt.

My father's office was covered in maps and items of pop culture. He began teaching the class in order to better inform those of us who wished to receive further education outside of Tidings about the rest of the world. For people who had never seen so much as a light switch or a car, it could be daunting.

The second room attached to his office had a small sitting room where a cot had been brought up for tonight. My father woke the moment I opened the door and sat up running a hand over his carefully trimmed goatee that retained all the raven color that had long left his hair.

"Gypsum? What's wrong?" he asked in a sleep thick voice before smoothing his pompadour away from his face.

"Dad, Ash and Sage went after Scar. Dahlia is locking down the university. She has men here guarding all the exits. They won't allow us to leave. I think they mean to imprison her," I told him and went into more detail about what I saw.

My father readied as I spoke. His lean dancer's form moved about the small room until he took off the long seax that rested on the plaque on the wall. He never used his weapons anymore. He taught; he didn't kill. I'd seen my father train a handful of times with the blade though and he was like a viper. Darting about in a graceful seamless dance with strikes you never saw coming. A shame really that all that talent was wasted telling ungrateful tyros about the DMV and job applications.

"I should have known better. I didn't question because of the tension between Ash and our family. None of the other provosts cared one way or the other when he asked us to stay late to go over our classes and not leave in case some tyros had a hard time adjusting. Tyros never have a hard time adjusting unless they're from outside Tidings. That is so rare we might see one outside student every five years. We have to alert Crag and Jackal. They would be the most vocal about a revolt and they will seek to silence them even if they are a Straumr and a Var." My father cursed and then apologized as he marched from the room.

I sucked in a sharp breath.

"What is it?" My father's dark eyes scanned the hall around me.

"Tawny. She's afraid and angry. She activated our bond," I said, unaccustomed to someone else's emotions in my mind.

Other than the day we first tried them out, we'd never had reason to use them. I was glad I knew she was okay, but I was rapidly discovering that her mood could fuse with my own. My heart was racing.

I retold what I saw in the portal room twice over before my father decided to rouse the provosts first and bring them all into Jackal's office. Eight provosts, three battle trainers, one headmistress, and me crammed into the small room when arguing erupted.

"Where is your wife?" River accused Fox.

"Nova is probably at the Straumr palace with her sister," Fox snapped back.

"He is too young to govern. Prone to childish fancies. So some girl does not want him, he would bring down our way of life because he has been scorned?" Boa Sunna asked scathingly.

"My niece is under attack as well. Ash is not the driving force behind the lockdown. This bickering gets us nowhere. I say we divide and root them out at once by any means necessary," Jackal said, gesturing with his hand as he sat cross-legged on the couch.

We had found Jackal and Crag together. Everyone knew the stoic eldest Straumr brother had fallen for Alder's brother who was several years his junior ending all hopes that Crag might one day be patriarch and Prime. He had been courting a few women at that time, but dropped all pretenses once Jackal came to be the Languages provost at Valla U. Neither the Vars nor the Straumrs approved.

"Agreed," my father was quick to announce.

Not everyone carried a weapon. These were the molders of young minds not the vanguard. Luckily, Crag, River, and Fox kept a healthy supply in their combined office.

"There are a few tyros who are ready. I can get them and those of you who don't go after the men at the doors can meet on the floor below the portal room so we can lock them," I explained.

They blinked at me as if they just remembered I was there until the cool eyed red head Wisteria, and Mica's mother, gave a brisk nod. "Sound idea. Magnolia and I will take the front doors with deadly force if necessary. I have no intention of letting them close our university again for fifteen years because of some lover's quarrel."

No one argued with her sentiment.

My father refused to let me go alone and secretly I was glad. Tawny was in a panic and suddenly she was in insurmountable pain. I tried to describe it to our father, but I felt as though my very soul was being ripped from my body. It wasn't a physical pain; it was an emotional anguish which I had never known the like. I hoped I'd never feel it first-hand.

"Steel or Scar. Your Shadow Breaker friends will have been bonded to Scar, ask them if their bonds snapped," my father said, swallowing. "Hurry. We have to get those portals back up so we can get to your mother and mine. Opal. By the Mother, the baby."

Spinel said a few things that led me to believe he'd known my father well and he certainly knew more than the average Guardian about Shadow Breakers which led me to believe there was a time before my mother that he'd known my father better than most.

My father picked up speed, and I trailed behind him. The Norns must have finally cut us a break because we narrowly missed running into a pair of masked men just outside the women's wing. If my father doubted my tale, he didn't after he saw the two men march past on patrol.

We slid past them once they rounded a corner and found the hall clear.

I opened the bedroom door to find everyone ready.

"The provosts are with us. We're going to head to the portal room and lock the portals. Those of you who wish to leave, may, but we intend to hold the university and keep it safe from any other attackers."

"We are ready," Mica said in her high falsetto.

On cat's paws, our group slinked along hallways and up the flights of stairs to meet the others. Tawny's emotions raging far away to the south all the while. Ro said her bond with Scar was still intact so that left Steel. I prayed Tawny was just being dramatic.

My heart lurched. "Beryl and Crimson. They're probably asleep in the greenhouse. I have to get them."

I'd completely forgotten about them. My father's dark eyes scanned mine.

"They're probably safer there than anywhere else. There's no way out except through the glass. We will have to barricade the greenhouse after we lock the portals."

I reluctantly agreed, and we set out once again.

"What is going on here?"

Malachite's force field shot up between us and the young man with skin the color of raw umber and long thick black hair that fell past his broad shoulders. The iridescent nimbus looked as if you could pop it with a poke of your finger, but I knew no weapon or *calling* could penetrate it. His round eyes so dark they looked void of color locked on my father.

My father drew himself up putting on his provost face and started to address the pajama clad student. It was a ruse. As soon as Malachite's force field fell, the young man shot out a fireball which I countered with a blast of wind he didn't expect. His body ignited and his screams tore through the hall.

None of us knew what to do next. I didn't think I was the only one who'd never watched a man die before. My dad had tried to extinguish the flames with water that steamed in the hall, but whatever talent the young man had made them burn until they incinerated everything in its path.

"How did you know he wasn't going to get a late-night snack?" Malachite asked me in disbelief.

"Onyx. He was a Stygian Knight. Scarlett warned me about him."

I stared at the young man only a year older than me I had just killed. I had killed tribesmen that were attacking me before, but never a man — a kid, really. Barely out of his teen years. Tawny's grief made it hard to breathe or was it my own?

I should have been shaking, feeling ill, something, but my nerves were still. I had a jolt of excitement just before I'd countered his *call*. Did that make me a psychopath?

My father placed his hand on my shoulder after he walked from the crispy corpse. "These friends of yours would have been as badly burned if he had succeeded. Great instincts, son," he said before we moved to the front of the group.

The provosts were lying in wait in an unused room. Crag's bald ebony head came into view when we neared and the provosts filed out. Resolve colored their faces. We would need it. We were outnumbered five to one, but we didn't know where loyalties laid with the other tyros.

As soon as we reached the level the ballroom and the portal room were on, we knew our discovery was imminent. The masked men were in the main hall with Dahlia and Basil. More men had joined them, things looked bleak.

"I have to get your mother. She is all alone," my father said as we waited around the corner for Crag's signal to charge.

Malachite cleared his throat. "Actually, Provost Sumar, Captain Dagr put a Breaker on his aunt when the Second was attacked."

My dad gave a tight distracted smile. Slate wasn't an easy guy to like, but my dad had always given him the benefit of the doubt because he was his best friend's son raised by his own mother and sister. There was pride in my father's face.

"I'll wait until we've got them beat," he said, giving me a reassuring smile.

I couldn't help but feel like I'd led all of these people to their deaths. Crag jumped out into the hall flashing a light so bright that when the masked men turned, they were blinded.

Our *calls* evaporated against them like mist. "They are wearing nix cuffs!" Ro cried as she parried a man wielding a long seax with her daggers.

Dahlia's eyes blazed, upper lip curling as she stood behind the line of fighting men. Blades flashed and sparked. She must not have felt the need to participate since we were grossly outnumbered with Magnolia and Wisteria having gone to rid the exits of their guards.

Fern Rot, who reminded me of my grandmother, used a pole arm she'd taken off the wall to beat away those nearest her. She'd positioned herself in front of her granddaughter, Mica, whose whip coiled around weapons' arms so others could dart in with their blades. Jade was one of those. She used two glinting short axes as if they were extensions of her arms.

The two Tio provosts fought beside their mother. Ford's claymore was given wide berth as he used both hands to swing with such force the men whose swords he connected with gritted their jarring teeth. Sky's left arm was nicked, blood dripped from his fingertips as he used a staff to whack and trip his opponents.

We neared the wide door to the portal room and five men marched forth from the bright white light. Hunter's predator eyes narrowed seeing us through the doorway and drew his blades.

"Secure the university. Incapacitate as many as you can!" Hunter shouted as he led the charge.

We retreated. My father at my side. He kept pushing me behind him as we fought. It was a paternal instinct I wasn't sure he was doing intentionally or not.

Hunter was in front of me and then he wasn't. I spun around in time to block his blade with my axe. He was a teleporter.

My father guarded my back as I spun back and forth trying to keep Hunter in front of me as he popped in and out of existence. Sounds of the fight all around me kept my senses muddled with the combination of Tawny's debilitating anguish.

Hunter's laughter mocked me as I spun to my right only to spin directly into his outstretched blade. I groaned, determined not to cry out and distract the others.

"Do not worry, Sumar. You shall meet your uncle in the afterlife," Hunter said with a twist of his lips.

I clamped a hand over the wound in my stomach. They never can quite describe how badly it feels to be gutted. How Scarlett had survived so many horrific wounds was beyond me. It was something that must be experienced to appreciate how excruciating it felt, but I wouldn't recommend it.

Hunter's bloody seax coiled back in his hand and I raised my axe to block his thrust.

Hunter's eyes went wide. His neck corded, mouth slack. He crashed to his knees and fell forward. An axe was buried in his skull. I lifted my head to find Zircon looking down at his dead brother. He yanked the axe from his brother's skull with a sickening sucking sound.

My father turned to me and pressed his hand over mine healing me. "He said Steel is dead."

It was the first thing that came to mind when the pain faded.

Zircon wiped the axe on his brother's back. "Bad blood. Him and my sister. Always trying to keep up with the schemes of greater families. Power at any cost will cost you everything."

He raised his aquamarine eyes to mine in his savage face, daring me to judge him. White light showered over us as a shadow loomed from one of the portal doors.

"It's Slate!" I yelled before anyone could attack him.

The seven-foot-tall beast man shifted its frightening horned head to me and flashed me finger long fangs in what I thought was a smile. He tossed back his head. His human mane of black waves fell from his head as his body rippled. An unearthly roar bellowed from his deep chest.

"I'm leaving now for your mother. Send Storm-pale to us if you need to send word. Start closing the portals now." My father embraced me as if for the last time and his mint scent blended with sweat and blood made me feel as though we faced the apocalypse. "You have saved hundreds if not thousands of lives tonight, Gypsum. I'm proud of you."

My throat clenched and I couldn't utter a word as he swung open a portal door and was swallowed by the white light.

"Start locking the portals!" I shouted to no one in particular but couldn't start doing them myself since I had no idea how to even begin.

Slate was ripping apart the last of the masked men. Zircon had gone with Beryl, who appeared towards the end of the fight, and Malachite to root out the other Stygian Knights. I started to heal those injured. By some miracle, none of ours had died.

Slate's charcoal grey body towered over me. "Do not forget the Prime's portal."

"Is it true? Is Steel dead?" I asked, trying to get a grip on what I was doing leaning over a tyro who must have heard the fight and came to our aid because I'd never seen him before.

There were a dozen more tyros that had rushed out in their pajamas with nothing but their blades to fight the masked men. That they'd chosen to fight with the provosts instead of against them spoke volumes of the kind of respect they held for them.

Silver human eyes in a beast's face softened as much as they could. "It is unlikely he survived. I must go. You did well, chief."

"Chief?" I asked, cocking my head.

Memory blocked Slate did not have the soft spot for me that old Slate did. He never spoke to me if he didn't have to.

"Memories. It was Ash all along," he growled with a snarl.

I inhaled sharply, "Does Scarlett know? Did you see her when you got them back?"

"She is with Tawny, Jett, and Quick. I do not know when this will blow over. Until then, keep the tyros safe. We are moving the portals into the arenas and trying to evacuate as many people from the town hearts as we can. Valla is overrun with Anguillan. Do not let anyone go there. Be brave," Slate said as he stalked back towards one of the open portals.

"Where are you going? What about Indi?" I called after him.

"She is with Sterling. Elivagar."

"Sterling?" My stomach twisted.

"Why?" Slate stopped, sensing my mood change and turned back to me.

"Sterling is with the Stygians," I whispered.

# CHAPTER
# TWENTY-NINE

The midnight sky turned a Byzantium purple as night slowly fell to day. We hadn't slept, and we were still running. We had to go deeper into the nameless woods beyond the cottages to try to lose Sage and his mix of twenty Stygians and Crathode. No Jorogumo were with him or we would have been caught ages ago. They could skitter across the ground twice as fast as we could run all except for Quick, but not in the state he was in after all the fighting.

"Come on, Tawny. We've got to keep going. Every step they fall behind is one closer we are to getting away," Jett said, urging her forward.

Our legs were stiff and tired. We long ago stopped healing one another's muscle aches for fear of draining our energy. At least Tawny had stopped crying. That was something. Guilt weighed heavy on my heart. Their sheer arrogance boiled my insides. They'd given us those precious minutes knowing even if we collected ourselves, they would still beat us.

Slate and Brass were safe and Steel was a crater. Tawny spoke enough to let us know Gypsum was safe and that he had been injured but was healed. Quick said Indigo was sleeping and had not been injured in the slightest. For some odd reason, that boosted my mood. At least one of us was unscathed.

The forest floor was flat covered with all types of frozen plants and dusted with a light layer of glittering snow that crunched with every step of our boots. There was no time to grieve. There was no time to think about all the things I would have done differently. There was no time to wonder if Sparrow and Hawk were reunited. If Pearl evacuated the town heart before they were ambushed. If anyone at Valla U was killed. If Thrimilci was entirely run over with Anguillan and Jorogumo. Would Spinel be arrested for having been close to me?

Every worst scenario ran through my mind as we walked in the bitter cold.

"Did anyone pack food?" Quick asked.

His stomach rumbled so loudly I could hear it over my breathing which was quite the feat. Tawny pulled out a set of apples from her pack and handed them to Jett. He tossed one back to Quick and started to eat one himself.

I thanked Quick for the half-eaten apple, took two bites and handed it back.

"You should eat," Quick said, knitting his brows.

"I've *called* too much. I need rest, not food," I murmured tonelessly.

He didn't argue. I was the only one still using my elemental ability to keep everyone from getting frostbite as we walked.

Amethyst and Cherry were safe, except Jett said they were extremely upset. Panicking, was the word he used. Since then, Jett had a short fuse. I couldn't blame him. I didn't blame any of them. I was trying to stay out of everyone's line of sight. Quick was the only one bothering to talk to me.

An early onset of survivor's guilt, I decided.

Where did Ash go? Was he burning Thrimilci to the ground or Elivagar? Tawny was so grief stricken by Steel, I doubted she had thought about what was happening in her lands at all.

"Is there some kind of castle manager or steward... a constable that would be looking after Elivagar's needs?"

My gravelly voice sounded forced as I tried to raise to draw Tawny's attention. She kept on, lumbering beside Jett, and I worked saliva into my throat so I could speak louder.

I repeated myself and she stopped. Jett paused to look at her, dark circles under his eyes from lack of sleep and exhaustion. Quick's weren't quite as bad, but his normally glittering eyes were puffy.

"Don't speak to me. For the rest of this nightmare, I don't want to hear your voice."

Tawny's shoulders moved as she gritted out the words and I frowned at her back. We never argued. Never fought. We'd been best friends from birth, closer than sisters. The tone she was using was better left for...well, how I imagined I would sound when I finally got Sage alone.

"I'm sorry, Tawny. I had no idea —"

She whirled around. Her milky white skin red and tear stained. Her wide hazel eyes bloodshot and much more swollen than Quick's. Her lips trembled as she spoke.

"You couldn't keep your legs closed. Ash? Are you sugarfooting me? *Ash*? What did you think would happen when you said, 'Whoops, didn't mean to lead you on after I let you fiddlestick me.'? Do you have to sleep with *everyone*?! Slate would have been with you if you weren't so busy sleeping with his best friend! Brass would have been with you if you hadn't been fooling around with his grandfather, or was it Cory or Ash? I can't keep track anymore! I'm lucky Steel is your uncle or you would've slept with him too or Jett or Gyps! Careful, Quick. You're the only one she hasn't invited into her bed."

Her chest rose and fell heavily as she seethed. If looks could kill... I worked my throat trying to loosen the lump that had formed under her diatribe. An awkward sob came out instead of words and Tawny spun around with a whirl of her cloak and started walking once again.

"Frigga's sweet grass, Tawny. Take it easy. She's pregnant for the Mother's sake," Quick said.

"So am I," Tawny practically snarled.

"What?" I asked, forgetting her warning.

"It's what Steel whispered to me before we parted. We've barely been trying for a month. I thought it would take longer," she said, sounding far away in her own thoughts and misery.

Jett veered to wrap an arm around her shoulder as they walked. I could hear him murmuring softly to her and sighed. Tawny wasn't the only one who thought those things, she was just the only one who didn't have to worry about me snapping back or slapping her. I doubted, if I lived long enough, she'd be the last.

"Do not listen to her. She has a tongue like a razor blade when she is upset," Quick murmured.

"I know," I said woodenly.

That tongue was always used to defend me, never against me. In high school, we were younger than all the other kids. No one bullied me, but if a catty girl had thought to say a comment in passing, Tawny was quick with a biting retort. Her reputation of being a spitfire preceded her when we'd gone to the default college all the kids who hadn't gone away to school had gone to. Don't mess with Tawny Dagr — Tawny Vetr, since she took her father's last name.

Movement caught my eye ahead. We were traveling south west to try to get back to the arena portal while staying away from the Ymir River. Then I was getting lifted off my feet by Quick. Jett scooped Tawny up and was running at full speed.

"Hold tight," Quick said breathlessly as he caught up to Jett.

I wound my arms around his neck. His longer strides took a sharp southern turn, and I saw the source of the movement. Through the forest of bare skeletal trees whose limbs did little to hide the grey cloudy sky, were a score of Jorogumo. It explained why there weren't any with Sage. He'd sent them ahead to trap us.

"We're running out of island," I warned.

"I think that is the idea. The Valkyries are straight south. We will try to claim sanctuary. Your and Tawny's pregnancies may help us after all," he said in a jostled voice. "Maybe Indigo and Sterling arrived there already." But Indigo hadn't moved.

They couldn't keep up their speed much longer, not while carrying us. We'd have to make a stand. There was no way we could outrun them. The segmented bodies of the Jorogumo were fully visible now with their pinchers and skittering legs. Some had human torsos of varying shades, some furred, others had a slick armored look to them. All had more sets of eyes than anyone should and none had hair. The Jorogumo that had the bodies of spiders, big round backs and bald human heads disturbed me the most. Their bodies should have been impossible.

Jett let out a whoop. "Straight ahead!"

A massive white gate barred our way. Tawny was shouting for someone to come open them far before we reached the curving white iron. Quick and I reached the gate and saw the guardhouses were empty. The sky was turning a brilliant golden orange with the sun's rise, but it was too early for the Valkyries.

Jett set Tawny down and started kicking the gates and screaming. Far beyond the gates we could make out a compound. We would be long dead before they reached us.

Tears of frustration poured down Tawny's cheeks.

Quick had started *calling* blades of air at the Jorogumo, but with how weakened he was, they barely penetrated their exoskeletons.

"A lake! Can Jorogumo swim?" I asked, springing my wrist blades.

"We're about to find out," Jett called back as he ran towards the end of the fence.

"It is the ocean, not a lake. There is nowhere left to go!" Quick shouted.

The Jorogumo were nearly to us. Sage's smug face was discernible as they grew closer with the Crathode claws snapping, readying for the kill. They would tear Jett and Quick to pieces.

Small stone slabs were skimmed by the ocean's water. Fifty yards from the shore, was an arch.

"I think it's a portal. I can open it," Tawny said, hopping from the shore and onto the first stone.

It looked like it would bob in the water, it shouldn't have been floating to begin with, but it stayed solidly in place. Tawny was hopping from stone to stone.

"How can you open it if it even is a portal? If not, we'll be trapped out there," Jett asked, hopping into the water behind her.

Quick shoved me towards the stones and I realized they were shaped like lily pads. This was intentional, that portal had to be like the one in Karkinos. It would only lead to and from one place.

"Orion had two access keys. One for him and one for Cassiopeia. He took hers back years ago so only he had the ability to open and lock portals in an instant," Tawny explained.

I hopped on the second stone and Quick leapt onto the first *calling* to deflect the cross bolts Sage was firing our way.

"Who has the other?" Jett asked stupidly.

"Steel," Tawny said, and I could *feel* her suffocating sorrow.

"Where will you go now? Ash said you were clever. He has *always* been wrong about you!" Sage called out to me.

Below the stone pads, the water was clear and so deep, I couldn't see the bottom. There was this chill that crept up my spine when I gazed at its watery depths. Something very dangerous lurked down there. This place was not for swimming.

Tawny was at the door and she placed her hand at the base of the door after testing it. It had been locked, but now it was glowing. Sage was shouting orders behind us. I waited on the stone lily pad behind Jett *calling* with every bit I had left to create a solid wall of air Sage's bolts relentlessly struck as he taunted.

"Run away! There is nowhere for you to go. Hunter was waiting for our signal and by now has secured Valla University with all the provosts inside. Gypsum will be a hostage along with all the other lesser family tyros *you* conveniently put in rooms together. Pearl, Spinel, Reed, Sparrow, Cordillera — everyone on the outside you hold dear was apprehended the moment Hunter relayed your noncompliance. Opal will be raised by my wife and me. Our grandmother is a Geol after all."

Sage was trying to distract us as the Crathode waded out into the water. Jett's face grew hard as he looked at Sage.

"Over my dead body," Jett ground out.

Sage pouty lips curled. "That is the idea. Yours and Cerise's while Amethyst is given to Hunter Snjar for all his good work. Even Canis draws a line at killing fertile greater family daughters. A greater family bride. A Geol? More than he could ever have dreamed. There will not be a soul to avenge your precious *Cherry* if you leave. Viper Enox was among our list of those to be apprehended. You have no one left. Elivagar is ripe for the taking. No one to defend it if you leave, Tawny. *But* the best is what we have planned for precious Indigo. How convenient for Sterling to be at the party knowing Regn would be accompanying her. Indigo was always a compliant daughter. Sterling will fill her belly with a barghest hybrid son and with the Dagr blood from Gypsum, we have all the pieces of the puzzle. Except for those stones you wear around your neck. Give them to me and we will let your children be birthed before we obliterate all your memories and give you to Ash as his own personal khoraz."

Sage reached out his hand as if I would toss my necklace to him. Quick had gone completely rigid.

"You are wrong. Sterling has never been a barghest with Indigo," Quick said in aggravation.

Sage's watery blue eyes looked amusedly at Quick. "Not *yet*, but we told him it was the only way we would let them be together and keep the child. He does not need to be in barghest form to plant his seed. You were more of a threat than he bargained for."

"It's open!" Tawny cried out.

"Quick! Don't listen to that asshole. He'll get his," Jett said.

Quick inhaled sharply and leapt to my stone pedestal with a twist of his big powerful body. Jett jumped in unison, grabbing Tawny under her arm. I swayed above the water and looked down to see a serpent with a mouth as big as I was tall barreling towards us. I yelped as Quick locked his arms around me and leapt once... twice and knocked into Jett, throwing all four of us through the silver arch.

Sage shouted as the white light embraced us.

# CHAPTER 30
# INDIGO

Silver's face, haggard and woeful flashed in my mind followed by Scarlett's. Hers was strained and afraid, her hair a wild nest around her beautiful face. Then there was Jett. Teeth gritted looking determined, but so tired.

I gasped and rolled into a ball. All my bonds snapped at once causing such a sharp pain it had forced me awake. Why was I sleeping?

"Indi. It is okay. You are safe." Sterling's reassuring voice soothed me, and I burst into tears.

"They're dead. They're all dead. Scar, Jett, and Silver."

I choked on Silver's name unable to believe that last night we'd been making love happier than either of us had ever been and this morning he was dead. I opened my eyes to find Sterling lying in the bed next to me. His violet eyes filled with sympathy. He held a murky blue drink in his hand and gave it to me. I was parched and didn't second guess the citrusy beverage.

"It is a cocktail of rousen and marawacian. I thought you might need a little time before you started to process all that happened. I am sorry, Indi," Sterling rasped.

I couldn't stop crying. The drink strangled me as I gulped it gagging in the process. Sterling took the glass from me and placed it on the nightstand. The bed was simple for Tidings, carved wood, but only queen sized with a bronze and ivory Damascus bedspread. The room wasn't tiny, but it wasn't like the sprawling rooms of a castle or palace.

"We are at the Haust cottage. They will not think to look for you so closely," he said leaning on his side again. "Indi, please do not cry. I promise to take care of you," he said softly and produced a kerchief for me.

I wiped at my nose and dabbed under my eyes. "I can't believe they're dead. What happened?" I squeaked out.

"After you fainted? Everyone ran. Your uncle hung back instead of Slate who was goaded by Sage into the battle early and I believe a rafter or the ceiling must have collapsed on him because he did not make it far from the cottage. I am sorry about your family."

A soft ray of sunlight cut through the clouds to come in the window across from the bed. I was having a hard time finding the silver lining in all this. My body was raked with sobs and Sterling pulled me against him. It was such a familiar place for me. He'd been holding me so intimately for years.

Sterling kissed the top of my head. "I missed you. I wish it were under different circumstances, but I am happy to get to hold you again."

There was no one to betray by letting myself be held and kissed. Silver was gone, they were all gone. What would I do now?

Sterling was still kissing me. He trailed his kisses down my cheek and over my lips, his body leaning over where I laid.

"I love you, Indi. Gods, I have missed you. I should have married you, family or not. Betrothal be damned. I will never live it down." His kisses pressed along my neck, his breath tickling the fine hairs making my skin prickle. "Let me soothe you. I want to comfort you." He breathed as he popped buttons open along my shirt.

If I tried to speak, a sob would tear free. Instead, I ran my hands down the hard muscles of his back. Sterling moaned against my mouth.

"I want you to be mine, Indigo. Only mine," Sterling said against my lips.

I shut my eyes. I would do anything to end the pain.

I fainted. How could I have done that to my family?

I was the second strongest after Scarlett and I had done nothing to help us escape. When Sage told her he had been the one to push our mother over the balcony and to ambush our father, stabbing Scarlett's unborn child in the same night it was like my mind rejected it so completely it had just shut down. I was raised with Sage as his adopted sister. He was cruel and callous, but a murderer? Even if I could understand why he thought he wanted to kill my mother, but our father? Was it because he made Jett heir over him? Sage couldn't be an heir, he had to know that, he didn't have the right temperament. Canis and Cygnus were brothers and Cygnus's rule never diminished Canis's in any way.

*Silver.*

No wonder Scarlett had been so adamant about Slate being alive. By the Mother, Scarlett and Jett. I'd lost everyone. Everyone except for Sterling.

He felt the moment I surrendered to him. His eyes so blue they were almost purple, glowed against his darkening skin. I watched as his ears grew pointed and mouth elongated into a snout. The bed bowed from the mass he put on as muscles bulged in his normally tightly muscled chest. A chest that was covered in sleek silvery grey fur.

There wasn't a series of snapping and popping of bone and sinew as he grew, but a smooth flowing transition. The only sign of exertion was a sheen of sweat over his fur. Not even when two sets of horns forced their way from his scalp, one set curling like a ram's, another jutting up like a goat's. A set of tusks for goring pushed from his jaw and he breathed heavily, his apprehension was palpable.

Scarlett made love to Slate like *this*?

"I have only ever made love to you and Diamond. I can do this with one woman for the rest of my life," Sterling said in an unusually coarse voice.

His human eyes above his canine like snout searched my face. We were one another's firsts. I had taken that from Diamond Natt. I relished taking something else away from Ash's sister even if she wasn't the one who orchestrated the ambush.

I cupped his furred face and carefully brought my mouth to his soft lipped snout. It was as much invitation I would give him before he introduced me to a claiming.

# CHAPTER 31

# GYPSUM

There were so many empty rooms at Valla U during classes. Crag and Sky were running the university for the time being and gave the tyros the week off, but intended on teaching classes, if a bit differently, as soon as they could.

I didn't bother knocking on the girls' door. I knew she wouldn't respond. It had been a bad day. The last two days had been terrible.

Basil was caught in the crossfire on the night of the ambush and was found dead in the carnage. We had killed the Patriarch Straumr and not even known it. Crag, River, and Fox were building his pyre in the greenhouse to hold a mass funeral for all the fallen men since they decided not to destroy the tunnel that led to it. We would need to keep growing food there to survive so we barricaded the stained glass as best we could and soon found that it had been made of the same material Scar used on her arenas. *Calling* couldn't penetrate the university.

Dahlia had gotten away.

After breakfast, I had sent out a message with Storm-pale to my father in Thrimilci and another with Drill-tooth to the Vanaheim arena. Storm-pale had been waiting for word from my father and I had gotten his letter within hours of him writing it. Pearl, Reed, and Spinel were having a clandestine meeting with Cordillera in Ostara at the Regn manor the night of the ambush and no one had heard from them since the portals were either closed or guarded.

My mother was safe. My father reached her in time and brought her and the Dagr staff out to the Sumar palace. When he went into the town, he evacuated as many as he could, sending them to the arena on the island. They had already been alerted somehow and were in a line for the portal gate with Solder shouting orders at the end.

The gods only knew what would have happened without the *calling* protected arenas. Problem was, Opal had gone missing. My father said the girls had shown up and were beside themselves. Amethyst had left again, but no one knew where. Cherry was alone. She was bonded to Jett and must have known he was dead too.

The Shadow Breakers, Brass, and Slate had gotten a few people out of Valla. There was no word from Elivagar. Mabon and Ostara were under Stygian control. Canis's control.

"Hey," I said, shutting the door behind me.

It had snowed and the stained-glass ceiling didn't allow any sunlight into the gloomy room. Mica pointed up to the stained glass. A man made of night and a woman made of day embraced in a sinuous line made up the colorful art.

"Wind Dagr and Storm Natt. Since then, Dagr and Natt lines have always been female. Slate breaks that tradition. I have heard you talking to Malachite about a project and pieces. You mean Storm's pieces, right? They almost ended our world. It seems like it is happening all over again, does it not? All for power. Because one person thinks they could do it better than another when working together would be the best for everyone. Stupid, really," Mica murmured, not bothering to move from her bed.

I stepped into the room and she scooted over on her bed that was nestled in the alcove between the braided yellow stone pillars. I kicked off my boots and laid down on my back next to her folding my hands on my stomach.

"How is my grandmother?" she asked in a small voice.

I swallowed. "Not good. They are setting up camp outside the university, preparing to try to starve us out. Our — their bodies are already on the pyre," I told her, and I felt the bed move as she nodded.

There was no longer any doubt. We were at the beginning of a civil war. If the trails of smoke into the air from the town's heart wasn't enough sign of the small rebellion that had been put down there, then Canis, Cygnus, and Dahlia parading out Reed and Pearl onto the university grounds before the gods and all the tyros had done it.

Spinel and Cordillera weren't with them and I held out hope that they were alive. When Drill-tooth returned from Vanaheim, I'd know for certain.

Canis demanded the university's surrender. If not, then they would execute the traitors.

*Traitors? The bastards.*

They had come up with a ludicrous list of accusations for almost every person I loved. They were convinced Steel was dead. Not just Steel though, but Jett, Quick, Scar, and Tawny as well. I could confirm Tawny. Her face bore the same expression in my nightmares as when our bond snapped. Malachite and Ro had both confirmed Quick and Scar.

I put that in the letter to my father and in the one I sent to where I hoped Cordillera had fled to at the Vanaheim arena.

Reed was Sky's father, Fern's husband, Mica's grandfather. Half his family was in the university. It wasn't hard to discern his feelings towards their demands. He'd hugged Pearl fiercely and a few rapid words were said between them before Reed held up his head regally to his descendants that crowded the windows of the castle where he was Second until a few months ago. He gave a slice of his head and dropped to his knees. Canis made a point of having a countdown until he received his answer, but no one gave him one.

Reed's body was burning on a pyre outside the university.

He gave us until noon before he marched Pearl out. The other tyros had made room for me so I could see her. She looked more dignified than any queen ever had, even on her knees in her fine dusky blue silk. Her emerald eyes found me and I had blinked at tears. She smiled in a way only grandmothers could that let you think everything would be all right.

Pearl's body was burning on a pyre beside Reed's.

I'd put that in the letter too. How do you tell your father his mother was beheaded on the lawn of our university by her scorned suitor? I was a coward and only watched until she looked away. I'd sank to the floor and covered my mouth with a hand. Then again, I didn't think she wanted me to witness her death. More than my fair share of nightmares replayed in my mind's eye and what I saw was enough to add to them.

"How are *you*?" Mica asked in her high falsetto voice.

I wondered idly if she sang. People thought of the most ridiculous things while under duress. I ran my hands over my unwashed hair, letting the copper beads slip past my fingers.

"Not good. I don't think Spinel escaped. I bet they brought him down to the arena and did the same thing to him there. Tell me they would've killed the provosts, a bunch of tyros... *something*," I asked her, sighing. "Tell me I didn't just watch my grandmother and great uncle die to hold on to a bunch of old stones. My sister is dead, her husband, my cousins, and my good friend. I need some good news." I tried to keep my voice from wavering. "My cousin who died... his daughter is missing."

Mica shifted on the bed, wafting the smell of loquat and orchids to my nose. It was a sweet, girlish scent that suited her. I could feel her deep brown eyes on the side of my face and I turned to meet them.

"Whoever controls the university, controls Tidings. It is the only access point to Karkinos and the seat of power. It is why the Prime's office is here. They could parade out whomever they wish and we never would have gotten the people to agree to give it up. I am sorry about your family. At least your parents are alive," she said, resting her palm over my laced hands.

Her ivory skin seemed luminescent in the dark room. A pink cupid's bow mouth seemed brighter against her fair skin. Her blunt cut bangs fell to the side where her fiery red hair laid like silk over her pillow. She was average height, but thin and elegant so it made her look taller.

"Keep telling me that. I just sent a message to my father about what happened. I'm not looking forward to the response," I confided.

She gave me a sympathetic smile. "My mom is lucky her twin and her family are here. There are a lot of children, and those who recently graduated who were at the Tio palace. I have no idea if they are all right."

"I'm sorry, Mica. I'm being selfish," I murmured as I started to swing my legs over her bed.

Her grip tightened over my hands. "Stay… for a short while longer. Please."

I followed the trail her tongue took along her lower lip. Everyone sought comfort in different ways. I wasn't upset with Ro or Malachite for their fling, but I wouldn't be going to Ro's bed anytime soon. Word was, he wasn't either. He didn't know if his family was alive and there was no way to find out.

I shifted on her bed and she let her hand fall from my chest as her eyes flitted between mine. I brushed her bangs over her face and bent my mouth down to hers. She inhaled sharply as she canted her chin up. My hair was unbound and fell over my shoulder to click softly as it framed the side of her face.

I could feel her heart pounding in her chest against my own. I waited for that moment. Her tongue slid along mine as I kissed her. Her hands rose to stroke my hair. Women couldn't seem to help the gesture.

Then I felt that moment. She melted. Her body simultaneously wriggling and offering itself to me.

My own desire shocked me. I liked Mica. Ro had given me crap about it when I saw her after the induction ceremony. The svelte red head wasn't my type, but she had something sweet and soft and, most importantly, genuine I couldn't resist. I wanted it for myself.

Balder's brow, I was becoming Slate.

She moaned against my mouth as I shifted on the bed to lower myself between her slim thighs. She kept her hands on my shoulders or in my hair as we kissed and I thought she must be nervous. That would explain why her pulse was racing.

I leaned back and pulled my shirt over my head and her eyes ran over my chest. I'd worked hard on my body the last two years. Every day without fail and the look on her face made it all worth it.

Damn I was glad Hunter hadn't killed me.

My hand slipped between us working on her pants as we kissed. Her skin was even softer than it looked and I could not stop touching it. She lifted her hips as I pushed her pants down. Her kisses grew more frenzied. Her high moans promised a symphony once things heated.

She still hadn't touched me. Maybe a little more warm-up before the game started.

I slid my lips from hers and gently rolled up her cotton shirt to reveal her flawless skin except for a sprinkling of freckles between her breasts that fit perfectly in my hand when I cupped them. She let out a shuddering breath as she squirmed.

*Now.*

I pushed my pants past my hips and took her hand from my face as I rose to kiss her again. I placed her palm against me and moaned. She gasped.

"I will go slow," I promised her.

She licked her lips and scanned my face. "I do not think I can..."

I smiled feeling a bit more than a little flattered. "I promise to wait until your body adjusts."

She shook her head, still holding me between my legs.

"We don't have to, Mica," I said, feeling like a pervert.

"No, I was shaking my head because... there are no others, Gypsum. I do not think..." Mica's eyes dropped, and I felt her run her fingertips over me as if to verify what she thought she saw.

"Oh," I said moronically, and shifted from her, pulling her shirt back down.

I began to dress in a hurry. I'd never been someone's first. There was Shale, but she'd been making love to Ama for years. She'd just not slept with a man. They'd made such crap out of Scarlett last year for not having a lover. I didn't think it was common place.

Mica was probably saving herself for a better husband and was feeling vulnerable. I was about to exploit that.

By the Mother, I *was* Slate.

"Don't worry about it. You should... save yourself for someone you love, Mica. Not some creep who invited himself into your bed you hadn't even kissed before." I offered her a smile over my shoulder as I tugged my shirt on and got up to collect her pants that I had kicked haphazardly onto the floor.

Mica didn't respond, but nodded, looking at her jumble of pants and underwear after she pulled a sheet over herself. I sat down on the bed next to her and kissed her cheek.

"I can still hang out here with you, if you want," I offered, but she shook her head.

I was ashamed to be relieved as I left her room.

# CHAPTER 32
# INDIGO

When our mother died. Scarlett was practically catatonic. She didn't talk for days and would only eat or venture out if Slate made her. I never understood it until half my family died.

Silver had been my rock when Sage killed our father and Scarlett's capture had kept us all distracted from the pain of his death. I wouldn't eat unless Sterling brought it to the bed. I only showered if he was with me, and I never spoke.

There was nothing to say.

I was grieving my sister, my brother, and the man I was going to marry. Sterling knew this but didn't seem to mind as he took care of me. We'd never spent so much consecutive time together and under different circumstances, I would have been elated. Sterling waited on me hand and foot. He'd had the upper hand in our relationship since day one and now he was making up for it.

He was more relaxed and comfortable than I'd ever seen him. No one to sneak in on us, catching us. The cynical voice in me had thought it was part of the appeal, but being with Silver taught me that the best days were lazy ones when we spent all day making love and talking about nothing. It was a thrill in itself to bask in someone's unconditional love for you.

His barghest form didn't bother me, though there was no such thing as love making with a beast like that. I hadn't taken another cocktail since the first morning. Three days later, I found my traitorous self happy to have Sterling to wake up beside.

And the sex.

Not in all our years together had he made love to me the way he had been. He *had* missed me. He knew he was losing me and it had made him appreciate what we had.

"I love you, Indi," Sterling breathed as he lifted his forehead from my sweat slicked shoulder.

I kissed him deeply. I didn't know if I would ever say those words to him again. Even if I did love him, it had changed. I ran my thumb along his high cheek bone and he withdrew with a lazy smile.

"You are so beautiful, Indigo. I cannot believe how much I have been missing. I feel good for once. Are you hungry?" Sterling asked, pulling the sheet with him as he shifted to lay beside me.

His fingertips brushed my hair from my face and I nodded. He kissed my lips and hopped from the bed. I would've given anything to have this with him a year ago. I watched him tug on his pants and give me an impish grin before swiping a hand over his shimmering chocolate brown hair that bespoke what we were up to on an hourly basis.

I curled up on my side and tried activating my bonds again once he left the room. He had been so determined to make me his, but Tio women were cursed. We were never allowed to love for long.

A pan clanked in the kitchen and footsteps pounded on the stairs. Sterling burst into the room and began to barricade the bedroom door.

"Indigo, I am so sorry. Get up, get dressed. You have to run. Please! Hurry!"

Sterling didn't have to say another word. I leapt from the bed and pulled on the clothes he'd laid out for me on the dresser in hopes I would want to get up one of these days. I stepped into my borrowed underwear and snug grey pants and managed to clasp the bra around my chest when shards of the door blasted over Sterling.

I grabbed my boots off the floor and was shrugging into a powder blue sweater when I was bound with ropes of air at the open window. I struggled against them, trying to cut through the *call*, but it was more than one man.

I clenched my jaw as Sage and Ash walked in followed by ten men including my grandfather and my great uncle. The ropes fell. I walked over to Sterling, knowing escape would be impossible from the four powerful men and began to remove the splintered shards from his skin and heal him.

"Come along, dear. We are running behind schedule. Your sister has gone and killed herself and lost us the pieces. We are going to try to find her body even if we have to kill that serpent and dive into the depths of the ocean to get them," Cygnus said, beckoning me over with a curl of his fingers.

It had been said Cygnus was dashing in his youth. Tall, blonde, blue eyed with a strong square jaw just like Jett and Alder. It was reflected in his looks even now.

Canis scoffed. "We shall send that octopus woman, Vanna'ra, into the depths."

I knew that name. She was the ring leader of the Merfolk who had betrayed their king to transport the portals to other islands giving the Minotaur, Jorogumo, and Crathode access to lands that were not theirs.

"I would rather die," I ground out, and held myself proudly as Sterling straightened at my side.

My first words I'd spoken in a week held steel.

Cygnus laughed. "You were always so much like your father. It was a wonder none of us knew your true patronage years ago. Why, we would have married the two of you straight away and avoided all of this ugly business."

"My father — your grandson murdered," I said through clenched teeth.

Cygnus smile slipped. "Not what I would have done or consented to. Alder was my heir and my son, but what is done is done."

Sage stepped forward with Ash and I retreated, wishing I had my bow on me. I'd lost it all in the cottage. *Calling* was futile, but I didn't care if I lived anymore.

"No! Indi!" Sterling cried, his face a mask of horror.

"Why not?"

I could *call* enough to burn all of them and myself with it. Canis looked coolly at Sterling.

"Yes, Haust. Why not, indeed?" he asked.

Sage's hand darted out and caught me around the middle. Not ungently, and he laughed.

"Well done, Sterling. I did not know if she would let you." Sage laughed, his slick hair catching the sunlight.

"She is pregnant." Ash had his finger tips on my wrist.

As I stood in my stunned stupor, I did not see him come up beside me.

"You promised," Sterling pleaded, pushing past Ash to stand beside me and drawing me away from Sage.

If there were such a thing as a good and evil twin, it could be said that Canis was evil, but Cygnus had never been good. He had only been less bad. When it came to finesse though, Cygnus was the one who took charge.

"She will not be harmed." He nodded. "As long as she does not resist, we will put her own in her old room where we can care for the child and as agreed, you may keep it and Indigo as your paramour until we can find her a suitable husband. We promised Amethyst to Hunter, but he was killed and all we have is you, dear."

"That was not what you promised. You said if we conceived, we could be on our own, unharmed, until you needed us. You said nothing about taking her away or about marrying her off. I will not lose her again," Sterling said threateningly.

"Sterling?"

My voice had come out a croak after not using it the past few days. Sterling spun, hearing the recrimination in the one word.

"Indi, they were going to attack, anyway. I had to find a way to protect you," he said in a rush as I backed away from him.

"You could have warned us," I accused.

Sterling's face fell with a heavy exhale. "You know who my mother and father are."

The betrayal was nearly as bad as the deaths themselves. "What do you plan to do with me?"

Cygnus shone an approving smile on me. "Let us go home. Unfortunately, it will take some time since all but the Valla gate are closed.

Clever little minx of a sister made the portals portable and they have all been brought into the arenas which are virtually indestructible thanks to Orion. She would have been a valuable ally." He shot Ash an irritated glance, who was brimming with indignation.

"I tried several times. I nearly succeeded until Quartz scared her off. She had given herself to me completely that night," Ash snapped.

"It is not our problem you cannot control your wife. You brought Scarlett to our attention, and it hinged on you keeping her close and compliant. What you *succeeded* in doing was making sure she would run right back into the arms of Dagr. You should have known about her bond to him so we would have had him prisoner in Karkinos as we speak. Without Hunter's teleporting, you will need to come up with another way to trap him alive long enough to die on the project. We have nine months thanks to Sterling delivering on his promises unlike you," Canis barked.

Ash fumed while Sage's pouty smirk needed a good slapping. My backhand caught him off guard and I shook my hand, dripping blood on the floor after cutting my knuckles on his teeth.

"You cunt!" Sage snarled as he lunged for me.

Sterling intercepted, shifting mid leap into the silver barghest, and pinned Sage to the floor. Sterling roared in his face gnashing his fangs.

"Never think to touch my mate again!" he rasped out.

None of the other men had lifted a finger as the scene played out. Cygnus looked at the beast man just under seven feet tall.

"It would appear there are some unforeseen consequences to our endeavors. Sterling, shift back, son. Your point is made. No one will raise a hand to her again as long as she complies. You must go back to your wife and run your island." Sterling was slowly becoming a young man again and began to protest until Cygnus held up a hand silencing him. "We will arrange visits with her every weekend on which you may spend two nights with her. Agreed?"

Sterling looked to me, but I wouldn't meet this eyes. "As long as she will have me," he said, clasping Cygnus's arm.

Sterling was put on a horse and told to ride back to Valla. He protested leaving without me, but there was no swaying them. Five men rode with him which I found reassuring. There were roaming bands of rebels in Valla they thought were either coming from the arena or were taking orders from them.

They had brought me my horse from Ostara whom I hadn't ridden in ages. I mustered a smile for Gullfaxi. The golden sheen of her buckskin coat stood out brilliantly even under the grey sky. The Akhal-Teke was graceful and intelligent. My grandfather knew this and had forced me to not only put on a nix torque around my throat, but her reigns were tied to his own as we set out back to Valla.

With nothing to say, I pulled the hood of my cloak up and prayed they gave me a cocktail before the day was through. I was alone again and in the enemy's clutches.

"I was told you were bonded to her. Is she truly dead, as Sage says? He tried to confirm it, but the portal door they found would not work for him. There was also the small matter of Jormungandr itself protecting the blasted thing." He cursed. "It killed a dozen Crathode before they retreated."

"The bond broke between me, Jett, and Scarlett and with Silver Regn and I." I told him flatly. "Good luck collecting those pieces. If I know Scarlett, she'd come back from hel to keep them from you for what you've done."

"Your grandmother Pearl and your great uncle Reed are both dead. I thought you should hear it from me before Sage says it in some spiteful manner. Silver's grandfather as well. We had quite the rebellion on our hands. We offered an exchange — Spinel for Slate. His daughter declined after a very eloquent speech made by Patriarch Regn. Slate was like a grandson to him, so he said in flowery words, and proceeded to declare your sister Freya herself. He said he would care for her in the afterlife if his wife allowed until his grandson Brass and Dagr joined her in the heavens. I suspect from his smirk that he meant more than his words implied. Your sister is a bit of a seductress to have impacted the illustrious Regn in such a way. He ran like a coward, but we have it on good authority that he is gone from this world for good."

His tone was conversational. It made his news worse. I wondered how Gypsum and Hawk were or if the girls had gotten away, but I wouldn't ask any questions. He was saying these things so I would know just how alone I was in this world.

He didn't need to rub it in. I already knew.

My sitting room was done in pale pinks and cream with a simple white coffee table. A little further in was a luxurious white and pink bed. All the castle was done in pastels and elegant Neo-classic architecture. I heard the lock click in the door behind me and I sniffed.

Where would I even go if I escaped unless there was something they weren't telling me? I could try to find Hawk. He was my only living relative left aside from Gypsum.

Tall, narrow windows stretched from floor to ceiling and I pulled back the blush-colored curtains aside.

Var castle sat atop a rock pillar at least a hundred stories into the air above a circular lake, long white stone bridges met the pillar and connected the castle to the lands of Ostara with their arching forms and metallic globes that lined the rails. Anguillan swam around the waters far below. They were keeping order with the Guardians who had gone over to Canis's side.

I crossed the room to the bathroom and ran the water in the porcelain claw-footed bathtub. A good soak would help me clear my head.

Good gods, I was pregnant.

After my bath, a hearty meal of chicken and wild rice soup with bits of carrot and potatoes waited for me on my coffee table with a bit of flaky bread that was still warm from the oven. I ate with gusto, finding myself famished and promptly climbed into bed.

I awoke and started.

My limbs were heavy with a type of lethargy. I couldn't *feel* anything.

My door unlocked as I stood to try to seek the attention of a Guardian to help me. It took a great effort to stand. The pewter nix torque was heavy on my collarbones as I stumbled around in my nightgown as the door opened.

Ash walked into the room and locked the door behind him. "Your sister..." He shook his head slowly. "She promised me an elemental child. She promised to marry me. What does she do? Makes me look like a fool. I made her Second to the Prime, and she left me. For what? That beast. She became his khoraz. I was hoping Sterling would not succeed. I wanted your womb for myself. I think it is only fair. *Her* sister. Good news for you, I do not take pleasure in harming women, though I would not have minded dispatching your sister with my own hands." His teeth gritted, and he sneered.

I should feel something. Fear, anger, nervous — anything.

My feet tripped over one another as I tried to make my way to the door and Ash caught me. He lifted my dead weight into his arms and carried me back to the bed to lay me down.

"What did you give me?" I asked, sounding drowsy.

"A bit more marawacian than rousen in your cocktail." He looked down at me and his nostrils flared. "You were untouchable. Sterling never asked for anything, but you. This will be our little secret. Do not worry, you will not need to lie. I am very good at memory blocks. You will never remember our hours together. I promise."

He climbed into bed with me and stroked the hair from my face. I needed my panic, my rage, and indignation. I'd settle for frustration. He bent his lips to mine and brushed them over with a featherlight kiss. I heard him swallow as he withdrew and rolled away from me onto his back.

"She is dead? Sage, Sterling, and Cygnus confirm it. The thought of making you my own khoraz, forcing you to have my elemental child, and taking you as my paramour seemed like a just idea. *Fair.*" He shifted to look at me and my hair scratched against the pillow as I faced him. "You are not her. You never will be." He swept his hands over his face and pressed his palms into his eyes.

I couldn't believe he would feel grief for Scarlett after what he'd done.

"I loved her very much. Love made a fool of me."

"Love makes fools of us all," I whispered unable to use the full force of my voice.

Ash peered at me from the corner of his eyes and pulled his hands from his face. "She would not forgive me if I took you. Perhaps she would find a way to haunt me if I did." He rose from the bed and walked around it, back to the door. "They are going to keep you heavily drugged, Indigo. They cannot afford you to have the will to fight and Sterling would not survive if I stole your memories." He held the doorknob and paused. "I never cared enough to wish your family harm. Slate though... when I find him, I will mount his head on a pike and preserve it so I may keep it for a century."

"Ash," I croaked, making him stop halfway into the hall.

He looked at me with furrowed brows.

"She wanted to love you, but you were too ambitious for her. She never wanted all of it. Just love and a family. They used you, Ash. You never needed them." I blinked slowly, having used all my energy for my speech.

Ash gave me a cool, bored look. "That is what she said as well. None of this will matter once we get the pieces in the project, Indigo. Lay there, let Sterling take you, and grow your babe. That is your only role in our scheme. A dumpsite for the beast's seed," he said cruelly, before slamming and locking the door behind him.

I couldn't even drum up sadness.

# CHAPTER 33
# JETT

They fell in a pile inside the portal door and one thing was obvious, it was not Elivagar as they planned.

Also, there was no longer a portal door.

"Where were you thinking of?" Jett asked Tawny.

Tawny turned around and he blinked. She was no longer in her cloak and weapons, but a glittering midnight blue gown fit for the Yuletide masquerade. She looked happier, her hair and makeup was done to the nines and she was glowing.

"Elivagar," she said, shaking her head and shrugging her shoulders.

Jett turned back to Quick and Scar and started. "Where is your shirt?"

Quick looked down and noticed he wore a pair of black training pants and black supple leather boots. That was all. Scarlett was wearing a dress he recognized. It was blush with a sweetheart neckline and layers upon layers of chiffon fabric.

"Your babies?" Jett asked, and she pressed her hands to a flat stomach.

Freya's burly boar, she looked ready for an Ausa Vatni. "I'm pregnant..." she said hesitantly.

Jett looked down at himself. Black on black. A traditional Thrimilci V-neck with stone toggle buttons. Where was his cloak? Weapons?

Where were they?

It was cloudless and blue. They stood on a knoll of long grass which led to a white sand beach with clear inviting waters. The land seemed to stretch out as far as the eye could see, but only past the water could they discern buildings. How did anyone get out there? Was there a boat or another portal?

Quick plucked a purple crocus from the rolling meadow that wasn't there a moment ago and tucked it behind Scarlett's ear. She smiled so stunningly Jett actually groaned.

"Where are we?" Scarlett asked as she laced her hand into Quick's.

Jett shook his head. "No idea. Those houses are a jumble of every kind I've ever seen in Tidings and a few I've seen back in the States. Where are all the people?"

Quick pointed to a dark-haired man walking from one freestanding stone archway to another. He was fair skinned with wide eyes, the kind that found a reason to smile in everything. He glanced to us and gave a curt wave before crossing into the gaping archway and disappeared.

"There are more over there. How do we get there?" Quick asked, gesturing to the island of homes.

Jett's thoughts were clear. He didn't have a worry in the world. A smile was plastered on his face, on all their faces.

"We should try those archways. One might be a portal back," Scarlett said, gesturing with her free hand.

"Back where? There is only here," Jett told her, looking confused.

"Jett, to Amethyst and Cherry, and Opal," she said, looking confused herself.

Jett knew who all of these people were, but they wouldn't need him. They would be better without him. Why did Scarlett and Quick get to hold hands and Jett and Tawny couldn't? Jett crossed over to the petite brunette and offered her his hand.

She was always so beautiful when she wasn't scowling. She only ever looked that way for Steel. *Steel.* The fragmented thought crashed over Jett like a wave and receded with the tide.

The thought was gone.

Jett kissed her hand, and she beamed brighter. She wasn't his usual type. He hadn't dated a girl under five foot seven ever — but exceptions could be made. Would that special smile be his? Would she grant access to places only one man had ever been before? Jett felt better than he had in his entire life. Buoyant even. Happiness infused the very air.

"Let's follow that guy," Scarlett suggested as she dragged Quick with her to the first gate.

Her feet were bare and suddenly her dress was white. Her wedding dress. Quick still didn't have a shirt on as he tramped over the long grass, chuckling behind her.

Jett sat in the Prime's office wearing the black robe of the station. The door opened and Fox walked in wearing the robe of the Second Scarlett designed.

"Sorry to bother you, Prime. The induction ceremony is beginning," Fox said with twinkling blue eyes.

Jett rose and followed Fox out.

Jett was Prime. Everyone looked up to him. His wives were each on an arm as they rubbed elbows with the other greater families. He had united all the great families and now there was peace in Tidings under his reign.

Jett stumbled out of the archway to find the other three staring at the stone arch. "What was that? The future?"

Scarlett pointed to the runes etched at the peak of the stone arch. Pride. That certainly explained a lot.

"Did everyone imagine being Prime?" Jett asked with a smirk.

Scarlett and Tawny shook their heads.

"I dreamed I raised the first female Prime," Tawny confessed.

"That mom and dad saw how great the arenas were and told me they were proud," Scarlett said, moving back to Quick to hold his hand.

"Prime." Quick nodded with a megawatt smile and a laugh.

Jett laughed too and scooped Tawny up as he ran suddenly barefoot over the long grass. "Which one has the food? I'm famished!" Jett called.

Scarlett and Quick raced behind them while laughing.

"Gluttony," Scarlett shouted, and Jett read the runes until they reached gluttony.

They stuffed themselves senseless.

"I'll race you there!" Scarlett shouted, unzipping the back of her dress as she ran towards the lake.

Quick threw back his head, his Adam's apple bobbing as he laughed heartily and in a blink, he was totally nude and charging towards the water.

"How did you? Hey! You're a cheater!" she said through her laughter and chased after Quick.

Her feet splashed at the shore before she dove in and swam out to where Quick wiped a hand over his face floating deep in the lake. He sunk down all of a sudden and Scarlett popped up beside him splashing water into his face as they both laughed until he wrapped her in his arms. She buried her face in the crook of his neck as he used his jaw to push her dampened hair from her throat.

Jett ran after Tawny towards the water. Her dark waves fanned out behind her to expose her curvy hips and trim waist. She glanced over her shoulder as she ran pulling strands away from her mouth and Jett caught her under her chest and swung her around as she giggled.

"You're going in!" Jett yelled.

"Don't you dare!" She giggled.

Jett tossed her as she squealed and she went under with a splash. Scarlett had climbed onto Quick's back with her arms around his neck and they both laughed as Tawny's head broke the surface of the lake.

She was still smiling as she wiped her heart-shaped face. "I'm going to get you for that."

"You could try!" Jett shouted before diving under and grabbing around her waist to pull her deeper into the lake.

Her toned legs kicked until Jett resurfaced, chuckling and helped her brush her thick hair from her fair face. "You nearly drowned me," she said, feigning anger.

Jett ducked his head and stole a kiss that made her smile bloom. "Never that," he promised.

Tawny's big hazel eyes scanned his face before she wrapped her arms around his neck and Jett floated back towards the shore. Somewhere behind them, he could hear Scarlett's laughter with Quick's. There wasn't a worry in the world.

Tawny rested her chin on his shoulder as the water lapped between them and gazed out at Quick and Scarlett. He was nuzzling her throat, having twisted her around so he could face her. She was trying to fend him off with smiles.

"I can't remember why. I just can't," she said, running her index finger down Quick's nose, making him groan.

"He's a good-looking man," Tawny said out of the blue.

"Better than me?" Jett asked wryly, and Tawny's head whipped to him.

Something like sorrow flitted through her eyes and then it was gone. She smiled brightly and Jett groaned. "No one's better than you," she said confidently.

Jett's feet righted on the lake bottom and he slid his hands up to the nape of her neck. Her eyelids slid low as Jett slanted his mouth over hers. An adorable moan sounded in her throat and Jett held her tighter so her soft body was crushed by his.

*"I would liken you to a night without stars were it not for your eyes. I would liken you to a sleep without dreams were it not for your songs."*

Not everything he quoted from Langston Hughes was tactless.

She pulled away and Jett breathed harshly as she started for the shore bounding on her tip toes in the water. Jett's heart was hammering in his chest as he watched the petite brunette until she slowed with the water at her thighs and cast him the steamiest glance he'd ever had directed his way.

Jett dove under the water and hurried after her. She was just reaching the shore when Jett caught her hips and kissed along her spine up to her shoulders. They fell down into the sand with Tawny panting.

"By the Mother," Jett breathed as her fingers clawed the wet sand, kissing Jett over her shoulder.

She arched her back to him and Jett shifted to straddle her calves as he lifted her hips. "Fuck, I've imagined doing this for too long," Jett grit out as he slid slowly between her legs while she pulsed around him.

Tawny bucked, moaning high as their frenzy grew wild.

"Oh gods!" She moaned after only a few moments and Jett couldn't hold back as she clenched him firmly inside her.

He could vaguely hear the giggling of Scarlett behind them.

"How many hours do you think we've been here?" Tawny asked, resting her head on Jett's stomach as she traced his palm with her finger tip.

This place made you want to love. To touch and to make others happy. No worries, no need to sleep, and despite their frequent visits to the Gluttony Gate, no need for food. They wore the same clothes every hour... every day?

"It's been a few days," Jett stated.

She sighed. "I guess."

They'd all hated the Sloth Gate. Then again, the island was like a Sloth Gate. They laid about all day doing nothing but laughing and talking and making love. Greed wasn't so bad. Jett and Tawny had the same dream, to make the island they reigned over the most prosperous. In Jett's, he has swam through a pool of golden daymarks.

"Where are the other two?"

Tawny had a hard time remembering their names now. Jett did at times except when he came out of the Lust gate. Then things were all too clear. Quick and Scarlett spent most of their time between the Lust and Wrath gates. Scarlett and Jett had the same dream in the Wrath gate. Tearing Sage apart limb from limb over and over again then going on a killing spree against all those involved with the Stygians. Canis, Ash, Hunter and the rest.

One day. Then the thought was gone.

Scarlett had gone into the Envy gate once and never went back. When Jett had gone into the Envy gate, he imagined himself as a myopic living a simple life in Scar's old apartment training people at a gym like she had. He was envious of Scarlett's myopic life.

"In the Lust Gate again," I mused.

"They should just make love to one another as we do," she said, rolling onto her stomach. "Come for a swim," she said, hopping up.

Her clothes were gone, revealing her creamy, porcelain skin. One thing about dating women who had been tall and thin, they didn't have her curves. Jett arched a brow at her and his clothes were gone. He curled up onto his knees before she could sprint away and rubbed his face between her full breasts with her giggling all the while. Jett pulled a pink nipple into his mouth and she wrapped her arms around his head.

"We are not making it to the water, are we?" Tawny asked.

Jett toppled her over onto her back, her dark waves fanning out around her as she looked up at him with dreamy hazel eyes. "We can go there next."

When you never tire, you *never* tired.

Jett lifted her supple thigh as he pushed into her, back rising off the grass as she moaned. Her fingers curled in the long blades as Jett moved, kissing her wide mouth. Her skin reddened so easily he always had to be gentle. Tough as she was, she was delicate, and he relished it.

"*Ah*, Tawny."

# THIRTY-FOUR

"Remind me again why we can't," Quick said.

"We can't," I said, unable to recall exactly why.

"I am already naked." I could hear the smile in his voice.

"Clothes come off with a thought. Don't act like you've accomplished some impossible feat," I teased.

I myself became naked the second he said it, as he knew I would. I thought of a man's white linen shirt. The kind a man would wear in Thrimilci. I'd worn it before, but I had to leave it with the Faunelle.

My hands roamed freely over Quick's torso letting my fingertips bump over the ridges of his tightly packed muscles. His hands roamed just as freely over my skin and I tried not to get swept away by it.

"Lower," Quick said playfully, and I laughed.

You laughed all the time here. Laugh, touch, taste, smell, no stress, no responsibility. I began calling it Utopia. Quick's memory was better than Jett and Tawny's. Those two often forgot about us for hours. Mine was the best.

It was a blessing and a curse. I knew I couldn't make love to Quick though I often forgot why. I knew I was supposed to take care of him, but I couldn't remember for whom half the time. We spent a lot of time in the arches particularly the Lust Gate because when we came out, we could think clearer. Neither of us were with who we thought about while in there.

Slate and Brass consumed my world in the Lust Gate. I relived every memory I had with them and changed memories that had ended poorly into ones that ended with me deliciously sated. Quick told me he remembered Indigo and one of us had to hold on to their memories so we wouldn't do what Tawny and Jett were doing.

What they were doing again.

There was no shame and Quick and Jett were often in the buff. It was whatever we thought of at that moment. I usually wore the dress Brass told me he liked best or the ivory nightie I knew Slate favored.

Jett and Tawny's lovemaking could go ceaselessly through the night. Then again, there had been times when I was the only to say it was night, the others said it was day. Quick's hands ran over my skin and I held him closer as I shut my eyes letting him nibble on my ear.

Touching felt good. You craved closeness in Utopia. The first time Jett and Tawny had sought comfort in one another, we had all been skinny dipping in the lake. Not having shame worked both ways as Quick and I held one another and had watched them.

We held one another often.

"Look, it's the ghost!" I called out as the man in the white, billowing cloak walked from one stone arch way to the next.

The arches were dangerous. Time was lost in them. In Envy, I had found I was envious of how effortless Quick and Indigo's love had been. I wanted it, too.

The dark-haired man walked past giving a little wave as he always did and I got up and raced over to him with my very best smile. The carpet of grass was cool, soft, and thick under my feet. The stars twinkled in the sky above us and the ghost stopped walking to face me. None of us had tried to speak to him before.

"Hi, I'm Scarlett Tio. What's your name?"

He was my age and had a lazy mischievous kind of grin that made his hazel eyes sparkle. "I... forgot... my name... awhile back."

"Why don't you come sit with me and my friends? We're new here," I explained.

Ghost shrugged and walked back with me once I clasped his hand. He stared at our hands.

"I cannot tell you how good it feels to have contact again. Not that I missed it, I did not know I missed it until now. A Tio you said? I knew a female Tio once."

His eyes had laugh lines — a good sign. He had the callouses of a man who was familiar with a quarterstaff, but he didn't carry one. Quick was in a pair of plain black pants when I returned to him with Ghost in tow. Quick's biceps bulged with his arms folded under his head.

"'Quick' Silver Regn. Charmed, I am sure." Quick flashed Ghost his incredible smile, and I laughed gesturing down to lay on the grassy knoll that rose above the beach.

Quick opened his arms, beckoning me forth, and I threw myself at him. His big hands caught me around my ribs and he rolled us so we both faced Ghost who had laid down beside us. I traced Ghost's features with the tip of my finger and he shut his eyes savoring being touched again.

"Regn... I went to Valla U with a Regn," Ghost said, nuzzling my palm.

Ghost sighed as he took my hand and rubbed it along his short cropped dark hair. Quick arched a brow at me in amusement. Touching was a drug in Utopia. Ghost's chest had a tightness to it as the white billowing cloak he usually wore disappeared and he was suddenly in a pair of burgundy swim shorts.

His body reminded me of Hawk's lean dancer's build, with dark hair that covered his chest and tapered down his stomach. Abruptly, I was in my sea foam green fringed bikini. Quick cocked his head as he looked down at me.

"I think you are supposed to be pregnant," Quick said, running his palm over my toned stomach to the inguz tattoo on my left hip.

I gave a little shrug and hopped to my feet. The stars in the sky grew brighter as I grabbed both Ghost's and Quick's hands, pulling them to them up, ignoring whatever Tawny was doing in Jett's lap, and leading them into the crystal lake.

"I do not swim. I..." Ghost broke off, looking towards the Lust Gate.

"I'll teach you to swim," I comforted him, beaming a smile his way as Quick scooped me off my feet carrying me into the water.

Ghost waited hesitantly on the white sands watching us. "I conceived my daughter in a hot spring. There is not a lot of water where I come from. Not warm enough to swim in."

Quick nuzzled my neck needing to feel closer, and I pressed my cheek to the top of his head. When I looked up, we had lost our Ghost.

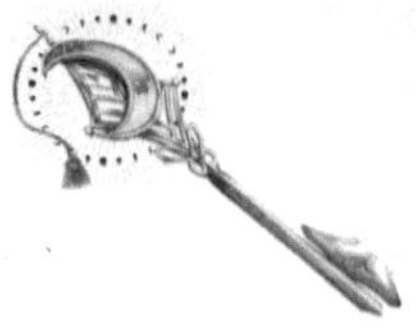

There was a change in the air. We all felt it and began to look around. A portal had formed out of thin air and a Valkyrie in beige robes walked through followed by a man I knew.

"Spinel?" Quick called out as he scrambled to his feet, forcing me up with him.

The Valkyrie had golden eyes that widened when she saw us. "You should not be here!" she cried in a silken voice despite her alarm. "I will send someone for you. Listen. You may visit the portals for as long as you need before you take the boat to the others." She gave her instructions to Spinel while keeping an eye on us. "Normally, I would spend a day with you so you did not forget, but circumstances have changed. I recommend leaving now. Good journey, Spinel Regn." She disappeared into the portal and it vanished with a flash of light.

Spinel's deep chocolate eyes caught on us and Quick grabbed my wrist as we watched decades melt from him right before our eyes. I blinked at tears that rolled over my lashes until a man our own age, far too similar to Brass but with a bearing like Quick's. Then he smiled. It was slow and spread easily with a rakishness that bespoke a Regn.

"You are alive," he said in his smooth deep voice and his eyes gleamed. "I am so sorry, young Scarlett."

For the first time, I was faster than Quick. I threw myself into his arms and felt the tears begin to fall.

"This brings me so much peace, but I must go," he whispered into my hair.

He reminded me so much of Brass, he even felt like him. "Don't leave me. Where do you have to go?" I asked through tears.

Spinel cupped my face. Streaks where tears had run over his olive cheeks led down to his anvil jaw.

"My time here is done. Take care of my grandsons." He pressed a hand to my belly. "And my great grandsons. You are a rare woman, young Scarlett. You remind me of my wife." He pressed his plump lips to my cheek and moved away from me to embrace Quick.

Quick's hand fisted in a young Spinel's navy Patriarch robe as he tried not to cry. "The Regn have always had nefarious reputations for womanizing, but what they do not say is that when we fall for a woman, there is only ever her in our hearts. I am proud of you. Robin would be proud of the man you have become, as would your father. Ask Brass to please forgive a covetous old man. I love you and your brothers. Perhaps one day we will rejoin."

Quick sucked in a deep breath as Spinel gave his back a pat and walked towards the waters. Jett and Tawny sat on the meadow watching as a canoe appeared from within the water. Without preamble, Spinel climbed in and I sought Quick's hand.

"Where's he going?" Tawny asked.

Spinel looked back and gave Quick and me a smile so bright my heart lurched. Quick held me tight to his body as the canoe drifted towards the buildings.

"Home," Quick said roughly, and he scooped me up into his arms. "Come to Lust gate. I need to remember."

"Remember what?" Jett asked in genuine confusion.

Quick's heart beat was like soothing ocean sounds for all the effect it had on lulling me to sleep. I was wrapped up tight in his big arms. Jett's back was pressed against mine with Tawny lying on his chest, both dressed for once when I caught the flicker of what I knew was Ghost's white cloak.

I smiled to myself while launching off of Quick and running towards Ghost before he could enter the Lust Gate.

"Elivagar!" I shouted, feigning breathlessness since you could never ran out of breath in Utopia.

Ghost stopped and blinked his big hazel eyes at me.

"Vetr," he replied, knitting his brows.

I nodded, smiling broader. "Right. The Vetrs are from Elivagar. Where you're from, right? Hot springs? Doesn't Elivagar have ice fields, but not water outside of the ocean that surrounds it and what's under the ice?"

"Vetr... My name. It is Ridge Vetr. Have you heard of me?"

He blinked wide hazel eyes I'd seen all my life back at me and my stomach managed to drop even in a world where you only felt boundless happiness.

"Tawny!" I shouted, not taking my eyes off of the ghost claiming to be Ridge Vetr. "If you're Ridge Vetr, tell me more about yourself. My mother was Wren Tio, deceased. My father, Alder Var, deceased. My grandmother is Pearl Tio —"

"Did Hawk marry her? I must be missing for five years in this world. What did my father do? Orion Vetr? I knew Lark was not your father. Did Wren give him another child?"

Ridge's eyes grew wider with excitement as he spoke. I could almost see his memories rising to his mind like bubbles once frozen, bursting at the surface of a lake. Tawny trudged over to where I stood, trying desperately to hold on to what I was feeling. It was slipping.

She ran a hand through her hair and imagined herself in a flowing crimson chiffon dress with a lazy smile. "What *are* you yelling about?" Tawny blinked at Ghost as she cocked her head. "Good morning, or whatever time of day it is for you."

My sense of urgency was slipping. "Tawny Vetr meet Ridge Vetr."

There wasn't much else I could think of to say in the moment.

While Ridge's went as wide as saucers, Tawny laughed even under

Ridge's scrutiny. "He's dead..." My name slipped her mind. "Killed by the Crathode while mom and I escaped from the cottages. Everyone knows that."

Ridge Vetr, Orion Vetr's son, slowly shook his head. "I drew them away. They followed me into the forest and I... stumbled into a portal. The more you want to forget, the sooner your memories disappear. I have held on to two things only; Sparrow, my wife, and my daughter, Tawny."

Tawny's eyes raked over Ridge, she had to see the same fairness of skin, the same wide hazel eyes, and wide mouth. "You would be twice the age you look. What are you... twenty-three, twenty-four? How would you get the portal open?"

"Twenty-four. With this."

Ridge pulled on a chain around his neck and produced an ivory auseklis pendant. Tawny snatched at it and yanked a matching pendant from within her bodice and held it up. They were identical.

"He said there were only two," she said softly.

"My mother and father's, and I have one. One thing you'll learn about Orion Vetr, he lies... a great deal." Ridge's eyes crinkled as he gave a wistful smile.

"Why did you forget so much? Where are we?"

I started to interrogate Ridge, whom if he was telling the truth, had been within the portal for twenty-odd years. Abruptly, the pressure in the air around us changed, and I looked around.

Quick and Jett leaned up on their elbows from where they laid on the lush grass watching us, or they were, because now they were gazing at a woman in thick cream robes cinched by a brown silk rope. Her cloak was pushed back to reveal her deeply tanned shaven head. Emerald eyes looked at us disapprovingly as she gestured for Quick and Jett to join us.

"I would have been here sooner, but there are many orphans being brought to us these days thanks to the war," she said, pursing her lips.

"Who —"

She cut Jett short with a flick of her fingers. "This is Disir, the sixth island. Forbidden for the young and most especially pregnant." She gave Tawny and I disappointed looks.

I looked down and my stomach was big, much bigger than when I'd last seen it and I yelped. Then it was gone. I whipped my head up to see if anyone saw my globe of a belly. They did.

"This island was created to only have access from the Valkyries who could lead those dying or wishing to leave the true world whether it be to simply live out their lives as they saw fit or to escape the inevitable changes outside of here. We are in a waiting room, so to speak, where you can live out your most sinful dreams until you are ready to meet the others."

She gestured across the lake to where the mismatched houses from every island were spread out. It was a whole other town out there filled with people. The leshy I found in Orion's dungeon had told me the island was forbidden. Probably because once here, you could be lost in it forever.

Spinel — I'd forgotten all about him.

"Now we really must be going. Time changes differently here. It is much slower than the true world," she continued.

"Are there Leshys here?" I asked, interrupting.

"Who cares about Leshy? If what he says is true, and he has maybe aged three years at most when he must be in his late forties, who knows how old we will be when we leave this place!"

Tawny was wearing her blood red gloves and quiver. Her recurve bow wrapped around the shoulder of her brown cloak. It was what she was wearing when we entered. She was feeling again. Normally, I would have been ecstatic, but then she looked at Jett and let out a low whimper.

"What have I done?"

"This one must have forgotten the quickest. It happens, dear. While you are close to me, your true feelings will surface. The oath I took becoming a Valkyrie prevents me and those around me from experiencing this island." She placed a hand on Tawny's shoulder.

"Who are you? You were at my mother's funereal and my father's. You spoke to my — Slate," I explained, and her smile deepened. "Do you know if Spinel is happy?"

"Come closer to me, dear. You are standing outside of my realm of influence and you need to focus."

I moved closer on the grass, the self-loathing rolled over me and I groaned.

"I am your great grandaunt. We are allowed to look after our descendants. To answer your previous question, this entire island is leshy fueled. They have their own portion invisible to Guardian eyes," she informed us.

"Great grandaunt? Pearl's aunt?" Jett asked, keeping a close watch of Tawny from the corner of his eye.

"Yes, I have heard the stories about me. They say I returned, when in fact, I never left. I was found by the Valkyries and stayed with them. My brother is your great grandfather, but he never married me because here I am," she stated with a smile that reminded me of Pearl's.

"Then who was raised by Leshys? Who was pretending to be you? Who carried the first stone piece to the Tios?"

*Slate. Brass. Indigo. Opal. Ash. Sage.*

Names ran through my head at warp speed and I started to feel sick. I'd been sleeping in Quick's arms, enjoying his company more than I ever should. Even though we'd never slept together or given more than a kiss, we'd done *a lot* of touching. All while Indigo was in the clutches of the enemy, while my entire family was suffering.

I felt like a monster.

"I do not know, Night's Child. What do *you* think? I was not the only greater family child to be raised outside of their ancestral home. Natt's are known for their double standards for paramours, as they are known for giving up the children born of those indiscretions. You have to leave. Too much time has passed already but prepare yourself for the aging process. Time catches up once you leave."

"Leave how?"

Quick was in his traveling gear checking blades and his pack. It was as if we never left the true world. Ridge never tore his eyes off Tawny as if she'd disappear if he blinked. Tawny was too busy losing herself to her grief again to notice Ridge.

"You merely need to think about your way home."

I was the first one through when the gleaming silver portal appeared behind the Valkyrie.

I thought about the Sumar palace when I went through the portal but was spit back out onto the stone lily pad in front of the silver portal. I hopped along the stone slabs until I reached the shore. Cramping pain across my middle doubled me over and I started groaning and wailing, unable to stop it.

Quick's arms swiftly moved me from the water's edge and away from the sea serpent's lair. I saw him through the slits of my eyes and started. He had a full dark beard and a head full head of hair. Tawny stood bowed over at the water's edge holding her stomach, gritting her teeth.

My stomach was growing beneath my hands, but I managed to gape as Jett's crewcut became a mop of hair that blended in with a beard. He bent over a fifth figure laying on the forest floor. Ridge's loud groans were nearly as bad as my own. He was aging twenty years in a minute.

I furrowed my brow as I placed my palms on my belly. It was hard and began to soften again like an involuntary muscle flex. My eyes widened. Quick's dark eyes were on my belly, or maybe my breasts which could now rest heavily on top of my belly.

"Sugarfoot! How long were we in there?" I meant to shout it, but it squeaked past my lips as I grit my teeth.

Suddenly, the Valkyrie was there. She brushed fingers over Ridge's back whose face relaxed the second she was past him and she knelt at my side with her palm on my roiling belly.

"Help me get her inside the gate. These babies are being born now," she said in a modulated tone that sounded far too calm to me. "You were in too long. Your body cannot take the change."

Jett was helping Tawny up who were both looking at me and when she straightened on wobbly feet, I nearly fainted. Her small belly protruded noticeably.

Quick scooped me off grass much greener than it was when we went in and cradled me to his chest as I groaned, following the Valkyrie to the white iron gates of their compound. Quick cursed and I felt fluid between my legs.

I was panicking. "Quick. It's too soon. I can't have the boys now. What about Brass? They won't make it. He needs to be here to see his sons."

Quick's face was pained. "Look around, Ms. Scarlett. We have been gone for months. It is spring. You may be a month or so early at most. I promise we will make sure they survive."

The Valkyrie opened the guardhouse door and hit the energy plate so the small room lit. She began pulling beige robes off shelves and piling them on the floor and gestured for Quick to lay me down.

"You should not make promises you cannot keep. She was far too thin to begin with and those babes have not had the necessary nourishment. Have you taken a moment to look at her face?" she asked in a stern whisper.

Quick rubbed a hand over his beard and thick glossy dark hair as he sat down on his heels. His normally manicured thick brows furrowed as he looked at my face and he busied himself with removing my damp pants.

Jett rushed in with a much more pregnant Tawny and Ridge. I was astonished to find his hair only as long as the other two men. The lines on his face deeper, but as a whole, not much different. Tawny looked thinner than she ever had in her life. I knew that must have been why Quick looked so concerned. The babies had taken what they needed from us, leaving us weakened.

"I groomed myself when I remembered. Apparently it has not been as long as I feared, though when I can take these boots off and clip my nails I will be grateful," Ridge said, giving us all a small smile and diffusing some of the tension.

I found myself nervously chuckling along with Quick. Jett was running his hands over his hair as he always used to do, but with much more hair to do it with. Tawny started crying, and I sought her hand with mine. She squeezed it tightly as I let out another wail as pain scraped down my hips.

The smell of the fight was on our clothes. Ridge wore a white cloak as he had in Disir, but it was blood stained and torn. His crimson padded jerkin was in tatters. In his left hand he carried a red stained wooden quarterstaff. Whatever cuts and bruises he suffered fighting the Crathode had been long healed and scarred.

Tawny raised her head to meet my eyes. "I didn't mean what I said. That you sleep with everyone." She swallowed hard. "I'm sorry."

I laughed breathlessly as Quick laid my pants over the wooden chair and the Valkyrie brought a bucket of water to where I laid on my back. She bent my knees up and Quick lifted my shoulders into his lap.

"Fill that with hot water," the Valkyrie said, gesturing to a wash basin on one of the shelves behind her to my brother so he wasn't standing helplessly over us.

Ridge closed the door and leaned against it as he watched with a concerned expression.

"I know. I shouldn't have been with Ash. I was feeling weak and was unbelievably stupid to think even for a nanosecond that I could be a second wife. Apparently, I'm a Natt and everyone knows Natt's don't share." I gave her a rueful smile, and she gave me a tight smile in return.

"I slept with your brother — a lot," she whispered.

My cheeks heated. I'd watched them in equal measure, without an ounce of shame until now.

"So have a lot of other women." I tried to perk up her mood.

She sobbed. "But I was only supposed to be with Steel. My husband, the father of my child. I don't even know if I have a home to go back to it's been so long they probably burned Elivagar to the ground or put one of those evil Natt twins in my place. *Fiddlestick*, Steel is dead!"

Jett was doing a good job of trying to pretend he wasn't the subject of her crying. He handed the Valkyrie the basin as she looked between my legs. The contractions had temporarily eased.

"My father is dead? What of my mother? Sparrow?" Ridge started to launch into a barrage of questions. "Elivagar is loyal to her ruler. If you are a Vetr, I take it my father made you the heir?" Ridge asked, stepping away from Jett to come towards us.

Tawny eyed him warily as she wiped her hands over her cheeks. "Orion is dead. I'm sorry. Your mother is still alive, but she's Hel incarnate. So are your sisters... and your nieces — that's why I'm the matriarch of Elivagar — or I was."

Ridge sucked in a deep breath and exhaled gustily. "There was no love lost between my father and me. It is difficult not being an ambitious son of an overly ambitious father. My marriage to your mother is the only thing I agreed to of his machinations — my mother and sisters included. It would seem he made the right choice for once making you his heir. You are... married? Carrying an heir?"

Ridge held out an ivory skinned hand and Tawny stared at it as if some dubious trick lay concealed within it. Finally, she nodded, and he placed his hand on her belly. My whole body warmed at his smile that could only be described as euphoric. A man living in darkness with only his mistakes to chase him who found the light and a new reason to live.

"A granddaughter. I am going to be a grandfather," Ridge murmured.

Tears sprung to my eyes as Tawny gave me a gaping look. She hadn't known until now what she was having.

"Congratulations," Quick and I said in unison.

Jett muttered something similar but wasn't prepared to start speaking to Tawny as yet. Jett was the one who had the affair. He had not one but two wives to answer to and who knew what their response would be, especially since Sage might have their daughter and Cherry would be very pregnant.

I stiffened, sucking in a sharp breath. "Gods! Why does it hurt in my legs?" I asked, clenching my teeth as another contraction caused unspeakable pain down my back and hips.

Tawny's eyes widened as she held her stomach and delved into me. "By the Mother, you're going to be a mother! Today! Your sons..." She gestured down. "One's right there," she squeaked.

I screamed. My pelvis felt like it was going to split in half.

"I don't even have any clothes for them or their cribs."

Hot tears burned my cheeks. It was a ridiculous statement brought on by the helplessness of my situation.

"We have everything you shall need," the Valkyrie reassured me.

She was between my legs with Jett holding a robe at the ready beside her. Tawny held my hand looking petrified with horror when she wasn't offering me smiles.

"My mom," I squeaked as another contraction strangled my words with the intense pain of a blade running down my spine. "Fiddlesticks!"

"One is crowning," The Valkyrie announced. "I am sorry Scarlett;

they are going to come fast. Your womb has not had the time to grow enough to hold them."

Ridge had retreated into introspection and Quick was whispering prayers that I didn't find in the least bit reassuring.

I was back to shaking my head in disbelief. Tawny focused on trying to get my breathing steady while squeezing my hand.

"3... 2... 1... *Push!*" The Valkyrie called to me, and I pushed with a cry.

"Oh my gods. Oh my gods," Tawny chanted beside me.

"Again. 3... 2... 1... *Push!*" the Valkyrie commanded, and I scrunched my chest to my thighs as I grunted with the exertion.

"I'm never having sex again!" I sobbed, and Jett laughed nervously along with Quick.

I wanted to choke them both.

"One more big push," The Valkyrie said, sweat glistening on her upper lip and her shaved scalp.

I nodded as she counted again and I gave it my all realizing I would have to do this all over again for my second son. A sense of peace came over me with relief as Tawny let out a little whimper slapping her hands over her mouth.

"Your son, Scarlett."

Jett took him from the woman and wiped him off using the basin to dip the robe into and dab gently over the squalling pink boy. I gaped as Jett held the umbilical cord for a stupefied Quick.

"You are the father's brother," Jett said with dampened cheeks.

Quick nodded numbly and used a blade from his boot to cut my son's cord. I looked to Tawny in a daze, she was sobbing as Jett handed me a crying babe with a mop of dark hair.

"My son," I breathed.

There was a hollow place in my heart that had formed with the death of my mother. I didn't know it was there until I looked down at my son and felt it fill. I would always miss my mother, but the unconditional love I received my entire life from her was now transferred to the little boy in my arms. I felt whole again and knew my heart would expand when my other son was born.

Which was happening *now*.

Giggling little girls woke me.

"Shoo! How did you get back in here?" The modulated voice of my great grandaunt held a hint of amusement as she ushered out the orphan girls.

I pushed myself up on my palms careful not to wake Quick and looked into the bassinet on my side of the double bed. We'd had to push two of the single mattresses together because Quick and I hadn't wanted to sleep alone. Tawny, Jett, and Ridge laid behind the screens that divided the large room in the Valkyrie compound.

My great grandaunt smiled brightly as she walked to the opposite side of the bed and picked up my other son. I cooed to the one I hovered over and picked him up. They were so small. I'd been petrified at first, but Lily assured me it was normal for preemies.

I sat back against the metal barred frame and slid the sleeves of my borrowed shift over my shoulders. Lily sang softly to my son as she came around the bed and helped me get him to latch so I could nurse them both at the same time.

"Such hungry little men. Is their father a big man?" Lily asked with shining emerald eyes.

"He is my size," Quick said in a sleep thick voice. He lifted his head from where he laid it on his folded arms while he rested on his stomach.

Tall windows lined the room at our heads that shone beams of light every few feet. I had never noticed how much gold was in Quick's eyes before. Lily smiled. She may not have understood Quick and my relationship, but she approved of him.

"Were the girls looking at the babies again?" I asked in a whisper.

Lily nodded. "We seldom get babies this young. Do you want me to have breakfast brought in before you leave?"

I sighed and nodded. Lily ran her finger over one of the boy's cheeks before she left. Quick rolled onto his side, tugging on his bushy beard.

"We can stay a few more days, Scarlett," he said in a hushed tone.

He was in awe of his nephews. They were identical. The five of us had gone over my sons, making sure they were perfectly perfect. They were.

"I wish we could, but —"

I swallowed hard and Quick gave my thigh a squeeze. We didn't need to go over it again. We were completely cut off from the world and had been in Disir for four months. The Valkyrie had no new information to give us. The short time Lily had gone into Disir to get us, made her lose two whole days.

We had been with the Valkyries for three days, and it was as much time as I could allow myself without feeling horribly guilty. Tawny came around the white fabric screen and yawned as she plopped down at our feet, rubbing her belly.

"I can't believe you get to skip nearly two trimesters and I have to do the last fatter half. You look thinner than before you got pregnant." Tawny pouted.

"So do you. Except your boobs are the size of melons," I teased, and she rolled her eyes.

"You're one to talk. Since your milk came in, those things are as big as my head. How are my nephews? Did you think of what you'll call them until their Ausa Vatni?" she asked.

My nursing was commonplace. No one gave it a second look. I could hold full conversations without them batting an eye. Tawny's cheeks were more defined than ever. Her arms and legs were thinner. The baby had taken all her fat right out of her. Tawny looked good with curves; she'd already informed us she planned on filling out again.

"It doesn't feel right without Brass having met them yet."

I sighed looking down at them. We didn't discuss the possibility that Brass might not be alive and if he was, that he could've moved on.

Jett shoved back the screen, opposite Tawny's, shirtless and ran his big hand through his dark blonde hair which curled around his ears. "They look like him. Him and Spinel," Jett teased, and Quick chuckled.

"Brass will love hearing that." Quick laughed. "Thankfully, at seventy his fertility had been long gone."

"He told me he was sixty-six." I wrinkled my nose as Quick chuckled.

Spinel going to the lands where Guardians retired was bittersweet. We were glad he wasn't dead, but never seeing him again was unimaginable. He never said why he was there in the first place, but it didn't bode well for the state of Tidings.

Quick took one of my sons who had finished nursing and I pulled up my shift before handing the other to Tawny who both began to burp them. Babies didn't need to be burped after breastfeeding, but I let them believe they were helping.

Ridge came around the corner running his fingers along his beard, his bare feet on the polished wood flooring. None of the men liked their newfound facial hair. I had also discovered that Quick usually kept his body hair to a minimum. He groomed more than I did.

"Today is the day?" Ridge asked, bracing his hands on the metal frame at our feet.

"Looks like. I better go say goodbye to my girlfriends," Quick joked as he gave my son to Jett and got up from the bed in nothing but his boxer briefs.

Jett rolled onto his back and held up my white clad son. "Uncle Quick needs to start wearing pants when he sleeps with mommy, doesn't he?"

Ridge chuckled as Quick passed behind him looking even more like an unscrupulous rogue than usual with his full beard. He had told fairytales to the little girls at night and more than a few had crushes on him. It wasn't hard to see why.

After I gave birth to my second son, the Valkyries had rushed out and took us inside. We were taken to the empty infirmary where I slept most of the first day except when I had to nurse. The world seemed at peace there, but they had told us their wards had doubled in the last four months.

The world outside was imploding. The Purge War was upon us.

# THIRTY-FIVE

"We were chased into the portal by Stygian Knights seeking to capture Scarlett and Tawny and kill Quick and me. The arenas are closest if they haven't been overrun. We don't have a choice," Jett said, checking his long seaxes over his black cloaked shoulders.

Quick rubbed his beard, looking back at the white closed gates of the Valkyrie compound. "We should keep these to disguise ourselves. All of Tidings knows I would not have a beard and this nest on my head. Entirely *un*Quick like. Do you girls have anything to help mask who you are? Take off any jewelry that might reveal you."

I thought to the short black bob I had in my pack and nodded. Not that anyone would recognize me with a baby strapped to my stomach. Tawny's belly barely allowed my other son to rest against her front. One had a blue band, and the other had a green band around their wrists so I knew which one was which. Green was born first. We'd have to be very careful at bath times.

We started walking arm in arm as we headed northwest along the ocean coast. My hair was tucked under my chin-length bob and Tawny had wrapped her long hair into a bun at her nape. I wore no jewelry. My Dagr solar cross ring was clinking against Alder's wedding band that I had taken back from Slate on my necklace with the stone pieces all tucked into my shirt. Tawny's ruby wedding ring, which she hadn't taken off since the day she married Steel, hung with her silver Yggdrasil necklace.

Trees ended abruptly off the sides to the craggy rocks below as the elevation slowly rose. Tawny began to explain Orion's death, and Sparrow and Hawk's marriage to Ridge who raptly listened, but I could feel the depth of his hurt. He'd missed so much to find Sparrow living happily with her first love. Him all but forgotten.

I fell back as we walked along the trees between Jett and Quick who had been speaking in quiet tones since Tawny had begun to warm up to Ridge. There was so much to process my head started to ache just thinking about all the stuff to think about.

Jett's face was a mask of anger with himself.

"If you've fallen back to lecture me, baby sis. Don't waste your breath. She has an excuse, I don't. I know that," he ground out.

We walked on, the moon following our walk with its rise. Ridge had begun to talk about himself and Sparrow before Tawny was born and Tawny was enraptured. Hearing first hand was entirely different from the second-hand opinions of Orion. I wasn't feeling too guilty about Quick. I wished I hadn't held him undressed so frequently and that we had been properly worried instead of the wonderful happiness we experienced together in Disir, but I felt without a doubt that I would have forgiven Indi if the positions were reversed.

"Do you know why Brass and I hit it off from the first time we spoke?"

Quick and Jett both looked at me with open faces of astonishment in the moonlight. I hadn't mentioned *those* two other than when I spoke about Brass and his sons. I was upset with their lack of goodbyes and their cold attitudes when I could've died that night. The judgment in their eyes at what Ash said, as if either of them had never before made a stupid decision when it came to women, couldn't or wouldn't be forgotten. I could name dozens of times in the last two years alone.

"Is this a trick question?" Quick asked, tugging at his short thick beard.

"He reads minds, you read emotions. You have to be honest with one another," Jett said without preamble.

I smiled internally knowing my brother would have figured out where I was going with this before I finished my thoughts. "Right. In Disir, you pushed away... events and people that brought you pain, making you forget. That's not why you feel like you do though, is it?"

Jett looked at me from the corner of his turquoise almond eye with a dry expression, and I continued.

"Can you think of any woman you wanted that you didn't have a chance with? Honestly? Tawny only wanted Steel. From the moment she met him, she fell for him. *Hard*. You had no chance. She isn't even your type, aside from the dark hair, but you were attracted to her before we got to Disir. I'm not judging. I find Quick attractive, but I've never *wanted* him. No offense, Quick."

Quick arched a brow with a smirk. "None taken, I think." A glimmer of his humor surfaced, and my mood boosted.

"What's your point, Scar? You're saying subconsciously I've wanted to sleep with Steel's wife? A man I consider my brother even if he is my uncle?" His tone was overly defensive, but I wasn't going to back down.

"You have the same eyes, skin tone, and hair color as Steel, some of your mannerisms are even the same. She went to you because you remind her of what she was unwilling to confront. Personally, what I learned with Slate is that someone isn't dead unless you've seen the body, but Tawny needed comfort and so did you. You wanted to see if you could get Tawny before Disir, that's why you feel so sugarfooty. I could *feel* it."

"Truth," Quick murmured as we walked.

Jett's hand scratched against the back of his head. "Now I know why you and Brass prefer not to date people. That is an annoying habit of knowing what people are feeling when they don't want to admit it to themselves." He cleared his throat when it didn't need it. "I did. Happy?"

"Far from it, big bro. You've got two wives who are probably worried sick about you and now you've got to tell them you had an affair. Tawny and Cherry are close. I'm hoping for all parties involved this is not going to go too terribly. They're open-minded women. I don't think you'll get away with it, but I don't think they'll leave you. How are you doing otherwise?" I asked.

He sighed. "I don't like tough love. I like *love*-love."

"We know," Quick muttered.

Jett sniffed a laugh. "By the Mother, that place was dangerous. Not good. If Sage has Opal..." Jett choked off unable to finish.

"Then we'll get her back," I assured him.

Jett finally turned his face to look down at me and cracked a smile. His eyes gleamed.

"How are you doing?"

"I've been better," I said, stifling a sigh as I rubbed Green's little foot.

We'd lost four months of our lives. Our loved ones had likely taken new lovers and we would have been forgotten or mourned as Ridge had been. None of us wanted to discuss it. None of us were good except for Ridge who had gained what he had left of his life back.

The scent of flowers hung in the warm air. The grass bent under our booted feet, and the sun was high. It was a gorgeous afternoon in Valla. The orphans had all come out to say goodbye when we left the compound. It was a happy goodbye. I planned to send them supplies as soon as I got the chance. People forgot how much there need was when it wasn't before their faces. I'd donate my time too, I'd decided. Not many women were joining the Valkyries since the portals had closed over twenty years ago.

"Seems unwise to be walking with two babies and a pregnant woman in this part of the forest. I do not believe the short one can run, perhaps a hasty waddle."

A man stepped out from behind a tree and grinned wickedly at me. I felt us all relax except for Ridge who didn't recognize Chafer as the blade of a man whose sharp tongue was twice as cutting as his features.

"I didn't miss you at all," I told him, determined not to get emotional about seeing Chafer. He would never let me live it down.

Chafer chuckled. I *felt* relief. Happiness even.

"Is everything okay?" I asked.

"Freya's burly boar, I never thought I would be glad to see your hideous face," Quick breathed.

"Your bonds broke. Come. Stygians roam these woods in the hopes of trying to capture me. We shall walk and talk." Chafer gestured for us to move on and four more men detached from the shadows.

Tawny was relaying the relationship between us all to Ridge and he stuck to her side as we walked. Something told me he'd be there as long as she let him and she appeared to be warming up to him. I wondered what Hawk would think about it.

"How did you find us? Our bonds broke?" I asked once we were back on our path to the arena.

Chafer nodded. "The night the war started. They are calling it the Purge War. I do not know how you all could be alive, but I am glad for it. If you repeat that to anyone I will deny it with my dying breath. *Please*, I could smell Quick's overbearing sandalwood and patchouli cologne even without a nose like Slate's. It did not help that you were all speaking loud enough for the Aves to hear you from here."

Quick gave me a look, he didn't believe what he'd just heard. "I do not understand how our bonds would have snapped. We were all alive."

"I saw both of your faces, as we do when bonds snap as well as Spinel's. There is not a soul who believes you are alive. It is best for now because those of us better known Guardians are hunted," Chafer said with a sneer.

"Why Purge War?" Jett asked tentatively.

Chafer's silence spoke volumes.

"Were... a lot of Guardians killed?" Tawny asked in a soft voice.

"Yes," Chafer answered in a clipped tone. "Before you ask, I know that Slate, Brass, Amethyst, Cerise, and Indigo are alive for certain. As well as your cousin that looks like an American native and his parents."

I *felt* fear and wrath so strongly I was sure it was my own.

"Where's Indigo?" Quick asked in a tone that dared Chafer to keep it from him.

"In Ostara under heavy guard. By all appearances, she seems in very good health. Hardly a prisoner at all, but she did try to escape once. That is why she is so heavily guarded now. Gypsum managed to get a message to her with that Goshawk of his, Storm-pale. Slate, Brass, and Lera planned a rescue and nearly succeeded until your lover interfered."

Chafer shot me a look.

"So you just left her there? In their clutches?" Jett came between

Quick and Chafer who stopped to eye Quick who had yanked his arm around.

"We lost ten Breakers trying to save one woman. For *you*... and you."

He looked to me. There was no love lost between Chafer and Jett. Chafer didn't like anyone who had been with Lera. We walked the rest of the way in silence.

# THIRTY-SIX

"Pearl and Reed, were the only ones publicly executed. They offered to trade Spinel for Slate, but after Spinel gave a speech about you he managed to flee into the woods. His bond broke two days later," Lera told us in her smoky voice.

As it turned out, Spinel used to run the Shadow Breakers and had been as bonded as the rest of us. Quick was telling her about our run in with Spinel and I'd never seen so much emotion from her.

I couldn't pull it together. My tears wouldn't stop, I felt so much sorrow my children's children would feel it. Every empath in a hundred miles radius would be clenching their teeth. I ran my thumbs over the thick waxy paper Lera handed me. Sketches of her, Slate, Brass, Chafer, as well as all those I loved like Gyps, Hawk, and Sparrow had been posted all over Tidings as enemies of the Guardians. Murder, treason, conspiracy, fraud, the ludicrous list of allegations went on and on.

"We do not know what would have happened to us if Brass and Slate had not warned us in time. We pulled in all the portal doors and evacuated as many Guardians as we could in Valla. Headquarters was destroyed. Valla University is under siege as is the Vetr castle and the Sumar palace. All the arenas are safe as are the greater family homes, but the Tio palace was overrun, as was the Dagr palace. We do not know how, but the Elivagar people were all evacuated. When we questioned them about who helped them, they said a man with a baby. He was cloaked and they could give no description. The castle is locked no one comes in or out and no word has been sent," Chafer reported so Lera could collect herself.

"But it appears whoever this man is with the baby is on our side?" Tawny pressed.

Vanaheim arena was crawling with refugees. The stadium was being used as a shelter for all those who had escaped Valla, whose star fortress design was being used as it had originally been intended. No one came in or out of Valla's heart without orders from the Prime. Thousands of people lived in what was supposed to be a recreational stadium.

Lera had looked better. Her normally polished appearance had a weary look to it as she sat behind her cherry wood desk. She always favored rich fabrics and reds, her office in Vanaheim reflected her taste. What didn't was the nugget sized ruby on her ring finger. Her and Chafer had more than five heaping helpings of death in the past few months and she had finally settled down with him even though they were twenty years apart. It was a good thing Guardians aged half as slow as myopics.

"It appears so. If not, it would be strange to save so many people from the Stygians. The mining town, Glitra, on the south side of the Frostfell Mountains remains. Mostly men and khorazes reside there, none were evacuated likely they were too far to be reached before the mystery man could close the portals. I have gone to the Niflheim arena, and it is wall to wall refugees. Worse so than it is here." Lera continued tapping her red nail on her lower lip and Blue in her lap.

That would be something. You had to step over sleeping bodies at the Vanaheim arena that crowded into the marbled halls. The dorm rooms that weren't taken by Breakers who had started bunking together, were given to families. The arena was rigidly policed with a zero-tolerance policy of no violence. Guardians could train in the arena if they chose to get out their aggressions, but that was all.

"How are you supporting all of these people?" I asked, finding something I could grasp onto.

Chafer sat on the edge of her desk and gave me a wry smile. "Your Uncle Hawk. The portal is usually closed, but every month Slate and Brass make a round to all the arenas and deliver what foods they grow in the conservatory. Technically, we would all be dead if you had not made these arenas. Of course, it is your fault for being a khoraz seductress to begin with."

I wondered what the last paper was that Lera had in front of her. Now I frowned as she gave Chafer an aggravated look and pushed the paper across the desk to me. The others huddled as I lifted to read it with Green sleeping in my arms.

<u>NOTICE</u>
By Order of the Prime

Scarlett Tio, former Second and wife of the Patriarch Dagr confessed to the seduction and subsequent murder of one Patriarch Haust with cooperation of Slate Dagr and Brass Regn to obtain Mabon lands for her Vigrid arenas. Anyone caught at the aforementioned arenas shall be arrested for conspiracy in league with one Scarlett Tio.

Mrs. Tio then murdered Patriarch Vetr after placing one Tawny Vetr in his seat of power. The Sumar family with Pearl Tio as its head, worked with the Tio and Regn families in order to purge the bloodlines and place her family in positions of power and displace the balance of power in Ostara by elevating the Regn.

Mrs. Tio used her considerable power to seduce the Prime into making her his Second and take command of Valla University.

All those that do not cease their rebellion with the former Second, a known khoraz elemental seductress trained in the most deadly skills of persuasion, will be executed.

*<u>Those Who Stand Accused of Treason are to be Arrested on <u>Sight:</u></u>*
*Slate Dagr Brass Regn Jackal Var*
*Gypsum Sumar Hawk Sumar River Straumr*
*Cordillera Blomi Chafer Fell Boa Sunna*
*Sparrow Dagr Magnolia Rot Asp Sandr*
*Wisteria Rot Fern Rot Viper Enox*
*Sky Tio Ford Tio Crag Straumr*
*Fox Straumr Butterfly Rot Coyote Regn*
*Cerise Kaldr Amethyst Geol Cyan Tio*
*Malachite Blao Solder Plaines Crimson Rot*

There were even more names. Mostly tyros at the university included on the list in case they escaped like Jade Kaldr, Zircon Snjar, Rosasite Sols, and Beryl Sunna. Everyone Gypsum associated with at the university. Crimson Rot was on the list, which I found surprising. Since when did she go against anything Ash said?

"Why is Solder on the list?" I asked.

Lera's lips curled. "Solder was the last man in before they locked the portal to the Muspelheim arena. They say he had slain dozens of Jorogumo himself before retreating."

I found I could still smile. Thrimilci had been evacuated for the most part, as had Elivagar and Valla. Lera had told us Minotaur swarmed Mabon before anyone could be evacuated except for the fifty people Viper trusted and brought there himself. Ostara was completely lost, only Coyote remained in case anyone sought refuge. Anguillan were everywhere in Valla too. The only reason Lera hadn't been arrested with Pearl, Spinel, and Reed was because Brass had made it to her at HQ in time.

I slapped down the notice and pulled the wig off my head. I needed a shower and to think about my next move. The people would hate me.

The khoraz seductress. How redundant.

Lera pulled out four rings, each one different, and placed them on her polished desk top. Ridge had gone to Valla U with Lera and she had nearly stumbled when she saw him. The two had been friends, everyone got along with Ridge Vetr. He was one of those men who knew how to speak to people to diffuse tensions. Lera had no problem letting him into her inner circle after their initial greeting.

"We tweaked the facial contorting rings with a girl whose talent is able to manipulate Leshy enchantments. She has proven invaluable. Those who travel outside the arenas use them. It changes your facial features and your voice so you cannot be recognized."

Lera took a clunky silver ring and slipped it onto her middle finger. Lera's appearance instantly altered. Her high arched dark brows became thicker and less manicured. Her wide red mouth became a small rosebud with less prominent cheekbones. Her olive skin had not changed, but her petite nose was longer. She was not an ugly woman, but a bit plain and inconspicuous. Lackluster dark eyes blinked at us and she smiled. The smile was all Lera.

"I assume you plan on leaving. You need the other piece from the Lycans and to rescue your sister. May I recommend cutting and coloring your hair?" She looked to me and Tawny, whose eyes bugged out.

"I'll keep it up," Tawny insisted.

I ran my fingers over my hair. "Can't I wear the wig?"

"It is too easy to yank off. Best color it at least," Quick said, giving me an apologetic smile.

I nodded with a sigh. "I have to get to Elivagar. I can go alone. I don't want anyone else risking their life for my stupidity. Everyone has done more than enough already. Everything I touch turns to sugarfoot."

"Quit whining. We have all lost people we care about in this war. They think you are dead, that works to your advantage. They have found the project, Scarlett. Canis is trying to find ways around needing the pieces since they disappeared with you." Chafer stabbed a finger towards me and Lera clasped her hand over it.

"We have digested this for months while they are only just finding out. We can speak more after a night's rest to process all we have told you. Delegate, not everyone believes the notices. Pearl and Reed Tio were well loved by their people. Thrimilci fought fiercely for their freedom," she stated and rose.

We rose with her. A Breaker stood at the door to accompany us to my office which wasn't being used. I stood and really looked at Lera and the way Chafer was protectively standing by her. Their dynamic had changed, she needed him.

"I'm sorry, Lera. About Spinel. I know he was targeted because of his affection for me and I cannot apologize enough for it."

Lera nodded. "My father would have been interested in you even if you were not a beautiful young woman. That you were, only made him more interested and the risk of death would have been too tempting to pass for him. He always said beautiful young women would be the death of him, I always assumed he meant it in a debauched way. *This* way, I may one day see him again." She gave me a rueful smile, and I tried to return it, but it felt tight and awkward on my lips. "I am glad you are alive, Scarlett. I am fond of you. If you are looking for my nephew and Slate —"

"I think it's better that they believe I'm dead. When I saw them last, they hated me for what I'd done. My death will have set them free. I can only imagine with everything that's happened they're hatred has only increased," I said, swallowing.

The others were waiting for me in the sprawling hall and could clearly hear our discussion. Chafer sniffed.

"You will find much has changed in the months you have been missing. You have never told us what happened..." Chafer trailed off.

"I want to... but I'm finding it difficult to describe," I admitted.

I wondered if Disir was forbidden to name aloud by Leshy magic. I had tried to talk about as had the others, but we became tongue tied and couldn't get the words out. Other than reassuring that Spinel was safe, but gone from them for now, we couldn't so much as pantomime the sprawling meadows and crystal waters or even name the gates.

"No matter. You are back and healthy." Lera looked to her great nephew, and I subconsciously rubbed Green's little arm. "They look like my father. I know this year's theme is precious stones and you and Spinel had a more than platonic relationship, but...

Lera asking me for something? The world really was spinning on a different axis.

"Balas and Spinel?" I said, unable to hide a smirk. "Brass will hate it."

"I think it suits them." Lera looked fondly down at Blue. "Balas? Do you like that name, little Regn?"

She didn't have children of her own and the way she looked at my son made me weepy all over again.

"Balas," I agreed and looked down to Green. "I guess that makes you Spinel. Good night, Lera," I said, before securing Spinel in my carrier and taking Balas from her hands.

"Scarlett. They were here yesterday. You just missed them," Lera called after me.

I fought back a strangled sob and followed the Breaker to my office where he had laid out food, fresh clothing, and towels so we could bathe.

After we showered and ate, our brains seemed to have not taken a moment's rest. Tawny's wild hormones got the best of her and Ridge swooped in to rub a comforting hand over her back as she cried. I'd seen Jett tear up, but never cry. Pearl was his mother. Our real mother had been with me when he grew up, and now he'd lost both.

The exhaustion of the trek to the arena and finding out all the horrible news that had happened as we lazed about made him not care that two other grown men were in the room. I took his head into my lap and rubbed his back until he fell asleep. Ridge had fallen asleep leaning against one of the pillars on the wall while Tawny was curled with her head in his lap.

I replaced my lap with a pillow and awkwardly crawled over to Quick who was sitting with his legs crossed, running his blade against a whetstone. I sank down beside him and clasped my hands over his, stopping his movements.

He had hugged me fiercely when I told them the names I'd chosen. Balas and Spinel were asleep beside Jett. I'd have to feed them in another two hours. Sometimes it felt like that's all I did, plus change diapers. One blessing had come from going to Vanaheim, I'd stocked up on diaper changing supplies.

"I would have saved her. I should have been here," he said as soon as the scraping stilled.

"Do you think Tawny or I could have made it with Jett alone?" I asked softly.

"Does not matter. I made my choice. Now I have to live with it."

He packed away his blades and whetstone as I *called* up a pillow and blankets. "I love you, Quick. Like a brother. You know that, don't you?"

"I know," he said, sighing.

I lowered myself down on one of the pillows over the blanket I used to pad my body from the floor. The corner of Quick's lip tugged as he watched me struggle to get comfortable and laid down beside me.

"I suppose I have slept beside you enough that this hardly makes a difference. Indigo has many things to hate me for, but helping you sleep will not be one of them. I am sorry I tried to bed you, Scarlett. I do not know what would have happened now if you had given in."

Quick brushed my freshly black dyed hair from my forehead and kissed it. He slipped his knee between mine and pulled me to him so my head rested partly on his chest. I threw my arm over his stomach and sighed.

"I am also sorry for all my groping," he whispered.

I chuckled. There had been a great deal of groping.

"What is so funny?" Quick murmured, sleep already claiming him. "I mean, aside from Lera naming your sons. I'd wager you never thought that would happen when you met."

I hummed agreement. "If you had told me that day you were a complete pervert in the prep room that I would be using you as a platonic body pillow, I would've called you a liar. Let's forget about it. We weren't making out, we didn't... touch *too* much."

"I will say this, you have a very nice rump. *There*, now we can pretend it never happened," he said with a bit of forced humor. "What do you think will happen with Jett?" he asked with a sigh.

"The girls will forgive him. If the girls have slept with someone else while they thought he was dead, he'd forgive them. Strange to think those three have a healthy relationship," I said dryly.

"You are probably right. The black hair looks good, Scarlett. Not the ring, but with your own green-blue eyes," Quick murmured absently.

The rumble of his voice with my ear against his chest made me feel heavy with sleep. "Keep talking, Quick. Your voice is soothing."

"If that is true, I will have to learn lullabies to sing to my children," Quick continued.

"Indi would like that. Feel free to practice on your nephews," I said thickly before succumbing to sleep.

# CHAPTER 37

# INDIGO

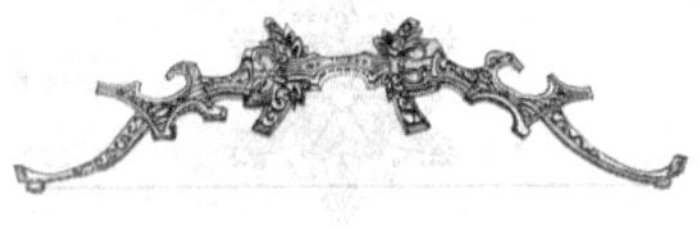

Sterling slowly dressed as I watched from where I laid on my bed, blush pink cotton sheets tossed over my hips. The marawacian/rousen cocktails had an unexpected side effect. It wasn't needed anymore, months of being Sterling's lover had trained me to be obedient to his every command. The moment he walked into the room, my nerves came alive and pleasure rolled me under. I couldn't look at him without wanting him to take me to bed. I had become a khoraz with the small amount of rousen I ingested in my cocktails at least four times a day to maintain my numbness.

Sterling's visits had to be approved by Cygnus. They had gone from eight days a month to ten, and, recently, they were allowing him to see me three days a week.

Sterling was miserable the first month when I wouldn't speak to him. He talked and talked, apologizing profusely as the bastard child grew in my belly. Then one day, Sterling came after one of Ash's strange angry visits. Ash had told me to give into Sterling because only he looked out for me. Sterling was useless without me and the change in him was evident, he claimed.

I found that despite my one-sided arguments with Ash and attempts to spoil what little joy I found, I enjoyed my days with Sterling. Sterling told me what was going on. That was how I knew the Goshawk was Gypsum's when it came to my tall, narrow window. Attached to its foot was a message from Brass. If I could get to the portal room, they had turned a man from the Stygians to help me escape.

It had been a disaster. The other men guarding the portal room saw me trying to sneak away, and the turncoat attempted to shove me through the portal. Unfortunately, I didn't know where I should be thinking of so when I thought of the Sumar palace, I was bounced back out into Ostara. The turncoat saw me and attempted it again as he held back four men with his spear until he was stabbed through the chest and fell into the portal. Shadow Breakers poured through the portal. trying to get to me. One of the men had already taken control of the nix torque I wore around the clock and used pain through it to bring me into submission.

The look on Brass and Slate's faces as they were forced back by the overwhelming swarm of Stygians actually made me feel better. Silver was dead, but his brothers would never rest until I was free. There were promises in those eyes that gave me hope.

Hope was a dangerous thing.

"You look beautiful, as always," Sterling said, sighing as he gazed down at me.

When my head was clear of the cocktail, which wasn't often, I plotted how to get to Brass or Hawk. Ash would try to come during those times because I could speak more. He never asked me to discuss things with him, but when he wanted an answer, I knew to give it right away. I didn't think he'd hurt me, but he could get someone who would.

I rolled lazily onto my back and his eyes flared to a deep purple. "By the Mother, Indigo. I do not know why I ever let you slip through my fingers."

He walked over to my bed and I silkily moved onto my knees to place a kiss on his lips. "Until next time," I said dreamily.

I smiled suggestively and laid back down on the bed feeling tired and sore from our vigorous afternoon together. I was asleep before he locked the door.

"Indigo, wake up."

My stepmother's cultured voice cut through my dreams like a hot knife and my eyes snapped open. I clutched my pink and cream blankets up over my naked body as she stood over me; blonde, statuesque, and the most beautiful woman I'd ever set eyes on. It was skin deep.

"Cygnus is allowing you to go for a ride today on Gullfaxi. Do not be late. Sage will be here to retrieve you in an hour."

She turned, her loose towheaded curls brushing the swanlike curve of her neck. I could've passed for her daughter. Before I found out I wasn't adopted I used to pretend she was, but she had made it clear I would never really be hers. Sage was the prince, and I was always treated as his live-in playmate until I became a woman. Then, I became a deal sweetener; the prize for the highest bidder.

My father never arranged suitors for me. I thought then that he didn't believe I could have an advantageous marriage, but now I knew it was because I was Wren's daughter. While I was his alone, it was as if he still had a piece of her. I loved my father all the more for it.

"I never want to see him again. I'd rather stay in my room," I said without the vehemence the statement needed.

I turned in my bed to face the newly barred windows so Gypsum's hawk couldn't get to me again. The nix torque was ice cold against my throat and I felt a sliver of sharp pain lace through me as Delta accessed the torque.

"That is no way to speak about your brother and the heir to Ostara. When Canis removes the usurpers from Valla University, he will be made Second. You should be kinder to him. Your life may hang in the balance once this child is born." Delta said threateningly but without a change in her prim tone.

Despite myself, I was excited about my baby. For years I had dreamed about having Sterling's children and now I was allowed to. I ran my palm over my swollen stomach and tried to imagine how I would look at the end of my pregnancy.

Aside from the bars and the torque, I hardly looked like a prisoner. I had daily baths, two attendants, I could roam the castle with my attendants as long as I stayed away from the portal room and could receive guests. It was my childhood all over again.

"What about you? Where do you fit in all of this *mother*? Did you know it was Sage who killed father and Wren?" I asked her and knew instantly I'd gone too far.

Delta had a vicious temper. She never should have had a child much less two. She used her *calling* instead of dirtying her hands, but I wore the nix torque. She wrenched me up by my arm as I tried to hang on to my blankets to cover myself. She was deceptively strong and taller than I was, outside of Tidings she would've been a glamorous model or some exceedingly rich man's trophy wife. Her pearly fair skin slightly reddened with her seldom seen rage.

"You ungrateful khoraz," she said in an arctic even tone. "We all know what you have become. A rousen addicted khoraz. What would your precious Sterling think if his true love was only bedding him because of rousen?"

An appalling mix of emotions swarmed me like biting mosquitoes. Pleasure at hearing Sterling's name, shame, knowing it would break his heart, and fury at hearing this ice-cold woman's knowledge of what I knew now they had done on purpose.

"Your son is a murderer. A spoiled sadistic mama's boy who couldn't convince our father he was worthy of being heir and had to kill my real brother, the true heir, to get his title back. How it must gall that he chose her son over yours," I snapped, uncaring what happened to me and hoping she didn't see the protective arm I wrapped around my belly.

She narrowed her frosty blue eyes. Delta's hand whipped around as she slapped me with a jarring sting across my cheek.

"It was never about me. Your father loved me in his way, but it was never how he loved that pitifully plain woman. You are lucky you inherited his looks. I was an obstacle between him and her — nothing more. A stepping stone to Canis and Cygnus's power and a means of revenge for Orion. You have no idea what they demanded I do."

"You would have done the same thing to me if I had married one of the merchants sons you paraded in front of me. After what you went through, why would you let them do that to me too? Why not help me be with Sterling if you knew how much we cared about one another?"

I had loved the glacial woman. All I ever wanted was her approval. For her to look at me once with the adoration she felt for Sage. If she had said a few encouraging words with a smile, I would have married whomever she wished.

Her smile was mocking on her pouty lips, the late morning sunlight lit her pale blue eyes like ice on fire. "Why do you deserve happiness and I do not? Who do you think asked Sage to have those who wronged me dispatched? I was meant to be a Prime's wife. Crag should have married me and he could have had Jackal at night, but no. He chose opprobrium. You *will* ride with Sage today and do whatever he wishes or I will have to send Sterling a messenger."

Her long-manicured nails dug into my arm as I tried to yank it away. I glared defiantly at her.

"You ruined your son. You made him a murderer. I knew he would never take the initiative to do something so drastic unless you or grandfather or Canis told him to. You are the only one who cared enough to have them murdered." I didn't know where my strength came from, my voice was oddly steady and lashed like a barbed barghest tail at her. "I would be careful about what you say about Jackal. Everyone who knows your son, knows his *true* inclinations. Jackal is the only one who has an ounce of compassion in this abhorrent family. I hate Sage and I hate you. Sterling will have to deal with it. Do what you will."

She slapped me again.

Her perfect white, blonde curl falling over her forehead as she cocked back her hand. This was new. She'd never struck me with her bare hands before and now she'd done it twice. *Thrice.* Both my cheeks stung as the blood rushed to them and her straight celestial nose wrinkled as she snarled. Her gorgeous face contorted with her rage.

She held my arm in one hand and I held my blankets with the other, I tried to pull away and duck my head as she cocked her hand back for a fourth swing and I bumped into the hope chest at the foot of my bed. I hadn't realized I'd been trying to retreat from her.

"Delta, dear. That is quite enough."

Ruby's reed like frame stood in the open doorway. It was my first visit from my father's mother. Her inky hair was pulled back in a ballet bun making her wide almond eyes, a Geol trademark, appear more angled below her prominent arched brows. Her sylphlike form glided into my bedroom as Delta released my bruised arm and used her *calling* to straighten her hair and gold and ivory laced caftan. Caftans were the traditional dress for women in Ostara. Not the bulky shapeless sacks worn ages ago, but heavily embroidered, richly layered works of art cinched with beautiful wide belts. Though, Delta would've looked gorgeous in a sack as well.

Delta seemed as angry with Ruby for interfering her brand of punishment as she did for my biting words. No one saw Delta out of control, she might have Sage kill Ruby for seeing her get carried away.

"My step daughter is my concern now that her father is deceased, Ruby. When I —"

"And my granddaughter is a woman now, a *pregnant* woman, possibly carrying an heir to the Haust since they are allowing Sterling to keep the boy. I will help Indigo get ready myself, thank you."

Ruby interrupted and dismissed Delta as I'd never seen anyone else do. Not even Canis crossed my stepmother. Cassiopeia treated her golden daughter as her ultimate accomplishment and had frequently visited to smooth roes between my father and her so no one else need be involved. My father had a history of short-term lovers I never understood and despised until I found out his history with my true mother.

Delta's shapely hips swayed as she walked past Ruby. "Sage will accompany you to the stables."

Ruby used her *calling* to shut the door as she crossed to my closet. I sank down on the bed. While I was showering, one of the servants would sweep in and remove all of my bedding and replace the vials I'd used that day. Of course they all knew what I was, nothing happened in that castle without them giving approval.

*Shame and lust.*

I understood why Scarlett railed against Slate for so long and finally grasped how hard it must have been for her to leave him once she was his khoraz. The torture of watching him with Amber those months and the pain of getting him back after being rescued only to have him not remember her.

Rousen was highly addictive, and I was now an addict. If I were ever to be rid of it, I would have to be weaned off as Slate had done for Scarlett. Her addiction had been much worse though I'd been addicted for longer. It would take weeks to wean me off and whomever helped me, I would become addicted to, too. As Scarlett was involuntarily aroused by Merfolk and barghests. I supposed that made me a barghest khoraz too.

Scarlett *had* been. Now she was dead. They were all dead.

Ruby swept back into the room careful to place the peach trimmed aquamarine caftan on my pale pink sofa. I sniffed derisively and Ruby's pursed her lips accentuating her high cheekbones.

"You think it is foolish to be well dressed and groomed? I know it is not traditional riding clothing, but you must look your absolute best. Now more than ever," Ruby chastised.

I looked at my rumpled bed, the elephant in the room as I sat there in my birthday suit. "For what? I was raised with Sage and grandfather hardly cares how I look," I said dryly.

Ruby stood in front of me and lifted my chin with her delicate finger tips. "Do you want a future, Indigo? You have the love of a Patriarch. You could be the second wife of the Patriarch since you carry his heir and you are of Tio blood and an elemental. Canis and Cygnus are nothing if not ambitious. They may be able to sway Cassiopeia and Dahlia into approving a second wife for Sterling."

Sterling's wife just a year too late.

"I don't know if it's his heir," I whispered.

My tears had long since been cried for Silver. I still felt the crush of my shattered heart, but my eyes remained dry.

Ruby looked thoughtfully down at me. "That does pose a problem, dear. You most certainly carry a son." I felt her delve into me to be certain. "The project will not work if it is not a barghest son. There are many ways to access the project, but without the right pieces, and the barghest baby... Canis may have to find yet another avenue."

Her lips tugged at that, she was no fan of Canis's, but my grandmother was a doormat — women in their place and men in power. She'd never spoken out against Cygnus. She was the epitome of passive aggressive. Her grand rebellion was giving Scarlett the lands to build her arena on, but that was actually quite a big deal.

"Could the child be ..."

"Silver Regn's."

Ruby nodded. "You loved that young man."

My heart was in the clutches of a razor clawed giant. Emotional pain could cause physical pain shading the old adage about sticks and stones breaking bones but not words, in a new light.

"I *do*."

# CHAPTER 38

# GYPSUM

Brass and Slate came through the only unlocked vine carved door of the Valla U portal room with supplies. I didn't know why they did it themselves when there were so many people in the arenas waiting for something to do.

"No progress with the Lycans?" I asked, taking the crate from Slate and passing it along the line of arms that stacked the supply crates along the yellow stoned wall.

We could have done it with our *calling* but it felt could to use our hands.

Slate grunted in negation. The Lycans wouldn't give anyone, but Night's Child the stone piece. Which meant either Indi or Scar. Since Scar was dead, there was only Indi. Brass and Slate had been staying with the Lycans in hiding at the northern most tip beyond the Igulbjorn Ice Cliffs of Elivagar since the Purge War began.

They looked feral. Slate had always had an animalistic edge, but four months of living with wolves had given Brass rough edges. His thick hair hung loose to his chest and a dark unkempt beard hid half his face. Slate's normally clean-shaven hard face had a shorter blue-black beard that made his eyes look almost devoid of color unless they flashed to silver. Needless to say, they flawlessly blended in with the Lycans.

They were harder since Scarlett, Quick, Jett, Steel, and Tawny died. We all were. As if armored scar tissue covered our hearts. The only thing we could do was not give up, defy Ash and Canis and the rest of the traitors. *That* and get back Indi. There was no word on where Opal was or who had evacuated Elivagar.

"How is Crimson?" Brass asked with a flash of bright white light as he brought in another crate.

"Ask her yourself."

I nodded over to where she hovered like a bumblebee around Beryl. Her palm pressed self-consciously to a nonexistent baby bump as Beryl stacked the crates for supplies and the few extra crates for the wedding decorations. Two things happened during war time I'd realized, all stemming from people not wanting to be alone and your mortality looming in the corners of your mind. Weddings and babies were inevitable.

"She looks very happy. It happened quickly," Brass noted.

Beryl smiled broadly crinkling his eyes as he kissed Crimson.

"They both are happy. It's a welcome respite during these times, a big wedding with all the bells and whistles." I tried to gauge how they were doing just by looking at them. "How are my parents?" I asked.

"They are as well as can be expected. We delivered Cherry to them; she is nearing the end of her pregnancy and should have the comforts of the palace. Opal has not been found. Amethyst refuses to return until the Lycans relinquish the piece," Brass said.

I stifled a sigh. The loss of a child had to be worse than the loss of a sister and I was still grieving Tawny's death. I would until I settled the score. How Slate and Brass must feel about losing Scarlett and their twins — I couldn't fathom. I didn't have a single memory without Scar and Tawny and now that they were gone I felt lost.

I asked the awkward question. "And how are you both?"

They lifted their heads in unison. They were spending too much time together. Slate's hand slid into his pocket where he kept the foot-long braid of Scar's golden hair. Creepy or romantic? It depended on who you asked.

"This is not how it was supposed to be."

Brass spoke for them both. Slate had taken an oath of silence until their war was over and Sage and the rest were ashes in the wind. Thank goodness Brass was a mind reader.

"Are you two staying for the wedding?" I asked.

"No, two nights. As usual, to collect any requests and deliver messages."

I nodded. It was the same every second Tuesday of the month. Two nights to deliver and receive, then they were gone again until next month. I watched the two men move past the line of tyros that seemed to unwittingly move out of their path. Tree-gold managed to walk between them without getting stepped on. She stopped and waited for me just outside the doorway. I had offered to take the skogkatt, but they said she did well in the tundra. Indigo's cat, Bee-gold would be lounging about the Sumar palace alone waiting for her mistress to return.

An elegant red head swept into view as soon as Brass and Slate turned the corner. Our dark eyes met; it was too late to look away. Mica smiled nervously at me, her flawless milky skin flushing. Thank goodness for my olive skin. I felt the heat in my cheeks as my blood drew to my face in response. I had tried to back pedal my relationship with Mica into friendship after assaulting her in her bedroom.

"Hey. Everything here for Crimson's wedding?" she asked, licking her lower lip as she looked down at the list I held filled with checked off items.

"Slate and Brass haven't failed us yet," I told her, offering a smile.

Her cheeks flushed again, and she dropped her eyes back to the list, her blunt bangs brushed her delicate brows. I watched her chest rise and fall, the smattering of freckles barely visible at the edge of her caftan's neckline like she'd been sprinkled with cinnamon. She didn't taste like cinnamon. She tasted like loquat, succulent and sweet and smelled of orchids. Her chest suddenly reddened, and I drew my eyes back to hers.

She'd caught me looking down her dress. *Fantastic.*

"Great. I shall inform the bride," she said in her falsetto voice.

I watched her walk away only to have Malachite's eyes and wry grin catch mine — the ass. I rolled my eyes as I folded up my list and shoved it into my standard Valla U black pants.

"That one wants you," Malachite teased.

"You're an idiot. Lots of women want me. I'm Patriarch Sumar now." I waggled my brows at him, and he chuckled.

"How could they resist such humble modesty?"

We chuckled together and Malachite moved to put away the supply crates before classes started. The provosts were as good as their word. After the first week, classes went as usual aside from the shift of tyros on watch to be sure Cygnus, Canis, and the rest of the traitors weren't up to no good outside of the yellow stoned castle walls. They'd started building siege machines.

*The sagamore will not give the pieces to anyone, but Night's Child. One of them. Grar Dyr grows impatient and Tiger Eyes grows reckless. They both look forward to death. Tiger Eyes lost his fertility after our last visit. He is not in a good way.*

I glanced down at Tree whose bright green eyes glazed intensely at me while she flicked her long-furred snowy tail. "Not now," I whispered, hoping no one saw me talking to the cat.

*They think I am too recognizable. They want to be rid of me, but they are whom Mistress loved. There is no one else. Convince them to let me stay.*

I scratched my temple, pushing my loose hair over my shoulder. "Done."

If cats could smile, Tree did and turned around the trot after her masters.

CHAPTER

# THIRTY-NINE

"Do I need to tell you that you shall need a horse? A camel, a carriage, or another mode of transportation with two young infants and a pregnant woman," Cordillera chastened.

I'd braided my inky locks in a crown around my head and slipped on the clunky silver ring Lera had worn yesterday as the plain dark-eyed girl with the rosebud mouth and the long, thin nose. Tawny had braided her hair similarly and slipped a white gold band with a solitaire opal stone at its center that transformed her face into a girl who looked like my facade's sister except she had a snub nose below her lackluster dark eyes.

I wore a brown empire waist chiffon dress with Balas strapped to my chest. Tawny was wearing a similar gown in navy with Spinel in her carrier. Lera offered to take care of them and find a wet nurse for me, but I'd declined. I wouldn't be doing any fighting. Not yet, at least.

Ridge was the only one not wearing a facial contortion ring. He'd been thought dead for twenty years, if someone recognized him without having spoken to him, they deserved to find us.

Jett's eyes were changed to hazel and his strong jaw now oblong with thin lips. He hated it. Quick was equally annoyed with his homely appearance; his new fleshy nose and hair lip. Because his tattoos were so recognizable, he'd had to wear a high-collared shirt even though we were headed into the desert. I was lucky the clunky silver ring covered my tiwaz tattoo.

No one would recognize us. We were four entirely different people plus Ridge, who was going anywhere Tawny was going. We filled our packs with supplies for the trek to the Wemic and Lera led us to the portal.

"I have a horse, Safanad. Slate's horse might be there too, Al-Fadee," I told her, checking on the stone pieces I'd sewn into my corset.

I couldn't wear them anywhere they might accidentally be seen anymore. My ivory sunburst, silver Celtic etched beads, the bronze and ebony beads, and the jade love rune were in my pack with the peacock feather and white eagle feather.

"Since when do you have mounts?" Tawny asked.

"Since Slate trained my Arabian mare as a wedding present," I murmured without looking up.

Jett filled the impending awkward silence that followed my statement. "We'll break into the stables. Helhest is in the stables too. Ridge can ride Sleipnir and Quick can ride Slate's mount. Tawny, do you have a horse?"

Sleipnir was Gypsum's sleek chestnut Arabian with white legs. Al-Fadee was Slate's impressive chestnut Arabian with a glossy black mane. I wondered if it would *let* Quick ride him. I hadn't ridden Safanad since Slate brought her to the Straumr palace when I procured the deeds for my arena. My Arabian mount was beautifully elegant with a white coat and black skin, I hoped she'd remember me.

Tawny's eyes widened. Jett and she had not addressed one another since we left Disir.

"*Um*, Banat Er Rih. Daughter of the wind," Tawny stammered. "I have a horse in Elivagar too if we can get to her. Grimhild is a black Noriker. Orion gave her to me when he named me his heir, she's good in the mountains," she rambled, her eyes flitting to Jett's and away again.

Jett wasn't any more comfortable than she was and only nodded at her verbose. "Quick will go to Muspelheim arena and rally the people there and we'll go to the tribes. It's settled."

Tawny pulled the auseklis over her head and licked her lips before handing it to Quick. "I might as well give this to you now."

Quick pulled it over his and ducked his head giving her a peck on her cheek. His smile was all Quick on that homely face.

"I promise to return it as soon as we meet again."

"We shall be ready when you come for us."

Chafer inclined his head to us as we stood before the white granite Roman arch that used to be at the bisecting bridges outside the arena. I rubbed my lips together and looked at the others with faces I was having a hard time adjusting to.

"I am not sure if you are aware, but after you give birth, your *calling* is unreliable. Do not exert yourself, delegate." Cordillera came as close to telling me to take care of myself as she would get before I walked into the portal.

"Business?"

I hadn't taken more than a step out from the portal when a hand halted me. The bright white light of the portal still blinded my eyes when a man's voice came from close beside me. I blinked several times, trying to adjust to the grey skies.

It rained two, maybe three times a year in Thrimilci. I looked back at the gate to be sure I got it right. That *was* the Thrimilci's portal gate.

"Fruit goods for Elivagar," I said not in my usual gravelly voice, but the masked girlish voice the contortion ring gave me.

My skin crawled as I looked around. The men guarding the gate were clad in black cloaks, Guardians with the valknut interlocking silver triangles on the back. Jorogumo skittered, huge and frightening along the white shimmering roads in between shops that normally bustled with activity but were now nearly abandoned. Not everyone had gotten away it appeared.

Four more bright flashes behind me announced my traveling companions. Normally, there was a constant flow of visitors between portals, but it seemed we made our first mistake. The Guardians watching the doors *felt* wary. I doubted many people left their home islands since the war began.

"I am traveling with my sister and father. He is my husband, and that is my brother-in-law in case she goes into labor. I could not leave our sons at home so young they require constant feeding."

The now fleshy nosed Quick with a hair lip was my acting husband and Jett with his oblong jaw and hazel eyes, my brother-in-law. Tawny's beady dull eyes widened at having to pretend Jett was her husband, but I couldn't very well do it. Ridge would be passable as our faux father with his dark hair and eyes, except he was too good looking to have fathered such plain girls. The goal was to not be noticeable, but we were the least attractive people I'd ever seen in Tidings.

The stern-looking guard watched Tawny rub her belly, she looked about four months pregnant. With luck, the guard knew nothing about pregnant women. The Guardian wrote something on a piece of parchment and pressed a stamp to it handing it over to me.

"Do not lose it. It is proof you have been questioned and have permission to be here for the next two days. You must present this when you return home or you will be arrested, if you lose it and are stopped, you will be arrested. You must stay with whom carries the authorization. Move along."

The Guardian stepped back and we hurried away. I rolled the parchment and placed it on the top of my pack. At the bottom, I had hidden my identifiable blades except for the short seax I had strapped to my thigh. Quick had attempted to comb his thick hair, but now I understood why he kept it short; it was hilariously unruly and the best he could do was tuck it behind his ears.

He took my arm as we walked towards the sprawling palace up the zig zagging roads that were lined by white stucco pueblos. A light drizzle began to fall the moment we began to ascend.

"Quick thinking, Ms. Scarlett."

I hissed. "We need knew names."

"Dibs on Jaw, as in Jawfish," Jett called in a scratchy voice totally unlike his deep bass.

Doors were shut, royal blue shutters, closed. Even the rooftop gardens had withered in homes that had been abandoned. I was glad Jett was feigning good spirits because our home island was downright depressing. The rain only added to our sour moods.

"I'm Ilisha and she's Scat," Tawny muttered rigidly with Jett on her arm.

"Try not to use contractions. I shall be Shark," Quick said in a guttural rumble unlike his smooth deep voice.

He flashed me a smile worthy of his usual face but looking strange with his hair lip projection.

"Those are the names she gave Spinel when we met," I explained, feeling an inexplicable squeeze of my heart.

"Fish? Is that the year before yours? I suppose I can keep with land formations. I shall be Dune," Ridge said from behind Tawny and Jett.

"Two years ahead of ours," Jett explained.

"Jaw, Shark, Dune, Ilisha, and Scat. We sound like a sideshow," Tawny grumbled as she watched a pair of shiny banded exoskeletons pass by in a flash of skittering legs.

"The stables are at the top. It may be harder than we expected to leave with the horses. How are you doing, *Scat*?" Jett asked as I gave him a dry look.

My calves were already aching from the uphill climb past the mosaic walls that wrapped around the home's gardens. There was no direct path to the palace other than the portals and the rain was making my dress stick uncomfortably to my skin.

"Hold in there. We will not be doing much walking once we get the horses," Quick reassured me.

I murmured something not even I understood as I contemplated everything that happened. The human body was amazing. It could take so much and keep going, I was in awe of my own hunk of bloody meat that beat in my chest. As broken as I felt, it kept going. I knew I couldn't begin to dwell on all the deaths that surrounded me or to let myself feel the hurt of the last time I'd seen Slate and Brass.

They were alive. That was enough. It was more than some people had.

"We should not activate our bonds," I said, trying to speak like the other Guardians.

"I thought the same thing. At first I thought Indigo might find it reassuring, but there is a chance knowing I am alive might jeopardize us. There is no sense in letting Brass know where I am and having him trying to come to us when we need to get to him," Quick said, sounding defeated.

"Gypsum is safe. I don't, I mean, *do not* want him trying to find me," Tawny said with a sigh.

Jett was silent. I imagined he nodded along with us.

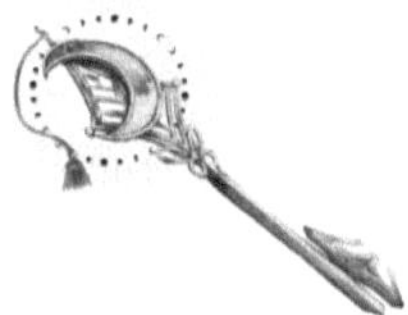

The Sumar palace was surrounded. A blend of Guardians and Jorogumo guarded along the smooth white stucco walls. No siege machines were evident as I thought there would be. Maybe they hoped to get the tyros and to hold them hostage until Hawk and Sparrow gave up. Canis wanted them out of the way and this suited him just fine. No one could contest his rule through Ash while imprisoned them in their own homes.

"Quick, *er*, Shark and I will round up the horses. Dune will stay with you girls." Jett's new hazel eyes looked around as we pressed ourselves to the garden wall of the nearest home before the road that ran even with the palace.

"Take the authorization papers. We will ride along the River Mani and go with you to the arena. After that, we will not have a need for the papers, anyway. You will need it in case you get caught before you get inside Muspelheim." I took out the rolled parchment and slipped it into Quick's pack.

"Thanks."

"Shark?"

I wrapped my hand around his wrist and he looked down at me

knitting his brows. I dropped my voice so the others wouldn't hear me and he slid along the wall with me.

"You may be tempted to use that auseklis key to gain access to the Var castle and rescue Indigo. *Please.* I am begging you not to. I promise, I want her as much as you do, but the only thing we have going for us is surprised. Where would we go if we rescue her and have not saved Thrimilci yet? We rid Thrimilci of this filth, we get the last piece, then we get back Elivagar on our way to the project. That is the plan. We need the last pieces from Canis, we will have to go to Ostara then, but we need a force behind us." I searched his big, dark projected eyes.

He clenched his jaw and dropped his eyes. "You remind me of Brass at times. Being an empath is a great deal like being a mind reader."

He didn't say it was a lie, which meant I was dead on, as I'd thought. I hugged Quick around his waist twisting my hips so Balas wouldn't be squished between us.

"You are a very good man, 'Quick' Silver Regn. Be safe. I promised my sister I would take care of you."

Quick kissed the top of my head and withdrew from me to step alongside Jett. I knew I had a part to play, but for stealth, Tawny and I were helpless with my sons strapped to us. Ridge moved to stand at the front of the wall.

"I shall heft you up, Ilisha, as they round the wall. Will you need help, Scat?" Ridge asked with his lips tugging to the side with amusement.

"No, this is the most access I've had to my body in ages," I confided.

"Thanks," Tawny said, giving Ridge a shy smile.

They'd talked until she'd fallen asleep. A chance she'd never thought she'd get. Tawny lost Steel but gained a chance to know the man who sired her and he seemed every bit the great man Sparrow said he had been.

"I hate being this close and having to leave. My mom and... dad on the other side of that stupid wall." Tawny eyed Ridge.

"I am not asking to replace Hawk; I only want to share in your life in any way you will allow. It would be nice if you could warm up to calling me father as well." Ridge wide hazel eyes looked back at Tawny who knit her brows and gave him a small smile of her projected rosebud mouth. "Here they come. Odin's eye!" Ridge blurted.

Safanad galloped on one side of Al-Fadee's shining chestnut flank while a riderless gray mare was to Quick's left. Jett rode atop a roan that must be Helhest with Gypsum's Sleipnir galloping alongside him. The gray must've been Banat Er Rih. By the Mother, I'd almost forgotten how noble the Arabian horses were.

High held tails, finely chiseled features, and beautifully arched necks — and thundering straight for us!

"Now!" Ridge shouted.

Using his *calling*, Ridge practically tossed Tawny by her hips into her saddle with her arm around Spinel in his carrier. Quick barely slowed, barreling past us. Tawny must have spent time riding in Elivagar because she swung into her seat gracefully unlike the plop I'd taken onto Safanad's back. I had almost no experience with horses, but Slate had trained her well.

"Hurry!" Jett shouted, dropping Sleipnir's reigns so Ridge could swing himself up.

"Not as young as I was yesterday," he said with a grunt as he righted himself on the saddle.

No sooner was Ridge on Sleipnir and we were breaking back into a gallop when the road was filled from wall to wall with Jorogumo. They scrambled like a wave of angry hornets from a kicked nest towards us. These were no hornets. These were six-foot-tall spider hybrids all with different degrees of paralytic poisons on those pinchers they snapped as they charged screeching towards us.

Our horses needed no other encouragement.

"Yah! Yah!" Jett shouted to Helhest.

Al-Fadee didn't like the other stallion in the lead and fought to race ahead of him. Quick started laughing and Tawny's beady eyes widened at me wondering if he'd lost his mind. Shadow Breakers laughed in the face of death. If we were caught in the swarm of inhuman shrieking spiders behind us, we'd be torn to bits before we could utter a word of defense.

"Head west! We are going to have to separate if we do not lose them," Quick shouted.

We'd discussed it as a worst-case scenario. I didn't want to continue on without Tawny. Her and Ridge would try to lead them away east, while Jett and I continued south into the desert and Quick went on to the arena. Tawny as bait put a bad taste in my mouth especially when she carried one of my sons.

I looked over at her and thought I could see the woman behind the contorted mask. Her eyes gleamed with the rush of adrenaline; her lips parted slightly as if her breaths were coming quicker. Dark locks of hair had fallen free of her crowning braid and whipped around her face. She looked wild and happy.

I saved my breath and urged Safanad on — faster, faster. She wanted to run. Hooves clopped on stone. Heads peeked out blurred pueblos as we thundered past, ducking back in when they saw what we brought with us.

"What did you do to piss them off?" Ridge called.

"Nothing. They think we are horse thieves and they are bored. I do not think they all want to be here. I heard them talking before we set the stable on fire. They were threatened. One said something about his daughters being taken away to breed, whatever that means," Quick shouted back.

We were drawing attention now.

"You burnt the stables down with all those poor horses inside!" I shouted, appalled with them.

"Do not be ridiculous. We freed them all and sent them trotting off to confuse the Guardians otherwise there would be even more chasing us." Jett laughed with his head thrown back.

We were finally being proactive about saving our people and it felt good. Better than anything Disir concocted for us to feel because it was real.

The road leveled off, so we were on the main street of Thrimilci. We raced past Hopper's shop, past Solder's Armored Armoire, and further still until the clattering of Jorogumo legs faded and we could no longer hear their chittering. Just before the white road ended and became sand, a wall of Guardians waited for us. They guarded the exit out of town and we had surprised them.

"Ride them down. If they are not with us, they are against us," Jett called, gritting his teeth hidden by his beard.

"*Or* they're doing their job!" Tawny yelled at him. "Help me, Scat!" She whipped her head to me and I knit my brows.

She started *calling* to create a wall of air around us while I used all of my strength to shoot a geyser like stream of water from my palms and into the center of their wall. The stones were slick from the rain that seemed to fall harder as the morning had gone on and the men fell into one another, slipping and sliding to get back on their feet.

Thunder cracked in the distance as we broke through the lines rushing past and free from the confines of the narrow roads. We didn't stop our race until Sumar palace was all we could make out clearly behind us.

We came to a fork in the figurative road and I found it hard to leave Quick. My nose burned with tears that wanted to force their way out from my eyes, but I refused to let them fall. His dark hair was matted to his forehead with sweat and the heavy downpour. By tomorrow it would all be dry and no one would even know it had rained.

"Four days. I will see you at the town entrance and we will win back your home." Quick promised me, his beard brushed my forehead as he spoke.

I nodded, not wanting to test my voice. He was my connection to Indi and to Brass and Slate. I had Jett, but it was different. Quick missed the same people I missed, felt the same pains. Jett had much different problems and yet the same.

I sucked in a deep fortifying breath and withdrew from his embrace offering a tight smile and wishing I was looking at his real face and not the projected one.

"You promised to stay safe. Indi will kill me if I lose you."

I was glad the ring contorted my voice, so it was hard to tell how badly it wavered.

"You have my word. Get out of here, Scat." He smiled. "Scat, Scat."

"So clever, Shark," I said laughing awkwardly and refused to look over my shoulder as I trotted Safanad to where the others waited after already saying their goodbyes.

Rain dripped off both Ridge and Jett's beards, hair longer than usual clung to their heads making us all look like drowned rats. The horses seemed to appreciate the rain, but it only made the usually dry air humid, thick, and uncomfortable to me.

The trip to Wemic lands took a day and a half on foot, with our horses in the rain, we reached the undulating red hills by early evening. I heard the ground change from sand to red rock as we reached the canyons before midnight.

It had rained all day only to stop moments before we reached the canyon. We hadn't stopped for food but ate while we walked the horses awhile. Seeds were the food of choice when traveling. We could grow anything as long as we had seeds.

I ate fresh plucked strawberries from the bush we'd grown in the desert. I tied the ends up of my dress and piled them in my makeshift bowl and ate out of it as I walked. Jett had started to walk closer to Tawny. Ridge, catching the hint, dropped back to walk with me.

When Tawny realized what was going on, she started and glared at Jett. "Haven't we spoken enough?"

"We did not do very much speaking if I remember correctly," Jett said playfully, but I could feel how nervous he was and how much he hated himself for having allowed himself to indulge in Tawny. The tension in his body was evident.

"That's not funny," she snapped. If it was daylight, we would have seen how red she had turned.

"No, it is not. You should practice speaking, Ilisha."

"Don't presume to tell me what to do just because I spent a few nights with you." Her voice warbled, and she yanked off her contortion ring. "I regret every time I was with you more than anything I have ever done in my life!" she hissed, looking and sounding like old Tawny again.

I pulled off my own ring and saw Jett do the same. Better the Wemic recognize us than not. They might spear first and ask questions later if four strangers came walking into their lands during war time.

"I understand. I'm sorry, Tawny. *Gods*, if I could take it back, I would. Steel was my big brother. I grew up with him and Slate and that's it. You know what I feel like right now having slept with his pregnant wife? A fucking asshole, that's what. I don't want you to forgive me, or for the girls to forgive me, I will never forgive *myself*." Jett's voice changed as he took off the ring.

It was still weird seeing him with so much hair.

Tawny watched him skeptically and then faced back towards the canyons. "I feel even worse because I enjoyed myself."

I cringed. Couldn't they keep their voices down?

Jett's head whipped towards her, his mouth agape. "Me too. I feel worse because I'd thought about bedding you before... while he was alive. Especially after you were caught in the undertow of Divine Beauty."

Tawny didn't look at him, her body bumping against her gray mare. "Me too. You two look alike in so many ways, it was hard not to. Like, imagining two Steels."

I could hear the smile in her voice and the implication of her words. I smiled myself and glanced at Ridge who was staring at the ground, his *calling* around his head causing wind to sound in his ears. He must have heard too much for his comfort.

Tawny sighed. "Despite all that. You know I'll never do it again, don't you?"

"You mean you don't want to be my third wife, Matriarch Vetr?"

He sounded like old Jett again and Tawny turned her head with a reluctant smile on her wide mouth. "You weren't *that* good, future Patriarch Var," she teased back, and Jett threw back his head and laughed.

"I am sorry, Tawny. If there's anything I can do to help..." he trailed off, sobering. "You *are* good enough as a wife." He glanced away, and it was Tawny's turn to gape.

"I think that's the worst marriage proposal I've ever heard," she said plainly. "I don't need a pity husband, but if I grow desperate enough… I'll ask Cherry and Amethyst before I let you know."

Jett nodded.

*"Let the rain kiss you. Let the rain beat upon your head with silver liquid drops. Let the rain sing you a lullaby. The rain makes still pools on the sidewalk. The rain makes running pools in the gutter. The rain plays a little sleep song on our roof at night. And I love the rain."*

"Is it safe?" Ridge whispered.

"My gods, is anything safe? If you mean have they stopped talking, then yes. Though I wish I had done what you had because I think I just heard my brother propose to my cousin and she said probably not but not no."

I wiped a hand over my real face and let my fingertips trail over my straight edged nose and my too full lips just delighting in being me for a while. I didn't think I would want to be me for a time, but it turned out I wasn't the only one who didn't have it together. I knew Jett and Tawny weren't in love by a long shot. Jett was doing the right thing by Tawny and she had never been with anyone else besides Steel and now Jett. Tawny could never be a third wife. If they didn't figure that out for themselves, then I would say something. Until then, I'd bite my tongue for once.

Ridge was an excellent story teller. His comedic timing was excellent and laughing felt better than the lust gate at this point. He had so many stories about Sparrow that I found myself missing my mother so badly my shoulders were curling unwittingly as if to protect my aching heart.

He had known our mother, our father, even Lark. Jett helped me back onto my horse and rode so he was close enough to touch as Ridge talked about how inseparable Wren and Sparrow were and how he wasn't the least bit surprised Tawny and I had grown up like sisters as they had.

I fed Balas and Spinel as I rode, stopping only to relieve we and change horrible cloth diapers. I needed some disposable Pampers stat. My only reprieve was that I had stopped bleeding from the birth. Jett said Amethyst was completely healed after two weeks and that Guardian women healed faster than other women.

I was lost in Ridge's stories when shadows shifted from within one of the canyons. I heard a laugh barked and then one of the shapes elongated in the moonlight.

"Rikke!" I shouted, waving and smiling like a lunatic.

Rikke looked just as pleased to see me as he waved back smiling with his cat-like muzzle full of sharp big cat teeth. His lime green eyes twinkling with their vertical pupils against his sleek black fur.

"Scarlett! It has been too long. I thought you were another contingent of those traitors come to try to force us to join them."

Rikke was bare chested, a loincloth as his only article of clothing with a beaded belt. His black hair was pulled back behind his pointed ears into a ponytail with feather fetishes adorned through it. He lifted me off Safanad with his soft clawed hands and laughed as my feet reached the red rock.

"What do you mean a contingent of traitors?" Jett asked, swinging himself to the ground.

Ridge was helping Tawny off her mare as Rikke greeted Jett by clasping his claw to the back of Jett's neck to press their foreheads together. "I will show you."

Jett shared an ominous side glance with me as Rikke led us down the canyon rocks they'd smoothed into a makeshift ramp over time so the horses could make the decent with us. Rikke smiled at me and down at my belly.

"You have never looked more lovely, Scarlett. Both pups are yours?"

"Yes. Balas and Spinel. Tawny is carrying Steel's daughter," I added, and Rikke laughed.

"I am happy to see..." He sniffed the top of my head deeply and his smile returned. "And smell you alive. We had an incident."

"Incident?" Tawny asked.

"Congratulations, Tawny." Rikke's eyes reflected against the moonlight. "I was sorry to hear about Steel, but you carry his legacy within you. That must bring you great joy."

Tawny's lips parted as she blinked at Rikke. Her hair had long ago fallen free from her braid and wisps floated around her heart-shaped face.

"Thank you, Rikke. I... I hadn't thought of it like that."

She *felt* optimistic, and I felt a joy of my own.

"Watch your step," Rikke said, and nodded ahead to his right.

A short low wail slipped from my throat. Heads. Dozens of them on pikes every few steps, rotting so a stench and flies swarmed the entrance of the Wemic lands. I gagged with my intake of air and saw Tawny whirl around to press her face into Ridge's chest.

"Seems drastic," Jett said, sidestepping what may have been a man with long, blonde hair.

"They said we were to swear fealty to the new Prime. That Scarlett, the Sumar, the Dagr, and the Tio were traitors and if we did not send them a hostage to ensure our compliance, they would eradicate our tribe. Our strike was preemptive. They wanted Tika. She is pregnant as well," he said, turning to smile back at me as his shoulder narrowly missed a dark-skinned man's head whose eyes had been eaten out of his rotting skull.

Tawny hadn't pulled her face away from Ridge as we followed Rikke through the dark. Our clothes had begun to dry, and the humidity was beginning to dissipate.

"This is Tawny's birth father, Ridge. You can trust him," I said, finally remembering my manners.

Rikke glanced over his shoulder. "Do you bear the mark?"

"Mark?" Ridge asked.

"Where have you been?" Rikke asked, coming to a stop to take the five of us in.

"Long story, but we haven't been around. Just pretend like we've been missing since it all started," I said. "What mark?"

"You shall see. A man and woman came here pretending to be you. Too bad for them, Keen knows your scent well," Rikke said, continuing between the craggy walls of the canyon.

Little round topped adobes were made right along the canyon walls. The canyon had opened up so a thin stream and vegetation ran along in the lifeline of the canyon. Little cat children were asleep in their adobes, none ran around as they did when we'd come in the past during the day.

"Why are you painted in black?" Jett noticed once Rikke was bathed in moonlight.

"I have been grieving you, Scarlett, Steel, his mate, Pearl, and the others who had died recently. The contingent came with the news."

Rikke waved a clawed hand behind him at the pikes. The fire pit stood at the center of the village. There were three smaller clay adobes for visiting Guardians and the largest adobe where the chief Reski lived with his wife the tigress Nata.

"I married," Rikke said, leading us to the Guardian adobes.

"Why didn't you say so when we met? Congratulations!" I reached on tiptoes to kiss his furry cheek, trying to avoid his tickling whiskers. "When do we meet her?"

Rikke looked away. "Tomorrow. Indigo changed me. Ama did, too," he said with a sad note in his tone.

I knit my brows and glanced at Jett who shrugged. I didn't know what one had to do with the other. I looked into the darkness of the adobe.

"I suppose no one is up now. I'm not sure I can sleep. Goodnight, Rikke." Jett shifted to place his arm loosely around my shoulders.

Rikke's feline face broke into a mischievous grin. "The wait until morning will be worth it, Scarlett. I promise you."

Jett followed me into the adobe that contained three beds and clay platforms and stuffed mattresses. "Want to share a bed?" Jett asked me.

I quirked a brow. "You're a bed hog."

Jett nocked up his chin and gave me a smug grin with his full lips. "So?"

He didn't want to sleep alone. One look at Tawny who had placed her pack beside the center bed told me she didn't want to either. It would be another night of bed hopping for me.

I peeled the wet dress from my body as the others readied for bed. The twins were fed and put to sleep in what was essentially a big clay bowl the Wemic supplied as cribs.

The skin of my belly was flat below my swollen breasts — I couldn't help staring. I should've still been pregnant and if not, double the size I currently was. I could count my ribs.

"Plan on putting a shirt on?" Jett joked.

I finished pulling the man's shirt I'd taken from the Vanaheim arena over my head. "My body has changed so much in such a short time. I don't feel like I was pregnant at all or like I'm a mother," I murmured, feeling an unfamiliar twinge I couldn't place. "I feel like I stole those little bundles."

I scooted up on the bed and beckoned Jett with my hands. Jett gave me a lopsided bearded smirk and crawled onto the stuffed mattress, pulling the sheet over him, placing his head in my lap. I began to stroke his head.

"You're pretty damn maternal, baby sis," he said with a sleep thick voice.

Balas and Spinel slept together between the beds. Their skin was taking a deep tan hue that reminded me of Brass. Their eyes were still the blue of newborns, but I had a feeling they would resemble their namesake as Brass did. They were such good boys, only crying when they were wet or hungry. I was a lucky mother.

I waited patiently until the sounds of his heavy breaths denoted his slumber. As I'd done before, I stealthily replaced my lap with a pillow and left the bed I shared with Jett for Tawny's. She was awake. I could *feel* her knot of muddled emotions.

"Feeling a little better?" I asked, sliding in beside her.

Her eyes flickered open. "What Rikke said resonated with me. I think I have to be more positive for my daughter's sake. Freya's burly boar, I'm going to have a daughter," she breathed. My lips curled into a big goofy grin. "Our children will only be a few months apart. For the record, my daughter is not allowed to date any Regn boys. I don't care how inbred the rest of Tidings is, but the Regn are trouble."

My smile infected her.

"And she'll have two grandfathers even if she doesn't have a father," she whispered.

"Do you think you'll remarry?" I asked her and immediately regretted my question.

She furrowed her brow. "I have to, don't I? That's why you looked for a second husband, we need the support. Someone to share in the responsibility, to come home to when we've had a stressful day. What do you think the end game is with all of this, Scar?"

"We have to do *something* with this project... works.... whatever to remove Ash, Sage, Canis, and Cygnus from power. Return the tribes to their native islands..."

She nodded. "An entire regime change. How are we supposed to do all of that? We're a couple of twenty-one-year-old girls with scattered allies, your brother, your sister's fiancée, and my long-dead-now-returned father are our only traveling companions. I can barely fight as pregnant as I am now and you've got to carry two premature babies."

"I thought you were going to be more positive," I jested, and she sighed.

The bed smelled like chamomile and lavender herbs that infused the stuffed mattress. "You're right. First, Thrimilci. Then, Elivagar. It's a good plan. While Gypsum holds the university, we have half of Valla. We have to go to him, Scar. I can't stand the idea of him thinking me dead, but I don't want to risk activating my bond and him leaving the safety of Valla U."

"After Thrimilci, I could use a heaping helping of good news from Chief."

Tawny's fingers inched towards my hand on the bed and we clasped hands. "I'm so glad we had a chance to remove the hair from our legs if I have to sleep in bed with you," I whispered, and was rewarded with Tawny's giggle.

"I saw you helping Quick remove his."

We both giggled as I gave an exaggerated groan. "I helped him remove it from a lot more than his legs." I feigned a shiver, and we shared another giggle.

"Poor Indi doesn't know she's marrying a gorilla."

Our giggling tapered off as weight lifted from our shoulders. We could pretend for a while that our world wasn't on its head.

One day at a time.

# FORTY

*Jett's soft lips part for his perfect white teeth as he tugs my nipple into his mouth. His tan cheeks hold a flush from our hours of lovemaking and I wrap my arms around his cropped blonde hair.*

*He tilts his head up and his hair is tousled, but he has those same turquoise almond eyes. When he smiles he looks like a model. Steel. We're in the pond below the cherry blossom tree at Valla U and he shakes the branches as we make love so petals fall like soft velvet pink snowflakes around us.*

*I whimper. I don't want this dream to end.*

*He withdraws from my kiss and he's Jett again. "Ah, Tawny!"*

*His neck cords as his strong arms fold me to him on the lush grass in Disir.*

I WATCH SPARROW RUN. *Tawny is bundled in her arms. She looks over her shoulder as the Crathode close in around me. Olive cheeks stained with tears; long wavy hair matted to the sides of her face. We should not have been here.*

*Father should have warned me what he was up to, now I have led my wife and newborn daughter to slaughter. This was supposed to be a family vacation.*

*"Go to Hawk!"*

*Anyone, but my mother and sisters. Cursed Natts. Cursed Vetrs.*

*My staff cannot kill the Crathode. I need only hang on until they our out of sight. I cannot resist looking over my shoulder at her. Her dark hair trailing behind her, Tawny's wide eyes peer at me and my staff lowers.*

*I am brought back to the now as a Crathode claw bites into my wrist and I almost release my staff. I summon as much calling as I am capable of and shoot fire all around me running blindly in the opposite direction of Sparrow.*

*I have to save them. All they have is me.*

My son bounces *on my knee with Opal shoving a book in my face. "Daddy read, please," she urges with those big blue eyes of hers.*

*Her dark mop of hair matches Thrush's as do their powder blue eyes like my father's. Another little girl comes running into the room where I sit on the rocking chair.*

*"Uncle Jett!" Her smile is wide like her mother's, but her eyes are turquoise like mine and her father's.*

*"Where's mommy?" I ask her.*

*"She's with Auntie Scar and Uncle Brass and Uncle Slate. Uncle Jett?" The girl's a spitfire like her mother. I wish her father could have met her.*

*"Are Auntie Scar and Uncle Brass and Uncle Slate like Mommy, Auntie Amethyst and Auntie Cherry with you?"*

*I shift uncomfortably in my chair. I knew this day was coming. There should've been more time. Scar comes into the room, her belly full again. She smiles as she rubs her chest from the heartburn.*

*"Yes, honey. I love Uncle Brass and Uncle Slate as Uncle Jett loves your mommy, Auntie Amethyst and Auntie Cherry. We are one big happy family."*

*Scar looks ravishing pregnant. Brass and Slate seek to keep her that way. Slate walks up behind her and kisses her neck.*

*"How are my bairn?" he asks with a broad smile.*

*"Giving me heartburn. Time to come out," Scar says, giving Slate a big lazy grin.*

*Brass carries a tray of sandwiches in with Tawny and the girls. Tawny leans down and presses a kiss to my lips and I bend to kiss her belly. Amethyst and Cherry take their turns and sit down on the cushions around the low table. Two golden eyed boys with thick dark hair chase one another into the room giggling all the way. Balas and Spinel never speak. They're both mind readers.*

*"Indi and Quick will be here in a few. Shrike was throwing a tantrum when we left," Scar said, holding Slate's hand as she lowered herself awkwardly onto one of the cushions.*

*As if on cue, Indi walked in. "Sorry, I know, I know. We're always late. Shrike is stubborn like his father."*

*Quick walks in toting the dark-haired junior scoundrel with our father's powder blue eyes. "The little prince has arrived!" Quick announced, and Shrike leapt from his arms and hit the ground running right into Balas who spun taking himself and Shrike down to the ground. Spinel throws himself on top of the pile.*

*All that was missing was Steel.*

*I'M WALKING THROUGH CARNAGE. I feel her, I hear her. My mother is standing in a white dress arms held out, her face distorted. She tells me I can fix this. I try not to look at the bodies, the battleground alongside Valla University. Not everyone is dead. Frozen angry faces stare up at angry faces on the castle, I can't even tell if the faces are human. They all look like monsters to me. The wind is whipping at me. I look up at the sky, even the sky is angry. Black clouds, lightening without rain. She's all around me. "You are night."*

*I stand in the middle of a circle, people around the edges, Slate lies in a pool of blood. Light and gushing wind blasts from my bod. My hair, my hands — everything shoots up. My mouth opens in a silent scream.*

SAND, sun, chamomile, lavender, and pine mingled with the scent of cool water as I sharply inhaled.

Tawny the dream beacon strikes again.

"By the Mother, I hate your dreams," Jett grumbled.

I didn't want to open my eyes. I wanted to go back to Jett's dream. It was only slightly awkward that Jett and Tawny dreamt about one another. I opened my eyes.

"Jett."

I shook my head. He had climbed into bed between Tawny and me. I rubbed my face gently as my mind focused.

"Sorry, I miss the girls," he said in a sleep thick voice.

He missed Opal too though he didn't say so. "You named Indi's son, but not my daughter?" Tawny asked, stretching.

She was a lot more comfortable in bed with Jett now. Jett shifted on the bed and I could hear the smug grin in his voice.

"It was a dream," Jett said.

"What about the one I was pregnant with?" she asked coyly.

I slid off the mattress, Ridge was already dressing, and I decided that was probably best. There was so much tension between Tawny and Jett I could jump into the air and stick in it. Ridge gave me a sympathetic look as he picked up Balas from the bowl and walked from the adobe.

"I don't know. I haven't consciously thought that far ahead," Jett said, his voice dropping. "Did you think of him while you were with me?"

I wanted to plug my ears and run from the room. Spinel fussed until I lifted him to me. Tawny wore a shirt that reached her knees and slid out of the bed.

"Of course I did," she said. "In Disir, it was whatever I imagined. You didn't act as he... did."

Tawny started to dress, and I left the adobe when Jett tossed back the sheet. Ridge stood speaking to two lion hybrid men. Chief Reski had wooden beads that hung from his mane of hair. Scars disappeared under a red eyepatch from the eye he lost when Slate was captured, his remaining golden eye was underlined by white fur. Black paint covered his cheek bones down to his whitened jaws and on his forehead into his hairline. He wore a loincloth as the Wemic did, women wearing cloth that covered their humanlike breasts unless they wore simple dresses.

Keen turned around, his black feline nose flaring as he caught my scent. He had gold fur covering his body that grew lighter under his chin and down his chest and stomach. Black paint swirled around his arms and shoulders. His golden eyes twinkled as he looked at me.

I walked over to him and he kissed my cheeks. His long golden hair pulled back with feather fetishes and scratched against my arm as I wound it around his neck to embrace him.

"It is very good to see you alive, Scarlett. We have been preparing. We expected Slate, but you are much better looking," he joked.

I laughed through my tears and he wiped them away with his padded thumbs. Tika swept in to embrace me and her belly rubbed against me as I held Spinel aside. The beautiful tigress's golden eyes gleamed when our hands met while touching her onyx plaited hair that hung down her back.

"Your sons are so handsome," Tika said.

"Thanks, they look like their father. You make a beautiful pregnant woman," I told her.

Nata didn't give us a moment before taking me up too. She and Nata looked identical except she had the bearing of a queen and had big, green glittering eyes.

Tikee's jolly laugh was music to my ears.

"I knew you were alive. I told them, while Slate lives and breathes, he would never let you slip away," he said in his deep bellowing voice.

The lynx man had ears long and high on his head reddish brown and spotted fur sticking straight out. He was also the burliest. I withdrew from Nata and started.

"Greetings. How does the day find you?"

I slapped my hand over my mouth. "Adal? In good health," I stammered remembering my manners. "How does the day find you?"

"Much better now that you have finally arrived. I told them, your death was not possible."

The Faunelle chieftain was half elk with fetishes that hung from his tall antlers. He was well-formed for a man, with a nose like a deer. Antlers stuck up from his tawny face with long hair that matched his short fur coat. He wore roughhewn pants, and a strap crossed over his chest that held a quiver as he leaned on a white staff that was topped with an oblong cage. A sheathed blade was strapped to his hip, his unstrung bow was resting against a stone seat.

He placed his hand on Raud's back, and I blinked. His wife was an elegant tawny doe with long fiery red hair that fell to the hips of her fringed halter sheath dress that rounded against her large pregnant belly. I repeated the greeting with Adal's lovely wife who had helped care for Indi and me after we wandered in the desert looking for Slate's body.

"I don't understand," I said in bewilderment as I looked around.

The Faunelle were like the Wemic. Where the Wemic had leopards, lions, tigers, and cheetahs. The Faunelle had moose, elk, antelope, and all different types of deer. They'd brought their children. Pudu deer girls ran with puma girls, panther boys wrestled with gazelles.

"When the traitors came, we sent an emissary to the Faunelle. They left their lands straight away," Keen said, wrapping an arm around Tika's shoulders.

Tika and Raud were both far along in their pregnancies. Tawny had come out of the adobe with Jett and a young leopard girl handed us all clay plates full of exotic fruits. We settled in around the ashes of last night's bonfire and began to eat.

Ridge sat between Tawny and I with Jett on my other side as Reski, Keen, and Adal filled us in. They'd been waiting for someone to show up until a man and woman came claiming to be me. Nata gave me a wrap to wear so I could feed the twins while they spoke. I wasn't sure where my modesty had gone.

"Rikke will bring them out in a moment," Keen said with a smirk.

"So you gathered to go to war for the Sumar?" Jett asked, having long forgotten his breakfast.

"To get back *our* home. We know what type of woman Scarlett is and anyone who would accuse her of the things they said she'd done, has to be in the wrong," Tika said, adding a nod to her statement.

I blushed. It wasn't all lies. More like embellishments. Tawny cursed drawing me from my introspection. I looked about the clear Thrimilci day, it was cooler in the canyon and not a hint of rain was around from the night.

"Delegate." I whipped my head around and scoffed.

Mirage wore a bandeau like top and skirt, her blonde hair brushed her bare shoulders. Hopper stood next to her; his tattoo arms bulged with hard, tan muscles. His midnight blue eyes raked over me, doubting what he saw.

"I felt your bond snap," he said gruffly.

"You brought her here pretending to be me?" I snapped.

Jett took the boys without asking. I was glad to have a fitted black tank top to wear with my snug khakis because I wanted to look fit in front of that woman. I charged towards her and Ridge scrambled to stop me, sensing my ire. She held up her hands in surrender and I sneered.

"I am sorry. I give up. What I have done to you — it was childish and catty," Mirage rushed out before I could pummel her.

"You slept with my husband, not once, but for two months just to hurt me! What kind of monster does that? I was pregnant with his child that I *lost*. What you did —" I choked off. "I am responsible for my own actions, but you helped him break me."

She blinked at me as my chest heaved. I couldn't believe what just poured from my lips. Hopper's usual perverse attitude was extremely subdued as he placed his right hand over his heart. Mirage mimicked the action as Rikke came to slide his arm around her waist.

"Your wife?" Tawny had stepped up beside Ridge and was giving Mirage an impressive glare.

I scoffed again. Rikke nodded. What he said made much more sense.

"It was a whirlwind romance," Mirage said, wrapping her arm around Rikke's waist so their bodies pressed against one another's.

I shook my head. "Okay." I turned back around, and Hopper grabbed my wrist.

He placed my palm over his pectoral. Hopper was stocky and his chest was covered in curly blonde hair. A red tattoo I'd briefly caught sight of was under my palm. Mirage had the same tattoo which I could see clearly on her chest. It was a deep red and black starburst with blazing flames around it.

"It is a Nordic compass, a sundial. It is the original sigil for the Tios. It is your sigil, the flames are like the Sumar sun, and it is red because..."

I interrupted Mirage. "Yes, I know my own name. Why would you both get that?"

"It is proof of our fealty to you. To taking down Canis and Ash and restoring order and balance. The symbol of the Red Seconds," Hopper explained.

He released my hand, and I ran my thumb over the black and red etches. "This isn't about me," I argued.

"It was the trigger. They would have done it in time, but *you* are who we can rally behind. Your memory, at first, but now you are here." Mirage finished.

Tawny and Jett were both looking at me as I slowly shook my head. "You came here trying to rally the tribes to save Thrimilci?"

Her wide mouth quirked. "We are from here."

"Who leads these... Red Seconds?" Jett asked, and Hopper chuckled. "Who else?"

I exhaled gustily and ran a hand over my face; Slate and Brass. It couldn't be anyone else.

"If your tribes are through waiting for action, we can leave as soon as they're ready," I told Adal and Reski.

I thought I would hear a list of reasons why would have to wait, but Keen immediately started barking orders. Adal called over a dark-coated moose man whose antlers were several feet higher over Tikee's head. The Faunelle were camped outside of the village and as soon as the moose man moved past the adobes, I heard the hustling of several people at once as they broke camp.

They'd been lying in wait for someone to lead them.

Mirage walked up beside me as I rubbed down Safanad's coat while the twins slept in the adobe. Lily had told me preemies slept a lot and fed a lot; both were true. I cast her a sidelong glance and rolled my eyes. She held water in her palm, letting Safanad's wedge shaped head bow down to drink from her palm.

"Your sons. They look just like captain... Brass."

I felt my eye twitch. "Did you project me for Brass too?"

"He hated me because you hated me."

I would not let her chase me away from my own fiddlesticking horse. We stood there in silence for several protracted minutes.

"He loves you, you know. I projected you in the prep room. I never had him as myself and he never stayed the night with me."

I sniffed derisively. "Go *away*. I don't care. What's done is done. Actually... I do have one question."

"Anything," she fired out.

"Were you able to sleep with him as a barghest because you looked like me?"

"We could do other things. I think that was why I was attracted to Rikke right away." Her smile was evident in her tone.

I hated her for her happiness. Hate was too weak a word.

I pressed my lips into a hard line so my chin wouldn't wobble. "We'll never be friends. Don't waste time trying. I'll never forgive you. The most you could hope for is that I don't kill you. The only reason I haven't is because Hopper and Rikke are friends of mine."

I couldn't stand to be near her another second. I turned around to find Jett so he could help me onto Safanad. It was hardly noon and our quasi-troops were eager to march. I couldn't believe it was happening so quickly. We would be a day earlier than planned and I prayed Quick hadn't run into any trouble. He knew to activate his Shadow Breaker tracker in case of an emergency so every second that passed and I didn't feel the pull to him was a blessing.

"I saw him after he got his memories back," Mirage called after me. "He was hunting me. I left the Vanaheim arena and went to Thrimilci, but he followed me there. Hopper spoke to him and convinced him not to kill me if I left to Mabon... the Folkvangr arena. I chose to come here to try to balance out all the harm I had done and I failed to do even that. If Rikke had not taken pity on me and Hopper our heads would be on those pikes. Keen is fiercely loyal to you... they all are. Slate and Brass were the first two to get the Red Seconds tattoos. We all sort of copied them."

"Get to the point," I snapped without turning around.

"He hated what he did to you. Hated himself, me, Brass, everyone for letting him be *that* way again. Did you see the khoraz brothel?" she asked.

"No," I spat.

"After it was evacuated, he burnt it down. People say he burnt down HQ too because that was where we were together," Mirage said in an unfamiliarly soft voice.

"He'd pass out from exhaustion if he went around torching all the places he'd had other women in," I muttered.

She chuckled. "You are right about that."

"It really doesn't matter. I don't need to hear these things. I have no intention of letting him know I'm alive. He can have his life, and I can have mine. Besides, knowing Slate, he's shacked up with some woman already and I'm long forgotten except for his vengeance."

Why was I still talking to her? I watched Tawny, Jett, and Ridge turn my way all ready to begin our trek and my adrenaline shot through me.

"I would not count on it. He is not doing well, you know. Brass? He is harder and angrier. An odd pair those two, blaming one another and yet inseparable. Maybe they have become lovers by now."

It was her attempt at a joke. Since I'd had them both at the same time, I didn't find it funny in the least. They would sooner grow gills and become Merfolk.

Tawny met me and her eyes trailed past as Mirage walked away. "What did that *skank* want?"

"Careful. You slept with a married man. Stones in glass houses and all that," I said, sighing.

Slate was a distraction. Brass was a distraction. I could afford neither.

Tawny cringed and stroked Banat Er Rih's gray coat. "I didn't touch him.... In the adobe, I mean. It was just a stupid dream. He *is* very sexy."

"Oh, *puke*. Please don't talk to me about my brother or my uncle being sexy. That being said, Jett is undoubtedly the best-looking man I have ever seen celebrity or otherwise. Steel, obviously, had those same characteristics since they were practically twins, but Steel was more wholesome." I smiled fondly at my mental image of Steel's open smile and air dried hair.

"There isn't a second that goes by that I don't miss him. I can't think straight. I joke and flirt with Jett because he distracts me... but that's all it is."

"He knows that, Tawns. Jett is far from stupid."

She nodded. "I don't know how you plotted out the arenas when you thought Slate was dead. I tried to put my shoes on the wrong feet earlier and began to cry when I couldn't."

"That's hormones, not grief," I jested.

Tawny lifted her shining eyes with a rueful smile. "Did you feel guilty about being with Brass while Slate was supposedly dead?"

"At first. Then I began to accept that he wasn't coming back and Brass could mourn with me. I fell deeply in love with him then," I confessed, and she sighed.

"What are you going to do about them, Scar?"

"Nothing. Sometimes, you've got to stop beating that dead horse. My horse is long dead. It's a skeleton. I'll always love them. I don't know how to stop. We've caused each other enough sorrow to last three lifetimes and I'm over it. I'm sure they are, too."

Jett walked over with both boys strapped into two padded leather carriers I got from the Valkyries. I swung onto Safanad's back and he passed me up Balas who I strapped to my back and then Spinel who nestled against my belly. He offered a boost to Tawny which she took with a smile and he glanced away.

He was practically wearing a sign that read *GUILTY*.

I took Safanad's reins in my hand and watched Jett swing onto Helhest's back. He'd combed his hair, so it was pushed away from his face and trimmed around the lips of his blonde beard so his full lips were seen. His long seaxes stuck up over his shoulder ready to draw blood.

"It doesn't feel like months. Steel died last week to me. You know?" Tawny sighed.

I did know. I felt as though it was only days ago that I saw Mirage in my bedroom after Pepper flayed my tattoos from my skin and tried to peel my breast like a banana.

Ridge hopped up on Sleipnir and the stallion tossed its head stomping white legs. He patted its sturdy chestnut flank and smiled up at us.

"Now we start a real war."

# FORTY-ONE

The snaking trail of two thousand marching Faunelle and Wemic were slow going. No one had been left behind. They didn't want to risk a counter attack and have only women and children left behind to defend themselves. I rode at the front of the train with the other riders, Adal, Raud, Reski, Keen, Tika, and Nata.

Though I insisted the pregnant women take turns riding, they refused, saying it wasn't their way. The children were excited. They ran within the mass of walking bodies laughing and playing at war. They were to stay back when the actual fighting began with me and Tawny. Ridge and Jett were discussing strategies the entire ride with the chief and chieftain cutting us out completely.

I knew I couldn't fight; Tawny hadn't looked shocked either. We would defend the other pregnant women and the children and in a strange turn of events, I was okay with that.

Mirage and Hopper had come with and walked with Rikke within the first group of Wemic that marched. Hopper got along with the

Wemic and appeared to have quite the following of female Wemic to vie for his affections.

Raud and Adal, who seemed to be two parts of the same serene person, moved forward to walk between Safanad and Helhest. The horses paid them no mind, they were well trained and glad to be out of the stables.

"He was alive," Raud said.

The Faunelle had been adamant Slate was alive when he was captured. "Yes. We rescued him from where he was unjustly imprisoned. I'd lost faith for a few days, but aside from a very angry scar on his face and the loss of his memories, he was unharmed."

"His memories have returned since, yes?" Raud asked, the chieftain's wife was light-footed even in her pregnant state.

I nodded absently, not wanting to go into details. "Did a contingent of Guardians come to your lands?" I asked her.

It was cooler at the southern tip of Thrimilci, but the Faunelle were adjusting to the heat as if they were Wemic. It helped that they wore lightweight roughhewn fabrics that were very breathable. The aggressive personalities of the Wemic were an odd mix with the calming presence of the Faunelle. I wondered what ripples this would cause in the future for Thrimilci.

"No. Adal believes the Guardians that visited the Wemic were meant to come to us after their dealings." She raised her doe eyes to mine and gave me a curious look. "It does not bother you that they have killed your people?"

"It was self-defense. My brother went through the packs the Wemic took from their bodies and found nix torque cuffs. I believe there would've been another massacre the Wemic would not have survived. If they took Nata and Tika as hostages, after Nekee's death, I doubt they would have rebelled. Guardians were created to do one thing — protect. These people who have taken over want power. Granted, we need authority to enforce protection, but what they have done is above and beyond what is acceptable. They want to imprison, subjugate... they've lost their purpose," I said tonelessly.

"Do you think you can reform them?" Raud asked in complete seriousness.

"I hope so. Most of them have been misguided, I think."

Ash would have been a great Prime despite his mean streak. Canis poisoned his mind, made him do things he wouldn't normally have done. Then he killed Steel. Ash would spend the rest of his miserable life in the bowels of Karkinos with Sage to join him. Cygnus would be stripped of his titles and sent there with them. Canis couldn't be left alive. The man was too devious. He would have to be executed and since I was positive he was the Stygian Knight commander, I had more than enough cause to validate it in my mind.

As much as I wanted revenge for my parents, I didn't want Ash and Sage to die. There was something final about death. Too easy. Too brutal. Sky Tio would make an excellent Prime when we waded through this disaster. I was already planning on what my quiet, secluded life would be like when we righted things. I would get a home by Solder and Katydid's. Out of the way, but in Thrimilci so I could be close to family.

Jett rode over to us after speaking to Adal and Reski. Reski had the right temperament for a chief, ferocious, but composed and Adal practically radiated tranquility. The two tribesmen's natures could not be more different, but they struck a perfect balance.

"We are keeping the slow pace and riding through the night so we can attack at first light. I'm riding ahead so Quick knows to be ready." Jett slipped on his tweaked facial distorter so he was the oblong faced hazel eyed man again. "See ya, Scat. Ilisha," he said in his faux scratchy voice.

"Jaw!" I called after him, and he reined in Helhest short to glance back. "Take care of yourself."

The air around me felt oppressive until Jett's projected hazel eyes glittered at me. "I'm not leaving you girls that easily, baby sis. We have a lot of rescuing to do before I can rest. Love you, Scar. You'd better not get in the fight."

"Love you," I whispered to his retreating back as he galloped his roan stallion into the twilight.

We passed through the red sandstone hills where I had been introduced to the Jorogumo for the first time. Events had come full circle, and we had to rid the Jorogumo that had infested our island. Problem was, I didn't want to murder tribesmen that may have only been there because their family was held hostage.

I sent out globes of light to help the moon light our way, falling to the midway point in our train. Tawny took up the rear, while Ridge stayed at the front so the entire train had a bit of light. I took two of the bigger children on Safanad with me and saw Ridge pick up a couple of young Faunelle boys who were swaying on their feet but were too heavy for their mom's arms. Tawny carried a baby in her arms and a toddler faced her on her gray mare's back so she could lay her head in Tawny's lap.

Most of the tribespeople had never been outside of their lands. Keen, Rikke, and only a handful of them had gone into Thrimilci's town proper. Mirage and Hopper added to our globes of lights. It reminded me of the Paper Lantern Festival in China and looked beautiful in the peaceful darkness of the quiet desert.

THE GOLDEN AND royal blue pointed domes of the Sumar palace reflected the rays on dawn like ripe apples on the tree. I got down off my horse with Ridge's help. He hadn't lost any of his jaunty smirk when he aged or that mischievous twinkle in his wide hazel eyes. Safanad sniffed Mirage as she swung her long leg over her back.

It was for the greater good.

"Do not be a hero, hang back," Hopper told her.

"She will not leave my side," Rikke promised with his hand on her leg.

Mirage's hair grew longer, darker, and wavy. Her skin tone deepened and her eyes became greener and the shape changed so there was a tilt to the corners instead of her wide set. Her lips swelled, cheekbones rose, and her breasts grew until I was looking at myself before I gave birth except much more pregnant than I had been able to grow.

I grit my teeth. Seeing her in my skin made my stomach churn.

"I will follow my orders to the letter," Mirage said, only looking at me.

Ridge helped me onto the back of Banat Er Rih behind Tawny before leaping back onto Sleipnir. It was the perfect time to change diapers and nurse the boys.

"Once we breach the walls, you may enter."

He used his heel to urge his horse forward with Mirage, their hooves were soundless in the hard packed sand. The children hung back as the Faunelle and Wemic spread out in a wave to crash into town. If Jett and Quick were on time, they'd be on the west end of Thrimilci waiting for Ridge's signal.

Crag would be disappointed at my lack of strategy participation.

Ridge rode out ahead. He'd made our war his own. I'd like to think if Orion was alive, he'd be on our side. I knew Ridge was doing it based on Tawny and our second-hand stories. Still, there he was in the vanguard.

"There are enemies knocking on our doors. They have infested our heart, demoralized our people, tried to take our wives and daughters, murdered our leaders. We have waited long enough to rid them from our home. Tonight, we take back our island."

Ridge trotted Gypsum's horse in front of our cheering ranks. Wemic roared, Faunelle stomped their hooves. The cacophony of noise made our horses skittish, and I held on tightly to the boys and decided it was time to slide them back into their carriers. Tawny balanced the little girls to the front of her and we faced the town entrances.

The column walked forward as one until we stood at the foot of the white shimmering roads that led through the town to the palace. Black cloaked Guardians crowded into the roads. Jorogumo swarmed behind them crawling over one another with their segmented bodies and too human faces.

Projected Scarlett galloped ahead with Ridge and came to a halt. "I am the leader of the Red Seconds. You know me as Scarlett Tio. The owner of Vigrid, wife of Patriarch Dagr, hand fasted to a Regn second son, daughter of spring and summer, Night's Child, Delegate to the Grand Mistress, Second to the Prime and beloved daughter of Alder Var and Wren Tio. I am here to reclaim my home. Those of you who wish to leave, may go. Take these with you, spread the word. Red Seconds are coming for the Stygian Knights."

Ridge and Mirage combined their *calling* to send baskets Faunelle and Wemic women made filled with red bands. We all took our own out and tied them around our biceps. The dawn had chosen a side. The sun rose to color the sky the same shade as my namesake.

"Leave through the portal and never return, stay, and put on the bands, or fight," Projected Scarlett said with her amplified voice and then used her *calling* to shoot fire engine red lightning into the air.

Ridge translated her words into the chittering of the Jorogumo.

I held my breath. Wemic and Faunelle shuffled their feet. Somewhere, a baby cried. My heart thundered in my ears waiting for a response from the traitors or from Jett and Quick.

Bright blue lightening flashed through the air and I slapped a hand over my mouth as a whimper escaped. Tawny reached behind and found my hand and gave it a squeeze. Quick and Jett had made it.

Suddenly, there was scrambling from inside Thrimilci. "Scar, look," Tawny breathed.

Jorogumo were leaving. There were a few Guardians picking up the red straps of fabric and tying them around their arms as they walked out to us. Someone pushed to the front in town. I was in such an optimistic mood; I never saw it coming.

The man who stood at the front of the line started *calling*. Fireballs struck the backs of the men walking towards us with their freshly dyed red bands. I screamed and found I wasn't the only one. Ridge fired a beam of blue lightening into the air.

It sounded like hundreds of drums all sounding at once. Battle cries melded together until I felt like my ears were bleeding. I pulled my sons' carriers around to my belly and covered their ears as best I could.

Quick and Jett would be attacking on the other side.

"They're wearing nix cuffs!" Tawny shouted.

The tribesmen had reached the town, and the clash had begun. I'd lost sight of the riders and all the tribesmen I knew. I hugged my sons and was never more grateful for them as the wave crashed into the beautiful town I'd grown to love. Shrieks reached us as we slowly followed the last of the Wemic to the edge of the town.

A stream of bodies could be seen fighting and running up the road that zigzagged up to the palace. We saw the moment Quick and Jett's Guardians joined the melee. The gates to the palace opened at the top of the cliff side and Tawny nearly fell off the horse. We couldn't make out who was who, but it was safe to say that Hawk would be leading the charge from the palace.

The battle was over in hours.

Banat Er Rih walked over the scattered bodies that littered the road like garbage. We'd left the other children at the town gates with the mothers before coming into the carnage. Blood, death, anger, and fear assaulted my empath abilities, and I dulled my emotions until I felt nothing.

Nothing, until I saw a human body... until I saw their face. Then horrible guilt when I was over joyed the gory body wasn't Jett or Quick's. Red stained the white roads, Guardians who had been in Muspelheim arena walked between the bodies of the injured and healed the few injured Guardians amongst the Jorogumo.

The day had begun to grow hot, making the smell of blood and what had voided from the bodies of the dead impossible to ignore. It was all of it punctuated by the low anguished shrieking from the Jorogumo and the pained wails of the few Guardians.

I gestured to a pair of Wemic, a snow leopard hybrid with grey eyes I'd seen several times before and a bobcat man that were dragging bodies into a row — the Red Seconds and Shadow Breakers with the Stygian Knight loyalists.

"Could you please help me down?" I asked in a tight voice.

The snow leopard man put his big, clawed hands on my hips and the bobcat helped Tawny down off Banat Er Rih. "Thanks..."

"Ginski," he said in a near roar.

I offered him a small smile. He was the one who had been with Ama and Shale before my wedding ceremony.

"Holler for us if we can help any of them," I told him as Tawny took my arm.

"Wemic do not *do* mercy."

Any dead was too many, but there weren't nearly as many bodies as I thought there would be. By the time we walked up through the roads to the palace gates, the battle was completely over. I kept both my sons at my chest in their carriers even though Tawny offered to take Balas. I needed them close.

We didn't take off our rings, and I walked through my mother's hometown as a stranger. As long as I wore the red band, I was left alone. Tawny and I wound our way into the Sumar palace, I could count on my fingers how many times I'd used the front entrance.

Tawny's arm was a constant source of comfort as we walked past the Red Seconds who had come from the arena. More red bands were passed out, and I internally thanked the Faunelle and Wemic for their thoughtfulness.

The scent of sun and sand permeated the tiled mosaic halls. "It feels surreal." Tawny whispered.

I nodded numbly.

No one noticed us as we walked into the dining room. Tawny froze on my arm.

Hawk stood rigidly as Ridge cupped Sparrow's face, kissing her. Cherry's thin figure was only slightly round and in her arms was a tiny bundle. Jett was trying to gently stop her from kissing all over his face as she cried. Quick stood off to the side with Hopper, Mirage as herself again, Solder, and Katydid. Cyan Tio walked from the Moroccan carved panels that closed the back of the room with the staff clad in white and royal blue bringing in platters of food.

I slid my ring off and Hawk spotted us. I heard him gasp, forgetting his wife in Ridge's arms. Tawny started bawling as Hawk wrapped his arms around both of us. I couldn't see through my bleary eyes.

"Thank the Mother, the gods, all of them. I did not think I would see you until the afterlife," Hawk whispered in a strangled tone.

"I love you, daddy," Tawny croaked out.

My throat wouldn't work to get my words out so I squeezed him all the tighter. At some point, Sparrow joined us and our words were indecipherable. I lifted my head to find Ridge's fair skin flushed, tears welled in the corner of his eyes as he watched his wife and daughter reunited.

"I... am overwhelmed," Sparrow uttered.

"I was gone, now I am back. I am glad you found happiness and raised our daughter to be the wonderful woman I have come to know over the last week. Hawk, thank you for taking care of my girls," Ridge said.

Hawk was at a loss. He stepped forward and offered Ridge his hand. The two men clasped forearms.

"I've been in love with Sparrow since we were kids, it was a foregone conclusion that I would take care of them. Whatever we can do to make your transition smooth," Hawk said his dark eyes scanning Ridge's face.

Ridge was only an inch or two taller than Hawk, their body types were the same. Dark eyes, dark hair — Sparrow had a type. It was strange to see her with the only other man she had been with.

"I do not plan to try to take her away from you," Ridge said with a smirk. "I spent two years with her while you spent twenty years and all the years before we signed our marriage contract. I cannot compete with that."

Sparrow smoothed her hair and wiped her cheeks. "We should discuss this in private."

Sparrow turned and noticed my sons for the first time. She cried out and covered her mouth. Hawk's mouth fell open as he looked at the two six-pound bundles at my chest.

"My sons. Balas and Spinel Regn, they're identical," I said in a hushed tone.

Sparrow started crying and took Balas out of his carrier. "I don't want to get them mixed up."

I laughed as I handed Spinel to Hawk whose eyes gleamed. "Spinel is in green and Balas is blue."

Sparrow watched as I crossed the room to Jett. "Jett, I'm so sorry."

Gods, I'd forgotten about Opal — Pearl.

A boulder was crushing my chest. My brother was crying and holding his son. He raised his eyes to me when I approached. There wasn't a chance I was getting my nephew away from him.

"He was born three days ago. I have a son," Jett said as his face muscles twitched and he sniffled, wriggling his nose.

I gazed down at my nephew. The pink squalling bundle was much bigger than my sons and he looked just like Jett but totally bald.

I hugged Cherry and wiped at my cheeks. "Congrats, Cherry."

"I'm calling him Junior for now," Cherry said as she looked over my shoulder to where Sparrow and Hawk were cooing over my boys.

I saw Quick trying to withdraw from the room and pulled away from Cherry to follow him. Tawny's eyes had locked on Cherry who was coming towards her for an embrace. If Cherry punched out Tawny in front of her parents plus her extra dad, I didn't want to hang around to see it.

Mirage and Hopper were sitting down to eat when I briefly greeted Solder and Katydid before chasing Quick down the hall. I caught up with him just before the portal room.

"Don't!" I called, out of breath.

Quick stopped and turned around as he slipped on his ring becoming the fleshy nosed man with a hair lip. "If it was Slate or Brass, would you wait?"

I searched his projected eyes and sighed. "Just promise if you're in over your head, you'll get out of there. I can't lose you too."

My voice trailed into a whisper. The corner of his mouth quirked, and he walked back to me. The blue starry light of the Sumar portal room twinkled all around us as he held me close.

"You are the adopted sister I never wanted," he teased. His words were muffled by my black hair. "I have to try."

I nodded.

By the Mother, why was it so hard to squeak the words out? He kissed the top of my head and I watched numbly as he used Tawny's auseklis to access the portal. He turned around one last time as he rose from his knees after putting the pendant in some hidden place.

I waggled my fingers as he gave me his patented panty dropping smile with his hair lip framed by a thick dark beard. I said a silent prayer to protect him and make his mission successful. It seemed as though getting Thrimilci and Indi back in one swoop would be too much to hope for.

# CHAPTER 42
# INDIGO

My door burst open and Sterling rolled me onto my back to hide my body. I peeked past his shoulder to find Cygnus and Delta in the room with a handful of Guardians clad in green and gold with their gold embroidered tree of life on their backs.

"What is the meaning of this?" Sterling growled.

I could feel his shift coming. He could not tolerate having anyone seeing me in a state of undress. Something to do with being my mate. Cygnus walked over my floral carpet to the edge of the bed while Delta disappeared into my closet. Sterling pulled the blush pink jacquard blankets over me as he slid, nude, out of bed.

He began to dress with his back to Cygnus, in front of the windows. He had locked the door. He always did. They had used their *calling* to break in.

Delta walked in with her swaying hips and long legs partially visible in the sheer front panel of her caftan skirt. She threw a jade-colored caftan with heavy ivory lace embroidery on the bed.

"Dress. You can no longer stay here," Delta ordered.

"Good. She is coming to Mabon with me," Sterling said, pulling a linen undershirt over his mussed-up chocolate hair.

"I am afraid not. Thrimilci is rebelling, they will likely attempt a rebellion in Valla next and if they find out you are here, they will come here. Unless you want the Red Seconds coming after her in Mabon?" Cygnus said, completely ignoring that he had caught Sterling and I in a postcoital embrace.

I pulled the caftan across the bed with the blankets shoved under my arms. "Where am I going?"

"With me."

Ash had slid into the open door and began dismissing the Guardians. My lips turned down at the sight of him, and Sterling whipped around.

"Indigo?" he asked in a rasping voice.

"Get dressed. We leave in two minutes," Cygnus said, sweeping from the room and taking Ash by the arm. "Delta," he called and her cool blue eyes ran from Ash to Sterling to me.

Sterling *called* the door closed and walked around the bed to stand before me. He nocked his chin up and looked down his nose at me.

"You have been seeing him?"

My lips parted. "He visits me once a week —"

Sterling's eyes glowed as his anger flared. He lunged at me, knocking me back on the bed, and pinned my arms down. Sterling had changed since I'd taken Silver as a lover but he had changed again when he made me his mate. I'd never known the possessive side of Sterling.

"Have you lain with him? Indi..." His chest rose and fell heavily, his jacquard satin jerkin hung open as he clenched his jaw.

"Sterling..," I said softly, too weak from the cocktails to speak fast enough. "Never."

His hand slid between us and my back bowed on the bed with a moan. "I love you, Indi. Tell me, *please*."

I roped my arms around his neck and kissed his soft lips. "Take me, mate."

"There is not enough time," he said, but was already pushing his pants over his hips.

I smiled. "Don't let them move me without you."

"They will not let me go. I have Diamond to take care of and Mabon to rule. The Minotaur are everywhere," he groaned out.

I shut my eyes. "You can care for Diamond *and* me if you took me as your second wife."

One thing Delta had taught me. Use what assets I had at my disposal. He was inside his favorite asset at the moment.

Sterling's teeth slid against my throat. "*Yes*. I want you, Indi. Be my wife. I will arrange things with Diamond. She has not been happy. I am with you and her lover is under siege."

"You have not been with her?" I asked, sliding my nails under his shirt.

"Not since I have been with you here," he rasped.

It was almost romantic.

Cygnus and Ash walked to either side of me as we walked through the gilt trimmed halls, past pastel rooms, and sage green clad servants. Gold chandeliers hung at intervals throughout the castle reminding me of the Regn manor.

I exhaled a shuddering breath and gingerly touched the nix torque around my throat. It felt ice cold against my fingers. The portal door swung open at the end of the hall with a flash a bright light. A man with thick, dark unruly hair that stuck up all around his head with a beard that matched, walked into the hall.

"That door is supposed to be locked, is it not?" Ash asked.

Cygnus froze. The bearded man was built like a tank, he had a wide shapeless nose and thin lips that curled when our eyes met. I knit my brows. I knew that smile. I knew that body. He reached up to his collar and casually scratched his throat. Black jagged tattoos peeked from under the shirt.

My breath caught. He opened his arms. I didn't think. I ran, picking up my skirts, my hair flying around my face.

"Silver!"

"Dove!"

Crippling pain shot through my nix torque and I was brought to my knees. The air was filled with fire and lightening. I couldn't stop shrieking. My head lifted to find the Guardians that were on watch at the door driving back the man who had Silver's smile and knew his pet name for me.

"Silver?"

"That is not Regn. Get up," Ash ground out. I clawed myself along the tiles until he scooped me up off the floor. "Indigo, have sense. You are pregnant," Ash snapped, and I went limp in his arms.

I watched the bearded man get wrestled to the floor.

"Dove?"

It *was* Silver. Wasn't it?

Silver was dead. My brother, sister, grandmother, uncle, cousin, and my love — all dead.

I dropped my head against Ash's shoulder and let him carry me away. If Silver were alive, he would've come months ago to rescue me. I sunk deep into the cocktail's lethargy.

Ash and Cygnus took me through the Ostara town portal. You could feel the tension and fear in the air as we rode through town.

"The Anguillan are scaring the townsfolk. What are they still doing here?" I asked as we bumped along in the carriage.

"Not enough Guardians to cover each island. Do you know who that man was?" Cygnus asked.

"No idea," I said absently.

Ash kept his hand on my knee and I faded to sleep.

MY LUNGS FROZE as I inhaled. My eyes shot open, and I gasped. There was nowhere else I could be except Elivagar. I was lying on a stuffed mattress in an ice cavern. I'd never been to the Frostfell Mountains where the Crathode lived before. Judging from the ice bars and the subzero temperatures, that's where they stashed me.

I shifted my stiff neck to find Ash sitting in the only chair in the corner of the tiny room. The ceiling was low, maybe seven feet high and I could see some of the other prisoners. I was the only human.

Ash watched me with cool celadon eyes. "This is where we keep the pregnant females. They will not find you here."

I shook as I pushed up into a seated position before him and he nodded towards the bed. I pulled up the blankets and Ash rose to his feet.

"This is only temporary quarters until we can reclaim Thrimilci." I decided the best recourse was to not argue with him but listen. "Reports are coming in that Scarlett was with them when they took the island."

I sucked in a harsh breath that seemed to freeze my lungs. Ash watched me keenly as he crossed to the barred metal door.

"No more Sterling. Hope you enjoyed him yesterday," Ash said, clanking the door shut behind him. "If I find out you lied, I will have to force myself to stick to my original plan. I *do* want my own elemental."

The clatter of a door woke me with a start. All of me was stiff and sore as I swung my bare feet onto the ice floor. I pulled the fur blankets tight around me.

No windows. No way to tell how long I'd been asleep since Ash left. I had no idea how long it had been since the bearded man broke into the Var castle. I had no idea how he could have gotten the door open since it was locked. I didn't think it was possible.

"Eat. You burn all your energy staying warm here."

I looked to the floor where a metal tray had been left, the food steamed on the plate. Lifting my head, I noticed a Jorogumo squatting against the wall in the cell next to me.

They'd imprisoned me.

I stepped off the bed and picked up the tray, scuttling back to the bed to eat. The only place it was warm was in bed. The Jorogumo blinked three sets of eyes on its pale white human face. She had crystalline legs and torso with a set of human arms. She had a fan of bleach blonde hair atop her head and her pinchers were smaller than most.

"I am Thre'ik. Welcome to the Beget Oubliette," she said with a twitch of her smooth lips.

Her looks would translate well into a human attractiveness. "The Beget Oubliette?"

"The men come in, impregnate us, then leave. Are you already pregnant or are they still trying? You are the only human here. Gestation is too long and unlikely to produce multiples," she said with a strange vibration in her throat.

My heart sank. I wasn't the only one they had bred. I prayed Sterling had been used as I was and didn't know about this place. My own family had used me.

"I'm around four months pregnant," I whispered as I dipped my crusty bread into my rapidly cooling stew. "Have you been here long?" I asked.

"Shorter than most. Six months. I am on my third sack." She almost sounded proud.

"What do they do with the babies?" I asked.

"They take them away. They are abominations. I have been bred with Merfolk, Gorgons, and Anguillan. What birth is this for you?" she asked.

"*Some* of us are trying to rest," growled a female from the opposite cell.

I looked across to a dark-haired woman with peach skin. She was Merfolk and gorgeous. I knew her name.

"Do not listen to Vanna'ra. She is one of the few who betrayed her people. She did not see this coming." Thre'ik laughed with a rattling noise in her throat.

"My name is Indigo. Indigo Tio," I whispered.

The Merfolk woman got to her bare feet with a blanket wrapped around her like a toga. Glossy black curls fell to her waist as eyes without any white searched my face from across the narrow hall. Her gills at the sides of her jaw flared.

"I mated with Steel Sumar, our ambassador. You know him or that khoraz, Scarlett Tio?" The Merfolk woman sneered as her black nails curled around the iced bars.

"Dead. They're both dead. My uncle and my sister." I swallowed and stared down at my empty bowl of stew.

"I am sorry. Traitors killed our own people. Guardians were with them, that was how I was taken captive. Many of the females here are Jorogumo, it is how they control the rest to fight their war." Thre'ik said, pulling a blanket over her bare torso.

"One human, two Merfolk, two Wemic, three Bjorn, seven Crathode, nine Minotaur, ten Anguillan, twelve Jorogumo, and fourteen Gorgons for sixty prisoners at their disposal. I have been here for over a year." Vanna'ra announced.

"Yes, yes. We all know how to count," Thre'ik said dryly, and I heard a round of chuckles.

I stood and got a better look at my prison. Cells upon cells of half-clad women from all different tribes filled the underground Beget Oubliette.

"How long has everyone been in here?" I asked numbly.

Thre'ik nodded her sharp face to her right. "There are Crathode who have been here for twenty years." She leaned in conspiratorially, "They built an army of abominations."

I hugged myself. Orion was written all over it. We had no idea how long this had been going on.

What could we do against an army?

# CHAPTER 43
# JETT

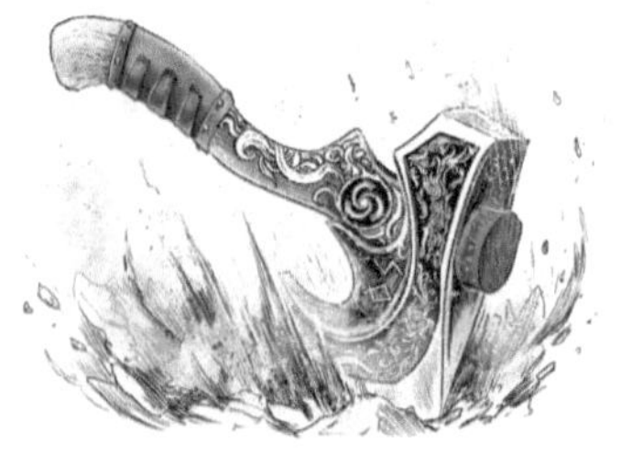

Tawny's eyes were like a faucet someone had broken the valve on. "I am so sorry. There is no excuse for my actions."

Cherry sat on their bed with her arms crossed over the soft swell of her belly. His son slept in a bassinet in the sitting room. By the Mother, what had he done?

Jett leaned against the bed pillar. He hadn't gotten a word in edgewise from the moment Tawny pulled them both to their wing of the Sumar palace. Cherry's full red stained lips were pursed as she stared at Tawny.

"Say something, please," Tawny begged.

Jett wanted to comfort her. Seeing her so upset, and being afraid to touch her in front of Cherry was torture. A bond had been forged in Disir, it was there when they returned and he had seen the change in Scarlett and Quick too. Not sexual — not *all* sexual, but a need to be near one another, to touch and be close.

"What do you have to say for yourself?" Cherry asked, turning her cobalt blue eyes on Jett.

"Nothing. I would take it back if I could. It was a whole other world; you would understand if you were there," Jett explained.

Tawny dried her wide hazel eyes. The slight uplift of her petite nose was red above her wide mouth. Jett did his best not to let his eyes linger over her soft lips.

Cherry stood and faced Jett. "You think you would have been forgiving if I was the one to have an affair with Tawny?"

Jett had asked himself this question a hundred times since leaving Disir. His answer was on the tip of his tongue.

"You have told me you would have slept with her if Amethyst agreed to it. If you were there, I would've been shocked if you hadn't."

Tawny looked at the two wide eyed. She was in over her head. Cherry walked over to Tawny and cupped her face.

"You can say no, Tawny, but I want you to say yes. My marriage depends on it." Tawny peered at Jett out of the corner of her eye. "Don't look to him. What did you do together?" Cherry asked.

Jett unfolded his arms and looked down at the two women. "Cherry, she's only been with Steel — before me."

"Everything," Tawny whispered, her milky white skin flushing.

"Don't worry, Tawny. Between Steel and Jett, your knowledge base must be vast. May I? Don't be nervous, We'll start slow."

Cherry grabbed the fabric of her skirts and Tawny tucked her waves behind her ears and looked over to Jett. His turquoise eyes twinkled as he watched Tawny give Cherry a slight nod. Cherry knew what she was about. It was a show for Jett.

"In this place, it was like a dream. It felt like there were no repercussions. This place makes the pain so much sharper. I miss him."

Cherry let the fabric of Tawny's drop and took her hand guiding her into the bed. She urged Tawny to lay down against the pillows.

"We all miss him. You won't have to do it alone. Your parents, Ridge, Jett, Amethyst, and I... Scarlett. We're all here... for all your needs," Cherry purred. She pulled over her shoulder as she unzipped the back of her dress and let it fall to the floor. "I look better when I didn't just have a baby."

"You know you look beautiful," Jett said wryly.

Cherry gave him a coy look over her shoulder as she climbed up the bed. Tawny's parted lips cast an alluring silhouette as Cherry pulled her dress over her head.

"What are you waiting for?"

"Cherry —"

Jett cut himself short. He should have expected this. Cherry would never leave him, there was so much love there that one infraction wouldn't destroy what they had. On the contrary, a new lover, one as gorgeous and unattainable as Tawny would excite her. Amethyst was another story, but Cherry was doing him a favor. With Tawny having made love to both Jett and Cherry, Amethyst was more likely to grant leniency.

Cherry's heavy breasts swayed between Tawny's creamy thighs. It'd been years since any of them had been with another. If they had agreed on a fourth person, they would have all shared that woman together.

"Tawny, I can't do certain things yet. Do you mind if Jett joins us?" Cherry purred, and Tawny shook her head, clearly in a stupor.

Jett shut the door behind him after checking on Junior. Tawny was gone and Cherry was sleeping, sated. He looked at the door down the hall and started down that way.

Jett swung open the door. Steel and Tawny's wing was like a ghost town. If Pearl had been alive, you could've used a white glove on the surfaces. With everything going on, dust coated every inch. On the coffee table, plans for a nursery with color swatches and wood samples lay spread out. They hadn't been living there since Orion died, but Pearl always kept it ready for them.

He wondered how Steel would feel about him having slept with his wife — *pregnant* wife. Cherry had given her a crash course on making love to a woman. Steel's perfect innocent wife fully immersed in his world of debauchery.

Jett shut the door. He wanted to take care of Tawny. He felt responsible for her. She was also sexy as hell since she wasn't glaring at him anymore. She had shone that special smile his way. The one she'd only given to Steel. Jett ran his hands over his bearded face.

They would comfort her as much as they could. In any way they could provide. Tawny would feel safe. They would bring her closer.

They wouldn't let her hurt alone. Steel would understand that much.

"Fuck. Steel," Jett groaned.

"Jett?" Tawny's voice came out small and pained from behind the couch.

Jett came around it to where she sat wrapped in their bedroom sheet. "You okay?"

*Stupid question.*

She shook her head.

Tawny leaned forward and brushed her lips across his cheek. Jett turned his face, a knee jerk reaction to when she puckered those gentle, but insistent lips his way. She sucked in sharply and pulled back looking at him with wide eyes. Her shoulder was on his.

He looked down his nose at her, broad chest rising and falling heavily as she looked through hooded, almond eyes. Jett leaned slightly forward and kissed her cheek letting his forehead rest to hers. She let out a heavy exhale.

"Why did you do that?" she breathed, not making an effort to withdraw her face from his.

"Returning the kiss," Jett whispered.

"Oh," she breathed, her lids growing heavy as she looked down to his lips.

"Are you cold?" he asked and slid his arm around her back, slowly rubbing it, the friction causing heat.

"A little. I miss him."

Jett slid his hand beneath the sheet. "Me too. We all do."

Breaths quickened. The sheet bunched around Jett's hand and Tawny softly moaned.

"Getting warmer?" Jett asked huskily as he looked down at her.

She scanned his eyes rubbing her lips together. "Do you think I'm a bad person?"

Jett scoffed softly. "What would that make me then?"

"I think you're very bad," she whispered.

Jett held his breath until the embarrassing moan stifled. He held her firmly as she made a little noise when he pressed his lips over hers. He couldn't make love to Cherry until she was healed from birthing their son but she had found other ways to get her pleasure. Cherry relished in her new lover until she passed out.

He pulled Tawny into his lap, she sat straddling him as they kissed, the blanket pooled around her hips. Oh, Freya's burly boar! Jett buried his face, and she held his head to her skin.

"We shouldn't be doing this without Cherry," she whispered, her hair brushing his shoulder as her head lolled.

"*I* shouldn't be doing this. You can do whatever you want," Jett murmured, unwilling to pull his face away from her chest.

His big hand cupped her backside and rocked her hips against him to her constant breathy moans. Cherry had enjoyed watching them together. She always had. Tawny was an eager student and a quick learner.

Things were clearer, they were more present. Jett pushed his boxer briefs down over his hips and parted from her pillowy breasts to see the expression on her face. Her lips were parted, her chest pink from his rough beard. She gave a little nod.

*Thank the gods.*

She bent up on her knees and slowly slid herself over him. "*Oh, Jett!*" she breathed when he was fully sheathed within her.

Jett sat up holding her in his embrace, a pose so intimate they could only be making love. Tawny was easy to please, her fingers curled against Jett's hair that was longer than usual as she moaned in his ear.

"*By the Mother,*" Jett grit out, driving deep inside her, kissing along her throat.

She panted in his arms. Jett shifted to lay her down and her chin canted up as Jett unfurled over her. *Gods,* she felt amazing. Her skin prickled as her muscles flexed around him and Jett groaned.

Sex flushed — she never looked better. He rolled off her and pulled her to his chest. She rested her slender palm on his chest as Jett laid back catching his breath. It was different from Disir.

Much different.

There was guilt. So much guilt. Opal was missing Amethyst still thought he was dead, and he had just fucked his uncle's wife in their suite.

"Jett?" she asked softly, raising up on her elbow.

Jett tried to control his face. It was spasming uncontrollably, and he touched his cheek. Dear Gods, was he crying?

"Jett. Hey... *hey*. It's okay." She pulled his face down to her memory foam-like breasts and started stroking his head.

"Fuck. I'm sorry," he said thickly.

She lifted his head and kissed the few tears that broke free. "It's okay. Tell me what's wrong?"

"What isn't wrong, Tawny? My daughter is missing, I'm cheating on my wives with my uncle's pregnant wife, and my sister is across enemy lines having the Gods only knows what happen to her. And Scarlett? Frigga's sweet grass, don't get me started." Jett's voice had steadily risen, but he stayed where she held him.

Her chest fell heavily with a sigh. "This isn't how it was in Disir. Everything is complicated here," she said, idly running her nails over his head. "Do you want to take a bath?"

Jett nodded. "Will you join me?"

"If you want," Tawny said, offering an empathetic smile.

"I want to cuddle your spectacular breasts that seem to have some kind of super power of instantly making me feel better."

Tawny gave him a rueful look and followed him out of the suite. They'd invite Cherry. She'd *really* like that.

They tried to recapture how they felt in Disir. Making love in the tub, tasting, touching, melding their bodies into one, but that blissful peace they felt in Disir had stayed there.

# FORTY-FOUR

"Quick!"

He staggered through the portal room door and turned, locking it behind him so whoever had chased him through couldn't follow. He was bleeding, his beard was singed, and his clothes were tattered with soot.

He was making a choked sound. I ran to him and started to run my hands over him delving as I went, healing the small wounds. Whatever was causing him to hyperventilate wasn't physical. I had sat right down and waited for him. He'd been gone only five minutes.

"She is alive — on rousen. She is pregnant! That Straumr *bastard.*" Quick turned around, removing his contortion ring, his teeth gritted.

"Rousen? That's impossible. Sterling —" I protested.

"He *lied.*"

Quick had me by my shoulders, he was completely healed, but there was something deeper going on. He scanned my face.

"She stopped. I called her Dove, and she stopped running towards me." He fisted his hands against his head and tugged on his beard. "I did not take off my ring or shave. How could she recognize me with this shit!" he yelled in frustration.

"Quick, it was smart. They can't know you're alive. It's the only advantage we have," I said, pulling his hands away from his hair before he tugged it out by the roots.

"They know *you* are alive," Quick accused.

I offered him a smile. "We decided they would think she was a fake. Without any of you to escort her, they won't believe she's me. She has to stay here to draw them away from Elivagar. Maybe it was an awkwardly shaped dress," I said weakly.

Quick furrowed his brow as his chocolate eyes searched mine with desperation. Blue lights shaded his face so he looked gaunt.

"They took Ama, Shale, Spinel, and now Indigo from me," he ground out. "Touch me, Scarlett. I need to be touched."

Quick was over a half a foot taller than me, he kissed along my cheeks as I tried to catch his hands. I felt his tears splash on my cheeks and a part of me wanted him to take me down this path. It was a path from which there was no return. If I didn't do it in Disir, I wouldn't in the real world.

Luckily, I loved Quick and I wouldn't let him do this to himself.

"Quick... Silver—"

His strong hand caught on the neckline of the men's shirt I wore and I yelped as I heard the fabric tear. Quick withdrew and looked down at what he'd done and tried to reattach the seam at my shoulder.

"Don't worry about it. It's fine," I said, trying to reassure him. I looked up at Quick, he'd finally cracked. "Come. I won't sleep with you, but I'll *sleep* with you. We can go to her room and pretend it's the last night we were here together until it's time for dinner."

Quick gave me a grateful smile, and I wrapped my arms around his waist letting my torn shirt fall open to reveal the strap of my bra.

"I am sorry," he croaked.

"Forget about it. You're just another massively inappropriate brother. There's nothing you can do to make me stop loving you. Nothing. You hear me?" I asked. "I can help you trim your hair and beard so you don't look so much like a feral gorilla."

He kissed the top of my head as we walked up the stairs to Indi's room. If I was Indi and Quick was Brass or Slate, I hoped Indi would take care of them.

"Where's Quick?" Jett asked when I came into the dining room.

Ridge sat in Steel's usual spot with Tawny in hers, then Cherry and Jett with their backs to the morning glories. Hawk sat in Pearl's seat at the head of the lightwood carved table. Sparrow sat to Hawk's right with me beside her. Solder, Katydid, Mirage, and Hopper were with us. Cyan Tio had his girlfriend at the very end where my stoic distant cousin seemed content to sit in silence.

A carved cream upholstered chair sat empty beside me.

My shower had felt incredible. We had Thrimilci back. The bodies were cleared from the roads and Guardians were washing blood away. The Muspelheim arena had been emptied and people were moving back into their homes. The Faunelle and Wemic had set up camp just outside of town in case the Stygians sent an army in retaliation.

Those were the good things.

Quick was right. All of those people were dead, Indi was captured, Pearl, Steel, Moon, Reed, Haarder, Cory, and my parents — the list was endless. We had taken a huge step in righting our world, but the empty seats were a reminder of the price we'd paid.

"He's asleep with his nephews. He went to Ostara and saw Indi. They have her heavily guarded. He's not doing very well," I said softly. "He also said she's visibly pregnant."

I sat down to the table. My orchid chiffon gown fit wonderfully. The Dagr palace had been ransacked. Guardians were being sent there to repair and restore. I'd asked a volunteer to bring back clothing for me and the boys.

"What! You let him go alone? Pregnant!"

Jett's palms slapped on the table top and I held onto my goblet so it wouldn't fall over. I spoke in a calm tone as I reached for a platter of pasta filled with black olives, red peppers, mozzarella, and basil and filled my plate.

"He had to try. He knew he wouldn't succeed. He got farther than he thought he would. He saw her. She appeared healthy," I murmured. "She's safe. They need her. We have other things to focus on at the moment."

I used tongs to pick up a chicken breast from another platter and topped my plate with an Italian dressing. Tension encased the room. Hawk and Sparrow wanted to know what we had planned. Ridge couldn't stop staring at Tawny and Sparrow. The discussion between Cherry, Jett, and Tawny must not have been as bad as she feared because the three of them seemed to have reconciled. It was better than they could have hoped for.

"I don't think we should stay the night. I want to see Gypsum and the Stygians are going to be monitoring the portals even closer if they're still open. Time is of the essence," Tawny said.

"I'm staying here," Cherry stated.

Jett and Tawny whipped around to her. "Are you sure?" Jett's face was etched with worry as he held his newborn son.

"I have a message for Tawny to give to Amethyst, but that's it," Cherry said, picking up her fork. "Unless you're leaving Balas and Spinel here, Scar?"

Everyone turned to me and my brows leapt to my hairline. "Leave them? I just had them and now I'm supposed to abandon them?" My voice reached higher and higher as I spoke and tears collected in the corners of my eyes.

"It does make the most sense. You want two preemies in the Illfuss Ice Fields of Elivagar?" Sparrow asked gently.

"I'm their aunt. My milk came in, I would wet nurse for them myself. You have to be there to get the piece from the Lycans," Cherry said, offering me a small sympathetic smile.

Katydid cleared her throat delicately. "Our son still nurses. If you approve, I would not mind helping with feedings."

Solder beamed at his wife. Peridot was asleep in their new rooms with a staff member. I didn't know how I felt about Brass's ex-lover nursing our sons.

Hawk sighed. "You know they have to stay. Brass will see them when he returns. It is the right thing to do Scarlett. You will miss them, it will be hardest on you, but I promise they will be loved and cared for."

I finally understood how my mother had truly felt in leaving Jett and Indigo behind. I wished I could hug her and thank her for giving me all the love she had for the three of us and to apologize to them for never knowing fully how deeply she loved them.

I nodded, blinking away tears. Katydid smiled pleasantly at me.

"I have a pump you can use so you do not lose your milk."

I had no idea what she was talking about and was glad when the subject changed.

The palace had the floral musky scent of Pearl in it. I wondered if she was the source of the scent or if the palace had infused her skin. Hawk began to tell us about what happened at Valla U, how Gypsum saw the Stygians because of Diamond, and how when he had come back to the Sumar palace with Sparrow, Pearl was nowhere to be found, and Slate had said Opal was gone. No one had claimed to have her.

Jett and Cherry were very quiet while he laid out the messages Storm-pale delivered from Gypsum describing the executions. Hearing about how Hawk was in the streets trying to evacuate the people into the arenas, how my grandmother was marched and executed in front of hundreds of people made my food curdle in my stomach.

"When do we activate the bonds?" Quick asked, walking into the dining room.

I had trimmed the back of his hair and put product in the top so it was a longer version of what he typically had; the beard was trimmed, so it flattered his anvil jaw. When you looked good, you felt good or so Tawny had always stressed.

He kissed the top of my head before sitting down. "Thank you."

He took the empty seat, and I gave him a lopsided smirk. "For which part?"

He leaned across the table to get his serving of dinner. "Take your pick. For turning me down, for taking care of me while I blubbered, for making sure I didn't go looking elsewhere, for helping to make me look mildly human."

"You're welcome... for all of it. The manscaping was for me, really. I understand now why you keep your hair short with that nest on your head. It was painful to look at," I said in a low tone.

Quick chuckled as he filled his plate as close to his old self as he was going to get without Indi back. Hawk and Sparrow had never looked so downtrodden. Not even when my mother died. The loss of Pearl and thinking they'd lost Tawny days apart had done a number on them.

"No bonds, not until we secure Elivagar then it won't matter once Tawny is reinstalled as her ruler. Unless... do you plan on becoming patriarch?" I asked Ridge who was startled out of his ogling of Sparrow to address me.

"No, not unless she wants my help. I could stay on as an advisor. I do not have anywhere else to live... unless that is a problem," Ridge added apprehensively.

"We will need to discuss your — *our* marriages to Sparrow at some point," Hawk said casually.

"I never thought I would see you again. When you told me to run, I did. I went to the Tio palace and took the portal to the Sumar. When word came back that you had been killed, that they thought we were all dead, Hawk took me to Chicago," Sparrow told him with such a pleading look she somehow looked as if she was groveling on her knees while sitting at the table.

Ridge had forgiven her the moment he'd seen her alive and well. "Sparrow, I am happy that you and our daughter are here now. Nothing else matters to me. I love you, Sparrow, and you, Tawny. I am intrigued about your son. Gypsum? Any grandson of Flint and son of Hawk Sumar must be one of the most honorable men to grace these islands... and handsome if he looks anything like his mother. Is he betrothed?"

"Gypsum?" Quick laughed. "Goodness, no. They were in Chicago until two years ago. He was inducted this year. Hard kid not to like. He will be one of the great ones."

Hawk and Sparrow both seemed pleased by Quick's impromptu endorsement. I licked my lips and tried to ignore Ridge's gaze.

"I never thought I would be this old. Alder and Wren's love children." He shook his head with a smirk. "I told Delta not to marry him, but all she saw was Willow as a Haust patriarch wife and she wanted to be the Var patriarch's wife if she couldn't be married to the Prime. I knew Alder well. Good man, quiet — introspective. Did not joke very much, but Jackal had taken more than his share of humor in that gene pool."

Ridge was coming with us. Solder and Katydid were returning home, but Mirage and Hopper would be staying in the palace to keep up their projection of me. Cyan and his girlfriend had nowhere else to go since the Tio palace had been overrun. Dinner was cathartic for us all. Long after we were supposed to be on our way, we stayed, catching up on everything that had happened and describing events at the cottages.

"I'm pregnant. Since no one else is mentioning it..." Tawny blurted out at one point, and Hawk looked at Quick, his hand fisting around his goblet. "Daddy, no!" she said, sounding appalled.

Quick only snorted. Hawk and Sparrow both turned on Jett with Ridge watching on with an amused expression on his fair face. It seemed to be the way his face rested.

"Jett Var?" Hawk ground out.

It would never matter how old she was, Tawny was forever his baby girl. I considered it a breakthrough he hadn't gotten up and decked him. Jett's face was beet red above his beard. To my surprise, Cherry placed her hand on both Tawny and Jett's hands where they rested on the table top.

"It's my understanding that the baby is Steel's, but we love Tawny and we've let her know she is welcomed in our marriage if Amethyst consents. Of course, it may be best she has a lesser family husband since Jett is heir as is Amethyst," she said pragmatically.

"Of course she's Steel's," Tawny snapped.

"She?" Sparrow squeaked, slapping her hands over her mouth.

Ridge's face split in a proud grin. "We are going to have a grand-daughter."

Sparrow and Hawk both stood along with Ridge and gave Tawny hugs as she began crying again.

"You have to go to Valla U and see Gypsum. He's trying to be strong, but it is hard to do with so many tyros grieving. He's found himself being someone the others look up to since his acts saved them," Sparrow said, wiping at tears. "You being alive and a niece will be just what he needs to keep the other tyros strong."

Saying goodbye was never easy. Saying goodbye after thinking your daughter, niece, nephew and the fiancée of your other niece were all dead was worse. It was Cherry's choice to stay. The right choice, we'd agreed, and I'd been there with her if I wasn't a pivotal piece of the puzzle.

Quick gave back the auseklis key and apologized to Tawny. She dismissed his apology telling him if she was in his position, she would've done the same. Sparrow had clung to Ridge as Hawk stood back, stoically watching the married couple embrace.

"Take care of our daughter. *Balder's brow*, you smell the same." She laughed nervously, and Ridge held her close.

I didn't want to eavesdrop, but I couldn't help myself. For once, I was glad of my nonexistent love life. I had no delusions about Brass or Slate. They were two extremely good-looking men leading a rebellion, of course women were throwing themselves at them. They did it before the two men had a great sob story about my death.

Ridge's eyes flitted up to Hawk who sighed and turned away. Sparrow gasped as Ridge kissed her. Quick gave me a nudge.

"Do you think that is what you look like? One kissing you, the other waiting his turn?"

"No. Slate was never good at waiting or taking turns," I said and found myself sounding wistful.

Not knowing what to do as Sparrow and Ridge kissed, Hawk walked over to me and pulled me into a hug careful not to squish Balas and Spinel in my arms. "Don't take unnecessary risks. Remember, they won't care about honor or fairness. If they have a chance to stab you in the back, they will. Trust no one, Scarlett. They have released creatures in the towns to keep the townsfolk from wandering. Slate and Brass were here four days ago and told us that on every island, monsters run the roads. They'd bred them specifically to keep fear in the people's hearts and to prevent an organized uprising. Not tribes, but demons and creatures they must have sold their souls for." Hawk warned. "If you hurry, you may catch them in Elivagar at the Niflheim arena. Unless you've moved on." Hawk spared a glance for Quick and I scoffed.

"Thank you for the warning and for the information, but things are better without any complications. They have what they need to do and until I need Slate's help, it's better we stay apart. I promised Indi I'd take care of Quick; I mean to follow through on that promise. I love you, Hawk," I said, squeezing him tight. "Ridge seems like a good man."

Hawk scoffed. "A good man who's moving in on my wife — his wife — I'm not sure about anything anymore. I love you too, Scarlett." He gave a solemn look to Spinel's little head. "There are times when I wish we never returned, but then I imagine this world without our help and know we did the right thing."

"Was it this bad?" I asked.

His lips turned down. "Sparrow was terrified and had this..." he smiled down at Spinel, "tiny bundle. I was supposed to go with her and return once we knew what was happening. Then the Red Kings." Hawk sighed. "We lost my father and my closest friends in a blink. The target on our backs — mine and Wren's for certain — would've put all of you in jeopardy. We couldn't convince my mother to leave. Slate's shift was unpredictable. They thought we were all dead. Steel would be heir to Thrimilci, Slate wouldn't be alone, and Jett could grow up on the lands he would inherit from Alder. It was safest to hide. We almost returned when we had Gypsum for the same reason that we let Jett stay in Tidings. Truthfully, I would've left you as well if I thought Wren could've handled it." Hawk brought his eyes up to mine. "The portals should've opened sooner. We would've known how bad it was and whether we could return. When they finally did, you were in college and Gyps was in high school. You were unlike those here *or* there; humble, kind, and what true Guardians were supposed to be. If things get bad, send word and run, Scarlett. Fight but don't die. We'll bring the twins back to Chicago and save those who can't stay here. We can help them there, too."

I pressed a kiss to the top of Spinel's dark head. The tears were not far behind as I gave him to Hawk.

"I have a role to play here. Running isn't an option for me," I whispered thickly.

"I don't wish this path for you... but I am so proud of you."

Quick rubbed Balas's cheek with the back of his finger as Sparrow came to collect him.

"We won't let anything happen to your sons. We won't let them out of our sight," Sparrow promised as she kissed my cheeks. "My, how Wren ever managed..." she choked off.

My mother lived a half-life. Never took another lover. Her only pleasure was me and her painting. I understood it better now. She sacrificed her life and happiness for everyone else's safety.

"We're moving your cribs from the Dagr palace into our wing tonight so I can do their night feedings. Katydid will be here in the morning so I can sleep. We've got it under control," Cherry promised.

I nodded and gave her a hug, sparing a kiss for Junior before Quick pulled me close and led me through the portal door.

CHAPTER 45

# GYPSUM

Celestine's ebony fingers were fluid as she played the lyre blending with my panpipe and one of the second-year men's bodhran drum. I'd asked Slate and Brass for some kind of string instrument and they'd brought a bowl-shaped lute another second-year man played during Crimson and Beryl's reception. It certainly made for an interesting modge-podge of eclectic music.

No dance floor had been erected. Tyros danced barefoot in the grass of the greenhouse with citrus and flowers blooming, mixing the sweetest scents. Moonlight shone through the bulbous stained-glass ceiling that seemed to drip down in the center like an inverted peak. Just about any kind of tree or flower I'd heard of grew in the greenhouse at Valla U.

The girls had strung together cherry blossoms from the trees that overlooked one of the three ponds and hung them in ropes from the trees like garland. Crimson wore a crown of delicate white star-like flowers in her hair that hung in shimmering red curls down her back.

436

Fern and Wisteria had hand sewn her dress from the fabrics Slate and Brass smuggled in. Beryl wore one of my own ivory satin jerkins since we couldn't make it to the Sunna manor.

Mica was her only bridesmaid; Cherry had donated a pale pink chiffon dress that matched the cherry blossoms for her to wear. She danced with Beryl in the mass of smiling swaying bodies of the tyros and even some of the provosts.

They needed this.

Morale was down, no one could see their family and Slate and Brass weren't able to reach anyone from Ostara. Hardly a handful of people had been evacuated from Mabon, but only because of Viper Enox. Cherry's dad was the Centaur ambassador and had gone into hiding after receiving several reports on Minotaur sightings around Mabon. On his way through town, he'd only told families he trusted not to turn on him to head to the arena.

Fifty Guardians saved. That was forty-nine more than Ostara.

We'd eaten on blankets off platters carried in by us, the whole feel of the wedding had been comfortable and quaint. Not what you'd expect when a greater and lesser family were bound together. They didn't have rings until Boa and Fern had both given up their own at the last minute. It was my favorite part of the entire day.

Until the drinking began.

I felt sorry for River and Crag who were watching the forces with a team of tyros. We could never entirely forget the mutant army outside of our walls. Canis sat in his command tent just outside of our reach with Dahlia around the clock waiting for our guard to be down for even an instant.

Mica made eye contact with me and I gave her a wink. She wore a white star flower in her hair that matched her creamy skin. Beryl had made me his best man, and we'd walked down the aisle together. I wasn't doing a very good job of avoiding her.

"Take a break. Have some fun." Malachite hovered behind me with a necklace of daisies.

I moved the panpipe from my lips for a moment. "Everyone else is having fun because I'm here playing for them. Why don't you go dance?" I returned to my playing and watched his squinty eyes crinkle as he looked at Celestine.

"Because Celestine refuses to dance with me. My feet have lost all rhythm while my heart aches," Malachite said, giving Celestine a salacious grin.

The dark beauty gave Malachite a smirk of her own. Malachite didn't have a type. *Woman*, was his type and during war time, there were a lot of lonely women.

"Ro looks sexy as hell."

Malachite nodded to where Rosasite danced with Zircon, her glossy black curls bounced as she hopped barefoot to the tune of our music. She was undoubtedly ravishing. Jade moved into sight taking Beryl's hand and Mica smiled dancing away.

"Do not be an idiot, Gyps," Malachite said, dropping his voice.

I pulled the panpipe away from my lips letting it fall against my chest from the twine I tied around my neck. I reached behind me and plucked a ranunculus the color of sunshine from the bed nearest me.

"One dance won't kill them," I said, waving to my fellow musicians and hurrying over to Mica before another took her as their partner.

Mica saw me coming and her cheeks instantly reddened. For a moment, I thought that the others stopped playing. I couldn't hear anything aside from the beating of my heart and the loud exhale of my breath as she blinked big brown eyes at me. The dancers blurred; she shone like the moon as I approached. Her smile was bright yet shy.

I held out the yellow flower to her. "Persian buttercup. Not as beautiful as you, but I doubt I'd find a flower in here that could come close." I knew my dimples pop into my cheeks when her color deepened as she plucked it from my fingers.

"Thank you, Gypsum," she said, adding the flower to her hair.

Music reentered my world. Swaying bodies appeared in my periphery. Where had they been moments ago?

I held out my hands to take her into my arms and her slender hand fit in mine, looking so small I thought I might crush it. I wondered if my callouses would scratch her soft skin as I took her in my arms and started to lead her around the grassy surface we'd designated as the dance floor.

She tripped over her dress as we spun and I picked up her hem for her, holding it in my hands as we moved. She licked her bright pink lips, and I realized I was staring at them.

"I thought you have been avoiding me," she said at random.

I kicked myself mentally and flashed her a reassuring smile. "No. I felt like a jerk for taking advantage of you. I wasn't sure you wanted me around after I assaulted you," I said ruefully.

She glanced away. By the Mother, I said something that upset her.

"I did not want you to leave... or to stop. I was trying to adjust your expectations," she said in a much cooler tone.

I'd watched Slate blow it enough times with Scar, to know I was getting nowhere fast. Still, my stomach was in my throat. She had wanted me to keep going. I scrambled for something... anything intelligent to say. Really, *anything* at all. Nothing was coming to my tongue.

"I didn't go to your room with expectations. It's better that we stopped, we were both in vulnerable places," I told her, praying for an end to this conversation.

"Are you still feeling vulnerable?" she asked, looking at me through her long fluttery lashes.

"No," I answered, feeling my stomach tighten and the overwhelming need to adjust myself.

She wouldn't ask. She wasn't that kind of woman. This was as close as she'd get to inviting me into her bed and judging from the unnatural shade she'd turned; she was hardly comfortable with what she *had* said. The question I posed to myself was whether I wanted the responsibility of her expectations hereafter. Diamond would be furious *and* she was Ro's roommate.

But, *Gods...* I wanted her.

Diamond was married. Who knew who Ro was with these days? I could have a future with Mica. Mom would love Mica and she was a Rot.

"Do you want to go somewhere quiet?" I asked her, unable to hide how my voice had dropped.

Her freckled chest rose with her inhale. "Yes."

I licked my lips and wrapped my hand around her wrist. I couldn't wait. I wanted her too. I had never wanted anything as badly as I did in that moment. Not even with Diamond. The first time I'd been with her, she'd seduced me. A myopic boy to rebel against her family's expectations. I felt like that was the only reason she was with me most days.

We wound through the bodies. I tried not to run or to make a scene. She seemed to be floating behind me with a dreamy expression on her face. Mica's hand squeezed mine and flashed her another smile praying it looked nothing like Malachite's had.

I turned back around and froze. Two young women stood at the entrance to the greenhouse. Both with long dark wavy hair that fell to their elbows, one with wide hazel eyes and a doll-like face, though you better not say that to her face, and the other with green-blue almond eyes and lips that always made her look petulant. Well, they had when we were younger. Now she looked sultry, and every man in Tidings had noticed. The beards on the two men with them did nothing to hide who they were, though the third man was a mystery.

I didn't remember dropping Mica's hand, but suddenly I was running towards Tawny and Scar. Tears streamed down their cheeks as they launched themselves into me. Thank goodness I wasn't as small as I used to be.

"You're alive," I said stupidly, and they both laughed through their tears.

Just like old times.

I didn't want to let them go, but they stepped aside so I could welcome Jett and Quick. There was a lot of back patting and stiff upper lips.

"Gyps, this is my birth father. Ridge Vetr," Tawny said, bringing a fair skinned man with dark hair and wide hazel eyes that looked just liked hers to me.

I shook his hand and found that he was scrutinizing everything about me. Not in a judging way, almost scientifically. He'd just discovered a living Dodo.

"Gypsum Sumar. Hawk and Sparrow's son. I can see them both in you. It is a pleasure," he said in earnest with a smile that held good humor in it.

"You saw my parents already? How are you alive? How are any of you alive? Odin's eye, I hope I'm not dreaming," I said, wiping a hand over my face.

Quick laughed with Jett as they slapped my back. "Looks like we came at the right time. Whose wedding?" Quick asked.

"Beryl Sunna and Crimson Rot. They fell in love; they're having a baby. It's been a crazy couple months," I said absently.

"Was that Mica Rot you were with?" Scarlett asked with a coy smile, and I cringed having forgotten her.

She was no longer behind me. Curse the gods. I would make it up to her.

It felt like only seconds had passed since I'd seen them walking into the greenhouse when I heard the music stop. Truly stop this time, as the others noticed who had come. Butterfly let out a strangled gasp as she ran to Quick.

"Coyote has been beside himself. He and the kids are the only ones in Ostara. We had another girl. I thank the Mother every day that they are safe, but he will not let Brass bring them here in case the Ostara townsfolk come to their senses and try to flee. *Oh*, Silver." The little red head clung to Quick, and he looked uncomfortable for probably the third time in his life.

The other provosts swarmed them and I was lost in the shuffle. I knew I would get them back, but now they had a story to tell. Scar had identical boys she named after Spinel. They tried to describe where they'd been and what they'd been up to. Beryl wrapped his arm around Crimson's shoulders as they listened.

They'd freed Thrimilci. The tyros cheered. They were full of great news except for Indi. Quick took Crimson out on the dance floor, *er*, grass, and Beryl swept Scarlett away. She looked thin for someone who had had twins a week past. Jett found Ro dancing and stole her from Zircon as Tawny moved to sit down with me. Ridge was surrounded by provosts who knew him from before. His story was unbelievable.

A life reclaimed. I couldn't imagine the emotions he must've felt at having it all torn from him because of his father. Only to return a score of years later and the world is falling apart. He was probably just happy to have Tawny. I would be. I was. She was alive.

"How's mom doing with her two husbands?" I asked Tawny.

Tawny laughed. "She's overwhelmed. Dad is handling it really well, even when Ridge kissed her — twice."

"Twice!"

She nodded with a smile. "Ridge is not a bad guy. Not like Orion. I like him, Gyps."

Mica and Malachite were dancing, and I forgot my panpipe. I would deserve it if he took her to our room tonight... but I wouldn't let that happen. Not Malachite and Mica.

"I'm sorry about Steel," I murmured. "How are you doing? Pregnant, I see."

"Not good. Steel and I are having a girl." She looked far away, and I didn't know how to take away her pain. "I've had a marriage proposal already though," she said, trying to keep things light.

"Oh yeah?"

"Jett." She looked at me from the corner of her eye.

I scoffed. "You a third wife? *Jett's* third wife? Steel's nephew? No way."

"I have been exploring that option but I made up my mind tonight. I'm not going to. I want to fall in love again. I know I got lucky with Steel, but I have to have faith that it can happen again," she said dreamily.

"Exploring?"

"Exploring," she confirmed and peeked at me from the corner of her eye.

I groaned. Tawny married the only man she'd been with and now she'd been with her second. Jett, who had two wives.

"May I have this dance, Matriarch Vetr?"

Ridge had finally broke free of the provosts and offered Tawny his hand. Tawny smiled and got to her feet. Scarlett took her place next to me as I picked up my panpipe.

"Mica has a big crush on you," she said with a fabulous coquettish smile.

I dropped my pipes again. "How are you, Scar?"

"Don't you mean Khoraz Seductress?" She sniffed derisively.

I gave her a wry smile. "Not everyone believes that garbage." I opened up my jerkin and showed her the deep red and black Nordic compass with blazing flames around it. "You'd be hard pressed to find a man in here without it over their hearts, some of the women got it too."

"You guys, too?" She feigned exasperation. "No? That the men who sleep with me either die or go crazy?" she asked, pursing her full lush lips. "I'm a Natt. That whole story about the missing Tio girl, Pearl's mother... it's baloney. Natt's are known for having affairs and leaving their bastard offspring with the Valkyries. Just like Pepper and Spear. Pearl's aunt, the girl that disappeared, told me. She's a Valkyrie. That means, Cassiopeia and Pearl were cousins. Don't think too hard on it, it starts to hurt your brain." She gave me a rueful smile as I gaped. "I didn't tell Hawk yet. He's got enough to deal with." She twirled a blade of grass between her fingers.

"That is one tangled web."

"It gets crazier. I think the Natt girl posing as our great grandma was lost where we were lost. I don't think she was raised by Leshys at all and something Lily, our real great aunt who was raised by the Valkyries, said about family looking after one another... I don't think our great grandma hallucinated this blue-eyed man. He must be our relative to have pulled her from... there." Her brow furrowed as she concentrated looking like she was on the cusp of something profound.

She shrugged with a sigh. "I guess the *how* of it doesn't matter. She got the piece and knew we were Natt's and that Pearl had to pass it along."

She'd lost me, but I gave her a reassuring smile, anyway. "Maybe you could break into Basil's history books and find out what Natt women could have been her mother. You could find out who the man was that way. He might know something if he's still around. He'd be super old though."

We were long lived. It was possible.

I picked my pipes back up and began to play again. Fox slid up, flashing his baby blues at Scarlett in a very *un*provost like way — *married* provost, at that. Scarlett's smile rose to her lips like blossoms opening their petals to the sun and she disappeared with him. Malachite groaned obnoxiously.

"The Second is possibly the sexiest woman I have laid eyes on. *I* would go crazy to rub my face between those —"

"Finish that sentence, Malachite and I will let my brother and our captain know." Quick snuck up behind Malachite who turned around to give a cocky smile.

"You two seem close," Malachite prodded, and Quick's smile darkened.

"She is like a very appealing, untouchable, adopted sister to me that I am extremely protective about."

Malachite nodded with his hands up in surrender and walked away to refresh his drink. Quick sat down beside me as I played.

"How have they been?" he asked, his tone changing.

"Not good. They're going crazy without her. They need to know she's alive, even if she doesn't want them back," I explained, rubbing my thumb over my lips. "Brass lost his fertility. Neither will so much as look at a woman."

Quick nodded and took a swig of his goblet. "We are going to the roof to show her in her elemental form. I will try to convince her to activate her bond. She is angry. She will not admit it, but she is so busy trying to make everyone else feel better. She does not want to admit that they hurt her *badly*. She blames herself for all of it."

"That's ridiculous. She'll know that when she goes to the window." I told him. "Jett slept with my sister?" I asked, and Quick laughed.

"Don't give her a hard time. It was a mess. She has been... exploring her sexuality," Quick said with a mischievous smirk.

"Gods, I don't want to know," I said, placing my pipes back to my mouth.

Scarlett stood in the window of Valla U and gasped.

"They're the monsters from my dream."

"By the Mother. They *are*," Jett breathed.

"They showed up two days ago. The purebred tribes were replaced by them. I know it's too dark to see them clearly, but they look like hybrids of hybrids. It's pretty terrifying. None of that *either or* like when humans and hybrids mate. These beasts are mutations." I grimaced.

The faces at that distance with only the campfires to light them, made the hybrids of hybrids look even more horrific. Jorogumo torsos had Merfolk nose*less* faces, Crathode had the sleek reptilian skin of the Gorgons. I'd tried to categorize the different types of creatures during the day and soon found there were at least ten different types predominantly mixed with Jorogumo and Crathode.

"They bred an army. Where could they have done this?" Jett asked in disbelief.

Crag leaned in the window frame next to theirs with Jackal. The moonlight shining on the men's faces.

"Elivagar. No one travels through the tundra. Ostara, the tribes are too volatile to explore," Crag offered.

Jackal scowled; the expression looked foreign on the tall knave's face. "The Natts. Guardians are too afraid to cross Cassiopeia."

"This has been coming a long time. Maybe even before we were born. Did you read anything about this in Orion's journals?" Scar asked Tawny.

"I didn't get very far. It's hard to read such horrible things about a person you loved, who you believed to be a good person... if an opportunist," she said knitting her brows together.

Ridge's jaw was clenched as he took in the scene below. Spring was in the air and you could smell the promise of new beginnings on the breeze.

"Orion knew. Nothing went on in Elivagar he was not aware of."

His statement was met with silence. They'd all been thinking it.

"Right. Let's get this over with," Scarlett said, sucking in a deep breath.

She was a roiling inferno inside a woman's body. Crag and Jackal helped her project her voice, and we all stepped back from the windows.

"I am the leader of the Red Seconds. You know me as Scarlett Tio. The owner of Vigrid, wife of Patriarch Dagr, hand fasted to a Regn second son, daughter of spring and summer, Night's Child, Delegate to the Grand Mistress, Second to the Prime and beloved daughter of Alder Var and Wren Tio. I am here to warn you who seek to upset the balance. Those of you who wish to leave, may go. Take these with you, spread the word. Red Seconds are coming for the Stygian Knights. It will take more than a siege to pry us from our seat of power." Her voice was disembodied as she addressed the masses below.

Canis and Dahlia stepped out of their command tent to listen. It might as well have been a palace for how they were dressed. We threw the red bands Quick and Jett had carried from Thrimilci then blew the wind so the bands would float into the army.

"Remind me why we're doing this again?" I asked in a whisper.

"Because Mirage is pretending to be her in Thrimilci, she is here and we are going to do it again in Elivagar. It is her legacy not her presence that they will fear. We need a face for this war, that is what she is. Not the khoraz seductress but the young vulnerable woman gifted by the Mother with special powers to help balance this world. They knew she would be powerful, that is why they smeared her name," Quick whispered back.

"Come, come. We all know the khoraz elemental was killed months ago. This ploy will not work," Dahlia said with her pinched face puckered into a sneer of a smile.

"I have risen as the voice of this rebellion against the powers that would end our way of life. You, hybrids of hybrids, all of you. Know that you have been bred for their purposes. I give you choice, while they give you war. I can find you a home where you can live peacefully. Where do you think they will put you once you serve their purpose?" she called out to them.

"That wasn't part of the script," Tawny hissed.

"Nice try, but it is more than likely that they have been brain washed." Jackal noted.

Canis raised his arms to show not one hybrid had shuffled. "You are not Scarlett Tio, you do not wear the pieces she covets. Give up. We will have you eventually, we need only wait for that one tyro who misses their mommy for our way in. We shall rain death and destruction down on your heads and it will be your fault alone. Why not give up the few we want and let life go back to the way it has always been? What are a handful of lives compared to hundreds?" Canis said in a crisp reasonable tone.

Jackal yanked Scarlett back, forgetting she was on fire, and hung halfway out the window. "You are a liar, sir! You would train these impressionable youths to follow you and Tidings would be bathed in your terror for generations. Just as they would be son you corrupted and if I had been a better uncle, I would have stopped you!"

Sage. By the Mother, that would be awful.

"Jackal, my boy. Quit this foolishness. You look like children who do not wish to bathe at night's end. Everyone knows when you are dirty, it is inevitable. Why prolong it? What if I promise to take care of your lover? Let you live in peace in a cottage on an island of your choosing? Have you not done enough damage to your family?" Canis coaxed.

I wanted to take his lips and move them for him. The way he kept his upper lip still as he breathed out clipped words caused me an irrational amount of irritation.

"My brother would rain down his ashes if I gave up his true family for the one you forced on him." Jackal sneered. "*You* are the one who forced Alder into a loveless marriage because *you* impregnated Cassiopeia. *You* told her to use Delta like a broodmare for the Straumrs because her sister could not bear children. You all blamed me as I was the one who stole Crag away from Delta's betrothal!"

Crag pulled Jackal away from the window as Dahlia hissed. "Moon was looking for a way to get Crag out of his betrothal because he refused to marry!"

Scarlett groaned and her flames faded so her skin went from fiery to a red ember like glow to her smooth, tan natural tone. Canis was right, she wasn't wearing her pieces or her fetishes.

"I think... my *calling* is on the fritz. Lera said this might happen. I didn't expect it to be painful," she ground out.

"It's too soon to be *calling* so much," Jett breathed and fell to his knees.

Scarlett groaned again, her throat straining, and Tawny took her hand. "Try to relax."

Quick fell beside Jett, Jackal placed his hand on her stomach and shared a worried look with Jett.

"You should not have heard that. Diamond is a good girl. I would not want her life up turned because of someone else's actions. Basil was her father. Crag was just the seed," Jackal muttered.

"I already knew. Is that why you did it? Because you had to get out of the betrothal?" she asked, looking to Crag.

Quick had moved her head into his lap as he kneeled on the granite floor. Scarlett held Tawny's hand.

"It was more complicated than that," Crag said, and she gave him a tight nod for him to continue. "I was betrothed for a short time to Delta.

We had not even announced it. Dahlia and Basil had been trying for years to conceive. Moon saw his chance to force children from me in order to break our marriage contract. He went to Cassiopeia who was already pregnant with Canis's children. Few knew of their affair. Orion offered not to disgrace her if she gave the children up and Canis promised one of his nephews to Delta since she would have to have two Natt/Straumr children in order to fulfill Dahlia and Basil's marriage contract. They sent Delta away while she was pregnant so no one would know. We conceived Diamond during Yuletide before the Red Kings Massacre."

Jackal knelt down to look over Scarlett's face, specifically her eyes. "Moon was a brilliant strategist. He saw an opportunity, and he took it. Cygnus only saw an advantageous marriage for Alder and another way to push out the Tio and Sumar. Everything they did was for power. The Tio scared them. They never did anything by their rules. They were the only ones who did not care if they married outside of the greater families." He got to his feet. "Niece, you are exhausted."

"When was the last time you slept?" Crag asked.

Guilty looks were shared all around. "We marched through the night," Jett admitted.

"No more of that. She needs to be kept hydrated and sleep regularly. Our *calling* does not heal the womb after births. She is weak. You all are... and skinny. You look like you have lost fifteen pounds you could not afford to lose," Jackal chastised.

"There are beds open in the men and women's wings," Crag directed. "Do not risk her healing to push."

Scarlett had fallen asleep at some point during Jackal's speech and Jett moved to pick her up off the ground. He staggered.

"Frigga's sweet grass, I thought she'd be heavier. Maybe a night of rest and a big breakfast tomorrow isn't a bad idea, though she'll be pretty pissed off."

Quick looked fondly at Scarlett and I narrowed my eyes at him. "Those weeks not eating did not affect us the same way because of the babies. She is a stubborn woman but forgiving. I will take her to the men's wing." Jett and Quick faced off as Quick angled to take her. "I do not trust myself with any other women. Scarlett keeps me sane," Quick said in a hushed tone.

Jett's eyes searched Quick's, and he exhaled gustily before turning over Scarlett to him. "I used to trust myself."

He let his eyes slide to Tawny, and she turned away. "My... father and I can take a separate room from yours and leave as soon as she wants in the morning."

I watched the four of them walk away with Scarlett's dyed black hair hanging as it swayed with Quick's steps. I had thought Scarlett's face looked thin, but compared to her chest, all of her seemed unusually slender. It was Tawny's gaunt cheeks and round belly that exposed just how emaciated they all were.

Crag placed a hand at Jackal's back. "What a good uncle you are."

Canis had said more after Jackal moved from the window, but it was all meaningless. As long as they hadn't used the pewter nix material for their siege machines, we were safe.

I left the two men to their shift at guard. Jackal kept Crag company, and I sought comfort in the scrape and step of my boots on the granite.

"What the world would have been like B.S.?"

I didn't see Ro hiding in the shadows of the alcove, but her voice rang clear.

B.S. was Before Scarlett.

"I don't have any B.S. memories. My life has always been enriched by her colorings. Are you lost? The party is back that way." I nodded ahead, and she detached from the shadows on my right.

She'd pulled up her ringlets, her eyes were full of devilry. Ro had given me the look before. For once, she wore a dress of our native Thrimilci. A deep purple that faded to black at the hem, she glided across the granite to me and smirked.

"I thought you would be deep in Mica by now," she purred.

I gave her a dry look, and she held up her thin creamy coffee hands in surrender.

"Who's warming your bed these nights, Ro?" I asked her, folding my arms across my chest.

Her eyes glittered in the dim hall. "Tonight? You, Chief. It has been awhile."

"Am I?" I asked, unable to hide my amusement or my unbidden lust.

I hadn't been with a woman since Diamond four months ago, aside from the intense make-out session I'd had with Mica.

*Gods, Mica.*

I should be with her. I wanted to be, but Diamond would be upset. Rosasite understood discretion and how to have a good time.

"If you play your cards right," she said, licking her pouty lips.

"I don't think we'll be making it to my bed, Ro," I told her, bending to pick her up around her thighs and she laughed, full and feminine as we reversed into the room whose doorway she'd just come from.

# CHAPTER 46
# JETT

Leftovers from the wedding served as the next day's breakfast. Even the cooks must sleep in every once in a while. Quick hadn't bothered making an excuse for crawling into bed beside Scarlett. Jett thought he was beginning to understand it. It was how he missed the girls and preferred to sleep between Indigo and Scarlett when they traveled... or Tawny and Scarlett when they let him.

They needed one another. Even just having had twins, with her reputation, men flocked to her. Women had flocked to Quick as long as Jett had known him. They kept one another from doing something stupid and regretful. He had never seen them so much as kiss in Disir and that would've been the place to do it without the guilt. The guilt came after.

Tawny had told Cherry before they'd left that she couldn't see herself as a third wife. Jett didn't blame her, but the fact remained that he had had an affair with her. Cherry had forgiven them, but Amethyst would be a different story.

They'd only left Valla U months before but had already outgrown it.

The busy chatting of young men and women playing puerile games with one another. Hearts would be broken and broken again in those halls. It was as if the world was oblivious of what went on outside of the walls. It comforted and frightened Jett.

"We should have left earlier." Scarlett said peevishly though it didn't stop her from buttering another piece of toast and putting it into her mouth.

Quick rubbed her back in small circles. Her surrogate husband immersed himself into the position guarding her as he would have Indigo without the intimacy, though there was a certain kind of intimacy between them.

Tawny seemed more comfortable since she'd made her decision. The fear of telling Amethyst looming before them shouldn't have been more frightening than what they faced should they fail to get to the project before Canis.

Gypsum watched Quick and Scarlett interactions and Jett's with Tawny. The kid was bright. He knew something was up.

Rosasite had laughed a little too loud and glanced a little too often since she sat on the bench down from them. Gypsum must have been with her last night. Chief had packed on more muscle, taller and more chiseled than his father. He was an old soul and had taken charge of things at Valla U as the voice of the students. The kid commanded respect, he'd make a great Patriarch.

"How do we know we can trust these people?" Tawny asked, looking around suspiciously at the tyros.

Gypsum's dimples popped in his cheeks as he pressed his lips together and looked down at the long table. "Every one of them was forced to take a blood oath. We couldn't risk anymore traitors."

Scarlett's eyes bugged. "What kind of oath, Gyps? Blood oaths are dangerous."

"Nothing crazy. Just that they wouldn't betray Valla U while they were tyros." He shrugged.

"Desperate times call for desperate measures," Quick said.

They changed into thick Elivagar clothing, padded jerkins, fur-lined cloaks, and thick wool socks for Jett and Quick. The girls wore woolen bell like dresses with what seemed like dozens of skirts beneath them. Scarlett was in a plain puce shade that buttoned snuggly to her flat belly with plain unadorned wooden buttons, Tawny was in a drab olive color that hung off her little bump, both girls had their hair braided around their heads like crowns.

Jett had attempted to smooth his wavy hair so it would lay flat against his head but gave up, content to let it curl around his ears for the time being. Once they took Elivagar, they could get rid of all the superfluous fuzz. Scarlett had helped Quick trim it so it had a sort of style, Jett liked to think he wasn't that vain.

Tawny hugged Gypsum one last time. Which was good since someone was going to have to get a crowbar to pry Butterfly from Quick. Jackal was busy teasing Scarlett who looked like she had needed the laughs he was giving her as Crag and Ridge stood to the side watching it all play out and speaking in low voices. The stoic eldest Straumr had picked back up with Ridge as if he'd been there all the while. It made sense that they would be friends; Ridge with his tension easing jokes and light-hearted demeanor and Crag, the serious, intense quiet type. Jett saw those same qualities in Jackal and Crag as a couple.

"Balder's brow! I almost forgot!" Gypsum practically shouted.

Jett mouthed *Balder's brow* in unison with Quick as they shared a smirk.

"What?" Scarlett asked, turning to him in the portal room of Valla U.

The doors were all locked until they used one that would take them to the Niflheim arena in Elivagar. Gypsum's puppy dog eyes were bright as he spoke excitedly to them.

"Storm-pale found the project. Drill-tooth is out there right now to confirm what he found, but... I think we've got it. Canis is always taking a mount somewhere south of here, at first we thought it was back to the portal, but Storm-pale followed him. It's on the coast of Valla. *Here.* On this island!" He looked around to see if anyone else had snuck into the long portal room once he had shouted out its location.

"Gypsum, that's fantastic!" Scarlett shouted back, too elated to monitor her tone.

"Don't thank me, thank Storm-pale."

"That reminds me. Where's Tree? She wasn't with Bee." Scarlett pursed her full lip to the side of her mouth looking concerned.

"She's with Slate and Brass. They were here a few days ago. She's well. They're all well... and they miss you," Gypsum added like he was dipping his toes in water that looked too hot for comfort.

Scarlett's face transformed as she slipped on her ring to test it again. "We'll see them when we reach the Lycans... if they're there," she said coolly.

Gypsum nodded. Water was too hot.

"Whoa!" Jett shouted at the sound of blades being drawn the second they stepped into the Niflheim arena.

The light of the portal caused spots of bright light to temporarily blind them.

"Thank the Mother I still have a chance to feel those lips," the polished voice of a man floated to Jett's ears.

"By the Mother, Lera let you run Niflheim?" Scarlett's voice sounded bored.

Jett's eyes adjusted to find them surrounded by men and women holding blades and bows. In front of Scarlett was a man even taller than Jett, but borderline lanky. His pale cheeks were gaunt with a smile that didn't touch his stormy eyes. He was looking down at Scarlett like she was brought there just for him.

"Where are your babies, Second? Are you healed enough for me?" His smile touched his eyes then and Jett decided he liked it better when it didn't.

Before Quick could pull his dagger, Scarlett slapped him across the face. It only excited him, he leered licking the blood from his lip.

"Get yourself under control, Styg," she snapped, shoving past him and he chased after her with long strides.

"*Gods*, I knew you would be a fighter." He chuckled as he followed after her. "I would willingly risk insanity or death to get you into my bed, girl."

Quick and Jett shared exasperated looks.

The Niflheim arena reflected their Draugr team. It was dark, the only lights came from faux torches that lined the grey walls to look like a medieval dungeon or the castle of some evil wizard. Scarlett sure had one wild imagination.

If you looked closely, you could see the floors were actually a matte granite. The walls were the same material but carved intricately so it looked aged. Niflheim was built right into a mountain.

"Does she know where she's going?" Tawny asked, skipping to try to keep up with her war path as Styg kept trying to convince her to take a brief intermission with him.

Finally, Styg stopped and pulled out a purple vial and Scarlett went rigid facing him. She was a recovering addict. Quick took a step forward, but Jett stopped him. She had to turn it down herself or she'd never know if she could. She took the vial from his hands and held it up to the torch light. The purple fluid glowed like a nefarious beacon.

"I haven't been intimate with a man for four months," she said as they watched her eyes dilate in the flickering flame. "I have wanted to. *Badly*."

Scarlett shook herself out of it and looked for Quick who took a shuffling step back. She smiled weakly at him. She chucked the vial against the wall.

Jett watched the rousen slide down and Quick let out a shuddering breath. "I would like to think we would have stopped each other before it went too far."

Jett placed a hand on his shoulder, it was bunched as if he restrained himself. Any doubt Jett had about whether they had crossed that line evaporated. Scarlett was a khoraz, Quick hadn't gone four months without a woman since he was fifteen. The restraint they'd shown in not indulging in one another was a testament to how hard they held onto their memories of Indigo, Slate, and Brass while they were in Disir.

"It's almost over," Jett told Quick who sighed.

# CHAPTER 47
# SLATE

Cold ale, khorazes, a soft bed, and hot palatable food — a man did not need more.

The mining town in the Frostfell Mountains that encircled the Vetr castle was the only other town inside of Elivagar aside from the town heart. It was the only one with bodies in it since the mysterious blackguard evacuated the town heart and shut up the castle's gates.

We should not have cared, less work for Brass and me, but it was our family's island to rule, not some usurper.

The Dark Dancer inn stank of ale, unwashed bodies, grit from the mines, and sex. Hardly any women were left. They were the first ones brought to Niflheim, so the ones that remained were in high demand. Most of which had been offering their services for a handful of nickel hunts before were now charging a silver crescent or two.

"You wouldn't have to pay," Brass said, giving me a sidelong glance as we sat at the bar deep in our ale.

*... With this face?*

*This face is a lifeboat; this is the face commanding and bearded, it asks no odds of the rest; this face is flavor'd fruit, ready for eating; this face of a healthy honest boy is the programme of all good. These faces bear testimony, slumbering or awak.; They show their descent from the Master himself. Off the word I have spoken, I except not one — red, white, black, are all deific; in each house is the ovum — it comes forth after a thousand years. Spots or cracks at the windows do not disturb me; tall and sufficient stand behind and make signs to me; I read the promise, and patiently wait. This is a full-grown lily's face. She speaks to the limber-hipp'd man near the garden pickets, come here, she blushingly cries — come nigh to me, limber-hipp'd man, stand at my side till I lean as high as I can upon you, fill me with albescent honey, bend down to me. Rub to me with your chafing beard, rub to my breast and shoulders...*

Brass chuckled. The ring gave me a hawk-like beak of a nose.

A night of rest on our way back without duties to fulfill every month is what we allowed ourselves. Humans posed less temptation than with the Lycan women eager for our seed. A mind reader and a barghest hybrid. They had snuck into our rooms at night trying to coax us into their beds. We had started rooming together and made our stance clear. Not until the war was over. Until she was avenged. Until they all were.

It was hard for us both. Brass's moods were dark even for me after he lost his fertility and myself who had not gone more than two months without a woman when Scarlett left our marriage. Before that was a week or two at most since I started. It had been since the night Scarlett found out about Mirage. The look of betrayal in her eyes was as fresh as if I had seen it yesterday when she called the guards on us and left with Ash. Brass had last been with Crimson. I had last been with Mirage. Torch was last touched by the fucking Straumr boy.

"Stop torturing yourself."

We both wore facial contortion rings that had been tweaked to change our features and voices. Both our eyes were a cool blue, his nose sloped with a rounded drip like tip and a thin mouth which did not matter since it was framed by an unruly beard. We both had unruly beards, his longer than mine.

*... What else is there to do?...*

Brass grunted and gestured for the blonde bar wench to refill our mugs. She showed an impressive amount of cleavage and should have been much cleaner as a Guardian with the ability to *call* water with a thought and a thread of energy.

"Is that all I can do for you, Scorpion?" she asked with a wink of her brown eyes.

"Yes. Thank you, Aardwolf," Brass said with a croaking voice far different from his own, nodding his head to her.

She wiped at one of the many stains on the counter with her dirty rag and sauntered away. Brass turned on his stool to face the dining area of the inn. A fireplace with a cauldron brewed stew directly across from us and the day shift of miners were filing in while the night shift filed out. They sat at the wooden booths that lined the wall or the rickety tables that were haphazardly scattered around the room. Upstairs were ten rooms seldom used for the night, but frequently for the hour.

It was one of three inns in Glitra. The Shadow Breakers used it when they needed to get out which wasn't allowed very often. The Dark Dancer was not a place you would catch an uppity greater family brat, so it was considered the safest.

I leaned my elbows on the counter as I drank my ale and watched a slender brunette with an apple shaped backside use one of the chairs to climb onto a table and start to sing a bawdy ballad she made up as she went along.

*... Care to wager when she falls?...*

"You mean *if*."

*... When...*

Brass chuckled again, foam from the ale saturated his bearded upper lip. There was no telling what I would have done without him after not only Scarlett had died with his children, but my brothers, the woman who raised me, and my cousins all left our world within two sorrowful days.

I would have gone on a rampage until they had put me down like a mad dog.

What we did instead with the Red Seconds was a better use of my energy. Scarlett would have approved.

"She would have, *Scarab*," Brass said, using the name I claimed while in town.

The wood door clattered against the wall as a man kicked it open carrying in a pregnant woman. He was a big man, as tall and wide as me with a dark blonde beard that could not hide his horse-like face.

"I can walk, Jaw," the woman hissed in his arms.

"Quiet, Ilisha. You have walked all day, no need to be brave. In fact, I would prefer if you let me and — your brother-in-law handle things, my dear sweet wife."

The man called Jaw gave the woman Ilisha a smirk she scowled at. She was a plain wall flower of a girl with small dark eyes and a snub nose above a small pouty mouth. Hair as dark and thick as Brass's wrapped around her head in a braid. Another couple, her sister by the resemblance they shared, and her husband entered the inn after them.

The sister was taller with a longer thinner nose which would explain her husband's hair lip and potato like nose. The older man though, he was what one expected from a Guardian. The two homely couples had found love, it would appear since I could scent the mother's milk from the sister. Both women bore the scents of their husbands so they spent a great deal of time together.

"I'm... I *am* pregnant, not helpless." The feisty woman kicked her skirts until Jaw nearly dropped her, and Brass chuckled.

*... Remind you of someone?...*

I smiled. The only kind of women with spirit around were the kind that tried to get you into bed. It had been a very long time since I smiled.

The sister walked over to the bar giving the room a cool gaze. She was not dressed as any of the other women were. She was clad in all white, her cloak was reversed so the inside was black and the white fur held to the outside. Her pants clung to well-shaped legs and curved hips that hinted at a backside made for squeezing. She must have recently birthed. Her breasts were larger than she was used to and was wearing a shirt made for a woman with a smaller chest with a padded corset that displayed a trim waist. She winced slightly as she kneaded her back and then stole a quick glance at her husband to be sure he did not see her pain.

Aardwolf sauntered over to the woman who looked her up and down. She was clean and well kept. She pushed back her cloak and removed her white leather gloves; she had an ample tan bosom that swelled at what should have been a modest neckline as she breathed.

"Hi, yes. I am hoping you have three rooms available. For me and my husband, my sister and hers and my father? Also, we would like to have dinner," she said, giving Aardwolf a thin-lipped smile.

"Where did you come from? I have not seen your like in these mountains before."

She placed her palms on the counter. Yes, a fighter this one. She had blades concealed all over her person. I could smell the metal. Her husband walked over with Jaw like her bodyguards. They had a deadly grace that bespoke their skill with weapons. Her husband raked Aardwolf with his eyes like he had found shit in his stew.

"Three rooms or two if you do not have the space. We will eat in our rooms," her husband said.

"Shark," she grit and she pulled him back a step to whisper, but with my heightened hearing, I could hear her. "How will we know who the man is if we do not listen to the people? We do not even know if they have heard about Thrimilci yet."

"I do not like how these men are looking at you, Scat and... Ilisha. Have you noticed there are no other women here other than khorazes?" Shark said, bending his head to her ear.

She leaned back, and I missed the look she gave him, but he groaned as he relented.

"We shall eat here in the common room," Shark said and slapped down two gold daymarks on the counter that Aardwolf quickly shoved into her bra. "For your intrigue." He winked at her and wrapped his arm around Scat's shoulders.

Ilisha and the father were heading towards the stairway as the other three walked along the bar past us. Both men gave us scathing untrusting glances I did not blame them for before Scat ran her small dark eyes past us.

*Warm spiced apples and vanilla.*

My gut hurt like a Centaur had kicked it and I shot to my feet. Brass got up because I did and the girl stared at us with her hand at her waist where a belt of daggers waited. Her husband was as big as Brass. He clenched his jaw and waited for me to say something.

Instead, Scat patted her husband's hand at her shoulder and took a step forward bending down without removing her eyes from me to the floor and righted herself. She moved between Brass and I, and I shut my eyes breathing her in. Freya's burly boar, she smelled like Scarlett.

"You dropped this," she whispered, and I saw what she placed on the bar.

The red swath of fabric Styg had shown us. There had been a rebellion in Thrimilci and they had chased out the invaders with Mirage acting as Scarlett. It was the first success our side had had in the war.

Brass smoothly took it from the counter and shoved it into a pocket. I grabbed her wrist, so small and delicate in my hand and she grit her teeth, looking at me.

"He wants to know how you know about it," Brass said, not taking his eyes off her companions who couldn't see how I grasped her.

"He has a mouth and a tongue he keeps using to lick his lips at me as if I was some choice dessert. He can ask me himself or release my arm. Is that how you repay kindness? With violence?" she asked coolly, not even bothering to struggle though I towered over her by a foot.

Brass chuckled, and she gaped at him. "He is mute, I am afraid."

A blade appeared in her other hand against the base of my cock and her husband shifted his body to block the rest of the inn from seeing our altercation. I sucked in a sharp breath. The beast wanted the alpha female.

"I would prefer not to kill either of you because I have seen too much death. But if you do not release my wrist, I will detach you from what is undoubtedly a pathetic thing before you can blink," she said in a rapid, hushed tone.

No one was paying attention. I was aroused beyond reason. The lyrics of the bawdy song caused bursts of raucous laughter that drowned us out. Brass placed his hand over mine and I released her with great effort.

*... My mistake. Apologize for me...*

"He is very sorry for the misunderstanding and would like to buy a round for you and your family when you come down to dinner," Brass said, sitting down.

Her blade withdrew.

"We can afford our own drinks," Shark said, wrapping his arm around his wife again.

"If he is sorry, he can say it himself." Scat sniffed and turned around to join the others who were already upstairs.

"She does smell like Scarlett, but don't you know better than to go feeling up other men's wives' wrists?" Brass chuckled at his own joke. "Especially ones who would rival a Breaker for her blade skills."

*... I do not think I can stay here. I cannot get her scent out of my lungs...*
Brass nodded. "If it makes you feel better. I gave her a good sniff too. Another round or two and we'll go to a different inn."
I nodded and glanced back up the stairs. She looked nothing like our Scarlett and yet the beast had rattled in its cage. That was never good.

# FORTY-EIGHT

Styg had been less than helpful with no way to expedite or trip through the Frostfell Mountains from the arena to the mining town. The whole point of going to the town was so that we could hear the latest gossip and hopefully get an idea of who was squatting in Tawny's castle.

Glitra Mines had a town bearing the same name Styg assured us we'd find people willing to talk. Men, he'd said since the women and children had been the first to be evacuated, but the nearest portal door had been in the arena so those who had escaped Glitra had to make the hike to Niflheim.

Secretly, very secretly, I was unbelievably relieved when Jett started to carry Tawny. They'd had to go slowly so she could walk with them from the most western coast of Elivagar where I had built the arena right into the mountainside, all the way to Glitra on the other side of the mountain. It had been a very unpleasant trek.

The longer it took, the longer I was away from my sons.

Katydid's handheld pump helped me relieve my aching breasts.

They constantly leaked and if I was going to nurse when I returned, I had to keep up with the pump.

We were going to try to procure a horse for Tawny so the rest of the trip wouldn't be at a snail's pace. She couldn't walk the entire way. Not unless Jett wanted to carry her across the Illfuss Ice Fields.

No more elemental shifting, and only using *calling* when I absolutely needed to was a temporary problem. In another few days, I'd be completely healed from birthing Balas and Spinel and things should go back to normal. My helpless frailty was driving me mad.

The inn was disgusting. I'd finally found where the unsavory characters congregated in Tidings along with the hard-working men and women of the Glitra Mines. The barkeep was a slutty older woman and her patrons were grimy with roaming eyes. Not that I wanted to lump them all in together, but it was obvious they hadn't seen a woman who wasn't throwing herself at them in some time.

The two men at the bar had proved that.

I'd been trying to be inconspicuous and failed. If the two men that had dropped the red band weren't murderers, then I was a hot pink Billy goat hybrid. Their scents had spiked even with my ring on. It had dumbfounded me.

They wore furs mounded on their backs so it had given them an imposing look, but I thought they must be heavily muscled under all those furs. Then the taller one had gripped my wrist like a vise. He emitted a powerful charge that nearly shocked my arm. When the other man spoke, there had been something that made my ears perk up. I thought I knew them, but that was impossible.

I'd never seen the two men before in my life and I was in no mood for any man to try to seduce me. I was far from reserved in my current state and my whole khoraz body was very aware of how long it had been since I'd been intimate.

When we'd gone down to dinner, they were gone. I was thankful because I thought Quick was going to kill them and, for once, I wasn't sure who would win.

"It's amazing how fast a place can deteriorate," I said, walking arm in arm with Quick down the darkened cobbled roads of Glitra.

"I doubt it was meticulously cared for before the Purge War, Scat,"

Quick said as we skirted a spot in the road where someone had regurgitated their food.

"News of Thrimilci's successful overthrow is trickling in. Styg said he'd sent in a few Breakers to plant the information and encourage an uprising when the time comes."

"We should meet up with the others. I do not like splitting up," Quick murmured, eyeing every shadow.

"We agreed we'd cover more ground this way. How else will we listen at both inns and find a horse?"

I squeezed closer to Quick's arm. He was taking the whole pretending to be my husband show seriously, and I appreciated how well cared for and safe he made me feel. I'd worn all my blades, having removed the gold work from my wrist blades so they were plain black and wrapped my short seax sheath in black fabric as well as the pommel so no one would see the golden Freya on them. I'd even taken the golden daymark belt buckle off for fear of being recognized.

The brick town was only two stories high at its tallest point without any street lamps. Most Guardians walked hunch shouldered either from exhaustion or because they were up to no good. I thanked the gods it was cold or the smell would've been putrid.

Quick pointed to a sign down the road.

"There. A stable. Apparently the only one in this God forsaken town," Quick grumbled.

I gave his side another squeeze. "Cheer up. We'll go back to the warm room, take a hot bath, and crawl into bed. I could even permit us to sleep in some," I promised.

Quick's lips curled, and he kissed my forehead. "I get it now. Why my brother fell for you... despite the complications of your life, you are wonderfully simple."

"Thank you, I think. Why don't you haggle? You'll get a better price without your wife hovering. This place isn't likely to give you a better deal because of me. They might try to get you to trade me for the horse," I told him with a wry smile.

"I don't like leaving you out here," Quick said, looking about.

"I won't go anywhere. I promise."

He pointed a finger at me. "You better not."

I gave him a swat as he walked into the front of the shop that was attached to the stable. Cold weather made people cranky or so I was learning. I *called* a barrel over to the side of the brick home next to the stable house, whose puffs of chimney smoke looked inviting.

I slid my finger against the stone pieces I'd sewn into my blade belt. I'd threaded my father's ring into my braid and hid it in my hair with the wooden oak leaf carved comb I'd received from the Leshy. I thought it was safe since no one knew I wore the comb in my nest of fetishes.

In two days, I would be reunited with Slate and Brass and they thought I was dead. If you squinted really tight, it looked like I was dreading seeing them again. What if they'd moved on? What if they were disappointed that I was back?

I rubbed my breasts as I hummed. The twins had liked it when I hummed. They liked when I laid down and Quick had his ring off speaking close to them.

A group of three men, more than the few stragglers that had passed by, came down the road and I pulled the hood of my cloak up. I straightened apprehensively until I realized one was a woman. A beautiful woman with short coppery curls and lush curves. They seemed unaffected by the cold as they walked nearer. A man with snow pale skin and inky black hair that curled around his ears. The third traveler was a forgettable looking man whose face was hidden in the cowl of his cloak.

The woman stopped and her head turned to look directly at me. She floated over to where I sat with her companions in tow. Her big, luminous eyes hitched on my belly.

"You had babes recently?"

Her voice was mesmerizing. She had a soft voice that hit her "H's" hard and rolled her "R's". I felt like a grubby toddler fumbling for words.

"About a week ago," I said, searching her eyes.

She made a contented sound in her throat as she shifted her head to her inky haired cohort. He made the slightest movement, and I noticed his eyes were blood red. I sucked in a sharp gasp to prepare my scream.

"Follow me," he said and my mind went blank.

I hopped off the barrel, feeling my feet move and my mind unable to form thoughts. I knew I was in trouble and needed to fight back. I dug deep. I had to get away.

The trance he'd put on me combined with the poor condition of the road helped me. I tripped over a gap in the cobbles and ran headlong into my slick haired abductor. He hissed like a cat as I caught my footing and broke into a run. It was too late to backtrack and scream for Quick.

I sprung my blades and pumped my legs as fast as I could trying to mind my footing. I couldn't go elemental or everyone would know I was in Elivagar if I didn't pass out from the effort. I'd have to fight, but the red-eyed man had some kind of hypnosis talent I had no defense against.

As a rule, bad guys should shout constantly as they chased you so you wouldn't feel the need to look over your shoulder to mark them. Things like, "Get her!'" or "Don't let her get away!". My abductors were as silent as the grave they likely intended on burying me in. I wasn't even sure the dark-haired one could *breathe*. I wasn't even sure they were human.

I cursed the gods as I slipped in the greasy remains of the upchucked dinner Quick and I skirted earlier. My teeth clacked together as my feet flew out from under me. I saw stars as my head hit the cobblestones and groaned. Without a doubt, I'd injured a vital part of myself.

The shadowed face of the third man hovered above me and yanked me to my feet. I rammed my blade into the soft flesh under his chin. He shrieked a high-pitched wail that was in no part human. The body shriveled away to dust as I turned to come face to face with the woman. I had no time to gape at the ashes on the cobbles.

Her upper lip was curled. A tail lashed from beneath her dress and my eyes widened. I launched myself forward aiming for her heart which I missed an inch. She clawed at my face screeching and I stabbed her over again in her chest. Pain exploded in my cheek as the inky haired man backhanded me sending me sailing.

My back skidded against the hard cobbles and I held my face groaning. Cramps rolled through my back and into my skull.

"Is that all you got?" I spat, staggering to my feet.

My philosophy on death was if you're going to be murdered, antagonize them so a least they'll do it quickly. If there wasn't healing, I would've died a half dozen times in my young life.

The inky haired man dragged me up by my throat and my feet kicked as I was lifted inches above the ground. His red eyes burned as tried to loosen his grip. I was going to have to *call* before I fell under his hypnosis again.

I blew a burst of razor-sharp air that blew us apart and his body writhed on the ground across from mine. I slowly sat up determined to crawl my way back to the stable. Quick had to know I was missing by now if the stable master wasn't trying to haggle him for all he was worth.

The inky haired man had the pallor of a slug as he rose to his feet. My mouth fell open and my stomach dropped to my boots. He should have been dead. He opened his mouth and moonlight gleamed off of elongated canines.

A thunk sounded and a cross bolt stuck out from the man's chest. I whipped my head around to find two men running towards me. I let out a shuddering breath and my head swam. I touched my fingers to my head and a thick red fluid clung to my unpolished nails. My head lolled and my body sank back down to the cobbles.

I shut my eyes and began to hum again. If I was going to die, I didn't want it to be listening to the sound of unwashed men's heavy breathing.

"She is alive," came a gruff voice. "She killed Lamia."

I felt a hand on my head and tried to pry my eyes open. "The Ijiraq too. Heal her. I like what I see and plan to see the rest of her. Over there," another man's voice said.

"Heal me," I said feebly as my body was dragged by my wrists against the frozen cobbles.

My head pulsed with the loss of blood as it lolled from the way I was unceremoniously dragged like yesterday's garbage.

My arms were released, and I cried out as my injured head hit the cobbles. There wasn't as much moonlight on the back of my lids. My vision was blurred, and I wasn't going to stay conscious for long. I grappled limply with the hands at my neckline and felt the fabric give. I clung to one of the man's hands and sent fire into his skin. He shouted and fell away as the second man laughed. I rolled dizzily until I hit a wall and felt the cold air against my chest as I blinked blood from my eyes to find the second man.

I spotted him and saw him raise his crossbow before he sent it sailing into the meat of my thigh. I cried out as I gripped the shaft. The first man shifted on the ground and he slammed his blade into my foot. I pulled two blades from my belt as the second man rushed me and heard them find homes in flesh with two curses.

I fell face first driving the arrow deeper into my thigh and felt my clarity dim as my world went from dark to blinding white with the intense sharp pain.

One of them nudged me over with a boot. "Heal me. I am going to fuck her bloody, the bitch." I felt a man yank on my pants.

A man's laughter fell short. "Mind your business. Go find your own woman."

"We want that one," said a croaky voice.

"She is taken."

"That is going to be a problem for you," the croaky voice said and I heard the *shing* of blades.

# CHAPTER 49

# SLATE

Three piles of dust signified the death of the creatures the Stygians had loosed in town. The two miscreants were gurgling as they died slowed deaths.

"Go find her husband. I doubt he would let her leave the inn alone. Get him and his friends at the Dark Dancer and take them where they were headed tonight," Brass said, resting his hands over her stomach.

"That is the Warden. The Stygians will want blood for this," Cabhan said in his human form as he leaned over one of the men.

"*Oh*, she smells delicious." Niall's glowing green eyes reflected the moonlight as he seared into memory the exposed woman Scat.

I bent down and pulled her torn shirt closed over her full breasts. It was the plain girl from the inn that smelled like Scarlett. Niall had kissed Scarlett and never let us forget it.

"That's why I need you to get her family out of town. Now go. He's probably running the roads right now looking for her. Tell him she's safely being taken out of town." Brass looked over her and pulled a bloody hair comb from her inky hair. "Give him this so he knows we have her. Careful, he seems dangerous."

Niall snorted and pocketed the wooden comb. The three Lycans were the only ones from the village who ventured so far south. No one would guess they were Lycans. Niall tossed his mane of black waves that were like my own when I had cared about my appearance.

Cabhan had married Niall's sister, the serious blonde man had steely, scrutinizing eyes that did not miss much. Lorcan was the lynch pin for the trio. He squatted by Scat's body and pushed her wisps of hair from her face.

"Her scent is familiar… it is like your mate." Lorcan turned his brown eyes up to ours and pushed his waist long braid back into his cloak as he stood. "See you three back at the village. I catch your scent," he said with a dimpled smirk.

I gave a low growl and Niall laughed. "If you do not want her, I will take her. She has great, plump —"

"She is married and if you haven't noticed by the fight she put up, not one to be trifled with. What you smell is your own scent. Have a little decency. Now go," Brass said in an aggravated tone my emotions mirrored.

The three Lycans started to trot away and Brass peeled off her boot to heal her foot. She gasped, and her gloved fingers curled in pain.

"My babies," she said in a high voice.

"Where's your husband?" Brass asked.

She shifted her head on the cobbles and I lifted it into my lap scooting to my knees. "He left me," she said with a pout.

Brass gave me a curious look.

*… She is not in her right mind…*

"The man Shark, he left you?" Brass asked.

"He's not my husband. He's at the stables trying to get a horse. Oh no!" She tried to shoot up, but I rested my palms on her shoulders.

She opened her brown eyes and blinked at us.

"The stable house!"

A howl answered Brass's shout.

"If you're going to rape me, make it fast," she said, nocking up her jaw as best she could.

Brass lifted his head from where he had been peeling down her bloodied pants to see the arrow in her thigh, his face incredulous. If we did not have our rings on, she would not have said such things. They were unscrupulous faces belonging to scoundrels or brigands. Brass rinsed his hands as he pulled her pants up over her hips with a jerk.

"Madam, I was trying to see your wound. Bits of fabric caught on the arrow as it entered your body and lodged in your bone. You're welcome," Brass said with so much indignation I felt myself smile for the second time that day.

"Usually before a man takes liberties with me, he at least buys me a drink," she said in a haughty tone.

Brass fought a smile. "I offered to buy you a drink earlier. You declined."

Recognition shown in her eyes and her pouty lips formed a perfect "O". "You are the ruffians from the inn!"

I could not stop my snort. Never had a woman forgotten she had met either of us. It was a new world.

Brass ran a hand over his face. "These *ruffians* saved your pretentious life."

*... She may be less caustic if you come out from between her legs...*

Brass looked to where he kneeled. He replaced her boot and stood, acknowledging her vulnerable position. I offered her my hands to help her into a sitting position and she took them without a word as I slowly helped her sit. She fell back against my chest, her silky hair against my chin.

The beast howled and rattled in its cage. I grit my teeth sucking in a breath.

"Thank you," she said, turning her head slightly to address me and her smooth skin rubbed up against my beard.

I wanted to feel her skin on mine.

She turned her head to Brass. "Both of you. If it is not too much trouble, could you help me back to the Dark Dancer?"

She was oblivious to the tear down to her taut belly. The swell of her breasts poured over the edges of the tattered fabric. Sitting as she was against my chest, I wanted to slide my palms over her shoulders and over that smooth tan skin to see if her peaks would be a paler pink like a kitten's nose or would they be dusky like a rose. When she was hale, I could ask her to spar and see where that would lead. She was strong, brazen, and could handle herself.

"Frigga's sweet grass, Scarab," Brass cursed.

I schooled my thoughts.

*... Ask her about her bairn...*

"You mentioned your babies? Did you have them with you? We can't take you to the Dark Dancer. Our friends went to the stables and are going to get your husband and friends and take them out of town tonight. Where are you headed? We'll take you there to meet them. You can't stay in Glitra, one of those men who attacked you ran this town for the Stygian Knights. There will be Guardians looking for him," Brass told her.

"No. They are with my uncle and aunt," she said looking away, and I scented her tears.

She hadn't cried when they attacked her, but she would because she missed her children. What a strange woman.

"We are headed north. Why would you help me? How would I know you are not taking me to some lair of yours where you can do something awful like those first three creatures intended?" she asked, taking her weight from my chest.

Brass gave her a smirk. "You could say we have a soft spot for helpless women. We are headed north anyway; it isn't that big a deal." He leaned forward with his deviant's face looking menacing. "If we wanted to do awful things to you, madam, I wouldn't have bothered healing you or killing those other two. We would've waited our turn."

He nodded to her shirt, and she pulled her fur-lined cloak around her chest. I caught her scent. It was fear. She had been abused before. I wondered if Brass could pick anything up from her mind, or if she was closed off as some people were.

"All I have is what you see. My husband had our coin and my pack is at the inn. I cannot pay you. I do not even have any food," she said licking her lower lip.

I stood and reached down under her arms and nearly tossed her, she weighed less than she looked with that thick cloak and being top heavy. Her thighs were toned and slender like what I had seen of her stomach. Fantastic legs, really.

Freya's burly boar, I could not be around that woman. Her scent had done terrible things to my vow of celibacy.

"We do it out of the kindness of our hearts. I promise you," Brass reassured her, straightening.

She looked over her bloodied and torn top. "I want to believe you. I know what the red band means that you dropped in the inn, but how can I be sure you will not take advantage of me in my sleep or the like? I do not have anything else to wear."

I slowly unbuckled my jerkin and tossed back my furs to show her the only tattoo I had gotten that was not functional; a deep red and black Nordic compass with blazing flames around it, the symbol of the Red Seconds.

Brass had pulled down his shirt to show his own over his heart. She turned to look at our matching tattoos.

"I heard the men who started the rebellion got it for the former Second. Quite the romantic gesture in her memory. Are those supposed to reassure me?" she asked.

"We of the Red Seconds are not rapers. Where is *your* mark?" Brass asked and dropped his cool blue eyes to her neckline.

"Should we not get going?" she asked, attempting to make herself look presentable which was not possible covered in blood as she was.

Brass and I shared a look, and I swept her legs out from under her. Her choices were simple, flail and fall or hold on and be carried. She gave an impressive scowl as we walked.

A light snow began to drift down lazily, as it always snowed in Elivagar. She pulled her cloak tightly around her and I felt the moment she relaxed. She believed I would not do anything immoral for the time being.

"You may sleep. He doesn't mind," Brass said, walking along beside us.

"What are you some kind of mind reader?" she asked combatively.

"I find it incredible you manage to be snide carried like a babe as you are. If you must know, we have known one another a long time and I know what he is thinking. It helps that I am an interrogator. Scarab and Scorpion," Brass said, lying.

She pursed her lips at him but did not argue. "I am Scat."

"So, the man Shark? Not your husband?" Brass asked slyly.

"Did I say that?" she asked in a coquettish tone and sighed gustily, "Well, I suppose you already know the truth. It is *like* we are married, but no."

"But you said your husband left you?" Brass pressed.

"Do you always interrogate strangers? I do not see why you need to know anything about my personal life to help me," she snapped.

Brass stopped and placed a hand to her face that she recoiled from. He *called* and she faded into a dreamless sleep.

"Why do I feel like I'm going to regret helping her?"

*... We are doing the right thing. Not liking your new face?...*

Women and men alike warmed to Brass with no effort on his part. He had a face you could trust. Not the face he wore now.

"Is she breaking your vow worthy?" Brass asked.

Snowflakes settled on her lashes. Her long nose did not look as long with her beady eyes closed.

*... No one is breaking any vows. I appreciate her scent and her spirit. What about you? Enjoy being a glutton for punishment?...*

Brass looked away fighting a smile. "I am. I like it when they are unavailable or uninterested. Poses a challenge."

*... I know. I caught your scent...*

"I'll flip you for her."

Brass dug out a silver crescent and tossed it into the air. It gleamed as it spun end over end and he caught them slapping it to the back of his hand.

"Crescent side you get to flirt with her with your grunts and looks."

*... We could share her...*

Brass chuckled. "Are we destined to share every woman for the rest of our lives?"

*... We need one woman before we can share every...*

In a pinch, we had a safe house at the edge of Glitra. Nothing special, but beds, a fireplace, and outside of the rounds the Stygians made at night.

I laid Scat on the mattress as Brass got a fire going. Her clothes were fine leather and wool. She was still in all white that was now splashed with her blood. Undressing her could pose problems, but letting her sleep-in blood-soaked wool was worse. I began to unlace her corset and could feel Brass's eyes on me.

*... I am going to clean the blood from her clothing. It is all she has...*

"I didn't say anything," Brass said in an amused tone.

I pulled off her gore-soaked gloves and rolled her from the thick corset holding it out to Brass.

*... Here. Make yourself useful...*

He took the leather corset and began to wipe the fabric with his *calling*. I unlaced her woolen shirt, pulling it over her head then unbuckled her short seax to pull off her pants and socks. I left her thick blade belt on with her white cotton boy shorts. I caught the hint of a tattoo under her belt and as I reached to lift it, Brass cleared his throat.

"Plan on covering her?" Brass said, furrowing his brow to look up at me.

I yanked the quilt over her and found a fresh towel then began to unbraid her hair to rinse out the blood. I held up the short seax so Brass could check it out and he looked impressed.

Brass began drying her shirt as I slid my hands up her thighs to replace her clean pants. I was doing my best not to look at her too closely, especially since the blasted woman was unconscious and apparently had little regard for bras.

"Are you going to stay here with her so she doesn't do something foolish like try to go back to her friends?" he asked, laying the clean corset and socks over a chair.

*... Four months and a volatile murderous woman is the one to catch my eye. No, I do not want to break my vow. I only want her because she reminds me of Scarlett...*

Brass nodded. "I feel the same. Come."

I lifted her up with my *calling* and pulled her shirt over her head before tucking her into bed. We locked her in the room and went to the front room and started another fire. Brass laid on the couch undressing to his pants and linen shirt. He threw me a cushion I placed under my head as I laid down in front of the fire, taking off all of my furs and boots. I slept in my pants alone. It was freeing not to have to wear all that clothing for once.

"I know I do not have to say it —"

*... Then do not...*

"She is married. She is wearing a wedding ring, if a hideous one. We do not need distractions right now. Not with our plans finally coming into fruition."

*... Take your own advice...*

"I plan to, brother."

It was a long while before the beast let me be and I fell to sleep. Brass was still tossing and turning when I faded into my dreams.

# CHAPTER
# FIFTY

Maybe I should have been more grateful. They did save me after all. After our first hostile interaction at the Dark Dancer, I was less inclined to kindness, and I hated feeling helpless. I supposed I could have killed one of the two men last night, but I would have probably bled out in that dead end if Scarab and Scorpion hadn't found me.

They said there were three other men with them and they were going to guide Tawny, Jett, Ridge, and Quick to where we needed to go. I couldn't activate my bond with Jett unless I wanted to let Indigo know where I was too.

I couldn't use much of my *calling*. It sucked all the energy from me which after everything I had been through lately, was too much for my body to handle. I hated to admit that in lieu of my family, I needed the two blackguards.

Scarab and Scorpion earned points with me when I awoke to blood free clothes and clean hair but lost them when I remembered that I hadn't worn a bra.

I laced my shirt as best I could with the tear and the corset over it then braided my hair into a single rope pulled over my shoulder. Alder's ring was still threaded into it so they must have overlooked it. They lost more points when I had to use my *calling* to unlock the bedroom door but regained a few when I saw my clean boots and socks.

In the front room, I found the two men asleep with the glowing embers of the fire burning out. I stoked the ashes putting another log on the fire.

Since they took care of me, I thought I would return the favor and start the day out on the right foot since I'd be spending the next two days with them. They were both big, muscled men with long dark hair and cool blue eyes. Brothers, I figured. The one called Scorpion had a long drip like nose and thin lips. Both men had dark unruly beards, Scarab's face was overshadowed by a beak of a nose. Still, they looked better than the unfortunate faces Quick and Jett wore.

Even better than my own. Which was why I couldn't understand why their scents spiked around me. I wasn't exactly pleasant and there was nothing remarkable about my appearance. It was baffling.

I looked for their packs and found one resting up against the couch where Scorpion laid with his corded arms crossed over his face as he slept. Scarab slept shirtless on the floor and I had to work saliva into my mouth, it had gone completely dry. Lately, I'd only been around men I couldn't touch. Judging from Scarab's scent, I *could* get away with touching him. Much more than the playful roaming I'd done with Quick in Disir. I could be touched too.

Scorpion's palms were up and I saw the callouses that graced the pads of his hands as if he was accustomed to blades. The scratch of those callouses would feel *fantastic* against my bare skin.

I squeezed my eyes shut, and I gave myself a mental kick. Filthy fiddlesticking khoraz. I had to focus.

I moved to the leather pack and lifted the flap, digging through to find food to make us for breakfast. I was rewarded with apples, berries, flakey bread, and a thick cream I tasted and found it to be butter. I sliced the bread and toasted it spreading the butter on its warm surface and sliced the apples placing it all on small wooden plates he'd had in his pack.

I worked as quietly as I could on the floor between the two men and arranged the breakfast for us. I was proud of my accomplishments and stood with a plate of buttered bread, apple slices, and a handful of berries for Scorpion. I could see his fine dusting of dark hair that I imagined covered his chest, peeking from the 'V' neck collar where his pecs met in a crease as I extended my hand to wake him.

My fingertips brushed along the curve of his hard bicep. His big hand snapped out, latching onto my wrist that held the plate, sending the food flying. I grit my teeth as he toppled me over and discovered a dagger at my throat. His dark hair was wild around his face, his muscles strained as he blinked down at me. His body pressed on top of mine, but he made a mistake. My other hand was free.

I *called* as much as I dared since he hadn't used air ropes and pulled my short seax. Slate had taught me a move he called 'the mount' that had nothing to do with our bedroom play. I flipped Scorpion onto his back and rammed my knees into his underarms as he grunted. I pushed his arms out and placed my arm wide, bracing it on the floor as I pressed my chest to the side of his face to restrain him. My blade was pointed towards his face where my hand splayed on the rug.

Movement beside us drew Scorpion's attention, and Scarab held up the plate I'd dropped in my periphery. Scorpion's body relaxed as he looked up at me from the corner of his eye.

"Try to pull your blade on me again and you will regret it," I bit off, and leaned back, putting my blade back in its sheath as I sat back on my heels.

His cool blue eyes glittered as he made no move to shift. I breathed deep for him. It'd been a while since I had a man beneath me. I looked away, careful not to show him my dilating pupils as I swung my leg over his chest and got to my feet.

"Enjoying the show? Do you plan on retiring from the Red Seconds?" I asked in a caustic tone.

Scarab chuckled in a tone higher than I'd expected from such a big man. Scorpion pushed up off the floor.

He looked defensively at me and I scowled. "I only touched you to wake you."

"For what?" he barked back.

Some silent communication passed between Scarab and him, and I bent to pick up the remaining two plates we'd almost landed atop. Scorpion's deeply tanned skin darkened as he watched me offer the plate to Scarab who took it with glittering blue eyes. I ignored the look and popped a berry into my mouth.

"Your breakfast. What you did not smash into my back, is on the floor. Scarab, how is your breakfast?" I asked, and turned to the man who had not dressed and towered above me.

I craned my head back to look at him and he lifted his plate to me with an inclination of his head. "I am glad you like it. I admit, I did take it from your pack, Scorpion so I hope you were not saving it."

I moved with my plate to sit on the couch he had leapt up from and began to eat off my lap. Scorpion used his *calling* to place it all on the plate and sat down beside me, not quite touching. Scarab contented himself to stretch out in front of the fire and eat on his side.

"My apologies. I did not mean to assault you," he muttered.

I scoffed and continued to eat.

Scarab beckoned me with a crook of his finger and I tried not to bite down on my lip. It was too come hither for me to be comfortable. I couldn't back down though so I pushed from the couch and stood in front of the lounging man. He placed his palm over my leg and I felt him delve.

"No damage done," Scorpion said grumpily. "I do not think I have been subdued by breasts before."

Scarab chuckled before I could snap at him and I sat back down on the couch.

I could feel Scorpion's eyes on my chest and turned to glare at him. "Your shirt." He gestured, and I put my plate aside to cover my quickly dampening top.

"Let us categorize this into the personal column, things we need not discuss," I said coolly, and stood from the couch.

The low heel of my boot caught, and I went stumbling back with my arms windmilling. I didn't land. Scorpion caught me under my arms and gently helped me onto the couch. His fingers ran down my ribs to my waist as he lifted me effortlessly to my feet.

"Thank you. I am out of sorts." I blushed at my uncharacteristic clumsiness.

Scorpions hands lingered as he withdrew and offered me a small smile. "It is good that we are here with you then."

"I just need a moment then I am ready to leave whenever you are," I said, going back into the modest bedroom.

"After breakfast, we'll set out," Scorpion agreed, collecting my plate and shoving them into his pack.

I shut the door behind me and took off my shirt and corset, cursing. My pump was in my pack back at the Dark Dancer. I tried to milk myself like a cow and was rewarded with the slowest trickle that ran down the swell of my breast and over my stomach. I groaned in frustration. They were rock hard and hurting.

There was a soft knock at the door. Either the two men hadn't spoken at all or they were unbelievably quiet even for a mute and a cache hole.

"Yes?" I asked peevishly as I crossed to the door.

"Is everything okay?" Scorpion asked.

I opened the door appalled at was I was going to ask. I looked at them both and weighed my options.

"Are either of you married?" I asked.

"He is, but she passed away at the start of the Purge War," Scorpion said arching a brow at me.

I licked my lips and nodded. Better the mute than the guy who was a huge jerk. I crooked a finger at Scarab.

"I need a favor. You *can* say no. Come in... please."

Scarab and Scorpion shared confused looks and the big man slid through the crack in the door. He started when he saw my state of undress and shook his head.

"I'm not coming on to you, you big Neanderthal!" I admonished. "Get down here. There is nothing sexual about this. I need help and what I need is in my pack with my friends that *you* said I couldn't get so you have to do this. Just spit it in this basin," I said, lifting the metal bowl from the end table.

He was still shaking his head.

"They're just breasts! Now get down on your knees and latch on. The sooner you finish, the sooner we can go... and don't look. Keep your eyes closed," I said stiffly.

His cool eyes dropped to my swollen chest, and he thumbed to the door. I shook my head.

"He pulled a knife on me. Besides, you can't talk to rub it in. *Please.* I wish I could say it would just be this once, but... I will need your help again. If I sat down would that make it easier? Look, I am fully aware of how odd this is. I'm not exactly thrilled about a complete stranger suckling from me," I said dryly.

He exhaled heavily and nodded to the bed. I didn't think he would like to be on his knees, but it was worth a shot. I laid down on the bed and carried the basin with me as he followed. Scarab's skin prickled as he stood above me and I was suddenly glad Tawny helped me remove all my superfluous hair as I patted my stomach for him to get comfortable.

The bed bowed with his weight as he settled between my legs and looked up at me where I'd propped myself up on the pillows. He licked his lips and lowered his mouth over my hard pearl. Before his eyes flickered down to my chest, I thought I saw the telltale widening of his pupil.

I dropped my head back and groaned as I let down.

Scarab jerked away, and I opened my eyes to see what the problem was. Apparently I'd squirted him with a rogue breast. Milk ran down his cheek into his beard and he shook his head as he laughed.

"Sorry," I said, mortified.

As if it wasn't awkward enough.

He placed his palm over the rogue breast as I folded my arms behind my head and bent his mouth down to finish. I shut my eyes and pretended not to feel his beard on the sensitive underside of my breast or the way his tongue swirled in a very *unnursing* like way.

"You're drinking it!" I accused, and he lifted his eyes to me dryly as he continued to suckle.

I shut my eyes again, unable to stifle the visceral response of a virile man with his lips against my skin.

"It's just weird is all. I guess there is nothing *not* weird about this." I sighed.

I felt him shift to the second one. His tongue slid over the milk trail that had rolled over my breast and my eyes snapped open.

"Hey!" I snapped, slapping the top of his head.

I swallowed. His scent was so strong I wasn't sure I could control myself. The fire the rousen created in my brain was already simmered. Those cool blue eyes dilated, and I gasped. I hadn't imagined it.

"You're a khoraz," I breathed.

He gripped my nipple between his teeth and sucked hard so I hissed with an intake of air. "I'm sorry. I didn't mean to insult you. I just never met a male khoraz before... I am too," I whispered and averted my eyes.

He reached up with his hand from where he laid bare chested on my belly and tapped the corner of my left eye. My pupils were likely dilated too. What a fine pair we made.

"How long has it been?" I asked, working moisture into my mouth.

He tapped the breast he cupped four times. Why was he cupping my breast again?

"Four days?" I asked, feeling relieved he'd had a recent fix of flesh.

He gave a gentle shake of his head, and my eyes widened.

"Four weeks?" I asked.

He shook again.

I laughed. "Four months?" He wasn't attractive for a Guardian, but he had some indiscernible quality that made me feel a tug to him.

He gave a little nod, and I gaped at him. "You're kidding. Why?" I asked, and he tapped his ring finger where a band wound around it.

Since his wife died.

"I'm sorry about your wife," I said softly, and he withdrew, wiping his mouth on the back of his hand.

I felt cold.

"It's done?" I asked, pushing up on my palms.

He nodded not looking at me and I grabbed my shirt off the bed, pulling it over my head. "I'm sorry for bringing it up. I lost loved ones in the Purge War too," I told him, hoping to make up for sticking my big foot in my mouth, but he just shut the door behind him as he left the bedroom.

I watched them move, such big men should have bumped into each other every once in a while, but it was like a choreographed dance. They'd done it dozens if not hundreds of times. One of them had cleaned my gloves and whatever spots of blood had been on my cloak. I clasped on my corset and looked to the two men as I sat on the couch.

"Does either of you have a sewing kit?" I asked.

To my surprise, Scorpion pulled out a thin wooden box that held buttons, needles and thread. I chose a white thread and began to mend the seam where my assailant had torn it along the lacing of my shirt. I looked up to find them leaning against the fireplace watching me and my cheeks heated.

"I thought I should do this now because it will be cold tonight," I said nervously.

Scarab grunted, slinging his pack over his head and Scorpion offered me a hand to help me off the couch. "Good idea. Have you ever stayed the night in the Illfuss Ice Fields?"

I laced up my shirt and replaced the needle. "No."

They stopped and looked at me, taking a measure of everything I wore. "If you get cold, don't be shy. We huddle for warmth and sleep together at night, or we won't wake up in the morning." Scorpion said, pulling a scarf from around his neck and walked over to me. He wound it around my head and raised it over my nose and mouth, then pulled my braid free and lifted up the hood of my cloak. "That will have to do."

I didn't often let others take care of me and the way he did it without asking and so efficiently left me dumbfounded. It was as if we'd been doing it for years. The pang in my heart had nothing to do with my two blackguards.

We were in a small cottage on the outskirts of the mining town when we emerged at early morning's light. My boots crunched on snow that had fallen overnight and frozen over at the low temperatures at dark. Alone with two strange men without my pack and unable to *call* more than a flame was not how I saw the trip going.

"We're going to have to skirt around the Frostfell Mountains to head north. We take this way to avoid the Natts, but it brings us close to the Crathode," Scorpion explained as we marched.

All I had to focus on was putting one foot in front of the other and I found myself tiring by early afternoon. This was the way we'd planned with Ridge who had thought skirting the Natt castle would be best too.

There wasn't any wind, but the cold was enough to make the men's noses and cheeks bright red despite their tan tone and even I who didn't feel cold had found the limit of my abilities. My face was actually cold.

"I should tell you... and I hope you appreciate the risk I am taking by confiding in you, but I can't *call* very much. Just in case we get into a scuffle, you should know." My voice was muffled by our heavy breaths and the scarf I wore.

"Hopefully we won't have a reason to fight. If it's so bad that we can't handle it, we're probably dead anyway," Scorpion retorted, and I frowned as I stepped over fallen rocks.

"How delightfully pragmatic," I grumbled under my breath.

Scarab went from idly running his thumb against something in his pocket, to whittling a piece of hand sized wood in otherwise complete silence.

The mountains of Frostfell loomed to our left as we trudged around them. The Vetr castle sat nestled on top of the highest peak with fanged snowcapped mountains all around.

"Do you know who sealed the castle?" I asked, looking at the magnificent place Tawny would raise her daughter.

"No. No one does," Scorpion said, and shared another secretive look with Scarab.

That was getting annoying, and I soon decided not to speak to either of them.

We ate as we walked for lunch. Scorpion passed out salted meat that I had to work my warm spit to chew and green roots he'd foraged as we walked. We did little talking, the freezing air would seep into our lungs from our mouths and we would find ourselves gasping for breath. Walking alone was strenuous without adding talking to the mix.

My heart lurched as we passed close to Elivagar's town heart. I fantasized about the puffs of chimney smoke that had always made the quaint village seem like a greeting card. It was too quiet, not even the dogs were left to roam. I supposed it was a good thing that it had been evacuated, I knew now that the three ghouls who had attacked me were some of the creatures the Stygians had loosed to terrify the people into staying indoors. I saw why it worked.

The woman, Lamia, and the shadowed man were known to hunt and devour children. The third was a run-of-the-mill vampire. If vampires could be called run of the mill.

As night fell, Scarab moved inconspicuously to stand on my left and slowly drove me towards Scorpion like a shepherd herding sheep. I knew what he was doing, and deep down I was grateful because I had too much pride to admit I needed warmth — proud and incredulous.

Scorpion wrapped an arm around my shoulders, pulling me under his cloak and *called* heat into us as we walked. Scarab's habit of rummaging in his pocket, turned out to be for a long braid he kept half hidden. I figured it was his wife's braid, it was kind of endearing.

They had a certain goal in mind where we would camp and I couldn't wait to get there. My feet were frozen, I had to make waste, and I was exhausted. They steered me to a mountainside and Scarab pulled out a folded white leather square he shook out and began to push stakes into the ground. It was a low, white tent that blended in like a snow drift against the mountain. I would only be able to kneel in it wasn't very high.

Scorpion gestured for me to climb in and I pushed back the flap crawled inside. The two men came in after me and I realized that the tent was only made for sleeping, and for two men not a third, even a woman.

"I saved the best for last. Tomorrow we have to hunt or fish," Scorpion said, pulling out flaky smoked whitefish wrapped in wax paper and heated it before giving me a fillet.

Our knees touched as we sat cross-legged in a triangle. I finished my fish and Scorpion produced the last apple and divided it into three pieces for each of us and I thanked him. I knew they must've been used to eating much more.

I excused myself and had one of the single most horrible experiences of my life as I made waste in the tundra with only my *calling* to cleanse me. I missed the toilet paper I secretly brought on every expedition. I finished up my nightly grooming by rubbing my finger over my teeth with some snow in lieu of brushing and huffed.

I couldn't meet their eyes as I crawled back inside the tent and attempted to make a pillow out of my arm. Scorpion laid down next to me and his eyes met mine. A globe of light from one of the two men's *calling* shadowed the tent.

"We always lay together to stay warm. We can't risk the fire so close to the village and the Crathode. Elivagar has long nights," he said, and I sat bolt upright.

"You two *lay* together? I thought you were brothers?" I asked doubtfully.

Sexuality and virility practically oozed off of them. I didn't believe it.

He made a face he had either practiced or genuinely meant. "Of course we do. We're comfortable with ourselves. Why wouldn't we if it keeps us warm?"

I gaped at him and heard Scarab chuckle behind me, but not in a way that made me think Scorpion was lying. Still, I would not be bedding two perfect strangers.

"Well, I guess I'm going to have to freeze to death. What kind of woman do you think I am?" I huffed.

"I thought you were the kind that wanted to stay alive!" he snapped. "I have never heard of anyone making it through the night alone, Scat," he said, turning serious.

I clenched my jaw. I could see the rationale behind it. If we three laid together, it would certainly generate a lot of heat that would linger in this small tent. Perhaps they were tired of one another and needed a little spice to their strange relationship. I didn't want to be anyone's spice, but I certainly didn't want to freeze to death so close to our goal.

If I closed my eyes, I could swear I caught the scent of my husband and my former lover; cinnamon and cloves. It had been months since I had been touched that way. Scarab and Scorpion were powerfully built men.

Hooking my finger in the tie, my braid loosened, and I caught my own scent. I wasn't very pretty with the distorter but they seemed to find me attractive. I shook out my hair and saw Scorpion watching me with wide eyes. I smiled internally.

They weren't the eyes of the men I loved. I stared down at my hands twisting my hair tie between my fingers. Two trains were placed into my hands and I looked up as Scarab sat back.

"Trains for your children. You can paint them or leave them as is," Scorpion explained.

Had he also shoved an exquisitely carved wooden ball down my throat?

"I have two sons. Thank you," I said, strangling the words out.

Scarab was shifting things in his pack to use it as a pillow when I held the trains in my fist and flung myself at him. I had to do it in a rush because taking the time to say something nice and work my way to a thank you would've made me chicken out at some point.

Hugging him was like embracing a DaVinci's David. The man was made of solid stone. No one had gotten my children a gift. Spinel had come with me to get their cribs, but Scarab had made my sons trains with his own two hands.

His confusion was palpable. The fact that I was tearing up must have been bewildering. Despite the cold, he smelled like sweat and man. I could detect the saltiness of his skin where my nose pressed in the crook off his neck. He'd taken off his furs and cloak. His jerkin was unbuckled to his sides and his Yggdrasil chain peeked from the brown padded fabric.

"Are you okay?" Scorpion asked in a soothing tone from behind me.

Readjusting my hold on Scarab's thick neck, I nodded where I leaned against him on my knees. "I won't have sex with either of you. I don't care how cold it gets," I muttered, my lips rubbed against Scarab's collarbone as I spoke.

I could feel them doing that quiet communication thing and pulled away. Scarab's deep-set eyes were a cool blue just like his friend's. He looked frightened of me.

"But, you can hold me... for warmth. I'll need your services again,

Scarab. If you do not mind," I added, and he took one of his big hands and wiped away my tears.

I pulled my face away yanking my shirt over my head and laid down on my back. I heard Scorpion suck in a sharp breath as Scarab urged me back up and drew my shirt down. He rolled it just over my chest before helping me lay back down leaving my discarded corset rolled above my head.

Scarab laid down between my legs and I felt his warm breath against my chest before he lowered his mouth over me. His other hand covered my breast from a possible geyser. I sighed and felt myself begin to thaw as the ache was alleviated from my chest. I didn't care that he drank it anymore. He was the only reason I would still be able to nurse when I got back to Balas and Spinel.

He *felt* so woeful I almost asked him what was wrong. *Almost.*

As he suckled, my lids grew heavy. I couldn't stay awake after the grueling day.

# CHAPTER 51
# SLATE

Scorpion left us in the tent to snare a hare and forage for roots and berries. He had not spoken before he left for fear of waking the sleeping woman. She had turned in the night and wrapped her slender arms around me. Her face was buried against my chest and I spent every minute since I awoke in the position wishing I had thought to bathe before we began our trek.

She stirred. Her hands running down my back to the seat of my pants. She purred, gripping full palm to fingers wriggling against me. My breath hitched. If I moved, I might reciprocate her firm hold. When was the last time a woman held me?

"Don't let me ruin your fun," Brass joked as he came into the tent.

Her eyes shot open and her hands released as if I scalded her. She pushed away scooting to the far corner of the rounded tent and pulled her knees up. Her body was tense like a cornered animal. The last day's events ran through her mind and her wild eyes narrowed at me as if I had coaxed her into copping a feel.

"Surprise. Eggs," Brass said, revealing the bird he must have followed to its nest and its contents.

"Scarab?" Her brow knit, and I nodded knowing she would need relief.

"We'll eat first while it's warm... then you can... do that," Scorpion said awkwardly.

Scat tramped behind them, politely refusing to walk with them. She had not spoken through breakfast no matter how much Brass coaxed — her walls up and reinforced around her. She lost a lot of pride in asking me to suckle from her. She did not like needing anyone.

"I can't get her out of my head," Brass whispered.

My instinctual response was to grunt.

*... You tripped her yesterday morning so you could hold her. If you promise not to play dirty, tonight can be your turn...*

"We could extend our trip, hold her for many nights." Brass chuckled.

*... A month into it she might grow suspicious...*

My lips curled as I glanced over my shoulder. Scat was not exceptionally attractive, but she had an indefinable quality that drew me — *us* — to her. It was not that she had the most succulent breasts I had had the privilege to put my lips to. It was hard not to grope and to keep it from crossing into amorous territory. She had whacked my head when I had temporarily lapsed.

I shoved my hand into my pocket and stroked Scarlett's braid. I felt a deep sadness settle in my chest with my guilt.

"Did she really goose you in there?" Brass asked.

*... It was more of a solid grip than a quick squeeze. I nearly forgot what it felt like to hold a woman...*

"As good as you remember?"

*... Better...*

Brass looked back at her and she lifted her head, feeling our eyes and gave a chilling gaze. We tried not to laugh as we turned back. She shoved the train she was fondling into her cloak pocket and tossed her mane of obsidian hair.

You would not have guessed it from the way she glowered, but you could not have shoved a nickel hunt between us as we laid in one another's arms only hours ago.

I had woken up harder than the feet of ice that lined Elivagar. It was infuriating. I wanted to take my ring off, for her to see me. For her to be cowed... then again, not. In the past, I thought it was my presence that made the wrong women attracted to me.

I gave his back a pat as we walked over the mountainous landscape.

*... The wound is too fresh to think about another woman in a serious way. I get the feeling Scat is not the love and leave kind...*

Brass sighed. "Not unless she is doing the leaving." He paused. "You know the only reason Scarlett and I saw each other again after we told her you were dead was because we were already together. She never would have let me get close otherwise."

*... I know, brother...*

In case the Stygians were looking for her. That was what we told ourselves.

That meant the longer way around. No more walking during meals. The tent only took a few moments to set up, we could eat in relative warmth. If she were Scarlett, we would be doing that and more.

Like Scarlett though, Scat protested the stop for lunch. She grudgingly ate the hare Brass snared and tried not to show her obvious discomfort; palms cupping and releasing swollen breasts. I briefly gave her relief while Brass tried to act like he was not jealous.

"There are hot springs south of the Crathode lands. We plan to stop for a bath," Brass told her, waiting to see if she would rise to the bait.

We sat hunched in the low tent in the valley between the Frostfell Mountains. My newest wood carving project for her sons was still a half-formed chunk of wood. We were at a crawl and the Lycans would be a half a day ahead with her companions.

"A hot bath?" she said, practically moaning. "We should have enough time for that."

I bent my head down to hide the curl of my lips and Brass had to look away before we started giggling like a couple of tyro girls. I saw her straighten in her haughtiest pose through my lashes.

"Two men hiking through the mountains with all the furs you wear, *living* in those boots. Baths should be more frequent." She sniffed. "Sweating... with all of your heavy breathing. I am just thankful neither of you snore," she said it peevishly, but whatever Brass saw in her mind did not seem irritated and neither did her scent or the way her skin had prickled across her chest.

She wriggled her hips where she sat and I looked to Brass. "You'd pay to see what I do right now," he said in a breath so low only I would hear.

*... About last night?...*

Brass nodded. "About this morning," he whispered.

She was staring, her beady eyes narrowed. "That is horribly annoying. I have excellent hearing and can pick up every few words of a one-sided conversation. You are a mind reader. I did not realize they were so common."

They were *not* common. There were five that we knew of, all distant descendants of the Regn line.

Brass searched her face, trying to discern if she was playing coy, but her scent said she was not. Grease slid along her little finger and down to her wrist and I watched its trickling trail to her sleeve. She slid her tongue from her mouth sliding up the path it took. The ghost of the trail that tongue followed made a tingling trail on my cock as I watched her. Scat's eyes flitted up as I returned to my own meal.

"There are no napkins," she said in an embarrassed whisper.

"I take it as a compliment. I have heard of finger licking good, but not wrist licking," Brass said, and I let my eyes drift to her as she suppressed a rueful smile.

"It is very good, thank you... again. Have you spent much time outside of Tidings? You use contractions."

Brass stilled. "Some. Just enough to expose myself to the culture. You?"

"I miss it," she whispered.

Scat was eager to arrive at the hot springs. The promise of a hot bath lit a fire under her and twice we had to redirect her path as she trudged ahead. The Vetr castle was fading away as we neared the Crathode lands.

Scat was practically hopping as she undressed. A rock made shelter for the Guardians who frequented the springs in better times, was there for our use. A single room without windows that had a low table, a dozen cushions, and two mattresses. We could hear the rustling of clothes being removed as we faced the wall while she undressed. It was warmer near the springs, no snow clung to the craggy stones and she emerged in Brass's borrowed black linen shirt with her short seax strapped to her thigh.

She was bare under the thin material; we could see the outline of her body within it and she folded her arms over her chest whose hardening peaks shown through the thin material with the small fire going in the fireplace.

"I see that there is only one hot spring deep enough to emerge ourselves. Can I assume we will not be taking turns?" she asked, dancing on her unpolished tip toes.

"You want to take turns?" Brass asked, smirking. "We will not take advantage of you. You have our word."

She pursed her lips, wondering if Brass was teasing her, and narrowed her eyes.

I gave her a wry look.

*... Unless you ask...*

Brass knit his brows. It had been a long time since he spoke to women he was interested in, he was rusty. I told myself I was not a complete scoundrel. She had thought we were lovers by the way Brass had phrased his words the first night. She thought he meant we slept together to stay warm and alive through the night. It was true, we were warmer than we had ever been during one of our expeditions with her. We had also slept more soundly than we had in ages.

Scat relaxed visibly before starting out towards the steaming pools of water. She wanted that hot bath more than she was concerned about her safety. Brass and I stripped our clothes and shared an exasperated look as we left on our pants before walking over to the springs.

There were several shallow springs scattered over the stony surface, a heavy steam mist hung over the pools. Scat had been right, there was only one small pool we could submerge ourselves in standing up. She cut through the surface wiping her hands over her face and smoothing back her hair with a bright smile.

It was the first time I had seen her smile.

Water pooled in her collar bones as she bobbed over to the edge, not having spotted us yet. The water was clearer than I remembered.

She was singing. She hummed, her body swaying in the fading light.

"*We* could take turns," Brass offered. I could not tell if he was jesting.

I sucked in a rough breath. It was a myopic song. Scarlett loved that song. She loved to make love to it. Brass picked up my thoughts and sighed.

"You're seeing her where you wish. It's a popular song."

I did not want to debate him. Scat and Scarlett were totally different people, I knew that. There were an uncanny amount of similarities, but it was more likely that I was stretching my imagination so Scat would fit Scarlett's shoes.

She stiffened as we cut through the mist and sank down to her chin, her torch song cut short. We began to remove our pants and she turned around, placing her palms on the stone edge. I whipped my head to Brass; he was staring too. She had hidden the delicious curve of her backside in all of that clothing, but now we could see it clear as day even in the twilight.

Brass and I dropped into the pool and I held out the bar of soap I brought for such trips. I felt like an awkward prepubescent boy.

She dunked herself, water cascading down her long raven waves, and turned around, carefully placing her hair over her chest, her dark narrow eyes skeptically looked at the soap I offered. She plucked it from my fingers and drifted back the short distance to the edge.

Scat sniffed the soap and sighed. "Are there scents that connect you to certain memories like a fish on a hook being reeled in and there is nothing you can do to fight it?" she asked wistfully.

Brass dipped his head back into the spring and made a sound of ascent. Her scent. It was the first time she had spoken in a kind, relaxed tone.

I nodded, dunking my head in the water.

She gripped the soap like a weapon in both her hands. "Cinnamon, cloves, and... what is the third scent?"

"Sweet woodruff," Brass answered.

"At least you will both smell good tonight," she said absently as she turned around and began to wash.

It was hard not to watch her body move with an unfettered view of her flawless skin. The water bent what lay below her hips though I spotted a tattoo that grew too hard to make out under the water.

I wanted her to look at me.

She drifted over and held out the soap. Scat was sad now. Whatever memories the scent of the soap invoked had brought her sorrow. I wanted to comfort her, to wrap my arms around her and ask her if I could help.

"Lost loved ones?" Brass asked her, and she lifted her gaze to him.

"Yes. Too many. Where is your wife?" she asked, nodding to the distorter ring he wore over his tiwaz ring tattoo. "I thought only Scarab was widowed?"

I rubbed my distorter ring. Scarlett had taken back her father's wedding band. I had my mother's ring, the one I had given her, that she had given back just that once as opposed to the half dozen foolish times I had given her back Alder's, in my pack. It was the access key to the arenas.

"No, not married. She turned me down. We were hand-fasted for as long as love lasted, but I don't think it lasted for her," Brass said with a rueful grin, thinking of all the mistakes he'd made to hurt her.

"Oh. I am sorry," she said, swallowing.

Melancholy fell over us, but the hot water was too good to leave. Scat bobbed with her eyes shut intent on becoming a prune before she went to back to the tent.

"Where you from? Not here. Your skin is dark and so is your hair. My guess would be Mabon since you have light eyes. Am I right? Though I cannot fathom why anyone from Mabon would be in the rebellion. Word is the townsfolk like Sterling Haust over his father," she asked, trying to lighten the mood.

Brass exhaled heavily and nodded, not liking having to lie to her. She gave an encouraging smile and my brows quirked. She was pretty when she smiled — very pretty. It helped that she was being friendly.

"Want to guess where I am from?" she urged.

"Thrimilci; dark hair, eyes, and skin. There or Valla," Brass said, matter of fact.

She gave a pout. "Thrimilci. I thought that would be harder."

She was not lying; it was refreshing since I was sure she was purposefully not volunteering information. Her teeth ran over her lower lip in a nervous habit and I imagined them as fuller lips, almost too full, and the way she would let it spring forth driving me wild.

The beast rattled the cage, and I held my breath until the feeling passed.

"We received word while we were in Glitra that a rebellion had risen in Thrimilci. The Sumar are back in charge and have rid themselves of the Stygians and the rogue tribes," Brass told her, testing a theory we shared.

Scat's rose bud mouth pressed tightly together and sighed. "My companions and I were there. I —" She looked at Brass suspiciously, "I know the chief's brother, he comes into Thrimilci every once in a great while to trade for goods and we went out to the Wemic lands." She glanced away, staring through the steam. "The Faunelle had already mobilized. They were just waiting for someone to lead them. We gave them the proper incentive to follow us back. They were the ones to make the red bands like the one you dropped in the inn. It was a short battle, most of the Jorogumo had been threatened into joining the Stygians."

We had known there was more to her and her companions than met the eye, but even this surpassed what we discussed. That begged the question, who was her quasi husband?

"With your husband?" Brass asked.

"I already told you, he is not my husband. My husband left me. I have nearly died half a hundred times without him. I could not care less what he thinks. He was not the last man I was with anyway," she snapped, obviously thinking he had implied more than he meant.

Which he had, but not about her husband.

"The last one you were with... you did not like them much?" Brass asked, trying to cool her hot temper.

"Them was a *him* and no. He was one of the biggest mistakes of my life." She sighed.

"My last as well. His too. Too many mistakes when lust is involved," Brass said, nodding to me.

She watched me intently deciding whether she would trust us. "I should tell you — my husband who left me — that is where I am going. I need him now. He is... with the Lycans. That is how far north I have to go...all the way," she said nervously and then rushed out the rest. "I understand if you cannot take me the whole way, if you could point me in the right direction, that should be enough. I do appreciate your help." She scanned our faces. "Since you are both Red Seconds, your help would be appreciated. I need to mobilize the Lycans into Elivagar and any other tribes that would be willing to join us in retaking the island. It is no easy task, I know, but someone has to try."

Brass had stopped breathing. There were not many men living with the Lycans. Two to be precise and she was looking at them.

"We have been there. What does he look like? We probably know him," Brass said.

I had a good idea of who she was going to describe.

She glanced away, struggling with trusting us. "Tall, broad shouldered, lots of muscles." I was not sure if she realized she was smiling. "He is hard to miss, very good looking with long black wavy hair and —"

"We know him," Brass said, cutting her off.

My insides boiled. I had grown insanely jealous with her every description. Fucking Niall. He was always taking up with women who had no idea he was a Lycan, but marrying them? Leaving one pregnant? He would take responsibility; I would make sure of it. How deceitful he had been, pretending not to know her in the alley!

Her eyes widened. "He does not want me anymore, but he is very possessive. I —" She bit her lip. "I would not want him to hurt either of you out of misplaced jealousy."

Brass snorted. "He is free to try."

I was too enraged to speak. It was Niall all right. I turned and lifted myself from the pool with Brass a heartbeat behind me. What was it about this woman that was making us act so out of character?

I picked up my discarded clothing and heard her stifled gasp. I cocked my head to catch her ogling. Her scent wound me tight, I was ensnared.

"I am sorry if I am asking too much," she said in a hushed tone, going through great pains not to drop her eyes as she peered at us.

"It's not you. It's your husband. Come. You shouldn't stay here alone." Brass held his clothes over himself and offered her a hand.

She strategically placed her long hair over her chest and took Brass's hand as he hoisted her up. Brass gasped. Quick was fast, I was faster, but Brass could keep up with us both.

He spun her around, dropping his clothes while pulling a blade he had concealed in his pants to her throat. She squeaked.

"Who are you?" he demanded, pressing her tightly to him with the blade biting into her skin.

She held his forearm and Brass did not see the fear and rage in her eyes. Oh yes, she had been abused before and she had no intention of letting it happen again. Brass would not attack her unless he saw something terrible when she willingly touched him. He was wrong though. She had been honest. That morning, he had told me he had seen a lot of Shadow Breaker information in her mind and Scarlett's arenas. Nothing to get my hackles up, but that suspicion that she was hiding something never ebbed.

Brass was harder than ever before, but not hard enough. She *called* her seax into her hand and sliced his thigh so he loosened his hold which allowed her to spin in his arms. She didn't try to get away as I thought she would. Instead she gripped him between the legs, pressing her blade against him with a clenched jaw as she flattened herself to him.

"I am not a spy. I just want to get back to my family," she ground out. "What did I tell you about pulling blades on me?"

Brass and I both sucked in sharp breaths. With a flick of her wrist she could geld Brass. There was no way I could stop her in time.

Brass's arms were still around her, his blade at the back of her neck now. Her head was craned back to meet his eyes. She was a ferocious woman with bite to back up that bark.

"I told you, you would regret it," she said in an even tone.

"She is no Stygian." I broke my vow of silence, and Scat glanced up, gaping at me and Brass pounced, knocking them both back into the water.

Scat was from Thrimilci so she was an avid swimmer, everyone from Thrimilci was, it was the best way to stay cool. Brass had strength against her as they grappled in the water. Brass grit his teeth as he pinned her against the edge of the spring. He snatched a fistful of her hair in his hand and his hips pressed up against her backside, her arm bent behind her back. She had fought dirty and Brass was losing a string of colorful curses.

I arched a brow at him when she stopped her struggling. They both huffed, dark hair clinging to wet skin.

... *What now, Casanova?*...

Brass looked to me and cursed. She would likely dive for her blade as soon as he let her go and castrate him.

... *Let her swear an oath*...

"Swear you won't betray the Red Seconds," Brass said roughly.

Scat struggled again and Brass pressed harder against her, bending her head back so she was likely lifted off her feet in the spring. Her struggle was not having the effect it should have on any of them.

"Go fuck yourself," she spat.

I tried not to chuckle as Brass looked to the heavens. She didn't beg, didn't plead. She would rather die than submit. He looked to me for his next move and then froze.

She arched her back and was wriggling her hips as much as she could with him pressed so firmly against her.

"What are you doing?" Brass ground out.

"What does it feel like I'm doing? Is this not what you wanted? I *feel* you, Scorpion. When was the last time you had a woman?" she breathed.

I held my clothes in front of me. It was a game. A convincing game, and Brass was at a loss. He was not so sure of his hold any longer.

"Stop that," he said stupidly, and I watched his pulse race in his throat.

"You know how to make me stop," she purred.

Brass cursed and let her go. She whirled around at him; her blade flew from the water as she lunged. Her *calling* wrapped him in ropes of air so he was bound as she kicked him in the stomach so he fell back in the water. I dropped my pants thinking I would have to save him from a girl half his size.

Scat dragged him up by a fistful of his hair as he had done to her and used her *calling* to throw him against the spring edge. Brass was not putting up a fight past breathing. She yanked back his head and put the blade to his throat. She had climbed him like a tree, her legs locked at his waist from behind so his head rested on her shoulder.

"I swear it," she whispered and spoke the words of the vow.

*"My name is not my own, it is borrowed from my ancestors. I must return it unstained. My honor is not my own, it is on loan from my descendants, I must give it to them unbroken. Our blood is not our own, it is a gift to generations yet unborn, we should carry it with responsibility."*

Scat was shaking. Her blade trembled in her hand against Brass's Adam's apple.

"You're right. I was wrong. I am deeply sorry, Scat," Brass said softly.

"Don't you *ever* touch me like that again. I won't do you the courtesy of warning you."

Her voice quavered. She had been sorely used in her life and I wanted to tear the throats out of every man whoever hurt her. As her blade came down, the ropes that bound Brass fell and she slid down his back.

He turned to her, and she stuck the blade in her thigh sheath. She had cut her own arm to say the oath. I sucked in a breath, thankful no one had lost any important appendages, like, either head, and picked my pants back up off the rocks.

"You said he was mute," she whispered.

"By choice. I am sorry, Scat," Brass murmured.

"I heard you the first time," she said but could not muster the rage needed for the words.

She took my hand when I offered to help her out of the spring. Her obsidian hair formed to the shape of her breasts.

Scat pulled Brass's thin shirt over her body and stalked over to the shelter, going inside alone. I began to dress as Brass ran his hand over his face.

"She's hiding more," Brass said, climbing out of the spring after finding his blade.

*... Perhaps...*

"I saw Pearl in her mind, the Wemic, Orion... Ash. She's bedded Ash," Brass said, dropping his tone.

I sneered. Who had he not fucked?

We crept into the shelter. She had not dressed and blood crusted her arm, but she was sleeping. Scat wore our scent, and I liked it on her even if she had slept with the Straumr boy.

"Freya's burly boar, I pulled a knife on a woman — *twice*," Brass whispered.

I chuckled.

*... Times have changed. You are being cautious. Did you notice her dialect change? She has been playing a part...*

He did not seem reassured by my words so I patted him on the back.

*... Make it up to her tomorrow...*

Brass sighed and pulled on his shorts and drew up his cloak as he knelt down in front of her. She had chosen to sleep on the right mattress. She fit along the curve of my body as I laid down behind her.

*... By the Mother, I wish you had not upset her...*

I wrapped my arm around her. It was the first night since I met her that she had not asked me to relieve her. Brass was using his shirt's edge to wipe the blood from her arm.

"Everyone assumes I am the smooth one," he said dryly as he healed her.

He walked over to the other mattress and laid down, taking off his ring. I was looking at the man I had known all my life. He rubbed his face.

"Fucking Niall," he cursed.

I grunted in agreement and ran my nose over her hair. She smelled like Scarlett and our soap.

"Cold?" Brass asked with an amused look.

*... No thanks to you...*

Scat stirred and before Brass could slip his ring on she opened her eyes. She let out a little moan and threw herself at him, pulling out of my arms. She was a lot stronger than she looked. Brass looked over at me as he tried to turn away. She had sprouted a dozen arms.

"*I miss you,*" she whispered in a whimper. Her hand pulled his ring down over his knuckle and his face transformed.

"Gods, forgive me," Brass murmured.

Scat's eyes shot wide, and she threw herself back so violently she collided into me. She drew a shuddering breath.

"Easy, Scat. You were dreaming," I said in a comforting tone.

Brass's chest heaved as he caught his breath. "I'm sorry about earlier, Scat. I would've stopped you now, but —"

"Stop talking!" she shouted.

She was making soft choking sounds, fighting a cry that welled over, turning to face me, away from Brass. I took her into my arms. No one sought me for comfort. Brass was the soothing one. They always went to him. We had done some kind of role reversal. I understood now why he did not mind being the one to comfort after I made a mess.

Brass looked at me so helplessly distressed I nearly laughed as he left the rock formed room to give her a minute. She sobbed quietly, and I carefully slid her back down on the bed. I was not sure she would let me, but to my surprise, she placed her hand over mine.

"I miss my fake husband and my sister and my brother. I even miss my horrible husband and my ex-lover." She sobbed.

"*Shh.* Scorpion did not mean to hurt you. War makes even the best men insane. He is a very good man. I swear it," I whispered to her in my absurd alto voice.

Women loved my voice, but the girlish alto the ring Styg gave me was ill suited to my size. Being mute had worked better.

She blinked up at me scanning my eyes. Never had I wanted to take my distortion ring off the badly as I did then.

"Your voice doesn't suit you," she said in a hushed tone, blinking those dark sad eyes at me.

My brows quirked. It was the second time I had spoken to her without realizing it. There was that vulnerability I had adored in Scarlett. Trying so hard to be strong, but when she was not, she bloomed and let you in. It was a rare gift for her to trust you enough to help her.

Before I knew what I was doing, my body was moving. My head bent down and slanted her mouth with mine. Her gasp was swallowed. Her body was electric, and I wondered if she felt it too. *I* needed her. I had to have *her*. Her soft body molded into mine.

Scat kissed me back. It was revolutionary.

She tugged my lower lip, stroking it with her tongue, hands running along my beard and into my hair so her nails scratched against my scalp. Scat's black hair fanned out around her head as I pushed up her chin up deepening the kiss.

Her pulse raced, I felt it throb in her throat where my hand cupped her jaw. She was panting. Her scent of warm spiced apples and vanilla — like a drug. I pushed her thighs apart with my hip and watched the thin material of her shirt shiver as she looked up in disbelief. Disbelief that she was allowing me to do it.

I growled as the beast broke through the bonds and I lost control.

She yelped as I tore open the shirt like a spider's web and felt my teeth elongate into the barghest's. Her breasts were heavy and soft in my hands. My cock was so hard I thought I would burst if I did not have her that instant. Her nipples hardened against my rough palm that were quickly becoming clawed.

"Scarab!"

The cold of the outside air rushed in with him as Brass grabbed my ankles and yanked me off Scat, dragging me onto the cold rocks. My claws dug into the floor, causing sparks as I shifted, her eyes were closed. Brass would not let go.

I shot to my feet, rounding on him. He held up a blade in each hand huffing with effort it took to pull me outside.

"Think about what you're doing," he said, trying to lure me away from the rock house.

I grit my teeth trying to regain control. I had not lost control like that since I felt Scarlett's bond snap. I fell to my knees fisting my hair in my hands, growling in frustration.

"Just breathe. How were you expecting that to end?"

He was making too much sense.

"I know," I growled.

Brass was right, I wanted her to be Scarlett so badly that I had started to envision her as we kissed. She felt like Scarlett to me, kissed like her, even the sweet scent of her sex smelled like her.

Scat moved inside the hollowed-out rock and poked out her head, one hand clasped at the tear in Brass's shirt.

"Scarab? Are you okay?" she asked in a sincere tone.

"He's fine. Why don't you go on to bed, Scat?" Brass urged in a gentle tone.

She flushed down to her chest. "Okay."

That was all she said and Brass and I were eating out of the palm of her hand. I decided then and there that we would help her convince the Lycan sagamore to bring his people to Elivagar's town even though he hadn't given us the piece.

"Wait," Brass called, and she appeared in the doorway again, looking ashamed. "Are you hungry, Scat?" he asked.

Her stomach rumbled audibly, and she gave a rueful smile. Brass followed her into the stone as I took steadying breaths.

"Are you mad at him? Don't be. It was... a mutual mistake. It won't happen again," Scat said in her high voice from inside.

"It is not my concern what the two of you do together. We have promised to take you where you need to go and I intend to do just that. Whatever you do." If Brass was trying to be indifferent, he was failing miserably.

"I'm sorry...a bout earlier too. I know how hard it is to be around someone who has so many secrets that you don't know what to believe anymore. Soon everything they say feels like a lie. I'm not lying about being on the side of the Red Seconds, Scorpion. I swear it on my sons."

"I believe you, Scat. I'm being hard on you because you remind me of someone I used to care about." Brass admitted and was met by silence.

The only sound was the crackling of the fire. Times like these made it good to be a Guardian or they would be lighting dried dung to warm their temporary homestead.

"Scorpion, would it be too much to ask for your help tonight?" she asked, sighing. "I may be testing Scarab's will a little too much." She dropped her voice. "Myself too."

"I think that will be fine, Scat."

Even I could hear the nerves in Brass's croaky voice.

She let out the little groan she did every time the milk began to flow, and I fisted my hands over my ears. It was better that way. I did not think I could stop myself from trying to take her again. Still, I brooded.

I waited until the shuffling signified Brass had finished. The rock was just high enough not to have to duck my head, the small fire was going where Brass and Scat sat eating left over hare. He held up the hare's crispy leg over his shoulder without looking which I took and crossed over to the bed I had assaulted her on.

"I apologize, Scat," I said before tearing the flesh from the hare's leg.

"Don't worry about it," she said then paused. "It's my fault too. I think I was half asleep... dreaming. Sorry."

I sighed. Of course she would have been discombobulated in order to lay with a man with a face like mine. She cleared her throat.

"Join us... won't you? If you want."

My brow quirked, and I rolled from the bed and my brooding to settle in opposite Brass. I *called* over what I had whittled on my walk from my pack and let it fall into her lap. Scat stopped chewing as she held the cloaked wooden Guardian in her hand.

I hoped she was not going to break into tears again. I hoped she was not crying because of the poor workmanship.

Her finger ran over the Guardian cloak. "Do you have children with your wife that passed away?" she asked in a faraway voice.

Pain lanced through me. It was not the physical kind, but the kind that made it difficult to formulate words or to croak them out of a clenched jaw. The unexpected question sucked the air from my lungs. What was worse than losing Scarlett, was losing her and our one chance to have a child. All hope that I would be a father... I had not even known I wanted to be one.

Scat lifted her gaze, eyes gleaming. "Did they pass too?" she asked barely louder than a whisper.

I nodded unable to grind out the words. She sighed.

"I'm sorry for asking such a personal question," Scat apologized.

She absently rubbed her belly and Brass watched the flames dance in the small soot filled alcove of a fireplace, unwilling to talk about the sons he lost. I wondered if he was thinking of Scarlett as I was.

"We've taken vows of celibacy," Brass said to himself, and seemed astonished the words had found a voice.

Scat blinked blankly at him. "I didn't mean to... Did you think I would...?"

She was back in her white pants and woolen shirt unlaced. Most of her chest was covered, but sitting so close to the fire as she was, the slightest change in her skin color showed and when she leaned forward...

She was a dusky rose.

"I have no intention of making you break your vows. Tonight was... has been... confusing. Do you have that sewing kit?" she asked, picking up the shirt I tore.

Brass held out a hand to open his pack and pull forth his sewing kit from his pack with his *calling*. She took it and moved to sit down at the fire with us as she sewed. She placed her heel on the hem of the tunic to keep it down between her legs. She pulled the thread between her lips before pushing it through the eye of the needle. Her hair fell over her bare shoulder as she hunched into her sewing. The collar of her tunic fell, lopsided, much too big for her slender neck when unlaced. Her hand moved gracefully, the flash of a tiny tattoo I could not see clearly. She had long elegant fingers that reminded me of Pearl.

She tied her thread in a knot and instead of slicing the end with her *calling*, she slid it between her teeth and bit down. I had never seen someone do things the myopic way. Guardians always used their *calling*. She had shown her adept use in *calling* despite what she said about being weak.

Scat held up her thin shirt and accessed her work with beady dark eyes. "It'll hold up until I can get my pack." She tossed it to Brass who seemed to finally realize that she had done it for him.

I tossed the bones of the hare into the fire. Brass and I would not fight over a woman again. I would be willing to share Scat once the war was over.

"Is it okay if I share a mattress with one of you? I will keep my hands to myself," she said with a wry lopsided smile.

*... I do not trust myself tonight...*

Brass nodded imperceptibly, "You're welcome to share with me."

Scat laid on the left mattress. Brass took one look at her alone under the thin blankets and got up to join her.

*... She is a khoraz. Careful with her...*

"As careful as you have been?" he chided.

# FIFTY-TWO

I shouldn't have allowed that.

I had been half asleep when thought Scorpion was Brass. When he spoke, I recognized Scorpion's voice, and it jarred me into reality. The anguish had rolled me under until all I wanted was to forget who I was and where I was and the impossible feat set before me.

Then Scarab had given me a look so raw and full of need I'd been speechless. It had been a very long time since I was kissed with such passion. Brass had done it on my desk at Vanaheim on that fateful day. Brass had a feeling of desperation while Scarab's was so forlorn and that *need...*

Best not to think about that.

My stomach hurt, I was so hungry. Breakfast was some kind of green root with fish Scarab had caught from the hole he carved in the ice early that morning. I had woken groggily with Scorpion's arms wrapped tightly around me; so tightly, I couldn't have moved if I wanted to. I was afraid to admit how it felt to be held by Scorpion... or to be looked at like *that* by Scarab. Scorpion was my human pump when he awoke.

I followed behind them. Hood drawn, scarf covering all but my eyes, as we made our way over the beginning of the Illfuss Ice Fields. Crathode lands were close to our right in underground caverns. There was no place to hide if they found out we were there, it was totally flat except for the snowdrifts which would only hide us if we squatted behind them.

The cold had worked its way into my bones. There was no getting warm until we were back inside. We had one more night in the Igulbjorn Cliffs and on the other side was the Lycans village. I could do one last day. Twenty-four more hours and I'd be back with my family and put the confusing mess behind me.

"We're going to break for lunch," Scorpion said, falling back.

They looked as big as the Risar cloaked in their furs. Mountains, not men that traveled over the ice daring anyone to get in their way. They reminded me of the men I loved and it hurt.

I nodded, wishing we would just keep walking. If we stopped, they would cloud my senses with their familiar scents. When they touched me, it felt like it was *them* touching me. If Scarab or Scorpion were to push a little, I would turn into a limp noodle and do whatever they wanted... even take an extended naked lunch that stretched into night.

Scarab set the tent up and we crawled inside. Scorpion passed me wax paper filled with nuts and the roasted pika Scarab had caught this morning while Scorpion tended to me. I thanked him and ate in silence mending as I chewed.

"How are you doing so far? Should we slow down?" Scorpion asked.

I took another bite. Things were awkward. We were too polite, like walking on eggshells.

"I'm fine."

"*Scat*," Scarab said my name like a plea.

I looked at him through my lashes. He wasn't traditionally good looking, but I found him attractive... them both attractive.

"We will help you... with whatever you need," he said with a nod of his head.

"Thank you," I said in earnest. "I need the sagamore to move his tribe to Elivagar's heart. There're too many Stygians and Crathode in town for the Shadow Breakers alone and if the Minotaur fight us we'll be vastly outnumbered."

Scorpion's thin lips rubbed together, and I thought of Brass. I smiled as I reached up and pulled his beard so his lips popped. His blue eyes went wide, and I fell back, unable to explain why I did it.

"We'll help you," Scorpion said, searching my face.

"It may have helped if you had not sewn your shirt all the way up."

Scarab was teasing me and easing the uncomfortable tension.... causing an altogether different tension. Scorpion was waiting for my reaction. I realized I'd been kneading my breasts. I would be grateful to have the pump Katydid gave me back when we met with the others.

I ran my fingers through my hair, trying to think of something to say.

"Well, there's still time to rip it again," I said in a playful tone, and Scorpion and Scarab both smiled as they ate.

Slate was probably going to kill them; I doubted Brass would hold his tongue when we reached the Lycan village. My mind wandered as I tried to grasp seeing them both again after how they treated me the last time I saw them. The night Ash told them we had been together and the disgust on their faces.

I heard the loud crack of ice splitting like logs bursting into splinters. Scarab jumped up, slinging his pack over his head with Scorpion's as he sliced through the bleached leather of the tent. Scorpion dove for me. His arms caught me under my own as my feet abruptly fell from beneath me.

There was no time to scream. Scorpion dug his fingers into my cloak, trying to gain purchase as I dangled there. The tent blinded me as it clung to us. I could hear Scarab dicing through the thick leather. Scorpion's face was strained, there was nowhere for me to grab and he was slowly sliding over the edge with me. I gave him an appreciative smile.

"Thank you," I whispered and sliced the leather directly beneath my feet so when I went, it wouldn't drag him with me.

"No!"

The tear of my cloak deafened my ears with my hair whipping around me as I free fell through the hole. I thought I would smash into the water or into the ice. Instead, hard segmented arms caught me.

I finally screamed.

It had been building in me since the night we left Elivagar when I'd been attacked. I needed to scream for so many reasons.

Round, black eyes looked down at me as they clamped their claws around my extremities like ice and just as hard. Their hard-shelled faces sneered with gnashing gashes for mouths with spike like teeth. They were speaking, but I couldn't understand them.

Jackal had been right about me. I was a useless translator.

Lightning struck all around me, the smell of crabmeat filled my nostrils and my stomach roiled knowing this was no Alaskan King crab leg scent. They shrieked, and I *called* fire. It couldn't be helped.

I was dropped flat on my back and I curled into a ball dodging away from the segmented legs that stomped all around me. My leg was pinched as a Crathode fell and I cried out. Scarab had dropped down and his blades sought the soft throats of the Crathode who did not go down without resistance.

Bodies were littered all around me. Scarab tossed the body that laid over my legs and scooped me off the ice, making me wince.

Scorpion dropped a rope from the hole above and Scarab put his foot in the loop of the rope. We were hoisted up, every jerk caused me to wince as it jostled my leg which was undoubtedly broken.

Scarab hopped over the side of the hole and I grit my teeth as he laid me down on the ice and placed his hand on my leg. I couldn't look, I could feel the damage. Then it faded as the warmth of his healing flooded through me.

"Scat, don't you ever look at me like that again!" Scorpion shouted at me as Scarab helped me sit up.

Scorpion's face was red with anger.

"I didn't want you feeling culpable. You don't owe me anything, Scorpion," I said as Scarab helped me to my feet. "I don't know why you're so angry."

Scorpion curled his hand into a fist in front of my face and grit his teeth. "I *am* responsible. The moment we agreed to take you, the second we saved your life we became responsible for *you*!"

The shredded tent was at the bottom of the hole. My clothing was bloodstained once again, and I was back where I was the first night I met them.

"I'm —"

"You find something worth dying for and you live for it! Your sons are worth living for!"

"Easy," Scarab said under his breath and Scorpion growled, marching away.

Scarab was slowly rubbing his palm along my back, urging warmth to seep into me. I was so sick of men and needing their stupid help. Why couldn't I have a team of super hardcore women to assist me?

I knew the answer. Ama and Shale were dead. Tawny was pregnant, Cherry just had a baby, and Indigo was in the hands of the enemy. The women I knew who were warriors were all fighting, but not with me for now.

"Which way to the Lycans?" I asked, pulling up my hood and shoving the scarf he lent me into Scorpion's chest.

"Do not be rash. We are all headed the same way. Scorpion has had a hard time with women and sacrifice."

"I'm not those women. Just because I'm with you doesn't give you any say in what I do. Which way?" I demanded, pulling my gloves from my cloak pocket and yanked them onto my fingers.

"Those mountains in the distance." Scarab pointed ahead. "Once we cross them, we shall be on Lycan land."

I nodded and started forth.

They spoke in low tones behind me as if to remind me that they could outpace me at any time of their choosing and they were only tolerating my tantrum because they could. My clothing was saturated in frozen Crathode blood.

I ducked my head, marching in the cold, my throat frozen from the windier north that blew a biting breeze directly into my nostrils. I thought as though I could feel my lungs crack off icicles with each breath. They assured me that on the other side of the ice cliffs, the temperature was that of a milder winter.

I was skeptical.

Grudgingly, I fell back and the two men opened up to bring me into their fold. Scarab coaxed me under his furs and I reluctantly pressed against him. We didn't discuss the morning's argument, and we didn't discuss the Crathode. They found us a cave safe from the wind and built a fire.

"We passed Bjorn lands. As far as we know, they are staying out of the war. Only the Crathode and Minotaur are involved," Scarab informed me as we huddled around the fire. "We could send an emissary to the Bjorn and plead our case."

"That makes the most sense," I agreed.

We needed bodies for our war. The Crathode had let us pass through their lands, but a couple thousand Lycans wouldn't cross their lands unharmed. The other option was to pass by the Natts. There was no clear path.

Scorpion had hunted and killed a caribou that now roasted over a pit constructed of rocks and string they'd had in their pack. The skin was stretched over more stones with string pulling it taut and Scarab had concocted some liquid he rubbed on the hide and sat drying it with his *calling* near the fire.

With a full stomach, I started to feel drowsy and wrapped my cloak around me as I leaned against my knees. Scorpion stood and dusted his hands off before pulling on his gloves.

"This is your first time in the Igulbjorn Ice Cliffs?" Scorpion asked, and I knit my brows at him.

"Yes, why?" I asked.

His lips twitched into a smile and he offered me his hand. "Come. I want to show you something."

I pursed my lips. "Are we going far? I have to clean my clothes."

"Not at all. Here. You can wear this for now."

Scorpion handed me a pair of his own pants and Scarab tossed me the tunic I borrowed the night before. I moved into the shadows of the cave and changed into the clothes they'd given me.

I *felt* when they both stole a look.

He was giddy as he held my hand and led me outside. We walked back the way we came so we could see the cliffs more clearly and Scorpion moved behind me and pointed. There was no need, it was the most beautiful thing I'd ever seen.

I grabbed his wrist as I gasped. "It's stunning, Scorpion," I breathed.

Green streaked through the night sky like a trail left by Mani's chariot. A brilliant red and vivid blue clouded around the emerald streak.

Scorpion's breath was next to my ear. "The northern lights. Almost as beautiful as fireworks. I wanted to apologize."

"Fireworks have nothing on this. There's nothing to apologize for. If I remember correctly, it was I who threw the tantrum."

"That's not what I'm apologizing for." He paused. "I guess it depends on who you're watching the northern lights with."

My cheeks flushed, and I wondered if he could feel my increase in heat. "No?"

"For being a bastard, drawing my blades on you, making you swear the blood vow, and shouting at you. It's a very long list. I haven't dealt with human women in some time. I think I've lost my touch," he said, and I bumped back against his chest.

I started to apologize but, he lifted his arms and loosely encircled me.

"You're a good man, Scorpion. Even if you yell a lot at women."

He pressed his face into my hair. "It's your scent. It's like my love's. When I shut my eyes, you could be her," he whispered. "I lost two children in the war."

I turned in his arms; his proximity invoked bewildering emotions I couldn't begin to sort. His eyes were hooded and I could see how he had grown to care for me. It was mind-boggling. I couldn't understand what would cause such a passionate man to find something in me he found appealing.

"We should get back. Tomorrow afternoon you'll finally be rid of me and you can go find a woman who makes the Northern lights better than fireworks."

"What if I've already found her?" he whispered and my stomach flipped, a roll of heat washed over me, pulling every pore tight in its path.

That was the nicest thing anyone had said to me in a long time.

"You think that because I'm the only human woman you've spent time with recently." I wondered if that was true and turned back to the aurora borealis.

"That's not it. I am hoping you feel it too and leave your bastard husband for us," Scorpion breathed.

"Us? It's not that simple, Scorpion. I..."

"You're still in love with him," he finished for me, and I nodded, furious with myself for being such a foolish girl to not only still be in love with Slate, but Brass as well.

A long moment stretched as we stood watching the lights, pretending I was nobody with another no one and I was free to enjoy the company of whomever I wished. That I had no responsibilities whatsoever.

Scorpion held me tighter to him. "You're the first woman I've held since Yuletide," he whispered almost to himself.

Lots of Guardians had made vows during Yuletide. It was tradition, even more so with the Purge War.

"I had hoped I would find love again one day. I know it will never be what it was with her, but I have to try. If not for my sake then for Scarab's, he's not been in a good way since the Purge War started. Since you came barreling into our lives, it's the most like himself I've seen him. He broke his vow of silence for you."

Scorpion turned me around to face him. Had he just said he had found love in me?

"He did it so I wouldn't stab you. You want me to be with you both?" I asked, furrowing my brow in disbelief.

His lips pulled into an embarrassed smile. "I know how it sounds, but that's what we've been doing, isn't it? It works, yes? He's my brother and I love him; I also know we haven't looked forward to each day the way we have since we met you."

I was completely flustered. Scorpion put a finger to my lips, and they puckered to kiss them on instinct. He smiled again.

"Think on it, Scat." He took his finger away, his cool blue eyes flitting between my eyes. "May I kiss you?"

I sucked in a breath to fortify myself. "Don't ask my permission. Try, and risk rejection." It was all happening so fast.

He slid his gloved fingers along my jaw and into my hair. His body seemed to curl around me as he bent to my lips. The scent of his cinnamon soap teased my heart and my eyes fluttered shut. Scorpion's lips brushed mine. I sucked in sharply at the soft touch like the beat of a butterfly's wings.

*Again*, I thought. *More.*

He brushed his lips past again, my inhale stole the oxygen from his mouth. I wanted to run my fingers through his hair but wrapped them around his back instead. Scorpion's mouth finally landed flush to mine and my tongue parted my lips, seeking his.

"Ask me," he breathed.

My heart was thudding in my chest. I wanted to, but I couldn't. Scorpion kissed me deeper, his body rubbing against mine as he held me.

"Please," he begged.

My fingers curled in the padded fabric of his jerkin. He wanted me to ask him to break his vow. As much as I wanted to be touched by this man *and* much to my dismay... his brother-in-arms, I couldn't. Not while Slate and Brass had no idea I was even alive.

"Scorpion, Scat! Come. Before your vital parts freeze off," Scarab called wryly.

Scarab stood in the mouth of the cave looking down at us where we stood a little ways away. From there, I could *feel* his amusement.

# CHAPTER 53
# SLATE

"You're going to think I'm crazy," Brass whispered once Scat had fallen asleep between them.

"I heard the two of you speaking. You are falling for her. That is why you are suspicious, why you shout at her. I understand."

The fire flickered casting shadows throughout the cave. Brass cradled her from behind, the firelight at their heads. One day, he would see her totally nude in the daylight so he could remember every inch of her.

"What about you?"

"What about me?" I asked.

"You have feelings for her."

"I will step aside. We both know my prophecy looms ahead. If I had been a better man, I never would have let Scarlett get involved at all."

My fingers brushed her raven hair from her brow. How did I ever think she was plain? How would she react tomorrow once she found out who we really were and what we looked like?

"Don't. We would have shared Scarlett. Scat will be no different. You deserve happiness, Slate," Brass said in a hushed whisper.

"Would I of? You are more confident of it than I. Once I retained my memories, I could have pushed you out of the picture."

Brass's mouth broke into a sly grin. "You could've tried. She fell in love with us both. The luckiest bastards in Tidings."

"Or unluckiest," I murmured, turning over onto my side.

Scat was not ours. She had been our ward for a few days. A few very memorable days of walking, shouting, and fighting. There *was* that very memorable kiss that was seared into my mind.

She had passed out snuggly between us as she had that second night. Where she belonged. It felt right.

Dread snuck up on me, Niall would claim her tomorrow and it all would fade.

Our feet dragged as we entered Lycan territory. Scat went through bouts of quiet contemplation to pushing to get to know us. Volunteering information did not come naturally to Brass or me. We had spent months hiding, living with false faces and false identities.

Scorpion and Scarab, the Red Second transporters.

Scat acted like a friend. Laughing and smiling, cracking jokes to get us to smile, but kept her distance. Brass could see the wall she had begun to put up around her trying to draw that line in the sand between lovers and friends since it had gotten muddied on our trek.

She had woken up before us, any doubt I had about Niall being her mate vanished. Scat was scrubbing our scent from herself in the cold, her tan skin held a pink hue from her fervent nail scratching as if she could remove a layer of skin with her washing. She asked me to be careful not to touch her much when I tended to her.

Only then had I acknowledged that I did not want her to go back to Niall. She wanted to pretend as if we had never happened. Niall would scent us on her, I would make sure of it. Then, Brass would finally have his happiness.

By the time we started to reach the thatch and stone longhouses of the Lycan village, her laughs were forced and our mood, gloomy. Niall would not allow her to be friends with us and would challenge us once he found out we had touched his mate.

It was not as frigid on top of the Igulbjorn Ice Cliffs. There were conifer trees that peppered the land offering the Lycans plenty of wood for the continuous burning fires.

Scat stared openly at the people walking around in human form clothed in the tartans they donned at home amongst the Lycan form who wore tartan kilts and tunics. She did not seem surprised, only interested. Cook fires were lit for dinner, and women in tube shaped woolen dresses with apron-skirts fastened by turtle brooches were washing dirty-faced children.

Scat stopped suddenly and I could hear her heart race. She turned to face us and gave Brass a firm hug. Saying goodbye was not our strong suit. Brass held her until his fingertips slid from her back as she pulled away. She crossed to me and did the same. Warm spiced apples and vanilla — she should be ours.

She gave a tight smile. "I can't thank you enough for bringing me here. I hope I see you again and that we can be friends."

*Friends.* The word all men dreaded from a woman they were falling for. Before we could answer, Niall came prowling out of the mead hall and spotted us. He let out a whoop and Scat whirled around.

"Niall!" she shouted, and he broke out into a salacious grin as she briskly walked to him.

Brass glanced over to me with a mixture of desperation, forlornness, and anger. We followed her at a distance until Niall scooped her up into his arms and planted a kiss on her lips with her giggling.

"I didn't think you would recognize me," she said with Niall's hands around her waist.

"I would know your scent anywhere. Fire of body and soul, more beautiful than Freya herself." He ran his hands through her long black waves that she had left loose as if to impress Niall.

Brass rolled his eyes, and I felt a hint of jealousy ripple through me. Niall looked past her to us and his emerald green eyes glittered as he pulled her in for a less chaste kiss.

"We have done our duty."

I bumped Brass with my elbow as he stood transfixed by Niall and Scat. He did not respond, only walked solemnly beside me as we went into the longhouse we used as a home.

Ours was one of the smallest thatch longhouses in the village, we had no intention of staying when we had come there.

Two beds, a table and chairs, a copper tub, dresser and basin. That was all. Brass immediately began stripping down to wash. It had taken two months to pull him out of his melancholy, I was brooding until four days ago. Brass was slipping back into his old habits; I could not stand to watch it happen again.

"Wash up. We have much to do today."

Brass was climbing into the copper tub he had filled with hot water. "I haven't had much rest. I plan on sleeping until morning as soon as I finish this bath."

"Then I will have to challenge Niall for her myself."

Brass's lips curled. "You *like* her."

"Trim that nest you call a beard. We will speak to her before I formally challenge him."

He ran a hand over his jaw and looked down at his distorter ring. "Do you think she'll be angry we lied about who we are? The husband and paramour of the Second?"

I filled the basin preparing to remove all of my facial hair, the wooden bowl next to the basin contained all of my silver etched beads, the ivory sunburst, solar cross, jumis, and the jade barghest fetish. I would thread them through my hair so she would see me for who I was.

"She will undoubtedly be furious." I *called* a thin blade and slid it along my jaw. "We will persuade her to forgive us."

"I'm glad you're so optimistic. This is a new look for you," Brass jested.

"You could use a little of it yourself."

I met his eyes in the mirror and he smiled ruefully before sliding back in the tub. "I *am* feeling optimistic."

Niall shut the door of the longhouse used for distinguished guests and honeymoons. I grit my teeth as he spotted us walking on the dirt path between houses. His green eyes glittered as he swaggered nearer.

"There you are. You think a shave and a bath will impress her?"

Niall smirked. He was the kind of man women would crawl over one another for a chance to be with him. He knew it. The sagamore's son was charismatic, deadly, and women thought he was good looking. Scat's perpetual caustic remarks would be her only defense against his advances *if* she wished to defend against him.

The beast roared inside me. Control was fleeting. Brass was too enraged to calm me.

"I challenge you for her," I ground out.

Niall's eyes widened and then slowly his lips curled into a smug smile. "The Grar Dyr wants to challenge *me* for that Guardian woman?" He looked around for witnesses and found a trio of women with their pups scampering around their skirts. "You women, you heard his challenge?" They nodded, confused. "Tomorrow, in shifted form. Lycan against barghest in the Ice Cliff Games. Winner claims the woman?"

"Done," I growled, wishing I had taken off my distorter ring.

Niall laughed, shaking his head and walked away. Amethyst emerged from the longhouse and gave us worried looks.

"You two should come back later," she said nervously. "We need to speak first."

Amethyst was not wearing black. She wore black every day. Black woolen dress, black apron-skirt, now she wore the deep purple of the Straumrs with a heather grey apron-skirt. If she had taken a lover while we were away, we had no room to judge.

"We have to speak to her first, then we'll come find you," Brass answered.

She sighed and pushed one of her obsidian locks back into the plaited braids she wore in the Lycan style. "Okay. Watch out for Niall, he's determined to work his way into her bed to spite you."

Strange way to put it, but it was good news. He had not lain with her. If she were mine, that would have been the first thing I did.

"Thank you, Amethyst," I said, and placed my hand on her shoulder.

She patted it with her slender hand and offered a smile. We started towards the door and paused.

Nothing was polished in the Lycan village, everything was exquisitely carved with care. Celtic braids roped around the door of the stone building.

"We'll explain and then reveal our true identities," Brass said again.

I grunted in agreement and pushed into the longhouse. A fat, furry white form darted in before me. Cursed skogkatt. Scarlett's cat Treegold followed us everywhere. We had tried to leave her at Valla U, but Gypsum had likely sent her through to the Niflheim arena the day the portal door would be open so she could continue to spy on us for him. As if we did not know the zoolinguist got information from the forty-pound beast.

Hide covered chairs, a dining table, and tapestries hung in the unlit front room. Screens separated the single long narrow room and the bedroom; she had all the comforts of home. She was moving about the room, lighting thick, squat, off white candles. A fireplace to the left made up of stones that built the larger longhouses blazed.

Vanilla scented candles and pine infused the gelid air reminding me of Yuletides from my childhood. Brass and I stepped up to the dividers and into the bedroom.

Long, caramel hair spilled down to her waist, she wore a thin thistle colored robe with sweeping sleeves that brushed her knees as she raised her arm to light each candle. With the fireplace behind her, we could see the outline of her legs within the robe; the diamond portal of light at the apex of her thighs, like a gateway to heaven beckoning us to enter.

She hummed as she blew out her *calling*.. My boot scuffed the wood planked floor and she spun around. Big turquoise almond eyes went wide with surprise. Her lush full lips pulled into a shy smile as she tucked caramel hair, not black, behind her ear. It made her high cheekbones round, her straight edged nose reddened slightly with embarrassment. She was the most breathtaking woman I had ever seen, and she was my wife.

"I can explain," she said, and crossed to the carved nightstand beside the huge, canopied bed hung with heavy teal panels.

She slipped on the clunky ring we assumed was her wedding band and she was Scat again. She ran her teeth over her bottom lip until it popped from her mouth. Gods, how I loved the way she did that.

"My real name is Scarlett Tio, or Natt as I'm now finding out," she mumbled. "I'm the Second, the Stygians think I'm dead. It's the only advantage I have. That's how I convinced the Wemic and Faunelle to follow me. We had a woman named Mirage pose as me to lead the troops, then my family and I went to Valla U. I spoke to Canis Var and Dahlia Natt as an elemental in an effort to confuse them and distract from my real goal. That's taking back Elivagar from whomever this man is in my cousin's seat of power. *Um*, that's how I found out I can't be an elemental again until I'm totally healed from giving birth to my sons." She gave a rueful smile and rubbed her flat belly. "The sagamore has a piece I need. Two more pieces are with Canis, but we're going to have to play that by ear before we go back to Valla and try to activate this *project*." She swept her hand over her hair and stepped towards us. "I have to go back to my husband and lay with him until I carry his son."

She sighed.

"I didn't want to lie to you." Her eyes flitted between us. "I've been called a Khoraz Seductress and so many twisted truths have been told about me. If you turned me in I would've been handed over to Ash Straumr and... I don't want to contemplate the things he would do to me. Then, I, *um*, was too afraid to reveal myself," she said with a long exhale, her palms held up. "Men have treated me like a novelty, like a doll to play with, like a womb to fill. My powers, my name, my face... I didn't have my name when you met me, I couldn't use my powers, and I couldn't use my appearance to sway you. Still, you offered to help me with no benefit to you, you protected me, and didn't ask for anything in return. You don't know what that means to me. You wanted *me*, for me and I wasn't even very nice." She gave a sheepish smile. "Say something. *Please*. I'm so very sorry."

Scarlett. She was there, standing before us. Not dead. Very much alive. We had been with her every single night for the last four nights.

Brass was just as stunned as I was. His bairn, my wife, my mate. I stepped forward and grabbed the front of her robe, yanking it open. Her unpolished fingers curled at her sides and I spotted the tattoo I had only caught glimpses of; the inguz rune and Shadow Breaker tracker she had put over the *KHORAZ* scar. Brass took her hand and removed her distorter ring, the tiwaz rune was hid underneath. The kenaz rune hid in the crease of her thumb and index finger, that left her EH rune. She struggled feebly against our inspection.

"Scorpion... Scarab... stop. If my husband sees you in here..."

Her husband. *Me*. I had given Niall a right to claim her in challenging him to the Ice Cliff Games.

Much was becoming clear.

Brass had sliced his own thumb and rubbed it on her ring finger sucking in a sharp gasp as her bond with him became active. I pulled on her full lip and did the same. Scarlett. My Scarlett. Bold, afraid, nervous, excited, and always so lustful though she tried desperately to control it. We had known Scat was a khoraz, she could do nothing to hide her dilating pupils when we kissed her.

As we were doing now...

She whimpered; brows knit. "You have to leave. It's not just my husband... I have, *had* a lover. My sons' father. He's here too, they'll both kill you."

I could not take another second of her rambling. My fist wound in her hair and Brass pulled her hands gently away from where she was trying to pull back up her robe.

This was going to take time.

A marbled Arctic fox rug was splayed before the fire place. Her eyes searched mine as I reversed her to it. Brass helped her lay down, and I released her hair.

I pushed back her robe over her shoulders to reveal her body, fully illuminated by the fireplace and the candles that lined the room. Her breaths came short, her skin prickled despite the warmth.

"I wasn't being dramatic. They *will* kill you. Leave now," she said, tilting her chin up, eyes shrinking to slits.

We could have told her the truth right away, but everything she said was true. Our family name, our genetics — she had wanted us even as nameless ruffians — *hideous* nameless ruffians. She was convinced I did not want her, I would prove her very, very wrong.

Her fingers were curled in the fox's white and grey fur. Her eyes gleamed. What had I done to make her so fearful of herself? Ah, yes. Many, *many* things I had yet to apologize for. The ripples of those actions extended far and wide.

Suddenly, I was afraid to reveal myself. It would be the last time as Scarab. When she was sated and sleepy, we would remove our distorter rings. Brass met my eyes, and it was agreed. We wait.

"You heard the lady."

A blade pierced the soft flesh just below my ear. I knew that voice.

"Don't try a gods be damned thing. You're lucky we haven't killed you already. Scar, you okay?"

I knew that voice as well. They would never let us forget the way they had snuck up on us.

"Jett! It's *fine*! Quick, get that blade out of Scarab's throat! These are the men who saved me."

Scarlett clasped her robe shut over her breasts, that were fuller than they were when I last saw her. Her body was thinner as if she had not been eating well. Slowly, cautiously I held my hands up and began to turn towards the two men.

"Can I help her up or will you stick me with that blade?" Brass asked, sounding beyond amused.

It *was* Quick and Jett, bearded with longer hair than I had ever seen them wear, but them.

Tawny and the older man from the Dark Dancer inn stood just beyond the screen. Quick cursed and lifted Scarlett up from under her arms and pulled her robe shut. Brass and I turned our heads, Jett's blade still at my throat.

Quick's eyes never dropped to Scarlett's spectacular bosom. He actually looked upset with her as he held up her chin and looked into her eyes probably checking to see if we drugged her with rousen.

"Did they hurt you, Scarlett? I will kill them if they touched you." Quick grit his teeth as he looked at us.

"Quick, stop," she said, yanking her chin away and holding her robe shut. "I have given them each a thank you kiss for escorting me here safely, that's it. This... is just a misunderstanding. I was just telling them I was expecting Slate and Brass to come storming in any minute now, though I was hoping for a proper bath beforehand." She ran her hand over her hair.

Amethyst must have helped her remove the color, a long dull job she must have done while we had shaved and bathed.

"She's married and has two sons at home. This is Scarlett Tio, you motherless bastards. Show some respect. Wait until her husband and paramour get here," Jett spat.

"Brass is the father of my children, my hand fasted — whatever he is, not my paramour," she interjected.

"That's right, in these lands he'd be her second husband!" Tawny called obviously displeased with us.

"Alright already!" Scarlett shouted.

She was having a quiet argument with Quick which he seemed very upset about. If he had slept with Scarlett, it was I who would be doing the killing.

"You are Shark? Her pretender husband. Did you bed her?" I nodded to Scarlett.

Scarlett's eyes bulged, and I got my answer, but Quick's face contorted into rage. "Do not presume to judge me! If anyone was getting into her bed, it was me!"

"Quick! You're not helping," Scarlett shouted back at him, and took him aside whispering, but I could still hear them as could Brass. "I'm sorry. Please don't be upset. They helped me, nothing more."

"Those two assholes from the inn. That is who you choose to cheat on my brother with?"

"As opposed to if I had given into you? That would have been better?" she asked dryly, and I shifted to stand, but Jett's blade dug deeper.

It was getting old fast.

"No!" he shouted and dropped his voice.

Jett and the others seemed used to Scarlett and Quick's private arguments. Some insane part of me grew jealous that they had grown close enough to have them. That they were common enough that no one made a move to stop them because they knew it would blow over. The only explanation was that they cared about one another and no matter how bad the argument got, they would walk away okay.

"That is not what I meant. This is coming out wrong. I caught you laying with two hideous men. You do not think I have moments of weakness?"

"I know you do, Quick, but you have them with *me* because I remind you of Indigo and part of you wants to hurt her because you know I'll always turn you down. I'm sorry, Quick. I let things get carried away with Scarab and Scorpion. They were caring and uncomplicated. They had no idea who I was, and it felt really good to be liked for being myself for *once*." She sighed and took a step towards Quick.

He anticipated her move and embraced her, kissing the top of her head. "I am sorry." He sighed. "I was worried about you. You disappeared, then those three men found me, shouting in the streets for you. I almost killed them."

"I'm not going to leave you. I promise. I'm like a bad penny, I keep turning up. Now leave me alone so I can take a really hot bath and use real moisturizer." She giggled in a sultry feminine way, and Quick's face relaxed as he smiled down at her.

Gods be good, Quick *did* love her.

"I've had enough of this," Brass ground out.

"Easy, scamp," Jett growled, pulling a second blade.

Quick released Scarlett and he sheathed his blades as she walked over and pushed Jett's blade from my throat.

"They promise never to try anything with me again. Don't you?" she said, giving an assuming nod over her shoulder to us.

"I promise to take you on every flat surface of this room as soon as these interlopers leave," I said, getting to my feet and removing my ring.

When she turned back to me, I knew Brass was standing behind me, his ring in his pocket. Her eyes flickered between them and then rolled up to the heavens as her body twent limp. Quick was faster than I was.

She was in his arms before I could blink and he was carrying her to the bed. Jett yanked me to him, slapping my back and laughing.

"I was going to kill you! Scarlett has terrible taste in men but those faces you were wearing — I thought she had finally lost it. You two looked particularly unsavory even for you. This handsome punim is much better," Jett said, pinching my cheek until I elbowed him off.

For all his joking, he scent told me just how happy he was to see us. He greeted Brass next as I walked over to Tawny. The little spitfire scowled, but I embraced her anyway.

"Cousin," I said, lifting her off her feet as she struggled. "I welcome your glower," I teased, and she scoffed.

"I guess I'm glad you're not dead either, but only because —" she broke off.

*Steel.* It felt like someone had stuck a blade in my heart and twisted it. It was too much to hope he would be with them too. I held her all the tighter and scented the salt of her tears and... Jett. Had the little fireball bedded her husband's brother? That would be an interesting turn in events. It would explain why Amethyst was not with them.

"Ridge Vetr." The fair skinned man stuck out his hand.

I took it, dubious of his introduction. "Slate Dagr, patriarch of the Dagr since your daughter is now the Vetr heir and your nephew through marriage," I stated, watching him carefully.

He had a mischievous air, not one who liked pranks or problems, but who preferred laughing to arguing and smiled often. He also did not seem to be lying. Tawny closely resembled him.

"Yes, so I have heard," Ridge said with a puckish grin.

The air was punched out of me as Quick hugged me from behind, lifting me from the floor and releasing me. He punched my shoulder as I turned around smiling like a fool.

"Dear sweet Gods, it *is* you. Like I told Brass, I have tried to lay with your precious Scarlett, but only once outside of... where we were. She turned me down flat. She is not the same woman she was, that was why I was so shocked she was putting up little resistance to you two trolls."

"Are you implying that my virtuous wife is a philanderer?" I growled, only half serious.

Quick laughed wickedly. "Never. Especially to your face. Besides, I have laid bared for all her eyes to feast upon and she still managed to say no. The maiden fair if ever there was one." Quick smirked.

"Silver, if you were not my brother I would kill you," Brass ground out and moved past me to greet Jett and the others.

I walked away as embraced and spoke excitedly to one another. Quick had laid Scarlett down on the furs that topped the square columned bed. Her long lean leg parted the robe to her upper thigh.

*My wife.*

I would get her whole explanation when she awoke *after* I made good on my promise to take her on every flat surface of the longhouse.

# BIBLIOGRAPHY


Hughes, Langston. "Final Curve."
*Selected Poems of Langston Hughes, January 1st,* 1959

Barrett Browning, Elizabeth. "A Woman's Shortcomings."
*Blackwood's Edinburgh Magazine,* October 1846

Shakespeare, William. "Romeo and Juliet."
*Authorized Quarto, Act 2, Scene 2.* 1594

Whitman, Walt. "A Hand-Mirror."
*Leaves of Grass,* 1848

Whitman, Walt. "All is Truth."
*Leaves of Grass,* 1848

Hughes, Langston. "The Weary Blues."
*Opportunity Magazine,* 1925

Hughes, Langston. "April Rain Song."
*The Brownies'' Book,* April 1921

Whitman, Walt. "A Leaf of Faces."
*Leaves of Grass,* 1848

# About the Author

For more of Tidings's world, family trees, quizzes, events, and news from Charli Rahe, please visit www.charlirahe.com and join Charli's Devils on Facebook.